DEDICATION

I dedicate my first novel to my best friend Christine, who left this earth far too early. I miss her every day. I want to thank some very special women who were very supportive and volunteered to be my focus group. With all my heart I thank Cheryl, Jo-Anne, and Monique for their comments, which I found very helpful. I also want to thank my amazing and truly gifted artist, Sarah Smith who created the most magical dust cover for this novel and will be doing all my dust covers.

Last, but by no means the least, I want to thank my son Craig who encouraged me not to give up even after receiving rejection letter after rejection letter. He wanted me to pursue my dream of being published and said one day it would happen. Tada!

List of Novels in this series

Book 1 – The Dream
Book 2 – The Wedding
Book 3 – The Return
Book 4 – The Holidays
Book 5 – The Final Goodbye
Book 6 – The Unexpected
Book 7 – The Arrival
Book 8 – The Visitors
Book 9 – The Passage of Time
Book 10 – The End is a New Beginning

Arada Self Publishing
C1139096

THE DREAM

By: Deborah L. Clouthier

Chapter 1

As I sat drinking my coffee waiting for my friend Roxie to arrive, I thought back about the last few years. I sold the house and moved a few times but was finally settled in this senior's condo complex on the south side of Stony. I won a large lottery the year after my ex passed and gave some to my son and set up a trust for my granddaughter. It was now time to concentrate on me and do the things I wanted. One of which was to get into better shape. I hired a personal trainer and worked out with her five days a week for an entire year. I really wanted to be well toned and at the end of that year I looked and felt a good twenty years younger. For the first time in a long time, I felt good. I was determined to exercise regularly and stay in shape.

A good friend from high school, Janet, and my best friend Christelle came out to help me get through the funeral arrangements of my late husband and it made it so much easier on me. I wanted to show my appreciation to them both and I kept my promise to Christelle and bought her a condo, the one she always wanted. For Janet, she and her husband Wade had Scottish ancestry and I offered to take them on a two-week holiday to Scotland. We went the following June after I won the money. I was remembering that holiday when we went to Scotland. We stayed at a hotel that seemed central to the places we wanted to go. Wade offered to do all the driving for us. We stopped in at a restaurant for lunch the day before we were to leave. The people at the hotel said it was a pretty good place to go and eat. We ordered our meal and then sat talking and laughing and remembering the places we had been and things we had seen.

I recalled that I had a weird feeling that somebody was staring at us, and I looked up and around. The restaurant was full, but everyone seemed to be paying attention to their meals except for three men on the other side of the room. Perhaps we were obvious tourists and stuck out like sore thumbs. I saw one man staring but the other two looked away when I looked over. I went back into our conversation and after we finished eating, I paid the bill, and we got up to leave. As we did, I noticed that one of the men kept staring at me. He had amazing eyes and was quite handsome. Remembering his eyes made me smile now as I drank my coffee.

"James who are you looking at?" Malcolm wanted to know why James was so distracted as they'd come to the restaurant to discuss business. James spotted her as soon as he sat down.

"Now that, is a beautiful woman." Angus and Malcolm turned around to look and looked away quickly when they saw her look over. He was going to go over and introduce himself, but they got up to leave before he could do so, and a large group of customers got up at the same time. For days, weeks and months all he could think about when he had moments alone was her. He could not get her out of his mind and after going to see his dear friend Annie who was a very well respect medium throughout the UK, he had his answers.

"James my dear, you have a woman on your mind. You can't stop thinking about her, yet you don't know who she is or where she is from. You will meet her again, but not for a little while. When the time is right, I shall let you know where you need to go to meet her again, but for now you are too involved with your business, and she is not ready."

Someone laughed, and it brought me back to the present. It was mid-April, and the days were getting warmer, and the sun was heating up the ground to rid it of the last remnants of winter. It was Monday morning, and I was meeting Roxie for coffee at a coffee shop not far from where I lived. I arrived before she did and got my coffee and a table by the window and sat facing the door, so I could watch for her to come in. She was back from California about a week where she went every winter to escape the cold. There was still a bit of snow here and there, but the sun was nice and warm. I saw her pull into the parking lot and got up to meet her. I finished my coffee but was going to get another one and one for her as well. When she came in, we went to sit at our table. The coffee shop was unusually full this morning and I was lucky to have grabbed a table when I did.

"I have some things to tell you but first tell me how your winter was." She told me all the things she'd done and the people and places she'd been and seen. She was not one to sit around and, from the sounds of it, she had been on the go from the day she had arrived.

"So, tell me what it is you must tell me. Is everything going, ok? You look amazing. What have you done to yourself? I swear you look younger, and you've lost weight. You're not sick, are you?" We talked about how I was doing since my husband passed as I had not seen her as she was away on a trip to Europe. I promised her that I was fine and that I'd been working hard to lose weight and get into better shape. Being able to afford to go for weekly facials and other beauty treatments made my skin look and feel amazing was also part of it. She was glad that I sold the house and was looking forward to seeing the new place. We were going to go there after we had coffee if there was time. As she was only back a short while, she still had lots of things to take care of.

Once we got the news out of the way, I started to tell her about this dream I'd been having. It was almost on a nightly basis for the last several months and it was weird. Not weird crazy but just odd that I couldn't shake this dream. I would only get bits of this dream, quick flashes of pictures. She sat listening to me go on about a tall handsome man named James who had a Scottish accent. We sat chatting for some time about the various flashes I was getting in the dream when I saw someone come through the door. He was tall, well dressed in a nice suit and tie, very handsome and he stood in line to get a coffee. He looked familiar. He started looking around the room as if he was meeting someone. He looked our way and started to come over.

"Ladies would you mind if I sat with you. The place seems to be full and the person I am supposed to meet doesn't seem to be here. Of course, we said he could sit. But before I could say a word, Roxie spoke to him.

"Hi, my name is Roxanne Lebrun, and this is Cassandra Harris. It sounds like you have a Scottish accent, not something we hear around here much." I could not speak; my head was going through the dream, and I thought I must still be asleep. Roxie was still talking to him asking him all sorts of things. I was sure that he was starting to regret sitting at our table. He was a little surprised at how many questions were being directed at him.

"My name is James, James Sutherland and I am from Scotland, but I work and live for the moment in Toronto." He sipped his coffee hoping that, and a few other answers would satisfy her curiosity. But after hearing my dream, Roxie went on. People loved to talk to her, she was originally from Holland and still, even after all these years of living here, still had a bit of an accent. But James started to ask her questions.

"You sound Dutch, are you here visiting, or do you live here." As he was asking the question to her, he kept looking at me as if we knew one another. She responded by telling him she left Holland when she was eighteen and lived here ever since.

"So, what is it you do love." Roxie called everyone love. Everyone smiled at her when she said that. It was all part of her charm. I finally found the courage to speak. "So, what business are you in?" He looked straight at me, and I swear that I had seen him somewhere before but just couldn't place where.

"I'm actually looking to locate a site for a few company startups in the area. I was supposed to meet with someone from the planning division from the county, but I must be early, or they are running late." He looked around again a couple of times.

"Why didn't you meet them at the municipal office, if you don't mind me asking." He looked around again and still nobody was showing up.

"I'm just going to make a quick call and see if there has been a mix up, so if you will excuse me a moment." He got up and went outside and made his call and while doing so Roxie and I looked at each other. I had a feeling I knew what she was thinking but indicated in the only way I could to not ask any more questions.

"It seems there was a mix up. They thought I was going to meet them at the municipal office, and I thought here, I guess I got the message wrong. I must be off then; they are waiting on me to take me to the industrial site. It was a pleasure to meet you both, perhaps we shall meet again." He got up and left. Moments after he was out the door, Roxie grabbed my arm.

"Oh, my goodness I cannot believe that you had that dream and in walks the guy from your dream. This must mean something. This is spooooky." I agreed it was and she looked at her watch. She had to run but she wanted to know more about the dream at another time. I said maybe she could come over and we could go out for dinner, or I could cook something up. As she dashed off, she said to call her in a day or two. I was about to leave myself when I noticed that the gentleman dropped one of his gloves on the floor. I picked it up and hurried outside to see if I could catch him, but he left. I was getting into my car when he pulled up beside me.

"I dropped one of my gloves inside." He was about to get out of his car, but I said that I noticed it and gave it to him. He smiled and said thank you and was about to leave and stopped.

“I know this is going to sound very forward of me but I’m going to be here for about a week getting things sorted out, and wondered if you would be willing to go out for dinner or lunch or even coffee with me? I would like to get a sense of the people here and the area and I presume you live in the area, and I thought you might be able to answer some questions for me that are not motivated by the people from the municipality.”

I hesitated for only a moment and said that perhaps we could meet for coffee here around 9:00 the next morning if that was okay with him. It would have been too awkward to go for lunch or dinner. He said that would work out well for him and he would see me at 9:00 the following morning. Having had this dream for what seemed months I seemed to recall that I would have coffee with him more than once. What was going on? Was I now clairvoyant or psychic? My intuition was always very strong, but I shrugged it off that it wasn’t anything more than a chance encounter. But how could I possibly have known he would be Scottish, and his name would be James. This really was too weird or as Roxie said ‘spooooky.’ I went home and picked up my dream journal. I got into the habit, at much insistence from my best friend Christelle, to jot things down that I would remember from my dreams each morning after I woke up. Was this really happening to me?

I preoccupied myself with visiting some of the other seniors in the condo building. All the other seniors were older than me, but they were still able to get around on their own without too much trouble. The condo building wasn't that old but there were some problems that were occurring. Often, I would sit with them and talk about how things were going and how they were doing. Some had family still in the area, but the majority did not. I organized walks for those who were up to it after I came back from the gym.

It got everyone out and in the fresh air and moving. There was an exercise room in the building, but it had very little equipment and what was there was not always operational. For those who didn't feel up to walking, I tried to encourage them to use whichever exercise machines were working. But most of them were always up for a walk. Every few weeks I would add an extra bit onto the walk until we'd gotten up to two kilometers in one direction. They were all very enthusiastic about it and never complained.

I went up to my place and made a few calls. Video chatting with my granddaughter was always the highlight of my day. I thought about moving back east now that I was on my own, but I was settled here. When I moved out here many years ago, it felt like I was coming home. I missed my son, daughter in law and granddaughter but Ayleen was now in school, and Ross and Lindsay were always so busy on the weekends. They promised to come out and visit soon, so I looked forward to that. Later that day my phone rang, and I had a feeling it would be Roxie and sure enough it was.

"How freaky was that. Did you two talk more after I left? You must tell me more about the dream." I let her know that James wanted to meet for coffee the next morning to get information on the area. I told her that he suggested lunch or dinner, but I thought it would be safer to go with coffee. I let her know a bit more about the dream. As I explained to her, I only ever saw flashes, nothing like a story or anything like that. We talked about other things and then I said I would have to go. It was bingo night in the party room. Normally I would not entertain going to it, but it was something my Mum always enjoyed, and I felt oddly close to her when I would go.

That night I wanted to see if I could get any more on the dream but all I would get is very quick flashes and before I knew it, I was fast asleep. Next morning, I got up got dressed and went over to the coffee shop. I didn't want to get too dressed up; it was after all just coffee. I put on a pair of jeans and one of my favourite red sweaters. It was still cool, so it would keep me warm, but I still took a light jacket. I fixed my hair, put on some makeup and I was out the door. I got to the coffee shop just before 9:00 but I could see that James was already inside. He waved me over to the table. There was hardly a soul in the place today. He already ordered my coffee, so I sat down. He was dressed a little more casually today in a shirt and tie with jeans and a sports jacket.

He had curly brown hair which he kept short at the sides, and it had a little grey here and there and amazing green eyes. I'd seen eyes like this before, but the man had a full beard and the man in front of me was clean shaven. Could this be him? He had a certain look about him; it was an air of confidence, I think. Over coffee and listening to him start to ask some questions, I took more notice of him. He had something of a tan which I am sure he got on some tropical island somewhere. He was a little over six feet tall and had a great build. He looked to be in his mid-fifties, but it was hard to tell.

"You look very nice today, Cassandra. So, tell me, what do you do with your days?" I told him that I was retired and was widowed. He offered his condolences, and I thanked him. He didn't ask me anything about my late husband which was good because I didn't want to talk about it. He asked if I lived close and I said that I had a condo not far from here. I didn't want to appear too nosey about him, so I tried to ask questions that were not too invasive.

"So how long did you say you were going to be here? You also mentioned you were going to be starting a few companies here in the industrial park. Did you find what you were looking for?" He looked at me and I felt like he was looking deep into my soul.

"I will be here for another four or five days assessing the site that I want to build on. I'm looking to set up several companies. My group of companies is quite large. I have several companies in Scotland, and I've been working with my business partner who runs his own company, and he thought that Alberta and in particular Parkland County would be a good place to expand given the economy in this area." So, he was going to build several different companies, but he hadn't decided which businesses he would move into them. I asked him if he immigrated to Canada to which he said no. He lived in Toronto because that was where his largest company was and was here only part of the year. His main residence was in Scotland, and he was not going to give up his homeland. We talked for several hours and then he looked at his watch and said he must leave for another appointment with the municipality.

"It was very nice to see you again." We both got up and went out to our vehicles. He wanted to know if we could meet for coffee again tomorrow and perhaps the next day. I said that would be fine. He seemed like a very nice person and was, without doubt, very interesting. We met each morning for the next few days and chatted about a variety of things. I told him that I was involved with the seniors in my condo complex by keeping them active going for long walks and that I worked out to stay in shape. We talked a bit more about the condo where I lived. I said it was very nice when I first bought it, but it was starting to have problems. The original owner sold the building, and the new owner was never there but had a manager who looked after the place. Unfortunately, it was not being well looked after although I was sure it wasn't the manager's fault. Things were starting to fall apart in other units, people were having issues with plumbing and peeling paint. My unit was a model unit when I bought it and I made sure to keep it well maintained. I enjoyed being around people and I felt like I was doing something productive by organizing walks with the residents of the building. He then switched topics onto other things that were happening in the area and within the province. Every day that we met for coffee it was just for an hour or two and then he had to leave. Today was Friday and he mentioned that he was going to be flying back to Toronto early the following morning.

"It is my hope that you would be open to have dinner with me tonight before I leave. I know it's very short notice, but I enjoy talking to you." I was nervous about being asked to dinner because I only just met him, but I suggested the restaurant that was very close to where I lived. He said that he knew where it was as he had been doing a lot of driving around over the last few days to get a feel for the area. We arranged to meet at the restaurant around 6:00 tonight. He offered to pick me up, but I said I would go in my car if that was okay. He understood and said he would see me later tonight.

I had a spa appointment to get to that I booked the week before and made it just in time. After my appointment was done, I decided to buy something new for dinner tonight. I didn't want to buy anything fancy, but I felt like I should wear a dress. I seldom went out at night and when I did it was with Roxie, and it was always casual. I stopped at a local dress shop to see what they had in. They had a lot of spring and summer things that were very nice, but some were just a bit too summery for this time of the year. There was still a chill in the air at night and it wasn't uncommon for us to get snow in April and May.

They had clearance on some of their winter things and I picked out a periwinkle light knit dress that fit perfectly and was lined so I would be warm enough in it. It came with a matching jacket which would give extra warmth in the event the restaurant was cool. I needed a new pair of shoes now because I didn't own anything that would go with the dress. It had been forever since I wore a pair of heels, and I was sure that if I bought a pair I would end up twisting my ankle. I played it safe and found a pair of beige wedge pumps which felt heavenly to wear. With my purchases in hand, I went home. I don't think I was in the door five minutes when the phone rang.

"So how was coffee, tell me everything." Roxie was eager to hear how things went. We both were guessing how old he was, and both agreed he was probably around fifty-five maybe a year or two older. Roxie thought this was perhaps fate and that this was the man for me. I wasn't looking at this as a romantic venture. He seemed nice and it would be nice to have a guy friend who was not interested in anything more than being a friend. I told her that he asked me for dinner tonight and we were meeting at the restaurant near my condo. I knew that she was happy for me because I rarely went out at night, and I said many times before that I was through with relationships after my husband passed away. I wanted to spend the rest of my life enjoying my son and his family and doing the things that I wanted to do.

"Sounds like he is interested in you though. How do you feel about him?" I assured her that I was not interested in him romantically and I doubted that he was interested in me romantically. Although I dreamt about someone like him, I did not dream of every moment of every day where he was in the picture. I would get little snapshots of him in my dreams like seeing him in the coffee shop. I knew that he was a successful businessman, that much I saw in my dreams, and I did see us having coffee every day for a week and I did see him asking me to dinner. I would get other flashes of him asking me to a large gala which I would have Roxie come to as well. I could only get so far into the dream before I would fall asleep and each night I would start right back at the beginning with only flashes of future events. We talked for almost an hour before I said that I had to go.

It was still early enough that I went for a walk with some of the seniors. I was very proud of them for continuing to work on staying fit and healthy. By the time we got back it was a bit later than I thought and I needed to take a fast shower. I didn't want to be late for dinner nor did I want to be too early. I got dressed put on some makeup, fixed my hair, took a last look at myself in the mirror and went out the door. It turned out we arrived at almost the same moment.

I was getting out of my car when he pulled into the parking lot. I walked to the entrance and waited for him as there was light rain starting. I told James earlier I would make the reservations if he was ok with that. I knew the owner and I asked for a table near the back in the private area. We were shown to our table and drinks were ordered. I asked for a small white wine as did he. James looked over the menu as did I. We placed our orders, and I gave a toast to him having a successful venture.

"This is a nice restaurant, although I can't say that I like the clear glass wall. I feel like I'm in a fishbowl." I had to agree, it was the one thing that I didn't like about this room, but I thought it would offer a measure of privacy in the event he was going to talk about his future business in the area.

"James, tell me a little more about yourself. Where in Scotland did you live? Are your parents still there? Do you have any brothers or sisters? What sorts of companies do you run?" I didn't want there to be long awkward silences until the food arrived. I wanted to see if anything would match up to my dream but also because I knew that Roxie was going to ask.

"Okay, I will answer your questions as long as I am permitted to ask you some." I agreed but said that if there were questions, I was asking or that he was going to ask me, that neither of us wanted to respond to that it would be okay to say we didn't want to talk about it. He agreed.

"I was born and raised in Dumbarton which is not far from Glasgow. I attended the University of Edinburgh and graduated at the top of my class in business and financial management. My parents are both deceased. My Dad, Patrick James had a glassmaking business that he started when he was in his twenties, and it did very well but one night in the winter when he was coming home, he skidded off the road and hit a tree. He and his brother, who was in the car with him and worked with him, were killed instantly. I was about fifteen at the time and it left just my Mum and me. I was planning to go to university in a couple of years. My Mum,

Cullodina Roxanne got breast cancer about two years before my father died although she never said anything to me about it until a year after my Dad died. She lived long enough to see me graduate with honours. My Uncle Duncan, my Mum's brother took over my Dad's business while I was at university and when I graduated, I took control. Duncan has a very successful real estate business of his own but ran both his company and my Dad's until I was ready to take over. The business was faltering a bit during that time, but I managed to make it very successful. A lot of people became very interested in glassware, stained glass, and other forms of glass so I was fortunate enough to make it very profitable at the right time." He took a sip of his wine and continued.

"There was a shipyard in the area that was going under, so I bought it with some of the profits and a small bank loan, changed the type of product that was being built and catered more to the super yacht industry, which was booming, and I doubled the number of people I employed. I paid the loan back long before it was due, and it was all profit from there on. I also took over a failing whisky company and changed the entire production area into something more modern and higher tech. I was fortunate enough that my uncle knew a retired master whisky maker who was renowned at his craft, and he agreed to help me with putting out a product that was a hit in no time. So, with these three companies I managed to turn them into enormous successes. Profits were way up, and it allowed me to branch out and invest in other ventures that, with some work and using the skills I learned, turned into very profitable companies. I eventually built a successful empire that has broadened its scope considerably. I am also partner with my best friend, in a company that has proven very successful as well. Suffice it to say I am doing very well." It sounded like he was extremely smart.

"Now it is my turn to ask you some questions if you feel that I have amply answered yours." I agreed that he had and said that he could ask me his questions.

"Do you have any children. Have you lived here all your life? What did you do before you retired? Do you have any brothers or sisters? What about your parents?" I smiled as the questions were similar to mine.

"I have been married twice. I have one son from my first marriage and he and his wife and my granddaughter live back east. My son works for a courier company and my daughter in law is a kindergarten teacher. My granddaughter is in grade one and she is the joy of my life, aside from my son of course. She makes me happy when I think of her. I spoil her as much as I can, and I do it without shame." I showed James a picture of her that I had on my cell phone, and he agreed she looked adorable.

"I moved here many years ago and continue living here because this is home for me now. I am set up here and I prefer the weather here to that of back east. I do not like the humidity they get back east which I am sure if you live in Toronto, you know what I mean. I lived there more than half of my life and when I got the opportunity to move out west with my job, I took it. I worked for a company for over thirty years in a field that I never really enjoyed. I retired a year or so earlier than I should have but I couldn't tolerate working in that environment any longer." I explained that I did not want to go into detail about my working years and hoped he would understand.

"As for my parents and siblings, well both of my parents are deceased. They both died of cancer. My Mum Natalie went very quickly and, in her sleep, and my Dad, Walter died several years later. He suffered a bit but died in his sleep as well. I think he went into a coma and never woke up. As for my siblings, I have an older sister and two younger brothers. I am close to my sister Sonya whom I keep in touch with on a regular basis. She has never come out here because she is afraid to fly so when I can go back east, I make a point of seeing her as much as I can." James could see that talking about my family was a difficult thing, so he did not pursue it further.

"I never had any brothers or sisters myself, but I have lots of cousins, so I am close with them. I see them whenever I am back in Scotland, and they have come over to visit me in Toronto a few times." Our meal arrived, and we talked about the food and the weather. We ordered coffee and James asked me more about my life.

"Well, let's see, I have some very wonderful friends, such as Roxie, who, as you noticed loves people and enjoys finding out about them, and my best friend Christelle lives back east, and she has been my best friend for a very long time. I wish I could see her more often, but we video chat and when I go back east, I always make time for her. I reconnected with a high school friend Janet, and we talk or text almost every day. I have another friend Judy who lives on the east coast, and we seldom see each other but we talk on the phone from time to time. I help the seniors where I live by taking them out for walks and keeping them moving and trying to ensure they stay healthy. It doesn't give me much of a workout, but I get that in at other times. I have a few hobbies that I enjoy like painting, stained glass, and knitting. I don't knit as much as I used to, but I do occasionally." I took a sip of water and smiled.

"I must admit my jaw dropped when you mentioned you have a glass company. I have loved stained glass since I was a child. I took a few classes in how to make things like sun catchers and I do okay, but I am by no means an expert, but I just love looking at stained glass. Painting I took up years ago. I went to a few paint nites. I'm not sure if you have ever heard of them but you go to a restaurant, and they have a painting which you have chosen in advance and paid for, and they teach you how to paint it. But I decided to try my hand at doing things on my own and every so often I try to paint a picture of a photo I have taken. Sometimes they work out and others not so much. But I enjoy it. They are just hobbies and that is all that I wanted them to be." He said he would like to see some of my work, but I had a feeling he was only humoring me. But I said that maybe someday I would. I asked him what time it was as I wasn't wearing a watch. When he said it was 9:30 I gasped?

"My I didn't realize that we've been here that long. I know you have an early flight tomorrow and you probably have some last-minute things you want to take care of. We should call it a night." James paid the bill, and we left the restaurant and went to my car.

"I would like to see you again when I come back if that is ok with you." I enjoyed his company, but I was worried that maybe he was wanting this to be more.

"James, I think you are a wonderful incredibly interesting man. Probably the most interesting man I have ever met. I don't want to sound full of myself, but I am not interested, at this point in my life, in having a romantic relationship. I would love to have you as a good friend if that is ok with you." He gave out a huge sigh of relief which he inwardly hoped was convincing.

"I would love to have you as a good friend. You never did ask me my status. I was married when I was much younger, but it ended very badly, and I guess it was lucky that we never had any children although I wanted them, but she did not. Fortunately for me, she married a Duke very soon after we divorced and before my businesses took off. I too am not interested in a romantic relationship at this point. I am extremely busy with my companies, and it is difficult to make time for a personal life which, for now, suits me. But I will say this in all honesty, you are the most interesting woman I have ever met."

I knew that he was being kind but if a handsome younger man wanted to compliment me, I was going to be gracious and accept it. Even though he was too polite to ask, I told him that I was sixty-three to which he said I looked not a day over fifty, which again, I accepted. He said that he was fifty-five, which I was not surprised about as that is what I guessed. He didn't look it though and I told him so.

We agreed that friendship was the right thing for us. We exchanged phone numbers and James said he would text me or call me when he knew he would be coming back and could arrange to meet up. I got in my car and drove home. James drove off to his hotel and would be leaving in the morning. I was glad that we reached an understanding. It would have made things awkward if he wanted more.

Back in his hotel suite and after packing his suitcases, James checked the time and put in a call to his uncle. He was mulling over what he said to Cassandra about being friends. He knew in his heart that he wanted more but they just met, and he did not want to push it. With her, he was not interested in a one-night stand. He knew almost from the second he saw her in Scotland and again now that she was someone that he wanted to know more about and wanted to see as much as possible.

"Duncan, it's me James, how are you? I know you are up early, so I thought I'd give you a call." It had been almost a month since he last spoke to his uncle, and they had a lot of catching up to do. James was informed on all his cousins and aunts and uncles. Duncan had been there for James when both his parents died. He helped him to understand more about his Dad's business and they talked endlessly about where James wanted to take the business. The fact that he succeeded and created a very large empire, his parents would have been ever so proud.

"I met a woman while I was here. She's amazing and I really like her. She's older than me but to look at her you wouldn't know it." James went on about how he met Cassandra and Roxanne and that he met her for coffee the rest of the week and just went out to dinner with her. He didn't think it necessary to tell Duncan that this was the woman he saw years ago in Scotland and couldn't stop thinking about.

"But it is complicated Duncan. She isn't interested in anything more than friendship. I think she has been badly hurt and if I move too quickly, she might run, and I really don't want that. She wants to be friends and, for now, I am okay with it. Maybe she will see that I am different." Duncan was empathetic and told James to take it slow.

"Now tell me about Roxanne, what was she like." James laughed and said that he thought Duncan would like Roxanne. From what he saw and what Cassandra said she was fun and full of energy. James talked a bit longer with Duncan and said that he would see him in a few weeks once he completed some business in Toronto.

I wanted to check James out online but there was also a part of me that didn't. I didn't want to influence whatever would come to me in a dream, so I decided not to. He said he built up quite an empire. Did I want to know just how big it was? Yes, of course, I did but I pushed down my curiosity and got ready for bed. It must have been the walk yesterday afternoon because I slept like a log. I gave Christelle a call the next morning to see how she was doing. She was getting over a nasty cold and needed to be careful because she could easily get pneumonia having had it a few times. She had another heart surgery a couple of years ago and I was very worried about her. I told her that I had lots I wanted to talk to her about but for now I just wanted her to get better. It was very important to me that she get better. I couldn't lose my best friend.

Later in the day my phone rang. I was surprised to hear James's voice. I asked him how his flight was, and he said it was fine. We talked for a little bit and then I said I had to go. Some of the seniors wanted to discuss some issues they were having with their units with the manager of the building, and they wanted me to be there. I felt it was the owner's not wanting to invest any money to keep the building in proper shape. He said he would give me a call in a few days because he was leaving for Scotland shortly. I asked if he was going to be there long.

"Not too long. I miss my aunts and uncles and my cousins, but I also have businesses there to run. I will be back in a couple of months or so, maybe sooner. I've made progress on buying the land I looked at, but the review process is going to take several months so I am using the opportunity to go and visit my family. I will give you a call when I am back in the country again. Take care."

I went down to the lobby and met the other seniors. We went into the manager's office and gave him the list of the problems that needed dealing with. Fortunately, I didn't have any in mine. My unit was the largest one in the building. The living room and bedrooms were large for a condo and the balconies on the top floor were all large enough to put a full-size patio table and chairs and still have room to walk around. It was one of the things that helped me to decide to buy the unit. Mr. Bradley was not a very likable man at the best of times and today he was in a very surly mood.

"Well, I can tell you that I won't be the one that will have to deal with any of your complaints for very much longer. You can take all of them up with the new manager who will be starting here in a few weeks. The building is in the process of being bought by another company and it is going through the paperwork to be finalized. It all came about quite suddenly, and I suspect that you will be getting a letter in a few weeks telling you about the changes. I will take your complaints and put them in the office for the new manager. I will be staying on until he arrives, but I've been instructed to only handle emergencies at this time until the sale is finalized. I want to say that I'm sorry that things have not been going well here but I was under strict instructions from the previous owners not to spend a lot of money on the place. They were not looking to make a go of this building and they wouldn't allow me to spend money on repairs if they weren't absolutely necessary. It was mostly a tax write-off for them. I am sure you will all be happy to see me go but I wanted you to know that it wasn't my fault. I regret how I have come across to some of you, but it really bothered me having to lie to all of you and I just couldn't look any of you in the eye." Everyone looked at one another and felt sorry for Mr. Bradley. They understood now why he was always walking around looking cross. I felt that something had to be said.

"Mr. Bradley, you should have told us what sort of position you were in. We would have understood and not felt the need to take it out on you. Now that we know, we wish you all the best and we hope that you will find another position somewhere where you will be happy." After hearing what I had to say he looked up and I think for the very first time, I saw him smile.

"You will be happy then to hear that I do have another job lined up. It won't take effect for several months perhaps even as much as a year, but the new owner has graciously offered me a generous severance package until the new job with his company starts. It has been a long time since I have had a nice long vacation and I plan to go and see my kids and grandkids out on the coast and stay with them until the new job starts." Everyone left and went back to their units. I asked if anyone was up for a good long walk, and a few were interested. I went up and changed into my work out gear and went back to the lobby. We did four brisk kilometers that afternoon. It was a great walk and by the time we got back everyone was ready to relax.

I gave my son a call to see if my granddaughter was up to having a video chat. Unfortunately, he said, she was over at a friend's place for the afternoon, but he would get her to call when she came in. I talked with Ross for a little bit. He was never one to talk much on the phone. I asked how his job was going and how Lindsay was doing. All was well he said but they were getting a lot of rain at night, and it was warmer than usual during the day. It was only April and already the heat was setting in. School was going to be finished for the year at the end of June and he was wondering if I wanted to go and visit for a few weeks. I had no plans for the beginning of July, so I agreed. They generally went away on a family vacation for ten days or so later on so going at the beginning of July would work best. He was going to talk to Lindsay and make sure she had nothing going on and he would get back to me.

It had been almost a year since I saw them. Ayleen was now six, going on seven, and she was quite her own person. Full of energy for her age and very sure of herself. Not in a spoiled way, just the cutest way possible for her to be. She was very smart for her age and had in fact been like that ever since she could talk. I was so looking forward to seeing them in person. I cleaned up my condo and then decided to give Janet a call. We texted each other almost every day but I hadn't talked to her on the phone in a few weeks. I never told Janet anything about meeting James in texts, but I did tell her about the dream and the few things that happened in the dream. I caught her when she was home, and her husband Wade was out of town for a few days. So, she had lots of time to talk. I told her about meeting James.

"Oh my God are you kidding me. You must be clairvoyant or something. How could you possibly have known this was going to happen? I don't even know where to start in asking questions, so start at the beginning and tell me everything." I told her how I was having coffee with Roxie, and I was telling Roxie about the dream and hadn't gotten too far into some of the details when in walked this guy with curly brown hair and green eyes and he asked to sit at our table because the place was full.

"I'm telling you I just about passed out. I couldn't say anything, but thankfully Roxie started the conversation. When I heard his Scottish accent I thought no, this can't be and then when Roxie introduced us, and he said his name was James, I'm telling you Janet I just about peed my pants." I went on to tell her about meeting him for coffee every day and then going out for dinner. We talked about him, and I mentioned what I learned about him through questions.

"He is very nice and very much a gentleman. He said he wanted to see me again when he came back but I didn't want to mislead him and had to be honest with him." Janet sounded disappointed and groaned.

“What on earth did you say. He sounds perfect why wouldn’t you want to see him again.” I smiled but it was a nice feeling to know she cared.

“I told him that I wasn’t interested in a romantic relationship. If he wanted to be friends, I would like that very much. He was relieved I think because he said that he wasn’t interested in a romantic relationship either. So, we are going to be friends and he said he would call me when he came back into the country which would be around mid-June.” I am not sure whether Janet agreed with my approach, but I knew she only wanted me to be happy.

Janet and I reconnected after my Dad passed away. We went to grade school and high school together but after high school her family moved to Sudbury. We had a bit of a falling out in high school and drifted apart. Years later, when my parents passed away, we reconnected. She wanted to talk about what happened in the past, but I said that the past was the past, leave it there. She said she missed me a lot and thought of me often and I said I missed her too. Janet emailed me some pictures of her and her two kids who were all grown up and her husband and the grandkids. When I saw the picture of her, I told her if she had walked up to me on the street, I would not have recognized her. She told me more about her life and how she met Wade, who just happened to be of Scottish heritage. We both laughed at that. From that day on we texted each other almost every day, even if it was just to say hi or good morning. I was so happy to have her back in my life especially prior to my ex passing away.

Life for me went on as it usually did with my days filled with going to the gym each morning, long walks with the seniors and having a spa day every two weeks. I took a self-defense course many years ago and every six months or so would go back for a refresher course and I was due to go back soon. It was now the end of April and, as Mr. Bradley indicated, we received letters from the new owner of the building. It was a corporation that now owned the building, and we were all assured that the building would be fixed, and all outstanding issues would be dealt with immediately. We were informed that the new manager was Mr. Patrick O'Leary and that he would introduce himself personally to each of the condo owners.

Weeks passed, and I'd been contemplating for some time about getting back to some of my hobbies again. I went to several paint nites over the next few weeks because I wanted to learn some new things. I wasn't really interested in taking an art class because I didn't want to start at the very beginning. I found someone through the paint nite sessions who would show me how to do certain things like clouds or different motions in water and I was happy with that and to pay her fee. But for now, I enjoyed seeing what I could do and most of the time I was happy with how things turned out. My daughter in law's birthday was coming up so I sent Lindsay off something for her birthday and a card and then started to box up my stained-glass stuff as Roxie was going to allow me to do some work out at her place.

Living in a condo it wasn't possible to do any stained glass, but I had a few things that I really wanted to do. When I had those completed over the next several days, I sold all my equipment to someone who was just starting out doing stained glass. I got her name from the place where I took my lessons and was happy to sell it to her. One afternoon, in late May, there was a knock at my door. I looked to see that it was Mr. Bradley, and he had another gentleman with him. I opened the door and asked them to come in.

"Afternoon Cassandra I'm just taking Mr. O'Leary around and introducing him to all of the folks. Seeing as how you are on the top floor; you are the last for me to introduce him to." Mr. O'Leary appeared to be in his mid-forties I thought. I asked him if he was familiar with managing a building such as this.

"Yes, ma'am I am. I managed a larger building in Toronto but moved out here for this job. My wife and I always wanted to live out west, so this was an opportunity we couldn't pass up." I asked him when he was going to be able to start doing some of the repairs like the painting and plumbing.

"Well ma'am I can do some painting, but the owner has actually asked me to bring in professional trades to bring the building back to a proper state and make sure that all of the condo owners were well taken care of. My job, for right now, is to get in the proper people and then ensure the building runs smoothly from then on. Oh, and something else I should inform you about as well, which I told all the other condo owners, the new owner has said that he will not be accepting any further HOA fees until further notice. He said that because the building was not being kept in a good state of repair, he was going to refund HOA fees from the time the previous owner took over from the original owner." I thought that was wonderful especially for the others as they were all on fixed incomes. But I wondered how the new owner was going to pay for any further upkeep of the building.

"Are we going to know who the new owner is? How are things going to get done if there are no fees to help pay for them?"

"Not to worry ma'am, the new owner I don't know personally; all I know is that the company that owns this building now is a numbered company from what I understand. I have only dealt with the human resources person who has assured me that everything will be taken care of. I guess the company must be doing well to make all the repairs, which are many and to no fault of Mr. Bradley here but the company, as I have been told, did not feel it was the fault of the condo owners to foot the bill for any repairs."

Well now I was really curious, and my gut was telling me who I thought the new owner was. I mentioned to James that the building had fallen into disrepair since the current owners took over from the original owner. I also mentioned that the current owner raised the HOA fees and some of the seniors were having a hard time financially. I had a feeling that it was James who bought the building but couldn't figure out why he would do such a thing. It didn't upset me that he did, in fact it was a very nice thing for him to have done. I wasn't hurting financially like some of them were and with the refund of the HOA fees for them was going to be a very good thing and that made me happy.

Repairs started taking place throughout the building over the coming weeks. It was starting to look wonderful again. The seniors were feeling so much better and got out more, which was also a good thing. I started to think about what I was going to do. Even though I'd only been in this condo for a little over a year, I stayed here largely because I was concerned about all of them, and I felt like I was their voice. This condo was quiet compared to some of the others I lived in, but now I knew they were going to be well looked after, I could move now if I wanted. I liked the area a lot, but I wasn't sure if I wanted to stay in a condo. There were some very nice homes in the area, but they were all too big for me. I loved the quietness of living in my own home without having neighbours below me. I missed seeing wildlife coming through and listening to the birds but owning another home, well, I wasn't sure I wanted that again.

It was getting late in the day, but it was staying light out later now, and it was a really nice day, so I decided to go for a long walk. Whenever I walked alone it was always a good opportunity for me to mull things over about what I was going to do with the rest of my life or sort out any problems I was having. I wasn't having many problems these days, but I was trying to sort out if I wanted to stay living at the condo or move on to a place of my own again. I decided to take a detour and walk through the various subdivisions in my area. The homes were very beautiful and some of them were more like mansions.

The road kept going through treed areas and it was so pretty, but I was starting to get tired, and I still had to walk back. The road finally ended and there was a large bush area that did not seem to be part of the subdivision. This would really be a pretty place to put a nice big house, but it didn't have any sign saying it was for sale. I got back to my place quite tired and had an early night. The following week was spent cleaning, running errands, and going for a spa treatment. Days went by and more and more repairs were being made to the building and I heard there was even a proposed new building being built on the other side of the grounds.

The following morning, I went to see Mr. O'Leary and asked about the new building. We went into his office, and he showed me the plans for the new building which was going to back up onto the treed area and the balconies would all be facing at the back. I was thinking maybe I would buy one of the new ones but still wasn't sure if I wanted to be in a condo. The building was going to be six stories and very modern. Mr. O'Leary showed me some concept floor plans for the top floor, and I thought it might be nice. I mentioned that I might be interested in one of the new units but asked if I could work with the architect to make mine a little bigger and a layout that I would be happy with.

"When do you think they will be ready. Are there more detailed plans I could look at." Mr. O'Leary didn't have anything more than some general floor plans. He said that some of them could change depending on what the owner wanted.

"They might be turning the whole top floor into much larger units but that is just a rumour I heard. I don't know if that is a fact or not. I have a feeling it isn't true because they want these kept for seniors and I am doubtful that anyone could afford the larger units. But I will give you the name of the architect so you can talk with him when you want." I went back up to my unit and had a quiet evening in. I woke in the middle of the night with yet another dream about James and slept restlessly the rest of the night.

I got up the next morning and ate breakfast and then I needed to work off the nervousness that the dream was giving me, so I did a very challenging hike. When I got back, I had a salad and sat on my balcony looking at the construction for the new building going up across the way. It certainly didn't take them long to get the foundation put in. I talked to Ross about moving and he asked why move to one that was across the field. It had me rethinking so I decided not to look at doing that. I spent the rest of the day cleaning up my condo, looking over things that I could toss out. I took a quick shower and decided to go out for dinner for a change. It was now the middle of June and a Friday night, and I asked Roxie if she wanted to join me, but she was watching her grandsons for the night. I envied her, I wished my son lived closer, but they loved where they were, and Ayleen made lots of friends at school. So, I was going to dinner by myself.

I got a text from James while I was getting ready to go and it was just to say hi and how were things going. I responded that things were fine and that I knew what he'd done about buying the building. We texted back and forth about how things were going and then I told him I was off to dinner at the restaurant nearby and would text another day. It was a beautiful June evening and I put on a pair of dressy navy pants and a newly bought chiffon blouse in shades of blue and went out. It was staying light now longer and longer. I rarely went to dinner at the restaurant so when Jason saw me, he was surprised to see me walk through the door.

"Cassandra, what a nice surprise to see you this evening. Would you like your usual table?" I said yes and followed him to the private seating area. I was amazed to see that they replaced the clear glass wall with a beautiful frosted blue glass. It looked incredible. It was quiet for a Friday night, which was unusual.

"Jason when did you replace the glass? This looks really nice, and I love the colour too." It was a very pretty royal blue that offered enough light for those in the main area during the day but privacy for those in the private area and at night it was especially pretty. Just as Jason was about to answer James walked in.

"Hi, mind if I join you for dinner?" I was surprised to see him but happy too. We hugged, kissed, and sat down.

"I just texted with you, why didn't you tell me you were back? I didn't think you would be back for a few more weeks." He sat down and ordered a drink and asked me if I wanted anything. I said no that I was fine with water.

"Well, I was going to tell you, but you said you were heading out the door in your text, so I thought I would show up and hope you wouldn't mind." I didn't mind and told him so. He asked me if I liked the new glass, and I said I did and then I realized that he must have had something to do with it.

"Did you put that in?" He admitted that he did. He spoke to Jason about it weeks ago and said that he would provide the glass free of charge and have it installed if Jason was agreeable. Apparently, there were other people who didn't liked the plain glass wall either.

"This is a new colour my glass company has come up with. Do you like it? What do you think of it being frosted and the rippled glass? That was a suggestion I had and fortunately it worked out well." I said I loved it, and it was so amazing to look at, especially in the evening. We ordered our meal and talked endlessly about his trip.

"Okay, so now tell me why you bought my condo building? It was a very nice thing to do, and the seniors are so happy now and the fact that you are not charging HOA fees and giving refunds, James, it is very generous of you, but I have to ask why?"

"I bought the condo building because I looked into it right after you said that it was not being run properly and saw that the people who owned it were less than honest and I don't like that, so I bought it. They were more than happy to sell, and I made it worth their while. There is enough property attached to the sale that I was able to get clearance from the municipality to build an additional building or two. I don't like seeing people, and especially seniors, being taken advantage of and who, for the most part, are on fixed incomes." I was impressed even more than I already was. James was an honourable man and generous as well.

"Well James I must say that I am very impressed, very impressed." He said he meant every word. His Dad was successful but not quite to his extent. But his Dad made it a point to always help out the community. He impressed upon him at a very early age that while it is a great thing to amass a great amount of money, it has little value if you have no value of yourself or your community. James always remembered that and promised himself that he would live up to that standard. We ate and laughed and discussed more what we'd been doing since we last saw each other.

"I did some stained-glass pieces, which I am happy to say, look not too bad. I sold all my equipment to someone who is newly starting the hobby. The pieces are sitting in my spare room at the moment and I'm hoping my son will like them so much he will want to put them in his home." I mentioned that someone gave me painting tips and I was going to get doing some of that over the next while.

"I am going to visit my son and his family at the beginning of July for a few weeks and then I will see what the fall will bring. I've been mulling over the idea of buying one of the new units in the new building, but I decided that if I'm going to move it will be to another place." James didn't want to ask where she was planning to move to in case it was out of the province.

"Have you got any plans for tomorrow? If not, I would like to show you something and I would like your thoughts on it. So, if you are not busy, I can pick you up around 11:00 tomorrow morning." I had no plans for the next day other than to video chat with Ayleen in the afternoon hopefully. I said as much to James, and he promised that he would have me back in lots of time to do that. It was getting late, and I was tired from my work out at the gym plus all the walking I did today.

"I am sorry, but I am going to have to make it an early night. I did a lot today and I am getting tired, I hope you don't mind." I asked Jason for my bill, but James said he would take care of it. I wanted to argue but he wouldn't hear of it. I said it was nice to have him back and I would see him tomorrow. I left before Jason brought the bill to the table. Jason opened the door for me and then took the bill in to James.

"She's a very nice woman and I would not like to see her get hurt." James looked at Jason a bit surprised but admired the fact that he was concerned about Cassandra.

"Not to worry, I like her a lot too and we are just good friends. I promise you I would never hurt her. That is something you will never have to worry about." The two shook hands and James paid the bill and went out to his car. He liked the idea that Jason was looking out for Cassandra. He was hoping that Cassandra would be happy that he was going to buy property in the area and that they could spend more time together. Admittedly he had an ulterior motive for doing it but if it didn't work out his way, he was still looking forward to being closer to her and being a friend.

When I got home, I was so tired. I was yawning the whole way from the restaurant. I put on my pjs, took off my makeup and I don't think my head even hit the pillow before I was asleep. I couldn't even recall dreaming which was really unusual. The next morning, I called Janet to see what was new with her.

"Nothing much, doing the same things. Wade is going out of town next week he thinks, for the entire week and possibly a bit more and my daughter is busy with work and my daughter in law and the boys are going on vacation, so I am on my own. What are you up to these days? Have you heard from James lately?"

I told her that he showed up unexpectedly last night at the restaurant where I was having dinner and that he bought my condo building and all the things that were happening with it. I also mentioned the new building that was going up and I was thinking of getting a new unit in the new building but decided against it. Janet asked why and I said because it didn't make any sense to move several hundred yards. I let her know that I was going to have to make our call short because James was coming by to take me out to show me something he was looking at buying and wanted my opinion.

"Well, that's interesting. What do you think he wants your opinion on?" I wasn't sure, but I would let her know when I found out. I asked her if she would like to come and visit for a few days if she could get the time off work. She would talk to her boss and Wade about it and let me know. We agreed to speak later that night.

I had my coffee and some toast and got dressed. I was going to try to squeeze in a walk, but Janet and I talked for a while and there was not enough time now. James texted me that he just pulled up, so I went down to meet him. He was driving a different car this time. My jaw dropped when I saw that he was driving a dark grey sports car which was a car that I absolutely loved. This was the car that I always wanted to be driven in. It was on my bucket list of things I wanted to do but didn't think would ever happen. He got out and opened my door for me and I got in the car and buckled up. I was tempted to get into the back and then tell him about my bucket list wish but decided against it. He wouldn't tell me where we were going when I asked him. He drove out and started to drive up into the exclusive subdivision. I didn't recall seeing any of the homes up for sale. It wasn't until James drove up to the end that I realized what he wanted my opinion on.

"What do you think of this property?" The property was lovely, and I said as much but I didn't realize it was for sale. I didn't know why he wanted my opinion on it, and I asked him why.

"I'm glad you like it because I bought it last week and there is a crew coming in a couple of days to start clearing some of the trees. The reason I asked you to have a look at it is because you and I are friends and I'm new to this area and I wanted to know if you knew anything about this particular spot. It isn't a serviced lot, but they have water and sewer lines in the subdivision so I'm going to have them run here. What would you say to taking a walk around and looking it over?"

We got out of the car and walked around the property a bit. It was really too big to walk the whole thing in the short amount of time we had. He knew I had to get back to video chat with Ayleen. I had no idea just how much property there was attached to the sale, but James said that in total it was six hundred and fifty acres. Two hundred acres went back to a large ravine and that was one of the property lines. There were two hundred acres on either side and fifty to the front. The property on the other side of the ravine was a reserve area so nobody would be building back there. It was mostly birch with some poplar and the odd oak tree. There were spruce near the back and around almost the entire perimeter of the property. I pointed out to him a bunch of Saskatoon bushes and what looked like a few crabapple trees but suggested he get someone in who knew fruit trees to say which it was. Depending on where he was looking to build his house, he would have to clear out a fair amount trees, but I told him that he could use the downed trees as firewood in the winter. With the spruce trees located where they were he would have year-round privacy not that there were any other homes close by.

"It's a beautiful spot James but where are you thinking of putting your house. You are at the end of the subdivision, so you don't have a neighbor close which gives you privacy but sometimes the winters here can be bad, and we can get a lot of snow. How far back are you looking at putting the house."

He said he took that into consideration but wasn't overly concerned about it. He was looking at setting the house back some distance from the road and showed me approximately where the house would go. It was quite a distance from the end of the subdivision road. He was going to build a caretaker's cottage and thought that would be best closer to the front entrance. The driveway was going to be long, but he would have the right equipment to ensure the road was cleared properly and it would be paved so it would make it easier to keep clean.

"What sort of house are you looking at building. The homes in this area are quite large and I think you would have to build something similar. Are you planning to have a pool? You would probably need to discuss all of this with whomever you are going to get to build your house." I asked him if he had a contractor yet to which he said no. He did have an architect in Toronto that was going to do up the plans in accordance with the local building code of course but a contractor he had not chosen as yet. I remembered seeing a young contractor on tv once and mentioned to James that I believed he lived in the Toronto area. He came across on the show as someone who was very knowledgeable about his trade and that he now had his own company and hired veterans as much as possible. James said he liked that idea and asked me the name of the guy and said he would look into him later on. But I still wasn't sure why he was building a home in this area and asked why.

"Well, I live about five months of the year in Canada, and I decided that I would like to have a home here instead of a suite at a hotel. I have a penthouse in Toronto when I am there but here, I have been living out of hotel suites and it can get a little old after a while. Since I am starting up companies here, I want to have a home. I have a pretty large estate in Scotland where I have staff that look after the place, but I also plan to have staff here as well, such as a housekeeper, chef and I'll have a caretaker who can look after the maintenance of the place. I have two different styles I am looking at, but I can bring over the plans and show you and you can give me your opinion."

I said that I would love to look at the plans but warned him that I'm the type of person who always likes to make changes to something that is already down on paper. It was something I always used to do dreaming of someday being able to build my dream home. I told him I was a big fan of Queen Anne style homes. I just loved wraparound porches, turrets, and wood fireplaces.

"I know wood fireplaces are not very environmentally friendly but with the winters we get it is always nice to have at least one in case of a power outage. I have often pictured decorating the porches for Christmas and I'm rambling a bit, sorry about that." He had a nice smile.

"Don't be silly it is nice to hear what you have always dreamed of; we are friends remember and if you can't share your dreams with friends who can you share them with. It's too bad you were never able to get that dream home. I think you would like my estate in

Scotland. It's a bit more traditional style than a Queen Anne I'm afraid. My Dad bought the estate when he started his own business. The estate was going into disrepair, so he got it for a very good price. My Mum loved the place as a child and she used to go for long walks on the estate when she was older, with permission of course. My Dad actually proposed to her at their special spot on the estate. He updated it and when he married my Mum, and they moved in. My Dad was fifteen years older than my Mum. She had me when she was nineteen and they had planned to have more children but each time she miscarried. She was having all sorts of female problems and had to have a hysterectomy at age twenty-five. I still live at the estate today or at least whenever I am back in Scotland. When I'm not there we let wedding planners use it for wedding photos. There are certain areas that are off limits though. We get lots of requests for weddings and it is quite picturesque. I think you would like it. You should come over with me sometime and I can show you my home." There was a very long silence after what he said. We only knew each other for such a short time. I didn't think it would be appropriate for me to fly to Scotland even though we were becoming good friends.

"You could ask Roxanne if she wanted to come along. I would love to show both my new friends my Scotland. I'd also like to ask if you and Roxanne would like to come to a gala in Toronto. It's one that I chair, and I would like to have you as my plus one. The gala is in August." James thought asking Roxanne to come along would make it easier for Cassandra to accept both trips.

"Can I think about it. I'm going to have my friend Janet out for a visit shortly and then I have the trip planned to visit my son which I just realized I have not even booked which is not at all like me." He said of course he completely understood me needing time to think about it. We arrived back at my place, and I was going to ask him up but given what we just talked about I thought maybe another time. Fortunately, I didn't have to come up with an excuse because his phone rang before I had a chance to say anything. He asked me to hang on a second. When he was done with his call, he said that he was going to have to go back to Toronto. Something came up that needed his urgent attention. He said he would call me when he was back, and we could talk more, and he could show me the plans.

I went up to my condo and tried to remember if this was part of the dream. I remembered something about going to Scotland, but I wasn't sure where in the dream it happened. It was all so confusing. I had my video chat with Ayleen which didn't last very long because she was going to a friend's house. I really needed to talk to Christelle, but I wasn't sure if she was over her cold, and I didn't like to get into things where I needed her advice when she wasn't well. I did call Roxie though and mentioned to her about the invitation to

Scotland and to the gala in Toronto. While she eagerly said yes to both, she said that it wouldn't be possible for her to go to Scotland until the beginning or middle of September. I told her I still wasn't sure if it was right to go given we were just new friends but that I would think about it.

I should probably have told James that I went to Scotland once with Janet and her husband and would make sure that I let him know the next time we spoke. I had my passport even before going to Scotland because I talked to the ladies about the five of us taking a trip to the Turks and Caicos. It was a trip that I had yet another dream about and it was something that I wanted to do and treat the ladies to thank them for sticking by me and being very supportive. At the time, I couldn't afford to do any such thing but when I won the money, it was possible. So many things had gone on from then until this point, and it wasn't possible to think seriously about it until now. It might not be all that I fantasized about, but I was hoping to arrange it for April of the following year if everything worked out.

Four of us were retired but Janet still worked, and it had to be done well enough in advance for her to take the time off. I stopped by a travel agent's office a year ago to pick up some travel info on the Turks and Caicos and the rentals that were available. They of course wanted to go over everything with me, but I said right now I was just at the thinking stage. They wanted my number, so they could follow up, but I didn't want to be hounded and politely refused to give it. I took the brochures home and put them on my coffee table and forgot to look at them again. I was going to call Janet back to see if she was going to be able to come for a visit, but she must have read my mind. When I picked up the phone she was on the other end.

"My goodness it didn't even ring. How are you? I have been thinking about your invitation and I would love to come for a few days. Wade's trip was changed to the second last week of June. So, if you still want me to come I can be there on the 20th?" I was thrilled she was coming.

"I know you have seen pictures of my new place, so I will be happy to have you here and see what you think. I'm still thinking about a move, but it is still at the thinking stage." We talked for another half hour or so. She said that she would text me the flight arrangements.

"I can't wait to come and see your new place. Is there any chance that I will get to meet James, your new friend?" I told her I wasn't sure. We went out that morning to look at some property he bought and was going to build a house on, but he got an urgent call and had to return to Toronto. I wasn't sure when he would be back. I told her I was paying for her trip and gave her my credit card info. She argued with me, but I insisted.

I was so looking forward to seeing Janet again and I wanted her to see that I was doing fine. Now that Janet was coming, I called Roxie back to see if she wanted to get together, maybe go for dinner at Jason's. She said she was free on Wednesday night when Janet would be here and would love to go for dinner. I was busy for the next few days cleaning and making sure that Janet's room was ready. I took the stained-glass pieces off the bed and put them in the closet in my room. When I bought the condo, I bought all new furniture and new beds. When I sold the house, and moved to the first condo, it was a stop gap, and I took furniture with me until I could figure out where I wanted to live.

When I bought this condo, I donated all the contents that I took from the house. The bedrooms in the new condo were large enough to put in king beds in each room and each bedroom had its own ensuite. I thought that I would get some new bedding for Janet. I knew her favourite colour was yellow, so I hit one of the big box stores that week and picked up the perfect bedding ensemble. I knew she would love it. The guest room was ready for her arrival on the 20th. The day before Janet was going to arrive, I went for a good long walk and spent some time with some of the other seniors. The change in them was remarkable now that things were improving in the building. They were all so much happier. I told them that I was having company this week and would not be doing our usual walks but hoped that they would keep it going.

I took the time in those few days prior to her coming to freeze a couple of casseroles. I knew we would be going out often, but I wanted us to have nights in as well. I spent the rest of the afternoon freshening up the rest of my condo. Janet's plane was going to be in late morning the next day. I was so excited the next morning to get to the airport I was an hour early. Fortunate for me that I did go early because her plane actually arrived half an hour early. I saw her coming down the stairs and ran to meet her.

"Oh, I am so glad to see you. How was your flight? Did Wade get away okay yesterday? Let's get your luggage and we'll head back to my place. Have you had anything to eat, maybe we could stop for a bite at the restaurant by my place for a quick something." She was going to be staying for seven days and I was happy about that. She brought only one piece of luggage, but it was a large piece.

"I wasn't sure what we might be doing or where we might be going so, I packed for just about anything. I even packed some workout clothes and runners because I know you said you do a lot of walking and go to the gym. My goodness you have lost weight. Are you ok?" Just then her luggage came down the chute and she grabbed it. I said we could talk more when we got in the car and driving back to my place. I told her she looked great, and it was so nice to have her here.

“You look wonderful Cassandra. You’ve lost a lot of weight from the last time I saw you but boy oh boy you look in great shape. I know you have been doing a lot of walking and going to the gym but surely you didn’t get that body by just walking alone.” I first of all thanked her for the compliment and I thanked her for not calling me Cassie. Of course, when we were younger that is what I went by but when I got older and moved out west, I went by my full name. I told her that I had been working with a personal trainer and I told her that I was working with weights and really toned myself up, but she didn’t know that I had a bit of cosmetic surgery done to get rid of some loose skin and flab around my stomach. It wasn’t a tummy tuck as much as it was removing excess flab that no amount of working out would have gotten rid of. I had that done after we got back from Scotland. I didn’t want to tell her about the self-defense courses I’d been going to because I didn’t want her to worry. She was satisfied that it was all due to hard work.

I was pointing out the different things as we were going by like the first ever pumper in the province and other things of note. It wasn’t too long before I was pulling into the parking lot of the restaurant. Jason saw me coming in the door and I introduced him to Janet. He showed us to my favourite table and gave us menus and brought some water. Janet commented on the blue frosted glass, and I told her that James arranged to replace the clear glass with this one at no cost to the owner of the restaurant. I said he didn't like the clear glass wall and I wasn't really a fan of it either, so he arranged for this to be put in.

"Wow that's impressive. So, when did you say he would be back in town and that I could meet him." I knew she was doing this out of concern for me, but we laughed. She knew about things in my marriage and the family situation, but I could never tell her everything. Maybe over the next few days I could do so but maybe not. We ordered our food and talked and talked. We were going to stay in that night and have dinner at home. I pulled out one of the frozen casseroles before I left for the airport. Lunch was great and after the bill was paid, we went over to my condo.

"I love the area and the condo building looks quite nice." The building had six floors and I lived on the top floor on the right side of the building. When I opened the door and showed Janet in, she was surprised.

"Oh, my goodness this is beautiful. You've done a great job on decorating. I love all the new furniture too. It is very you." I showed her into her room, and she burst out laughing.

"My favourite colour. I love the bedding and I love the king-sized bed. The condo is much bigger than it looks from the outside. This is really a nice place. I am so happy that you are here." I left her to unpack her things and I got out some red wine and we sat on the couch and talked. I poured us each a glass of wine.

She really liked the place, and I was happy. It was a nice afternoon and we decided to sit out on the balcony. She commented that it was a larger balcony than most you see on apartment buildings or condos which I said was one of the reasons I liked the place and bought it. We sat catching up on what was new in her life, and I let her know that Roxie was going to meet us at the same restaurant we had lunch at on Wednesday night for dinner. She was looking forward to meeting Roxie. It started to rain a bit, so we went back in. She noticed the travel brochures on the coffee table.

"Are you still thinking about going to the Turks and Caicos?" I said that I was, but I wanted to see if she would be able to get time off in April. She didn't think it would be a problem, so I called Christelle to see if she still wanted to go and she said absolutely. I got in touch with Judy, and she said she was good to go too. I let each of them know that I wasn't going to do anything until at least September or October, so we still had time to talk things over but to make sure they locked down the dates.

Janet was tired. She was yawning a fair bit. I put the casserole in the oven and set the table. It only took forty-five minutes to cook so she could get to bed early. I showed her the stained-glass pieces I did, and she loved them. She wanted to know what I was going to do with them, and I told her I wasn't sure just yet. If I moved into the new place, I might be able to work with the contractor to install them as a transom over the doors. She thought that was a great idea.

Dinner finished, and dishes washed and put away we both got our pjs on and sat to talk. My phone started to buzz. It was a text from James saying he was going to be back in town on Wednesday. I texted back saying my school friend Janet was in for a visit and that Roxie, Janet and I were going to go for dinner at Jason's on Wednesday night. Janet said that I should invite him and so I did. He said he would love to meet my school friend and to see Roxanne again. He called her Roxanne even though Roxie insisted he call her Roxie. But he said he liked Roxanne, as it reminded him of his Mum whose middle name was Roxanne, so she couldn't argue with that.

We got up the next morning and had coffee and cereal on the balcony. We decided to go for a walk and then we would go and do some shopping. She'd never been to the big mall and wanted to go. We only did a quick walk because I knew we would be doing more walking at the mall. I texted Roxie the day before to ask if she wanted to join us. She said she was going to be at her place in the city, and I told her we would be at the mall around 11:00. She said she would meet us at the entrance by the big box store. When we arrived, Roxie was already waiting for us inside. I introduced her to Janet, and it was like the two of them had known one another for years. Janet was wondering what we were wearing for dinner on Wednesday. She brought some dressy pants and wondered if that was ok. I thought about it and said that we should get dressed up. I said that this was going to be my treat and while they tried to argue the point, I was having nothing to do with it. They gave in and we had fun.

We stopped in at one of the nicer women's stores on the top floor and looked at some things. Janet and I were both looking at some really nice dresses. Roxie seldom wore dresses and said she would prefer a nice pant suit and started looking at those. She picked out a really beautiful black silk pant suit with a wide leg and tuxedo lapels. She chose a lovely green silk blouse to try with it. Janet picked out a pretty yellow silk dress with short sleeves and went to the change room. I looked around at some of the dresses but wasn't seeing anything I wanted. The sales lady said that she got some new things but hadn't put them out yet but would bring them out for me to have a look at. She brought out the most beautiful yellow, orange, and red chiffon dress. It had short sleeves and felt like a cloud. I said I would try it on. Janet and Roxie already had their outfits on and were out in the change area waiting for me. I could hear them commenting on each other's outfit. I came out and they both gasped.

"Oh my God that is absolutely stunning on you." They both said it at the same time. They both looked amazing in what they'd chosen too. Roxie looked fabulous and she kept looking at herself in the mirror. Janet always looked great in whatever she wore but she looked like a million dollars in that yellow silk dress. I took care of the purchases, and we went to get new shoes. They wanted to argue about paying for those too, but I said no, it was my treat. Roxie found a pair of green silk pumps very close to the colour of her blouse that would look great. They had a small bow covered in black crystals. The heel was not too high, and she said they were great to walk in.

Janet loved shoes and admitted she could never resist buying them when she went shopping. There was a yellow silk sandal that she was looking at. It had a mix of yellow and chocolate crystals on the straps of the sandal. She looked them over and I thought she was going to try them on, but she put them down. I went over and picked them up. I think she put them down because of the price. They were pretty expensive designer sandals and she said she couldn't let me buy them. She would look around for something else. I said that she was going to get them. Roxie's heels were almost as much.

I wasn't sure what I was going to get. I was very leery of wearing heels, but I thought I would at least give them a try as long as they weren't too high. I walked over and saw an orange pair of open toed pumps with yellow and red crystals. The heel was about two and a half inches high, so I tried them on. They were very expensive, but I guess when you buy expensive shoes you get a better fit. I showed them to the ladies and they both agreed they would look great with my dress. It was the first time I ever truly splurged on a dress and shoes.

The last stop was at a kiosk that sold crystal jewelry. Roxie and I went in once before and jokingly picked out pieces we liked. Janet's eyes popped when she looked around. I knew Roxie liked the black and white necklace and earrings. I was looking for something that I knew would go with mine and picked out white crystals shaped stars. There were three across the front and the drop earrings had one each. It was perfect. Janet was looking at a necklace with a large yellow crystal centre stone and smaller chocolate-coloured ones around it and smaller yellow and chocolate crystals along the rope of the necklace. I knew she had a problem with certain types of metals but the earrings for all of us were in twenty-four carat gold, so I was sure there wouldn't be a problem. The earrings with her set were studs with a large yellow crystal surrounded by chocolate crystals. Neither of them was going to argue about me paying because they knew it was pointless.

We decided to have lunch in the mall for which Roxie said she was paying. Janet wanted to pay half, but Roxie said no, she was on vacation, and she wouldn't hear of her paying. We laughed a lot during lunch, and I was ever so pleased that they both got along. We talked about the trip next April. Roxie said she would definitely be back from down south but wouldn't bother unpacking her luggage. We laughed and laughed. I said that I should text James and let him know we were getting dressed up for dinner. He replied that he appreciated the heads up. I asked Janet if she wanted to look around a bit more. Roxie said she had to get back home as her grandsons were stopping by after school. She thanked me ever so much for the nice things and was looking forward to Wednesday night.

"And of course, meeting that gorgeous James again. Janet wait till you see him. He's an absolute dreamboat." She kissed us goodbye and left.

We walked around the mall for about another hour. Janet couldn't believe how big it was. She admitted she was getting a bit tired and wanted to know if we could go back to my place and relax for a bit. We drove back and got home late afternoon. We ate a fairly large lunch so neither one of us was very hungry. We decided to have a sandwich for dinner. We sat in front of the tv and watched a couple of shows before heading off to bed. Next morning, we had our usual coffee on the balcony, but it was only toast this morning. I brought out some of my Saskatoon jam which Janet loved. We went out for a walk, and I took her into the subdivision where James bought the property.

"Wow this is a huge piece of land. Look at all the trees and oh my goodness there is a deer." There were actually a few of them but they took off as soon as they spotted us. I showed her where I thought James was going to put his house and we looked all around. There were a lot of trees already down, but I mentioned he was going to keep what came down to burn in his fireplace.

"Have you seen what kind of a house he is going to build. I can only imagine what it is going to look like. All of the homes in here must be extremely expensive." I agreed with her. We speculated on what they cost but could only guess that they were in the millions. We walked back to my condo, and I introduced Janet to some of the seniors who were in the lobby when we arrived. We talked with them for a while before going back up to my place.

"I really love it here. You have such a nice place and good neighbours. I am so happy for you. You finally have a good life now."

Janet jumped into the shower while I did a bit of cleaning up. When she got out, I took one. We were meeting Roxie and James at the restaurant at 6:30 tonight. We did our hair, put on our makeup, and got our new frocks on. We looked at each other and said we looked great. It was time to leave. I texted Roxie earlier to let her know we were getting ready and would meet her at the restaurant. She responded back that she was already dressed and getting ready to head out.

Janet and I went down to the garage and got in my car and drove over to the restaurant. When we arrived Roxie and James were already there. When we walked in Jason escorted us into the private area. All of the other tables were taken out and there was just our table set for four in the middle of the room. I looked at Jason and asked him what was up with the one table. He said that he thought perhaps I would like to have the room to myself and my guests. He was such a thoughtful person. James stood up as we entered. I introduced Janet, who I must admit giggled a little when she was introduced. Roxie got up too and gave each of us a hug and kiss.

"You ladies look absolutely amazing this evening. I ordered some champagne. I hope that is ok with each of you." My goodness who could resist champagne, even Roxie had a small glass. I asked her when she got here.

"Actually, James called me and said he would pick me up. I have to say I have never been in that kind of sports car before. It was quite a thrill and best of all I get to go home with Prince Charming." I'd never seen Roxie with such a happy look on her face, at least not for a very long time. James made a toast to having great friends and family, a toast that we could all agree on.

I filled Janet in on much of James's info like family and where in Scotland he was from when she first arrived. James brought up that he hired the guy I told him about to build his house and the caretakers house and all the other buildings. He told him to hire as many workers as he would need because he wanted everything done and ready to move in by the end of October. While I thought giving George only a little over three months to build James's enormous house, garage for the house, a caretaker cottage was a big ask, James said he was going to pay him well and would give him a bonus if he met the date. Roxie was unaware that James bought property but winked at me which was her way of letting me know 'told you.'

"James I am not sure if Cassandra mentioned this or not, but my husband has Scottish heritage and so does my Mom. Cassandra actually took my husband and me over about a year after her husband died to thank us for helping her with the funeral." James looked at me with a puzzled look and said that I never mentioned to him that I'd been before even though he knew I had.

Janet and James talked for a long time it seemed. He said he would like to invite them both over to his home in Scotland whenever that could be arranged. He also asked her and Wade to the same gala that he was inviting Roxie and me to. I could hear him asking her whether she worked and what Wade did.

"Wade is retired from the provincial government, but he still works for them a couple of days a week. I work with a company that does copyright work for artificial intelligence but would love to retire. Unfortunately, I don't get a pension through my work, so I have to keep working for quite a while yet. But I would love to retire as all the other ladies are retired and we want to travel and go places." I could tell that James was thinking something and was going to change the subject, but he spoke before I had a chance.

"Are you committed to staying with the company you are with, or would you consider a job change? I ask this because I think I might have something I could offer you. I would not expect you to move, you could work from home mostly, but you would have to make a trip at least once every two weeks to meet with my vice president to go over the policies. I should warn you though I have a lot of companies and holdings and a lot of policies, so you are going to have your hands full. I'm willing to make it more than worth your while. You will have generous benefits and I will personally top up your pension, since you currently don't have one, so that when you are ready to retire you will be going with a full pension from my company. When you are ready to retire, I will need you to train someone or several people in the Toronto office to take over things. It would of course require you to be there during the week, but you can fly home on the weekends. Does that sound like something you might be interested in?"

Janet was speechless and so was I. She didn't know what to say and I could tell that she was really moved by the offer. This was one of the nicest things I'd ever seen anyone do. When she was finally able to say something, she spoke with a nervous voice.

"I will need to think about it and talk to Wade and then to my employer. But I don't see Wade objecting and I only have to give two weeks' notice to my employer, but I still need to talk to them. Is that ok with you?" Of course, James understood and gave Janet his card and said to call him whenever she made up her mind. I could see she was almost in tears, so I said I needed to go to the ladies room and asked her to come. Roxie didn't mind having James to herself. When we got into the ladies room Janet started to cry a bit. I started to laugh.

"You will ruin your mascara, stop crying. I guess I don't have to ask if you are going to take the job. It is a dream job for you, and I know you would be very good at it." She had to text Wade and let him know that she needed to talk to him tomorrow at noon. She was a little shaky when she was texting, which made me laugh a little.

"I think I need some wine; can we order some when we get back. Wow, this is unbelievable, I don't even know what to say. He is really something and Roxie wasn't kidding he is gorgeous. You can't let this guy get away and I can see in your eyes when you look at him, that there is a little bit more than just friends in that look. Wow I am stunned at the job offer." I admitted that I was a bit attracted to him but with my past I wasn't ready to get involved with anyone. It was still too painful to think of giving my heart over to someone again.

"Janet, he is seven years younger than me. What could I possible offer him? I know he has always wanted children and that is never going to happen with me obviously. I want to stay friends for now and see how I feel down the road. If he moves on it won't hurt." Tears dried up, face looking like new, we went back out to our table. I asked Jason on the way through if he would bring a glass of good Cabernet Sauvignon for Janet. He said he would bring one right over. James and Roxie looked like they were deep in conversation, laughing and talking.

"I asked Jason to bring Janet a glass of red wine. She felt after that amazing job offer you gave her she needed it." We all laughed, and Jason brought the wine.

It was a wonderful evening and at 8:00 it was still light out. I asked everyone to come back to my place for coffee and asked James if he wanted to show us his house plans if he had them with him. Given Roxie came with James, she of course couldn't refuse, and she didn't want to. She was having a wonderful time.

We left the restaurant shortly after 8:00 and went over to my place. After parking the car in the underground garage Janet and I went up to the lobby to wait for James and Roxie. They were not long walking through the door. It would be the first time Roxie was in the building and she was commenting on how much she liked it. Neither of them had been in my place so I was a little nervous to have James there. The place was clean of course but still I was a bit nervous. I made the coffee and brought the pot, mugs, cream, and sugar to the coffee table. Everyone grabbed a cup as they came through. James brought up the house plans and I cleared off the dining room table.

James walked over but paused at the travel brochure as he was getting his coffee. He laid out the first set of plans on the table. The house was enormous to say the least, but it was a very traditional looking house, not dissimilar to some of the other houses in the area. There were seven bedrooms and seven ensuite baths with a half bath down by the study. It had a very large dining room for formal occasions, a very large living room with a smaller dining room off the kitchen, which was in my opinion, every chef's dream kitchen, with a medium sized family room off the kitchen. All of the bedrooms were large with walk in closets, but the master bedroom was really big. It was at the back of the house and there was a private balcony that would be overlooking the forest. It was a beautiful design but not my taste.

The next plan he pulled out was a Queen Anne design with a wide wrap around veranda. It was really pretty. This one also had the same features as the other, same style of kitchen, living room, bedrooms but the difference in this one was the balcony off the master suite. It ran almost half the length of the back of the house. There was a wood fireplace in the living area and the family room had a gas fireplace as well as in the master bedroom. The traditional only had one fireplace in the family room. I guess he could have added more but I really liked this one better. He had colour prints of what the front of each house would look like. The traditional was in a really nice grey stone which I liked a lot. The Queen Anne was of course in that orange red schoolhouse brick which I much preferred.

"I didn't know you liked the Queen Anne style James. They are both very beautiful homes and very big. Have you decided which one you like the most." If the truth were known, he said he preferred traditional style as a rule, but he had to admit that when he looked at putting the Queen Anne on his property with all of the trees around it, it had great appeal to him. The fact that Cassandra loved the Queen Anne was a bonus.

“I wasn’t sure to be honest. I had the architect go out and look at the property and he came up with these two possibilities. He did say that he thought the Queen Anne would look perfect with the trees but of course it was my decision to make. I actually sat out there looking at both designs trying to envision what they would look like in all of the seasons, and I have to admit, the architect was right, the Queen Anne looked the best. So, ladies do you think looking at this design, is there anything you would change?” Oh dear, the way the architect had things laid out was for the most part really nice but given the size of the house and the layout of the bedrooms upstairs, I would have added a huge four-season room at the back with glass all around to take in all of the beauty. I would probably make the master a little bit bigger and run the balcony for the master the full length of the sunroom. I mean a house that size, you want to make sure you have a really big walk-in closet, if he decided to resell, and the ensuite bath had to be like going to a spa with a large double shower and rainwater shower heads. I hadn’t realized that I was taking so long to answer, and James was looking at me.

“You’ve redesigned the house haven’t you.” He laughed and asked me what it was I would change. I told him it was more add than change. I suggested the four-season room the full length of the back of the house and the other ladies quickly agreed saying it would be a wonderful place to have a party with the trees in the background. Then I said that I would make the master bedroom bigger and have a really large walk-in closet for future resale and really go all out in the bathroom and run the balcony for the master the full length at the back. James penciled in my ideas and said that he rather liked them. He asked if there was anything else to which I responded no because I thought the rest of the house was very nice the way it was.

"Okay I will pass this along to the architect and if he agrees, get the changes made. I like them a lot and as you say it would be a nice place to have a party and especially at Christmas." Roxie and Janet both expressed their thoughts at that idea. They were already thinking of where the Christmas tree could go. James put the plans away and we sat in the living room having coffee. It was such a wonderful, pleasant night I asked them if they would like to sit on the balcony. We adjusted the chairs, so we could watch the sun go down further in the sky.

"I noticed a travel brochure of the Turks and Caicos on your coffee table Cassandra, are you planning a vacation soon?" Janet went in and got the brochure and showed it to Roxie. Of course, Roxie was delighted to see where we would be going. With each turn of the page, she oohed and aahed at the villas and the water.

"I have been talking to Janet, Roxie, Christelle and Judy about going on a two-week vacation for a long time now. It was always just a fanciful dream but then I won the lottery. A lot of things happened between then and now, but now, it is going to happen. I haven't decided what villa yet, but we are trying to plan it for mid-April of next year. But I'm worried about what they are advertising and whether that is what it actually looks like. If we can choose a couple of options I want to see if I can get current photos of the place, but I have to see what the others think." Roxie was going through the brochure, liking every one that she saw. Janet was much the same. They would have been happy with anything I think. James had his tablet with him, and he pulled it out and searched for something. When he found it, he showed it to me?

"As it just so happens, I own a villa on Turks and Caicos in Grace Bay. It is probably larger than you were looking at, but you are welcome to use it if you want. I won't be going there in April as I have business in Germany with my business partner. Other members of my family use it as well but none of them will be going at that time either, so you are welcome to use it if you like. You can also use my plane to fly you down, although it would probably be best if you could all meet in one location and go from there." He showed me the pictures of his villa, more like a mansion and it was, to say the least, beautiful.

The views were breathtaking, and it had a very large infinity pool and upstairs the balconies were large and looked out onto the ocean. He said that he would arrange for us to have a driver at our service whenever we wanted to go anywhere. He also had a chef and housekeeper that would take care of us. Janet and Roxie took the tablet and were looking through the photos. All I could hear from them were gasps and giggles.

"James the place is gorgeous, but I can't ask you to do that. I have money and I can afford this trip now. I can't really explain why this is something important to me, but I have to pay for this myself. I want to show these ladies how much they mean to me." I wasn't sure what to do. I didn't want to hurt his feelings and refuse but we were friends, new friends and I didn't want this to look like I was taking advantage of him. I think James could sense my dilemma.

"Ok, I understand how you feel, and I don't want to upset you so let me propose this, I will rent the villa to you then, if that will make it easier, but it will be at the price I set, and you can't argue. I insist you use my plane though as it will be more comfortable, and you won't have to worry about delays or that sort of thing. The driver, chef and housekeeper come as part of the rental package, no arguing. I will be going to Scotland before heading to Germany, so I could actually drop you off and pick you up on the way back. Would you be agreeable to that?" He was making it impossible for me to refuse and he had Janet and Roxie on his side.

"It is not fair that you two are on his side. I will agree as long as the rental price is fair, and I will arrange to fly the ladies here a day or two ahead of when you are ready to leave for Scotland, so we will be in one place. If you will tell me what price you are going to charge me, then perhaps we can come to an agreement." James laughed but he was happy. He knew that if he said too low a figure she would not agree and even though he knew she had won a lot of money he didn't want her to give any of it to him. Although he would not tell her this, he would donate it to a charity in her name.

"Okay, so looking at the rates of the other villas you were looking at, based on that, what about four thousand Canadian a week. If that is too much, I can drop the price, because we're friends and all." He smiled, and I knew he was doing that, so I wouldn't refuse. I told him that would be fine. The other villas were double that and more for a week and in US dollars and I had no idea what they looked like. At least I knew that James's villa was beautiful and would be just as it looked like in the photos. I contacted Judy and Christelle and told them to keep the middle two weeks in April free for our holiday. They hooted and hollered with excitement. I told them I would send them more info and photos later.

I asked James to email me the photos he had of the villa and any other info that I would need so I could share it with the others. Janet and Roxie were clapping with excitement. It was getting late, and James and Roxie had to leave. James was flying to Toronto to meet with his architect and then attend to business. He reminded Janet not to forget to call him when she made her decision and Roxie, well she reminded us that she was going home with Prince Charming.

We walked them down to the lobby, but before he left, Janet wanted to get pictures of us all dressed up. We took several photos from all our phones. We hugged and kissed them goodnight. It was the first time James and I had kissed on the lips even though it was very brief. Any other time we met it had been on the cheek. It tingled and as they went out the door my hand went to my lips.

"Come on you, it is time to go back upstairs, and you and I are going to have a talk about you and James." Roxie felt like a queen sitting in James's car, but it wasn't long before she felt she had to have a talk with James.

"James, I think you are a truly wonderful man. I also think that you like Cassandra a lot more than you are letting on. I believe that you have the best of intentions where she is concerned but I am going to say this because I care about her. She has been through a lot, and I mean a lot, especially with her late husband. I'm not going to get into details because that is something for her to talk about, not me. But I know more than she knows I know but I'm not saying anything to her about that either. Maybe it isn't right for me to say this to you, but I like you and I think you would be great for her. She has had her heart crushed into a million pieces more times than is right, promises made were broken like they meant nothing, and trust was violated. Cassandra holds trust as something more valuable than anything. You break trust with her and that is it. James, I am not going to ask you what your intentions are, as I said I think you are what she needs, but you hurt her, and you will have a lot of people in your face faster than you can think. I hope that you won't be angry that I had to say what I had to say." James thought about it for a few minutes and pulled the car into a parking lot in Spruce Grove. He turned in his seat and turned on the interior light to look at Roxie because he wanted her to see his face.

"Roxanne, I am not offended by you saying what you did. In fact, I am grateful, not just that you said it but that you care so much for Cassandra. I will be very honest with you; I don't want to be just her friend. I want to be more than that. From the second that I saw her at that coffee shop my heart stopped. I saw the two of you sharing something and the smile she had on her face, and I could hear her laughter, my very soul was still. She has hinted at things from her past but frankly I don't want to know about them. If she wants to talk about them, I will listen, but I will never ask her about them. I care very deeply for her and for now that is all I will say. But I am, for now, respecting her wishes." Roxie was elated to hear this. For weeks now she suspected that Cassandra felt more for James than she was letting on and even tonight she caught her stealing a look at him without him noticing. It was the look in her eyes that gave her away, but it was there for only a second and it was gone.

"Okay, Cassandra so let's you and I talk or maybe I'll do more of the talking and you listen, and I don't want you thinking it is the wine either because I only had one glass. I know you like James more than you are letting on. It is me here now, your friend and somebody who cares about you. I saw the look in your eyes when James kissed you good night. It was brief, and I gather the first time, but I saw the look in your eyes. I think you more than like him, but you are afraid to admit it. You are afraid to put that trust in someone else again because you are afraid you are going to get hurt. I was never around to see what happened with your marriage, but I know that you tried, and I know that even when you said that you had given up, you still hoped that things would turn around. It seemed for a while that it was, but perhaps that was because he knew he was going to die, and he wanted to make amends for the way he treated you all those years. I have only just met James, but I believe with all my heart he is honest and good and will treat you right, the way you deserve to be treated. Don't let your fear keep you from the one man who is so right for you." I knew Janet was only concerned and wanted what was best for me, but I didn't know what I wanted. I sensed that James wanted to be more than friends, but I knew that he was being respectful and not violating my wishes. It was easy being around him, but I didn't know what his life was like on a day-to-day basis. He had an empire to run and even admitted that having a personal life was not easy.

"I hear what you are saying, and I believe that James is everything that you say and more. My marriage was hard. Not saying that everything that went wrong was all his fault because it wasn't. But he broke my trust repeatedly and even though I said I would forgive and forget it was hard for me to do. He broke so many promises and each time I forgave him. It got to the point I couldn't forgive anymore because I didn't care why he had to say he was sorry. I know he tried at the end before he passed but it was too little too late. I don't know why our marriage was the way it was. It could have been so much better, but I don't think he wanted it to be better and that is what hurt the most. I told him as much days before he died. I needed him to know that I stopped loving him a very long time ago. There was too much hurt over too long a period. My heart was broken into a million pieces because I truly loved him when we were first together. Since he passed, I have been careful with my heart and with my soul. Yes, the moment I saw James, my heart stopped, and I couldn't breathe. If we met under other circumstances I might not be so hesitant, but for my own sake, I must tread carefully. Am I falling in love with him, I don't know, it is way too early to say, but I am not going to leap into anything. I need to do this my way and in my own time. Can you please trust me that I will handle this right? If it is meant to be it will be." Janet listened to what I had to say and hugged me at the end. She knew that I would have to do this my way. We talked more about the vacation and the day. It was a revealing day for me at least. We both went off to bed, but I had so much going through my mind that it took me a while to relax. The sun was coming up earlier each day. I was used to it, but Janet was not. She came out to the kitchen rubbing her eyes.

"What time did the sun come up for heaven's sake. I need coffee and lots of it." I laughed and handed her a cup, and we went to the living room and sat down. We decided to go out for breakfast and of course we went to Jason's. We both dressed casually and got to the restaurant shortly after 8:00 that morning. We ordered as soon as we could because Janet had to be back at my place, so she could call Wade at noon his time.

"Have you decided on taking James's offer. It would be an amazing job for you and being able to work from home with only having to travel once every two weeks. You and Wade could make a mini vacation out of it if you wanted. Go and see some shows when you are in Toronto." Janet was sipping her coffee and before she could say anything the food arrived. We sat eating and I waited for her to talk.

"It is too good to pass up. When I told James what I did for my company, I guess he felt confident enough that I could handle what he wanted me to do. I'm pretty sure Wade will be on board with it. He would never say no to such a great offer for me. Things at my office are ok but the one girl who works there could take over what I was doing. I'm going to say yes as long as Wade is ok with it." I was very happy for her, and I knew she would be great at the job. We finished eating and went back to my place. I went onto the balcony while she put in the call to Wade.

I didn't want to eavesdrop, so I closed the door. I sat looking out at the skyline thinking of our earlier conversation. What was I going to do? I really had to ponder that one. I had my back to the living room, so I had no idea how the conversation with Wade was going. The door opened, and Janet came out.

"Wade thinks it will be an amazing opportunity. I told him about the benefits and pension and the salary, and he said that I couldn't refuse. It was the opportunity of a lifetime. He told me to accept it without even hesitating. My goodness I can't believe this. I will be making more money that I ever thought I would, and I will actually have a really good pension when I retire. I don't even know what to say. I have to thank you because if you hadn't had your dream, if James hadn't come through that door, none of this would have happened for me. I am grateful to him of course but I owe you the greatest thanks. I know I said a lot the other day and I hope that I didn't overstep but I really think this is the guy for you. Don't use age as an excuse not to be with him because it doesn't seem to matter to him one little bit. Personally, I think he's head over heels in love with you, but that's just my opinion." I was happy she was going to accept the job.

I suggested that we go for a good long hike and hoped she was up for it. She said she was indeed and thought that she could walk home and back, she was so excited. I settled for doing four kms and walking through the subdivision where James was going to build. I stood and looked at the property envisioning the Queen Anne home nestled in among the trees. I could only imagine what it was going to look like in the fall. The colours of the trees changed from year to year in colour variations depending on how much rain or lack thereof that we got. I then tried to imagine what it would look like with big snowflakes falling. A smile crossed my face, which Janet took note of.

"It will be pretty decorated at Christmas with all the lights and decorations. You will have to send me a picture." We continued on our walk and by the time we got back we were both tired. We were staying in for the night. We had fresh wild BC sockeye salmon with a nice garden salad for our dinner. We had club soda to drink and toasted to her new job. Janet wanted to go back to the mall tomorrow to get some things for the grandkids. We hit the sack and planned to get up around 9:00 the following morning.

Chapter 2

The next morning, we got up, had coffee and some toast, and went to the mall. She really wanted to get them a t-shirt that had Stony Plain on it, because that is where we were, but we were having a hard time finding them. Fortunately, we came across a place in the mall that made up t-shirts with whatever you wanted on them. They actually had a graphic of Stony Plain and some of the murals, so she got a few of those made up. We walked around to a few more stores and stopped and had a big lunch. I picked up some costume jewelry from one of the stores for Ayleen. She was more careful now about the things she wore, and I knew she would like some new things.

By the time we got home it was late, but we were still full from lunch. I brought out some cheese and crackers and some coffee. We sat out on the balcony and watched the sun slowly setting. I opened up my laptop and saw that I had an email from James. He forwarded me lots of photos of his villa and included a list of the amenities nearby. He made a few suggestions of places to go and things to do just in case we were interested.

"Oh, darn I wonder if I will be able to take the two weeks off if I start working for James. Maybe I should call him now and accept. Do you think it is too late to call?" I looked at the time stamp of the email and he just sent it. It was still early enough back east so I suggested she call him on his cell. He answered the phone almost immediately.

“Hi James, it’s Janet. I hope I am not calling too late. I spoke to Wade and if you are still offering me the job, I would like to accept. I do have one immediate concern though. I hope this isn’t going to look bad, but will I still be able to have the two weeks off in April to go with Cassandra and the others on vacation? If you say no that’s okay, I will understand.” She had her fingers crossed hoping it wasn’t going to be an issue. She had her phone on speaker, so I was able to hear the conversation.

“It won’t be a problem at all. I am glad that you are accepting. I gather you will have to give your present employer two weeks’ notice. Perhaps I could have you come to Toronto, and I can show you what you will be handling, give you an idea of what and where the office is. You can bring Wade along as well; it will give me a chance to meet him. It’s the end of June, let’s put a start date for you after the holiday in August. That will give you time to give your notice and get yourself set up at home. I will arrange for you to have a company credit card sent to you. You will use it to book your flight for you and Wade and I will arrange for your accommodations. If you can send me your home email address and other particulars such as home address and phone number in a reply email that I sent to Cassandra, I can get some things going. I look forward to seeing you at the beginning of August." Janet thanked James and hung up. She was jumping up and down for glee. She started to cry again.

"He wants me to send a reply email on the one he sent you giving him some of my info. I'm going to start after the Civic holiday. I will have to hand in my resignation letter as soon as I get back. He said there was no problem me going on the holiday we arranged. I felt kinda bad asking for the time off already, but he said there was no problem. Can you, the next time, you talk to him, make sure he is really ok with that. I told him it was ok if he said it wouldn't be possible." I laughed at her and reminded her that she had her phone on speaker, and I heard everything he said. I reassured her that if James said he was fine with it, I was sure that he was, but I knew it was going to bother her until I did have a chance to ask. We looked through the photos again. I forwarded them on to each of the other ladies. We sat looking at the sun setting again and then we decided to turn in for the night.

It was Saturday and Janet's last day visiting. We went for a walk in the morning with some of the seniors. They liked Janet a lot and told her to come back soon. It was a rather warm day and we decided to do a little driving around. We drove through Stony and the Grove and then I drove back to the old house. It was someone else's home now and I was happy that I got all the work done on it that I wanted. It felt good seeing a happy family in it. We took a drive out to Roxie's country home and had a short visit with her. It was getting late in the afternoon by the time I drove back to my place. I thought I saw James's car in the parking lot. I pulled into the parking garage and went up to my unit and sure enough James was waiting at my door. He was wearing jeans, a shirt and sports jacket.

"Well, hello I didn't know you were in town. I thought from your email you were still in Toronto. Do you want to come in?" He said he did, and he said hello to Janet. He said he was in Toronto until this morning. He had to come out and deal with some construction issues involving the new business sites. He knew it was Janet's last day here and he didn't want to spoil any plans that we had but he was eager to show me something. I looked at Janet and she looked at me with that 'see' look in her eyes.

"I think I mentioned I am partners with a friend of mine, and we have a cosmetics company in Germany. We decided to build a lab here, but he has controlling interest and runs the company. The products are all top of the line and we have products for every age group. But we were talking on a video call, and I asked him what he thought about doing a specific line for those over sixty. I can't say that I am all that familiar with women's makeup, but I thought perhaps we could try something completely out of the box." Janet and I were both intrigued.

"We are going to build a lab here and produce the same line of high-end cosmetics using the same research as the company in Germany. It would be a partnership with him of course but the twist would be that in all of the major and medium sized malls, we could set up kiosks and have makeup artists selling the cosmetics but, and here is the twist, showing the seniors what to buy and how to apply it. They would walk them through on how to do a daytime look and an evening look. We could offer them a senior's discount of course but the quality of the product they are getting is exceptional. What is your reaction to this idea?" He was asking the both of us but looking more to me for my answer.

Wow was my first reaction. I was sure that nothing of the kind existed at least not that I was aware of. I knew some did makeup, but they charged for it. Even though I'd worn makeup for a good part of my life, I said that I wouldn't mind having an expert show me the way to do it properly. Even Janet said she had never heard of anything quite like it. James of course was not going to say that building the cosmetics labs was already the reason why he was in Alberta aside from Cassandra.

"Clearly you have given this a lot of thought. I think it is an awesome idea and I would even go to one of the kiosks. I'm sure that I could learn a thing or two."

Janet said the same thing. James said he was going to work on getting a lab set up as soon as the building was ready, which he figured would be in another month. Once they saw how the kiosks were received, they would look at setting up more across Canada and throughout Europe. I told him that I was sure a lot of the seniors here would certainly go, and I really hoped that it would be successful. He was getting up to leave and I asked him if he wanted to join us for dinner. It was going to be a casual night for the two of us because Janet's flight was mid-morning, and we weren't planning on staying out late.

"If I won't be imposing. It will be nice to have dinner with you and with, of course, my newest employee. Janet and I freshened up a bit then we went out. James said we could go in his car, and finally, at last, I got to sit in the back seat of the sports car. I wasn't going to let Janet sit back there by herself. We got in and I couldn't resist what I was going to say.

"Once around the block James." James turned around and looked at me and we laughed, and he asked how long I had been holding that one in. I said it was something on my bucket list for a long, long time and now I could check it off. James laughed again and said he was going to have to get a look at that bucket list and see what else was on there. I laughed and mentioned a few things like going for a horse drawn carriage ride in the snow, when big flakes are coming down, being on a big expensive yacht in the middle of the Mediterranean, retracing my father's footsteps during the war and ending up where he and his unit liberated the town, I said I had never, as a child, sat on Santa's knee to say what I wanted for Christmas, and even though I was well beyond the age of doing so, I still wanted to do it. I really didn't have a big list, but they were things that meant a lot to me. I even talked to Roxie once about doing a river boat cruise in Germany as long as we could get to that one town.

We went, of course, to Jason's and of course, Jason seated us at a table in the private area. Janet and I had a half glass of wine, her red and me white, James ordered whisky which he told us came from his distillery. James talked to Jason a few weeks ago about trying out his product and he provided him with a couple of boxes of his company's whisky. We talked about a lot of things like favourite shows, the weather and even the job Janet would be doing. Our meal came, and we ate and talked about other things in life. James paid the bill even though I protested, and we left and went back to my place. He walked us into the lobby. Janet said she wanted to get a picture of the three of us, so James having a much longer arm, took the photo.

"I am going to leave you ladies here as I am sure that you want to spend the last few hours together. I will see you both soon I hope. Have a wonderful night and Janet have a safe trip back home." He turned and went back out the door and we went up to my unit. We got our pjs on and had some tea. She texted Wade before it was too late to do so and then we sat on the sofa and talked.

"I am going to miss you. When are you leaving to visit Ross? Have you told him anything about James?" I was going to miss her too. It was so nice having her visit on happier terms and I was so happy that she was going to be starting a new job. Visiting Ross was going to be the beginning of July. She pulled out her cell and said she would send me the photo, which she did. It was a very nice picture, but Janet couldn't help but notice that James's arm was around me a little more than around her.

"Oh, don't make too much of that please. It is probably because you are now an employee, and I am a good friend." I tried to make light of it, but Janet was not going to let it go.

"Why can't you see that the two of you like each other more than you will admit. You have known each other for a little more than two months, why does it have to be longer if you know you are right for each other? Not to get too weird about my new employer but he's handsome as all get out, he's tall and in great shape and that deep Scottish accent. You have to admit that gives you butterflies." I laughed. It was hard to argue that point. He did have a very sexy voice and he was handsome, and he was in great shape. My head was spinning a little bit. I didn't want to talk any more about James. Janet was leaving the next morning, and we took out the photos of the villa and looked everything over. It was a beautiful place. I heard back from Christelle about it. She thought the place was amazing and who was this James that I hadn't told her about. I sent her back a quick email which I knew she wouldn't get until the following morning telling her I would explain everything on the phone.

We got up the next morning and had coffee and some toast. Janet's flight was going to leave at 11 am so I wanted to make sure that she was at the airport in lots of time. She didn't want me to come in even though I was quite prepared to park and sit with her until she had to go through security. But she said no she didn't want to cry when she left, so I dropped her off, gave her a big hug and said I would see her again soon. When I got back home, I gave Christelle a call to see if she had time to chat.

"No, you are going to video call with me because I need to see your face when you tell me about this person." I hung up, opened up my laptop and put in a video call to her.

"Ok, so why haven't you told me about this person. Why am I just hearing about him now?" She wasn't angry with me especially when I explained that I didn't want to get into long conversations on the phone because she hadn't been well. She was ok with my reason but still wanted to know all about him. I explained first my dream and how I would get flashes of this person and how I would meet him, but everything was just flashes of moments together. I then told her about being in the coffee shop with Roxie and in walks the guy from my dream and everything that had happened from that point on.

"How weird is that don't you think. I mean really it was a dream and for all I know I am still dreaming. You know me Christelle better than anyone and you know that I am not ready for any type of relationship. You know how hard it was before and what I went through, all of it." She listened to me talk as she always did, and she was watching me. I asked what she thought.

"Well, first of all I don't get any feeling that he is anything but a nice guy. In fact, I get the feeling and my guide is telling me that he is a really nice guy. I know what you went through, and I know you said that you would never get involved with a man again. But things change you know that. The universe has a way of giving us what we need when we need it, not when we want it. The fact that you have been having dreams about this guy down to the very thing of him being Scottish, to me, is not something that you should ignore. I haven't met him, but he sounds like he likes you and I think you like him, but you are afraid to open your heart." I said that I was going to be coming back east in two weeks arriving on a Saturday, and maybe we could get together during the week and talk. I showed her a picture that Janet took of the three of us, but she said that it wasn't clear enough on her computer. I told her that I was so glad she was better because it was driving me crazy not being able to talk to her about all of this. I said I wanted to go out for a walk, so we hung up.

It was still early afternoon and I really needed to clear my head. I went out and walked and walked. So many thoughts going through my head. I hadn't realized that I ended up at James's property until I was standing at the end of the road. This place was so pretty. I turned around and walked back home. By the time I got home it was late. Janet sent me a text to say she arrived safely and was going to make it an early night. I thought that was a good idea and after having a light dinner and watching a little tv, I did the same. I thought I would dream more about James, but I didn't. I wasn't getting any more flashes. All I dreamt about was how things had been up to this point. I called Christelle again the next morning and told her that I was not getting any more flashes of future things other than what I had told her.

"Perhaps the universe has decided to keep some things a mystery for you, you never know." We talked for a little bit longer as she had to go for a doctor's appointment in a couple of hours. I spent the day cleaning my condo and visiting some of the seniors. James texted to say that he was heading out of town and would call when he was back. I went on a few walks with the seniors over the next week. I had a lot to think about these days and I spent many restless nights trying to figure out how I felt. The first few days of July flew by, and I was now approaching the date I was to be leaving and I still hadn't booked my flight. I was worried that maybe I wasn't going to get a flight and would have to look at another airline.

It was Tuesday morning, and I had my coffee and some toast for breakfast, but I was restless and decided to go and do a bit of shopping for my trip which was going to be in a few days. I still had a casserole in the freezer that Janet and I had not eaten, so I took it out before I left and thought I would have it for dinner tonight. I video chatted with Ayleen many times and she talked about things she wanted for her birthday which was not until October. I think she was giving hints to Gramma that she would like these things sooner than her birthday. She made me laugh. I decided to stroll around the mall and see if there was anything I could pick up for my trip.

I wouldn't bring a lot of stuff with me because we seldom went out. Lindsay, Ayleen, and I would go grocery shopping but that was about the extent of our outings. Now that they had a beautiful home with a little bit of treed property around it, they liked to stay at home and entertain. It was going to be hot but hopefully not too humid back east. Thankfully, their new home had air conditioning. I picked out a few sleeveless tops and capris and a couple of summer dresses. I hardly wore dresses in the past but lately I liked wearing them. I bought some new sandals and then I looked for a few things for Ayleen. I never bought things for Ross or Lindsay because they were hard to buy for.

What I would like to buy Lindsay was not necessarily something she would like, so I stopped buying them clothes a long time ago and gave them gift cards instead. But Ayleen was easy to buy for, she loved anything and everything. I picked out a couple of outfits for her that would go with the new jewelry I bought her. It was well past lunch when I was finished so I stopped at one of the restaurants in the mall and had a light lunch. I got back to my car and was going to start it when my cell rang. It was James and he was returning to Edmonton and wanted to know if I was free for dinner. It would be about another hour and half before he landed.

"I am free but how about we eat at my place. I have a chicken casserole out that I was going to put in the oven. Why don't you come by, and we can dine in for a change?" He agreed and said that he would text me when he landed. The drive from the airport was about forty-five minutes to an hour depending on traffic. I got home in lots of time, took a quick shower, fixed my hair, and put on a bit of makeup. It was a nice July day and I thought about eating on the balcony, but it looked like it might rain. I set the table and when I got his text, I put the casserole in the oven. Almost forty-five minutes later he buzzed to let me know he arrived, and I let him in. When he knocked on the door I opened it and he looked really tired.

We hugged and kissed on the cheek. I asked him if he would like a drink and he asked what I had. I told him that I asked Jason for a bottle of his whisky which he happily gave to me and said that he would have just a small bit because he was tired. I let him know that I talked to Roxie about Scotland and the gala, and she wanted to go to both, so if he still wanted us to go we could but not to Scotland until September. He said he still did and that was good with him. He was in Toronto the day after Janet left and then had to fly to Scotland and then to Germany and then to France on business.

He looked out the window at the building that was going up across the way. He was happy that progress was being made and in the next few months there would be a model suite. The casserole was done so we sat and ate and talked about his trip. It sounded exhausting, but he said it was never usually like that. He wasn't sure why so many things all happened at the same time, but they did and fortunately it was easily resolved. Some of the business was in cosmetics and some was with his glass and whisky business, which he said were doing extremely well. He had a very lucrative high tech security company, which he ran out of Toronto. I asked him if he wanted another drink, but he declined. We finished dinner and I made coffee. We sat on the sofa relaxing and talking. I could tell he was starting to get a little sleepy.

"James why don't you sleep here in the spare room. You are too exhausted to drive back to your hotel unless you want to take a cab and then come back tomorrow for your car. I don't want you falling asleep at the wheel." He admitted he was really tired, and he did have his luggage in the car. He went down to get it. I put the dishes on the counter to wash up in a minute. I stripped the bed after Janet left so I got out the other comforter and fresh sheets and made up the bed again. I wasn't sure if James was a fan of yellow, so I was glad that I had a comforter that was black and gray. I put gray sheets on and finished when James came back up. I gave him my key for the building and my door, so he didn't have to ring. He put his luggage in the spare room and came back out to the kitchen. I finished filling the sink and put the dishes in.

"Why don't you use the dishwasher? You have one, don't you?" I assured him that I did but I only ever used that when I had a lot more dishes to do. When it was just me or one other person I preferred to wash and dry them myself. I started to wash, and he picked up the towel to dry. I was going to object, but he insisted on helping. The kitchen wasn't really small but with him being in it, it seemed smaller. The dishes were done and put away. I asked if he was interested in watching the news. He said he was, so we sat again on the sofa, and I turned to the news.

It was getting late, but it was still a bit light out. James's eyes started to close so I suggested that he head off to bed. I realized he was probably on a few different time zones, but it was still a bit early for me. He readily agreed and went off to the spare room and closed the door. It seemed so odd having him in my home, sleeping just a wall away.

I watched the rest of the news and shut off the tv. I was still not tired, but I got my pjs on and went onto the balcony. It was a warm night and I had on a sleeveless top and short pj bottoms that had cats on them. I thought it was silly at the time that I bought them, but I couldn't resist. I put on a light robe because the breeze picked up a little. There was a storm off in the distance and the odd flash of lightning and the rumble of thunder, but I thought it was still miles away. I loved a good storm as long as it wasn't a damaging one. The storm was coming closer, so I decided to go inside. Just as I was walking away from the balcony door a loud crack hit very close. It startled me, and I screamed a bit.

James came running out with only a pair of long pj bottoms on. He asked if I was alright and I said yes, it was just the lightning hit close and it startled me. I apologized for waking him. He said that I hadn't it was the lightning hit that woke him but then he heard me scream. I pulled my robe tighter and apologized for letting out a scream. I tried so very hard not to look at him in only his pj bottoms. His shoulders, I knew were broad, but I had no idea that he would look that great. He went into the spare room, grabbed a t-shirt, and put it on. He must have realized I felt a little uneasy with him being half naked. I felt butterflies in my stomach which I had not felt in a very, very long time. I said I was going to head off to bed, but he said that he was awake now and if I didn't mind he was going to stay up for a little bit. I said that was okay and went off to my bedroom and shut the door. I laid in bed thinking about him and as hard as I tried to get him out of my thoughts I couldn't.

James sat on the sofa with a glass of water in hand. Normally jet lag didn't bother him because he travelled so much but it did this time for some reason. The storm was moving on, and the clouds cleared and let the full moon shine through. It lit up the living room enough that he could see the pictures of her son and granddaughter that were around the room. Her son looked like her and her granddaughter did a bit too. There was a picture of all of them from a Christmas past. It was easy to see that it was her favourite time of the year just by the smile on her face. There was a painting on the wall that he hadn't noticed before. It was a winter scene showing a horse drawn carriage with a couple going down a snow-covered road. It oddly looked similar to the road into his new property but that was probably a road similar to a lot of roads in the area. He noticed a photo album on the end table and picked it up and looked through it.

There were lots of pictures of Cassandra and her granddaughter, her son and daughter in law. There were also pictures of her parents and her sister he guessed and some photos of her other friends. Some of the pictures were taken many years ago. She looked very different from how she looked now. He could see the pain and sorrow on her face from years ago. There were oddly no pictures of her late husband. He felt like he'd been doing something he shouldn't, so he put the album back where it was. James realized that he had been sitting there for almost two hours. He was heading back to his room when he heard her crying. He knocked on the door, but she didn't answer. He knocked again, and she came to the door. It was obvious there were tears in her eyes still although she tried to dry them.

"Is everything ok Cassandra? I heard you crying." I explained that it was just a bad dream, and I was ok. He asked me if I was sure, and I said yes but I knew he wasn't convinced. I was going to tell him about the dream, but it was too personal, and it was about the past. He said if I was sure I was ok he would head back to bed. I was not ok, but I didn't want to say anything to him. I didn't know if I wanted James to know about my past. I eventually fell back asleep again and got up at my normal time. I put on my robe and opened my door. I could smell coffee and James was in the kitchen pouring himself a cup. He saw me coming out and poured me one as well. Even though it was early, the sun was well up and we sat out on the balcony. He had on a t-shirt thankfully. I felt a little bit shy about what I was wearing. I think James could sense.

"Listen Cassandra, I am not going to throw you on the table and ravish you. We are friends remember. I want you to feel at ease around me even if you are wearing the cutest pj bottoms I have ever seen." He laughed, and I slapped him playfully. That actually made me more at ease around him. We drank more coffee and he said he was going to make pancakes if I had what he needed. He told me what he wanted, and I put everything out for him and went back out onto the balcony. Not because I wanted to but because I was ordered to leave the kitchen, jokingly of course. I was sitting drinking my coffee when my phone rang. I went in to get the cordless phone. It was Christelle.

"Hi Christelle, how are you? Is everything ok?" She said that it was, but she felt like she had to give me a call. I took the phone out onto the balcony. I told her that James came by the day before and I asked him for dinner.

"He was so exhausted from his business trips that I didn't want him to drive to the hotel, so he stayed in the spare room." I said that he was now making breakfast, pancakes and I wasn't sure how it was going because I was asked to leave the kitchen.

"Well, well that is interesting. I guess I know why I was supposed to call then. Too bad I didn't video call I could have gotten a look at him." We talked for a few minutes and James popped his head out to say that breakfast was almost ready. I said it was Christelle and did he want to say hi. I was surprised when he took the phone from my hand and started talking to her. I could only imagine how shocked she was.

I went into the living room and saw that even the table was set, and very nicely. He poured me out a glass of orange juice and put three pancakes on my plate. He cooked up some sausage as well and I took a couple of those. He finished talking to Christelle and put the phone back in its cradle. He sat down and told me to dig in. I wasn't sure what to expect but these were about the best pancakes I ever had. He made them from scratch, and they were so light and airy. I didn't like anything but maple syrup on mine, but he put some of the Saskatoon jam on his. He said he liked the jam, and I told him it was mine. He said it was great and asked if I could give him some. I said of course I had lots.

"But you will be able to have some made from your own berries once you build your house. You have a lot of Saskatoon bushes on your property don't forget."

We finished eating breakfast and did up the dishes. James was a pretty darn good cook.

"Do you have time to go for a walk. Perhaps we can swing by my property. The site has been cleared where the house is going." I said that I had nothing planned for the day. While he was taking a shower, I cleaned up the dining room and living room a bit. When James came out in a pair of shorts and t-shirt, I was a little flustered. He had great legs. I said I was going to go and take a shower and then we could head out.

I came out wearing one of my new tops and capris. James already put on his runners and was waiting at the door with sunglasses on. I put on my runners, grabbed my keys and my sunglasses and we were off. I took a bottle of water for each of us as I wasn't sure how long we were going to walk. Once down in the lobby, there were a few of the seniors sitting on the lounge chairs that were added to the lobby. I stopped and introduced James and told them that he was the owner of the building. They thanked him for making all the repairs and for all that he'd done. He was gracious and kind to each of them and that really warmed my heart.

We went out and started walking in the direction of the road to his property, but he wanted to walk a bit further. I took him on the trail I normally went by myself. It was too challenging a trail for the seniors, but I knew it would be a piece of cake for James. We walked for about five kms and turned and walked back and went down the road to his property. I would have walked further but I knew that he was still tired from his long trip and not completely rested. When we walked around more, I pointed out to him that he also had raspberries. He said that at one time there had been a farmhouse here so that was probably where they came from. Now that he knew where they were he said, he would make sure that they were not cut down. We walked back to my condo and took the elevator up to my unit. I gave him a glass of water and we sat for a bit on the balcony.

"I could stay here all day, but I have to get back to my hotel, shower, and change. I have a meeting this evening and I need to take care of a couple of things before I have to go back to Toronto." He finished his water, collected his suitcases, and gave me a kiss on the cheek and went out the door and gone. I didn't know what he and Christelle talked about, so I gave her a call. She answered on the second ring.

"I had a feeling you would be calling me. Has James left or is he still there?" I said he left and was curious to know what they talked about.

"Oh, he was just saying that it was nice to get a chance to say hi and that he hoped that we would meet someday soon. I have to say that I like him even though I haven't met him. I got a very good feeling from him and so do my guides. He has a very sexy voice and as we were talking my guides were giving me a message. I'm not sure you want to hear it or not but here is what they said: "he is for her." They kept saying that over and over. I hate to tell you this my girl, but he is the man for you, and I have that from the highest authority." It wasn't that I was doubting her. The more I was around James, the more I liked him and felt at ease with him. I was starting to feel like we were old friends and not just someone whom I met only months ago. I told her that his pancakes were amazing, and I told her about me screaming when the lightning hit last night so close and James coming out into the living room with just pj bottoms on.

"I really had to fight a feeling to do all sorts of things which I will not go into. Being a woman of my age, I try not to think about those things anymore." Christelle laughed at me.

"You're not dead my dear and from the sounds of it he is a sexy man, and he likes you a lot. I don't think he would have objected to anything you were thinking of doing to him." She laughed at me. I knew I was being very silly and that she was right, but I was still not ready even if my hormones were. I told her I would see her next Tuesday if she was free. She said she was, and we arranged to meet at our usual place. I went into the spare room and laid down on the bed and hugged the sheets and comforter around me. I got up feeling very foolish and stripped the bed and washed the sheets. I put everything away in the linen closet. James left his t-shirt in the bathroom. I put that in my room and was thinking of wearing it tonight.

I was leaving on Saturday in the morning, but I still hadn't booked my flight for some crazy reason. I knew that waiting until the last minute like this I might be out of luck, especially with the airline that I wanted to fly. I was busy with Janet being here and other things, named James and it completely slipped my mind. I checked flights for Saturday hoping that there would be openings. Fortunately, there were but there were only a couple of seats left. I was about to book when my phone rang. It was James and he said that he thought he might have left his t-shirt in the bathroom. I said I found it and would give it to him next time I saw him.

"I know you are going back east to see your son Saturday and I had an idea. I am going back to Toronto Saturday, and I thought if you hadn't booked your flight or if you had, I could drop you off. It's only an hour from Toronto by air so not a big deal and you could return my t-shirt, not that it is important as I do have others." I said that I was actually just looking at booking as it did escape my mind with Janet's visit.

"Then don't book anything. You can come with me and maybe, if I have time, I can meet your son, daughter in law and granddaughter, if you are ok with that. By the way, we deplane from the private terminal, so your son will be cleared at the gate to drive in once the plane has stopped and he can pick you up right at the plane. You will have to let him know that, so he doesn't think he has to go into the airport." I hadn't mentioned anything about James to Ross. I wasn't sure if I should, but knowing James from being around him, I knew he was going to make a point of meeting Ross. It suddenly hit me, and I asked him if he had his own plane because he wanted me to go to the private terminal. He laughed and said he did, and he mentioned it before, but I said it probably didn't register. I agreed to the flight and would let Ross know where to go when he arrived. I gave James his last name and mentioned that I would have his t-shirt washed and ironed. He laughed and said that he would pick me up at 10:00 in the morning on Saturday.

I put his t-shirt on the washer to wash but decided that I was going to wear it that night. I don't know why but I just wanted to. That night I put it on I can't even describe the feeling I felt when I was wearing it around the living room. I took a selfie of me wearing it because I wanted a memory I could keep. Next day I did some washing, James's t-shirt included and did some packing. Cleaned the bathrooms and bedrooms and video chatted with Ayleen. She was excited to see me and even Ross got on for a bit. We talked about how things were going and what the weather was like. He said it wasn't too bad and it wasn't supposed to be humid when I was there.

"Um, I'm not sure how to bring this up but I have a guy friend. I met him a few months ago and we see each other whenever he is here, which is actually quite often now that I think of it. He is flying me back east and said that if he had time, he would like to meet all of you." It was hard to read how Ross would feel about it. I told him a bit more about James and that he was actually a really nice guy. I mentioned he was younger than me but that was not something Ross was worried about.

"Hang on a second. Did you say 'he' was flying you back here? Does this guy have his own plane?" I told him that James was pretty well off and that he had a huge business empire. The plane was his but that was beside the point. I said he was Scottish and that I liked him. I wanted to know if he would be agreeable to meeting him and I hoped that he would be ok with that. I usually took them out for dinner the day I arrived, but I assured him that James would not be joining us. He agreed that it was ok to meet him if he was able to take the time. I told him what James said about going to the private terminal to pick me up and would have to tell security at the gate who he was and that he was meeting James Sutherland's plane. Ayleen came back on and asked me who James was. She wasn't far away and heard the conversation. She wanted to know if he was my boyfriend. I had to explain to her that people my age didn't have boyfriends. She was a smart little girl and picked up on things quickly. I explained to her that he was a new friend and someone that Gramma liked a lot and that he wanted to meet them.

"Sounds good Gramma, looking forward to seeing your boyfriend." She blew kisses, giggled, and waved and as she always did, hit the red button before I had a chance to say anything. What a character that little girl was. I was leaving in two days, and I wanted to ensure that the condo was neat and tidy and gave my plants some water. On Friday I finished the last of my packing and had my luggage by the door. I let Mr. O'Leary know that I would be out of town for a couple of weeks, and I gave him the key to my mailbox and asked if he would be kind enough to put my mail on the table inside the door. He had a key for my door as he did for all the other condo owners, and I felt comfortable enough with him putting my mail in.

The days were getting shorter now. The sun was setting earlier each day and that heralded the oncoming of fall and the end to summer. I went for a walk later than I would normally do but it was such a nice afternoon, I wanted to get a good long walk in. I got back home, took a shower, and had a couple bowls of cereal. I wanted to use up the rest of the milk before I left. I hadn't heard from James all day but that was okay. I knew he was trying to get some business details looked after before going back to Toronto.

I sat out on the balcony for the longest time reflecting on my life and where I was now. There were things I regretted but it was what it was. I didn't want to look back anymore, I spent the last year or so going forward, and I was at peace now and for the first time, happy. I texted Janet and let her know that I was flying back east with James. He was returning to Toronto, and he said it would not be out of his way. I know that she wanted to talk on the phone, but I wanted to have an early night and I really didn't want to get into a long conversation about James.

He was already occupying my thoughts a lot these days. It was already after 9:00 pm and I got my pjs on and watched a little of the news. The weather forecast for back east was looking like it was going to be nice, not too hot and no humidity was being forecasted. I was getting into bed when I got a text from James wishing me a good night and he would be at my place to pick me up at 9:00 the following morning. I responded back to him that was fine with me and said good night.

My bag was already packed so it was not something I would have to worry about in the morning. I slept soundly and woke to my alarm. I never set my alarm normally, but I wanted to make sure that I didn't sleep in. I took a shower, dried my hair, styled it, and put on some makeup. I decided to wear some dress pants and a sleeveless blouse all of which were new. The pants were white cotton, and the chiffon blouse was pinks, oranges, and reds, very summery. I had a red sweater that I brought with me in case it was cool on the plane. I wore a pair of red flats with a cute bow. I never ate or drank coffee before I would fly. It wasn't that I had a weak stomach I just didn't like to use the bathroom on the plane. I went onto the balcony and waited for James to arrive. He texted me that he was in the parking lot and would be up in a minute. He buzzed, and I let him in. I opened my door so that he could come in without knocking. I was in the bathroom checking my hair when he walked in.

"Hello, I'm here. I see you are all set to go so let's hit the road." He asked me in the elevator if I was excited about seeing my family, to which I said yes. He wanted to know if I had eaten, to which I responded no. I didn't usually eat before I flew, which had nothing to do with stomach issues but more using plane bathrooms.

"Well, the bathroom on my plane is much nicer than on commercial flights. I thought maybe we could have some coffee and a fresh fruit plate or whatever you like. We are going to have salads for lunch if that is ok with you. I don't generally like eating a heavy meal on the plane either." I said that would be wonderful. I missed having my coffee and fruit sounded just fine. We talked about the weather, and it was going to be a nice day for flying. I told James that I mentioned to my son that he wanted to meet them. I had to confess that I hadn't mentioned anything about James until now. He looked at me with a puzzled look.

"Is there a reason why you haven't mentioned me to your family? Not that it upsets me or anything, but I am curious why." I explained that I was afraid to say anything because we were new friends, and I didn't tell my son who all my friends were. However, since James said he wanted to meet them, I felt I had to say something about him. James laughed.

"So, what did you tell your son about me? It doesn't matter if you told him I had money, that sort of thing doesn't bother me." I explained that I had told him a few things such as him being Scottish and younger than me and that yes, he had money.

"Of course, my granddaughter was listening and came back on the phone and asked me who James was and I said that you were a very nice man whom I liked a lot. She wanted to know if you were my boyfriend. She's six going on seven so you have to expect that kind of thing from her. She is a smart little girl, although she would not want to be called little. She says she's a big girl and of course she is right." James smiled and laughed when he heard what she had said. He said his younger cousins were always saying things like that and being children, they had no filters. It was never anything bad mind you, he said, but it did make their parents blush a little. We both were laughing at that point. James did not overlooked that she told her granddaughter and son that she liked him a lot. He was happy at the thought that she felt more comfortable around him and maybe she was willing to pursue more than just being friends. We arrived at the airport just before 10:00. James pulled up to security, showed his identification and we went out to the tarmac. There was parking available for VIPs which James pulled into.

"Don't we have to go through a security check and have our baggage scanned?" He said no it wasn't done for private jets.

"Generally, people with larger private jets like mine don't go through a security process. In some countries they require it but for the places that I generally fly into and out of, there is no requirement. I pay for the privilege of having access to the private terminal, so the onus is put on me to make sure that I follow the rules, which I always do. But when I am coming into or out of Scotland, Canada or Germany, Customs always comes onboard to do a passport check. When we land in Scotland, Customs will come onboard and when we return to Canada they will come onboard." He got my luggage out of the trunk and pulled out his briefcase. I asked him where his luggage was, and he said it was already on the plane. The flight crew were staying at the same hotel, and he gave his luggage to the captain to take on board. He took mine out of the back of the car and put them by the stairs. We went up the steps and one of the flight attendants greeted us.

"Good morning sir, Ms. Harris welcome on board." The flight attendant stood back and let us come in and go down the aisle. This was all new to me. I'd never been on a private plane before. I took the time to look around. The interior was really jaw dropping. Clearly James spent a lot on this plane and had it designed to his specifications. The seats were like sitting in a recliner and so very comfortable. I asked him if I could take a quick look around and he expected I would. He was not lying about the bathroom. It was gorgeous, the whole plane was gorgeous. It could easily seat thirty or forty people quite comfortably. I returned to my seat and told James it was a beautiful plane, and I was speechless. I guess he could tell I'd never been on a private plane before.

We took off and shortly after we reached our flying altitude, the flight attendants brought us coffee and some fresh fruit. James introduced me to each of them prior to taking off. He said that each of his flight crews worked for him for a long time, but they were not, however, his only flight crew. The captain for this flight was Charles and his first officer was Randy. The flight attendants were Maria and Janine. James explained that because of the amount of travel he did he had to have three pilots and three first officer and six flight attendants. He had one crew that flew within Canada, and another based in Toronto that flew over to Scotland and a final crew that he used to fly within Europe.

"As you can probably guess I do a lot of flying on business and I prefer to be comfortable. But at the rate my family is growing, my cousins who are married with kids who will eventually be having kids, I may have to order a larger plane. My Mum has a brother Duncan that I already mentioned, and she has a sister, Fenella and my Dad had one brother Alistair. My Uncle Duncan never married because he said he never found the right woman. My Aunt Fenella and her husband Dr. Callum Sinclair have a son Angus who married Catherine Williams and they have three daughters and a son. Their two oldest girls, Fiona and Laren are seventeen-year-old identical twins and are attending the University of Edinburgh, then Skye is thirteen and Cailean turned seven in June. He and Ayleen are close in age. My Dad's brother Alistair died in the same car accident as my father. His wife, my Aunt Alisa has a son Malcolm and a daughter Glynnis. Her son Malcolm married Fiona Crawford and they have two sons, Cameron, and Donald age seventeen also twins, not identical and also attending the University of Edinburgh. Alisa's daughter Glynnis married Gowan Carmichael, and they have a boy Errol who is sixteen and a girl, Mackenzie who is fifteen. Fenella, Angus, Alisa, and Malcolm work for me. Catherine, Fiona and Glynnis are stay at home mums for now. Callum is a surgeon at one of the biggest hospitals in Glasgow and Gowan works at a very prestigious law firm in Glasgow, and he does most of my legal work. At least once a year we plan a family vacation. Sometimes it is during the school break or when school is finished. Fiona and Laren are studying to be research scientists and Cameron and Donald are studying business like I did. All of them are in the top of their class and I will not be surprised if they all graduate with honours." He pulled out his tablet and showed me some pictures of his family.

There were quite a few redheads with blue eyes. James's Mum was very pretty. It was my guess that he got his brown curly hair and green eyes from her. His Dad had reddish with green eyes. His Uncle Duncan had reddish brown hair with blue eyes and his Aunt Fenella had reddish hair and green eyes. There was a picture of his Uncle Alistair and his wife Alisa. Alistair had brown hair and blue eyes and Alisa was a redhead with blue eyes. All of the cousins except for Cailean had reddish hair and blue eyes. Cailean took after James and had curly brown hair and green eyes. I think James probably had a soft spot for Cailean, but I was sure he never favoured one over the other.

"They are a wonderful looking bunch James. I will have to show you some of my family pictures when we go back." James had to confess that he looked through her album and he hoped she didn't mind. It was the night he stayed there and was up for a couple of hours after she went to bed. Cassandra assured him that she didn't mind. I told him a bit more about my family.

"My Dad, Walter was born in Canada and my Mum Natalie was born in England. They met during the war and married when it was over. My Dad travelled by train once up into Scotland and stopped at a town called Arnprior. He was wearing his Canadian military uniform so when he stopped in at a pub, and they saw he was from Canada, everyone bought him a pint. He lived in Arnprior, Ontario for a short period of his life so he wanted to check the place out he said. My Mom was born and raised in London. She was a war bride and at the end of the war she came over on the Queen Mary. She was very brave to have left her home at such a young age to move to Canada and start a life there. I have the utmost respect for her being so daring. I have three other siblings, but I only keep in touch with my sister Sonya on a regular basis. My family story is a complicated one." James could see that even after all these years it still hit me whenever I spoke of them, so he did not ask any further questions about my family.

We sat silently for a few minutes drinking our coffee. Time passed quickly, and it was already lunch. James asked me before we left my place what kind of salad I wanted, and we both decided on a chef salad with an herb dressing. Maria brought our salads and asked if there was anything we wanted to drink. We both had water. We talked through our meal. James asked more about my son and daughter in law. He said he thought he knew a lot about my granddaughter because I talked about her a lot. I had to laugh because I really did talk about her a lot. I told him of the first time I met Lindsay and the time she had stayed the night at my home. I thought she was going to sleep in the spare room but silly me I woke up and realized she was with Ross downstairs.

"I remember saying to them when they were sitting on the couch in the living room that I would have appreciated a heads up about sleeping arrangements. I think Lindsay thought I was angry because she didn't say too much. I told her I was joking, sort of, and she was ok after that. To be honest, I couldn't have been happier with the girl he chose. They really are perfect for each other. I remember at their wedding reception each of the parents were asked to say something. When the microphone was passed to me, I had nothing written out and I thought I would be able to get through the speech without crying but I didn't. It wasn't something I wanted to do but Ross said everyone else was, so I didn't have much of a choice. Not something I ever want to do again, speak in front of a crowd." We finished our salads, and the captain came out to say that we were only about forty-five minutes from landing. He went back into the cockpit and Janine the other flight attendant took away our dishes. It was actually nice to eat off actual china and not plastic.

"Tell me what else is on your bucket list?" I didn't think he would remember that, but I told him it was not a bucket list before I die type of thing, it was a bucket list of things that I have never done and wanted to. Some of it was rather silly and I told him he wasn't allowed to laugh. He promised that he wouldn't.

"I don't have a lot of things at least I don't think I do. I started the list some years ago and after my husband died, I came across it and I started to think of all the things that I wanted to do and never had. I think I mentioned the sports car which I can now cross off my list, thank you. There was the horse drawn carriage in winter, the yacht which I must admit I only put down last year. I have always wanted to go to Aruba. I was able to go to Hawaii once, so I was able to cross that off. I am a bit of a Christmas ornament fanatic and I have always wanted to go to Austria or Germany to buy ornaments at the Christmas markets. I know it's silly because I could easily get them online but being among the atmosphere is what I am wanting. I have always wanted to try a particular champagne bottled in the year I was born but it is so expensive, and I thought if I didn't like it my God what a terrible thing. Then there is, well there is other stuff, but you get the idea. I want to apologize for not having told you I went to Scotland once before. It was several years ago and frankly I don't remember too much about the trip. I was trying to get my life back to a point of normal, but I wanted to show Janet and Wade my appreciation for being so helpful and quite frankly the whole trip was a bit of a blur." He said there was no need to apologize and perhaps this time I would look at it with different eyes.

I wasn't going to tell James that I never ever had a proper proposal where the man got down on one knee and proposed with a beautiful ring. I'm not into these spectator proposals that you see where the man skywrites 'will you marry me' or does so in front of a huge crowd. I want him to ask me in private and I most definitely don't want to read it. Been married twice and not once did I get my dream proposal. The captain informed us we were getting ready to land, so we buckled up and waited to touch down. By the time we came to a full stop it was just after 4:30 pm.

I sent Ross a text letting him know the approximate landing time before we departed, and it was right on time. I figured by the time I got through the introductions and James had a chance to talk it would be closer to 5:00 before we left the airport and by got to the restaurant around 5:30 or so. The plane taxied around to where it was to stay until departure again. When the stairs were brought to the door, Maria opened it. James and I got up. He grabbed my luggage which was put up front in the storage area and I followed him down the stairs. Ross, Lindsay, and Ayleen were getting out of the car which was parked in the VIP area. When I was at the bottom of the stairs Ayleen came running over.

“Gramma, Gramma I am so glad you are here.” She gave me a big hug and a kiss and then stood beside me a little shy of James who came down the stairs. Ross and Lindsay came over and I hugged and kissed each of them. Ayleen was wearing a really pretty cotton pink dress and Ross was wearing jeans and a dress shirt and Lindsay was wearing dress pants and a blouse.

“Ross, Lindsay, Ayleen this is James Sutherland.” James shook each of their hands and crouched down to shake Ayleen’s. Ayleen had grown some since I last saw her, but James of course was very much taller.

“It is a great pleasure to meet you Ayleen. Your Gramma talks about you all the time.” I wasn’t sure what she was thinking. She looked at him and I could tell her mind was forming an opinion. James stood up and started to talk with Ross and Lindsay. Ayleen was looking up the stairs into the plane. James took notice.

“Would you like to come onboard and have a look Ayleen.” Of course, she nodded yes. She was a curious child. James asked Ross and Lindsay to come onboard as well. Janine greeted Ayleen and I took her into the cockpit to meet the pilots. She came out and went into the body of the plane looking all around. She was fascinated with it I could tell. I could also tell that Ross and Lindsay were both impressed too. They both said it was a beautiful plane. Ayleen came back and took my hand.

"Gramma I have to use the washroom. Can you take me." She was so much like her father, and I told him as much. I showed her where the washroom was. She was old enough to use it by herself. When she came out, she walked back to her parents. James was talking to Ross and Lindsay.

"Mr. Sutherland, I like your plane a lot. Maybe I can go up in it sometime, up in air." James said that he would love to have her as a guest. We got off the plane again and walked over to the car. Ross and Lindsay shook James's hand once again saying it was very nice to meet him. Ayleen waited for me.

"Gramma aren't you going to give Mr. Sutherland a kiss goodbye. We have to go and eat now. Goodbye Mr. Sutherland. I like you very much. C'mon Gramma give him a hug and kiss goodbye." She got in the car but was not yet buckled up. I gave James a hug and kiss on the cheek and thanked him for the trip.

"No Gramma, you are supposed to kiss your boyfriend on the lips not on the cheek. I thought you said you liked him a lot." Well out of the mouths of babes. James pulled me close.

"Now what is this that you have been telling your granddaughter." He laughed and pulled me toward him and kissed me. I could hear Ayleen in the background woohooing. It was a little embarrassing. James laughed and went back up the stairs to the plane. I got in the backseat with Ayleen. I told her that Gramma was embarrassed by that.

"But Gramma you said you liked him, and I can tell he really likes you. You should marry him. I like him, and I would like to have him as a Grandpa." Ross laughed, and Lindsay shook her head laughing.

"Well Ayleen I am not sure if I want to get married again. I like James a lot, but I don't think either one of us is looking to get married." Ross made a snort, and I asked him what that was for.

"Mum, seriously, the way he looks at you and you at him. Are you seriously going to tell me that you are just friends?" He did that air quotes that Ayleen always used to do.

"Why are you letting what happened to you in the past stop you from being happy with someone? Don't use age as an excuse either because that guy is clearly into you, and you don't want to see it. I mean seriously he flew you here out of his way." We were just getting ready to leave when James knocked on my window and I put it down.

"It seems that I am going to have to fly back to Scotland instead of going to Toronto. The crew that flies me overseas is in Toronto and can't get a flight here for a day, so we are going to be staying in Ottawa for at least a day or two." Ayleen was clapping her hands and asked him to join us for dinner. Clearly, she liked him. Ross said that it was fine if he wanted to join us, it wasn't anything fancy though. James thanked him and Ayleen for the invitation but said that he was going with the crew to the hotel. He said he would give me a call in the morning. He waved bye and winked at Ayleen, and we took off from the airport.

"Gramma I like the way he talks. Where is he from? Can we go visit him at his home?" I explained that James was Scottish and was born in Scotland. He had a big home there, but he travelled all over the world and he was going to be building a home near Gramma. Ross turned around and looked at me.

"And you don't see that he's interested in you, really?" Ayleen then asked her Dad if they could go and visit him in Scotland. She didn't know where Scotland was but thought it would be fun to fly on his plane to Scotland. We got to the restaurant, ordered our meals and I had a glass of wine. I wasn't terribly hungry, but this was their favourite restaurant, so we had seafood. Ayleen was a bit of a picky eater when she was around four but finally liked seafood. It was getting late by the time we finished. I paid the bill, and we got back on the road. Ross didn't like driving in the city, so Lindsay did most of the driving.

We got to their place around 8:00. Ayleen was still pretty excited from being on the plane. Her first time so she was talking constantly about it. I loved their new home. They looked around at several before they settled on this one. It was close enough to Almonte so that Ayleen didn't have far to go to school. It made it easy for Ross and Lindsay too because they both worked in Almonte. It was close enough for Ayleen to have friends close by but not too close that Ross and Lindsay didn't get the privacy and treed property they always wanted. I was happy to pay what it cost, and it also had a bedroom just for me. Ayleen took me up to my room and left me to unpack my clothes. Ross came up and sat on the edge of the bed. He never did this, so I was curious why he was now.

"Listen Mum, in all seriousness, if you like this guy don't let anything hold you back. I know what it was like before for you and I know how badly your heart was broken. But this guy seems genuine, and I really do think he likes you a lot. Not that I was comfortable seeing my sixty-three-year-old mother kissing another man, but I could tell the two of you belong together." I sat down next to him on the edge of the bed.

"Ross I am going to be honest with you. I do like him a lot and I think I may be falling in love with him. I know that makes you uncomfortable hearing your mother saying that, but it was hard for me to get to this point. It wasn't only my heart that was broken but my trust and you know how much I place on giving my trust to someone. It didn't have to be that way, but he couldn't accept me as a wife even though he was the one who wanted to marry me. We both know the reasons for that, but I always thought he would come around. But he didn't and now he's gone, and that part of my life is over. I am happy now with my life for the first time in a very long time and since James has come into my life, I think I could be even happier. But that kiss you saw at the airport was the first one, so I am not going to rush into anything." Ross agreed that I should go at my own pace but reminded me, as only he could, I was after all sixty-three and didn't have a lot of good years left. I slapped him on the backside, and he left laughing.

Ayleen came in and said that my phone was ringing. I took it from her, and it was James. He wanted to let me know what hotel he was at and if we were free, he could take us out for dinner on Monday. His flight to Scotland was going to be leaving at 11:00 pm Monday night and he wanted to get together before he left, if it was ok. I told him I would call him back after I spoke to Ross and Lindsay because I had no idea what the plans were for the next couple of days. I went downstairs to see what their plans were. Ross said they really didn't have anything set in stone. Because it was summer holidays, Lindsay was off, and Ross booked the first week I was there. I said that James wanted to take us out to dinner on Monday night if we were agreeable.

"I told you; he hasn't even been away from you for two hours and he's calling you to see you again. Tell him we are good with that. Just let us know where and we can meet him." I told Ross not to be such a brat, but he laughed at me. I gave James a call back and said that we would love to have dinner with him and where could we meet him. He wanted to pick us up, but Lindsay said that it would be easier to go in their car. Ayleen came running into the living room with a pretty dress in her hand.

"Gramma, Gramma look what I am going to wear when we go out with Mr. Sutherland." James could hear her and laughed. He named the restaurant and Lindsay knew where it was. We set a time, and I said good night to James.

"Wow that's an expensive place. We have obviously never been there before. I wonder if there is a dress code." Lindsay looked it up online and there was a dress code. She said that Ross didn't own a suit since he lost all his weight, and she didn't have anything suitable to wear either since she lost weight.

"That's an easy fix. We will go shopping tomorrow and I will get Ross a suit and you a dress or pant suit, whatever you want. Ayleen already has her pretty dress, so we don't need to worry about anything for her. Let's go early tomorrow so we can get any alterations made as quickly as possible if necessary." We decided to go to the closest big mall as it had a wide variety of shops for both men and women. Ross and Ayleen sat and watched a little tv and then he took her up for her bath and bedtime story. Lindsay and I sat in the kitchen having a glass of wine. She didn't drink often but I picked up some wine before coming.

"I know that Ross has already given you his opinion, but I would like to throw in my two cents if I may. Ross doesn't know all the things you went through because I promised you, I would never say anything. I didn't tell him anything, not even after he passed away. But I have to agree with Ross, this guy seems to like you a lot and I think he will treat you the way you should have always been treated. I am not going to say what you should do because that choice is yours to make and you alone, but I can honestly tell you from the brief time that we met him, if you did decide to make a life with him, we would include him in our lives. I don't know if that factors into your decision or not, but I wanted you to know that we like him." It meant a lot to me, and I told her so. They never allowed my late husband to know Ayleen because neither one of them liked him and they didn't want Ayleen to know him. But as I said to Ross it was complicated and I didn't want to jump into it.

"My life is pretty good now. I don't have to worry about finances anymore and neither do you guys. I don't want his family to think I am after his money because I am not. I have enough to live on for the rest of my days and I have trust funds set aside for you guys. You know he stayed at my place one night, in the spare room of course. He just returned from business in several countries, and he wanted to go for dinner. We ate at my place, and he was literally falling asleep on the couch, so I told him to sleep in the spare room. I am not comparing James to him because there is no comparison. James is caring and kind and everything any woman would want in a man. We've talked a lot, and I told him once that there were probably scores of much younger women who would do anything to be at his side, but he brushed it off and said he wasn't interested in any other woman. At the time I didn't think much of it, but I guess I should." We finished our wine; I gave Lindsay a hug good night and I went up to my room. Ayleen came running out to give me a hug and kiss good night. I hugged Ross good night and went into my bedroom and shut the door. I was tired and wanted to get a good night's sleep. I drifted off in no time. The next morning there was a little knock at my door.

"Gramma are you awake yet. Can I come in?" I was awake and had been awake for a little while and opened the door to let her in. I asked if Mommy and Daddy were up yet, and she said not yet. I put on my robe, and we went downstairs. I made myself some coffee and we each had a bowl of her favourite cereal. By the time we finished Ross and Lindsay were up. Lindsay took a shower and said Ross was in the shower and would be down soon. She made herself a coffee and sat at the table with us.

"Mommy, Gramma and I had cereal." Lindsay laughed and said she could see that. It was only a few minutes later that Ross came downstairs, showered, and dressed in jean shorts and a shirt. As he was getting a glass of orange juice I went up to take my own shower. It was a bit warmer today, so I decided to wear a pair of shorts myself and a sleeveless top. Lindsay dressed similarly, and Ayleen put on a cotton sleeveless dress. We were out the door by 10:00 and at the mall by 10:45.

"Who do we shop for first?" Lindsay said that we should do Ross first in case his suit needed to be altered and hopefully they could do it while we were shopping. I was willing to pay extra to get it done so I was pretty sure they wouldn't refuse. There were a couple of men's stores, but I suggested we try the more expensive one first as we were more likely to get faster alterations done. We walked in and a young man asked if he could help with anything. Ross never used to like having store attendants follow him around, but he told the guy what he was looking for and took him over to show him a few options.

They had a wide variety of summer colours in stock. I asked if it was possible to get alterations done right away as we were on a short time frame. I knew I would have to pay extra for that, but he said it shouldn't be a problem as long as the alterations weren't extensive. He tried on a light grey wool designer suit, but it didn't really suit him. I asked him to try on a navy designer suit which looked really good on him. The jacket fit him perfectly and wouldn't need alterations, but the pants had to be taken up a bit. The sales agent picked out a white Egyptian cotton shirt and a multi-coloured tie in blues. Ross looked amazing in it. Even though it was a wool blend, the sales agent said it would keep its shape and it wasn't a heavy weight wool and he would not be too hot in it. Ross said he didn't feel warm in it at all. The alterations would take about an hour or so, so we said we would be back. We then went to look for something for Lindsay. She wasn't really one to wear a dress or skirt, but I think because Ross was wearing a suit and tie she thought she would look at what would look good on her. We stopped in at one of the more upscale women's stores.

Lindsay looked through the racks and found a couple of things she wanted to try on. She came out in a lace overlay sheath designer dress. It was a deep coral colour and looked amazing. She went back into the change room and tried on the other dress which was a simple cotton green and blue print. We all agreed she looked amazing in the coral dress. We picked out some jewelry that would complement it. I didn't bring anything quite so fancy because I didn't think we would be going out much. I too had to look for something to wear tomorrow night. I picked out a red silk halter pleated dress. I brought the star necklace and earrings with me that I bought at the mall at home and thought they would look great with the dress.

Next, we had to get shoes. We went into a well-known shoe store. There were two sales agents available. Ross went with one to find shoes that would look good with his navy suit. Lindsay, Ayleen, and I went with the other sales agent. Lindsay showed her the dress and the girl said she knew the perfect shoe. Lindsay never wore heels which she told the girl. She brought back a very stylish pair of wedge sandals that were a nude colour with coral crystal patterns in them. I said they would go great with the dress. My dress was red, so it wasn't going to be hard to find a pair of shoes to wear. I went with a nude colour sling back sandal.

"Gramma can I get a new pair of shoes to wear with my pretty dress. I want to get all dressed up nice like you, Mommy and Daddy." Well of course I could not refuse her. We went over to the little girl's section, and she saw a pair that had purple on it. Purple was her favourite colour. The white wedges were not very high and had little crystal purple flowers. It had a strap on them, so she would be able to keep them on. Her dress was a white organza with big purple flowers on it. At the time Lindsay was not happy because she would have to get it dry cleaned but it was such a cute dress when I saw it I had to get it. She was won over when she saw it on her. Ayleen also had to have some jewelry, but I told her that I brought her some and it was still in my luggage. There was a nice necklace that would go perfectly with her dress.

We went back to pick up Ross's suit and then stopped for a quick bite of lunch. Ross was going to barbecue for dinner, so we didn't eat a big lunch. Heading back home I suggested to Lindsay that we go and get our hair done and a mani and pedi for me, her, and Ayleen. Ayleen was old enough now to have nail polish on her fingernails and not just her toes. I looked up the number of a place we could go to in Almonte and they had an opening for the three of us at 1:00 tomorrow afternoon. There were three stylists available that would each do our hair and three estheticians to do our mani/pedis.

We got home to their place just before it started to rain. It didn't rain long but it was long enough to cool the temperature down a bit, which I was happy about. Ayleen and I played a couple of her games while Ross and Lindsay got things organized for dinner. My sister stopped by just in time to have a bite. She wasn't going to stay but Ross insisted she stay and have dinner with us. Ayleen went out to help Ross or maybe it was just to watch him cook. I poured Sonya some iced tea and we sat in the living room chatting. She finally sold her home that she lived in for so long after her husband passed away. She was looking happier now and she even gained a little weight which was actually good because she was too thin, I thought. She bought a really nice condo in Carleton Place. She made some friends and was happy with her life.

"I'm even going to get up the nerve and get on a plane and come out and see you whenever it is good for you." I was thrilled that she was willing to do that. She was comfortable enough financially, but I said I would get her tickets and that maybe we could do it for Thanksgiving if that would work for her. She wasn't sure she would want to leave Rhonda at Thanksgiving, so I suggested she invite her to come along. That way she would have someone to talk to on the plane. I said that if Nicole and Austin could make it, they could come too.

"Are you sure you have the room. I thought you only had a two bedroom. Where would everyone sleep?" I said it was no big deal. The condo building had a family suite that was a two bedroom and two bath that I could rent for a few days and Nicole, Austin and Rhonda could stay in there. She could have my spare room. I sent Mr. O'Leary a quick text to make sure that it was available and that I wanted to book it for five days. I knew it wouldn't be a problem with the building manager.

"Well, if Rhonda can get a few days off and Nicole and Austin are able to come, I'm okay with Thanksgiving." It was agreed. I would pay for the flights for them even though she said she could get her own.

"I want to do this please. I have money now, so it isn't a problem. So please be agreeable to this ok." She thought about it for a few minutes. Sonya never liked to impose on anyone and never liked to feel indebted.

"Well alright as long as we can book first class." We laughed because I knew she was saying that jokingly, but I said that they could book first class for sure. She asked me what I was up to, so I told her about James. She was shocked because I said I never wanted to get involved with another man again. I told her I'd only known him since April, but we'd been spending a lot of time together even though he was a very busy person. She wanted to know more so I told her that he was Scottish, tall, and very handsome. I showed her the picture of me, James, and Janet. I knew she was wondering if there had been anything going on, but I assured her that we were only friends. I did tell her that he was seven years younger.

"Well good for you then. I wish I could find someone seven years younger who was a decent person." Maybe James has a friend I said, and we both laughed. It was so nice to see her laughing and enjoying our time together. Lindsay made a couple of salads to go with the burgers that Ross was bringing in. The table was set, and we sat down to dig in.

"Auntie Sonya did Gramma tell you that Mr. Sutherland brought Gramma on his plane. I went inside, it is very cool, and Mr. Sutherland said that I could go up in the plane one day." Sonya looked at me with her mouth open.

"No Ayleen, Gramma left that little detail out. Just how rich is this guy and I certainly hope he does have a friend." I explained a bit more about James and what he did. I said that I would ask him if he had a friend who was maybe just a little older than him. Sonya said that if he had a friend who was around sixty that was okay with her. I'd like to think that Ayleen didn't understand what was being said, but the smirk on her face told me otherwise. Mr. O'Leary texted me back that the suite was available and blocked it off for me. It was on the same floor as my unit, so we would all be close. The meal was good, but Sonya said she had to get back home. She hadn't planned on staying as long as did, but she was glad she did. She thanked Ross and Lindsay for letting her stay and they of course said she was welcome any time. I offered to help Lindsay clean up, but she said that she and Ross would look after it. I went up to my room to get out the necklace for Ayleen. She bounded up the stairs not long after.

"Gramma what is it like to get engaged." I asked her what brought that up and she said that she heard Mommy and Daddy talking about it. I sat her down and even though I said that it was something she should talk to Mommy about she said she wanted to talk to me about it too.

"Well Ayleen, when are older and you meet the right guy, I think you will know. You know you are a very smart girl and I hope that you are going to work on getting the best education you can first. Gramma put aside some money to help pay for your education, a really good one at a good university, so just know that you can do anything you want. But enjoy life first Ayleen, see the world or as much of it as you can. If you meet the right guy and he really loves you, then he should make sure that he saves up enough money to buy you the perfect ring. You know when I was young, perhaps a little older than you, I always dreamed of the man who was going to ask me to marry him. I pictured him getting down on one knee and proposing. I think it should be special, perhaps going on a picnic to a special spot, just the two of us and just before we are ready to leave, he gets down on his knee and opens up the box with the ring in it and it is so beautiful. But that was my dream, Ayleen. I hope that one day you will find the right man but for now, you are only six, going on seven, and you have your whole life ahead of you." I wasn't sure that answered her question, but she seemed to be okay with it. She went into her room to look at her dress and new shoes. She loved the necklace and put it on to show Mommy and Daddy. Lindsay came upstairs laughing saying she didn't want to take it off. It was time for her to have a bath, so she was going to have to take it off. She got into her pjs and toddled off down to be with Ross. She was such a happy little girl. I showed Lindsay the necklace and earrings I was going to wear. She liked them a lot.

"Maybe I can get something similar for you. It would make a nice Christmas gift. Speaking of which, are you going to come out this year." She said it might be possible, but she wasn't sure if Ross booked any time off between Christmas and New Years and would have to see if he did. They hadn't been out for Christmas in a long time, and I was hoping that this year they would. I got my pjs on and put on my robe and went downstairs. Lindsay talked to Ross about Christmas.

"Is James going to be there?" I looked at him oddly and said I didn't think so. I was sure he spent Christmas with his family in Scotland, so I doubted he would be here. I mentioned to Ross that James had a distillery back in Scotland and that he made a very nice whisky, not that I drank a lot of it, but I did taste it.

"Really nice stuff. I have a bottle at my place. I know you don't drink whisky a lot, but you might like this." Ross wasn't a big drinker nor was Lindsay but during the holidays or a special occasion they had a drink or two. Lindsay was usually the designated driver, so she rarely got the chance to drink around the holidays.

"We were at Lindsay's parent's last year and went to my Dad's on Boxing Day, so I guess if I can get some time off, we could go. We'd have to look at booking as soon as I know though because flights at that time fill up. Well Ayleen's ears perked up at the talk of going on a plane.

"Are we going on Mr. Sutherland's plane Gramma? Are we going to your place for Christmas?" Now she was all excited and it was almost time for her to go to bed. I said I would have to talk to Mommy and Daddy more about it and she would know in lots of time. She gave everyone a hug and kiss goodnight and Lindsay took her up to tuck her in. Ross and I talked a little bit more about it. He thought because Christmas and Boxing day fell on a Saturday and Sunday, which meant he would get the Monday and Tuesday off, that he could probably arrange to take off the previous Thursday and Friday and maybe the following Wednesday and Thursday. He would have to talk to his supervisor when he went back to work. They weren't planning on going on a vacation this year, so he didn't think it would be a problem. I asked why they weren't taking their usual holiday at the end of August.

He said it was going to fall right when it was Lindsay's parents fortieth wedding anniversary and so they couldn't get away. So maybe he would be able to stay until at least New Year's Day. We never celebrated New Year's together, ever, so this would be wonderful if they could stay that long. With New Year's Day falling on a Saturday, he would get Monday off, so they could fly back on the Sunday and have a full day to rest. Lindsay and Ayleen were not going back to school until the week later, so it would work out great. I wasn't going to get my hopes up though, but it looked like it would be very promising. I went to bed that night with great expectations for the holiday season.

Next morning, we were up by 9:00 and downstairs tucking into breakfast when my phone rang. It was James. He wanted to make sure we were still on for dinner that night. I said an emphatic yes and that Ayleen was going to be dressed up in purple. James said he like purple very much and was looking forward to seeing us at 6:00. He remembered that I didn't like to eat too late in the evening. I helped Lindsay do some cleaning and Ross and Ayleen went to get the car washed and waxed.

They got back in time for a light lunch which was leftover salads from yesterday and cold cuts. We left at

12:30 to make our appointments at 1:00. We got our hair done first and since we had taken showers that morning and Ayleen had her hair shampooed and conditioned the night before, they only had to style our hair. Mine didn't take long to do. Lindsay had hers put in a long French braid and Ayleen was having hers made curly. Both Lindsay and Ayleen had a natural curl in their hair so when Ayleen got hers done it was pretty curly. She liked it because the hair stylist put a really cute purple sparkly bow in her hair at the back. We had our nails and toes done next. Ayleen wanted purple, Lindsay went with a coral colour to match her dress and I went with red to match mine. My nails had grown a bit and were just a bit too long, so the manicurist filed them down a little, but she said she didn't want to do too much because the longer nail with the red was going to look really good.

We had enough time for Lindsay to get some makeup done. She never wore a lot, but I said that this was special, so she got herself all done up. I had my makeup at home and would do myself once I got there. Beauty taken care of, I paid the bill and we drove home. Ayleen kept trying to look at herself in the mirror. She didn't usually have her hair this curly, but I had a feeling now that she saw how it looked, she might just be getting Mommy to do it more often. When we got home, I went up and applied my makeup. When I was done, I got dressed, put on a little my favourite French perfume and went downstairs. Ross was already down there.

“Ross you look so handsome in that suit. I am glad you went with that colour and not the grey one.” He said that I looked very nice. Then Lindsay and Ayleen came down the stairs. Lindsay looked amazing in that dress and Ayleen looked like a little princess. Ross told them each how pretty they looked. We stopped only long enough to take a group shot with each of our phones and then went out the door. We got to the restaurant in good time and parked not far from the entrance. I wasn’t sure if we were here ahead of James or not but as I got in and was about to say who we were meeting, James came over to get us.

“Ross, love the suit, looks good. Lindsay, you look very lovely and Miss Ayleen well you look just like a princess.” He pointed to our table and Ross, Lindsay and Ayleen started over. James turned around and looked at me.

“Now what can I say about the lady in red. You look stunning.” He gave me a kiss on the cheek, and we went to the table. James ordered some champagne. Lindsay was going to decline but I said that I would be the designated driver tonight. Both she and Ross had a glass of champagne, Ayleen had some sparkling water as did I.

“So, James, my Mum said that you have your own whisky. I will have to give it a try when we go out at Christmas. At least that is what the plans are right now. I have to make sure I can get the time off at work." James said that the restaurant carried his whisky if he wanted to have a shot with him. Ross was not going to decline. The menus came, and we looked over what there was. Ross and Lindsay decided on the prime rib because they rarely came to such an expensive restaurant. I ordered the lamb and Ayleen chose the chicken with rice. James ordered a steak medium rare. He offered Lindsay more champagne, and she had another glass. Ross and James had another shot of whisky. Ross paced himself and made that his last shot.

"It goes down really smooth but I'm going to make this my last shot if that's ok. I don't think Lindsay will be having another glass of champagne because I think it is starting to get to her." We laughed and agreed that the rest of the evening would be sparkling water for the rest of the night.

It wasn't long before our meals came out and we ate and talked about a variety of things. James asked Lindsay how she liked being a kindergarten teacher. She told him that she loved it and it was great that she was actually at the same school that Ayleen went to, so they travelled to school together. He asked her about the school funding and if it was well funded. I wasn't sure where he was going with this, but I had a feeling.

"It's actually quite good. The school board is looking to get funding for the kids from grade two to eight to learn how to do coding on computers. They have computers in the school but would need new ones just for them to learn. It is a new program that was introduced in most of the schools so that kids, at an early age, understand programming and how it works. They have one teacher who comes in part time to show them but right now it isn't enough for them to be at par with some of the other schools." I could see the wheels in James's brain turning and I knew that before Lindsay and Ayleen went back to school that they would have those computers and dedicated teachers to teach them coding.

He could see that I knew what he was thinking, and he just raised his eyebrows as if to say 'what.' The meal was over, and the waiter asked if we wanted dessert. I was full of course but Ayleen asked what the dessert was, so the waiter went and got the dessert tray to show her. There were a few things on there that I knew she couldn't have because of the alcohol content but there was a chocolate mousse that she wanted. She was the only one having dessert, the rest of us were full.

"I have really enjoyed having you for dinner and I hope that we can do it again in the not-too-distant future. Especially with you Ayleen because I think you are the most adorable young lady." James was genuine in his comment about her. James paid the bill, and we got up to go. Ayleen pulled on James's hand to take him to one side. She wanted to say something to him. We thought it was cute and gave her the privacy to say what she wanted. He knelt down to hear what she wanted to say.

"Mr. Sutherlands are you going to marry Gramma because if you are you should take her on a picnic, just the two of you with cheese and crackers." James looked at her and winked and said he would definitely keep that in mind. She gave him a big hug and kiss. I think James was a little overwhelmed by it but hugged her right back.

"Thank you so much Mr. Sutherland for dinner. I loved the dessert." James said she was welcome, and it was ok if she wanted to call him James. She looked at Lindsay to ask if it was ok and Lindsay nodded yes. We walked out to the car together. Ross shook his hand and Lindsay gave him and hug and said thanks. They got in the car and got Ayleen settled. By the time we finished it was almost 8:30 and she would no doubt fall asleep on the way home.

"Thank you, James, for a wonderful evening. I really appreciate you including my family for dinner." He said no thanks were needed and he really enjoyed being around them.

"That little one, she does tug at the heart strings doesn't she." I completely agreed with him, gave him a hug and kiss on the cheek and got in the driver's seat. I was familiar enough with this part of the city to at least get us out on the road. Lindsay sat up front and said she would tell me where to turn off to get on the highway. James motioned for the driver to come forward. He knew that he would be having a drink or two and didn't want to drive himself, so he ordered car service. The car service picked them up at the airport and would be taking them back to the airport later in the evening.

On the drive home everyone was still full. Ayleen got quiet and we knew it wouldn't be long before she fell asleep. Lindsay told me which turn off to take and it within minutes we were on the highway and heading back to their place. Normally I didn't like driving at night, but my vision was much better now and for the most part the highway was well lit. Ross fell silent in the back as well. Perhaps the glass of champagne and the two shots of whisky helped with that. Lindsay was talking in a low voice, so she wouldn't wake up the two in the back.

"I had a really nice time tonight, thank you for that and for getting us new things to wear. I will say it again that I think James is a very nice man and I think you should go with your heart." Although she said she wasn't going to say what I should do, she admitted she was now because she was watching James all night.

"He was looking at you with such a look in his eyes. I could tell he respects you and thinks the world of you." I was thinking about what she was saying.

"When I go back home, I will be there only about a week and James invited me and my friend Roxie, Janet, and her husband Wade to a charity gala in Toronto at some big hotel. I said that we would go, and I am actually looking forward to it. Then, and I haven't told Ross about this, he asked both Roxie and I to go to Scotland for a couple of weeks in September. I'll be back about a week or two before Thanksgiving just in time for Sonya, Rhonda, Nicole, and Austin to come to visit. I knew you guys wouldn't be able to get that much time off, so I hope you don't mind I didn't ask you guys first." Ross stirred in the back. I thought he was asleep, but he only had his eyes closed.

"Hmm you are going to his home in Scotland, sounds great. Just remember to bring me back a case of that whisky. We are not upset you didn't invite us for Thanksgiving. We are going for Christmas remember and it doesn't bother me a bit that my wife was staring at another man all night." Lindsay laughed because she knew he was kidding which he really was.

I got up the next morning ready to go and visit with Christelle. We always met at the mall which was halfway between us. I offered to pick her up, but she said it was easier to take the bus. We set a time for 11:30. I arrived right at 11:30 and walked through to the mall. She was sitting waiting for me to arrive. She hadn't noticed me approaching so I came up and sat down beside her.

"Oh, my goodness, you look so different. I never would have recognized you. You've lost a lot of weight, but you look amazing. You'll have to tell me about your secret on how you lost the weight." We laughed and started to walk back to the restaurant. I asked her how she was feeling after her surgery. She said it was okay now but was hoping that she would never have to go for another one at least not for a long time. We laughed and joked all the way to the restaurant. We chose a booth to sit at because it was easier for her.

"Ok so show me the pictures of James. I want to see what this guy looks like." I pulled out my phone and showed her the picture of me, Janet, and James but also the picture from dinner last night with Ross, Lindsay, and Ayleen and the one with Roxie, Janet, me, and James. She commented on how good we all looked and especially how cute Ayleen was.

"My goodness Ayleen has grown since the last time I saw her. She looks so pretty in that purple dress. But all of you look really nice. Ross and Lindsay have lost weight and they both look really nice all dressed up. Ross cleans up well doesn't he." I was waiting for her to make a comment about James, but she was taking her time getting to it.

"Ok so now about James. My guides were talking in my ear as I was looking at the photos and they were all saying yes, yes and applauding. Surely you can see that Ross likes him because he has a big smile on his face, and you can tell that Ayleen likes him too because in a couple of the pictures she kept looking up at him smiling. And of course, you are glowing. I love what all of you are wearing. Oh, look at you, the lady in red, sexy. I'll bet James had something nice to say. So, now that I have a clearer picture of him, I have to say that I do like him. I mean who wouldn't he is very handsome and as I said the vibe is good." I agreed that we looked really good that night and I admitted that I was really starting to like James more than just as a friend. But I changed the subject and we talked about the trip in April. I had more pictures of his villa to show, and she was giddy with excitement at the thought of going.

"I wish it was now. It looks really beautiful. It will be great to see Judy again and I can't wait to meet Janet and Roxie. I am so excited about going." We talked for the next hour and then wandered back out into the mall and looked in at a few shops. Of course, whenever I was back east and went to visit Christelle I always stopped at the Chinese place close by to pick up two dozen of their famous egg rolls. I just loved them, but I could eat two dozen by myself, so it was always a treat.

We stopped in front of a couple of clothing stores and Christelle said that she would have to pick up a few things before the trip. We went and sat in a corner to chat, and we had a talk about how I lost weight. She knew that I won the lottery, but she didn't know that I hired a personal training and worked my ass off. It took a year to get rid of all the weight I gained, and I kept working out to tone everything up with the exercises and weights. I said that I did have to have a little cosmetic work done to get rid of loose flab which the work out was not getting rid of.

I did the same for Ross and Lindsay; hired them a personal trainer to help them lose their weight and got them really good work out machines so they could continue to work out often. She already knew about the self-defense classes but didn't realize that all the work outs and weights that I continued to do was because of that. I said that I was going to put in my order for the egg rolls and that I was going to have to get back. Although there were no plans for dinner that night, I knew that everyone was going to love the egg rolls. We hugged and kissed each other. I hated it when I had to leave.

"You are my best friend in the whole world, and nobody knows me as well as you do. You know that I miss you all the time and you are going to have to come back out and visit me and see my new place." Christelle agreed that she would love to come out for a visit, but we would talk about it another time. I left and said I would give her a call the next day. Driving back to Ross's place gave me some time to think about what Christelle said. Maybe I was being too protective of myself. James never did anything in the months I had known him to prove that he was anything less than honest and respectful.

The rest of my time with Ross, Lindsay and Ayleen flew by but I was going home on Saturday. I got a text from James saying that they would be at the airport at 3:00 on Saturday to pick me up. Sonya wanted us to come over to her place for my last day there. She was a great cook and was going to make a roast of venison. We agreed we wouldn't tell Ayleen what it was though because we didn't want her to think that Sonya killed Bambi.

We arrived at her condo at 4:00 on Friday afternoon as requested. She was on the top floor and her unit overlooked the water. It wasn't a huge place, but she didn't want a big place. It was a two bedroom two and half bath. Her dining room was big enough to hold six people easily. I asked her if the furniture was all new because I didn't remember seeing this when I went to her place years ago. She said everything was new, she sold the house furnished. We changed the subject and talked about her condo.

"It smells great in here and I love your place." It was easy to see that she was so much happier now. She knew that I was going to have an early night, so she set dinner for 5:30. Sonya was a fabulous cook, and she made the best pies which were on the counter and which Ayleen had been eyeing. The girls had a glass of wine, Ross was now the designated driver. The meal was great, and the berry pie was scrumptious. Ayleen had ice cream with hers. The dishes were all put in the dishwasher, and we sat having some coffee and talking.

"Nicole and Austin will be able to make it for Thanksgiving and Rhonda as well. I'm really looking forward to it now even though I am still a bit nervous to fly." I was thrilled she was coming and said that the family suite was booked for Nicole, Austin, and Rhonda.

My condo was larger than all the others on the floor, so they had to build a smaller unit with two decent sized bedrooms, a smaller kitchen and living room to accommodate the change. It was right next to my unit which was something that I was happy about, not having a neighbor right on the other side of the wall all the time. But I had to admit that everyone in the building was very courteous and didn't make a lot of noise.

"I am so happy. It will be great to see Nicole again. I haven't seen her since Jerome died and I haven't seen Rhonda since Mom died. This is going to be great. I am going to put in an order for my turkey when I get back." Rhonda and Sonya were going to come a few days before Thanksgiving to avoid the crush of people travelling, which was great and Nicole and Austin would be able to make it on Friday before Thanksgiving. I was excited and looking forward to it.

We left Sonya's at 7:00 and went back to Ross's. We talked about her new place on the way back. Ayleen was commenting on being able to look at the water from so high up. We got home, and it was such a nice evening we went for a short walk. When we got back from the walk, Ayleen was starting to yawn so Lindsay took her up for her bath and to get her pjs on. We had no plans for the next day other than to just hang around the house. Lindsay's parents were going to come for lunch. It would be nice to see them again too. I asked Ross and Lindsay not to say anything about James, at least not for now. They both agreed but they couldn't guarantee about Ayleen.

The next morning was bright and warm. It was already plus twenty-five, so I decided to wear one of my summer dresses. Ayleen came into my room as I was putting on some makeup. This would be my chance to have a private word with her about James. I said that I needed to talk with her about something and she came in and sat down on the bed with me.

"Gramma is not ready for a bunch of people to know about James, so can I please ask you not to say anything when Grand'Mere and Gramps come. Can you please do that for Gramma. It isn't that it is a secret, but Gramma is not ready for anyone to know about James, yet ok." She agreed that she wouldn't say anything. She ran off downstairs while I finished getting ready.

Ross was making Lindsay and Ayleen's breakfast and asked me if I wanted anything. I said I would have toast, coffee, and orange juice as I wasn't really that hungry. Ayleen was happily finishing off her cereal but spilled some milk on her dress. Lindsay took her up to change her into another one. Ross worked this past week and spoke to his supervisor about taking the time off at Christmas. His supervisor said it wasn't a problem for him to take off the time he wanted. There was a relief person that would do the route for him while he was away.

That is wonderful. I am so looking forward to seeing Ayleen on Christmas morning." It will be the first time that we have spent Christmas together in many years. Ross and Lindsay came once when I lived in Edmonton but since Ayleen was born they were not able to come. They couldn't afford the time off work, or the cost of the airfare and I wasn't in a position to pay for their tickets either. I always had a fresh tree at Christmas and Ross said that he was looking forward to it as they always had a fake tree.

Ayleen came bounding down the stairs and sat back at the table to finish her juice. She was now wearing one of the pink dresses I got her. Pink was her second favourite colour, which she let everyone know all the time. Lindsay's parents arrived at 11:00. They were a bit early, but Lindsay told them that we had to leave to take me back to the airport no later than 1:00. We went out and sat on the front porch talking while Ayleen was on her swing set. She kept asking Ross to push her, which we all knew was just a game because she was old enough now to get the swing to go up high.

Lindsay's Mom brought a tossed salad and Lindsay and I had prepared a pasta salad after breakfast. Ross and Lindsay's Dad went to fire up the barbecue. We were going to have burgers with salads. I told Ross that I was only having some tossed salad because I didn't want anything heavy when I flew.

Ayleen, as promised, didn't say anything about James although she almost blurted something out a couple of times. She was good though, she caught herself and being the smart little girl she was, changed the subject. Lindsay's Mom never thought anything of it. The burgers were ready, so we sat down. Lindsay's Dad asked me how things were going. They sent condolence cards when my husband died but they knew that I was not heartbroken about it.

"Things are going great. I moved into a new condo last year which I just love. It has mostly seniors in it, which is ok. At least I don't have to worry about noise or loud parties." Everyone laughed at that. They knew I won money, and I kept my promise to them to help them out for all that they had done for Ross and Lindsay. We agreed at the time that we wouldn't talk about it further.

It was nearing 1:00 and I went up and got my luggage. Lindsay's Mom offered to do the dishes while we were gone but Lindsay said she was going to put them in the dishwasher. They wished me a safe flight and left. We didn't really have to leave at 1:00 but in order not to raise questions we said 1:00.

We put everything away, Ross put my luggage in the car, and we left just before 2:00. It would give us lots of time to get to the airport. Ayleen didn't say too much on the trip to the airport. I asked her if anything was wrong, and she said no. Ross said that she was probably going to miss me.

"You know Ayleen, you and Mommy and Daddy are coming to see me for Christmas this year. Won't that be exciting, and I bet you are going to get lots and lots of gifts." Ross said that she still believed in Santa, and I was glad about that as so many kids around her age didn't.

"Gramma is James going to be at your place for Christmas?" I reminded her that I already told her that I didn't think so because he spent Christmas with his family in Scotland.

"Well, it would have been nice. I like him a lot." I could see Lindsay looking at me in the rearview mirror with raised eyebrows. Ross was chuckling to himself. They both made it very clear that they thought James liked me a lot and that I like him a lot.

Ayleen was busy looking out the window as we drove on the highway. I fell silent too for a bit. Finally, we arrived at the airport and Lindsay drove to the gate to go to the private terminal. She pulled the car into the VIP parking. James's plane was already there, and the stairs were in place at the door of the plane. James stood at the top and waved everyone to come onboard. Ross carried my luggage and left it at the bottom of the stairs. Ayleen ran up to James and he picked her up.

"My word you look very pretty in your pink dress, and I love those sparkly sandals." Ayleen informed him that Gramma bought them for her.

"Gramma has very good taste doesn't she. Ross, I brought you a case of my whisky and Lindsay, I brought you a castle line lace tablecloth, for those special occasions." Ayleen was watching and looking but said nothing.

“Ayleen, I didn’t forget you. I brought you a skirt made of my tartan. Normally it is ankle length, but I had it made to the knee. It has a white blouse and black vest. This is traditionally what young girls of your age would wear in Scotland on special occasions. Ayleen looked at the gifts from James. She took the skirt out to look at it by placing it against her.

“Thank you very much James this is so pretty, but when should I wear it?” Since James said it was for special occasions she knew it wasn’t something she could wear to school. Lindsay said that she would wear it at Christmas at Gramma’s. Ross and Lindsay thanked James for the gifts.

“James are you going to come to Gramma’s for Christmas?’ Even though I said that he would be with his family she had to ask. James said that he had plans to be with his family in Scotland but if things changed, he would definitely let her know. She seemed happy with that and went and sat in one of the seats.

The captain popped his head out to say that they were ready to go whenever he was. I walked Ross, Lindsay, and Ayleen back down. James waited at the top of the stairs as he gave them hugs and kisses bye from the plane. I hugged each of them goodbye and gave Ayleen a big kiss. I hated saying goodbye to them as it was always hard for me to leave.

Tears were falling down my cheeks as I went up the stairs. James hugged me, and we got onto the plane. I got a tissue out and I thought he was going to say something, but I was glad that he didn't. We saw Lindsay pull out of the VIP parking and back out the gate. I could see Ayleen's face and her hands waving. We buckled up and the captain started to taxi out onto the runway. Once we were up in the air, Maria came around to ask if we wanted drinks. I said that I would have a small bit of James whisky, which I think shocked him. He asked for a glass as well. She brought them to our table and went back to the front.

"It is hard to leave them after visiting. I feel like I'm always leaving them behind and it has been harder since Ayleen came along. But things are different now, they are coming for Christmas and maybe they will come more often." I felt a bit better, and the whisky was helping a bit. We talked about how his trip was and how his family was. I told him that my sister Sonya and her family were coming for Thanksgiving.

"So how are things coming along with the house or have you been too busy to check up on that." While his trip back to Scotland had been a busy one, he said that he was getting regular updates from George. He was doing a wonderful job and finished the caretaker's cottage and the Quonset. The house was already completely framed, and the roof was going on next week. The garage was also nearly finished. Everything was coming along great and even a little ahead of schedule.

James had an interior designer, Christina, who was going to help to complete the interior of the house. She sent him a number of layouts which he pulled out to show me. He wanted to go with a warm country feel to the house. Queen Anne homes typically had a lot of wood in them, but James didn't want it to feel quite so dark, but I suggested that if it had a warmer tone, it would look good as long as there wasn't too much of it. One thing he didn't want was wallpaper, which I told him I was happy about because I hated wallpaper. He pulled out each board of each room that the designer did up.

We looked through all of the different layouts and picked out the colour schemes for each room. I told him that I liked the coffered ceilings in the rooms they were in and the beamed ceilings as well. There were paint swatches and fabric swatches of varying colours, so we tried them all to see what looked best. I said what I thought would look nice, but I was not an interior designer and maybe she would have a different opinion, but James liked them too and hoped that it would all work.

We looked at the design for the kitchen and for the most part the layout I didn't have a problem with.

The one drawing had white cabinets with a dark granite countertop and accenting backsplash. He could tell by the look on my face that I didn't like it. I told him I didn't like white cabinets, but it was of course his house and his choice. He admitted he wasn't fond of white either but couldn't decide between the really dark cabinets and the warm brown ones.

I thought the pecan-coloured cabinets would look nice with a light brown fleck in the dark brown natural stone countertop with a brown and tan backsplash would be nice. The designer included a lot of samples of countertop and backsplash as well as samples of the cabinetry. We looked at them as a set and James agreed it looked very nice. We picked out all the swatches, tiles, and paint colours for every room and closed the book. Janine came and got the book and put it in the storage cabinet.

"I couldn't have done that without your help. I think the designer will agree with the choices we picked out, but we shall see. Hopefully, it will all go together and work out perfectly. I think keeping the paint colour for the most part in rich warm tones was a good idea. There is going to be lots of traditional plaster work done on the ceiling especially around the light fixtures. I'm going to leave the light fixtures up to the designer to pick out. I don't want to be bothered picking every light fixture for every room. I do agree with you about using natural stone instead of granite. It is much easier to look after and requires little care. Once she has made these changes, I can show you the revisions and see if you like them." I told him that it wasn't necessary to get my opinion on this because it was his house, but he said that he valued my opinion and wanted to make sure that I would like it.

"You'll be coming over a lot I hope, and I don't want you to turn your nose up when you walk into a room." He laughed because that wasn't something I did and of course he knew that. I appreciated his confidence in my opinion. He asked if I was hungry for anything, and I said no but if he was, to go ahead and eat. I mentioned to James that I met with Christelle and showed her the pictures I had of him and my family. He had a curious look on his face.

"She thought you were very handsome and was getting good vibes from all her guides." I explained to him that she was a master reiki and very spiritual. She was also very intuitive and could see spirits from time to time. I thought maybe he would laugh at that, but he didn't.

"I have a very dear friend who is very much like a grandmother to me. She lives in the village, and she is a very well-respected medium. All the best mediums come from Scotland you know." He told me more about her and how he met her. He was finishing university at age twenty-two and was having coffee in a small café and she noticed him and came over to give him a reading.

She was fifty-six at the time and what she told him he thought was quite interesting. But he never said what it was that she told him. Both sets of his grandparents died by the time he was fourteen, so he didn't have a grandparental figure in his life. Annie was her name he said, and she took an instant liking to him. She was now in her late eighties, and he saw her as often as he could when he went back to Scotland.

The captain said that they were getting ready to land so we buckled back up. Once we landed, I texted Ross to say we got back safe, and sound and I texted Janet to let her know I was home. The sun was still up a bit in the sky when we landed. James grabbed my luggage, and we went down the stairs and to his car. The flight attendants brought down James's luggage and briefcases and put them beside his car. They were going to have a couple of weeks off before they had to fly again to Toronto.

The plane was taxied to the parking spot for it, which I couldn't believe that planes had, but anyway, it was going to remain there for another two weeks. Maintenance would be done during that time James said and the flight crew were each flying to their respective homes on commercial flights. Luggage and briefcases safely stowed in the trunk of the car; we left the airport.

Even though I missed the kids, it was good to be back home. I let out a sigh as we were driving away from the airport.

"Good to be home again, isn't it. I get the same feeling when I go back to Scotland. Why don't we stop and have dinner and then I can take you home? That is if you are not too tired." I wasn't tired, but I was worried he was after all the travelling he just finished. He said he was fine, and we went to the restaurant. James called ahead to make sure we could get our table in the private room. By the time we pulled into the restaurant parking lot it was just after 6:00.

We were seated at our table, and both decided to have water and no alcohol. I wasn't overly hungry, so I ordered something light. James was hungry, so he ordered a steak. We talked a bit more about the house. James got a couple of texts which he looked at briefly. The gala in Toronto was in two weeks and I was going to have to give Roxie a call in the morning to make sure she was still going to come. The plan was to go to Toronto a few days ahead of the gala. James had a seven-bedroom seven-bathroom penthouse in a very exclusive building. I didn't object to staying there and I was sure that Roxie wouldn't.

Chapter 3

Our meals came, and we sat in silence eating. I didn't want any dessert, but I did want a coffee. James had one as well and we talked a bit about the charity he was involved in. His company was the lead sponsor for the event although he admitted that he left a lot of the organization up to his personal assistant. James was a major contributor to this charity and had been ever since he started living in Toronto. The charity allowed him to meet with a lot of influential people in Toronto and the area which was good for business he said.

"Roxie, Janet, and I will have to go shopping for something to wear. It sounds like it is quite lavish, and I know that nothing I have recently bought would be suitable. It is good we are going a few days ahead of time, it will give us a chance to go to a few stores." It was at that moment when James pulled out a credit card with my name on it. I looked at him with a very puzzled look.

"I asked you, Roxanne, Janet, and Wade to come to this as my guests and I want you to use that credit card to get whatever you want. Right now, it has a two hundred- and fifty-thousand-dollar limit on it but that can be increased if necessary. Oh, and by the way, don't buy any jewelry for whatever you end up getting to wear, I have taken care of that. You will, however, have to let me know what colour all of you are wearing." I was going to protest but he would not let me, and I don't think I even had the words to say anything when he said what the limit was. We finished our coffee; James paid the bill and we left for my place. He was tired I knew and frankly so was I. I was finally starting to admit to myself that I had feelings for him, but I wasn't sure if he felt the same.

"James, I know you are tired; why don't you stay at my place, in the spare room for tonight anyway. We are both rather tired and even though it is not terribly late, I don't want to see you drive another forty-five minutes back into the city." James agreed he was tired and said that he would like to stay. He grabbed one of my suitcases and his and I took my other one and we went into the lobby. It was empty at the time, which I admit I was thankful for. The seniors in the building were all very respectful of each other's privacy, but I didn't want to give them the wrong idea.

We got up to my floor and to my door. I unlocked it and we went in. There was a bit of mail on my table and the key for my mailbox was there as well. I would have to thank Mr. O'Leary in the morning. I hadn't remade the bed before I left so it took me a few minutes to do that. While I was making the bed James was in the living room responding to his texts. I came out and told him the room was ready and there were fresh towels in the bathroom if he wanted to take a shower. He said that he would and went into the spare room and shut the door. I took the opportunity to call Roxie and let her know I was home but also to make sure she was still going to come to the gala in Toronto.

"You bet I am but if it is going to be that fancy, I will have to get something new because I don't think my pant suit would be appropriate. So how was your trip and how was little Ayleen?" I told her all about the trip and said I had lots of pictures to show her. I also told her that James was going to pay for our dresses with the credit card he gave me tonight. I told her that I didn't want it, but he insisted. I wasn't going to tell her though that James was spending the night because I didn't want her to jump to conclusions. I asked her if she wanted to get together during the week for lunch and she said she would call in a few days as she had been babysitting her grandsons and once they were gone she had a couple of days when she had appointments. I said that I would wait for her call. I hung up just as James was coming out of the bedroom with his pj pants on and a t shirt.

I said that I was going to take a quick shower too and if he wanted to have some wine, the red was on the counter and the white in the fridge. He got out a couple of wine glasses and poured himself a white wine. He knew that Cassandra didn't really care for red, so he went with white. He was just about finished his glass when she came out of the shower wearing her pjs with her robe tied very tightly around her waist. He laughed to himself thinking of the last time he had seen her in pjs. He went into the kitchen and poured her some wine and himself a bit more. We sat on the couch and looked over the designer's book once again going through each room. We both still agreed with the choices we made on the plane, and he put the book in the bedroom.

James had an aerial view of the property, and it really provided a good view of how large the property was. He was going to put in a paved walking path all around the edge of the property and have street lights put in every fifty feet or so. He was also putting in outdoor electrical outlets along either side of the driveway so that he could put lighting in the trees at Christmas. It all sounded so wonderful. It was still early, and we decided to watch a movie on tv.

We scanned through the movie channel to see what was on and went with a comedy. It was a safe choice because everything else was either a romance or slash and burn type movie, which I did not care for. The movie was over at 10:00 and we both said we enjoyed it. I shut off the tv and said that I was going to hit the sack. I took the wine glasses to the kitchen and set them on the counter. James was tired as well and was waiting for me to come out of the kitchen. I could feel the butterflies building up in my stomach. He was leaning against the wall that was between the two bedroom doors. As I approached, he looked at me and pulled me towards him.

"I don't know about you, but I think I am about done with being just friends and I would like this to be more, if that is ok with you." Before I could say anything, he bent down and kissed me. A very passionate but controlled kiss. I think that he had his answer by the way I kissed him back. He looked at me smiled, kissed my nose, and went into the spare room and closed the door. I went into my bedroom and closed my door. I knew that my heart was pounding because I could hear it. He certainly knew how to kiss, no question about that. I laid in bed awake for the longest time before falling asleep.

James knew that he was taking a chance kissing her the way he did, but he felt that things between them had changed and was sure that she would not reject him. She didn't, and he was very happy about that. He didn't want to go further than the kiss though, at least not tonight. He knew he was going to have a rough night ahead, but it was a rough night he was willing to endure.

James was still in the bedroom when I got up and went to make coffee. I didn't have anything in the fridge to make breakfast and thought perhaps we could go and have brunch at the restaurant. When James came out he looked like he just got out of the shower because his hair was still wet. It got really curly when it was wet, and he looked so good this morning in his jeans and short sleeved shirt. I handed him a cup of coffee and he gave me a kiss on the lips and said good morning. I thought that I had to say something about the kiss last night.

"Listen, about that kiss and what you said, I would like to be more than friends too. I would be foolish to try and deny that I don't like you. I think the way I kissed you back rather confirmed that." He laughed and pulled me into his arms and kissed me again.

"You had better go and get dressed before I have other ideas. I want to be respectful and not rush you, so go get dressed and we will go out and have breakfast. I think it is probably wise that we are around other people today." While he was finishing his coffee and making another I went off to the shower. That was probably the fastest shower I'd ever taken. I didn't want to linger because I knew that if I did I would not be alone for long. I dried my hair and put the flat iron through it. Put on a little makeup because I don't like to wear a lot during the day. I went with jeans as well and a short sleeve top. James put his sneakers on and was waiting by the door with his suitcase in hand. I slipped on my sandals, and we went out.

I don't know why but the sky looked bluer, and the sun shone brighter for some reason today. The parking lot was rather full but James, as usual, called ahead while I was in the shower to reserve our table. We talked while we waited for the food to arrive. James was going to be meeting with George to go over the progress on the house and talk about any issues that he had. He then was going to meet with the designer in the afternoon to go over the designs for the house. He asked me if I wanted to come along but I said that I had to go and get some groceries and wanted to check in on some of the seniors. He dropped me off at my place when we finished eating and I went up to my unit. I was actually rather giddy. I made up my grocery list and went to the grocery store. I wasn't sure what plans James had for the next couple of weeks, but I knew that he was going to be here in town because the plane was undergoing an inspection.

I spent the rest of the next two weeks checking in on the seniors, having a day at the spa, doing laundry, and working out at the gym since I hadn't been in a while. I also put in a call to Mason my self-defense trainer to ask when I could get into a class. He said when the next classes were starting, and I put it in my calendar. I thought perhaps I would see James on Friday night, but he said he was going to be tied up in meetings all weekend. But we did talk about what the designer said about our changes. I got back from grocery shopping and just after I put the groceries away I got a call from James. He wanted to know if I could meet up with the interior designer to look at the lighting.

"She really liked your suggested changes and thought perhaps you might have some interesting choices for the lighting. It isn't something I want to deal with, so you would be doing me a huge favour going over this with her. I will be happy with whatever you choose so you can tell her once you've picked them out to go ahead and get them. You don't need to check with me first. I will be out at the industrial site handling some issues there and then over to the house. Can you give her a call to figure out where to meet? I'll text you here name and number. Have fun." I was thinking about the lighting fixtures and had a thought about art glass for all the ceiling fixtures and the hardware in a brushed pewter. The art glass could come from his company in Scotland. I wanted to first find out whether there was someone there who could do that sort of thing. I had to give James a quick call back.

"One question James, do you have artisans at your glass company who can do antique art glass. I was thinking that you could go with a Victorian look and have a lot of the glass done in Scotland. It was just a thought but before I speak to the designer, I would need to know if that is possible." James liked the idea a lot and it would incorporate a bit more of Scotland product in the home. He said that there were several of them who could do that easily and they actually did it at the factory and would get the designer to contact them.

I gave Christina a call on Saturday and said that if she was free, we could do this at my place. Regrettably, she was tied up Saturday but said that she was free on Sunday. I suggested that she come to my place, and we could go over things here. At least it would give us the room to spread things out. She said that she would bring all the room layouts with her, and we could look at the lighting in each room and of course the hallways. I spent the rest of the day cleaning up and after dinner had an early night. Christina arrived promptly at 9:00 the next morning and I let her in. I wasn't sure what to expect. She had a bit of an accent when we spoke on the phone, but I wasn't sure where it was from. She was standing at my door with two very large portfolios in her hands.

"Oh, my goodness, please come in. Let me help you with those." She gave me one of the portfolios and I could see that she was looking around. She was in her mid-thirties, around five nine, black hair, blue eyes and very pretty. I think she was surprised to see what I looked like because she looked a little taken aback when I opened the door. I suggested that we lay the things out on the dining room table.

"I like the way you have decorated your place; it is very charming." I wasn't sure if that was a good thing or a bad thing, but I let it go. I mentioned that I thought going with Victorian lighting would be nice but wanted her thoughts.

"My goodness you must have been reading my mind. I thought we could do more things with that era than with the Queen Anne. I like the way you think, what are your thoughts? Let's take it room by room, hallway by hallway." I mentioned to her that I thought art glass would be great to go with and that I talked with James, and she could get it from his glass company in Scotland.

"He said that he had several artisans who could do the glass for shades and bowls without any problem. I thought that the entrance would need something big which I am sure you have already thought of and please don't hesitate to say no to anything I suggest. I personally am not a big fan of chandeliers but that is just me. However, I have been looking at different things online and I picked out one that I thought might look good in the front entrance. You would have to see where you can get the hardware done but maybe you know of some antique places that would have the fixture and put in a new shade or bowl from James's glass company." I showed Christina the different things I chose and wasn't too sure about what type of hardware to go with, but maybe brushed pewter would look good.

She looked at the large piece and then the different shades that I picked out. I thought that because James had the glass company, we should try to make full use of the different colours of shades, bowls, and wall sconces and even table lamps. I thought as well that there could be some stained-glass door lites perhaps or even some stained-glass transoms, but I was worried maybe that was too much glass. Christina was looking at all of the things that I put in front of her, and I could tell that she liked my ideas.

"I like your ideas a lot. I don't think we want stained glass in every door but perhaps the two side lites at the front door would look good although not too much colour there because the doors are the centre piece. I mean if we can get all of this done up before the end of October, which is what he wants, I think it is a great idea and I like the idea of the transoms too. I hadn't thought of doing that and it would be a great way to incorporate more of the Scotland charm." We went through each room and hallway and selected what style of shade and bowl would look best. We selected the styles of table lamps for each room but when we got to James's office, I said that we should definitely keep that very masculine.

She brought with her the different types of hardware, and we picked out the dark pewter for the lights. Now it came to the kitchen, and I was not sure what to do there. I like kitchens to be light and bright but again that was my preference. There were two dining rooms, a large more formal one for big occasions and a smaller one for a small gathering. Christina recommended not going with too heavy a fixture. Even though she knew I wasn't a fan of chandeliers she showed me a photo of one that was actually quite nice although I didn't like the swans on it.

“Don’t worry, I know where I can get two that don’t have those on them, but it looks the same as this one. I should also show you the lighting that I selected for the exterior. Because it is brick and James mentioned he didn’t want white or cream, I found these Victorian black that look like the old gas streetlights. What do you think of those for all of the exteriors including on the garage?” They were perfect and exactly what I would have chosen. I hadn’t realized that we had been doing work on the light fixtures for four hours and it was almost 1:00.

“Christina, would you like to have lunch with me. There is a restaurant very close to here and I would like to take you for lunch, you must be hungry because I know I am.” She said that it would be nice, and we could go in her car if that was ok. We carried the portfolios down to her car and I showed her where the restaurant was. Because it was mid-week there was hardly anyone there. Jason saw me come in and showed us to our table in the private area. He left us with menus and water after having asked us if we wanted anything else to drink. We both said no, and we looked over the menus. I told Christina that the frosted blue glass was from James’s company.

“It is really pretty, maybe we could use some of that same glass for the lighting or maybe the door lites. I have to say Cassandra, you surprised me when you opened the door. James spoke about you all the time when we met to talk about the designs. I must admit that I was expecting someone younger. Although I must say you don't look your age. I realize that perhaps that wasn't very professional, but I get the impression you are the type of person who appreciates honesty." I said I wasn't offended and that yes, I do appreciate honesty.

We both agreed that it was going to be nice working together on the house. We ate our meal and after coffee Christina dropped me back at my place. When I got up to my suite, I gave Christelle a call. We talked for a bit, and I told her that James and I had our first big passionate kiss. She laughed and said that she was not surprised but I told her that was as far as it had gone. She knew that I was going to the gala in Toronto in another week and that plans were made for me and Roxie to go to Scotland in September. I also told her about Sonya and her family coming for Thanksgiving and Ross, Lindsay and Ayleen coming for Christmas.

"I want lots of pictures of everything and don't be afraid to give into your heart. I really believe that this is the person who is going to treat you like a queen. But I do have a confession to make." I laughed and asked what she did that she needed to confess.

"I should have told you that James, when he was in Ottawa, asked me to meet with him. I was glad that he did because it gave me a chance to see his energy, which I have to tell you is great. We talked for a couple of hours but even though I said that you have not been treated well in the past, I did not go into any detail. That is for you to decide if you want to tell him anything, but I don't think he wants to know from what he said. He didn't want to bring the past into his relationship with you and I think that is wise." We both laughed at the comment about being treated like a queen because she knew that was not what I wanted. I hadn't realized that James met her, but I was happy that he did, and I thought it was so much in his character to do that. We said no more about what they discussed.

"His designer was just here, and we went over all the lighting for the interior of the house. I wasn't sure if she was going to like me putting in my two cents, but she really liked my ideas. Most of the glass is going to be done at his glass company in Scotland. The overall theme for the lighting is Victorian and James said that he was leaving me to pick it out. I just hope that he isn't going to be sorry he did that. Christina, his designer said that it would look really good with the interior, and she was sure James would agree completely. She was also surprised when she met me. She thought by the way James kept talking about me that I was younger but maybe that is just what she was expecting for someone like James." We talked for a little while longer and then I said I had to go out for a walk.

For the next week I spent my time brushing up on my self-defense skills. It was a crash course, and it was exhausting but I felt great at the end of it. Mason scolded me a little for not keeping up with my weights, but I said how busy I'd been and was forgiven. Not that he was really angry with me. I also video chatted with Ayleen and had a spa day at the end of my course. I decided to drive to James's house to see the progress on it. I thought maybe James would be there, but he wasn't. George did see me coming and of course James mentioned me. He introduced himself and asked if I wanted a tour and of course I said yes.

"I guess I should thank you for the referral. James said that you recommended me from seeing me on tv. I really appreciate the confidence you put in my skills." I told him that it was my pleasure, and I knew he was going to do a great job. From seeing him on tv I liked the way he did things, and I just had a feeling he was honest and would not skip corners. The house was really coming together. The staircase was in and while I had a feeling what it was like I had no idea how grand it was going to be. Just inside the front entrance on the left was going to be James's study. It was quite large, and the bookcases were in. I loved all the hardwoods that were down.

"I like the idea that you used just the right amount of wood on the walls so that it isn't overpowering. It really looks wonderful." He took me into the other rooms which had the floors down but were covered so they wouldn't get marked up. The painters were in and doing the rooms. I was concerned that the blue in the dining room was going to be too dark, but it was stunning. All of the colours downstairs were beautiful. We went into the kitchen to have a look around. The cabinets were being installed and they were awesome. I told George I was glad that James went with them up to the ceiling as there was nothing worse than having to climb up and clean between the cabinet and the ceiling. George laughed because I think he knew that James would not be doing the cleaning. We took a quick tour upstairs and into each of the rooms. The double doors to the master were amazing and he had the frame done above the doors for the stained-glass piece that would be installed much later. The room was so big with a fireplace on one wall. The walk-in closet was done, and I had to laugh at the size which was just about the size of my condo. The master bath was going to be grand as well.

"I asked James if he would let me pick out the colour scheme here. I know the two of you had something selected, but I have some ideas and I think it is going to look really good. I hope you will like it." I told him that I thought it was amazing what he had done in the house so far. I could see that there was a free form tub near the window, but he scooted me out because he wanted it to be a surprise when it was done. I did notice that there was a large towel closet which I had never seen before.

"I love the towel closet idea that is amazing, and I take it that it was your idea. Good job. Nothing worse than taking a shower and realizing that you have to run into the hallway to grab a fresh towel. I like that a lot." George was pleased that I liked everything, and we finished the tour. We went back downstairs and out onto the wrap around deck. It was really something and it led all the way around to the fully glassed-in room. There were doors on either end of this room. I hadn't realized it was going to be so large. The view from this room was amazing. It would be great to sit and watch all the wildlife coming and going.

"James said this was your idea for the enclosed glass sunroom although it is probably the biggest sunroom I have ever seen. The original blueprints had it being fifteen feet wide, but I spoke with James and the architect and said that it needed to be wider. I presume that this will be where a lot of time is spent year-round." It was beautiful, and it was the only room in the house that had slate flooring. George picked out the slate for this room in tones of beige and a bit of grey. The walls were painted a nice shade of grey, not too dark to make it look institutional but a warm grey that would look good at any time of the year.

"My goodness the number of windows alone must have cost a fortune." George said nothing of course and I did not expect him to. Everything was beautiful, and I said he was doing an amazing job. I knew he had to get back at it, so I left him and went back on my condo. I spent the rest of the day doing some ironing and video chatting with Ayleen who called unexpectedly and asked if James was with me. She made me laugh but it ended my day great, and I slept that night really well.

I gave Roxie a call the next morning to see what she was up to. She was leaving the city and heading out to her country place. I asked if she wanted to meet up and we could have dinner. She generally spent a few days in the city doing all her running around with errands and appointments. But she liked to be out at her country place for a really nice long weekend.

“I would like that love but nothing fancy, I’m in my capris and a tank top.” I said we could have dinner at my place since I bought groceries, I at least had food in the house. I knew she didn’t like night driving and the days were getting shorter, so I suggested we eat early. I made up a salmon casserole and put it in the oven. By the time Roxie arrived it would be done. She arrived about twenty minutes early and we sat having a coffee on the balcony.

“I’m looking forward to next week going to Toronto. I’ve never been there before. It’s too bad we won’t be there for long; it would be nice to have a tour but maybe another time. So, we have to get all gussied up, I have to say I am looking forward to that.” We were sitting down to eat and there was a knock at the door. I was surprised to see James there but told him to come in.

"We are just having a bite to eat do you want to join us. It's a casserole nothing fancy." James came in and said he would like that. He saw Roxie and went over to say hello. Roxie wanted a hug which she got.

"We were sitting here talking about going to Toronto and I was saying that I have never been before and wished it was for a bit longer but I'm happy with the four days." I set a plate for James, and he helped himself to the casserole. I asked him if wanted some wine, but he said water was fine.

"If you ladies want to go to Toronto on Wednesday, that is ok with me. It will give me a chance to go to the office and handle a few things. It will also give you a day extra to go shopping for your evening gowns. The charity gala is Saturday night so perhaps on Friday we could do a little touring around. My Uncle Duncan came in from Scotland and is going to be there, so I can introduce you to him and he can come on the tour too if that is ok." I gave a look to James as much to say, 'what are you doing' but he just winked at me and continued eating.

Roxie said she had to go out to her country place and take care of a couple of things out there and make sure that she could arrange for her neighbours to water plants and keep an eye on the place. She could be ready to go Wednesday if that worked for me. We agreed that we would leave Wednesday morning at 10:00 for the airport and Roxie would come to my place and leave her car and I would drive us to the airport. James would let the captain know about the earlier departure. Janet and Wade were coming as well, and they were arriving on Wednesday night. The rest of the meal we talked about my trip back east and I showed Roxie the pictures. She was surprised to see James in some of them but said nothing. She asked James how the house was coming, and he showed her pictures of the progress so far.

"Wow that's big. I had no idea it was going to be that big." James said that he would take her on a tour once we got back from Toronto if there was time. She was very much looking forward to that. We finished eating and I cleared the table. We had coffee and sat out on the balcony. Roxie liked it out here because she could check everything out. She made me laugh. James said he was going to have to say goodnight. He had some calls to make when he got back to his hotel and Roxie decided to leave at the same time. I went down with them to the front door in the lobby. I think James could sense that I didn't want a big kiss or anything in front of Roxie, so he gave me a hug and kiss on the cheek.

Back up in my unit I pulled out my smaller piece of luggage and put it on the bed in the spare room. It was the middle of August, but it could still be quite warm in

Toronto and humid. I made sure to mention that to Roxie, so she could pack accordingly. James suggested that maybe if there was time we could see a Broadway show, but it wasn't anything that we would have to get too dressed up for. I put a light colour beige dress pants on the bed and picked a red silk blouse to go with it. I also put some jeans and some capris on the bed too with tops to go with them. We would be flying back by ourselves on Monday because James had business to attend to for the next few weeks in Toronto. I took out a pair of dressy black pants and jacket and matched it with a light blue chiffon top.

I had flats that I could wear most of the time, my nude wedge sandals to go with the black suit and a pair of red espadrilles to go with the beige pants and red top. I kept everything on the bed in case I changed my mind on anything. James said not to bring shampoo or anything like that, there was lots in the penthouse, and he was arranging for us to have someone come in and do our hair and makeup on Saturday afternoon for the gala. I spent the rest of the evening watching some tv. I called Roxie just to confirm the time she needed to be at my place, and I told her that I reserved a parking spot for her in the underground parking. I mentioned that we were having someone do our hair and makeup on Saturday which she thought was great.

"I feel like royalty, I am not use to it, but I have to say I love it." We both laughed because it had been a long time since either of us had been so well taken care of. I gave Janet a call to have a chat before leaving for Toronto. I told her about the credit card James gave me for us to buy what we needed for the gala. It was going to be nice having extra people that I would know. I mentioned that we were leaving tomorrow because Roxie wanted to see a bit of Toronto and James had some work he needed to get done at the office.

"I am so looking forward to this. I can't believe that James is being so generous. Do you have an idea of what colour you want to wear? I think I would like to see if I can find something in a midnight blue, but I am open to whatever." I had been giving this some thought but hadn't made up my mind. I too was going to have to wait and see what the stores had.

"James's personal assistant sent me an email with the store that she thought would be best to go to for our gowns as they had a wide variety of designer gowns. We could also get Wade's tux at the same store and our shoes. She also mentioned a spa close by where we could go for mani/pedis, facials and massages. She made an appointment for the three of us for Saturday morning. She already contacted the clothing store to ensure that any alterations that any of us needed could be done the same day." I gave Janet the website address, so she could look as well but she would wait to see what I was going to pick out first.

"I'll check it out and have a look at the tuxes for Wade. We will try to keep it all within reason. It looks like Thursday morning we will be going to pick out what we are going to wear and Saturday morning we are going to the spa, which leaves us with a full day on Friday." I told her that James arranged for us to have dinner at the penthouse when we arrived and that he had a personal chef on call. James thought maybe after a busy day we would appreciate being together and relaxing.

"His personal assistant is seeing if she can get us tickets for the opera on Friday night, so I am going to bring the red dress I bought in Ottawa and I will tell Roxie to pack the black silk suit she bought for dinner here with you. I don't know if you want to wear the yellow silk again or not, but I leave that up to you. I am not going to say anything to Roxie until we get to Toronto about wearing a gown that cost a lot because I'm afraid she may back out of coming if I tell her that. I think James is trying to play matchmaker for his uncle because he is going to be with us in Toronto. I've seen pictures of him, and he is quite a handsome man. I think James said he was sixty-eight and he is a smidge shorter than James from what I saw. Roxie just turned sixty-nine in January, so I don't think she will mind being with a man a year younger." I had to get my things packed and said that we would see each other tomorrow.

I had my red dress in a garment bag and put my shoes and clutch in my luggage. I hope that I packed what I would need but I could get anything in Toronto if I had to. I left a message for Mr. O'Leary that I would be out of town again for six days and asked if he would look after my mail once again. I knew he would do so without a problem and said I would leave the key for my mailbox on the table by the door. When I first got into bed my head was swimming with things, wondering if I had forgotten anything. My cell was buzzing. It was a text from James wondering if I were still awake and if he could call. I texted back that I was just getting into bed but still awake. He called the land line because he knew that I preferred to speak on that instead of the cell.

"I wanted to say goodnight and thank you for the great meal the other day. I am really looking forward to you being in Toronto with me, and the others too of course, but more you. I know you were wondering about my uncle. I think that he and Roxanne would get along very well and who knows maybe they will become a couple. Speaking of which, when I introduce you to people, I would like to say that you are my girlfriend, although I don't know if people say that anymore, but I can work on the proper term, but I just wanted to make sure that was ok with you." I told him that I was fine with that and that I too was not sure what the proper term was, but I expressed that I didn't like partner as it seemed very neutral.

"Goodnight, James, see you tomorrow at the airport." My stomach was full of butterflies, and I was incredibly happy about it. Morning arrived very quickly. I was having the most wonderful thoughts about James, but it was time to get up, take a shower and get ready. Mr. O'Leary texted me back saying it was not a problem and he would take care of things. I decided to have a quick video chat with Ayleen. She was all excited about going back to school and into grade two. She was growing up so fast and I missed so much of her when she was small. But it was not the time to dwell on the past.

"Gramma are you going to be with James? Are you going to come and visit me before I go back to school? Mommy says it is ok if you do and you can bring James too." I told her that I would love to come but I was going to be with another one of my friends called Roxie and that James was going to be very busy in Toronto until we went to Scotland. She asked me to hang on and went to talk to Lindsay.

"Mommy said you can bring Roxie and she can sleep in my room, and I will sleep with you, if that is ok with you and Roxie." I said I would ask Roxie when she came by this morning and see what she would like to do. But I said if we did it could only be for a couple of days because Roxie had to get back home, and we couldn't keep James's plane away from him. That seemed to appease her, but she knew that it was not for sure. We talked for a little bit longer and I said that I had to go and get some things done and I would see her soon hopefully.

I gave Roxie a quick call as it was still a few hours before she was to be at my place. I asked her if she wanted to go to Ottawa with me for a couple of days and visit with Ross, Lindsay, and Ayleen. I explained that Ayleen was giving up her bed for her, but she was going to sleep with me, a big treat not only for me but her. She said she would love to. I said it would only be for a couple of days because I didn't think we could tie up James's plane more than that. She would throw a few extra changes of clothes in her luggage just in case and be at my place shortly.

I made coffee for myself and had some cereal. I went down to hopefully have a chat with some of the other seniors to see how they were all doing. Some were decorating the lobby in a fall/thanksgiving theme. It was nice to see them happy. I was talking with them for a couple of hours and saw Roxie come in. I got in her car, and we went down to the garage. I pointed to the spot I reserved for her. It was just a few spots away from my car. We put her luggage in my car; went up to my place and grabbed my luggage and then off to the airport.

"I am so excited. I was telling my neighbours about going to Toronto on a private plane. They were all envious of me." She was definitely enjoying the feeling. I said that she was going to love the plane it was very luxurious. Traffic was light, and we were at the airport about twenty minutes early. I went to the security gate, gave my name, and showed my identification and we went through. I parked my car in the VIP spot, beside James's car. We got our luggage out, set it beside the stairs and went up the stairs to the plane. Janine greeted us. James was waiting for us in the cabin. He introduced Roxie to the flight crew, and we walked back into the plane.

"Wow is this ever something. Holy cow look at these seats, wow." I told her to go have a look at the bathroom and all I could hear was wow, wow. Maria was waiting beside us and laughing. When Roxie came out, she sat in the seat opposite James and me.

"Once we have lifted off, I will come back for beverage orders and let you know what we have for lunch." They had to follow proper procedure and go through the same security instructions as you would get on a commercial flight. Once that was done, the captain taxied out onto the runway, and we were off. Maria came back and asked us what we wanted to drink. She left us with the menu for lunch and would bring us back coffee and water. Since James didn't know what Roxie would want, he asked for a variety of things to be available. I went with the chef salad as it was so good last time and a small bowl of mixed fruit. Both James and Roxie decided to have the same thing.

"So, Roxanne, do you like my plane?" He was laughing because he heard her when she came onboard.

She said yes of course and was looking forward to the vacation in Toronto. I told her some of the itinerary on the trip to the airport. Our lunches came, and we sat eating and talking about the weather. James asked if we were still going to go with him to Scotland in September and of course Roxie answered yes for both of us. James excused himself to go to the washroom. Roxie took the opportunity to say something.

"This, Cassandra, this is for you. This is what you deserve and the way he treats you is how you should be treated. This is long overdue for you, so I hope that you are not keeping him at arm's length." I only had time to tell her I wasn't and that we already had our first big kiss. But before she could comment on that James returned. We talked about the dates for Scotland. I mentioned that I needed to be back by the last week in September to get things ready for my sister and her kids came. I hadn't the chance to tell James that she was going to be coming for sure.

"It is the first time she is going to get on a plane, I think. She is nervous, but her daughter Rhonda will be with her. Nicole and Austin will be coming down from up north. I haven't seen her kids who are not kids anymore but I haven't seen them for an awfully long time and especially Nicole and I've never met Austin. Rhonda is in the internet security field but I'm not sure what her position is right now. Austin is in sales for a mining company, and Nicole I think works in human resources for a major oil company. At least that is what I think they all do. Sonya is widowed and has been alone for some time, but she has her own place now and seems to like it. I thought for sure she would not want to get involved with anyone again, but she said she did, so I said I would keep my eyes open for her." I showed James a picture of her, of course, with the idea that he would have a friend that maybe I could arrange to introduce her to. But he didn't say anything. Janine brought around more coffee and took away our plates. Roxie commented that it was so nice to be eating off actual plates again and not plastic.

"James, tell me about your home in Scotland. Do you have a large family there?" Roxie was able to divert the conversation after there had been an awkward silence. This was a topic that James obviously liked to talk about. He pulled out his tablet and showed Roxie the pictures of his home in Scotland and his family. These I'd already seen so I listened as she asked him question after question.

"Who is this good-looking guy standing next to you?" James said that it was his Uncle Duncan whom she was going to meet when we got to the penthouse. She looked at me with a look similar to the time I made a dessert for her at a dinner party many years ago. It was a look of a little girl who was given the key to the candy store. Inwardly I was glad because I knew that James was going to try to pair them off.

The captain announced that we were on approach to Toronto International. James put his tablet away and we buckled ourselves back up. Janine cleared away the coffee cups and we settled in for the landing. James had a limo waiting for us. I was never in a limo before and from the sounds coming from Roxie, I gathered she hadn't either. The driver took our bags and put them in the trunk. James looked like he was a bit upset but said nothing. We arrived at his penthouse and got in the elevator to go up. The private elevator opened up to his own lobby. He grabbed our suitcases and set them off the elevator and then carried our luggage down the hallway. He opened the door and let us in to his penthouse and went back to grab more luggage.

It was stunning to say the least. It was very modern, more than I was expecting but the outdoor space was spectacular. It had a beautiful view of the skyline which had to be simply breathtaking at night. James showed us to our bedrooms which were stunning and the two we were in had its own door to the outdoor space. I hung up my things and put away things in the drawers in the closet. It looked very lonely in this big closet with just the few items I had. I went back into the living room and James was pouring himself a drink. He still had a rather pensive look on his face.

“Is something wrong James. Did I say something that upset you?” He looked at me with a look of astonishment.

“No, of course you didn’t. I was just trying to think of someone that I knew who we could introduce to your sister. I know a lot of pretty stand-up guys but from the way you talked about her I was trying to think of someone who was perfect for her. Do you think she would be willing to move if it were the right guy?” I said that I didn’t think so. She and her youngest daughter were pretty close, and she wouldn’t move too far away from her. Her other daughter on the other hand lived long distances away for a long time. He admitted that might make it a bit more difficult because he had someone in mind, but they would be moving to Toronto from Germany. Roxie came out and told James that she just loved his place. I think she was beginning to realize that she had overused ‘wow’ and had to come up with something else. James said that while the style of the penthouse was what he loved, the only thing that he really changed was all of the furniture.

“Most of the furniture was white leather and I am not a big fan of white leather, so I asked Christina my interior designer to replace the furniture, so it is a little less sterile looking.” I thought that it was very warm and inviting what he had gone with. He was pouring me a glass of white wine and Roxie was going to have tea when his uncle came in. I was so curious how Roxie would react when she actually met him, which as it turned out was now because he was just coming through the door.

"Uncle, I would like to introduce you to Cassandra, and this is Roxanne. Ladies, this is my Uncle Duncan, and he is going to be with us here and going to the gala with us on Saturday night." James poured Duncan a whisky and he sat beside Roxie on the sofa. I sat in a chair as did James.

"It is such a great pleasure to meet you both. James has talked nonstop about you Cassandra and Roxanne; he has said wonderful things about you. So are you ladies looking forward to this gala on Saturday? I expect that you will look very lovely, and Roxanne I hope that you will allow me the honour of escorting you to this event. I hope you like to dance because I really enjoy it." Roxie said that she would like that very much and she loved dancing. James motioned for me to go out with him to the terrace.

"Let's give them a few moments to get acquainted shall we. Besides, I want you to myself." He pulled me towards him and kissed me. "I have been waiting to do that for far too long. I hope that you have told everyone that we are now together because I don't want to have to avoid kissing you the way I want to." I said that Janet and now Roxie knew that we were a couple. James would have kept me on the terrace longer, but I said that we should go in. He got a text from the driver that Wade and Janet arrived, and he was showing them up to the penthouse. Introductions were done all over again. I never met Wade except when he poked his head in when Janet and I were on a video call. Wade wasn't a big drinker, but James poured him a glass of wine. James showed them to their bedroom and left them to unpack. They returned about fifteen minutes later and James showed them around as he did with us when we arrived. We were out on the terrace, the ladies sort of off to one side and the men the other.

"Oh my, can you believe this place. It is stunning. Look at the view." Janet was quite taken with the penthouse but who wouldn't be? Roxie and Janet were both looking at one another and then looking at me unsure what to say.

"Yes, you both know that James and I kissed. I know the two of you are about to explode because you didn't know if the other knew, but you both know." They laughed and of course asking me how it all came about. I demurely declined to say much because I didn't think I should. The guys came over to rejoin us and Duncan was telling Roxie that he was living in a wing on the estate of James's in Scotland. He was happy that we were going to be going over and would be there to welcome us when we arrived.

"It is too bad Janet that you and Wade won't be able to make it in September but perhaps the next time, we can all get together and have a good time." Wade accepted and agreed for them both.

Right at that moment, James's personal chef, Antoine, arrived to prepare our meal. James introduced him and then he went off to the kitchen to prepare dinner which he said would be ready in about an hour and a half. James said that we hoped we all liked salmon because that was what was on the menu. Everyone said they did. I was still working on my wine, Roxie on her tea and Janet on a glass of red wine that James poured for her. James, Duncan, and Wade went over to the bar, and each had another whisky, but Wade declined any more wine. It gave me a few minutes to chat, which James could see that I wanted so he made sure that Duncan was out of ear shot.

"Roxie, what do you think about Duncan. He is quite a charmer, isn't he? You don't mind going to the gala with him because if you do, I can say something to James." She assured me that she was more than happy with the arrangement and in fact was quite taken with him. She found out that he was a bachelor and that he liked to travel, enjoyed gardening and we already knew from their earlier conversation that he liked dancing. All the things that Roxie loved to do. I made the comment that they were made for each other and as soon as I had it out of my mouth, I worried I had said the wrong thing.

She assured me that it was fine, she was ok with the fact that James was playing matchmaker. Janet said that he was quite handsome and looked a lot like James. Roxie looked over and then kind of giggled.

"I could do a lot worse you know." We started to laugh, and I asked Roxie if she remembered the time we went to that store in Stony and I teased her that she was flirting with a gentleman about how tall he was. At first, she hadn't remembered but then she did and started to laugh. The men came over and asked what we were laughing about, and I said that we were laughing about the lines women our age used to flirt with other men. Everyone got a laugh out of that. We sat talking back and forth with one another. Dinner, we were told was ready if we wanted to go into the dining room.

The table was beautifully set with lovely flowers as a centerpiece. James knew that I didn't eat rice, so he had a garlic mashed potato for me and the others had the choice of rice or garlic potato. The meal was fabulous. Wine was served with the meal, and I had half a glass as did Roxie and Janet. It was a wonderful meal with great conversation. The chef prepared a fresh berry crumble with crème fraiche which looked amazing, but I was already too full. Everyone enjoyed their coffee. By the time dinner was finished it was getting late and everyone was getting a little tired. James and I sat up for a little while together on the lounge outside on the terrace. It was a beautiful night; clear skies and the stars were out. I didn't think they would be visible in the city but perhaps being up thirty floors had something to do with it.

"Thank you, James, for being so nice to my friends and family. You are making me a very, very happy person." He pulled me closer to him and we watched the stars. A really good meteor went by and lit up the sky. I told him that I always wanted to go to an observatory to look through their big telescope to look at the stars and perhaps even find the one that had been named after me. He hadn't realized that I had a star.

"It was probably one of the nicest gifts I ever got from my Dad. He knew how much I loved stars and he got it for me the year before he passed away. So many nights I would get up in the middle of the night because I couldn't sleep, and I would sit and look at the stars and make wishes. Sounds a bit wistful doesn't it but I could stare at the stars for hours and hours." James did not think it was wistful at all but said that he was wondering what more was on that bucket list. I told him that there were a lot of things that would probably sound very silly and was not keen on saying what they were, but he wanted to know.

"Tell me one thing that you have always wanted to do which you think is too silly to tell me." I recalled what he said to me months ago and I thought well, if I can't share my wishes with him, who can I share them with.

"I know this is going to come across as sad and it is, but I never went to my high school prom. I know it's sad isn't, but nobody ever asked me, and it was something that I wanted very badly at the time. I was even dating someone at the time. We'd been going together for a few years, but he would never ask me to the prom. We went to a Christmas dance once and another girl kept flirting with him all night. It made me a little angry I must say. It was my final year in high school, and he still wouldn't take me. I got a job right after I finished school and we were still dating but I found out that he cheated on me with someone else, got her pregnant and they got married. I never trusted another guy after that, not for a very long time. Not until my late husband and not since." The conversation was turning a little too deep and I stopped talking.

"Cassandra, I hope that you know you can trust me. I know that maybe you have heard the words before, but I promise you I will never break your trust. Obviously, those words when spoken to you before were shallow and meant nothing from the one giving them; but I will never break your trust. I gathered that things in your last marriage were less than happy, and I am not going to ask you about it. For me it is in the past and this is now, and I want to make you happy now and from this point forward. I hope that you believe me when I say that." I turned to look at him and I could see in his eyes that he meant every word of it to his very soul. I leaned forward and kissed him. He took me in his arms and kissed me thoroughly. We parted and looked at each other.

"Perhaps we should both head off to bed." James gave me a mischievous look and I said our own beds. We walked back in, and he left me at my bedroom door. I reflected on my past and I had always been the one to initiate things, say I love you first, hint at getting married, be the first to suggest making love, but when I thought about that, it occurred to me that it was never making love, it was just sex. James was making the first moves, the first kiss, the first one to say that he wanted us to be more than friends and more a couple. I fell asleep and before I realized it, it was morning. Janet and Wade were up and already out for a long walk and now having coffee on the terrace with Roxie and Duncan and James was making a few calls. I, apparently, was the last one to get up. I hurried and took a quick shower and got dressed.

"I am so sorry. I can't believe I slept in and made you wait." James came over and kissed me good morning. Janet tapped Wade on the chest as did Roxie with Duncan. James told me not to worry and poured me a coffee. The chef placed scrambled eggs, bacon, sausage, and toast on the sideboard in heating trays. Everyone grabbed a plate and served themselves.

James and Duncan had their tuxes already for the gala, so they did not need to go out. They were going to go over some business while we were out getting our evening attire. James said that the mall we were going to wasn't that far away, but the limo was downstairs waiting when we were ready. It was well past 9:30 by the time we finished eating and having coffee. Janet, Roxie, Wade, and I gathered our things, and we went downstairs. James gave me a key for the elevator and the door to the penthouse so that I would not have to call up to him to get entry. He also gave me another soft kiss before we went out the door.

It wasn't more than a ten-minute drive to the mall, and we were, at least the ladies, very excited to see what was in store for us. We left Wade at the men's apparel with a sales agent named Lawrence who was waiting for him apparently. He was going to look after him and assured us that we would approve of the choice that was made. We walked a little further down the mall to the store which we were suggested to go in. When we arrived, a personal shopper named Jackie was there, at Mina, James's personal assistant's request to take us to the designer floor to select our gowns. She offered us champagne once we got there but it was a bit too early in the day for us, so we declined. She suggested that we look around for a bit on our own and then she would help us to select something.

"Um Roxie, I don't want you to look at the price of anything ok. James gave me a very loaded credit card and said that we were to buy what we wanted and not to think about price. So are we all agreed that we are not going to let the price of something stop us from looking fabulous for our men, agreed?" They both agreed and started to look around.

Janet said that she would like something in red and went off to look at gowns that were in red. Roxie and I were both thinking about black, but I was open to maybe green or even blue. Janet asked for Jackie's help with the dress she was looking for. We both looked at their website and had a rough idea of what we wanted but whether it was going to look good on us was another matter. Roxie was definite that she wanted black for herself. I was looking around and found the dress I saw online. It was even prettier in person and one of the girls on the floor took it and placed it in a dressing room. There was a blue one I saw that had soft petals on it and I thought maybe it might look good. I found it and the girl put it in the dressing room as well.

I also looked online at something that I thought Roxie might like. I was looking through the racks and found it and showed it to her. Her face said that she liked it and the girl took it to another dressing room. Jackie found the dress that Janet was interested in. It was the one I sent her a picture of thinking it was nice and would look great on her. But I told her to also try the navy one that I saw. I described it to Jackie, and she knew immediately which one I was referring to. She brought it back and place it and the red one in a dressing room for Janet.

"Ladies if you require any assistance, please let me know and I will come in and help you." My dressing room was in the middle of Janet's and Roxie's. I could hear Roxie muttering about the price. I reminded her that we all agreed, and she said nothing more.

Roxie asked Jackie for some help zipping up the dress and she went in to help her. I was hoping that when she went out to look at herself in the mirror, she would like it. Since Jackie was helping her first, I waited to put my dress on because I knew I was going to need a hand. I could hear Roxie exiting the room and Janet asked for a bit of help before I had a chance. She was going to try on the navy dress first and leave the red one last. I waited for them to finish. When Janet exited, Jackie came in to help me.

There wasn't a sound out there and I was worried that they didn't like what they had on, and this was going to take longer. I tried on the royal blue dress first. When I came out, they were looking at themselves in the full-length mirrors. Roxie said that she loved her dress and it fit perfectly. She was not interested in trying anything else on. Janet wasn't sure she liked the navy and went to try on the red lace dress. I thought I liked the blue, but I too decided to go back in and try on the black one. Roxie waited for us to finish. I don't think she wanted to take off the dress yet. She kept looking at herself in the mirror. Janet came out in her red dress and Roxie whistled. I had a feeling that Janet was going to go with the red one. A few minutes later, I came out in the black one. Janet saw it online, so she knew what the back looked like. Again, Roxie gave out a little whistle.

"Wait till you see the back of it, turn around Cassandra and show Roxie." I did, and Roxie was shocked. I don't think she expected me to wear something quite like that.

"Wow, I think you look fabulous, and I think James is going to pass out when he sees the back of that dress. I think we all look lovely, but we are going to need shoes. We can't go barefoot." Jackie already picked out a few different styles for us to try on.

She had a couple of black ones for me to try on but the pair I thought about she didn't have with her. I asked her if she had them in the store and she said that they did and went to get them. I also asked her to bring the crystal pumps for Janet. I tried on the black ones that I first picked out. They were very nice, and they would go well with the black dress. Jackie returned with the three pair I asked her to get. Roxie put on the pumps and was very happy with them. There was just a little something in the pattern of the shoe to make them stand out. Janet was leery about the pumps I thought would look good. She was going to go with a red satin pump with a crystal encrusted buckle, but they didn't stand out. They blended with the dress. She tried on the pumps I chose, and they looked fabulous with the dress. Then I tried on the slings I chose and while I was nervous, they were going to be too high; they were extremely comfortable.

"I don't think I will be able to walk five kilometers in these but that is not what I'm wearing them for." We agreed that we would be comfortable in the shoes, and we looked amazing. I had Jackie take a picture of us so that I could send it to Ayleen. We didn't have our hair or makeup done but we still looked pretty good. The girl who helped with our dresses took them and put each one in a garment bag. The shoes were put in boxes and in cloth bags. We each needed to have our dresses shortened a bit. We were not the tall models that most of the designer dresses were made for. Jackie said that they would all be shortened by the end of the day and would be delivered to James's penthouse. We were going to take our shoes with us.

After I paid for the purchases, we left and went to find Wade. Wade selected an Italian designer tux with a white silk shirt and black silk bowtie. Wade liked the choice as did Janet. Normally she helped Wade pick out suits, but she left the decision in the very capable hands of Lawrence. I paid for Wade's tux and let the limo driver know we were ready. He met us at the front door of the mall, and we drove back to James's place. I was surprised that it only took us three hours to get all that done. When we got back and went up to the penthouse, Duncan let us know that James went into the office.

"He didn't think he was going to be too long but suggested just in case that I take all of you out to lunch. We are going to a wonderful restaurant in the downtown area; I hope that is ok with you. I have been a couple of times and the food is quite good." We deposited our shoe bags in our rooms and followed Duncan back down to the limo. He gave the address to the limo driver, and we were off. Duncan texted James to let him know where we were going in case, he was able to join us. We arrived and sat at a table that Duncan reserved for us. The waiter brought water for everyone and said our server would be with us shortly. Only seconds passed, and the server was there with menus which she gave to each of us.

"Can I get anyone anything from the bar." Everyone declined and said that water was fine. We looked over the menu and chose what we wanted. Duncan had a text from James.

"He apologizes profusely but he can't get out of the meeting he is in. You would think being the boss he could stop for lunch, but he has been working on this deal for a long time and was only able to meet with the people today. He promises that tomorrow, he will be all ours." The waitress took our orders and we talked about our shopping spree.

It was quite the spree. I don't think I have ever spent that much in three hours in my entire life. Wade, Roxie, and I got into a side conversation about what he did when he was working. Janet and Duncan got into a conversation about Scotland. She mentioned where her husband's and mother's family came from, and Duncan knew the areas well. There were still some O'Hagan's in the area, and he knew of a Marsh but wasn't sure if any of them were related. We finished eating and Duncan paid the bill. We got back into the limo and returned to the penthouse. We sat out on the terrace talking and looking at the view. Duncan excused himself because he had a little business to attend to himself. We assured him it was not a problem. It was only 1:30 so Wade and Janet changed and went for a long walk. Duncan was still handling some business, so Roxie and I sat out on the terrace enjoying the late August afternoon.

"You and Duncan seem to be getting along. He is a very nice man and successful from the sounds of it. Do you think you will see more of him?" Roxie didn't say anything for a little bit.

"I like him, he's nice and I can't say what will happen. I never know from one day to the next what I'm going to be doing, you know that. I take one day at a time, but I do think he is a very nice man." We sat in silence enjoying the view. The sun was getting a little hot, so we moved into the shaded area. Duncan came out apologizing again for leaving us. He had a tray of iced tea that he offered to us, and we sat talking.

"Duncan, if I am not being too forward or too personal, may I ask you a question? Why is it that a wonderful handsome man like you has never been married?" Duncan said he didn't mind the question at all.

"When James's dad and uncle died very young, I took over the company until James was finished university. I tried to be there for him when he needed the guidance of a father figure. He's a good lad that James. I had a business of my own to run and it would have been unfair to any woman for me to be gone as much as I was at the time. I started my working day early and didn't finish until quite late. There was constant travel and living out of hotels. There wasn't a company plane back then, so it was always commercial flights, which from time to time, were delayed. I never knew when I would be back home. Back in those days there wasn't the technology there is today, so while I dated some very nice women over the years, I never found one that I thought I would like to spend the rest of my days with, but I have not given up hope." As he said that he cast a glance at Roxie, which she did not notice but I did. At that moment James came in, apologizing for having to do business. He got himself a glass of iced tea and we sat talking. I asked him where the gala was taking place, realizing that I had not asked him.

"It will be at a major hotel in the downtown core in the nicest ballroom I've been in. It is quite beautiful there, but I don't want to spoil it for you. So, tell me, what colour is everyone's dress for the gala tomorrow? I have a jeweler coming by Saturday afternoon around 2:00 with something for each of you to pick out. It is only being loaned for the gala so have fun with it. Hans has assured me though that there will be a wide assortment of things but if there is something in particular you want for your dress, let me know and I will ask him to bring it along. He's an old friend so I am sure he will accommodate whatever you need." I told James what colour each of us was wearing and that for myself I would like to try emeralds, Roxie wanted something black, and I knew Janet would want rubies. I also said that because of the neckline on her dress that any necklace would have to be something that sits high up.

"I thought that if she couldn't wear a necklace that perhaps she could wear a gold cuff with rubies on it, so if you could see if that is possible." James said he would contact Hans and let him know the choices.

"At least that will narrow things down a bit for him and he won't have to send back to his store for things." At that moment Janet and Wade came back in. They quickly went to take a shower and then joined us on the terrace. James brought out iced tea for them and refilled everyone's glasses. The sun was now setting over the city skyline.

"Janet, we were just discussing the jewelry and I mentioned to James about the ruby cuff that we talked about, but I also said that if there was a necklace that could sit up high, because of the dress neckline, you said you would like that. But I am sure he will bring several things in rubies for you to choose from." She said she was going to be thrilled with whatever she picked out.

James was unable to get tickets for a Broadway show or the opera on Friday as he had hoped but tonight, we were going to go out on the town for a very nice dinner at a very exclusive restaurant. I was glad that we brought something nice to wear, even if we had worn it before. Reservations were made for 6:30 that night so it gave the women enough time to do our hair and makeup and get changed.

The men were sitting in the living room in their suits waiting for us to come out. The ladies hadn't seen the red dress that I bought in Ottawa so when we came out into the hallway, we looked at what the other had on. Janet chose to bring a metal grey sheath dress that she looked fabulous in. Roxie wore the black silk pantsuit but bought a pale blue silk blouse, for a change up. The men stood when we came into the living room. They said we look fabulous, and we told them they looked handsome.

James texted the limo driver to pull up front. We went down in the elevator and out into the limo. The drive to the restaurant took about twenty-five minutes. James and I were sitting at the back of the limo, Roxie and Duncan were on the side and Janet and Wade were at the front. My heart was racing a little. James leaned over and said that he loved my perfume. I liked my favourite French perfume and wore it often. Janet was wearing something from a famous designer and Roxie was wearing a similar fragrance. I was a little worried that we would smell like the perfume counter at one of the largest retail stores, but we seemed to blend nicely. James was close enough that I could smell his cologne. I didn't know what it was, but it had a woodsy scent to it, maybe it was sandalwood.

We arrived at the restaurant and once inside we got in the elevator and went up to the fifty-fourth floor. I had never been up that high in a building before and it was a little scary. Roxie was very nervous as well. We were shown to our table which fortunately was not right by the window but gave us a pretty decent view of Toronto Island. It was quite a nice place very upscale. The wine steward came to see if we wanted wine. James, Duncan, Roxie, Wade, and I had white, Janet had red.

After looking over the menus, we placed our orders. James proposed a toast.

“Here is to wonderful friends and family and to a wonderful night.” We cheered to that and started to talk about the gala. It was, as James told me, a charity that his company had been involved with shortly after he lived in Toronto. It was to benefit the sick children’s hospital and the funding from this event was one of their biggest donations. Duncan attended a similar event back in Scotland for the children’s hospital each spring.

“James is not always able to attend the one in Scotland, but we give sizeable donations and that is what it is about anyway.” Our food arrived, and we ate happily. The food was excellent, and the presentation was fabulous. The chef came out to see if we were enjoying the meal. He knew James, but I was thinking that there were few people who didn’t know James. We told him it was fabulous, and he told us to enjoy. I finished every bit on my plate, but I was full and had no room for dessert, which I am sure would have been equally impressive and tasty. Nobody else wanted dessert so we had coffee only. I leaned over to James.

“Thank you for such a wonderful evening.” I very nearly told him that I loved him, but I was not going to be the first one to say it. I held that one back even though it was how I felt. He smiled and said that it was his pleasure. We finished our coffee; James paid the bill, and we went back down in the elevator to the limo.

"Oooh I have to say that I am glad to be back down on the ground. That was pretty high up and while I am not afraid of heights that left me a little unbalanced." Janet and I echoed Roxie's comments. Back at the penthouse, James put on some coffee. We sat in the living room, and everyone was pleasantly full. I helped James bring the coffee into the living room and before he sat down, he asked Janet if he could speak to her.

"I just have one little business thing to take care of with Janet and I promise no more business for the rest of the time you are here." He asked her to go out onto the terrace with him. He had his tablet in hand, so I didn't think anything of it. Wade was asking Duncan about Scotland and Roxie was listening to him regale things that happened when he was younger. He was a very good storyteller. James took Janet to an area on the terrace that could not be seen from where we were sitting. He got her to sit down beside him.

"You have to promise me you will not say anything about what I am going to tell you. You can't react to it either, promise me." She promised and waited to hear what he was going to say.

"I am going to ask Cassandra to marry me when we go to Scotland. I know it might sound a bit quick, but

I have been in love with her from the moment I saw her. I have already spoken to Ross for his approval. He said that while I didn't need to ask, he appreciated that I did and gave me his full support. Something that I never mentioned to Cassandra while we were in Ottawa, I made a point to meet up with her friend Christelle. She is a very nice lady, smart, intuitive, and very charming and I told her my plan. She was thrilled." He could see that Janet was going to react and he put his finger up to his lips to keep her quiet.

"You have to stay quiet I don't want her to know. I am asking you to maybe give me some ideas on what sort of ring she might like. I was going to get white diamonds, but I think that she would prefer something else. Would you have any idea what she wants, has she ever talked about it?" Janet said that they had actually talked about rings when she went to visit.

"I showed her the ring I got from Wade, and I asked her what her ring was like from her late husband." Janet paused now and wasn't sure she should say what she had been told but she thought maybe James should know.

"I don't know if I should tell you this or not but, when I asked her about her engagement ring, she said that she asked her late husband for one many times after they first were married. They were talking about what to get each other for Christmas and he had been drinking all day and when he saw it on her list of what he could get her for Christmas he said she wasn't worth it." Janet cringed when she saw how James reacted to hearing that. He got tense and his face went white.

"You know; I know that you are not supposed to speak ill of the dead, but I am really starting to hate this guy and I don't use that word very often." Janet said she had to agree.

"But we were looking at things online and she was saying that she had always dreamed of a yellow diamond surrounded by white diamonds. We looked at a few and they were all quite stunning but we both knew they were also very expensive. I think the ones she liked the most were the natural fancy yellow diamonds, but I don't want to show you what she looked at because then she will know that I said something. I think you should pick it out yourself, although I will tell you she didn't want anything too large. She is not that kind of person, and she thinks the really large diamonds don't look real. I don't know her ring size, but if you can make sure that there are some ring choices in what your jeweler is bringing over, I can get her to try on one or two to see what size and what size of stone to go with. I just have to say hallelujah, I am so happy you are going to ask her. If you are worried as to how she will respond, I think you are pretty safe. I'm not going to ask how you are going to do it either, but I know it will be romantic. I do know that she hates public proposals." James agreed that he did not want to see what she had looked at, he wanted to surprise her but the idea about finding out what size was a good idea.

"As for the place, well Ayleen gave me a clue about how to do it, so I think I will go with what she recommended. Not going to say what that was, that is between me and Ayleen. So not a word ok. You can tell Wade when you go back home but not a word to anyone else, promise." Janet promised she wouldn't say anything. They went back in and joined the others.

"Ok business done for the rest of the time. Does anyone want more coffee?" Everyone declined. Janet and Wade went off to bed. I was tired too as was James. Roxie and Duncan stayed up for a little bit. At the door to my bedroom James kissed me goodnight.

"Right now, I wish that we didn't have company here." He kissed me again. I smiled and said good night and slept like a baby. I got up the next morning before anyone and started making coffee. The chef arrived and started putting breakfast together in the kitchen. We chatted for a little bit, and I really liked Antoine. Today was going to be a day of touring around and we spent all day doing that. We saw just about every major landmark there was to see in Toronto and my feet were aching by the time we got back. Antoine made a fabulous seafood pasta that everyone enjoyed. We went and sat out on the terrace until one by one we started yawning.

I don't know about the rest of you, but I am beat and I'm heading to bed." The others said they were tired too and went to bed as well. James walked me to my bedroom and kissed me goodnight.

The next morning, I got up early again and sat in the living room. James came out and gave me a kiss good morning. Janet and Wade were next out into the kitchen to grab coffee. I looked down the hallway to see if Roxie was coming and I saw her and Duncan coming out of her room together. In fact, we all saw it, but we pretended that we saw nothing so as not to embarrass them. I turned and looked at James and he gave a soft chuckle. They grabbed coffee and we sat down for breakfast. James tried to get the conversation going because the lull in the air was excruciating. I wasn't sure what to say, I didn't want to look at Roxie because I didn't want her to be embarrassed. It was then that Roxie broke the silence.

"Oh, c'mon you guys; we are all over sixty here at least most of us are. You don't have to pretend that you didn't see Duncan coming out of my room this morning. Life is too short not to enjoy it. We like each other, and we have fun." Everyone burst out laughing not because of what she had said but more because it was a relief not to have to pretend.

Today was the day of the gala. Our dresses arrived Thursday night as Jackie promised. She brought them herself and got us to try them on with our shoes to make sure they were perfect which they were, and we hung them up in our closets. Wade's tux looked amazing on him, according to Janet. After breakfast I took the ladies to the spa. Our appointments were for 9:00 so we ate quickly and then got ready. James, or rather his personal assistant, already arranged for some people to come to his penthouse to do our hair and makeup. Today was going to be a busy day for the ladies.

"While we ladies are getting ourselves all prettied up, what are you guys going to do to keep yourselves busy?" James and Wade were going to go for a run. Duncan was going to catch up on the news until they returned and then they were going to watch a football match, or soccer as it is called in Canada. The limo driver came up to say he was ready to take us to our appointment. We gathered our things and went out the door. Janet and I said nothing to Roxie on the way down as the limo driver was in the elevator but once we got in the limo.

"Roxie, you little vixen. Here you both are trying to get me to admit that I am in love with James and for the last couple of days you have been cozying up with Duncan." She knew that we weren't teasing her, well maybe a little but she knew that I was especially happy for her. We didn't say any more about it. We got to the spa, checked in and each went off for our facials, then we had our massages. The massages were only for a half hour but that was enough. We met in a private room for our mani/pedis. Janet knew that she was going to go with red, I was going with green, and Roxie was thinking of black, but we talked her out of it. She went instead with gold because there was a touch of gold in her shoes. It was four hours by the time we were finished and back in the limo heading back to the penthouse. The hair stylists and makeup artists were coming at 4:00 so we had time to go back and sit with the guys.

The gala tonight was a dinner/dance affair with some speeches of course and as James put it, it was mostly to encourage people to write big cheques. When I knew that we were going to this gala I arranged with Janet and Roxie, when Janet came to visit me, to have an account opened up in their names, separate from their own accounts into which I deposited a large sum of money for them to write a cheque for the charity. This way, they could use the donation on their tax returns and hopefully get a refund.

They insisted they would give me the refund, but I told them to put it away for their grandkids. Janet told Wade about the arrangement and while he didn't feel right about it, he came around to the idea. I didn't want them to feel any embarrassment at the gala. The guys sat in front of the tv watching the match and we sat in another section on the terrace. We didn't mind at all as it gave us a chance to just relax, something we were not used to. We took showers when we got back from the spa, to get any oil off from the massages and to have clean hair when the stylists came.

Right at 2:00, Hans, James's jeweler friend showed up with the jewelry. I asked the guys to go out onto the terrace because we didn't want them seeing our dresses before this evening. We brought our dresses out and showed Hans what we were wearing because who better than a jewelry expert to ask what would go well. I said I would like emeralds and he pulled out an emerald and diamond necklace and earrings that took my breath away. I thought it was too much, but he insisted it would look beautiful with my dress. I don't like wearing anything on my wrists, not even a watch but he had an emerald and diamond flexible bracelet that he asked me to try. He said it would look good with the dress, but if I chose at the last minute not to wear it to leave it in James's safe. Janet suggested maybe an emerald ring.

I was going to put it on the right hand, but she said to put it on the left because the bracelet was on my right wrist. It fit perfectly and was not too large a stone. I said that I liked it a lot, but Hans said, and winked at Janet, that it was probably too much and to go with the necklace, earrings, and bracelet. For Roxie he brought a necklace of black and white diamonds with matching earrings. For Janet he brought a ruby and diamond necklace that would sit just above her collar bone and earrings that had a large ruby drop. Because Janet's dress was sleeveless, he suggested the gold cuff with rubies and diamonds. With our jewelry picked out, Hans packed up his case, waved goodbye to James and the other men and left.

We took our dresses and jewelry back into our rooms. James let us know that the hair and makeup stylists arrived. Since the light was starting to change outside, we each went into our own bedrooms and more specifically the bathrooms to have our hair and makeup done. The stylists and makeup artists got the chance to see what we were wearing and did our hair and makeup to complement the dresses. My stylists were Tanya and Carmen. I told them how old I was which they said they couldn't believe but it was only because I didn't want anything that didn't suit me.

They both agreed that my hair should be in a loose messy French braid. I let it grow a little and it was now touching my shoulders. It wasn't snow white, but it wasn't grey either. I guess depending on the light it could look white or a very light blonde with white. I looked at them when they said messy, but they said not to worry, it was just a way to describe a look, but it was very sexy. While Tanya was working on my hair, Carmen got busy laying out the makeup. She looked at my eyes, brows, lashes, and skin.

"Your eyes from a distance look like they are hazel, but I think they are green and not hazel. I don't need to do much with your brows as they are a perfect shape; maybe just a little brow pencil and your lashes are a really good length. I have to say you have probably the nicest skin I have ever seen for someone your age." I said that my eyes were green, and I generally wore a plum eye shadow which really made them green.

She agreed that would be what she would go with. Tanya wouldn't let me look at my hair until after everything was done. My back was to the mirror, so I gave in to it and let them work their magic. Carmen said she was going to go with just a little bit of a smoky look but not too much. She wanted to keep the look age appropriate but still sexy. The red lipstick was the last thing to go on and Carmen said it would not come off if I kissed anyone. I could see the look on Tanya's face and was a little worried. I was concerned that red for someone my age wouldn't look appropriate.

"No, you look so beautiful, wait until you see." Carmen told me to turn around and look. At first, I didn't recognize myself. But looking closer, the makeup was flawless, and I looked really good. Tanya stayed in the room to help me zip up the back of my dress. I put on a little perfume while Carmen went to see if the others were done.

"Since this is Mr. Sutherland's gala, we want you to be the last one to come out." I put on my dress and Tanya did up the zipper. I put on the necklace, earrings, and cuff and then my shoes and stood in front of the mirror. Tanya was clapping with excitement.

"He will faint when he sees you. You are stunning in that dress." I was not a vain person, but I had to agree that I looked pretty darned good. Carmen came in and said that the other ladies were out into the living room, and it was now my turn. I could hear the guys saying how pretty they looked. When James saw me, he stopped talking. He came over and said that I was stunning. Janet told him to check out the back of the dress, which he did.

"Wow and wow, I don't think I have ever used that word in my life, but wow." I think I blushed a little, at least it felt like I was blushing. I asked Tanya if she would take a picture of us with my phone before she left. Janet took out her phone and so did Roxie. I told James I would send him a copy if he wanted one. He said that he most certainly did, but he wanted a picture of the two of us.

James pulled me as close to him as he could. Tanya said that I should turn slightly so that the back of my dress was just visible in the photo. The stylists left feeling very happy with how we looked. Roxie and Janet looked amazing. The men looked very handsome in their tuxes. Wade dressed in another room because Janet didn't want him to see her until she was done. So even she was stunned to see Wade in his Italian designer tux. The dinner was to start at 6:30 and it was now 5:45.

"We should leave because the traffic may be a little heavy. There is going to be a red carpet and photos taken, just so you are prepared. I don't care for them, but it is a small price to pay for a good cause. If everyone is ready, we should get going." James helped me into the limo and then got in beside me. Wade did the same for Janet and then finally Duncan for Roxie. The traffic was a little heavy, but we made it in good time. People were starting to arrive and getting their photos taken.

When James got out of the limo, the flashes started going off. They were a bit blinding at first but once you knew not to look directly at the photographers, it was not so hard on the eyes. Some of the photographers were yelling at James to say who he was with, but we just continued on in. Apparently, these were the paparazzi, the photographers hired for the event were inside. We stood as a group for a photo and then the photographer asked for one of only James and me. Because he didn't ask who I was I assumed James already said who he was bringing.

Inside the hotel, I looked around and it took my breath away. We were blown away at how beautiful the inside was. The ballroom we were in was even more lovely. James took us around and introduced us to many of the people who were standing inside. I had no idea how James was going to introduce me. I told him that he could say girlfriend if that made it easier, so that was how I was introduced. I could tell that some of the women were looking at me and no doubt were wondering why James was with an older woman. But what other people thought about our ages didn't bother me and I doubted very much that any of them would say anything to James.

We sat at the table that was reserved for us. It was a table of ten so there were going to be four more people sitting with us. One couple was James's senior vice president of business development, Peter Gallagher, and his wife Bonnie. He was about the same age as James and his wife I think was a few years younger. The other couple was a CEO of a major manufacturing company in Toronto, Thomas Christie, and his wife Monica. They too were roughly the same age as James. We greeted one another and once everyone was seated, the MC of the event asked James to come up and say a few words. He got up onto the stage at the podium. There was a band in the background, but the stage light was focused on James.

"Good evening, ladies and gentlemen. I want to thank all of you for coming here this evening in support of a very worthwhile cause, the children's hospital. Now I am not going to make a long speech because I see that the chef is standing there letting me know that the dinner is about ready to be served, so I will keep this short. There will be some young people in blue t- shirts from the hospital foundation coming around throughout the evening to gather up all those great big cheques that I hope all of you have written. I also want to let you know that this is my last year co-hosting this event. I have done it with great joy for the last five years, but it is time to let someone else take over for a bit and I am happy to say that Thomas Christie the CEO of Tri-Globe Corp has offered to do just that. I will still be giving generously to this charity, but I have other things that I wish to devote myself to. I want to thank all of the people from the hospital foundation for all the hard work that they have done to make this the success it always is and last but not least, my personal assistant Mina Costas for being my presence on the committee and for the hard work and long hours she has put in. We have a great orchestra here so have a good time tonight, enjoy the meal and later there will be dancing for all those who wish to do so. Thank you." There was a round of applause for James as he walked back to our table. People were shaking his hand and thanking him for all his contributions.

The meal was very well organized. I don't think I've ever seen such a large wait staff in my life. Everyone was being asked whether they wanted chicken, fish, or beef. There were probably around three hundred people attending so while it could have easily been chaos, it was all very well organized. The meal took about two hours to complete. Dishes were cleared without so much as a knife hitting the floor. The orchestra started to play, and James stood up and asked me to dance. We never danced together before, and I was very nervous. Mr. Christie and his wife got up as well. James could tell I was nervous.

"If you have to, you can stand on my feet, so you can follow me." He chuckled but it was the right thing to say to ease the nerves. I told him that I hadn't danced in such a very long time, and he would have to forgive me if I actually did step on his toes.

It was a slow waltz and James was a great dancer. He made it very easy to follow his lead. Within moments everyone else got up to dance. It felt much better to have everyone up on the floor; at least I didn't feel like I was the centre of attention. We danced a few more dances and then James took me around the room to introduce me to more of the people he knew. He didn't know everyone that attended this event, but he knew a good number of them.

For some it was the event to be seen at but others it was an important event for a worthy cause. Not that the ones who wanted to be seen didn't give a donation because they did. James held my hand the whole time we walked around. Mr. Christie and his wife Monica were also making the rounds. We came to one table where James introduced me to some very high-level lawyers and judges. One of the women who was with an older gentleman was looking at me and then at James.

"James darling, I haven't seen you in months where have you been." She was getting up to give him a kiss, but James held her back and shook her hand. It was obvious she was trying to let me know that she knew James and on a personal level. We moved on to another table and another. There was another slow song being played and James took me back onto the dance floor.

"I'm sorry about that. She is the daughter of one of the judges that I took out once and I swear nothing happened. It was something arranged by the judge to which I regret ever having agreed to because she called me non-stop for weeks and weeks and even showed up at my office. She couldn't get into my offices, and I changed my phone number after she kept calling." I could see that he was uncomfortable but inwardly I was enjoying it. When he looked down, he could see the smirk on my face.

"It didn't bother me. You didn't have to explain. I could see she was doing that to try and get a reaction out of me. It was kind of interesting to watch you explain it though. You looked like a cat on a hot plate." We both laughed, and he leaned over and kissed me. A flash went off and I looked around to see that a photographer had taken our picture. James laughed and said now we were going to be on the front page of the gossip pages. The photographer he said was reputable, but he was known from time to time to sell pictures to the rag mags.

We got back to our table. There was wine, but I wasn't in the mood to drink. Janet had one glass of red wine with her meal and that was it. Nobody was really interested in drinking in our group. The evening went on for several more hours. We agreed prior to going that we would try to leave at 11:00, which we did. Janet and I stopped in at the ladies' room on our way out. The girl who tried to give James a kiss came in just as we were getting ready to leave. She was tall, blonde, and buxom and dripping in jewels.

It looked like she was going to say something to me, but I think the look I gave her was warning enough not to. Janet asked me what that was about, and I said that she was someone James dated once but she was more interested in him than he was in her. We left and rejoined our group. James saw that she had gone into the ladies' room and had a look of concern on his face. I assured him that it was fine, and nothing was said.

We returned back to the penthouse. James poured a whisky for himself and Duncan. Wade had soda water as did Roxie. I decided to have a glass of wine as did Janet. I wanted to get a shot of just James and I, so I took him out onto the terrace. The lamps were lit and provided more than enough light. I gave him my phone because his arms were longer. We got close and he took the photo. In fact, he took several and even one of him kissing me. I pulled away because while the others could not see us, I did not want to remain on the terrace too long alone with James. He pulled me back into his arms.

"Cassandra, I love you, with all my heart I love you. I want you to know that and I mean it with every fiber of my being." I looked at him through misty eyes. I was so filled with joy I couldn't speak but I knew that I had to, or he would think that I didn't feel the same way.

"James, I am in love with you too. It took me a lot of soul searching and time to let that fill my heart, but it did, and I love you." He kissed me again and again. I pushed him back and said we had to go back in, or they would be wondering what we were up to. Only Duncan was in the living room. We asked him where the others were, and he said that they'd gone to change because they wanted to have coffee on the terrace and didn't want to ruin their dresses.

"I said I would wait for you two love birds to come back in, so you wouldn't think we had gone to bed." Duncan chuckled to himself. James, Duncan, and I went to get into our casual clothes as well. I hung up my dress and fell backwards on the bed. I was so giddy with hearing that James loved me. He actually said he loved me. I got up and was going to take my makeup off but decided that I would do that before going to bed. There was a knock on my door. It was Janet.

"We decided to get into our jammies and sit on the terrace and have coffee. Kind of like a slumber party." She could see that I was smiling from ear to ear and wanted to know why, although I think she probably had a good idea. I told her that James said he loved me, and I told him that I loved him too. I went into the bathroom and put on my cotton pj bottoms and t-shirt top. I brought a robe with me and put that on over top. Everyone felt comfortable enough with one another now to sit around in pjs.

James brought cups and a pot of coffee out onto the terrace. Duncan was obviously a little more formal with his knee length silk smoking jacket and pjs. Roxie was wearing satin pjs and a satin robe, Wade and James were in t-shirts and cotton full length pj bottoms. Janet had on cotton pjs and a robe the same as me.

It was warm out, but James started the gas fire pit anyway, just to keep the chill off. Everyone had a throw to lay over themselves for extra warmth. Roxie immediately suggested we have s'mores but unfortunately James didn't have what was needed. We agreed that next time, he needed to be prepared. Laughing and joking we had a good time. I was snuggled up to James, Janet to Wade and Roxie, surprisingly to Duncan.

Roxie was thinking of campfire songs and ghost stories that we could tell. While nobody was willing to sing, James and Duncan were more than willing to share a few ghost stories. They were stories told of people seeing ghosts walking on the moors in Scotland. Things like that didn't bother me but I whispered to James not to tell of any at his estate or Roxie wouldn't go. Janet mentioned the ghost walks that she and Wade did on a trip once and that people often said they saw the ghosts of the original owners.

One story led into another, and I could tell that Roxie was getting a little unnerved. Roxie was the first to say that she was going to head off to bed. All those stories of ghosts had spooked her a bit. It was then that Duncan said he would go with her to make sure she was okay. I poked James in the ribs and we both laughed. Janet and Wade stayed up for another twenty minutes and they went off to bed.

"You know I think that you and I are the only ones not sleeping together in this penthouse." I knew that James was joking, and I laughed. We stayed curled up together in front of the fire. He lowered some of the lights so that it was mostly the light from the fire surrounding us. It was so nice to be here with him like this. I think that James had a feeling I was thinking about what he said.

"Cassandra, I am not in any rush to get you in my bed. I commend Duncan for being so brave and Wade and Janet are married, but I am not in any hurry. When that moment happens, I want us to be alone or at least not with people on the other side of the wall. So don't fret ok." I thanked him for understanding. I started to fall asleep in his arms and said that I should go to bed. He kissed me and reluctantly let me go.

The next morning, Janet and Wade were heading home. We had a wonderful breakfast together. The chef prepared my favourite, eggs benedict, which the ladies had. The guys had eggs and bacon or sausage. The food was great, and we said thank you to the chef. Wade brought out their luggage and the driver came to the door and took them down to put them in the limo.

We hugged and kissed goodbye. It was so much fun with them. Janet said she would text me when they were home. When they left, we went out onto the terrace to take in the view. James asked if we wanted to see more of the sights. We said yes and decided on the museum and the art gallery. The kid in Roxie would have wanted to go to the amusement park but we went with the museum and gallery. Since we had a really large breakfast, we chose to skip lunch and have a nice dinner at the penthouse. We left it to the chef to decide with the exception being that Roxie did not like lamb. We grabbed our handbags from our bedrooms and met James and Duncan at the door.

We chose to go to the museum first and the art gallery last. There was an Egyptian exhibit on that I was happy to see. For the next two and half hours we toured the museum. Then it was off to the art gallery. James pointed out landmarks as we drove by them. While I enjoyed the museum, I was really looking forward to the art gallery. I wasn't knowledgeable at all about art, but I knew who some of the masters were and while they did not have any of their paintings at the time, we would still see some very good art. Neither Roxie nor I had been to the art gallery in Edmonton, so we said we would have to go for sure when we got back.

Some of the art I just didn't get but it was art. Duncan and Roxie went off in one direction and James and I went off in another. James wanted to get a couple of painting for the house, and he asked me what I thought. He pointed to one that was a very colourful painting of a skyline. The colours were very vibrant and joyful and we both liked it. I walked along and came upon one that was a field of poppies. I immediately thought of my Dad and a tear fell down my cheek. James asked me what was wrong, and I told him what the picture reminded me of.

"My Dad went back to France for the 70th anniversary in May and my two brothers went with him. My youngest brother is a pretty good photographer, and he took a picture of my Dad standing in a field of poppies, so this sort of reminded me of that. He didn't fully realize it, but he was quite ill on that trip, and he was diagnosed with terminal cancer later that year. He died one month after he was told how long he had." He gave me a long hug and then we caught up with Duncan and Roxie. Roxie looked at me and had a look of concern. I said I was ok, just a memory of my Dad. Roxie and I went to the ladies' room before leaving.

"Duncan keep the ladies occupied would you, I want to go back and buy those two paintings we looked at but don't let on that is what I'm doing ok." Duncan agreed and when we came out, he said that James had gone to the men's' room. Even though James returned from a completely different direction of where the men's washroom was, it made me curious, but I didn't ask.

James texted his chef that we were returning so he knew when to start preparing everything. James said he was preparing a roast of venison and hoped that was ok with us. I was fine with it as I loved venison. Roxie never had venison, so James texted Antoine the meat choice was good but to ensure that it was not too rare for Roxie or myself.

It was going on 6:00 pm by the time we got back. We went to wash up as Antoine said that everything would be ready in about twenty minutes. James poured a whisky for himself and Duncan. I said that I would have half a glass of red wine with the meal and Roxie said she would have a little bit of red wine too. She was not a drinker at all but on occasion on a hot day she liked a nice cold beer. Duncan and James laughed and said that if she wanted a beer, she could have one. She said it was ok she would have a bit of wine.

The meal was wonderful. The venison was beautifully cooked with roasted potatoes and carrots. It was absolutely delicious, and I ate every bite. Roxie was a little hesitant at first but dug in and liked it better than beef. Dessert, if we wished was a homemade coconut ice cream with mango sauce. It sounded divine and everyone had some. Coffee was served on the terrace. Antoine cleared the dishes and put everything in the dishwasher. When it was finished, he put everything away, signaled to James that he was leaving and the four of us sat quietly enjoying the evening sky.

"We go back home tomorrow Roxie are you ready to get back?" She was a bit ambivalent about it, but she promised to look after her grandsons for a week while her son and his wife took a small vacation. We would only be home for about two weeks before we were off to Scotland for two weeks. I had to disappoint Ayleen about coming to visit. When I explained that James's uncle needed the plane to take him back home to Scotland, she seemed ok with it.

I mentioned to James that I had never been on a plane as much as I had been in the last few months. I couldn't imagine what it was like for them having to do this all the time. They had to have been exhausted. Both James and Duncan said that they were used to it as they'd been doing it for many years. It was part of doing business and of course it helped when you had your own plane and could stretch out and sleep undisturbed when you needed to.

"I am really looking forward to going back to Scotland though. The first time I ever got on a plane was when I went to Cancun for two weeks. I went to Portugal once for a couple of weeks and I did travel a little bit with my job, but it was always within Canada and of course I flew back east a few times to visit my parents and my son and his family. But those were, for the most part, spread out over many years between trips. I am very much looking forward to this one." Roxie was looking forward to it too. Our flight back was at noon. James and Duncan unfortunately could not go with us as they had business to attend to and when the plane returned, it was taking Duncan back to Scotland. I was packing my things and James knocked and came in. He shut the door behind him.

"Anything I can help you with?" he said with a smile on his face. I looked at him and smiled. He sat me down on the bed beside him and kissed me. I looked at him and kissed him back.

"I'm sorry that I can't go to the airport with you, but I have to get some business things taken care of. I hope you don't mind?" I assured him that I didn't, and we got up off the bed. I had to finish packing, but he pulled me into his arms and kissed me so passionately that I thought my knees were going to give out.

"I love you so much you know." I said I knew, and I felt the same way. All of the jewelry that we had worn the night of the gala was being returned to Hans today. It was in James's safe, and he was planning to drop it off on his way to work. James planned to keep the emeralds and diamonds Cassandra wore but wasn't going to tell her yet. We hugged each other for a very long time. I wasn't going to see him until he came to pick us up for the trip to Scotland.

"I will miss you so much, I hope you know that." I knew that as well and we hugged again. James took my things out to the front door. Duncan and Roxie were already out there and waiting. The driver knocked on the door, took our things downstairs and we took one last look out on the terrace. We hugged them goodbye and went down in the elevator. I didn't want to cry because I was sure if I did, Roxie would so I fought back the tears. It was about an hour drive to the airport. We sat together in the back. We didn't say too much on the ride to the airport. We got to the plane and our luggage was put by the stairs and loaded by the handler. Janine went through the security procedures and when she was done, Roxie and I had a talk.

"James told me he loved me, and I told him I loved him." Roxie was elated. I hadn't the opportunity to tell her until now. She wanted to know what was going to happen now and I said I didn't know. I was happy that he said it first. I didn't want to ask her about her and Duncan because I knew she was in a bit of turmoil about it. I think she was worried about how her son would react.

We talked about the gala and looked at the pictures that were taken of us on our phones. James said he would send copies of the ones taken by the photographer. I could see that Roxie was thinking about Duncan. I didn't ask anything after we saw them coming out of her room in the morning other than the little bit of teasing in the limo. I presumed that they spent the next couple of nights together, but I wasn't asking. We sat quietly until Roxie brought it up.

"I like Duncan a lot, obviously, but I'm not sure how Mitchell is going to react to me getting so close to someone so quickly. I know that he will be concerned that he may be after my money, but I will assure him that Duncan has way more than me, way more. Murray has been gone for a long time now and while it took me years to get over that, I think I am ready to move on and be with someone. I don't want to live the rest of my life alone and Duncan and I have fun together." I know she was looking at me for advice. I thought for a few minutes before saying anything.

"Roxie, what you do with your life is your business. I am sure that when Mitchell knows that you are happy, and that Duncan isn't after your money, he will come around. He will of course want to meet him and talk to him, just as Ross did when he met James. We both have many more years to live and I for one am not going to go it alone and you have said you don't want to either. I know I said that I was not interested in another relationship but then James came into my life. The fact that I dreamt about him and then there he was. I don't know if God put him in my path, but James loves me, and I love him, and I am not going to let that go. I don't know what your feelings are for Duncan nor his for you, but don't you think it is worth it to find out? You might be surprised and the two of you end up getting married." She laughed at that because she knew that was not where things were between them, but she also did not say where things were at. She would be seeing him again in Scotland and would use that opportunity to find out how things stood.

"What is it the kids say these days, friends with benefits." We both burst out laughing. Janine brought us each a chef salad and water. We ate and laughed and talked about what to bring to Scotland. I checked last week to see what the typical weather was like in September.

"It is actually not too bad. It can go up to plus sixteen during the day and down to plus nine at night, balmy weather for us or as we say here in Alberta, shorts weather. We should probably pack a rain jacket of some sort as the online report said that it can rain a fair bit. We are going to be there for two weeks, so I am going to pack jeans and warm sweaters, some dress pants and some long sleeve and short sleeve blouses, just to be safe. We should probably go shopping for a couple of dressy things since James and Duncan have already seen what we have. James also mentioned that they dress for family Sunday dinner the majority of the time. I have some things, but I think I want something new. We can arrange to go shopping the week before we go, that way I can check the temps and we can adjust our wardrobe accordingly. How does that sound to you?" She thought for a moment. "I will agree to that if you let me buy my own things." I said that I would even though I said she didn't have to.

"I know, and you have been so great buying us things and James too. But I can afford to buy my things. I know for you having money is sort of new and I'm so happy for you that you don't have to worry anymore, but I'm still pretty solid financially so I can look after myself." All of a sudden it hit me that I still had James's credit card. We did some pretty decent damage to it, but nothing was anywhere close to the limit.

"Oh my God, I will have to text him and let him know that I still have it. I will cut it up when I get back to my place." We ate the rest of our salad and drank our water. We both got a little sleepy and put our seats back and dozed off. We must have been sound asleep because we didn't realize that Janine put a blanket on each of us. There was a little bit of turbulence which made us sit up. Maria came back and asked us to put our seat belts on and seats up. It wasn't anything serious just a bit of a storm that we were going through in Saskatchewan. That meant that we were almost home.

An hour later, the captain was telling the attendants to prepare for landing. It was good to be home, but I missed James. We put our luggage in the trunk of my car and went back to my place. It was 2:00 in the afternoon by the time we landed and 3:00 by the time I got back to my place. I transferred Roxie's luggage into her car and asked if she wanted to come up for tea, but she wanted to get home herself.

I texted James that I just parked my car in the garage and was going up to my unit and could he call me in about fifteen minutes. I then texted Ross to say I was home safe and sound and Janet as well. She said she would give me a call tonight. I got up to my unit, took my luggage into my room and hung up my beautiful gown. I was looking through the mail when the phone rang. It was James right on cue.

"James, it is so good to hear your voice. How has your day been going? I forgot to give you back that credit card you gave me, so I will cut it up into a million pieces." It was good to hear his voice, but he sounded tired. He said there was no need for me to cut up the card, that I should hang onto it. I told him I was nervous with it, but he said not to worry it was insured. I felt better knowing that.

"I miss you already and I would love to talk to you longer, but I have to get to a meeting. I'm glad you made it home safely and if I am not too late, I will give you a call later. I love you Cassandra, talk later." I said I loved him too and hung up. I looked through my mail and there was nothing of much interest.

I gave Sonya a quick call to say I was home and said I would send pictures of the gala. I told her that James was going to talk to one of his friends to see if he was interested in a blind date. We laughed at the notion of that but that was what it probably was going to be. She wanted to know if I knew who it was.

"I am not sure who it is. James said he had to see if he could work out a couple of things first. The guy though is not married. I think he was a long time ago though." She asked me if I saw a picture, but I said no because James said he didn't want to do that until he was sure that he could work things out. Anyway, I told her I would try to find out more when we went to Scotland. I didn't want to say anything to her about James telling me he loved me because I knew that she was lonely a little bit and I thought it would make her sad.

"I will call you when I come back from Scotland. We are leaving in two weeks, and I have a lot of things to do. We ate like kings and queens, and I need to work off a few of those calories. I will give you a call soon." I hung up and finished putting my things away. It was getting late, and I made a quick dash to the grocery store to pick up a few things. I took a shower, got into my pjs, and had some soup and a sandwich.

I put in a call to Janet, and we talked about the trip. She showed her dress to her parents and the photos from the gala. She was going to get a print made of her and Wade to put with their other family photos. I said that I was getting tired and would talk to her tomorrow. James texted and said he was going to be later than planned and would call me tomorrow for sure. I texted back to him that I loved him and to not work too late. He sent me back a kiss. I put my head down on the pillow and thought I was going to have such sweet dreams, but I was out like a light.

The next morning after having toast and coffee I gave Christelle a call to tell her all about the gala and that James told me he loved me. She was very happy for me, and we talked for about an hour. She had a doctor's appointment to get to, so we hung up and then I went down to the lobby to see who was up for a walk.

Only a couple of the ladies were there but they were heading out for a walk and said they would join me. I told them all about the gala and they were so happy for me. They stopped at about two kms and said they were going to go back, but I continued on. I took the road down to James's house and when I walked up, I couldn't believe how much was done. George was not there I was told by a supervisor as he was off picking up some special lighting. Christina was, and we walked through the house. So much had been done and it looked amazing. The shades and bowls arrived and were put up. They were stunning, and I was really happy.

"That was such a brilliant idea of yours. Doesn't that chandelier in the entrance just make your jaw drop." I had to admit that it did. I had no idea these were going to be so beautiful. I mean I hoped they would because James was trusting me but this far exceeded my wildest expectations. The downstairs was pretty much done. There were a few touch ups on the paint but nothing serious. The kitchen was like something out of a magazine. Christina did an amazing job and I told her so.

"Well thank you but you had a big hand in all of it. You helped to choose a lot of what you see. I filled in with decorative details, but you and James did a great job on choosing the paint and flooring and a lot of other things." I wanted to go up and see how the master suite looked but George was not finished yet and he put up a sign that nobody was allowed in.

I respected that and went down to see how the sunroom looked. Christina said that George's choice of slate flooring was perfect. The windows were so big, and they let in so much light. Christina picked out the furniture which was perfect for the room. The navy sofas were big and comfortable with accent recliners in a lighter blue with yellow pillows for that pop of sunshine.

There was a specific area that the Christmas tree would go in but for now there was a large armchair that could be moved to another spot when needed. There wasn't a fireplace in this room which was ok because this was going to be the party room, where the tree would go and where kids could run and not worry about knocking things over. Everything looked perfect.

"James will be so happy with everything and from the looks of things it will all be done by the end of October as he requested." Christina thought that they might be done a lot earlier but thought that the end of October was a very safe date to go with.

As yet there was no art on the walls. Christina felt that art was a very personal thing and was leaving that up to James. She mentioned that he already had a couple of pieces and would probably look for some when he came to Edmonton. There was of course some of the glass art from his company, which was not set out yet because she didn't want it to get broken, but she showed me several pieces. They were all beautiful, everything was just beautiful.

I left her to get on with finishing things up and I walked back to my place. It seemed very small now compared to James's home. There wasn't a soul in the lobby, so I went straight up to my unit. I did a bit of cleaning, had a light dinner, and sat and watched tv. Wasn't expecting to hear from James and I didn't.

I was out like a light as soon as my head hit the pillow. The next morning as I was sitting down to have coffee, I got a text from James. He didn't have time to call as he was going into yet another marathon meeting. There was a possibility he was going to have to go to Germany to work over some details on the cosmetics idea. He would know more tomorrow and let me know.

I felt a little restless and went for a drive. I thought maybe I would head to the mall and go and do a little personal shopping. I didn't want to do it with Roxie, so I thought since I had nothing better to do for the day that's what I would do. It didn't take me long to get to the mall.

I wanted to get a few sexy things, nothing wildly inappropriate for my age but maybe some lace bras and panties, some warm pjs in case it was cold as well as a robe that wasn't bulky and one or two nighties that were a little sexy. I took everything home, tried it on and made sure that the pjs fit. Threw everything in the wash and when it was dry, I put it in my luggage. I wasn't planning on wearing it before then.

The rest of the day went by quickly. I was going to go for a walk, but it started to rain a little at first and then it was coming down really hard, so I did an hour on the exercise machine in the exercise room. I worked up a good sweat and went up to take a shower and then got into my pjs.

I sent James a text, saying that I missed him and that it was raining cats and dogs. I wasn't expecting him to text back so quickly. He was going to video chat. I was already in my pjs, ones that were full leg and long sleeve. The rain made the air cool and damp. It was the one time that I missed having a fireplace. James's call came in and I answered.

"Hello sweetheart, how are you?" I told him I was fine and that I went to see the house and it was really coming along. I wasn't going to say that nobody ever called me sweetheart before. He looked very tired.

"James, you look worn out. I can only imagine how much you will be looking forward to going back to Scotland." I didn't want to keep him long because he looked about ready to fall asleep, but he wanted to see me.

“I miss you too and I wish I were curling up on the sofa with you, but I do have to go to Germany tomorrow. I’ll be gone for about two weeks. Do you think that you and Roxie would be ready to leave on Wednesday instead of Saturday? I do have some things to take care of back home and it would make it much easier if I just flew directly to Edmonton from Germany on Monday. I have to give the crew at least forty-eight hours rest and then we can leave on Wednesday evening, arriving in Scotland Thursday morning. Would that be ok?” I thought it would be fine and would call Roxie in the morning and text him and let him know.

He wanted to talk longer but he was falling asleep. I blew him a kiss and said good night. There was a lot of thunder and lightning, but it wasn’t too bad. I fell asleep eventually waking up to grey skies. I gave Roxie a quick call the next morning to see if leaving Wednesday was ok and she said it was. We agreed to go shopping on Friday before because she would be back in the city, and we could go to the different malls if we needed to.

I gave Ross a call to let him know that I was going to Scotland a few days early and also to see if I could video chat with Ayleen before I left. I would text him a day or two ahead. I knew that they would busy over the next few weeks with her parent’s anniversary. I finished my breakfast and went out for a walk. Most of the seniors were returning from their walks so I went by myself. I did a hard trail today, but it felt good by the time I got back. I took a quick shower and gave Christelle a call.

"How are you doing, did you get the pictures I emailed you of the gala? I got the one of James and I on the terrace in a frame and put it with the rest of my family photos. I also wanted to let you know that we are going to Scotland a few days earlier than was originally planned. James is heading to Germany and then when he gets back, he would like to leave after a few days' rest for the crew. He's got some business to attend to before he can spend all his time with us, showing us around." She got the pictures and thought they were beautiful.

"You look so happy, and I am so happy for you. He's a good man Cassandra and he will be honest and respectful and be good to you. You can count on him, and he will have your back no matter what." It was important to me that they liked each other, and I told her that. She liked my late husband at first but saw the way he was treating me and disliked him intensely. But as she would often say, he was going to have to reconcile that once he crossed over. I changed the subject and said that I didn't want to speak of him anymore. I told her that I went shopping for some lingerie, nothing crazy though.

"I'm not twenty-five and even though I have a pretty good body, I am not going to try to dress like a twenty-five-year-old. I have one short satin nightie that could be called sexy but the rest of the stuff I got was more for comfort. I am not and never have been into all the skimpy underwear, but I did pick up some lacy bras in a few colours with some similar coloured lace briefs. She was laughing.

"So, thongs are not your thing. Having a piece of thread up your butt is not your style." We both laughed hysterically at the thought of me wearing something like that. Never going to happen. I bid her a good evening and made myself something to eat. I knew that James was already in Germany and that he would be so busy he would probably not have time to call but he would at least text me a good night.

For the next couple of weeks, I went to the gym every day to work out. I went to the spa a few times and had a massage, facial and a mani/pedi several days before we were to leave. It was Friday morning, five days before we were to leave. I had toast and coffee and Roxie texted to say that she would meet me at the mall at 10:00. If we didn't get all that we needed there we could go to a couple of other malls.

On my list of the things that I wanted were several warm sweaters, several pair of dress pants and blouses to go with them, a good raincoat that I could easily pack, some warm socks, a few pairs of warm pants, maybe in light wool and a dressy pant suit that I could wear if we were going out. I updated my entire wardrobe because I didn't want anything from my past coming with me except those things that meant the most to me. I had a fair amount of clothes now for every season, but I wanted a few new things for the trip.

With my list in hand, I drove to the mall to meet Roxie. As usual she was waiting just inside the door. I gave her a hug and said I had my list. She laughed and said she had one too and off we went. All of the stores had their fall clothes out, so we knew that wasn't going to be a problem.

We went first to one of the big retailers and I found a couple of sweaters that I liked and wool pants that I could mix and match with them, dress pants, and blouses. Roxie was going all out because she didn't normally need much in the way of fall attire because she always went south before it got too cold. She picked out six really nice sweaters, some blouses and eight pairs of dressy pants.

We left there and went to the other big retailer to get some warm socks. I already picked up my pjs that I was bringing but she wanted to get some warm ones to wear. She picked up three sets of warm pjs and a nice robe that she could wear to lounge around in.

I said that I wanted to get a nice pant suit, so we went off to another store. I found a really nice navy silk suit that I matched with a silk blouse in pale pinks. But there was a dark green organza dress with long sleeves, v neck and a full skirt that I had to try on.

Roxie handed over the dressing room door a royal blue lace sheath dress with long sleeves and a round neck. I came out in the green one first and looked in the mirror, I knew I was going to buy it. I said I was going to try on the royal blue one but told her she had to get a nice dress to wear for our last evening there.

Roxie thought she should get another pant suit as well since she already wore the black one. She got one in dark grey wool that she paired with a red chiffon blouse. She was still going to bring the black one, so she thought she would get another silk blouse only in white. She chose a blouse that had multi-coloured flecks in it because just a plain white didn't look as good on her. She picked out a long sleeve modest v neck dark brown crepe dress.

We came out at the same time. She looked really pretty in this dress, and I liked this royal blue one. I stopped at the shoe store and picked out a pair of black satin peep toe pumps with a leaf pattern in green crystals, and a royal blue leather pump that matched the dress perfectly and Roxie got an alligator look leather pump in dark brown and a gold clasp on it.

The only thing left on my list was the warm raincoat which I found in a bright royal blue. I loved the colour and bought it. Roxie got one in a different style and in black. I asked if there was anything more she wanted to get, and she said that she thought she was done.

We had lunch and then she had to go to get some things taken care of before Wednesday. She wanted to know how long the flight was and I said about seven hours I thought. I went home and let Ross know I was back, so Ayleen and I could video chat. Within minutes she was calling me.

"Hi Gramma. Daddy said you are going to Scotland on Wednesday. I wish I were going; it sounds like fun." I said that yes, I was and hopefully she and Mommy and Daddy could go with me one day. She cheered up after hearing that. I asked her how her day went yesterday and of course she gave me all the details. I laughed at some of the things she said. I missed those days when Ross was young, but I was getting to relive them with Ayleen.

We talked for about an hour and then she said she had to go because it was dinner time. She blew kisses for me and for James she said. I told her I would pass them along. She giggled at that. She was such a happy girl and had been from the start. She was so much like Ross when he was her age.

I made myself something to eat and sat watching the news. James texted to say hello and that he was working late. I knew that James was going to be staying with me when he arrived on Monday. His house would definitely be ready by the end of October and possibly even the middle of October so there was no point in him booking hotels.

I had the things that I bought this morning laid out on the bed in the spare room. I had several pairs of shoes put out as well. I had runners and some dress shoes, but I wasn't going to bring the ones that I bought for the gala. I put aside some flats to wear and thought that we should get some sort of rubber boots or hiking boots if we were going to be out walking on the moors.

I would have to ask James about that as maybe hiking boots would be better. I didn't own a pair and I wasn't sure if Roxie did. I went to bed that night tired but happy. I spent the next two days of the weekend finalizing my clothes to bring, arranging for my mail, to once again be taken care of by Mr. O'Leary and letting some of the seniors know that I was going to Scotland. They wished me a good trip.

Chapter 4

It was Monday morning and James sent me a text saying that he would be back in Edmonton around 2:00 that afternoon and would come directly to my place if that was ok. I texted back yes of course it was. I knew he was going to be tired, so I picked up some things at the grocery store to make him dinner. I wasn't the greatest cook in the world, but I could follow a recipe and for the most part, my cooking was pretty good. I decided to make beef bourgeon. It was something that I wanted to try for years and picked up what I needed. It was a time-consuming meal that took almost four hours to make. If it didn't work out, we could get something from Jason's. I had all of the ingredients cut up and ready and was going to wait until James arrived before starting.

It was around 1:00 in the afternoon when James texted to say he was leaving the airport. I texted him back that I would meet him in the lobby so that he could get the garage key from me and put his car in the spot beside my car. We would be going in my car to the airport because I was sure that not all our luggage would fit in his sports car. About forty-five minutes later he texted to say he was downstairs. I went down and gave him the key and said I would wait for him upstairs.

I left my door open so that he could come right in. He brought up a medium sized overnight bag because he knew he was staying with me. He set it down near the bedroom door and came over and gave me the biggest hug and an even bigger kiss. He noticed that I had the stuff for dinner on the counter and asked what we were having. When I said beef bourgeon, he said he would help. He made it a few times himself and so he felt comfortable helping me with it. We worked well together in the kitchen getting all of the ingredients going. It was now going to take two and a half hours, so we grabbed some water and sat on the couch.

"So, tell me how did things go in Germany? It occurred to me that we have never, in all the times that we have talked, discussed our likes and dislikes very thoroughly and I have never found out all of the business in which you are involved." I knew that he was tired, but he said as for the business, he would give me a copy of the company's portfolio. He had one, but it was on the plane.

"Things in Germany went well and as for likes and dislikes, I don't have a lot of dislikes. I am willing to eat just about anything at least once, the exceptions being split pea soup, anything that slithers or crawls on the ground. I, for the most part, can get along with anyone until they prove otherwise. As for likes, well you are at the very top of my list, but that is a love not a like. I don't think there is any colour that I don't like. I like comedies and documentaries, not so keen on war movies or ones that are gratuitously violent. I love to travel but would prefer it more for pleasure than business as I do enough of that. I love holidays and being with family. That is pretty much it for me what are your likes and dislikes." I crossed my legs and sat looking at him.

"Well, I dislike sauerkraut. I can't stand the smell of it or look of it. I am not a picky eater, but I too will not eat split pea soup, there's a story there from childhood which I won't go into. I don't like anything that slithers or crawls on the ground except escargot. I have never tried haggis, but I would be willing to try it once. I won't eat eel to me that is like eating a snake, wretched things. I don't like public speaking or surprises in public or even in front of family. I don't like, nor will I tolerate anyone speaking negatively about my son or granddaughter. To me those are fighting words. I say to people if you have something that you don't like about my son, keep it to yourself and I have said so to my father, Christelle and Janet. Sorry, this is making me sound awful, but you have a right to know these things. Maybe you will turn tail and run but I believe in being honest and upfront. I don't like beating around the bush if I don't have to. I like to get right to the point, saves a lot of needless worry and time, tactfully of course. As for likes, well I do love you and you are also at the top of my list along with my son, daughter in law and granddaughter. I love to look at the stars and watch the aurora when it happens. I love it in winter when there has been a lot of ice fog and the tree branches are heavy with hoarfrost and then the sun comes out, spectacular to see. I love sheets that have been washed and hung on the line in a cold spring breeze. I have been quoted as saying that it is better than sex sleeping in those sheets. I am actually pretty easy going and not hard to please, at least I don't think I am. I have been told that I am very patient, and I can be pretty funny, although I don't let many people see that side of me. There is probably more but I'll let you digest that." James suddenly burst out laughing and pulled me beside him.

"My darling Cassandra, if you think fresh smelling sheets that have been hung out in a spring breeze are better than sex, you have never been made love to properly and by the right man. No, I am not going to turn tail and run. I too like honesty and getting to the point. I am sure that as we are together more and more, we will discover more about each other. That is part of the excitement don't you think? I promise I will never embarrass you by surprising you in front of a bunch of people. That is actually a good thing to know. Speaking of which, when is your birthday? I don't think I ever asked you that. Mine is November 8th and you have probably guessed I was born in '60." I looked at him with amazement and told him that mine was Nov 6th and the year is '53. It was rather interesting that we were both born in the same month.

"I guess that makes us both Scorpios. I have all the birthdays I am to remember on my phone, and I put them on the calendar that is on the fridge. But if you want to know Ayleen's, Ross's, and Lindsay's, I'll send them to you, but they are on the calendar on the fridge. Oh, by the way Ayleen sent you a big kiss when I video chatted the other day and I said I would pass it on." I leaned over and kissed him. He loved that she thought of him. We checked on dinner and added the vegetables. I couldn't believe we just talked about likes and dislikes for over two hours. I set the table, using the new china that I bought when I moved in. I got out some wine glasses and water glasses. The table was set now, we just had to wait for the vegetables to cook. James noticed that I had some flowers on the dining table and commented on them.

"I buy flowers for my parent's birthdays every year. Since we are leaving for Scotland on Wednesday, I thought I would get them now so that I could enjoy them. I don't send flowers to their grave anymore; they always get thrown out the day they arrive so now I have them here. I will put them down in the lobby when we go and ask Mr. O'Leary to throw them out when they are done. It just occurred to me that your birthday and mine are the same dates as my parents. How weird is that?" James said that when he looked through the photo album, he noticed that my Dad was a veteran, but he could see that it was still difficult to talk about, so he let it go. James started to put his bag in the spare room but saw that there were a lot of clothes on the bed.

"James, you can put your things in my room. You don't need to sleep in the spare room unless you prefer to. I mean whatever you want." James put his bag in my room.

"Whatever I want is to be with you always, but I don't want to rush you. I am patient as well; I think we are very suited for one another don't you." I had to agree with him. We were very comfortable with one another, and I found it was wonderful to be around him. James poured us each a glass of red wine and sat out on the balcony waiting for the vegetables to cook.

"Such a big difference from the terrace you have in Toronto isn't it. The vegetables should be done in about twenty minutes. I like watching the sunset at this time of the year too. The sky is coloured in oranges, pinks, purples, and greyish blues. I guess I like colours too." We sat together enjoying the last remaining bit of the sunset. I said that Roxie called to say that she would come in early if that was ok. I knew she didn't like driving at night, so I suggested that she come for dinner, and we could go across to the restaurant. James was nodding that that was a good idea.

Roxie agreed and said she would be at my place at 5:00 on Wednesday. I called Mr. O'Leary to see if I could reserve another stall in the garage and he said it was fine. The beef bourgeons was ready. I made up a plate for James and myself and took it to the table. I bought some rolls to go with the meal; Scottish baps which were hard to find but I was able to get them at a grocery store in the city when I went shopping with Roxie. James topped up our wine and we sat down to have a wonderful meal.

"Wow this is good; we make a good team in the kitchen James." He agreed totally. We both did up the dishes, me washing and him drying and putting away. I had just enough milk for cereal the next day, which was good for James.

"Best that I get used to eating cereal as I am sure that Ayleen will want some whenever she comes to visit." We laughed but I had to agree, she loved cereal. We sat finishing the last of our wine and watching some tv. James wanted to take a shower so went into the bedroom to get his things out to put in the bathroom. I was mulling over what to wear for bed and thought if this was going to be our first time, wearing my usual was just not going to do.

I went into the spare bedroom and picked out the blue floral satin chemise with matching robe. I was wondering what to do about underwear. Damn what a dilemma to be in. Do I wear them or not? I had a cotton pair in the same colour. He was going to be out of the shower in no time and I had to decide. I decided not to wear any. Oh goodness I hope that I wasn't making a fool of myself. I put them in my room. I didn't even know what side of the bed he slept on for heaven's sake, so I couldn't put them under my pillow. This was starting to be a disaster which I thought somewhere down the road I would laugh hysterically about. I went back out into the living room until James came out in his t-shirt and long cotton pj bottoms. Why was it always so easy for men, ugh!

"James if you don't mind, I think I will take a quick shower. All I can smell on me is food. I won't be long. You can watch tv or put on some music if you like. James shut off the tv and put on some soft music. He gathered by the CDs she had that she was not a fan of jazz, something he would have to remember. He liked jazz and listened to it often when he was alone in the car. She had some orchestral CDs and James put those on. He kept the volume low, just enough to say it was on.

On my way in to take a shower I grabbed the chemise and robe. My hands were literally shaking when I put it on. My biggest fear was that I was going to look ridiculous but when I took a look in the mirror, I looked pretty good. I dried my hair and put on some face cream, then a little squirt of my favourite French perfume. With a deep breath I opened the door. James turned down the lights and lit a few candles, thank God, he was not going to see me in glaring light. When I came out into the living room James had his back to me. He was looking at CDs but then he turned around. He was staring for what seemed the longest time. I did look ridiculous. I almost started to cry.

"My God you are breathtaking. I just want to look at you." He came forward and pulled me into his arms. He raised my chin and kissed me the most tender kiss I ever had in my life. He then picked me up and carried me into the bedroom. He lowered my feet to the floor and kissed me again. He pulled off his t-shirt and undid my robe. It fell to the floor in a quiet whisper beside his t-shirt. His kisses were on my neck and on my shoulder. He lowered one strap of the chemise and then the other. It too fell to the floor in a silent whisper. James carried me to the bed, pulled back the bed covers and lowered me down gently. His eyes were burning with passion; his hands were following every curve of my body. I too was letting my hands explore his body and I wasn't sure when, but he removed his pj bottoms and was lying next to me beneath the covers.

"You are so beautiful. I love you so much. I want you so much." His kisses were the most passionate I had ever experienced in my life. He was kissing me everywhere. He held my hands as our bodies met. I untangled my fingers from his and ran my hands up and down his back. His kisses were nonstop, and I didn't want them to stop. I wrapped my legs around his waist and kissed him back with all that I had. He was not in a rush, but the heat built up between us and we each cried out the others name. He slowly rolled to one side and pulled me close. My cheek was on his chest which was now damp from our love making. James was rubbing my back with one hand and pulling my face up, so he could kiss me again.

"I would like to say that I could do that all night, but I am so tired from travelling, I just don't think I can. I hope that is ok with you." I said I understood. I would have been happy to sleep with the scent of him on me, but I got up to go to take a shower. The heat and steam from the water was enveloping me. I could feel James's arms go around me as water was dripping down my body.

"I think I found my second wind." He gave a soft laugh and turned me towards him. While the love he made to me in bed was slow and sensual, he was now backing me up to the shower wall and his passion quickly grew. The kisses were hotter, needier. My nails dug into his back which only seemed to spur him on more. We both let out primal cries that had been, for too long, held back in both of us. I stood back down from having my legs wrapped around him once again. We looked at each other and smiled and laughed, that kind of laugh when you just enjoyed the best sex of your life.

"Now that was definitely better than those sheets off the line." We both laughed hysterically when I said that.

"I told you, you just had to have the right man making love to you." We got out of the shower, dried ourselves off. I went out to blow out all the candles and turn off the music and went back to bed. James held me in his arms, and we cuddled all night. It was glorious to wake up to him next to me. I got up quietly because he was still sound asleep. I used the bathroom in the spare room not to wake him. I put on my regular pjs that I slept in and put on a robe, went out to the kitchen, and made some coffee. I sat on the sofa and closed my eyes thinking about last night. I was so worried that I was going to disappoint him. I don't think I did but I wasn't sure. It had been a very, very long time for me at least; with James I wasn't sure. I must have been very lost in thought because I didn't hear him come out of the bedroom.

"You looked a million miles away just now. What were you thinking?" I told him what I was thinking. I was going to be honest and not hide my fears.

"I was worried that maybe you might have been disappointed. It has been a long time for me and, well you know, a woman worries about those things." He gathered me up into his arms and kissed me and hugged me.

"You could never disappoint me, ever and don't ever forget that. You were amazing, and it is not only women who worry about those sorts of things you know. I was a little worried too, but I think that we both did pretty good don't you think." I knew he was teasing me now. I told him he was amazing as well. He went and got himself a coffee and sat down beside me.

"In case you were wondering, it has been a long time for me as well. While, yes, I am a guy, I was too busy to get involved with anyone and my days of one-night stands ended a very, very long time ago. Also, to put your mind at ease, and I know you are not concerned, but I did get some tests done to make sure I had nothing transmittable. I have the proof of that if you want to see it." I told him it was not necessary and that I'd done the same thing after my husband died.

"I really don't want to go into my relationship with him, but he cheated on me more than once not long after we got married. He always denied that he did, but I stopped sleeping with him after I found out. I did the tests for my own peace of mind, but I too have the results if you want to see them. Fortunately for me, I didn't catch anything." We both agreed that we didn't need to see any test results.

We had our coffee and some cereal and orange juice. We got dressed and went for a walk over to his house. The caretaker's cottage was completely done. We went in and looked around. It was very cozy and wasn't really that small. It was a four bedroom two and a half bath with a decent sized living room, good sized kitchen and dining room and laundry/mud room area. We went out and looked at the Quonset, which was very big, but it was set back a bit, so it didn't stick out like a sore thumb.

We walked up the driveway to the house. We took a quick peak in at the four-car garage. It was a garage so nothing much really to look at. The view of the house was very impressive. We walked up the steps to the wrap around porch and to the front door. The double front door was a deep red with two beautiful stained-glass side lites. To me a red door was impressive, and I was glad that James went with it. Black was so common for front doors these days and red was good chi or so I heard. We went inside and there was still work being done. Christina was not there at the moment but then she didn't know we were coming by. George greeted us as he was coming down the stairs.

"James, Cassandra such a nice surprise to see both of you. Want me to show you around and I can tell you what is left to be done. We should be finished here the week of Thanksgiving or maybe the end of September. The majority of the light shades and bowls have been installed. There are still a few of the sconces that have to be installed, but that should be done in the next week or so. Christina came up with a couple of different ideas for a couple of the lamp shades, so it is taking a little bit longer to get those done. Why don't we start with your study which is right here?" James went in and looked around.

I saw it when it was nearly finished, and I thought he was going to really love it. The paint on the walls was a dark green and with the warm woods of the bookcases and flooring, it felt very warm and masculine. His desk arrived but they had not put it in place yet. The armchairs that were going to go in front were off to the side. His desk chair was off to the side as well. He stood in various areas in the room and said that he wanted his desk in front of the windows facing the door.

George made note of that and said it would be done tomorrow and the rest of the room put in place. There was a half bath and a large coat closet on the other side of his study. We then went across the foyer to the large living room. I think aside from the sunroom, this was my favourite room. It was probably the only room in the house where we chose a light colour of paint for the walls. It was a light sky blue with double crown molding that had gold accents in it to tie it in with the dining room. The hardwood floor was the same as throughout the house, a warm pecan colour.

The fireplace was the centerpiece in the room. The mantle was long and had plaster bracket accents.

The fireplace was made out of grey and bluish grey stone, it was very beautiful, and it was the only fireplace in the house that was wood burning. The furniture was not due to arrive until the end of September. I saw some of the pieces from pictures that Christina had shown me. I thought it was going to look perfect. The sofas were soft colours of grey with blue and gold coloured accent pillows. The armchairs were in blue and gold colours with accent pillows in grey.

The area rug was a Turkish Kilim rug, and it was down, but the coffee table was not on it yet. The rug had a gold border with a small navy and white pattern on it and the centre of it was predominantly navy with a gold, lighter blue, green and white pattern all over it. It suited the room very well. We went around to all of the other rooms and then upstairs. There were seven bedrooms including the master. George wanted to keep the master bedroom until the end. Each of the bedrooms were large enough to accommodate a king or queen bed in them but they had kings, and the rooms were still quite spacious. Most of the ensuite bathrooms had a large shower, double vanity, and toilet.

One bedroom I recalled was to have had a bathtub and shower with vanity and toilet. They were all done with the beds in them, but no bedding was yet on the beds. Christina was trying to go with a theme in each room but hadn't yet thought of what theme was going to be in the one bedroom that had the tub/shower combo.

James told her not to finish that room yet. The queen size bed set was leaning against a wall that had yet to be painted. We then went down the hallway that led across to the master suite. There was a large linen closet on the same side as the master bedroom. It was supposed to have been a smaller bedroom, but George talked to James, and they made it into a huge linen closet and storage area.

All the other bedrooms were down the hall, with three bedrooms on each side. George opened the double doors and we walked in. This was the only room that was completely finished. It was stunning. The huge king bed was along one wall in the bedroom and was the largest king I had ever seen. The bedding was dark grey with green leaves on brown branches. The sheets were a sage green. It looked so comfortable I almost crawled into it.

The walk-in closet was now completed, and George went with a soft warm brown for the cabinetry, because as he heard I didn't like white. The lights were pot lights, which I wasn't overly keen on, but it was a closet and having anything else in there would not have been as good. It was very large to say the least. There was a window seat at the largest window in the bedroom that overlooked the wooded area. There were garden doors that led out onto the largest upper balcony I have ever seen.

Next, he opened the double doors to the master ensuite. It took my breath away. It was like walking into a very expensive spa. The oversized double shower, with glass doors, had light grey slate on the walls and floors of the shower with a blue/black and darker grey wide glass tile band around the shower. There were two rainwater shower heads and other spray heads which I was not sure what they did but George said they were for steam. The free form tub I saw earlier was near the window at the back.

I was not into taking baths as a rule, but it was always nice once in a while to soak in a tub. Since there would never be neighbours, there were no window coverings in this room. The toilet was in an enclosed area which was always a nice feature. The towel closet had been completed and it was the same warm brown wood. There was of course the larger walk-in linen closet in the hallway that would be for bed linens, comforters, and the like.

I think what surprised me about this room more than anything was the colour of the paint on the walls. It was not what James and I had originally picked out. George thought that the colour, which was called Rosemary sprig with neutral tone trims, would suit better than the dark grey we'd chosen. Because the bathroom had tones of grey and the walls were grey, he thought this colour would look better.

"I showed it to the interior designer, and she agreed with my choice, so I hope you like it. If you don't, we can always go back to the grey you wanted." James looked at me and I had to agree, it was a really nice colour. The stone on the gas fireplace was varying tones of green slate and dark grey slate so it blended well. We took another look in the sunroom and James was really happy that he went with it wider. We finished looking around and then walked back out and down the driveway. James pointed out where all the outlets were along the drive because the landscaping company had them hidden by planting small shrubs in front of them. If he hadn't said they were there, I would not have known.

"Let's go for a walk around the walking path, I want to show you the lights I picked out for them." I thought that Christina and I had picked out all of the lighting, but James wanted to choose this lighting himself. They were spaced out far enough that there wouldn't be a dark area between the glow of each lamp. They almost matched the lights that Christina picked out for the exterior lighting but looked familiar, but I couldn't place where I'd seen them before. It would be good to cross country ski in the winter.

"It is all so pretty, and it will be nice to walk it all the way around, but not today. I'm getting a bit tired." We walked back to my place, and it was almost 1:00. Neither of us was that hungry so we had sandwiches and coffee. After we ate, James wanted to get a few business things taken care of. While he did that, I went into the spare room and packed my luggage for the trip to Scotland. I realized when I had two pieces of big luggage packed that I was probably overdoing it, but I would rather have on hand than have to run out and buy at the last minute.

I put the luggage by the door in the spare room. James was still going through some work matters and I texted Ross to see if Ayleen was up for a video chat before I left tomorrow. He said that she was, and he would get her to call right back. It was only a moment or two later when she called in.

"Hello Gramma, how are you? Daddy said you are leaving to go to Scotland tomorrow night. Is James with you now? Can I say hi." I said that yes, I was leaving tomorrow and that yes James was here, but he was doing some business right now. James was at the dining table but smiled and came over to talk to her.

"Hello Ayleen, how are you? What have you been doing since I saw you last?" He spent the next fifteen minutes listening to her talking and talking about all the things that she had done. He was laughing and joking with her, which I knew she thoroughly enjoyed.

"I have some things to finish up right now, so I am going to pass you back to Gramma and you can continue talking to her." She blew him a bunch of kisses and he blew them back. He handed me my tablet and I could see her giggling to herself. She started to whisper.

"Gramma I hope you and James get married so I can call him Grandpa instead of James. I would really like to do that." While James pretended he was busy and didn't hear that, I knew that he overheard because he had to clear his throat a couple of times. I knew that meant a lot to him. I told her I would bring her and Mommy and Daddy something back from Scotland. She wanted to know what, but I said that I didn't know yet. I told her I loved her and blew her kisses.

"I love you too Gramma and you too James. Bye." James was smiling at her last words. He was busy for another few hours. We were going to have leftover beef bourgeon for dinner.

"I am almost done taking care of the things that I need to. I am sure we can figure out something we can do to occupy ourselves until dinner." I knew he was teasing, but then maybe he wasn't. By the time he actually finished his work, because one email lead into another and another it was almost 6:00. I took out the beef bourgeon and put it in the oven to reheat. James was finished now with his business and helped me to set the table. We ate and enjoyed the leftover beef bourgeon.

"I meant to ask you about whether we should bring hiking boots if we are going to go for walks. I should have asked you earlier but forgot until now." James said that wasn't a problem, he would ask Duncan to go out and pick up both Roxie and I a pair. Because I'd been shoe shopping with Roxie a couple of times, I already knew what size she wore so I gave him that information. James sent Duncan off a text and asked him to get us each a pair of hiking boots. Duncan wanted to know if we had something in mind and I said to make sure they were comfortable. Style wasn't really an issue for either of us for that.

"It must be all that walking we did today, but I am a bit tired." I knew that he was attributing his fatigue to what we did last night. We both laughed, and he took my hand and kissed it, because we both knew we were thinking the same thing. I made us coffee and we sat in the living room. James put on some music, and he took me by the hand, and we danced to a couple of songs. When the songs were over, we sat and finished our coffee.

"I think I should give Roxie a quick call and make sure she is still going to be here at 5:00 tomorrow." He could tell I was looking for some reason to slow things down a bit. Roxie answered on the third ring and said that she would most definitely be there at 5:00. We were going to go to Jason's for dinner, relax a bit at my place and then head to the airport for 10:00. I sat back down again beside James.

"I really want to make love to you right now but if you don't want to." Before James could finish what, he was going to say I went into his arms and kissed him." I could feel the passion in him just as I was sure that he could feel it in me. He took me into the bedroom, shut the door and before long we were both undressed and in bed making love. It was the same sweet love that he had made the previous night. There was no hurry, no urgency to it, it was slow, it was sweet, and it was exhilarating. We fell asleep in each other's embrace and woke up very much in the same position.

"Good morning sweetheart. I have to say last night was, well I don't know if I have anything that would adequately describe the way that we were together. I think magical is pretty close though." He kissed me on the lips and on the nose and jumped out of bed and into the shower. I was reveling in what happened last night. Making love until the wee hours of the morning, we both slept in, and it was now 10:00. James was going to make pancakes again for me. I had just enough eggs and milk left. He came out of the shower with just a towel wrapped around his waist. I looked at him with a look and he knew what it meant.

"Vixen, out of bed with you or we will be there all day and I don't think Roxanne would be interested in an x-rated show when she gets here." He took his towel off and snapped it at me. He didn't hit me; it was a playful move, but I jumped into the shower. I came out, got dressed in jeans and a light sweater. It was what I was planning to wear on the flight over. I sprayed some of my favourite French perfume on under my sweater.

James had on a pair of jeans as well and a black shirt, but had the sleeves rolled up while he was preparing the pancakes. I poured coffee for myself and made another one for him. We both liked to have two cups of coffee in the morning. I kissed the middle of his back and wrapped my arms around him. I didn't realize that I was that close to the stove and burned my hand a little on the pan. I pulled back quickly and ran it under some cold water.

"Oh my God are you okay. Let me see how bad it is." It wasn't bad, I pulled away in time and it was just a little burn. I went into the bathroom and put some ointment on it. He was standing beside me holding onto my hand.

"James it's ok really. It isn't even blistering. I've had worse burns than this, no need to worry about it. The redness will be gone in a couple of hours. He kissed me repeatedly apologizing for me getting burned. I told him it was my own fault and not his.

"That will teach me not to try to get amorous in the kitchen when you are cooking." The tension was lifted, and he relaxed. He went back into the kitchen, forbidding me to come in now. I set the table and got my coffee and sat on the sofa. The pancakes were ready, and we sat down to eat. He kept looking at my hand to make sure it was okay. I showed him that the redness was already going away, and he felt better.

James took my suitcases down and packed them in my car. We were taking it to the airport as it was more practical than his car. Roxie was going to be here in a few hours, so I cleaned up the kitchen and stripped my bed. I thought that I may as well wash the bedding and a few other things while we were waiting. While I was doing that James got back on his tablet and did a bit of work. He put on some music but kept it low. I wanted to give Christelle a quick call before I forgot.

"Hi Christelle, how are you?" She said she was fine but wanted to video chat. I said I would call her back in a minute. I sat beside James on the sofa and dialed in to video chat with her.

"Ok there you are, and I see that James is with you. Hello James, how are you? You both look very happy. What time does your flight leave for Scotland?" James said hello back to Christelle and asked her how she was doing. She said that it was nice to see him again and she was doing ok. She told me already that they met in Ottawa. We both talked with her for about half an hour. I told her we were leaving my place at around 9 pm to go to the airport. Our flight was leaving at 10:00. She told us to have a wonderful trip and make lots of memories. I ended the call and put my laptop away. James finished the stuff that he was doing and there was still another hour before Roxie arrived.

"I've been thinking. You know how you mentioned that one of the things on your bucket list was to go to Austria or Germany to go to the Christmas markets, well I was thinking that we could do a trip maybe at the end of November. Would you like to do that? I could ask Janet and Wade to come along too, it would give me a chance to show her the office in Germany and then we could spend the rest of the time shopping, eating, and having fun." I said it sounded wonderful. James would get his personal assistant Mina to make all the hotel and other arrangements. I texted Janet to say that I wanted to video chat with her for a few minutes. She was available, and I called her right away.

"James is inviting you and Wade to come with us to Austria and Germany at the end of November to go shopping for Christmas ornaments, but we will do other things too. Do you want to come with us?" James said it would also be a good opportunity to show her the Germany office, so in a way it is a business/pleasure trip. Janet was absolutely onboard with it, and I could hear

Wade from the kitchen woohooing, so I knew he was good to go. It was settled, the four of us were going to Austria and Germany at the end of November.

"I will get Mina to send you all of the details. It will be easy for us to stop and pick you up in Sudbury and then we can go from there. We will go to Berlin in Germany as there is a very big Christmas market there and then Vienna Austria. Just make sure that your passports are current and will not expire while we are away ok. Don't want to run into any problems. It will be a fun trip I think." Janet said she and Wade were going to check out the markets online just to see what was there. We hung up saying we'd talk after we got back from Scotland.

"You make me very happy; do you know that. This has been a big dream of mine for a long time. I hope you are prepared for all the ornaments I plan to buy. I'm a little bit of a fanatic when it comes to them." He was happy to make me happy. Roxie called to say she was in the parking lot downstairs. I went down and went into the parking garage with her.

I told her about the trip to Austria and Germany. She parked in the spot a few places down from my car. She too had two pieces of big luggage. It was a good thing we didn't have to bring shampoo and the like otherwise we would have more. But there wasn't a restriction on the number of pieces of luggage anyway.

We both laughed at that. Back upstairs, James met us at the door. He gave Roxie a hug and a kiss and went inside.

"Cassandra told me you guys are going to Austria and Germany at the end of November. Gee too bad I am going back down south because I would love to go. But I have to go south, I'm going to sell my trailer. This will be my last trip down now. I like the warm weather, but I miss Mitchell and the kids and now that they are older, they are a lot more fun at Christmas. Not that they weren't when they were little but now I can do more things with them. It would be nice to go but maybe next year." Of course, James would love her to come, and he could always get Duncan to meet us, but Roxie said no, she had to take care of the stuff down in California. James assured her that there would definitely be more trips because he doubted that we would be able to bring back all the ornaments in one go.

"But I am going to make a valiant effort to bring as many back as I can, but of course we will go back again, and Duncan and you can come." Now it was time to go and have dinner. Roxie was dressed in jeans and a sweater too. We went back down to the garage and got in the sports car. This time I sat up front. Roxie giggled.

"Once around the block please James." We burst out laughing and drove across the road to the restaurant. James fit so easily into my life, like he'd always been there. He got along so well with my friends, and it was real. He was a good man, and I was so happy that I was in love with him.

We took our time eating because it was going to be a long flight and we would not arrive in Scotland until morning. We ate leisurely over appetizers and then onto the main course and then of course dessert and coffee. By the time we finished it was nearly 7:00. James paid the bill, and we went back to my place to freshen up. James checked in with the flight crew to make sure that we were going to be leaving on time.

"If you ladies like we can actually leave before 10:00, which would mean we could leave for the airport now and we can lift off around 9:00 pm. We agreed that instead of sitting around waiting we would leave now. We got to the airport at 8:30. James took our luggage from the back of my suv and put them by the stairs. His were already stowed except for the bag he had at my place.

The flight crew was different this time because they were flying us to Scotland. The captain was Michael, the first officer Corey and this time the flight attendants were both male, Drew and Ian. We settled into our seats and waiting for takeoff. Right at 9:00 we were cleared to go. The plane taxied out onto the runway, and we were off. We listened to the usual security flight process and then waited until we had reached flying altitude. It didn't take us long to get up to 44,000 feet. There were no clouds so the stars were visible. Drew brought an ice bucket back with three champagne flutes. I looked at him and wondered why we were having champagne.

"You said you wanted to try this champagne, so I was able to get a bottle of '53 from Jason who knew someone. It has been properly chilled, so let us get Drew to open it and pour it and we will toast to a wonderful trip." I could not believe that James would do this. I was so worried that he had spent thousands and thousands of dollars on this, and I didn't know if I would even like it. We clinked our glasses, and I took a sip. James waited for my opinion.

"Oh, my goodness this is so good. I mean that really. I'm not just saying it because I know it costs thousands of dollars either. I am so happy I like it." Roxie almost choked when she heard what it could cost. I told her not to spill any and we laughed.

Since we already had a big meal, James asked the crew to have on hand different cheeses and crackers. We would be having breakfast on the plane before landing. He hoped we were ok with scrambled eggs, sausage, and toast and of course lots of coffee. Roxie didn't have any more champagne, but James and I drank the rest of it. I was not going to lose a bubble.

Roxie was starting to nod off and Ian brought her a blanket and pillow. Ian asked her to keep her seat belt on as we had to touch down in Toronto to take on more fuel. He brought blankets and pillows for James and me, but we set them aside and moved up to the middle of the plane. We spoke softly not to wake Roxie, but she was fast asleep.

"James this was such a thoughtful and very expensive thing for you to do, but you must promise me you won't do that again. I don't want people to think that the only reason I am with you is for your money." He listened to me thoughtfully.

"Cassandra, anyone who thinks that you are with me because of my money is an idiot and I will happily tell them so. I love you and I want to do these things for you. It makes me happy because I can see how happy it makes you. But no, I will not be buying this very expensive champagne every week, that is a little extravagant even for my taste. I love that you care so much about this, but please don't worry about it ok. This was a special occasion and something I wanted to do." That said, the matter was put to rest. James remembered that I wanted to see his business portfolio and he pulled out a large folder and gave it to me. He turned on his tablet as there were some things he downloaded that he wanted to go through. We sat together, him working on his tablet and me going through the portfolio.

The first page dealt with the security company that he owned. It was, as James said, quite large. He hired some of the smartest computer people in the world to work on a variety of different types of security and computer programs. From home to industry and even government departments, James was involved in it. He had contracts from several large police organizations and a few others. In home security, which was something I was more interested in reading about, as the stuff with the police and governments was not very detailed, for obvious reasons.

I wondered if he was going to install this kind of security in his home in Stony. I looked at the pages on the glass company that his Dad started, the whisky company too and then the shipyards that he modernized. Page after page, business after business, James either owned the company outright or was partners in others. It was mind boggling how he was able to manage all of this, but he obviously did because he was an enormous success. He finished what he was working on and saw that I was finishing his portfolio. He wanted to know what I thought.

"What I think is that you are a very, very successful, very smart businessman and you manage to handle all of these companies extremely well. I think that your Dad would be very proud of you, your Mum too. You are amazing James, and I am proud of you as well."

That meant a lot to him to hear her say that to him. It had been hard long days and no doubt that if they had met when he was just starting out, he wasn't so sure they would have lasted. He sacrificed a lot to get where he was today and if luck was still on his side, he would be able to ease back a bit. We were getting ready to touch down in Toronto and Drew went to get Rosie to put her seat back up. She fell back asleep again after we took off from Toronto. James and I kept talking.

"All of those trips to Toronto on business, I was doing a lot of interviewing of prospective managers and vice presidents. My portfolio is large, and it keeps getting larger because new opportunities are made available all the time. Some companies I have sold off because in my view it was coming to the end of what I could do with it. I need to delegate more which I am starting to do. That's why I have been on a mad hiring run over the last few months. I have good people who work for me and who want to work for me. I pay extremely well, and I am willing to let them run with things. They know to always reach out to me when they need guidance and not to wait until things go badly. I have a very good rapport with my senior team. Mina is also training staff to help her out and to even take over some things. She has been my right hand for so long and I am glad that she is not looking to leave any time soon. She would be very hard to replace, and she knows that." We talked a little bit more, but I was getting tired and so was James. We went back to our seats, buckled ourselves in and drew the blankets over us and cuddled together as much as it was possible to in an airplane seat.

Drew turned off all the lights so that we could go to sleep. He and Ian relaxed and took turns having cat naps I was told before James, and I fell asleep. The flight was uneventful, and sunlight was starting to come through the windows. Roxie woke up and stretched. She couldn't believe that she had fallen asleep so quickly and even after waking up in Toronto she fell back asleep so quickly. She went to the washroom up front, and James went to the one in back. She returned before James did.

"Did you guys get any sleep or did you cuddle up on the sofa seats all night." I said we got to sleep an hour after we left Toronto. James had a few things to go through on his tablet and I was looking through his company's portfolio. From the prospectus, it looked like his net worth was in the multi-multi-billion dollars. Roxie gasped and so did I.

I knew James was wealthy, but I had no idea he was worth that much. James came back, and I went to wash up and splash some water on my face and redo my makeup. When I came back out Drew was bringing coffee and Ian was getting the scrambled eggs, sausage, and toast ready. Roxie commented on how good the coffee tasted and then we were served breakfast.

“Thanks love, this looks really good.” We ate and talked, and Roxie wanted to know what the plans were for our time in Scotland. James said that first Duncan was going to pick them up at the airport. Then we went back to his estate to get settled in and look around. A light lunch was going to be around 1:00 and dinner would be at 6:30 or 6:00 depending on how tired we were.

It was going to be a big time change for Roxie and me, so he thought that perhaps going to bed early would be wise. We were due to land in about an hour. We finished breakfast, Ian cleared things away and we had a last cup of coffee. Roxie and I were both looking out the window and could see land. James said that we were probably just south of Glasgow.

I was getting nervous. I was going to be meeting James’s family and I really wanted to make a good impression. James held my hand and said things were going to be fine and not to worry. Already he knew me well enough to know when I was worried. The captain told the flight attendants to prepare for arrival. We put our seats back in the upright position and made sure our seat belts were buckled. Ian took James’s briefcase and stored it up front.

There were no overhead bins in this plane. Anything that had to be stowed away was put in a large cabinet up front. We could hear the landing gear going down and we were starting to make the descent. Touchdown was the smoothest I had ever had on a plane. Just as James said, Duncan was standing by the car waiting for us to deplane. He waved at Roxie, and she waved back. He came up the stairs and helped her down. Although James called her Roxanne, she asked Duncan to call her Roxie, which he did.

"Roxie, I am so happy to see you. Welcome to Scotland, both of you. James was it a good flight?" James said that it was. The luggage was removed and was also placed by the stairs. James grabbed his briefcase and my luggage and Duncan grabbed Roxie's. James, it seemed had even more luggage than we did so he made a couple of trips.

When the luggage was safely put in the back of the large suv that Duncan came in, Roxie got up front with him and James and I got in the back. As we were driving along, James was pointing out landmarks to Roxie and me as he wanted Duncan to concentrate on driving. The roads in Scotland were good but this was a busy time of the day and as in most other places not everyone in Scotland was a good driver. It was only a twenty-five-minute drive James said and we drove through some very pretty places.

It was not long before Duncan was driving up the road to James's estate. He said it was big and he was not exaggerating. The estate was situated on eight hundred acres of land. His estate had an actual running farm of sheep, beef cattle, which are called Galloway cows and chickens.

We drove by the farmer's home and the barns and other outbuildings which were in immaculate shape. He didn't have a lot of cattle or sheep; it was more like a hobby farm. But it provided most of the meat that they ate James said. The home itself was much like a castle. This was the traditional style that James said he preferred, and it very much suited the surrounding. The land was largely fields with trees a good distance away from the house. There were a few trees around the house but that was more for shade I think in the summer. When we arrived, a gentleman came out to greet us.

"Good morning ladies, you go right on in, and I will bring all the luggage in. It is good to have you home sir." James introduced us to William who was the butler and driver. The rest of his staff would be inside, and they were. They were waiting at the door to take our things. There was the housekeeper Mrs. O'Toole and her daughters, Annie, and Beth. They helped to keep the house in perfect order. There was also the chef, Barclay, who James said was probably the best chef in all of the UK. He thanked James for the compliment.

The luggage was taken upstairs by the girls and put in the bedrooms. They asked if we wanted them to unpack for us, but Roxie and I said we could do it shortly. James showed us around downstairs. He had a massive living room which he said many a party was held in. The dining room was equally big, and the dining table was the longest I had ever seen. He showed us his study, a small sitting room, and a small dining room and through to the kitchen.

Everything was big and beautifully decorated. Then he showed us the games room which was so big my jaw dropped. James mentioned that there were seven bedrooms and seven ensuites upstairs. He whispered that he didn't want me or Roxie to be embarrassed so he had our things put in separate bedrooms. Mine was right beside his and Roxie's was across from Duncan's. Whether that changed during the course of the visit was up to Roxie, and of course me.

He took us up to our rooms. The hallway was decorated in a traditional style. My bedroom was beside his. He opened the door, and the king bed was against the wall of the room. The bedding was in colours of lavender. The walls were painted in a light lavender colour with lots of white trim but there was wallpaper behind the bed with huge purple flowers. The bathroom was pretty, single vanity, claw foot tub and a good-sized shower.

I took my things from my luggage and hung them in the walk-in closet and put the rest in the drawers. Shoes were placed on the shoe racks, and I noticed that my hiking boots were there as well. There was one huge window in the room that had a long cushion on it. Good for sitting on to read a book or look at stars I thought. There was a knock at my door. It was Roxie wondering what my room was like. Her room was in red and white, not particularly a colour she would have gone with, but it isn't her home. We went down to Roxie's room, so I could have a look. The one large wall was painted a dark red and the rest was wallpapered with large red flowers. Her bed was king size too and her bathroom similar to mine only it had red accents and white walls.

"See, this is why I don't like wallpaper. It is not what I thought James would have. I wonder what the rest of the bedrooms are like. We walked back down the hallway to the main staircase. There was apparently another staircase, Roxie said that was near Duncan's room.

"I guess for those midnight snacks." We both giggled. Duncan was every bit as tall as James, but he had a little bit of girth to him. Nothing that I couldn't work out taking him on walks every morning I thought. James was waiting for us downstairs. We joined him in the smaller sitting room. It was nearing 1:00 now and lunch was going to be served shortly. James had a fire going in the fireplace. The house had been retrofitted with proper plumbing and electrical according to my recollection of what James said. I sat beside James and

Roxie sat in an armchair. He asked how we liked our rooms.

"They are very lovely James, and this fire is nice and inviting." He had it on for that purpose only because he updated the boilers a few years ago, so the house was not damp and cold like most of them.

"It gives a nice ambiance, but you didn't really answer my question about how you liked your rooms. I apologize if they look a little outdated. I redid mine and Duncan's long ago, but the others are seldom used and frankly I haven't gotten around to it. So how badly do they need to be changed." I looked at Roxie and she wasn't going to say a word, I could just tell. I guess it was left to me. I gave her that look that said 'chicken,' but she just laughed. I could hear her mutter under her breath 'better you than me love.'

"Ok, so you know I am going to be honest with you, which is what you love about me right? First, in our rooms, please get rid of that sixties wallpaper. I haven't seen any of the other rooms but if they have wallpaper too, get rid of it. Take a page from the house you built back in Stony, change up the lighting a bit. You can still keep it period but maybe swap out the shades with new ones but have the vintage look. Go with richer colours and lots of white trim, but I am sure if you got Christina in here, she would be saying the same things. I'm not an interior designer so I know that while I can give an opinion on paint colours, Christina would be a better person to deal with." James was laughing but in a good way. He knew that I detested wallpaper but then so did he. He apologized to Roxie for the room she was in.

"I completely agree with you, the place needs a bit more updating, but have a look in my room and Duncan's and tell me if that is more what you are thinking of. I had a designer from Glasgow come and do those two rooms, but I will say that they are more masculine." As lunch was almost ready, I said we could have a look after if that was ok. James agreed and walked us to the small dining room.

We sat at the table, and we were served soup with a freshly baked roll. James said that it was cock-a-leekie soup a traditional soup of Scotland. Depending on the region though it varied in the ingredients. I was sure that Roxie never had it before. I knew that I hadn't, but I was game to give it a go. I could see Roxie waiting for me to go first.

"This is very good, a heartier version of chicken soup." I wasn't too keen on the bacon being in it, but I knew that I would not be having it every day. Roxie liked it as well. We ate our soup in relative silence. James said that the evening meal was typically the biggest meal in his home. He was generally out on business all day, so it was different for the chef to have him home during a weekday.

"James what are the plans for us while we are here. We are anxious to see your Scotland, at least as much as we can see in the two weeks we are here. I am sure to do it proper justice we would need to be here longer." First, he was going to show us around his property later today, which he would do on the buggy, which we found out later was a golf cart.

Tomorrow he was going to take us into town to show us some of the shops that we might like to visit and go back to later by ourselves and the local gardens; then on Monday we were going into Glasgow where he was going to show us his glass company, the shipyard, and the distillery. Then he had plans to take us to a museum, an art gallery and to show us a few of the churches that same afternoon, because he knew I would appreciate the stained-glass windows. There would also be evenings out as well. But he didn't want to overload us, this was of course, just the first of what he hoped would be many visits.

"I know you want to pick up some souvenirs to take back and there are three of the places that you will go to nearby that should provide what you want. They have a lot of made in Scotland items and something that I think Ayleen will like is the Loch Lomond Bear. It's cute and maybe she doesn't need it, but it would be a cute keepsake for her. I think that Duncan is planning to take Roxie on an outing on Saturday for the day, just the two of them so I thought that perhaps you and I could spend the day walking around, maybe have a picnic, if that is ok. But on Sunday we will be having the whole family over for a family dinner. You will get to meet the lot of them. We always dress up for Sunday dinner but nothing too formal." It sounded like we were going to be busy almost every day our first week there. I said that the picnic sounded like a nice idea.

It took about three hours to go all around the property, stopping every so often to look out at the beautiful views. There was enough time before dinner to sit in the smaller sitting room in front of the fire and have a glass of wine. Duncan recalled that Roxie said she preferred beer, so he offered her a glass of a light ale. Duncan and James both had a whisky.

"Duncan where are you planning to take Roxie on Saturday?" Duncan had a blank look on his face and looked quickly at James. James reminded him that he said that he wanted to show Roxie where he grew up in Duntocher.

"Yes, that's right, sorry I guess I was working out in my head all the touring that we were going to be doing and clean forgot about that. There is a lot of history to the village, and I think that you will enjoy walking around. It isn't very big, so we can easily take our time walking." Roxie said that she would love to go and see where he grew up. James said that it was also where his Mum grew up and Duncan's sister Fenella who had now become the matriarch of the family. The chef entered and said that dinner was served if we were ready.

"I thought perhaps this being your first night here we would eat a bit early and then you could retire early. I am sure that the time change is going to hit you fairly soon." The smaller dining room which James and Duncan used was set with beautiful china, crystal wine glasses and water glasses. The flower arrangement was very pretty with Scottish thistle, heather, and white roses. The meal was brought in, and Barclay said what we were having.

"The meal this evening is roasted grouse, black pudding and griddled green vegetables. Ladies if you are not familiar with black pudding it is commonly called blood sausage. I also have garlic mashed potato. I hope you enjoy." I was happy with the black pudding. I hadn't had blood sausage in a very long time, so I had that as did Roxie. Everything tasted wonderful. The roasted grouse I had not had for decades and decades, but this was done better than anything I had ever had. We chose to have water instead of wine.

"This is very yummy, and I have not had blood sausage or black pudding I should say since my Dad was alive. He loved it and had it a couple of times a year. Brings back some good memories for me." Roxie said that it was good, but she wouldn't want to eat it more than once or twice a year. Annie came in to take away our plates when we were done.

Barclay then brought in dessert which was Cranachan with raspberries and shortbread. James said that Scotland was known for its shortbread, and this was some of the best he'd ever had. Roxie didn't care what the Cranachan was, she dug in. It was delicious and by the time I finished I was pleasantly full. We adjourned to the sitting room for coffee. Roxie and I chose to have coffee while the men had whisky. Both Roxie and I grew a little quiet.

"I think you ladies are ready to hit the sack. You've both gotten awfully quiet." We admitted that fatigue was setting in. Duncan walked Roxie up to her room and James walked me up to mine. But first he wanted to show me his room, which as he said was more up-to-update.

He opened the door, and I walked in. The room was very large, and the four-poster king bed was definitely a statement piece. The wood he said came from large, leafed lime trees which was somewhat rare in the area now. The walls were painted a dark grey with double crown molding in white. The down filled comforter on the bed was white with a lighter grey pattern which surprised me.

The flooring was a rich oak plank stained to a dark brown colour or maybe that was the natural colour I wasn't sure. There were two large windows that let in a lot of light, although it was dark now, I was sure it would be a very bright room. He had dark grey drapes with a gold leaf pattern in them. The master bath was large and had a double sized shower with rainwater shower heads. The walls in the shower were a dark taupe natural stone. The long vanity was taupe natural stone and matching venetian mirrors. The flooring was a natural stone in a darker taupe colour. The one large window had a window seat, which I thought was unusual but very cute.

"James, I really like this room. Whoever you got to do this; you should get to do the other rooms as well. I love the natural stone in the bathroom, the colour is very rich looking and the window seat is a cute idea. But I would not have guessed you to go with a white bed cover, that surprised me, but it fits in the room, and it doesn't scream masculine, but it is very you I think." James was happy that I liked the room and agreed the other rooms needed updating. He said he would contact the designer and perhaps get her to come in while I was still here, and we could bounce ideas off each other. I said I would like that very much.

"You know you can sleep in here with me if you want, you don't have to stay in the other room. I will leave that to you to decide. We are not teenagers who have to hide the fact that we have slept together but I want you to feel comfortable." It didn't take me long to decide and we went into the other room and gathered my things and moved them into his. Since I had not slept in the bed it did not need to be changed.

"I have a feeling that Roxie is going to want out of her room as well. I don't think she could look at those big red flowers for long." James laughed as he saw that Roxie was doing the exact same thing that I was. He pointed down the hall and we waved and smiled at both her and Duncan.

James had a few things to take care of downstairs in his study and said he would be up in about an hour or so. I said I was going to take a shower, put on my pjs, and get into bed. I put all my things away in James's walk-in closet where he cleared out a spot for me and a couple of drawers. He had a lot of clothes, but he was an important businessman, so it only stood to reason.

Things put away, I pulled out my silk camisole top and matching long pj bottoms and took them into the bathroom. The water felt good after that long plane ride and long day. I dried my hair and sat at the window for a bit. It was a cloudy night so there was no chance of seeing any stars. It looked as though it was even raining so I grabbed my e-reader thinking that I would be able to tackle one of the many books I downloaded before coming.

I think I got through the first few pages before my eyes started to get heavy. I curled up on the right side of the bed because I knew James preferred the left and drifted off. I had no idea how long I was asleep before I could feel James's body close to mine. I stirred a bit and looked over at him.

"I didn't mean to wake you, close your eyes and go to sleep." He kissed me on the lips, and I cuddled into him. When I woke the next morning, James was looking down at me and smiling.

"Why are you smiling, I wasn't snoring was I?" He assured me that I hadn't been snoring. He was watching me sleep.

"I hope that doesn't sound creepy, but you look like an angel when you sleep." I thought it was sweet and said so.

"What time is it; the sun seems to be up. I hope I didn't oversleep." James looked at his watch and said it was 7:00, still early if I wanted to sleep for another hour. I said no and that what I would really like to do is go for a good long power walk. He wanted to join me, and we could walk out over the moors if I was up to it. I was indeed. We dressed in layers and put on our hiking boots. We went out the door only to find that Roxie and Duncan were already up and went for a short walk up the road. They were going in to have breakfast and we would eat when we got back.

The scenery was breathtaking and the walk challenging but I was up for it. It felt good to work the muscles. We walked out and about and around for a good hour and a half and then walked back. The air was fresh and had a bit of a bite to it which I loved. We got back and waved to Roxie and Duncan who were in the sitting room.

We went up to James's room, stripped out of our clothes and got in the shower. He had a wonderful smelling soap that I lathered all over him and he used my body wash and did likewise to me. It was a very sensual moment for both of us, but we refrained from giving into our desire because we knew that people were waiting for us downstairs.

Towel dried, hair dried and into clean clothes. I chose to wear a pair of black wool dress pants and a white cashmere V-neck sweater. I ran the flat iron through my hair, sprayed on some of my favourite French perfume, chose a gold necklace and gold star drop earrings. I had a pair of grey and black flats that I put on. I was ready to go back downstairs.

James chose a pair of black casual pants and a plum shirt. He held open the door and we went downstairs. Duncan was at the sideboard pouring himself and Roxie another cup of coffee when we went into the dining room. There were lots of freshly made scones with homemade jam, something called a friar's omelet which sounded interesting and of course toad in the hole which I heard my parents talk about. I decided to go with the friar's omelet with blackberries. James had the same with multi-grain toast. The coffee tasted very good after that long brisk walk.

"Where did you two go after you left us. Knowing you, Cassandra, you probably did a six-kilometer hike. I hope you were able to keep up James. She's a pretty fast walker." James laughed and said he had no trouble keeping up, saying my legs were shorter. A remark which got him a little jab in the ribs.

"It was a wonderful walk; the breeze was brisk and made me want to walk faster. The views were stunning. Why is it that everything looks so much greener here?" A comment to which both Duncan and James replied at the same time.

"Because its Scotland." We laughed and enjoyed our breakfast. Duncan and Roxie ate an hour ago but sat at the table with us having coffee. I could see a look of complete satisfaction on James's face, and I felt it too.

The touring was to start today. We drove into town and stopped at all three gift stores that James recommended. I did end up getting the Loch Lomond

Bear for Ayleen. It was too cute to pass up. I thought I would pick up Sonya a lace tablecloth similar to what James brought for Lindsay. There were some beautiful sweaters, so I picked out a V-neck sweater for Lindsay in a beige colour with a dark brown fleck.

They also had a red and black Celtic swirl scarf that I thought she would like because it was the colours of her favourite football team. For Ross, I got him a traditional Scottish Skeen with a green stone hilt. I wasn't sure how I was going to get this home though because it was a knife. James said he would take care of it for me.

I picked Ayleen up a peter rabbit tartan tam and scarf set and also a girl's silk tartan dress. I wanted to order it in James's family tartan, the old Sutherland which I could do, but it would take a full three weeks for it to be ready. It would be nice to have it for her to wear at Christmas. James said he would look after bringing that as well.

Roxie and Duncan wandered off looking at a bunch of things, which Roxie thought would be nice for her grandsons and Mitchell and Maria. She had a lot of friends to consider too while she was shopping. But I suggested that maybe for them she could bring back some traditional Scottish shortbread or perhaps a scarf. We wandered around from shop to shop until it was lunchtime.

James suggested a nice little restaurant that he often went to when he was younger, and it looked like it did a good business and James said that the menu was good. We were lucky that there was a table for four as we walked in and nobody else was in line. Water was brought to the table, and we looked through the menus. I knew that I was going to have the fish and chips. James and Duncan had fish and chips as well and Roxie had chicken pie.

The meal was good and there were now a lot of people in the restaurant. It felt like a lot of looks were coming our way but maybe it was because Roxie and I definitely looked like tourists. James must have been well known there as well as Duncan because the chef came out to say hello. James introduced Roxie and I but didn't say who we were to them, which was ok with me. James paid the bill and we left to go back to his home.

"I think I got everything I was looking to get but it will still be nice to check a few things out in Glasgow when we go. James when did you say we were going there?" He said if things went as planned that we would be going the following Monday and Tuesday because there was too much to see in one day.

"There are so many churches that I don't think we would get to them all, so I think that I will select the one cathedral as it has some very beautiful stained-glass windows. Then we shall go to the art gallery and a cultural building. I think after we have done that, we shall see how you both feel and go from there." It all sounded wonderful. We drove back to James's home and by that time it was late in the afternoon. Roxie and I took our packages up to our rooms and came back downstairs. But before we did, Roxie took me aside.

"I have to tell you something. Duncan wants to meet Mitchell, Maria, and the kids. I talked to Mitchell a bit about Duncan before we left. I thought he would be upset because he was so close to Murray, but he seemed to be ok with me seeing someone. He is going to come back with us on the plane and spend some time with me at my place in the city. I think I'm ready to sell the country place now. I've had a couple different people inquire about it and they seem to be very interested in it. They want to make it into a retreat for kids who have been abused and I thought, why not. It is time to move on and start new things and Duncan seems to want to come along." I gave her a huge hug and said that I was happy for her. I was thrilled. She and Duncan really got along well, and they enjoyed so many of the same things. I wished her only to be happy.

She and Duncan were going out doing their own thing tomorrow while James had a picnic planned for the two of us. Downstairs the men were in the sitting room. They were not having whisky as they normally did but rather coffee. It seemed out two coffee a day limit was gone out the window. A fresh pot was sitting on the sideboard and James gave one to both Roxie and me. We sat talking about the day and how much we enjoyed going in to all the little shops.

"I am sure that you guys weren't as keen on it as Roxie and I were, but I want to thank you for doing it. It will be wonderful to go into Glasgow next week. We are both really looking forward to it. Do you think maybe we could go to Edinburgh one day as well?" Even though I had been to both places before I was really looking forward to going back. James said that would be very possible. He could show us the university he attended, and he would give us a list of other places for us to select where we wanted to go. I was happy to visit any museum or art gallery or major cathedral. Roxie was happy to go anywhere, she loved to look around.

"You are both very easy women to please. So perhaps we shall play it by ear and go wherever the wind takes us." I wondered what was on the menu for dinner this evening. Barclay let James know that we were having Scottish beef fillet with wild mushrooms and tarragon mash, green vegetables and roasted red pepper sauce. It sounded wonderful and I was looking forward to it.

"The family will be here on Sunday night for a family meal. You will get the chance to try haggis because that will be on the menu but only if you wish to try it. Barclay is doing it up special because you've never had it. Generally, it is only served on major holidays like Christmas, and we try to have it when we have a big family dinner. It isn't everyone's cup of tea. Everyone is looking forward to meeting both of you. Maybe once they have, they will stop blowing up our phones wanting to know more about each of you." We laughed at that, and I told James he could have sent them some of the pictures from the gala. He said he had but that didn't seem to satisfy some of them.

At 6:30 Barclay let us know that dinner was ready if we were. Red wine was served but Roxie and I only had half a glass. The meal was so delicious I ate every bite. Barclay made a wonderful dessert, but I was too full. Roxie enjoyed it and said it was very light. But I was still too full. We went back into the sitting room to have coffee and enjoy the fire that was lit. It was a nice clear evening and I wanted to go out and view the stars. James and I went out onto the large terrace off the sitting room. It was getting a little cool, so James went in and grabbed a nice warm wool shawl for me. He had on a sports jacket, so he said he was fine.

"The stars are pretty tonight. The constellations are different here than at home. It is nice to see the different ones." James was not looking at the stars but at me. When I turned to look at him, he kissed me. He liked the stars too he said but he preferred to look at me. We stood looking at the stars for a few more minutes and then went in. Duncan and Roxie were sitting beside each other on the sofa, talking. It wasn't that late, but I was starting to get tired. Roxie said that she was getting a little tired too and that perhaps jet lag was starting to hit us. James kissed me and said he would be up later as did Duncan for Roxie. We walked up the stairs arm in arm.

"You know Roxie, I think we are very lucky ladies and have found two of the most amazing and wonderful men in the whole world." We laughed, but she agreed. Roxie went down one hallway, and I went down the other. I got into my same pjs that I wore the night before and went to the window to look out at the stars once again. I wished with all my heart that James was the right man for me. I went to bed and crawled under the covers. I was more tired than I thought and fell fast asleep.

"Duncan you and Roxie seem to be quite happy with each other. You said that you were planning to come back with us because you told Roxie you wanted to meet her son and his family. Sounds like you are serious about her." Duncan said that he was but neither he nor Roxie wanted to rush into anything, at least not right away. He wanted to see how things would go with her son and go from there.

"So, what are your plans for tomorrow, as if I didn't already know. Cassandra is a wonderful lady, James; I don't think I have ever seen you this happy before." James admitted that he was going to ask

Cassandra to marry him at the picnic tomorrow. He showed Duncan the ring. Duncan gave a low whistle.

"That must have set you back a wee bit lad." James said it did, but he would have happily spent ten times as much.

"I know she is going to like it because I asked Janet if she knew what sort of ring she wanted. They actually talked about the subject once, so I know this is what she would want. She isn't materialistic though Duncan. She wears a lot of simple jewelry; she's not a clothes horse and she doesn't own hundreds of shoes. She has more than enough money of her own and doesn't need mine, but I want to do things for her. Her last marriage, from what everyone has told me was really bad. I know there are two sides to every story, but I don't think for a moment that she deserved what he put her through. I don't want to know anything about her past either. I want to leave it there and not bring up old hurtful memories for her." Duncan agreed that the past should remain in the past but if she wanted to tell him maybe he should listen, if that is what she wanted.

"James, I have to say that you know there are going to be some members of the family who are going to strongly suggest that you get a prenup agreement. It is not my business how much money she has but you are worth billions, and I am sure that is going to be pointed out to you. I see that you love her, and I am not getting involved in this matter, but you know I stand behind you all the way. It is your money James, and you can do what you want with it, but just be prepared for some to say something on Sunday. Hopefully, they will not say anything in Cassandra's presence." This had also crossed James's mind. He thought perhaps that Gowan would definitely bring up the subject. While he got along with all of his family, Alisa had always been very vocal about money matters when he married the first time. He listened to her then and was grateful that he had, but he was not going to listen again.

"I am sure that Alisa and Gowan will have something to say about it, and I will let them say their peace, but I am not doing a prenup agreement. I trust Cassandra and I know that this will never be an issue for us. Anyway, I need to get through tomorrow and hope that she says yes. It will be moot if she doesn't." James and Duncan went off to bed.

James got changed in the closet and took to heart what Duncan said, that this was the happiest he had ever seen him. It was true, it was the happiest he had ever been. He could not recall laughing as much and having as much fun, but it was not only that. He truly enjoyed being in her presence, sitting together or watching the stars.

He was, for the first time in his life, content. He adored Ayleen and he and Ross seemed to have hit it off.

He didn't think that Ross would ever call him Dad and that was ok he didn't need to. But to have little Ayleen call him Grandpa made his heart sing. He went into the bedroom quietly as he could see that Cassandra was already asleep and he didn't want to wake her. He knew that she was tired especially after all the walking around they did today. He carefully crawled in beside her. She stirred a bit, and he was able to snuggle up to her without her waking.

"I am a very, very lucky man." James fell asleep and both slept right through until 7:00 the next morning. James was cuddled up with his arm around me, and for a few minutes, I snuggled in closer to him. He laughed in my ear.

"You keep doing that with your cute behind and it will be longer before we get downstairs." I rolled over to look at him. His hair was tussled, but he looked so very handsome. His hair was short and well-kept and had a lot of waves in it. I was sure if he let it grow out any it would be really curly. He had a beautiful, shaped face and a bit of a square jaw, a perfect shaped nose and beautifully set eyes and they were such a beautiful green. He was rugged in a sense and had a bit of stubble this morning, but he was always clean shaven.

"Then I say let's take a little longer going downstairs." James pulled me on top of him and this time I kissed him with all the passion I had in me. It heightened his passion as it did mine. He returned my kiss with one of his own that had hunger and desire in it.

"You do have a way of bringing out the primal in me Cassandra." He was a skilled lover and I hoped that I matched him. We hit the showers and would have lingered but we knew that we had to get downstairs. It would have been wonderful to be alone and not have to rush. We got downstairs just as Roxie and Duncan were heading out the door. We apologized for taking so long.

"Not to worry love, I am sure that you slept in." She winked, and she and Duncan left for the day. I was actually quite hungry. James poured us coffee and since breakfast these days was a casual thing, we took our time over coffee.

"James, do you think Barclay would make me eggs benedict. I have a craving for them." He went into the kitchen and came back out moments later.

"He said he would be happy to make them, and I am having them as well. Let's have one of his famous scones and more coffee until our breakfast is ready." The scones were the flakiest I'd ever had, and they were nice and warm. The coffee was really good this morning. A Columbian blend James said, and it was one of his favourites.

It wasn't long before Barclay brought out our eggs benedict. They looked absolutely wonderful. I think I would have licked the plate if I was alone, they were that good. When breakfast was finished James said he had a couple of things to take care of. It was still a bit too early to send out texts, but I had all of them prepared to send when I knew it was a good time to send them. I set a reminder on my phone to send them out just after lunch.

All my messages composed; I walked out onto the huge terrace. It was really beautiful here. There was a large grill at one end of the terrace and numerous tables and chairs. Obviously, James and his family spent many a day out here when the weather was nice. I could see the lake from the terrace and a gazebo off in the distance. It seemed an odd place to have a gazebo but maybe that was where James's Dad proposed to his Mum. He said that he often went out there to sit and look out over the lake and felt oddly close to them there. James came out and said he called the designer to come over to go over the other bedrooms.

"It's 9:00 and we have three and a half hours until we go on our picnic, so I thought that it would be good to do this while you are here. I hope that is ok with you." It was ok with me, but I said that he had to help too, which he said he would.

"I've been thinking that maybe all that needs doing in each room or at least from what I could see of the rooms Roxie, and I were going to be in, is taking off the wallpaper, a change of paint and maybe some different light fixtures. The bathrooms seemed to be okay for the most part and I don't think you want to start ripping out vanities, maybe just update the fixtures to go with whatever theme the room is going to be." The designer, Julia, arrived within half an hour, and we went first up to the room that I was in supposed to be in. We discussed paint options and of course removing all wallpaper.

"I suggest perhaps going with a deeper richer shade of lavender. I think all the ceilings should be white, but that is how I like them. The flooring is good as is but maybe put an area rug in an accent colour which I will leave to you. What do you think?" I think James was deferring all this to me, but he liked the idea with going with richer colours. Julia had colour swatches with her and I chose the colour that I thought would look good.

She liked the colour and picked out some accent colours. The vanity in the bathroom was granite and it was a nice colour, so all that needed doing in there was maybe switching out the fixtures for something in a brushed pewter and painting the walls white and accenting with deep purples. Julia liked the choices but would maybe come up with another option for the bathroom paint. I said that was ok as I really was not the expert.

Next, we did the room Roxie was in. Since there was already red in the room, it would be a question now of removing the wallpaper and putting up a feature wall of bead board or some type of paneling in a lighter colour or perhaps even grey. We looked through Julia's swatches and chose a gunmetal grey that would look great against the red. We went through all of the rooms and did much the same either enhancing the main colour by making it a warmer, richer version of the colour and going with more updated accent colours. The rest of the bedrooms also had wallpaper which were very busy.

"Mr. Sutherland, I will do up layout boards and pick out the colours with fabric swatches and accent swatches along with different fixtures for the bathrooms and lighting on what we just spoke about and bring them back to you at the beginning of next week for any changes and approval. If that is agreeable to you then I will leave and get started on this right away. I am very happy that you are making these changes." James said that would be fine and we walked back downstairs, and he showed Julia out.

"I'm glad that is done, and I totally agree with you, the rooms were very outdated, and I like that you wanted to go with heritage colours. I think it is just the face lift that the interior of the place needed. What do you say we go on that picnic I promised you? It is now 1:00 and Barclay has put together a hamper with some wine I think, cheese and crackers, little sandwiches, and some fruit so we have a choice of what we want to nibble on. I will go and get it and we can hop in the buggy and go to my favourite spot." James returned with a really large hamper that looked big enough to feed four people.

The buggy was brought around to the front door. James put the hamper in the back, and we drove to his favourite spot. It dawned on me as we were going along that he was going out to the gazebo. It took about twenty minutes to get out there as the buggy was not very fast. It was a very pretty spot, and the gazebo was large and had bench seats, but James took the hamper out onto a small knoll and laid out a very large blanket. He placed the hamper off to one side and we sat down. He took a couple of wine glasses out of the hamper, poured us each a glass and we sat back and looked out over the lake.

"This is probably my most favourite spot on the whole property. My Dad built this gazebo for my Mum, and they would come out here often when I was a baby and a youngster, and we would have picnics. I feel very close to them here and I wanted to share this with you. We don't want to let this wine go to our heads so let's have some of these fancy little sandwiches and cheese." We ate in silence for a bit.

"James tell me more about your parents and you as a little boy. But only if it is not painful." He said that it wasn't. It was a very happy time in his life he said. Even though his Dad worked very hard, he always made a point to spend quality family time.

"My Mum was a beautiful, kind person. She helped in the community all the time. She treated the staff like family and not servants. She never complained about anything, not even when she got sick. We would have long talks about everything. I think she was trying to get in all the things that she wanted to teach me about life in the little time she had. My Dad could never say no to her, and he never did. It wasn't that my Mum was materialistic and wanted all sorts of things, quite the opposite in fact. He was demanding at work but not in a negative way. His employees knew that he expected the very best from them and they gave him their very best. He treated his employees fairly and paid them very well. They were loyal to him, and he was loyal to them. If someone came to work sick, he would tell them to go home with pay because he didn't want everyone else getting sick. That's something that I do as well." He smiled and continued with his story.

"Christmas was a special time for us as a family. Christmas morning was always the three of us. There were always lots of presents under the tree but not always the biggest latest flashy thing that was out. I would get things I wanted of course but I never asked for much. My Mum taught me that it was better to give than to receive. But every year my Dad would buy my Mum a piece of jewelry, nothing big or flashy but it was always diamonds of some sort and of the highest quality. She loved brooches because she said they always dressed up anything. I kept quite a few of the things that she loved the most. She gave other things to her sister for her and to hand down to her children and grandchildren and to Duncan for him to give to his wife. Their marriage was a true love story from beginning to end." I could see that he felt immensely proud of his parents, and he carried the best of both of them with him every day.

"That was a very nice memory you shared with me, and I appreciate it so much. I would have liked them very much I think." James said that they would have loved me. We spent a good four hours over lunch eating the sandwiches and most of the cheese while we shared stories of our childhoods and teenage years laughing at all the silly things we did. There were fruit slices that we ate as we watched a pair of swans on the lake that had their almost full-grown goslings with them. It was a very peaceful moment. James was leaning back on one arm as I sat looking out over the lake.

"It is so tranquil here and I think I actually feel your parent's energy. I may not have told you this, but I took the first level of reiki many, many years ago and there are times when I can feel a different energy nearby. I hope that doesn't make me sound like a bit crazy.

Christelle has her master level and I only have my first level, but she has been, over the years, teaching me a few things. You are not looking at me like I've got two heads, so I guess that is a good thing." James laughed and said he didn't think anything of the kind. He read up on reiki many years ago and his good friend Annie in addition to being a respected medium is also a master in reiki.

"She helped me with a few sports related injuries after university. I totally believe in the practice, so you don't need to hide things from me. I love everything about you." We finished the last of the wine and got up to fold the blanket and put it in the hamper. I finished folding it and set it in the hamper when James said we forgot something. I turned around to see him on one knee with a ring box in his hand opened to the most beautiful ring I have ever seen.

"Oh my God James what are you doing?" He looked at me and laughed softly.

"Cassandra, you are the love of my life, will you please say that you will marry me and make me the happiest man alive." I was shocked and couldn't say anything. I could see he was getting a little nervous.

"James, before I answer you, I feel that I have to tell you about my last marriage." He stood up and stopped me before I could say anymore.

"I don't want to know about your past. It is the past and we are now. Your friends, who love you so much, have said a few things here and there. When I spoke to Christelle she wouldn't tell me everything because she said that was for you to say but she said that you gave that marriage everything you could. So no, I don't want to know what happened. It isn't important to me to know what happened or who he was or what took place in your marriage. I trust you and I love you with my whole being. We are here together, and I want to spend the rest of my life with you if you will have me. So please say yes." So many things were going through my mind. I didn't want to bring the past into what was now. This was good, and I was the happiest I have ever been. I looked at James and tears were streaming down my face.

"Yes, I will marry you. I love you so much" After he put the ring on my finger my mind was swirling, and I said the first thing that I thought of.

"I want you to draw up a prenup agreement. I don't want your family to think I am after your money. I know you know I am not, but I don't want there to be any question or doubts on their parts." He held up the finger he just put the ring on and kissed it. He said that he was not doing any prenup agreement. While I tried to argue the point, he was not going to hear of it. He kissed me again and that was the last that we spoke of it. He swung me around and was so happy. We were both giddy with excitement.

"James, this ring is so beautiful. How did you know to pick out a yellow diamond?" He said that he wasn't sure what to do but spoke to Janet and she had told him about when she was at my place and that we got to talking about rings. He had no idea what size to get because he wanted to make sure it would fit, and Janet suggested that when Hans brought over the jewelry to ask him to include a ring with a stone of five carats and six to see what size fit and to make sure the stone size suited my hand. I started to remember that evening and of course it all made sense now.

"Wow that was clever and I will have to have a chat with Janet. But bringing me on a picnic was a little girl dream of mine that I am sure I never shared with you or Janet. Why did you choose this way to propose?" James confessed that Ayleen told him about what I said to her.

"She was very specific, that little one, nobody else around and there had to be wine and cheese. She cracks me up that little girl is so adorable." I recalled the conversation I had with her but never thought she would say anything about it.

"I guess this was written in the stars wasn't it." James agreed and kissed me as I admired my ring. He told me that it was a six-carat natural fancy yellow diamond in case I wanted to know. That made it even more special because it was something I always wanted. We put the hamper back in the buggy and drove back to his home. I don't think I was ever so happy as I was at that moment. James took the hamper out of the back, and we walked into the house together. Duncan and Roxie were in the sitting room, back from their outing into town. We walked in together and stood at the door.

"I have an announcement to make, I asked Cassandra to marry me, and she said yes." There were shouts of excitement but not the surprise that I thought there would be. I looked at Roxie and she admitted that Duncan told her while they were out what James was going to do.

"Let me see the ring. Wow this is beautiful. I have never seen a yellow diamond before. This is absolutely stunning. I am so very happy for you; you deserve all the happiness this man wants to give to you." Duncan was handing out glasses of champagne to each of us to make a toast.

"I, we, wish you all the happiness in the world. I want to say that James has found the perfect person and I know that his parents would whole heartedly approve. Welcome to the family my dear." Duncan kissed me on the cheek and gave me a big hug and James as well. Roxie gave us hugs and kisses too. I was still in a euphoric state and wasn't even sure that I was walking on the ground. I had to sit down, or I thought I was going to faint. Roxie sat down beside me. I thought all of this was just a dream and I had to pinch myself to see if it was.

"Have you guys thought about a date yet or is that too soon to even be thinking about." I said that we hadn't gotten around to that, and we would probably talk about it later. James looked so happy he was almost glowing. He left the room and came back moments later.

"I let Barclay know that we will be dining out this evening. This is a day for celebration, and we should celebrate it properly. Ladies, I hope you brought something special with you to wear out for a special evening. I will let William know that we are going into Glasgow to dinner. I will make reservations for us at my favourite restaurant in their private dining room. It is now 5:30 and it will take us about forty-five minutes to get there, so if you ladies want to go up and change, as will Duncan and I, we can hopefully be sitting down to eat at 6:30 pm." I was still in a bit of a daze and went upstairs with Roxie. I was trying to remember what I packed that would be suitable to wear because my head was still floating. Roxie knew she was going to wear the grey suit she bought and the white blouse.

When I got into James's bedroom and into the closet, I remembered that I brought the green dress. I put on the dress as James was coming into the bedroom. He helped to zip up the dress and said that he had something that would look good with it. I slipped into my shoes and went into the bathroom to apply some makeup. I sprayed on some of my favourite French perfume and when I came out, James was already dressed in a navy suit with a light blue shirt and tie with greens and blues in it. He opened up a jewelry box and held out a beautiful brooch. It had emeralds, diamonds, and pearls in the shape of a flower blossom, at least that is what it looked like to me. It was beautiful.

"This was my Mum's and I want you to have it. It will look very beautiful on your dress, which I have to say you look stunning in." He pinned the brooch on my dress. I had a look at it in the mirror and he was right, it looked beautiful on the dress.

We went downstairs, and Duncan and Roxie were waiting. Duncan was wearing a black suit with a red silk shirt and black tie. Roxie had on her grey suit and white blouse. They both looked really good together. I showed Roxie the brooch that James gave me. She loved it and said it looked really good on the dress.

But Duncan gave Roxie something as well. He gave her a beautiful black and white diamond bracelet which looked amazing on. We were both very spoiled women. I had no idea that James had a limo in Scotland but there it was on the drive. William opened the door to the limo for us and we got in. James and I sat at the back and Roxie and Duncan at the front. It was as James said about a forty-five-minute drive to the restaurant.

When we arrived and entered the restaurant, the waiter showed us to the private area. It was private in that there were glass walls on one side which let you see into the rest of the restaurant. It would have been too closed in if it had all been walls.

It was not an overly big room, but big enough for a table of four or six with room to walk around. James spoke to the waiter before he left. The waiter returned shortly after with a bucket of ice and champagne. I noticed that it was my favourite champagne. I looked at James and smiled.

"You said that it was ok to have this for special occasions and our engagement is a special occasion." He had me there and while it was very extravagant, it was definitely a special occasion. Duncan was leaning over whispering to James and James turned to look out into the restaurant and turned back with a not so happy look on his face.

"James what's wrong. You look like you just ate something that didn't agree with you." He said that his ex-wife and her husband were in the restaurant, and she noticed us come in.

"You would think that Glasgow would be big enough that we wouldn't have run into them, but she is coming this way, why I don't know but she is." The door opened and in walked a very tall, young, and beautiful woman.

"James, it has been too long since we have seen you. Duncan nice to see you again. James, are you going to introduce us to your guests." Behind his ex-wife was her husband the Duke. That much James told me.

"Cassandra, Roxanne, this is Victoria and her husband Duke Edward Davidson. Victoria this is my fiancée Cassandra and her good friend Roxanne." Victoria's eyes shot up when James said that we were engaged. I was not sure how one addressed a Duke or Duchess who I gathered she was.

"Well James you are a lucky man. Your fiancée is very beautiful, and I can see that you are very happy. I wish you both the best and I can see that this is a night of celebration, so we won't intrude any longer." Before I could say a word, they went back out of the room. I looked at Roxie and she looked at me. It did not go unnoticed by me or Roxie that Victoria saw my ring.

"Well, that was rather different. She does seem to command a room doesn't she." We looked at one another and laughed, not at her of course, that would have been rude, but more at the situation. We decided to order Kobe beef. Duncan stood up to make a toast.

"To James and Cassandra, may they live a long and happy life together." James gave me a kiss and the topic of when the wedding was to happen was brought up again by Roxie. James thought about it and suggested an answer.

"We obviously haven't had time to think about it, or at least Cassandra and I have not discussed it but, I would like it to be as soon as possible. Cassandra, what do you think about having a spring wedding, just a small one of family and friends? We could have it here in Scotland at the estate or if you prefer, we can do it back in Alberta, I am happy to go with whatever you want." I barely had time to wrap my brain around the ring that was sitting on my finger.

"I am still a bit in the afterglow of James putting this ring on my finger. But I agree with James that spring would be a lovely time and as long as I can get the family I want to come and my friends, I am fine with having it here. But we will need some help with this because I don't think even as organized as I am that I can do this from the other side of the ocean." James said that he would contact the best wedding planner in Glasgow and the leg work could be done by them. Our meal came, and we talked about what sort of theme we would have.

"This has all seemed like a dream to me and a fantasy come true. I know that it is not the first wedding for either James or I, and I would really like your opinions on this, but I would like to have an ethereal theme, with lots of tulle and soft lights and lots of flowers. I don't mean people with wings or anything like that, a softer vibe for the décor. Am I being silly." James said that I was not and if that is what I wanted, that is what it would be. I tried to explain further what I meant, and I could see that once I'd done that, both Duncan and Roxie knew what I meant.

"Oh, I get it now, that sounds perfect. You want everything soft and flowy; I get it now. I guess depending on where you have it set, that should be easy enough to do." I knew where James wanted to have it.

"I know James would like to have it at the gazebo, but I am thinking that it is a long way to bathrooms and there are going to be some children. I know that's James's favourite spot and it is where he proposed to me, so perhaps we could take pictures there but have the actual wedding ceremony on the terrace. The gazebo overlooks the lake and I think if we time it at the right time of day, we can get some beautiful photos. We could add lights and tulle around the gazebo to make it romantic." James loved the idea and said we would discuss an actual date later.

We enjoyed the rest of the evening. The drive home was quiet. I think we were all full still from dinner but it might have also been the bottles of champagne that we drank. James would have ordered a third, but I had to ask him not to. I nestled in his arms the whole ride back to his home. It was late by the time we got back, and the house was quiet. Duncan and Roxie said good night and went upstairs. James and I went out onto the terrace.

"I hope that it was ok for me to say that I wanted to get married sooner than later. I know you had no idea I was going to propose, and you look like you have been in a blissful state of shock all day, but I hope you are ok with spring." I said that I was but that perhaps we should look at setting a date so that he could arrange his business calendar and I would have enough time to get a dress.

"Oh my, a dress, James I have no idea what I should wear. I've been married twice before, and I have no idea what would be appropriate. White is obviously out but I don't know what to go with, short, long, in between. I think I need to talk to the ladies and see what I should do. Oh, my goodness, I will have to text them tomorrow and let them know." James laughed and pulled me close to him.

"Don't get all stressed out about this. We will get done what needs to be done. I am not going to say anything to you about the dress other than I would like to see you wear something long. I'm a bit of a traditionalist in case you hadn't noticed. Maybe that goes against convention, but we are not conventional people. Wouldn't you agree?" I had to agree with him on that score. There was nothing conventional about us at all. I admitted that I had a vision of what I wanted.

"I will ask a designer friend of mine to come to the house and you can describe what it is that you want and hopefully he can put it into a sketch. His name is Gerard, and he is quite good. I can ask him to come on Wednesday if you like?" It sounded perfect. I wasn't sure if what I had in my head was even possible.

"But with Thanksgiving coming up and Christmas and New Year's, I wouldn't be able to come back over until after that. I know you go back and forth a lot, so I'd have to work coming on one of your trips back and that might not give the designer enough time. I just need a day or two to think this through and I can come up with a plan." James had no doubt that I would, but he needed to put my mind to rest on a couple of things.

"You can rest easy; I am planning to have Christmas with you in our new home. I hope you caught that because I can say it again, our home. I know Ross, Lindsay and Ayleen are coming out and it would make me so happy to see that little girl on Christmas morning. Besides, there is more room at our new home than in your condo. If that's ok with you of course?" I gave James a hug.

"Of course, it is okay with me." I had been mentally planning how the house would look at Christmas, but I wasn't going to be able to decorate it. I said that I would like to have Christina's help if that was ok.

"I do ok, but I could never decorate a house that big. I would like her expert eye to help tie it all together. I don't know what sort of decorations you like, but I like things to have a homey feel to them. I am not into plastic trees. I have always had a real tree and there is a place in the Grove where we can get one of the best trees for Christmas. We are planning on the trip to Germany and Austria for ornaments, so it will be all new and ours. I'm getting a bit ahead of myself aren't I." James laughed and loved the energy she had.

We went upstairs to bed. It had been a long day and James, at least, was tired and maybe a little inebriated. He wasn't concerned I would refuse his proposal, well perhaps a little but maybe more because he hadn't realized that he was pretty tensed up for most of the day.

Running into his ex was not a joyful experience either but it was bound to happen at some point. He was relieved that she didn't make a big scene like she normally would do. We changed into our pjs and got into bed and James held me close.

We both took some headache pills to ward off the headaches we both knew we were going to have in the morning. We fell asleep not long after our heads hit the pillow.

I woke next morning to the sun peering in through the drapes. It was 6 am and James was still sound asleep. I carefully got out of bed and put on my robe and went downstairs. My head was a little fuzzy but not as bad as I knew James would be. I think after seeing his ex like that he drank a little more champagne than he actually intended to and having that shot of whisky right after she walked out of the dining room probably added to why he was still asleep.

I went down to the kitchen and Barclay said that the coffee was ready and in the small sitting room. I grabbed a muffin and was eating that as I walked to the sitting room. When I went in, I saw that Roxie was up as well and was pouring herself a coffee. She poured me one and we sat down in the chairs by the fireplace where William had a small fire going and it felt warm and cozy.

Chapter 5

"Morning love, I guess we are the early birds today. How do you feel this morning? I know Duncan was still sound asleep when I got up and came down. I gather James is still asleep." I nodded yes and took a sip of coffee and was starting to feel more awake.

"Did you and James stay up late? Did you come to any decisions on a date or anything?" The coffee felt good and perhaps that little ache I had in my head had just a little something to do with the champagne and the excitement.

"A date, no not yet but I was thinking maybe the end of April or beginning of May, but I will have to talk to James about what the weather is like and at least perhaps narrow down the month. He will have to check his calendar too because I know he books things well in advance. James is arranging for a designer friend of his to come by on Wednesday so that I can give him my ideas about a dress. James said he would like me to wear a long one, so I will do that. I know that I want it in a soft beige with lace and tulle. I can sort of see it in front of me. Too bad I can't draw so I could at least help the designer. You will come won't you and I want Janet and Wade, Christelle and my sister Sonya and her daughters Rhonda and Nicole and her boyfriend Austin, Ross,

Lindsay, and Ayleen. I will have to see if Judy is able to make it. She would be coming solo I think because Jack never travels overseas. Oh no, we have that trip to the Turks and Caicos planned for April. Well, that settles it the wedding will have to be in May. At least we will have a nice tan." We chuckled at that. James and Duncan came into the sitting room. James had on his pjs and a t shirt, but Duncan was wearing pants and a sweater.

"What have you two ladies been up to this early in the morning. My head is buzzing a little and I need coffee. I think we had a bit too much champagne." James sat beside me on the sofa and Duncan sat in a chair close to Roxie and gave her a kiss. It was nice to see that Duncan cared about her.

"Roxie and I were just talking about dates, and I remembered that I had the trip planned to the Turks and Caicos with the ladies in April. Would the weather be good here in May? I have no idea, so I am going to have to defer to you on that one." James remembered too when I mentioned the Turks and Caicos. That had completely slipped his mind as well.

"May is a much better month, less chance of rain and we tend to get more sunshine in that month. But you and I can look at the calendar and select a date later. Right now, I am famished, and I can smell food." As if right on cue, William came in to say that breakfast was ready if we wanted to go to the small dining room. Barclay was bringing out hot plates with a variety of foods. There were waffles, eggs, bacon, sausage, and smoked salmon omelet, which James said he loved. I decided to give it a try and it was very tasty, but it seemed odd to have fish for breakfast. We sat and ate over the course of two hours.

Roxie and I went up to shower and change as we planned to go off into town by ourselves to do a little shopping. James and Duncan were going to use the opportunity to go into his factory and get a bit of work done. Back downstairs in jeans and a sweater and Roxie the same, we went out to William who had the suv out to take us where we wanted. He was a very kind man and worked for James for a long time. He said he lived in Scotland all his life and for the most part worked for James.

"If I am not speaking out of turn ma'am, I would like to congratulate you and Mr. James on your engagement. He's a good man and you make him very happy." I said thank you and that he was not speaking out of turn. I was pleased that he was happy for us. When we went shopping the day after we got here, it had been mostly gifts for others but today we were looking for things for us. I really wanted to get a few of the traditional Scottish made wool sweaters. I bought a really nice Finglas throw and got something for Janet, Christelle, Judy and Sonya. We toured around to a few other stores, bought a few more things and then went back to James's house. It was just about 1:00 when we returned.

"I think I'm going to need another suitcase if I buy any more things. I'm going to have to stop buying as I sure I am dangerously close to the duty-free limit." Roxie said that she was too. We took our bags upstairs and put them away and went back down. James and Duncan were still not back. Just as I sat down, James called.

"I am sorry sweetheart, but Duncan and I are going to tied up here until at least 4:00. I know that the family is coming for dinner tonight and we will probably all arrive together. I feel bad leaving you and Roxanne by yourselves. I promise that I will make it up to you when I get home." I told him not to be worried we understood and would amuse ourselves.

"I won't ask you how you plan to make it up to me, but I will be looking forward to it." He laughed and said he had to run into a meeting.

"Roxie, it looks like we are on our own for lunch as James and Duncan won't be here until dinner tonight. Let's wander into the kitchen and see what Barclay has and decide what we would like. I'd like to have something a little lighter myself, maybe a salad with grilled chicken. What about you?" The meals since we arrived were pretty big and the family dinner later that evening was going to be another big meal.

"I agree Cassandra let's just have something light for a change. Maybe tomorrow morning we can go for a walk. Maybe not the power walks you're used to, but I need to get a little exercise to keep my girlish figure." We laughed and went into the kitchen. Barclay was just getting off the phone.

"Afternoon ladies, I've just heard that James and Duncan won't be back until later this evening. I was just about to find the two of you to see what you would like to have for lunch." Roxie and I sat on the stools at the huge island in the kitchen.

"We would actually like to have a garden salad if that is possible. I know that the family dinner is going to be more than one course, so perhaps we could just go easy for lunch." Barclay said that he would fix that up, no problem and if we wanted, he could have it ready shortly.

"I don't know how you ladies feel about partridge, but William got a few early this morning and I could grill those up instead of chicken if you like." I hadn't had partridge since I was a teenager and that sounded delicious to me. Roxie said that she hadn't ever had partridge but if it was half as good as the grouse that was served the other day, she would like it as well.

Lunch plans set, Roxie and I went out onto the terrace. The sun was nice and warm with just a light breeze. We made ourselves a coffee before leaving the kitchen and it was nice to sit out on the comfy chairs and enjoy the afternoon relaxing.

"It's very pretty here isn't it, Roxie? But I don't know if I could live here permanently. It is hard enough living out west and being that far away from Ross and Ayleen. I don't think I could have an entire ocean parting us. It isn't something that James and I have talked about. He did mention once that he was not going to leave Scotland forever, but I guess it's something we will have to discuss. A bit concerning don't you think?" Roxie understood where I was coming from. She didn't think she could live far away from her family either. Now that she decided to stop going south in the winter and selling the country place, she had a lot to think about too.

"Gotta tell you kiddo, Duncan does make me happy, but I don't see him immigrating to Canada just for me. I do think though that James would do it for you. He loves you so much and he wants to make you happy. I think he'd do that if it was necessary." I wasn't sure what to do. James and I never really talked about it. I would be happy to come here for a few months of the year, but I don't think I could split my time to be home six months and here six months. Something that I was going to have to talk to James about tonight. Barclay let us know that our salads were ready if we wanted to go into the dining room. Neither of us wanted anything to drink except for water. Barclay brought in our salads and hoped we would enjoy our meal. We dug in, first tasting the partridge which was perfect. Roxie said she liked it too. We talked a bit about the weather and the places we had seen so far.

"I believe on Monday and Tuesday we are going to Glasgow again but this time to see some of the sites. We can have a look around at some of the shops too, but I don't think there is much more that I want to get. I might look for a scarf or something when we go to Edinburgh on Friday. James wants to show us the university he went to. Wednesday James has a designer friend coming by to help with the design of the wedding dress. I've been thinking about that a little. Do you think it would be inappropriate if I had the same kind of back as I did in the black dress I wore at the gala?" Roxie's eyes opened wide.

"I think that would look lovely but maybe not go quite so low. You don't want to shock the family. I am sure James would love it but given you are concerned about appropriateness, maybe have the dip a little higher up. I liked that dress, the style of it looked really good on you. I don't think I'm going to be picking up much else either, but I like your idea of getting a scarf. I may do that for some of my friends, just something small that packs easy." The salads were wonderful, and we ate every bite.

We took our coffee into the sitting room where William was adding a bit more wood to the fire to keep it going. We sat in the chairs on either side of the fire and enjoyed the crackle and pop. It was almost 5:00 so we went upstairs to change for dinner. James came into the bedroom just as I was buttoning up my blouse. I decided to wear the navy pant suit I bought. James changed into a pair of dress pants and a sports jacket. As we were getting dressed, he said it had been a long day but got a lot accomplished.

"James, I know you are tired, and we have to go downstairs because people are going to be arriving, but something we haven't talked about is where we are going to live. I know we have the house, but I know that you said once that you didn't want to immigrate to Canada. I am a little worried because I feel the same way about immigrating to Scotland. I don't want to live an entire ocean away from Ayleen. I hope that doesn't make me sound like I am being hard to deal with, but I am more than willing to come here for several months of the year, just not half the year. I know this home is important to you and you love Scotland so if you want to take back the ring, I will understand." James was on the bed tying up his shoes and bolted upright when I said that.

"Sweetheart, I don't want the ring back and I have been thinking about this for a little while. One of the reasons I was working so long today was because I wanted to set things up so that I could work strictly in Canada. I had to have a meeting with my family who works in each of the companies here to talk about how things were going to be handled. Fenella's son Angus and Alisa's son Malcolm are going to head up the companies here. They have both been basically in charge of things when I am away, so they are going to take a larger role. Fenella and Alisa sit on the board for the companies here in Scotland and will ensure that things are run smoothly. I will still have to come back once in a while when major decisions have to be made. Malcolm and Angus understand that they don't own the company, they are just running it for me. I will announce all of the changes at dinner." He got me to sit on the edge of the bed beside him so he could finish what he wanted to say.

"I am going to continue to run the office out of Toronto and will be going there on a bi-weekly basis. I have good vice presidents that handle the day-to-day things, but my presence is still required. The companies that I am partnered in are run by my partners. I will have to fly to Germany and France for board meetings but those are typically only held three times year or if something comes up on an urgent basis. I never expected that you would uproot your life because you agreed to marry me. You have a son, daughter in law and granddaughter and I know that even living out west is hard for you because you don't see them as often as you want so I would never ask you to move here. I love you with all my heart and soul Cassandra and I am more than happy to move my life to Canada. It is not a difficult decision for me, my heart is where you are. I had a very long talk with Fenella about this. She is like a second Mum to me, and I value her opinion above anyone else in the family. She agrees with me that moving is the right thing to do. She sees how happy; how joyously happy you make me. You don't need to worry about anything. I asked Gowan to get working on the immigration papers. Hopefully, it won't be a long process and the government will approve me quickly given that I have and am building businesses there. But it may take a few months before it all comes together, or it may take longer. We can deal with it as and when things happen. If I have to return to Scotland after a few months for a bit, well, I can deal with that because I know that you love me, and it is more than worth it." I was stunned by what James said. I had no idea that he was even thinking of doing this let alone actually having things in the works.

"James are you sure you want to do this. I mean really sure. I would hate for this to be an issue for us somewhere down the road." James assured me that this was what he wanted to do. Fenella was going to ensure that the estate was looked after and running smoothly.

"Malcolm and his wife Fiona said that they would move in, that way I wouldn't have to let any of the staff go. Duncan will still have his room and of course mine or rather ours will still be here. We can come any time we want; the estate still belongs to me. Malcolm is going to be here so that it runs smoothly, and the staff stay employed. Everything is falling into place so don't worry that I am being forced to make decisions that I don't want to." I felt much better now that he had laid everything out.

We went downstairs as it was time for me to meet his family. Duncan and Roxie were already down there and obviously been introduced to everyone. Everyone was in the large living room. James first introduced me to Fenella, who from the pictures I saw of his Mum, looked just like her. Then the rest of the introductions were made. Having seen their pictures on James's tablet I was able to match up the name to the face easily. William came into the room to announce that dinner was being served.

We went into the large dining room. The table was beautifully set and there were floral centerpieces down the center of the very long table. James sat at one end of the table with me on his right and Fenella on his left. Duncan sat at the other end with Roxie on his right. Roxie could engage anyone in conversation, so I was not worried at her being so far down the table away from me, plus she had Duncan to look after her. Champagne was poured for those old enough and sparkling water for those who weren't. Fenella stood up to make a toast.

"First, I wish to congratulate James and Cassandra on their engagement. Yes, some of you are not aware that he proposed to Cassandra yesterday. While it may be true that we know little about her, we do know James well and I, as the spokeswoman for this family, and someone who has been like a Mum to James all these years, knows that he is truly happy. James, I can honestly say that I have never seen you this happy ever. Cassandra, I hope that we shall have some time while you are here to get to know one another a little. I can see by the way the two of you look at one another that you are right for each other. So, here is to James and Cassandra, may their lives be filled with much love, much laughter, and much joy." It was a beautiful toast and James thanked Fenella as did I. Everyone cheered to us and wished us the same. James stood up to thank everyone.

"All of you know that I don't like making long speeches. We want to thank all of you for your kind wishes on our engagement. Cassandra and I have only talked briefly about a date to get married, but it will be here in Scotland next spring, most likely in May. The actual day itself we have not yet picked. I thank all of you for coming and I know that Barclay has prepared a wonderful feast for all of us so let's enjoy." At each plate there was a place card letting us know what was being served.

The first course was carrot and orange soup. This was followed by a garden salad and then the main course which was a variety of different choices. There was of course the haggis that James said would definitely be served, Chicken Bonnie Prince Charlie, which had Drambuie in it so, not for the kids, they had Chicken in the Heather, Dundee Lamb Chops, which I knew Roxie would pass on, she was not a fan of lamb, and venison in red wine. Barclay brought out the haggis and put it in front of James.

The tradition was that the master of the house made the first cut in the haggis and had the first taste before it was served to anyone else. For dessert there was a wide selection, Tantallon cakes, sticky toffee pudding, Montrose cakes and iced cherry cake. Everything sounded quite delicious. One course followed another. James and Fenella were in conversation and Angus was sitting beside me. He was Fenella's only child. He was probably around the same age as Ross.

"Cassandra how are you liking your time in Scotland. Where have you been so far?" He seemed like a very nice man, and it was nice talking with him. I told him that I had been here once before but for this visit, we'd gone into Dumbarton the day after we arrived and that we were going to Glasgow to shop and sightsee on Monday and possibly Tuesday, Friday we were going to Edinburgh and the rest of the time would be spent going wherever.

"Other than the visits to Glasgow and Edinburgh nothing is set in stone. When James is available, we will do things together with Duncan and Roxie and when he and Duncan are tied up with business, Roxie and I can manage on our own. It is a very beautiful country; the estate is quite grand." Angus agreed that it was quite a grand estate. Catherine leaned forward and asked if Roxie and I would like to have tea one day and combine it with a day at the spa.

"That sounds wonderful. I am sure that Roxie would love it too. Perhaps we could arrange something for late morning on Thursday. James has his interior designer coming in first thing in the morning to show us the renovations that she is going to do in the other bedrooms. Malcolm perhaps you and Fiona would like to be here as well since you will be living here. I hope that you were not a fan of the wallpaper because that is all going, I'm afraid." Fiona was elated as was Malcolm. They both disliked the wallpaper but since it was not their home, they couldn't say anything.

"Good for you getting James to update the house. It is long overdue and while I know Malcolm would like to be here, he has an out of town meeting that day, but I would love to come if James is ok with that." James overheard the conversation and said that he would love her to come. Fenella asked if it was ok for her to come as well, which James said was fine.

"Catherine dear I know that you asked Cassandra and Roxanne to go for tea and a spa afternoon, perhaps, if it is ok with the three of you, the rest of us could come along and that way we can have a fun ladies' day. But that is of course if it is ok with Cassandra and Roxanne. I don't want you to think we are ganging up on you or anything. It would be a good time for us to get to know each other. We can discuss it more in the living room over coffee if you are agreeable." I thought that would be fine and it would give Roxie an opportunity to see if she wanted to go as well. Since she was getting close to Duncan and this was his family too, I was sure she would agree.

"Well ladies if that all works out then the day will be on me, I insist. Fenella can you please look after that, and I will settle up with you later." Fenella agreed and would speak with James later. The meal was absolutely amazing, and I did try the haggis. It wasn't as bad as I thought it would be although I can't say that I would make a steady diet of it. After everyone finished dessert, we adjourned to the living room. The younger ones went off to the games room to play some games and watch tv.

Coffee and tea were set up on the sideboard. This room was much bigger, but we sat in one area so that we could chat easily. I mentioned to Roxie the invitation on Thursday to go to tea and the spa and she was all for it. There were so many places to sit in this room. James and I sat on a love seat, Roxie and Duncan sat in armchairs near each other and everyone else filled in around us. A fire was lit in the large fireplace, so it made the large room feel a bit cozy. James stood up to talk to the grownups in the room.

"Now that it is just the adults, I wanted to let everyone know that I will be immigrating to Canada with Cassandra. I asked Gowan to start the immigration process for me. Malcolm and Fiona have agreed to live on the estate, which came at a good time for them because their house needs major renovations. Angus and Malcolm are going to be heading up the companies here, but I retain ownership and will be available when needed. Fenella is going to continue in her position on the board of directors for the shipyard, the glass company, and the distillery. I have complete faith in the three of them to work together and keep things running smoothly. Alisa will continue being the head artist at the glass company but will be answering to Angus and Malcolm, but she is also on the board. Now, just so that this doesn't come up later, I am not asking Cassandra for a prenup even though she was insisting on it. Not that I feel I need to tell you this because it is between Cassandra and I, but I am saying right now that the matter is not up for discussion. Now let's continue to enjoy the rest of the evening." I wasn't sure about anyone else, but I was certainly surprised that he brought it up in front of the whole family.

I noticed that there was a change in the conversation in the room with some. It felt a little awkward, but conversations kept going. Fenella and Alisa asked what part of Canada I lived in and when I mentioned where they said they'd never been to Alberta. It was getting late, and the kids were getting restless or maybe a little bored, I wasn't sure. The parents said it was time to leave. Alisa came with Malcolm and Fiona, so she left when they did. Glynnis and Gowan and their kids left shortly after them as did Angus and Catherine and their kids left. There was only Fenella and her husband Callum left along with me, James, Roxie, and Duncan.

"James now that the others have left, and I don't want this to look like I am talking behind their backs but did someone already say something to you about a prenup." James poured himself a whisky and sat beside me with Fenella on the other side of him.

"Gowan raised it when I was arranging for the immigration papers. I told him flat out that I was not hearing anything about it. Cassandra is not after my money. When I proposed to her she said that she wanted one because she didn't want any of you to think she was after my money. But I said no. As I said to Duncan last week and to Gowan the other day, this is my decision. We met by a complete fluke at a coffee shop. While I was already in love with her the moment I saw her, she only wanted to be friends. I don't wish to come across as sounding harsh and I apologize if I am, but I had to be quite firm with Gowan. You know that I have the greatest respect for you Fenella. You have been like a Mum to me, and I have always appreciated your advice, but I hope that you are not going to oppose me on this." Fenella took his hand in hers.

"James, my dear, I would never oppose you on anything. I do not doubt that you love Cassandra, and she loves you and if you tell me that this is not an issue then it is not an issue. I will speak with Alisa and Gowan and reinforce the matter. I think that Alisa comes at this with the best of intentions and so does Gowan, but he sometimes thinks more like a lawyer than he does as a member of the family. So don't the two of you think about it another minute." I think once that was said that everyone gave a sigh of relief. There had been a little tension in the air after James gave his speech in the living room and I for one was glad that it was now more relaxed. As Fenella spoke to James, I went to talk with her husband Callum who had been talking with Duncan and Roxie.

"Callum, James told me that you are a surgeon, what is your specialty?" He was a neurosurgeon and really enjoyed what he did. He'd been at the top hospital in Glasgow for thirty-five years but was going to start scaling back on his surgical work and do some teaching. He mentioned that he had been to Canada, Toronto a few times for conferences.

"Cassandra don't let what was said here tonight upset you. James is a good man and his first wife, well, she liked to live the high life, so you will have to forgive us if we are a little bit protective of James. But I will say this, he looks very happy and when he looks at you, there is no question in my mind he loves you a great deal. Fenella will handle the others. They listen to her when she speaks and that will be the end of it. Let's just enjoy the rest of the evening shall we." It was nice to know that Fenella and Callum at least were in my corner. We sat talking and laughing for at least another two hours.

"Well James, I think Fenella and I will be off. I have rounds tomorrow morning. Congratulations to both of you." We walked them to the door and hugged and kissed them good night. James and I walked hand in hand back into the sitting room. Duncan and Roxie were going to call it a night as well. James and I sat near the fire and talked about the evening.

"I'm sorry if I didn't prepare you for what I was going to say tonight. When Gowan approached me about it, I knew that he and Alisa had been talking. I know it was out of concern, but they should know me better. I hope that I didn't embarrass you. If I did, I am very sorry." I said that he hadn't embarrassed me. It would have been nice to have had a heads up, but it was over and done with. We went upstairs to bed. I was actually exhausted from the tension I was under. James was tired too. I think having to sort all of these things out was hard on him. We got ready for bed and lay in each other's arms.

"Thank you, James, for agreeing to move to Canada. I don't want anyone to think I am forcing you to do this. I love you so much." James kissed my forehead and we both fell asleep. We got up early the next morning, had breakfast and went out for a good long power walk. It was nice to have the time together and getting in a good work out. James suggested that we do the moors a bit, which was challenging but exhilarating. When we got back Duncan and Roxie were on the terrace having coffee. It looked like it was going to be a really beautiful day but there were rain clouds in the distance.

"Good morning you two. Enjoying the sunshine while we have it, I see." James bent down to give Roxie a good morning kiss. Duncan and Roxie had been sitting for about a half hour having coffee.

"You two look like you've had a good work out. Roxie and I are going to walk down to the farm and see if the hens have laid enough eggs for Barclay. He wants to do Scottish eggs for the meal tonight, so I said we would go have a look." They were off after they finished the last of their coffee.

"See you later kids. By the way Cassandra, your phone was ringing. I didn't see who was calling so you may want to check." I went into the sitting room which was where I left my phone. The call was from Ross. He also texted to say it wasn't urgent. Ayleen wanted to talk. Before I put in a call to Ayleen, I sent off a text to Christelle and Janet that James proposed, and I said yes, and I would call them soon. When I was done with that, I looked at the time back in Ottawa and put in a video call to Ayleen.

"Hello Gramma, how is Scotland? I miss you and how is James. I miss him too. Are you bringing me anything back from Scotland?" I smiled because I was sure that was probably her primary reason for calling although I knew she didn't let on to Ross. I could hear Ross chide her a bit for asking that.

"Hello Ayleen, I miss you too. James is right here. Scotland is very nice and maybe you will be able to see it someday soon. Yes, Gramma has some things for you, but you will see them when I come home. We are going to stop by there for a couple of days. But we will stay in a hotel because Roxie and Duncan are coming too. I'm going to let you chat with James for a little bit because he wants to say hi, but I need to speak to Daddy right after ok so don't hang up." James took the phone and was listening to Ayleen ask all kinds of questions. He was so good with her, patient and teased her too. She said she had to go so Ross took the phone.

"I am sure that it probably comes as no surprise to you, but James proposed, and I said yes. We are both very happy and looking at holding the wedding here in Scotland in May of next year. We want all of you to come of course, so hopefully that won't be an issue." He congratulated both of us although he said he knew it was coming because James had talked to him.

"Don't think it will be an issue for me. Lindsay and Ayleen will still be in school, but it's grade two and I don't think it will be a problem if she is gone for a week or two. Not like she has exams to write." We could hear Ayleen cheering in the background and she poked her head back on the phone.

"James did you do it at a picnic like we talked about." James laughed and said that yes, he did. He followed her instructions to the letter. Ross was laughing wanting to know what that was about. James told him.

"I guess she knew something before we did. We are all very happy for you and we look forward to seeing you in another week. Enjoy the rest of your holiday and congratulations again. Ayleen do you want to say goodbye." She did but she also wanted to see my ring. I held it up to the phone for her to see.

"Ooooh pretty. Daddy says I have to hang up now. Bye Gramma, bye Grandpa, see you soon." The call ended. I looked at James and I thought he was about to cry.

"Are you ok." He said he was, but Ayleen called him Grandpa and that meant a lot to him. I kissed him and hugged him.

"I don't think Ross is going to call you Dad, but with Ross you never know. Sometimes he surprises even me, not always a good surprise but not always bad either." Roxie and Duncan came back with a basket full of eggs and took them to the kitchen.

It was getting later in the day than we planned, and William pulled the suv around the front for James. Today we were going into Glasgow. We would first be getting the tour of the companies, they were not that far from each other and then we would have dinner in Glasgow, do a bit of shopping. But first we had to take a shower and change our clothes and have lunch. When we finished, Roxie and I went up to our bedrooms to freshen up and grab our handbags. James and Duncan were waiting for us at the bottom of the stairs.

We got in the suv and the first place we stopped was the shipyard. They were currently working on a really large yacht for a Saudi Prince. I was going to ask where the water was for them but remembered that it had water on all sides. We were able to peek inside at the interior of the yacht but there was still a lot to do. The operation that James had running here was much larger than I thought. He employed a hundred people full-time.

We left there and went to the distillery. This was a smaller complex than the shipyard. The inside of the building was very modern and the equipment, James said, was top of the line. The master distiller who was an old acquaintance of Duncan's came over to greet us.

"Stewart, I'd like to introduce you to my fiancée Cassandra and her friend Roxanne. Ladies this is Stewart, and he is the master distiller here. The whisky he makes is the finest anywhere." Stewart greeted us and congratulated James and me. He took us on a tour of the operation. I thought that being in a distillery would really smell of alcohol, but it wasn't that bad, so that surprised me. James employed about fifty people here full time and doubled around holidays.

The last tour was of the glass company, which was something I was really looking forward to. But we stopped at a local restaurant to have a glass of wine or in Roxie's case a light beer and realized I had eaten there the first time I came to Scotland with Janet and Wade.

It took about fifteen minutes to get to the glass company and this was a larger complex. There were eighty people hired full-time and the place was very busy. He showed us where the glass was rolled out, where the colours were put in and where the glass blowing operation was. The place was hot to say the least but for me that was ok. There was another section where there were lampworkers that made molds for lamp shades, bowls, and table lamps.

I thanked them for all the beautiful shades and bowls they did for our home in Canada. We stopped at the ovens where they were blowing glass. James introduced us to one of the glassmiths. They all knew that James got engaged so the glassmith was in the process of creating a nuptial bowl. It was exquisite. It would be finished by the time we were ready to head back to Canada.

"Oh, my goodness I could stay here and watch them all day. They do such beautiful work. I am so jealous of their talent." Roxie was fascinated by it as well. She saw a fused vase that she thought was really pretty. James said that she could have it.

"We will have it sent to the plane and that way you won't have to carry it around." She thanked James very much for the lovely gift. James went up to the office as he wanted to talk to Angus about the items that he wanted taken care of. We waited for him at the car. He came out about twenty minutes later and we got in. It was still early so James took us to the cathedral he wanted us to see. It was open to the public, so we walked in and walked around without saying a word. The windows were breathtaking, and I stood for the longest time in front of each one.

"I know I'm holding everyone up. These are such beautiful works of art." We continued walking around the cathedral and left to go for dinner. James asked us where we would like to go and named off several places. As soon as he said the names of two famous women tv chefs, both Roxie and I said we had to go there.

"I used to watch those two on tv all the time. I know they are both gone now but what a pair they were. This is going to be an adventure for sure." James mentioned that there were several restaurants with their name attached to them, but we were going to the one that was bigger. We walked in and it was very cozy with the oak and mahogany, and I was surprised to see stained glass windows. We got a seat in a back corner. A waiter came and gave us water and menus.

"Seafood is their main thing here. It is always fresh, but as you know they were famous for the amount of butter they used in their recipes. It is not quite so laden with butter these days, of course depending on what you get. Does anyone want wine with their meal?"

We all said no so and when the waiter came back, we gave our food order. Everyone was having a different type of seafood, me the sea bream because I never tried it before, James the halibut, Roxie the scallops and Duncan the prawns. A fresh pot of coffee was brought to the table. James poured everyone a cup and we talked about the day so far.

"I have to say the glass company is my favourite, I really could watch them work all day long." Roxie said the same but she also liked seeing the yachts. From what James was telling us when we were there, they could handle building two large luxury yachts at once, more if they were smaller. It takes about two years to finish one.

Our meals came, and we dug in. The sea bream had a taste similar to that of sea bass. I only ever had sea bass a couple of times but liked it. We finished our meal, and we were asked if we wanted dessert. I thought Roxie was going to have something, but she declined. By the time we left the restaurant it was after 7:00. James took a different route back to his estate to let us see more of the countryside.

"It is really very pretty here, and I love all the little towns. Nothing seems to be very far away from Glasgow or other major cities. My goodness, look, there is a place called Renfrew. My Dad lived in Renfrew when he was younger, of course in Ontario not Scotland. Maybe the next time I come over James, could we drive up to Arnprior, if that's possible." James said of course and perhaps it could be done when Ross, Lindsay and Ayleen came for the wedding.

"I am sure they would get a kick out of seeing places of similar names as in Ontario. I looked into Arnprior here in Scotland and it seems the Arnprior in Ontario was named after the hamlet in Scotland. Small world isn't it." I found that very interesting how closely connected we really were. I didn't know if my Dad ever knew that, but it was an interesting historical fact. We were in no rush to get back to the estate, so we took a few detours on the way. Duncan knew a fair bit about the local towns, as did James, but he let Duncan do all the talking while he did the driving. We got back to the estate about 8:30 and I took my handbag up to our room.

"I have been dying to get you alone all day. I want to give you something and yes, I know you said you didn't want me buying you all kinds of things, but I think you will like this. I had it made just for you." James gave me a jewelry box which, when I opened it, it took my breath away.

"Now I know you already have a star way up in the sky with your name on it, and knowing how much you love stars, I had a local jeweler who is a friend make this one. Behind each diamond star is a name and you will note that one of the stars is blue and yes, they are diamonds. There is your name, mine, Ross's, Lindsay's, and Ayleen's. She is the blue star as blue stars are young stars. I hope that you like it. There are earrings as well but there is only the one star on them." It was absolutely stunning.

"James, this is so beautiful, and I truly love it. I really love it and I will wear it all the time, well not in the shower but all the rest of the time. Won't Ayleen be happy to know that she is the most expensive one. She may not understand that now, but I am sure when she gets older, she will. This is truly beautiful. You are spoiling me so much and I know that you are going to say that you like doing that but promise me that you will only give gifts on occasions. Please, say that you will agree to that. I know that you don't care what people think and normally I don't either, but I am new to your family, and I don't want them to think I'm materialistic or high maintenance." James agreed if only to keep me happy. We went back downstairs to join Roxie and Duncan in the sitting room. It was starting to rain outside so Duncan got a fire going to warm up the room.

"Roxie, look what James gave me. Isn't this the most beautiful thing. It has our names on the back and look at Ayleen's. If I didn't tell him to stop spoiling me, I think he would do things every day." Roxie thought it was stunning and she looked like she had something she wanted to say.

"Duncan has asked me to marry him, but we are not telling anyone until after we go back home, and he meets the kids. We also didn't want to ruin your engagement by saying anything. But I am excited." I told her not to feel that way, I was very happy for her and for Duncan and I know that James was too.

She showed me the ring Duncan gave her. He hid the ring in the basket of eggs this morning and as they were putting the eggs into a bowl in the kitchen, she saw the ring box. Duncan took it out and asked her to marry him. She said yes, and he put the four-carat white, princess cut diamond with a black baguette diamond on either side on her finger. It was a gorgeous ring, and I could tell that she was in love with it and Duncan.

"This calls for champagne. I will run down to the wine cellar and bring up a bottle of bubbly. Duncan, I am very happy for you. It took you all this time to find the right woman and I think your choice is outstanding." While Duncan and James went down to the cellar for the champagne, I had a chance to talk a little more with Roxie.

"Wow, I could see that you and Duncan were getting closer and closer, but I didn't think this was going to happen. What do you think Mitchell will say? I know you said that he was ok with you seeing someone, but how is he going to feel when you tell him that you are going to marry Duncan. I hope he is happy for you,

Roxie. You deserve to be with someone like Duncan. He will be good to you and you both enjoy a lot of the same things. Have you discussed where you are going to live, or have you gotten around to that yet? I know it is all so overwhelming, but you will figure it out." She was on the verge of tears, but I told her not to cry. If Duncan saw her crying, he would think something was terribly wrong.

"No love nothing is wrong. I am just very happy. Duncan is a good man. Murray was too but they are very different. I think he is going to retire, sell his real estate firm, or have one of the nephews run it. He has to talk to James about all of that given that he is now going to move to Canada." Just at that point Duncan and James returned. They brought in a bucket of ice and put the champagne in to chill. It was already in a chilled room in the cellar, but James wanted it to sit for a few minutes in the ice bucket.

"Duncan and I had a wee chat downstairs in the cellar. He asked me if I was interested in buying his real estate company and I said that I was. I am always looking to branch out and I am going to get Catherine to run it. She's had her realtors license for years but when she had the kids, she opted to stay home with them. He's going to chat with her now that Cailean is in school and give her the opportunity to get back into the business. That will free up Duncan to go wherever Roxanne wants to live or go." Now Roxie was crying. Duncan went to her and held her.

"Roxie, my love please don't cry. This is a good thing. I want to spend the rest of my days with you, and I don't want to have to travel back and forth for business. I want to be with you." She said she wasn't crying because she was sad but because she was so very happy. It sounded like Duncan would also be immigrating to Canada. James popped the champagne and poured each a glass.

"Here is to Duncan and Roxanne, we wish you both a long and happy life together." We hugged and kissed, and I was ever so happy for her. We finished the champagne in the sitting room to talk more about the day we had and if it was still on to go back to Glasgow after breakfast tomorrow. Before we realized it was well past 11:00 and everyone went up to bed. As I was getting my pjs on I asked James what he thought about the news.

"It has been quite a day hasn't it, in fact quite a week. I had no idea Duncan was going to do that, he never said a word to me. But he has been a bachelor for a long time, and I was worried that he would never find someone to grow old with. I am so very happy that he and Roxanne are together. I like her a lot." I agreed with James that it was good news and I too, was very happy for both of them.

"What did you have in mind for tomorrow. I don't think either Roxie or I need to do any more shopping. We could make a half day of it unless there was something specific you wanted to do. There was an art gallery he wanted to take us to or more particularly me to. He'd been in it many times and liked some of the artists and one in particular.

"But I will let you wander around and see if you come up with the two I like." The champagne made me very sleepy, and I curled up to James and fell asleep. It took him a little longer to drift off. I woke to the sound of distant thunder. It was still very early, and James rolled over and had his back to me. I put my hand under his t-shirt and ran my hand along his side. He rolled towards me and as I looked into his amazing eyes my hand just kept wandering. I could see the passion building in his eyes. He put me on my back slowly removed my camisole and then my bottoms. I got him out of his t-shirt and pj bottoms as well. We took the time to let our hands explore each other's bodies, building the fire within each of us.

"James, I need you, I want you so badly, please make love to me." It was all he could do to go slow, to build up our passion even higher but he couldn't hold out any longer. Our cries of ecstasy were drowned out by the loud cracks of lightning and thunder. We lay in each other's arms, passion fulfilled. We got into the shower, and it began all over again. I could not contain the fire he had ignited in me. James backed me against the shower wall and again and again I cried out in ecstasy which only inflamed his passion further. Our final cry of fulfillment left us both shaky and clinging to each other. He kissed me tenderly and then smiled.

"You are amazing and without doubt my dear, you have to admit that was better than sleeping in sheets off the clothesline in spring." He laughed and kissed me. I jabbed him in the ribs.

"James, you had to know I was so worried that I would not be able to satisfy you, but I guess I was worried over nothing." He assured me that I more than satisfied him and he kissed me as he washed me with my body wash, and I did the same for him with his soap that I liked the smell of so much. We took longer in the shower than we realized and quickly dried off and got dressed. It was still early but Duncan and Roxie were already in the dining room.

"Morning you two, we just got up ourselves. Looks like it is going to be a rainy day. Won't be doing too much walking around outside today. What have we decided we are going to do." Duncan was pouring us coffee. We were both pretty hungry but tried not to be obvious about it. I could see from the look in Roxie's eye and the smirk on her face that we weren't hiding anything. James gratefully broke the awkward silence.

"The only place that I want to go to is the art gallery to show Cassandra a couple of pieces of art, but that shouldn't take us long there. I suggest that we visit the two big tourist places that show a lot of the history of Scotland, and they have different exhibitions in and out all the time. You can also buy prints there too and they have a café where we can have a bite to eat if we are hungry. I know that you said you didn't want to buy any more things, but I think you have to visit the cashmere place further north. If you want to get scarves or socks or hats that won't take up room, that would be the place to get them. The raw product comes from Mongolia, the rest of it is done in Scotland." At the sound of cashmere, I didn't think Roxie was going to buy but I told her if there was something she saw that she loved, that I would get it for her. We decided to go to the three places and then come back to the estate.

The historical places were fascinating, and I learned a lot about how things were in the early days in Scotland. It was quite a large place, and the glass enclosed building was nice as the rain was coming down quite hard now. We grabbed some coffee and looked around. It took about an hour and half to do the complete tour. We left there to go to the gallery that James wanted to go to. He wasn't going to tell me which ones he liked so it took some time to look through the different artists before I settled on ones that I liked. I told James which ones I liked, and he said they were the same ones he was thinking of but said he was going to think about the paintings and let them know.

We finished off by going to the cashmere place. I knew that Roxie wouldn't buy anything on her own, so I told her to look for hats for the boys and scarves for Mitchell and Maria. She picked out a cashmere hat that came in two different colours but the same look, so the boys wouldn't fight. She picked out a cashmere muted check scarf for Mitchell and a cashmere tipped scarf for Maria. I picked out cashmere scarves and sweaters for all of my friends, Janet, Sonya, Rhonda, Nicole, and Austin as well as for Ross, Lindsay, and Ayleen but I also got her the tweed child's cap because she loved hats. I took my things and Roxie's to the cashier. I took out my card, but James gave the cashier his instead.

"Either you let me use my card or you use the one I gave you in Toronto. The limit on that will remain as it was before you used it in Toronto. If there is more you want to get, shop. If I can't spoil you with diamonds and other expensive things, then let me do this. I want to, and Duncan is going to do the same for Roxanne, who will probably protest just like you, but Duncan is just as stubborn as I am." He smiled that smile, and I knew that I was not going to win. I could see Roxie having the same discussion with Duncan and even putting the things down, but he picked them back up. He put his arms around her and while we tried not to listen, they were not that far away.

"Roxie my love, we are going to be married and you know that I am very well off. What I have is yours when you need it. Please, let me buy the items you have. You have not let me buy you a thing other than that ring so I'm going to insist, but in a nice way of course." James was right, Duncan could be very stubborn but in a loving and supportive way. Roxie finally gave in, and they looked around for a few more things.

"I am about shopped out. I have no idea how I am going to get all of this into my two suitcases. I will probably have to buy another one. I know you are in the same boat Roxie so maybe we will make that our only purchase in Edinburg when we go there on Friday. James, I hope you know where we can pick up some luggage." We left with our many shopping bags and put them in the car and drove back home. The rain finally stopped, and the sun was popping out. I asked James if he was up for a good hike. We took our things upstairs and we changed into some sweatpants, sweater with a t-shirt underneath. Because it could possibly cool off, we took our lined jackets with us.

We went down the road towards the farm and off down the road. We must have walked a good five kms and decided to head back because more rain clouds were coming in. We were steps away from the house when the sky opened up. We got drenched before we even got to the door. We took off our wet shoes, tried to wring out as much water in the entrance door outside before entering. We dashed off upstairs to strip out of our wet clothes and take a hot shower. I could not believe how hard that rain came down and how cold it was. I was shivering in James's arms as the hot water poured over the both of us. We finally warmed up and got out of the shower and toweled off. I gathered up our wet clothes and took them downstairs to the laundry. We went into the sitting room where Duncan and Roxie were both enjoying a Gaelic coffee although I didn't know at the time that Roxie's was a virgin Gaelic coffee.

"You two look like you could use one of these. Sit down, Roxie give Cassandra one of those warm blankets and you too James. You might be used to the weather, but you don't want to end up with the chills, so wrap yourselves up and I'll get you that coffee." It took him only moments to come back with the hot confection.

"Wow, now that's what I call coffee. I could easily get drunk on these, so I will only have one more." James laughed because he knew how strong they were. He motioned to Duncan to use a little less whisky. The chill had finally gone out of my body, and I was starting to feel quite warm inside.

"I think perhaps that I will ask Barclay to fix up some soup for the two of us and then I think I will get this one off to bed." James went and got the chicken soup which we had sitting by the fire.

While James was in the kitchen, he asked Barclay to set up the dining room for Duncan and Roxanne with the best china, some beautiful flower arrangement on the table and sparkling water in an ice bucket. He knew that Roxanne didn't drink a lot and didn't want to force champagne on her. He wanted the room to be romantic for them so that they could celebrate their engagement together just the two of them.

We finished our soup and James could tell I was getting sleepy. He bid both Roxanne and Duncan a good night and helped me up the stairs. The Gaelic coffee hit me because I drank it down too fast, and I was probably going to have a bit of a headache in the morning. James got me into my pjs and then got me to drink some water and take a couple of pills for the headache I knew I'd have in the morning before putting me to bed.

He lit the fire in the fireplace to make the room comfortable. He got into his pjs as well and had to admit that the cold rain got to him a bit. Once the fire was at a good heat, he put the grate in front and climbed into bed beside me. I snuggled up to him and he put his arm around me. He kissed me on the lips, but I was already asleep.

James grabbed his tablet and started to look at a few emails. He took care of the ones that were easily dealt with and sent Mina an email letting her know that he had proposed to Cassandra, and she said yes. He also let her know that he would be immigrating to Canada and that Gowan was working on the papers. But he wanted her to get in touch with him and make sure that everything was done as quickly as possible. He told her that he thought Gowan might try to delay it.

Of the emails that he needed to deal with as soon as possible, he asked her to set up meetings for Wednesday afternoon and Thursday. Hopefully, he could get them taken care of in those two days but if not, he could stay in Toronto the rest of the week. One of the emails she forwarded him was to let him know that the house was finished, and that Christina had finalized the last of the decorating. It was ready for him to move into weeks ahead of schedule. Mina already interviewed people for the house staff he needed. She found a family, Mr., and Mrs. John Davidson, who were in their forties. They came highly recommended and had previously worked for people that James knew in Toronto. He read their resume that she forwarded.

They were looking to move out west to be closer to other family. They have two daughters and a son, Marlene, Julie, and Max, respectively. The kids were in their mid-teens and could help the mother do the housekeeping on weekends and the son could help the father with the outside work. During the week, she found three local people who could help and would report to Mrs. Davidson. She found a chef Jonathan Parsons in

Edmonton who came highly recommended and was willing to look for a place near the house. James said that he would see about getting a temporary spot for the chef in the condo building where Cassandra lived. Even though it was supposed to be strictly for seniors, he was sure that they would not object to a temporary non-senior on the premises.

James sent an email to Mina letting her know that he would be in Edmonton Tuesday morning and would fly to Toronto late Wednesday morning. She responded saying that she would arrange to have George, the contractor, and Christina, the interior designer at the house late afternoon on Tuesday, giving him a chance to perhaps get some sleep. He said that would work fine and if he was able to get some sleep on the plane on the trip back, they could arrange to meet earlier. She attached a few reports that he needed to look over and could deal with once he was back in the office.

The last email had to do with the swap of his senior vice president of human resources in the Germany office with the vice president in the Toronto office. Both men were agreeable to the swap. Both were Canadians and knew this was part of how James ran his organization. Often, he would move some of his major executives around to give them experience in other countries. It took James a bit of persuasion to get them both to agree to it though. Richard who was sixty-three wanted his nephew who was forty-two and the director of marketing in the Germany office to move with him.

Richard's wife died ten years earlier and he didn't want to leave Mark on his own even though he was a grown man. He had been leading a bit of a reckless life over the last few years because of the loss of his mother, who was Richard's sister. Brock Moore and his family were more than happy to have the opportunity to live in Germany. He had a young family and the chance to live in a different county was something they were all looking forward to. But the move had to be made before the start of the new school year.

Richard and Brock were able to have two months together in Germany to go over each other's work. James had to do a bit of juggling for the director of marketing in Toronto, but he managed to work out a deal with Perry Lewis who also took his family over. He and his wife Mary had a son in university who was quite excited to be finishing his degree abroad. He had emails from all of them saying that the transition was going very smoothly.

James had an ulterior motive for making this move. He's known Richard ever since he took over his Dad's business and he was a really good man. He wasn't sure how he was going to arrange it, but he was hoping to introduce him to Cassandra's sister Sonya. He knew that Cassandra was having her sister and her family for

Thanksgiving and thought perhaps he might be able to arrange a visit to Toronto where they could meet. He would see if Cassandra's niece could bring her mother to Toronto, and they could stay at the penthouse. He would have to talk to her in the morning about it. He shut off his tablet, curled up to Cassandra and fell asleep. I woke up the next morning with a slight headache well more than a slight headache. Knowing of course that it had to have been the coffee I drank the night before. I flopped back onto the pillow and James was awake and he was laughing. I had my hands over my eyes that felt like they were on fire.

"Would you like another Gaelic coffee, a bit of the hair of the dog." I groaned and got up to go to the bathroom. I came back into the bedroom and James got out of bed and went off to the bathroom. I took off my pjs and went into the shower.

James went to get his tablet to check to see if Mina had responded back to his email but there was nothing yet. I finished in the shower and James got in and took a quick shower. I put on a pair of black wool pants and a red V-neck sweater and the star necklace and earrings that I got from James, brushed my teeth, and applied a bit of makeup. James was drying himself off as I was putting a flat iron through my hair. I loved to look at him, he was in very good shape.

"You keep staring at me and we will be heading right back to bed. You know the designer is coming this morning to talk about your wedding dress. I think we should finish getting dressed and head downstairs." I turned around to finish my hair but before he left the bathroom, he playfully slapped my bottom and kissed my neck. James put on a pair of jeans and a navy sweater. After finishing in the bathroom, we both went downstairs together. Duncan and Roxie were not down yet. We went into the dining room and poured ourselves some coffee. I decided to eat very light as my stomach was protesting a bit this morning. Duncan and Roxie came in just as we were eating.

"Morning love how are you both this morning. No ill effects from that cold rain I hope." There were none I said and any ill effects that I was feeling were from the coffee the night before. Next time I wouldn't drink it down quite so quickly. Duncan wanted to know what everyone's plans were for the day. He had some business to attend to in Glasgow and was hoping that Roxie could do something with me.

"Roxie, the designer is coming by today for the dress and I would love to have your input. Maybe you can get him to design something for you for your wedding, which you have not said when it would be." Nothing was being decided until after they went back to see her family. But she said we had not even set a date for ours, which was true. James took out his tablet to look at his calendar. Since we already said it would be the month of May, there was just the actual day to pick.

"Cassandra what would you say about May 1st. We can have the wedding here like we planned and then we can go on our honeymoon, how does that sound? We can see that everyone gets flown back home on my plane, because I would not want to disappoint Ayleen and then we can leave from Ottawa." That sounded wonderful to me, and I was sure that Ayleen would love being on the plane.

"But we need to discuss where we are going, don't we?" James said that he was taking care of that, and it would be a surprise for me. I asked how I was going to find out what to pack. It was months away from that happening and James said they could talk about it more when the date got closer. The designer was coming by at 10:00. Duncan wanted to get going so he could be back by dinner. He gave Roxie a hug and kiss and said he would see her later. James said he had some work to take care of and went off to his study. That left Roxie and I to our own devices.

"I know you said you haven't talked about a date yet with Duncan, but you can still see what the designer might come up with for you. I am fairly certain that James is going to ask Duncan to be his best man if he has not already done so and I presume he will ask Ross to be a groomsman. I don't really want to have a large wedding party; I want to keep it small and simple. I'll ask James about that in a little bit. Not sure if he wants Angus and Malcolm to be in the wedding party. He has lots of friends, but I guess because of his work he is always on the go. He mentioned once or twice about a best friend, the partner he has in Germany. We've talked so much but I don't know who he is. Wow, what an oversight on my part." Roxie had to go upstairs to the bathroom, so I took the opportunity to go into James's study to talk to him. He was just ending a phone call.

"James, I have never asked you who your best friend is or who you plan to have standing for you at our wedding. Roxie and I were just talking about it, or rather I was to her, and I realized I never asked you what his name was." I went over to sit on the edge of his desk.

"I never thought to bring it up myself. It's Quinn Drummond, and he is my partner in the company in Germany. While I majored in business and finance and minored in computer science, he was majoring in chemistry and minoring in botany sciences. When we graduated, he came up with the idea for a cosmetics company and since he was making a move to Germany that is where we set it up. He runs the company, and I am his partner. Quinn has fifty-one percent of the company and I have forty-nine percent. We've been through some interesting times and gotten each other into trouble and out of it but that was during our university days. He is happily married with four wonderful boys and a beautiful German wife, Charlotte. He was shocked when I told him that I was going to ask you to marry me but only because he thought I turned into a confirmed bachelor. He was best man at my first wedding, but he detested Victoria. He tried to tell me that all she cared about was money but of course I was young and as the saying goes, love is blind. I just started to make a lot of money, but it didn't take me long to realize what a horrible mistake I made, and we know how that ended. But I did ask him to be my best man and Duncan is going to be in the wedding party as well. I was planning on asking Ross as well, but I don't know how big you want this to be. We should probably get that settled first." I said I would like to keep it small if possible. I hadn't said anything to Roxie yet because I wasn't sure what he was going to do.

"I want to ask Christelle if she will be the matron of honour, but I have a feeling that she will say she would prefer to be a guest only. I will have to talk to her first, but if she declines, then I will ask Janet. I know she won't be insulted to be second choice; she knows Christelle is my best friend. Then I can ask Roxie, whom I am sure will agree and if you have Ross I will ask Lindsay. Ayleen will want to be flower girl and perhaps you could ask Cailean to be ring boy. That would keep it small enough. What do you think?" He was in total agreement. He would send Ross a text letting him know he wanted to talk to him, and I would do the same with Lindsay.

"I was thinking that perhaps we could ask the designer to do up the wedding party dresses as well. If they want to wear different styles but the same colour that is ok with me. Ross has the navy suit I bought him, which he can wear unless you have a tradition of the men wearing kilts. Hmm not sure Ross would agree to that though. You might have to twist his arm." James said they could work that out and it was tradition to wear a kilt and it was something that was important to him, and he would buy the men all new suits to change into after the ceremony was over. I left him to go back into the sitting room. Roxie came downstairs as I walked in.

"I talked to James and his best friend is Quinn Drummond who he has asked to be his best man, but he already asked Duncan to be a groomsman and he's going to ask Ross as well. I know that Christelle will be happy I asked her to be my matron of honour, but I know she will decline. I will ask Janet. I would love for you to be a bridesmaid and you can walk with Duncan and I'll ask Lindsay as well and she will be with Ross. James is going to ask Cailean to be ring boy and I'm going to have Ayleen as flower girl. This keeps it small like I want. When the designer comes, after he has sketched out what I have in my head for my dress, I can ask him to do up some designs for the maid of honour and bridesmaids. I don't care if they are different styles, but I do want them to be all the same colour. I know Ayleen is going to want purple and sparkly, so we will have to figure out a colour that will compliment that and all of you can agree to. Does that sound ok with you?" Roxie said she would be happy to be in the wedding party and she didn't care too much what colour we went with.

The wedding was going to be in May, but I didn't want the colours to be pastel. I was never fond of pastel colours but only because they washed me out. I thought perhaps going with either a green or blue shade might work well with everyone's complexion and age but just where in those spectrums we would have to see. Roxie and I talked over colours, and she was always a fan of blue over green. We would have to see what the designer thought. James told me he was very well known in Europe and had a showing every year at some of the biggest fashion shows. William came into the sitting room to say that the designer arrived. He showed him into the sitting room.

"Hello Gerard, I'm Cassandra and this is my friend Roxie." We sat down in the sitting room where it was small and cozy.

"James is in his study working and said he would come out after we were done. I'm not sure how much he told you, but the wedding party is going to be small, three on each side and I am hoping that in addition to doing up my dress that I can ask you to do the others plus a flower girl. James said he wants me to wear a long dress which I am going to do. I want it to be a soft shade of beige that is far enough away from white or ivory. I have a vision in my head which I am going to try to describe to you and I am apologizing straight up if it is confusing." Gerard said that he ran into this all the time dealing with a vision in a bride's mind and he was actually quite good at putting something down that was quite close.

"First give me some details of what your ideas are and then we can discuss what fabrics would work. I would be happy to do the wedding party as well. If you have ideas of colours or styles or not, I can work with that too. But first give me some ideas of what you want." I showed him the picture of the black dress I wore to the gala. He said that I looked stunning in it, and he knew that designer. I said that I would like to have something of a similar back but perhaps not quite so low but not a keyhole back. I wanted the lace bodice to be tight fitting but not all the way down. I liked the sheath but perhaps maybe just a little more volume in the skirt but not as much as a modified A-line. I wanted illusion long sleeves with crystals on the sleeves and bodice but not the rest of the dress. I was thinking perhaps a lace overlay with tulle under or chiffon." Gerard was busy doing sketches. He was very fast. He did up three different looks with three different backs.

"You are better at describing what you want than you think. I love the idea of the illusion sleeves and a lace bodice and just having crystals there. I was thinking that this all-over lace back that zips up, but you won't see the zipper. It will make it very easy to get in and out of. I think this style with a bit more volume than a sheath would work best, and I would go with the tulle and the lace overlay. Maybe we can make something for you in a chiffon for your honeymoon dress to go away in. Do you know where you are going?" I said that no I didn't James was keeping it a secret.

"I will speak to him and come up with something that will obviously be a surprise to you, but it will fit you perfectly because I will have your measurements from your wedding gown. We will go more on the cream to a very light beige for the colour. Perhaps even go a shade or two lighter for the tulle to give a contrast. It will be stunning. Of the three here, which do you like best." I had to agree with him on the one he said would look best. He had some swatches with him, and we picked out the linen colour for the dress and an alabaster for the tulle.

"This linen colour will be beautiful and I have it in lace and the colour for the tulle as well. This is going to look stunning on you. So now we have you sort of squared away, what would you like for the wedding party." I said that Roxie was going to be a bridesmaid, but I had to nail down the matron of honour and my daughter in law was going to be a bridesmaid as well and my granddaughter the flower girl.

"She loves purple and sparkles, so we will have to decide what will go well with that. Hers doesn't have to be a dark purple, it can be more between an amethyst and violet. For the others, I will defer to your expertise on whether to go with a green colour or a blue colour, but Roxie will be the oldest in the party so perhaps you could sketch something that you think would look good on her and maybe while you are doing that, I will give Christelle a call and then Janet to get this sorted out." So as Gerard was sketching and showing things to Roxie I put in a call to Christelle.

"Christelle, I know it's early, but I have a designer here to sketch out my wedding dress and I would like to ask you to be my matron of honour. The wedding is going to be May 1st and I know you will come of course." She asked me not to be disappointed, but she would prefer to be a guest.

"Congratulations first of all. I am so happy for you and James. Being a matron of honour is a special honour, but it also is a busy one. I hope you are not disappointed that I would prefer to be a guest and enjoy your wedding." I told her I was not disappointed as I had a feeling that she would prefer to be a guest, but she was my best friend, and I could not ask anyone but her first. I told her that I would call her again in a couple of days. I put in a call to Janet next and asked her.

"Congratulations to you and James. I am so excited for you both. I'm honoured that you are asking me to be matron of honour, but don't you want to ask Christelle. She's your best friend and I completely understand you wanting to have her." I explained that I asked Christelle, but she didn't feel like she would be up to it.

"I hope you are not insulted that I am asking you second, but I knew Christelle was going to decline but I had to ask her first. I hope you understand." Janet understood perfectly and said she would love to be my matron of honour. I said that I was with the designer now going over the sketch for my dress, which we had settled on and now going through the sketches for the wedding party.

"I'm going to show him what you wore at the gala, so he has a sense of what you look like and what would look good on you. I'll do the same for Lindsay as she is the other one I'm asking and of course Ayleen as flower girl. I will text you what he sketches and hopefully before he leaves today we can settle on something. If the dresses are different styles that doesn't bother me, but everyone is going to be the same colour. I hope that is ok with you." She said of course it was and would be watching her phone for the sketches. Next, I put in a quick call to Lindsay, who was getting ready to leave for school. She said that James already called Ross and he agreed and that she would love to be in the wedding party. Ayleen was close by and wanted to talk.

"Gramma am I going to be in the wedding party too?" I told her of course she was going to be the flower girl. She wanted to know what a flower girl did, and I said that Mommy would explain it to her.

"Can I wear purple and sparkles on my dress." I laughed and said that I already decided on that, and she was so very happy and laughing about that. Lindsay came back on, and I said I would send sketches to her on her phone and of Ayleen's dress too. Again, I said that all the dresses did not have to be the same, but I wanted them all the same colour. I did however want everyone to have the same sleeve length, so they were all going to have to either agree on three quarter or short sleeve. I didn't want a mish mash of sleeve lengths. I sat back down with Roxie and the designer. I showed him a picture of Janet in her dress and of Lindsay and Ayleen in their dresses when we had gone to dinner.

"Oh, isn't this little one adorable. My goodness I could use her in some catalogue work she is so photogenic and look how she knows how to look for the camera. I'm going to have to meet this little one when they come for the wedding. I've done up a spring collection of young girls' apparel for a major magazine and I would love to put her in a couple of the pieces. But we can discuss that later. Ok now that I have seen the other ladies, this is what I would recommend. I suggest we go with a modified A-line for them. Their dresses will have a bit fuller skirt than yours but that is what you want when you look at the photos. Normally it would be the reverse but, in this case, we are doing it the opposite way. Everyone seems to like and look good in darker colours so perhaps we could go with blue, perhaps in a sapphire or maybe a shade lighter. I think going with a three-quarter sleeve would be best as well." Gerard did up several sketches. We looked them over and I asked Roxie which one she liked best.

"They are all very pretty but if I had to single one out, I have to say that I like this one with the belt in a darker blue shade and a little bling. I think it is very pretty and I am sure it will suit me well." Gerard said that it would suit her very well. I took a picture of the four designs and sent them to Janet and Lindsay without telling them which one Roxie chose. Then Gerard looked at what he was going to do for Ayleen.

"I suggest something knee length for her maybe a little longer. You don't want her tripping in a long dress. I am looking at what she wore here, and I think perhaps doing something in a violet organza as well with a tulle underskirt. Not too much tulle, you don't want her to look like she's wearing a tutu but enough for her to have some fun. He sketched something with three quarter sleeves for her with a similar darker violet belt so that it would match the other ladies. Her belt would have lots of sparkles on it as well. I took a picture of that one and sent it off to Lindsay. Janet texted back that she liked the one in blue with the darker belt and three-quarter sleeves. I was going to wait until Lindsay texted back before I said anything just in case she chose something else. Moments later I got a text from Lindsay, and she chose the same dress in the blue and Ayleen, she said, just loved the sparkly belt for hers and she loved the colour.

"Awesome so we are all set on the design and colour. You ladies are all so very easy to please. I wish I had more like you. My job would be ever so much less stressful. I love that little girl and I am serious about wanting to have her wear something for my magazine shoot. Can you please mention it to her parents and see if they would be open to it? I am willing to pay her well for doing it and if they are open to letting her do other shots as well. My spring/summer collection is already done, and I have the perfect dress in mind for her, but I am nearing the end of my fall/winter designs and if you can convince her parents, I will make up something just for her to wear in the next layout. Anyway, I will let you ask them, and you can let me know. Ok ladies, so we are finished here I think, now I will go and talk to James about the honeymoon. I've done your measurements, and I will have to get the measurements of the other ladies. I will have to see if I can snag a flight with James at some point and visit each of them and get this done. I don't trust measurements taken by someone else. I would rather do that myself that way there are no foul ups. It was lovely to meet you both and Cassandra you are going to look stunning in this dress." I asked Gerard if he would do one more design.

.

"Roxie and Duncan are getting married, but they haven't set a date. But since you are here I thought perhaps you could design her a wedding dress." He said he was happy to do that. He and Roxie worked together to come up with something that would be perfect for her. She was going to look very pretty. Now that he was done with both of us, he went off to James's study to have a chat with him.

"I am so happy that everyone liked the same dress. Everyone is going to look so pretty in that color.

We will have to find matching colour shoes. I should ask Gerard to give me some colour swatches for your dresses, so you can look for the shoes. I don't care whether they are different. I want you to get something comfortable and because I am asking all of you, I am paying for the shoes and the dresses of course, so you will have to let me know if you can find them. If not, we will have to get them made to order." Gerard came out of James's office with James. I asked him for colour swatches, so we could get shoes, but he said he would take care of that if everyone was ok with it. I looked at Roxie who said fine as long as the heel was not too high. Janet could wear heels higher, but Lindsay never wore heels much so hers would have to be a wedge. He said that was not a problem he would do sketches and send them to me for the ladies to choose from. He wanted the shoes to be silk, so they had to be custom made. He could get our shoes sizes while he was here and would have to ask for the others to get them done at a shoe store, so they would be accurate.

"Please make sure they go to a good quality shoe store, so the measurement is properly done." I assured him I would take care of it and text him with the sizes. Because we were easy to work with Gerard was done everything by 1:00. Duncan was coming in as Gerard was going out. James asked Barclay to do up soup and sandwiches and hoped that was ok with everyone. The meal for dinner was going to be Scottish pies and it was going to be served at 6:00.

James was done with his business, so we decided to go for a walk after lunch. We asked Duncan and Roxie if they wanted to come so the four of us set out on a nice long walk down past the farm and then up the road in the opposite direction. We only walked two kms and then turned around and walked back. It was a leisurely stroll, not the power walks that James and I had been doing almost every day. Roxie tried to get James to say where we were going on our honeymoon, but he wasn't saying anything. He hadn't even told Duncan just in case she tried to get it out of him.

+

“I tried love. Guess you are just going to have to wait.” I said it was ok. This was a surprise I was ok with. James and I walked hand in hand as did Duncan and Roxie. By the time we got back it was just after 4:00. Roxie, Duncan, and James went into the sitting room. I said I wanted to go to the kitchen to talk to Barclay.

“Barclay, can I ask you to give me the recipes of some of James’s favourite meals. I am sure that most ingredients are the same but if there is anything that you put in that is particular to Scotland, perhaps I can take some back with me. As I am sure you know, James built a house near where I live, and he has his personal assistant looking for a chef.” Barclay was pleased that I asked for the recipes, and he would be sure to have them all done up along with any specific ingredient that could not be obtained in Canada ready for when we were to leave. I thanked him for being so kind to do this.

“It is my pleasure. James has told me that one of your favourite meals is chicken and dumplings. I make a very good one if I say so myself and I would be happy to make that up for you one night if that will be fine with you.” I said that I would love that very much.

The days were getting a bit cooler, and it rained most evenings. It was very thoughtful of Barclay to do that. I went back out into the sitting room to join the others. Duncan offered me a drink, but I declined. I had tea instead as did Roxie. Duncan decided to have coffee instead and so did James. There was always a fresh pot of coffee on the sideboard along with hot water and a variety of teas.

"Barclay is going to make chicken and dumplings one night for dinner. James you told him that it was my favourite, I appreciate that. Roxie, I hope that is ok with you as well." She loved chicken and dumplings, sometimes a little too much. I laughed and said that it was good comfort food and now it was getting cooler and raining at night, it would warm us all up. Duncan and James decided to have a game of snooker. They wanted Roxie and I to play but I was not good at the game so declined. Roxie said that she would play if I did, so I said I would.

"Do not blame me if I put a tear in the felt. You will have to explain the rules too as we go. I haven't played in a long time." Roxie said she never played but was game to try.

I played with James and Duncan and Roxie paired up. Duncan broke first and put in a couple of balls, so he continued. Then it was James's turn. He started to do a run on the table. Obviously, he was a very good player. He missed a shot and then it was Roxie's turn. She shocked the hell out of herself when she put the ball in. It went into the wrong pocket and was the wrong ball, but she put a ball in. Then it was my turn. I managed successfully to sink two balls in the right pocket but missed on the third.

"Well, well you are not a bad player sweetheart. I'll give you some lessons if you like." I said that it wasn't really something I liked playing. I think he could read that it was bringing up a past memory, so he cleaned off the rest of the balls when it came to his turn and the game ended. Duncan wanted to have a rematch, but I said that I would prefer to sit and watch if that was ok. Roxie picked up on my vibe and said she would sit out too. She sat beside me on the bar stools, and we watched James and Duncan play.

"Sorry love I forgot you used to have a pool table. I remember you telling me about all the times he had his friend over, and they got stinking drunk. I should have remembered that when you didn't want to play. I'm so sorry." I said not to worry about it. It was in the past and it was not something I thought I would have to deal with because I didn't know James had a games room. The gentlemen played a few very spirited games. Duncan would raze James and James would raze Duncan. It great to see that these two men loved each other deeply.

"It is nice to see the two of them together having fun isn't it. They are like brothers more than a father and son figure don't you think." Roxie agreed. I could see that she was very much in love with Duncan. She rarely took her eyes off of him.

"Any thoughts where you two might like to live. Duncan is selling the business to James, and he is letting Catherine take over the running of the business. I know you have said that you want to wait until you bring him to meet the kids, but I am sure that in all the alone times the two of you have had, you have at least talked about it." She said that they had and that I would probably be surprised.

"I like having a home with a yard where my grandsons can play, and I can go out and sit and watch birds and the like. Because Duncan owned a real estate company he has been looking into properties. A house in a subdivision on an acreage not far from your house may be going up for sale. The owners have been talking to a realtor but haven't decided when they want to sell. They have it tentatively listed but not ready yet to put it up on the internet. Realtors get access to property listings before they go out to the public. It is about a kilometer down the road from where you live." I was delighted to hear that they were considering moving close by.

"I hadn't really thought about moving there but it is between my country place and the city, and I have my doctor there and it probably makes sense. Duncan showed me the pictures of it, and it looks really nice. Not too big mind you but big enough that I can have the boys stay once in a while. I remember driving by that subdivision and there are lots of trees and the properties are a good size. Houses are not on top of one another. That's why he went into the office earlier because he wanted to see if he could put a hold on it until we went back so we could go and see it. If I like the house he's going to buy it for us." I was so happy for her. I knew that she liked her condo in the city because it was close to the kids, but the neighbours were close to each other which is something that I don't think Duncan would have put up with for any extended period of time. Moving out by us was a happy medium and it put Duncan and James in close proximity to each other. While James was relatively used to being in Canada, it would be a change for Duncan. It would be good for him to have James nearby.

"You don't mind moving there Roxie? I think it would be good for Duncan and if you decided later on that you wanted to be back in the city you could find something else. I know how much you like the country but being way out where your country place was is a bit too far and isolated for you. I think, for the time being, this might be a happy medium to go with." She was sure that it would suit them both just fine and agreed that being closer was much better.

It was almost 6:00 and Barclay announced that dinner would be served shortly. We went into the dining room and Roxie, and I had water while Duncan and

James had whisky. Barclay served each of us a Scotch pie and they smelled divine. We dug in and they tasted absolutely wonderful. The mashed potatoes and grilled asparagus were perfect as well. I ate too much and was full. There was an assortment of small desserts that Barclay did up, but I passed. We took our coffee in the sitting room as usual.

"Listen you two if you don't mind, we want to keep our engagement a secret for a little bit. I know that Fiona and Fenella are coming by tomorrow, so I really don't want this to get out yet. I am respecting Roxie's wish to first talk to her son. She will take her ring up to our room while they are here. That won't be a room that you and the interior designer go into so, if that is ok with you we would appreciate it." We completely understood their position and would say nothing. It was turning out to be a nice evening, a bit on the cool side but still a very nice evening.

James went out to the terrace and lit the fire pit. We took warm blankets and put on a warm sweater and went outside. The sky was clear and all you could see were stars and more stars. The moon was coming up over the trees and it was full and bright. James brought out the pot of coffee and filled everyone's mug. It was so nice to sit and chat by a fire. After a couple of hours Roxie said she was ready to hit the sack.

"Thank you love; it has been a wonderful day. It has been a wonderful holiday here and I am so glad I came." She gave James and I a hug and kiss goodnight and she and Duncan went upstairs. James and I were sitting in a love seat looking out as the moon rose higher and we sat in silence for some time.

"James do you think Duncan will be happy in Canada? I mean he has lived his whole life here in Scotland and it is going to be a big adjustment for him." James put his arm around me, and I cuddled into him.

"He will be fine because he will be with the woman he loves. Duncan has dated a few women in his day, but I have never seen him as happy as he is with Roxanne. Surely with your ability to see a person's energy you have picked up on that." I said I had but it didn't always mean that it would be an easy thing. As we sat watching the moon and the fire, I caught a scent on the air. I'd smelled this before, but I just couldn't place where.

"What is it sweetheart, did you see something." I looked at him and wondered if maybe the scent was coming from James.

"No, I didn't see anything, but I got this whiff of a scent. I know I have smelled it before, but I can't place where. It's a floral scent but I just can't recall what floral. Very bizarre. This happened to me once when I was doing my first level of reiki. The lady who was teaching us said that she had a spirit guide who had a strong musk smell. I can't tolerate the smell of musk as it gives me a headache. But as she was taking us through a guided exercise I could smell musk, like someone had sprayed it right in front of me. It was gross, but she was surprised when I told her. Anyway, just now I could smell something, but I don't know what it was." James put out the fire.

We got up, he put his arm around me, and we went into the house. I carried in the blankets and put them on the sofa. We walked arm in arm up the stairs. Once we got into bed, we fell asleep until morning. Today Roxie and I were going to be meeting the other women in Glasgow for tea and a spa day. Catherine arranged everything and all we had to do was show up.

William was going to drive us and would then return when we were finished. Roxie and I had enough time to have some breakfast before we had to head out. James and Duncan were going to do some things on their own today, what they would not say. We got into the car at 9:30 and drove to the spa. I was rather looking forward to being pampered for the next several hours. Catherine arranged massages, body wraps, facials and mani/pedis, it was going to be a very relaxing day. We arrived at one of the few luxury spas from what Catherine said that was strictly a spa and not a hotel. It was very exclusive and from the outside looked very impressive. Catherine met us as we went in.

"I am so glad to see you both. The others are already here and waiting for us in the back. Just to let you know, we are going to start with massages first, then we will have a facial and then a body wrap to cleanse any toxins, then we will all be together in a private room for lunch and then on to a private room where we will have mani's and pedis. I hope you ladies are ok with that. If so let's go back and meet the others and then we can start our day." Catherine took us back in the waiting area where Fenella, Alisa, Fiona and Glynnis were waiting. We hugged each other and then went off to change into our robes to start the day. The massages, facials and the body wrap were an hour, and the mani/pedis an hour each. Catherine had it all arranged down to almost the minute. I loved a well-organized day.

The massage was great. It felt good to have my muscles worked and I told the massage therapist to go at them and not take it easy. She did just that and it really felt good to have the knots in my shoulders worked out. The facial was invigorating, and the body wrap was very relaxing. I didn't realize having so much seaweed wrapped around me would feel so good. After our body wraps, we got dressed again and went into a small private room to have tea and sandwiches. I sat between Fenella and Catherine and Roxie sat between Fiona and Glynnis. Catherine asked how it was going so far.

"That facial was really good, and I loved the seaweed wrap. I feel whatever toxins I may have had, didn't stand a chance. It was very invigorating." Roxie said she was having a good time too and really enjoyed her facial.

"I don't really do this very much back home, I've always been on the go so much, but I have to say that I think I'm going to do a little more me time when I get back." The others laughed at that, and the door opened. We thought it was to bring in more tea but standing in the doorway was Victoria, James's ex. We looked at her, but it was Fenella who spoke.

"Victoria this is a private party. So please don't cause a scene and leave." She looked at Fenella and could see that Fenella was not to be crossed.

"My apologies to all, I thought this was the room I was to go in for my massage." It was easy to see that she was staring at me and for a second, I almost felt sorry for her. I felt I needed to say something.

"No harm done Victoria, enjoy your massage." She turned and left, and we didn't say anything more about the interruption. Our lunch finished, we went off for our mani's and pedis. We started with the pedis first so that our toes would have lots of time to dry before we had to put our shoes back on. I chose an iridescent green for my nails and toes. As we were sitting, having our feet thoroughly pampered, it was Catherine who broke the awkward silence.

"That was rather odd Victoria showing up at the spa today of all days. Seems pretty weird that she would have come to this spa today don't you think Fenella." Fenella did not strike me as a woman who would gossip about such things and said so.

"Ladies I would prefer not to speculate on why she was here. I know that she has been here many times and maybe it just happened that we all came on the same day. I for one am not going to discuss it further and I hope the rest of you won't either. Let's just enjoy the balance of our day shall we." And that was the end of the discussion about Victoria. It was nearing 5:30 by the time we were finished. Catherine put in a call to William to come back to get us. We sat in the waiting room together giving out nails a further chance to dry completely. Fenella asked Roxie and I what our plans were for tomorrow.

"James is taking us to Edinburgh, and we are going to tour the university and then a few other places that he said he thought we would enjoy. I am quite looking forward to it. We have not seen all of Scotland, but we are seeing enough that we want to come back and see more." Fenella was happy that the trip was going well. William arrived, and everyone left the spa at the same time. Roxie and I went back to the estate.

"That was quite the day wasn't it. I could have enjoyed a much longer massage, but I was happy with everything. What about you Roxie?" She enjoyed the day as well but the ex showing up was quite a surprise on that day of all days.

"Well like Fenella said, I'm not going to speculate on why and how. I'm not concerned about her at all." We arrived home just after 6:00 and went into the sitting room to join James and Duncan.

"Ladies, did you have a good day and were you well pampered I hope." I said that we did and I for one was actually looking forward to dinner. I wanted to go up and change as I wore a pair of jeans and a blouse to the spa. I was putting on a pair of wool slacks and a silk blouse when James came into the bedroom.

"Roxanne mentioned that Victoria showed up. I hope she didn't cause any problems." I assured him that she didn't. Fenella made it very clear that she would not tolerate it just by her tone. James was still a bit upset.

"I guess I should have expected something like this. Victoria and Fiona are friends, and I am sure that it was Fiona who said that you would be at the spa today.

I'll have a word with Fiona about family loyalty." I asked James not to do that.

"I am sure the Fenella has already had words with her. Let's leave it at that please James. I doubt that we will have to worry about anything happening again. I feel sorry for her James. It is obvious just from the encounters that I have had with her that she never really got over you. I'm not asking why you split up. It's irrelevant but perhaps she regrets it. I know you don't but maybe she does. I feel a bit sorry for her that's all." James hugged me and kissed me.

"You have a very good heart." I thanked him but assured him if she was trying to get him back, I wouldn't have such a great heart. He laughed and put his arm around me, and we went back downstairs to join Duncan and Roxie for dinner. Barclay prepared a roast of beef with mashed potatoes and a variety of vegetables. It was a very good meal. While Duncan and Roxie sat by the fire after dinner, James and I put on our jackets and went for a walk around the house.

"James remember me telling you about that scent the other night when we were on the terrace. It must have been Fenella because I could smell the same smell today when we were together. Perhaps it lingered from the dinner on Sunday." James thought about it for a second and then remembered something.

"My Mum used to wear the same fragrance as Fenella, but I don't think Fenella came out to the terrace on Sunday." I thought for a moment and then reminded him of me smelling the musk that time and perhaps it was his Mum who was letting me know she was near. James smiled and was happy at the thought. We went in and upstairs to bed. It had been a long day but a relaxing one and I was looking forward to a good night's sleep. James wanted to get in a run in the morning which he told me about before we drifted off to sleep.

When I felt James getting out of bed and looked outside it was barely light out. I groaned and he gave me a kiss on the cheek on his way out the bedroom door. I slept for another hour and heard James come back into our bedroom. He was sweating and his sweatshirt was soaked but I knew that he was thinking about Victoria showing up. He took everything off and jumped in the shower. I was sorely tempted to join him, but I thought it would make us late for breakfast.

I got up and washed up and got ready to go downstairs. James was done in the shower and shaved and dressed and we left the bedroom at the same time. We had breakfast with Duncan and Roxie. Roxie looked at me with a look of what was wrong with James. I shook my head hoping that she would let it go. James was quiet and even Duncan picked up on his mood.

“Everything ok James, you are awfully quiet this morning?” James assured him everything was fine, just had a bit of a restless night. I could see Roxie touching Duncan’s arm to say let it go, which he did. After we finished breakfast, the guys went for a good long walk.

“Is everything ok between you two?” I told Roxie things were fine. Nothing to be worried about. They came back after about an hour.

“It is very near lunch time; what do you say we take a short trip into town and have lunch at a pub. It isn’t anything we’ve done yet and the local pubs here all have great food, but we must not spoil the dinner for tonight. Are we agreed.” We all agreed to have a light lunch. The pub wasn’t that far away and while there was a good crowd we were still able to get a table.

People waved to James and Duncan as we walked to our table. Their family lived here for a long time, so it would have been unusual if they were not known in the area. The waitress brought water and menus and asked if we wanted anything to drink. James and Duncan had whisky, but Roxie and I stuck with water. When she came back with their whisky, we gave her our orders.

Everyone was having a chef salad, which we were told we could have with chicken or partridge in it. We all chose the partridge. The pub was similar to ones I had been in when I went to London a few years ago to see where my Mum grew up. A bit on the dark side and a little noisy. It didn't take long for our salads to come. They were quite large and there was a good amount of partridge. They were delicious and we each finished ours to the last bit of lettuce.

The waitress came back and asked if we wanted anything else. James said that the bill would be fine. He paid that on the way out and we walked around the town for a little bit. It was very quaint and had a lot of history. The streets were clean, and the houses were well kept. We did another stroll around the town and then back to the car and home. James looked very happy, and I was sure it was pride in being able to show me his home and where he grew up. Because it was still early we drove into Duntocher where Duncan, Fenella, and James's Mum grew up. Roxie had already been, but she was happy to go back.

This too was a small village and so we got out and walked around. Duncan pointed to the house that they used to live in when he was a small lad. It wasn't a big home, but it was a good size and was well kept and it was easy to see all the memories flooding over Duncan's face.

We got back in the car and drove home. It was nearing dinner time, and I was really looking forward to Barclay's version of chicken and dumplings. We ran upstairs to wash up and I changed from my bulky sweater to a green silk blouse I brought. James liked the colour on me. He changed his bulky sweater to a black cashmere pullover. He looked good in anything, and yet nothing as well. We got back downstairs just as Barclay was saying that dinner was ready. I could hardly wait until he put my plate in front of me. It looked and smelled divine. He had some warm crusty bread to go with it. I put some pepper on mine and took my first bite of the dumplings. They were so delicious, and the chicken tasted so good too. I ate ravenously and used the bread to dip in the sauce. Roxie was doing much the same.

"I guess I don't need to ask you if you liked it." I looked up a little embarrassed. I knew James was teasing but I literally would have licked my plate if they were not there. I scooped up the last of the sauce with my bread, licking my lips.

"It was so good, and I could probably eat another, but I won't. This has always been my favourite dish. My Dad used to make it for me to make me feel better. I remember once calling him up and telling him I wasn't feeling well, and he would make it for me. That was a good memory and he made good chicken and dumplings." James asked me if I wanted more but I said no I didn't want to be uncomfortably full. Again, there were an assortment of little cakes and squares which I did help myself to after everyone was done their meal.

We took a small plate of desserts with us into the sitting room where we had our coffee. Some of the desserts had some alcohol in them some had a lot. While they were all good, I didn't want to have too much.

"Today was a nice day guys, thanks for taking us around and showing us all the little places you used to live and hang out in. It was very nice indeed." Roxie seconded that. I wanted to go for a walk around the house. James brought me a jacket and one for himself and we excused ourselves and went for a walk. The night was crisp and clear, and stars were out in the billions. We were even lucky enough to see a few meteors shooting across the sky.

"Did you make a wish?" I looked up at James and told him I got my wish many months ago when he walked through the door at the coffee shop. He put his arm around me, and we continued on our walk. It was chilly out, but it was nice to walk off the dumplings. James laughed at me, he actually thought I was going to lick the plate.

"Hey if you hadn't been there I would have. It was that good. My Dad's was good too but a different good if you know what I mean." He did indeed, and we walked around the house one more time and then went in.

"James what plans have you for tomorrow. I know we are going to Edinburgh for you to show the ladies the university and I think Cassandra and Roxie want to pick up another piece of luggage. Did you have anything else in mind?" James didn't think that there would be enough time to do much looking so perhaps going to a place up near the north where he knew they sold a lot of luggage at good prices would be the place to go after going to the university. We were all tired and went to bed at the same time.

The next morning, we had breakfast and went to Edinburgh. The tour of the university took about two hours. I didn't think it was going to take that long but James kept running into professors he had and of course he had to introduce his fiancée and they remembered Duncan, and he introduced his fiancé. It was nice to see that they were all proud of the success he had become.

We went up north to the luggage place. James also decided to show us where the royal yacht sat. He said that there was a good Italian restaurant close by if we wanted to stop there for lunch. Roxie and I looked at each other. While it was great to be getting a taste of Scotland cuisine, it would sure be nice to eat something completely different. It didn't go unnoticed by James who just laughed.

"Getting a little tired of Scottish cuisine are you. I don't blame you. When you are not used to eating it, it can leave you wanting a change. I can ask Barclay to do something perhaps a little different for the family meal on Sunday. It will be the farewell dinner for the family for you two, so I think it only fair we have something different. I think Barclay can do up some Canadian dishes quite easily. I will have a chat with him." I asked James not to do that, perhaps we could arrange to do that when my family came over for the wedding. That way we could bring along some of the things necessary that were not available here. James agreed, and we went to see where the royal yacht was. It was quite an impressive ship. It was also our first view of the Firth of Forth. It was so expansive. We drove over to the marine esplanade and took in the sea air. It helped to build up our appetites.

We got to the restaurant which was quite lovely, and they had a very extensive menu. It was a hard choice, but I went with the fettucine alfredo, Roxie chose the lasagna and James had the carbonara and Duncan had the panzerotti funghi. The food was delicious and so filling. Everything was really good, but we pushed back from the table quite full. It will be a light dinner tonight.

James called Barclay when we left the restaurant to say that we would probably have sandwiches for dinner tonight with cheese and fruit slices. We started back to the estate, taking our time going another route to see more of the sights of Scotland. After leaving Edinburgh we drove to Falkirk and Stirling and up to

Perth and over to Arnprior and then back down to Dumbarton. It was a long road trip, but we got to see so much of the countryside, and it was nice to see Arnprior.

"Maybe the next time we come over and stay a bit longer we can explore some of the small towns and villages. Both Roxie and I enjoy that sort of thing, so I hope you guys don't mind being tour guides." James and Duncan both said that they would like nothing better. It was 6:30 by the time we walked in the front door. Barclay laid out the sandwiches, cheeses, and fruit trays for us to pick and choose from. We made a plate for ourselves, took it into the sitting room, with a fire going in the fireplace. It made for a relaxing end to a long day in the car. It was a chilly night, but I wanted to go out on the terrace. James grabbed our jackets, and we stood out there and I looked around.

"This is a beautiful place James, are you sure you want to move to Canada. I feel like I am tearing you away from this. I don't want you to regret it later." He wrapped his arms around me and assured me that I wasn't tearing him away from anything.

"Let's settle this so we don't have to talk about it again ok. I want to be with you. I love you and where you are is where I want to be. I know that you don't want to live so far away from Ross and Ayleen. I understand that. Don't forget they are my family now too and I want to get to know them as much as I can and living across an ocean isn't going to make that as practical as just a three or four hour flight. So please know that I want to be with you in Canada. Now, if we have settled that I know we are not going anywhere on Saturday, I would like to bring Annie over. She has been texting me that she wants to meet you and I thought perhaps we could have her over for lunch. If you agree I will go and pick her up and bring her here. What do you say?" I absolutely wanted to meet Annie, not just because she was a famous medium, but because she was the closest thing that James had to a grandmother, and he thought so much of her.

"Absolutely I want to meet her. In the little you have talked about her she sounds like a very interesting person, and she clearly adores you so how could I not want to meet her." So now that that was settled, and I promised not to raise the move to Canada again, we went back in. Duncan and Roxie already went upstairs so we did the same. The night air was chilly, and it would be good to get into a warm bed. I laid my head on James's chest, and he had his arm around me. I turned to look at him and he had such a serene look about him. I kissed him and said goodnight and we fell asleep in each other's arms.

Today was the day the interior designer was coming back with the layout boards of each bedroom upstairs. We finished breakfast and were having coffee in the sitting room talking about our upcoming weddings. The interior designer was scheduled to come at 11:00 this morning and Fiona and Fenella were going to come by at 10:30 am. It was not long after we finished our coffee that that Fiona came in. She said that Fenella called her to say she wouldn't be able to make it after all. Fiona was a bit early, and Roxie hadn't a chance to take her ring off. She looked at all of us and asked what was going on. I didn't like lying about anything, but I also didn't want further questions asked because Duncan and Roxie didn't want anyone to know about their engagement.

"I was just scolding James and Duncan for passing gas and told them they should ease up on the black pudding and whisky." Fiona looked at us and burst out laughing. The doorbell rang, and Fiona said she would get it. James looked at me and tried to hold back the laughter.

"Wow you are quick on your feet but did really have to say that." I apologized to James and then to Duncan, but it was the only thing I could think of to shut down the questions as to why Duncan and Roxie seemed to be fussing about when she came in. Fiona came back in with Julia who introduced herself to Fiona at the door. We decided to go into the dining room so that we could lay out all the drawings of the rooms. Once they were laid out we looked at each of them. The rooms looked really beautiful, and she was right to change the wall paint in the one bathroom from what I suggested. We gathered up the layouts and took them upstairs and went into each room.

"As you will see I have also done layouts for the hallways. They seemed a bit dark, and I thought if we were going to introduce new colours in the bedrooms that we should try to lighten up the hallways as well. I know this carpet James is very expensive, but it has, in some areas, seen better days. Perhaps we can work with a reputable carpet dealer and see if there is a way to make a large area rug for one or more of the rooms out of it and replace this with new carpet. But let's first go into the lavender room. I'm using these names just to identify them. You don't have to call them that if you don't want to." Julia proceeded to describe to us what she suggested in each room.

She like my suggestion for a strong lavender colour and paired it with a cream colour. She didn't think it necessary to change any of the bed coverings but had suggestions if we did. If we kept the existing coverings she had samples that would pull everything together. She updated all of the bathroom fixtures and the lighting. She liked the suggestion of using James's glass company to get new table lamps, shades or bowls and did stop in and discussed this with Alisa.

"She is a very skilled artist, whom I understand, does all the drawing for all of the glass work at your company James. She is quite brilliant." After having looked at all of the rooms and all of the bathrooms she opted to keep with one type of bathroom fixture. The brushed pewter seemed the best choice, so she went with that. In some bathrooms the vanities are granite and in others marble. A bit of a mish mash but she thought the brushed pewter would tie in nicely.

"If there is anything that you disagree with, please say so. None of this is fixed in stone and I am very open to further suggestions." We all agreed with what we saw so far. Room after room Julia explained the choices and how doing this or that would tie the whole room together. The ideas she had for the hallways were brilliant and would definitely make it much lighter.

"I can say that I am happy with the choices. Fiona are you ok with what is being changed here. I need you to like it as well since you and Malcolm will be living here for a couple years. I can tell that Cassandra loves it, so I need to know you are ok with it." Fiona loved it all and the only suggestion she had was for the bed covers in the room she and Malcolm would occupy.

"James if it is ok with you, I would like to go with the suggestions that Julia made for the room we will be sleeping in. I realize that the fabrics are quite expensive, but I think that we would like something a little more modern. Is that ok with you. I know all of this is going to be quite expensive and I don't want to add to it, so I hope it is ok." James assured her that it was not a problem. Fiona and Malcolm would not be moving in until the middle of November, so it gave Julia enough time to get everything done. No major items were being touched so doing the painting, updating the bathroom fixtures, lighting and new carpeting should be done in about a month and half. It would be ready for when they moved in.

With that settled we went back downstairs. James asked Fiona if she had time for a coffee, but she said she had to run as she had other errands to do before Malcolm came home from work. Roxie and Duncan stayed out of the way and so Fiona didn't notice the ring on Roxie's hand. I think staying seated and having her left hand under her leg probably helped with that.

"Well, that took a bit longer than I thought but I like what she proposed, and I am happy that it will all be done before Malcolm and Fiona move in. Cameron and Donald won't be home until the Christmas break, so it will make things easy for Malcolm and Fiona. Lunch with Annie was now turning into dinner. James let her know that he would pick her up at 5:00 and bring her to the house. Duncan had a few things to tend to so Roxie and I sat near the fire and chatted.

"I think I mentioned to you that Annie is a medium. I recall you saying to me once that you would like to see one. I don't know if she will read anything on us. I'm not going to ask for one, but I will be happy if she says something. Would you be ok with that or would you rather not?" Roxie was ok with it but would see how the evening went. James left right after Fiona and Julia left. We saw him coming up the steps to the front door. Annie MacKay was a very graceful, somewhat tall elderly woman. She had an air about her that was serene to me. James brought her into the sitting room and introduced her to us.

"Annie this is my fiancée Cassandra, and this is Duncan's fiancée Roxanne. Ladies this is my dear friend Annie MacKay. Dinner won't be for another half hour; can I get you some tea Annie." She said that would be lovely. Roxie and I already had tea and so James filled our cups up. Annie sat in an armchair across from the sofa.

"I have been wanting to meet you for some time now, but James has kept you busy taking you on a tour here and there. But I am happy to finally meet you, and you as well Roxanne. I don't know if James told you, but I am a medium, someone who can get messages from the other side and other things as well. You have an energy about you Cassandra, but I think you know that. It is a very bright light around you. It is not something that I see around many people, but with you it is very bright." I smiled and said that years ago I took a level in reiki, but she said that it was more than that and perhaps she and I could discuss it another time. She then looked at

Roxie but even I could sense that Roxie was a little nervous, so Annie left it for now.

"You know I told James he was going to meet someone in Canada on a business trip. I even saw him going for coffee, which James told me that is how you met. But I get the feeling you sort of knew you were going to meet someone that day at the coffee shop, in fact I think you had a dream about it, and you were telling Roxanne about this dream when James walked in." Roxie was intrigued now but I was not surprised she knew, in fact, I think I already knew she knew.

"James mentioned that you smelled Cullodina's perfume the other day and of another instance when you had that happen. You have a strong ability, but I also get the feeling that you don't want to pursue it as a career choice. That is ok my dear, it is not everyone's cup of tea. I myself rather enjoy it. It is always interesting to see the faces of people who come in as skeptics and go out as believers. I don't try to get people to understand, I just tell them what I see. But Roxanne, I see two people who have apologies for you. They handled a few situations badly and apologize for what they put you through. But they are very happy you are with Duncan. He's a good man Roxanne and you will have no concerns with him, and your son and his family will love him once they know him." I think that put Roxie's mind at ease because she finally seemed to relax.

It was like a weight being lifted from her and she was happier. Barclay came in to say that dinner was being served. James helped Annie to the dining room and seated her to his left and I was at his right. Roxie sat beside Annie and Duncan was beside her. The meal this evening was a chicken dish with chili and curry in it, but it wasn't too spicy Barclay said. There were oatmeal potatoes which we had not had but James said were Annie's favourite and seasoned vegetables.

"Barclay has prepared Annie's favourite dessert, so we must make sure to save some room for that. It's a raspberry whisky cheesecake, but not to worry, not too heavy on the whisky. I think you ladies will enjoy it." We sat eating and talking back and forth. Annie asked to see my ring and then Roxie's.

"They are both very beautiful rings, and you look very happy. James and Duncan, you treat your women properly at all times and spoil them as much as possible, even though they say they don't want you to. You must let him spoil you Cassandra, you have deserved this for such a very long time. You know that, so let him spoil you for a little while." I said I would try for which James, I could see, was happy.

Chapter 6

The meal was very good, and the dessert was as James said, excellent and not too much whisky. Roxie thoroughly enjoyed the dessert. We went into the sitting room to have our usual coffee after the meal. Annie declined any coffee as it kept her up at night. We talked about the wedding and James mentioned when it would be. Annie said it was going to be a beautiful day according to her guides. After a half hour, James said that he would take her home before it got too late for her. We walked her to the front door and hugged her goodbye.

"I shall see all of you again when the wedding takes place. I plan to be in the front row for that and I can't wait to meet that little granddaughter of yours. James has talked endlessly about her and loves her dearly. Goodnight all of you. See you again soon." Duncan, Roxie, and I walked back into the sitting room to talk about the evening. I liked Annie a lot. She had a very peaceful feeling about her, and I think she helped to put something to rest for Roxie.

"She is a very interesting woman. I have to admit I put up my guard up when she first sat down. I guess I was afraid of what she might say but I felt a load taken off when she said what she did. I hope that I wasn't being too reserved with you, I was really fretting about the kids." Duncan assured her that he was not concerned, and he understood completely how she was feeling but now they were more relaxed around each other. Duncan and Roxie decided to go up to bed while I waited for James to come in. He came into the sitting room a little more than a half hour later and shuddered a bit.

"Starting to get chilly out there. I see Duncan and Roxanne have gone off to bed. If you are tired we can go up as well, but I would like to sit in front of the fire for a bit, get the chill out. Annie likes you a lot. We had a nice conversation on the way home." James sat in front of the fire reflecting on the talk in the car.

"James, she is a lovely woman with a very big heart which she gives wholeheartedly when she is in love. But she was badly hurt before by her late husband. He hid things from her and drank too much and made things seem like they were her fault and not his. He is taking ownership of that now though, but he nearly destroyed her. Love her deeply and hug her a lot, but always stand by her no matter what, no matter if she is wrong, she needs to know that you are in her corner. I don't think that will be something that ever comes up, but trust is vital to her. I know you are an honourable man, and I can see how much you love her. I see also that she doesn't want to be spoiled with diamonds and the like but spoil her in ways that will mean so very much more to her. Get to work on that list of hers. She has a gift but fears using it. But I can help her with that in a way that I think she will appreciate. She has good and loyal friends and one in particular that she trusts with her very soul. It is good that this friend likes you and sees the good in you. She is a very gifted one so when you need advice, ask her, she will, knowing all Cassandra's past, steer you in the right direction. You have always been a very patient man, someone able to see things others cannot, this has helped you enormously in your business. Now apply a little of that to her. She has been abused my dear by people who said they loved her. It is sad my dear, very sad and I will not say what it was, but you know me well enough to follow my advice. Your parents are very happy with her in your life. She can be a great partner in more ways than one. Ah we are here. Thank you for the wonderful evening. I know you are going to Canada but will be back often, so I shall see you when I see you but do keep in touch." James kissed Annie on the cheek, got out and opened her door and saw her safely inside.

He thought very long and hard about what she said, and it was true. Cassandra did not want diamonds and lots of clothes, she was not into all that, but he would get her special things on special days. Her birthday was coming up soon and he wanted to work on taking her to an observatory. He would have to ask Mina to look into it for him. She had a star and even though it was a gift from her Dad, he was going to make it possible for her to see it. That, he knew, would make her extremely happy. For now, he just wanted to get through the Thanksgiving holiday with her family.

“Hello, James, are you in there. You were obviously a million miles away. Is everything ok?” He was more than ok he said and nothing to be worried about. He took my hand, and we went upstairs. We changed into their pjs and crawled into bed beside each other.

“I love you with all my heart and soul Cassandra and I will spend eternity to make you the happiest ever.” I did not question why he said that. I had a feeling that Annie may have said something to him on the drive to her place. I pulled his arm around me, and we hugged each other. I could hear his slow breathing and I knew he had fallen asleep. I felt secure in his arms. It finally dawned on me this was the first time I had ever felt secure. I drifted off with a smile on my face. There were no set plans for today. It was Sunday and the family was coming for dinner at 6:00. We had breakfast together and then James and I went for a long hike. It was challenging and took an hour and a half one way, but it was worth it. We stood together at the top of a large knoll overlooking the estate and beyond.

“This is invigorating don’t you agree? The air is crisp and fresh much like the air in late November or early spring at home. But we should probably head back don’t you think?” James wanted to stand and look around for a bit. He took a few photos of us and of just me. My cheeks were rosy, and my eyes were bright. He pulled me to him and hugged me and with a kiss on the lips, we went back. There were still many hours before the family would start showing up. James and I jumped into the shower. We toweled off and I got a bit of a leg cramp.

"Yikes I guess I over did it." I was massaging it, but James made me lay on the bed and massaged the leg, trying to work out the cramp. It felt good and the cramp was gone but I let him continue to massage my leg for a little bit. I think he realized what I was doing and slapped my rear.

"We don't have time for this, we have to get ready, but I promise I will give you a full massage later." I agreed to that. I loved to get a massage and who better than James to give me one. I said I was counting on it, and he had better do a good job.

"I will have you know that along with my many other talents I took a massage course, and I was quite good at it. At least that's what all the ladies said." Now I hit him on the rear, and he took off into the closet to get dressed. We got dressed in jeans and sweaters and went down to the sitting room. We had lunch and then James had to check on some work things and went to his office. Duncan and Roxie dressed up and went for a walk and I wandered around the house going from one room to the other. James came in search of me and said we should think about getting ready for dinner. Duncan and Roxie came back, and they were going to head up to get ready as well. James saw that I was going to wear the royal blue dress and went into the safe which was in the closet.

“Here, these will look lovely with that dress. I know you don’t want to be given lots of jewels, but these were also my Mum’s, and they will look remarkable with this dress. I think Duncan has something for Roxanne to wear as well that belonged to my Mum. She gave him a few things as well hoping that he would someday find a wife to wear them.” I got into my dress, fixed my hair, and did my makeup. I got James to zip me up and he helped with the necklace. It was stunning. A large sapphire pendant surrounded by diamonds and a diamond and sapphire strand around the neck. It was princess length and fit perfectly. The sapphire and diamond drop earrings were the same as the pendant. I turned around for James to see.

“They look stunning on you, but you make anything look stunning.” James had on a dark grey suit with a light grey silk shirt and dark grey tie. He looked amazing and I told him so. We went out and saw that Duncan and Roxie were coming down the hallway. She was wearing her dark brown crepe dress and Duncan was wearing a black suit, white shirt, and black tie. They looked amazing too and just as James said, Roxie was wearing a strand of pearls with a large chocolate diamond pendant with matching earrings. It was beautiful, and she had such a smile on her face now. We went down to the sounds of people arriving. Everyone was dressed up this evening because it was our last night together. Fenella and Callum were the first to arrive and then the rest not long after. Dinner was going to be at 6:00. Everyone went into the larger living room to sit and chat. William brought around glasses of white and red wine as well as whisky. Fenella came over to speak with me.

"Cassandra that necklace looks lovely on you and Roxanne's looks good on her as well. Listen I wanted you to know that I spoke with Fiona. She let it drop when she was having lunch with Victoria that we were having that day at the spa. She said she didn't do it intentionally; it came up when Victoria wanted her to go shopping. In any event, it amounted to nothing, so I hope you weren't upset." I told her that I wasn't, and I mentioned that I told James about it.

"He was going to talk to Fiona, but I said that you probably already handled it. Let's not talk about it anymore ok, it is in the past." We clinked our wine glasses and rejoined the others. Roxie was having a lot of fun with everyone talking to each person there and having fun with the kids. It was quite a change in her since Annie visited. Even Duncan was smiling and laughing more. James came over to stand behind me. He bent down to kiss my neck. My reaction was instant. He laughed and took my hand, and we went over to talk with Malcolm and Fiona.

"Malcolm has Fiona told you of all the changes. She seems to be very happy with them. As you know we are leaving tomorrow so if you want to start moving things in here next week, please feel free to do so. I'm sure you would like to be in before St. Andrew's Day." Malcolm said that Fiona had filled him in on the changes and that yes, they would indeed like to move in before the end of November.

"James, I know that St. Andrew's Day is not a typical holiday that we observe but I thought perhaps we might like to start doing so. Angus and I were talking, and we thought that it would be a nice thing to do for the staff when we take over for you. Not that you were not good with your staff, far from it, but it will help them to be more accepting of us I think. You are very big shoes to fill, and you know all of your employees are very loyal to you, so we thought this might start us off on the right foot." James saw their point and said that he thought it was a good idea. Making it a paid holiday was a good first move on their parts. James was always very good to all of his employees with generous benefits and salaries.

"You are absolutely right, talk with human resources and make sure that all employees get the day off with pay. But no more talk of business tonight, this is a family occasion so let's enjoy." Barclay came in to announce that dinner was being served. William and Mrs. O'Toole's two daughters Annie and Beth helped to serve everyone. Wine glasses were filled, water glasses for the younger ones and a toast from James.

"Once again, we are here as a family having a lovely meal. Tomorrow, Cassandra, Roxanne, Duncan, and I shall be heading back to Canada. As I mentioned to some of you, I will be spending Christmas and New Year's with them this year and perhaps, in following years, some of you can join us in Canada. We shall work it out going back and forth. You know that I love each and every one of you and you will always be in my heart. I am just a phone call or video call away which you are used to using with me being away on business. So let us enjoy this wonderful meal and have fun." There were cheers to his speech but also some tears. I was starting to feel a little bad, but Fenella looked at me with a look of happiness for James.

"Don't fret Cassandra, this is good for all of us and especially for James. He has his own family now, something he has always wanted. We have to learn to share him, and we will." That made me feel better. The evening went on with Callum playing the piano and the kids playing and dancing. It was a wonderful evening. The meal long over, now the younger ones were getting quiet. Angus and Catherine were the first ones to say they should get the kids home, followed closely by

Glynnis and Gowan. The rest of us sat in the smaller sitting room and Fenella told us some stories about her sister Cullodina and her husband Patrick James. I was sure that the stories had been told many times before, but they were new to me and Roxie.

"My Dad was not so certain that they should have gotten married. Cullodina was only eighteen and Patrick was thirty-three. He was concerned that she had not seen enough or dated enough. But Cullodina knew that Patrick was the man she wanted to spend the rest of her life with. She had a way of making our Dad see her side of it. She was a very good negotiator even at eighteen. Something James inherited I think. Their wedding was beautiful, and they were very happy. James came along the next year, and he was the pride and joy of both my sister and her husband. But life has a way of stepping in doesn't it and putting challenges before us. But it has made us a strong family and we are here for each other through thick and thin. Cassandra you now have us as your family." It was a very gracious thing to say, and I thanked her so very much and all of them as well for being so accepting of me. Roxie went into the larger living room to retrieve her bag. Fenella saw that she had done so and followed her.

"Roxanne, I hear congratulations are in order. Yes, Roxanne I know. Duncan has never been able to hide anything from me. He never could when we were children and not now. I won't say anything to anyone because that is the way you want it until you see your son. But I am very happy for my brother. You have brought him a level of happiness I have never seen in him, and I want to thank you for that. It makes me feel good to know that he has someone to spend the rest of his life with." Fenella hugged Roxie who had a few tears. Fenella gave her a hanky to dry them. They returned to the sitting room together. I could see that she looked like she was upset but came over to say everything was fine. She said Fenella knew but would not say anything and that she was very happy for them both. It was now going on 10:00 and it was time, Fenella said, for them to leave.

"Come everyone, they are going to have a long day tomorrow and I think they want to spend their last evening together quietly. Everyone say goodnight and let's go home." Hugs and kisses were shared and then everyone was gone. The staff cleaned up and they also left.

"I don't know about you, but I think James and I are going to head off to bed." James looked puzzled but when he saw the look in my eyes, he realized that I was giving Roxie and Duncan a chance to be alone. We got into our bedroom and James wanted to know why we left them downstairs.

"Fenella knows, and I think Roxie wants to let Duncan know that she said something to her. I think they just wanted to sit by the fire and enjoy being in each other's arms right now. Besides, you promised me a massage." He had indeed promised her that. I went into the bathroom, took off my makeup, gave James the jewels to put back in the safe, got my pjs on and then laid on the bed. He came in with his t shirt on and his long pj bottoms.

"I'm sorry but this is not how you get a massage. Off with the pjs." James got some lavender scented oil from the bathroom. I put a few towels under me so as not to get oil on the sheets. He lit a fire in the fireplace, and it gave a warm glow in the room. He put some oil on his hands and massaged my back working out any knots that were there. Then he massaged my legs to work out any lingering cramps from the hike early in the day. His hands were strong but gentle. He rolled me over and sat me up against the headboard and started to massage my feet.

"Oh God that feels good. I love having foot massages, but I could never get them done. I was always afraid I was going to sound like I was having an orgasm. Man, that feels good." James was laughing and enjoying it himself. I was naked as could be and yet he was not looking to have sex. He was simply interested in giving me a massage from head to toe. He took a towel and removed any oil and then put my pjs back on me.

"Ok now curl up against me and we shall go to sleep. Next time it is my turn." I promised him I would do my best and we chuckled and fell asleep. When we got up in the morning, James took out some suitcases of his to pack his clothes. He sent several boxes of his clothes over several weeks ago which were being stored at the house. He pulled out my suitcases for me to start packing my things.

"We will go down and have breakfast and then come up and finish packing. That way we can relax the rest of the day until we have to leave for the airport. Does that sound ok to you?" It did, so we got dressed in jeans and sweaters and went down for breakfast. Duncan and Roxie met us on the stairs. We mentioned the plan and they said they were planning the same thing. Barclay came into the dining room with some fresh coffee. There were scones put on the table with butter.

"Today is going to be a special breakfast for all of you. This is a multi-course meal so pace yourselves. Lunch today is going to be roast pheasant with roasted potatoes and seasoned vegetables and lots of little desserts and dinner is cobb salad. Enjoy, the first plate is coming out soon." The first plate was eggs benedict, and I ate them with gusto. The next was a couple of pancakes with a honey sauce which was very good, then came arbroath toasties which were smoked haddock, egg, and cheese on grilled bread, very tasty as well, then smoked salmon omelet and finally toad in the hole. We took a little of everything, well some things a little more of than others. The fish dishes were excellent, but I would have liked them on their own as a main dish. It was all very good, and we left the table very full. We took coffee upstairs with us so that we could do our packing.

"James, I cannot believe all the stuff I have. I am so glad I got that extra piece of luggage. Everything is going to fit but only by a little. Do you think we will have time to go for a short walk?" He thought that we would for sure. The hiking boots James got for us we were leaving behind for future visits. The weather was getting colder, and we had some heavier jackets to wear when we were out walking. Those too we were leaving behind for future visits. A good thing too because I could not have fit it into my luggage. I closed up two of them and left one open to throw in my brush and makeup bag. I didn't have to bring a flat iron as James made sure there was one in the bathroom.

"I sent three large boxes of clothes several weeks ago and I still have to bring along four suitcases. You thought yours was bad. I knew I had a lot of clothes, but I didn't think I was quite this bad." I laughed at him and said he was very high maintenance. He wrestled me to the floor in the closet and had a burning look in his eyes. He pulled off my sweater and removed my jeans. I took off his sweater and threw it in the corner and he took off his jeans. He held me in his arms and kissed me and then kissed my neck in that spot that always drove me crazy.

The reaction to that kiss was instant. I had my arms around his neck, and we were both removing each other's remaining clothes. This was passion and lust rolled into one. James put my legs around his waist drawing me into him. The urgency for both of us was undeniable. We lay on the floor panting; James over top of me leaning on his right forearm.

"That was very enjoyable. I hope you enjoyed it as much as I did." I kissed him and said I did, could he not tell. He kissed my nose and said yes, he could, multiple times. We got up, went to the bathroom, and then got dressed again.

Duncan and Roxie were already out for a walk down to the farm to collect eggs. It was their morning ritual to do together, and they enjoyed it. It was, after all, how Duncan proposed. James and I put on our jackets and went out towards the gazebo. We wanted to spend time looking out over the lake and remembering how special this spot was. We were there for a couple of hours enjoying the solitude of the surroundings. We got back in time to go in for lunch. We were having wild mushroom soup as the first course with warm rolls. The soup smelled wonderful, and it was nice and creamy. The rolls were warm, and the butter melted in them. The soup bowls were cleared, and warm plates put in front of us. Moments later, Barclay brought out the roast pheasant which he cut and served to us. William followed with the roast potatoes and the seasoned vegetable. The gravy with the pheasant was very aromatic. There was an assortment of pickled beets, olives, and cheeses to choose from as well.

"This is like a mini Thanksgiving here isn't it Roxie. This looks very delicious, and I can't wait to taste everything." I knew James was going to make a toast, as was tradition in the house, but I asked him if I could do it this once. He said of course. I took my glass of wine and raised it.

"This has been a wonderful time, not just for me but for Roxie too. You are both the most wonderful gentlemen, and your family has been so kind to the both of us. I look forward to years and years of times like this with you James. I love you so much and I thank you for coming into my life." Roxie seconded that but for Duncan of course. James and Duncan were touched by the toast. James leaned over to kiss me, and Duncan leaned over to kiss Roxie. The meal was as I had thought it was going to be absolutely delicious. Everything from the pheasant to the desserts that we had later on were wonderful. We were both famished and ate hungrily. We thanked Barclay for a wonderful meal and all the wonderful meals he had prepared.

"My word you two were eating like you didn't have a huge breakfast not a few hours ago." We looked at Duncan and then each other. Roxie gently slapped Duncan on the chest, and he realized what he had said.

We burst out laughing. We went into the sitting room to sit by the fire and have tea while the guys had coffee.

"Did you get everything packed Roxie? I can't believe how much stuff I'm bringing back with me, but James has even more. He sent several boxes ahead several weeks ago. He has left some things in his closet because he will be coming back from time to time on business." Roxie filled her bags to the brim and only had enough room to put her hygiene stuff in.

"I'm thankful we are not going commercial because it would cost us a lot to bring all this stuff back." We knew that we would have to pay duty on some of the things we bought, but James said he would handle the forms for us since he had done it more times than he could care to mention. We spent the next while taking photos. James and I in front of the fireplace, Duncan, and Roxie and then Roxie and me. There were so many photos to go through when we got home. James wanted to finish up a bit of business and Duncan and Roxie took a walk around the grounds. I sent Janet a text letting her know we were heading to the airport soon and I would text once I got home. I then sent Ross and Christelle a text saying the same thing.

I was by myself, so I wandered around the house. This was James's home from the time he was born, and it was a beautiful home. I was not worried about him coming to Canada, we settled all that but perhaps we could come again in August with Ross, Lindsay, and Ayleen to have a proper family holiday. That was something that I never really did with Ross. Mostly because money was always an issue and then when it was no longer an issue for me, we hadn't got around to arranging anything. I sat in the middle of the staircase imagining Ayleen dancing around, Ross and James going for long hikes over the moors and Lindsay and I taking Ayleen shopping. I was very lost in thought and didn't notice James sit down beside me.

"Where were you just now?" I told him what I was thinking.

"That sounds like an excellent plan to me. I'm sure that Ross will be able to take off a couple of weeks in August. They are only taking a week for the wedding, so we can definitely try to make it work. I would really like to talk to him and see if he is happy where he is, at work I mean. I could offer him a much better paying job with much better benefits, but I need to know where his passion is." It was a wonderful thought.

"They have both had trying times and it has always been hard for them financially. It has been better since they have money now and they own their own home and they don't have to worry as much, but I want Ross to feel like he is doing it himself and not relying on their savings or their trusts. I mean they don't ask for anything because they were able to get current in everything and paid off anything owed. I set up a trust for the three of them. I also gave them a sizeable amount of money to put in a savings account that they could go to when they needed. I wanted them to be debt free so that they didn't always have to say no they couldn't afford to go to the show or Ross take Lindsay out for their anniversary. Maybe a lot of people don't realize how much that bothered the two of them, but I knew. They don't walk around now with slumped shoulders, and they are actually happier." James was happy that I was able to do that and wanted to talk about it more later.

"I know that Ross loves cooking but I don't want him to say he wants to be a chef. That is not what I want to see for him. Those are long hours, and it isn't great for a family. He is a good cook, but he would have a long way to go to become a great chef. He is a hard worker and whatever his job is, he does it to the best of his ability. I don't have an answer for you I'm afraid. I know he loves me, and we are close but for the longest time we struggled with each other. It is getting better but there are still moments. I have some regrets where he is concerned but those are things for me to work out. What time did Barclay say dinner was going to be?" He said 6:00 but he was not going to let this conversation end. He would have to think about what he could do. It was clear from the catch in her throat that she and Ross struggled, and he was going to see what he could do to help. We sat on the steps and held each other. Duncan and Roxie came in through the side door into the sitting room and saw us.

"I think maybe we should give them a few more minutes. It looks like that was a difficult moment." Duncan agreed, and they sat quietly by the fire. They heard us coming towards them.

"Hi, you two, we just came in a moment ago and we're warming by the fire. Picked a few dozen eggs for Barclay. I think we should get those into the kitchen Duncan, don't you?" He agreed and picked up the basket and off they went. We sat by the fire in the seats that Duncan and Roxie vacated. I knew that I was putting a bit of a damper on the rest of the day, and I had to change it.

"I'm sorry about that James. I didn't mean to bring the day down. Sometimes when it comes to Ross there are things that just really get to me. But I am an optimist most of the time, so I am going to focus on the day and the future not the past." James smiled and agreed but I knew that he was thinking about what I said.

Duncan returned to say that Barclay was going to start serving dinner. The salads were wonderful and light enough that we wouldn't be too full on the plane. We went back upstairs to finish the rest of our packing and bring our suitcases down. Since Roxie was going to be selling her trailer down in the states, Duncan packed some clothes for the weather there. He also sent off several boxes of clothes that he would need for Canada to James's house which were put in storage. The suitcases sat at the front door. It looked like a small army was moving out and it was rather funny. We weren't leaving for the airport for a few more hours so we took the opportunity to go for a good walk. It was nice the four of us walking together but Duncan and Roxie only went as far as the farm and returned to the house. It was very chilly, but James and I were dressed warmly and continued on for a bit.

"I've only been here two weeks and I'm going to miss this place, so I can imagine how you feel. But I know we will be back often so that is the silver lining as they say. I know you are going to be busy running back and forth to Toronto and elsewhere, I'm ok with that. Maybe I can even go with you sometimes and do some shopping or visit museums and art galleries. I don't want you to worry about that, about me being alone for stretches of time. I'm used to it, and I find things to do. I wanted you to know that ok because I don't want you to worry about going to work." James pulled me close, and we walked arm in arm back to the house.

"I do appreciate you saying that, and I know you can take care of yourself. I would like it if you could travel with me whenever you feel you want to, and I will do my best not to work excessive hours like I have in the past. What do you say we have some champagne before we leave and yes it will be your favourite Cassandra?" It sounded like a great idea. James texted Barclay to bring a bottle up from the cellar and put it in the sitting room in an ice bucket with four glasses. It took us about half an hour to get back to the house and as we were going into the sitting room, Duncan popped the champagne.

"Good idea James let's celebrate to the four of us on a new adventure in life. But I want to say that for me, this is going to be the best adventure ever and I get to do it with you Roxie." It was a touching thing to say, and I could see Roxie get caught up in it. William loaded all our luggage into the limo and was waiting to take us to the airport. We finished the champagne, said goodbye to Barclay, and left. It wasn't a terribly long drive to the airport but once we got there, getting all our baggage onto the plane took a bit of time.

We boarded the plane at 10:00 bound for home. James completed the duty free forms for Canadian Customs. We were over by a bit, but he would look after paying the tax for us. It was now nearing the end of September and the leaves were starting to turn here and they would probably have already turned at home. Hopefully, there would still be some so that we could see what the colours would look like against the house. This was yet another flight crew that worked for James. The captain was Peter, and the first officer was Daniel. The flight attendants were Rachel and Martin. We went through the usual safety process and then when we got up to altitude, Rachel asked us what we would like to drink. We wanted water which she brought to us. Martin brought blankets and pillows. Duncan and Roxie went up front because they were getting tired and wanted to sleep. James and I stayed at the back. The lights were turned out in the cabin except for a small light at our seat.

"I really enjoyed my time in Scotland James, and I love your family." I knew James was happy that I was accepted not that it would have changed anything, but he knew his family would have loved me.

"Annie and you really hit it off. I'm glad about that. She means a lot to me. It was good to see Fenella happy for us as well. It will be fun to have them over for a holiday. Mind you not all of them at the same time." I could see that Duncan and Roxie drifted off. I leaned over to kiss James.

"I think we should try to get some sleep, don't you?" He agreed, and we pulled our blankets around us, and I laid my head on James's shoulder, and we drifted off to sleep. I could feel James stirring and lifted my head. We'd been flying for about five hours according to James's watch, but it was still a bit dark.

"Sorry sweetheart, nature call." While he went to the bathroom I sat up looking out the window. Daylight was just starting to show its signs. James returned and then I went to the bathroom. I didn't want to use the bathroom at the front in case I woke Duncan and Roxie. When I returned to my seat, James had his tablet open and going through some documents. Before takeoff he would always go through his emails and download anything that required him to read and go over. In addition to the lab that was being built in the industrial area, James was setting up a geothermal site but had not, as yet, decided on what he was going to put into the largest of the buildings.

"I've been thinking about the place where you and Roxanne bought your scarves and things, at that place up north. They import all the raw material from Mongolia and then process it from that raw state to the finished product. That allows them to say made in Scotland. I have been noticing a trend now for a few years where people, more and more, want to buy made in their own country. I was thinking maybe I could do the same thing and put a textile plant at that other building. I would have to talk to the owner of the cashmere store and get some details from them, but I think it might work. I am sure that there are probably local raw materials that can be had in Alberta that we could process to a finished product. What do you think about the idea?" I thought it was a great idea. It would be quite a boost to the economy and create a lot of jobs. James was going to look into it more but thought it could be profitable. Daylight was getting brighter, and I could see that Duncan and Roxie were now stirring. They took turns using the washroom to freshen up and then came to join us. James asked Rachel to get breakfast going because everyone was up now. As she was doing that Martin brought around a pot of coffee.

"Morning you guys; did you get some sleep. I slept like a rock, and I think Duncan did too." We said that we both slept well and had only been up a short while. The coffee was good, and we sipped in silence for a moment or two. I mentioned that James was going to set up a textile business similar to the one where we bought all the cashmere scarves. Duncan thought about it and agreed it would probably work well. We had to touch down in Ottawa to refuel but got right back up in the air.

"I think it will work out well, but it is going to take some time to get all of the equipment in and the proper people. There might be training needed for some. Fortunately, the shell of the building is there so that won't delay it." Duncan and James discussed business matters while Roxie and I drank our coffee. It was interesting to watch James discuss business to see how his mind worked out different issues that could come up. He really had a unique talent which was obvious because of his success.

The smell of eggs and sausage wafted through the cabin. Rachel and Martin served us our plates which looked so good along with a side dish of fruit cocktail and more coffee. We ate in silence enjoying the meal and by the time I was finished I was quite full. I got up to go to the bathroom to freshen up and Roxie did the same. We returned to the guys talking more business, but they stopped when we sat down. Rachel offered more coffee, but we all declined. The plates and cutlery were cleared away. The flight was very smooth with little turbulence. The original plan was to stop in Ottawa for a couple of days, but we changed our minds prior to leaving and only did it to refuel. I let Ross know so that Ayleen would not be disappointed, which of course she was, but we would be seeing them at Christmas. Roxie and I took a lot of pictures, and we were going through them making sure we noted where they were taken. We laughed at some of the candid shots. There were photos of the family dinners and of our night out to celebrate our engagement. There was one that Duncan took on my phone of James and I with my hand up on his chest showing my ring. It was a really good photo.

“I think I will get this one printed and framed. It’s a nice shot of the two of us don’t you think James.” He looked at the photo and agreed.

“We will have to start a family wall in the house. I like the photo taken of us at the gala too. I really liked that dress. We will have to find an occasion for you to wear it again. Maybe New Year’s Eve we can have a big party at the house. Everyone dresses up and Roxie you can bring your family too. Ross, Lindsay, and Ayleen will still be there. I think it would be fun and what a great way to bring in the new year." It sounded like fun, but we could talk more about it after Thanksgiving.

"Let's get Thanksgiving out of the way first ok but if we are going to make it semi-formal, we have to make sure that will suit everyone. I think we should say business suits and not tuxes but if the ladies want to wear a long dress they can." Roxie was going to check with Mitchell to make sure they had no plans.

"We don't normally do much at New Year's because I'm never usually here and I know that Cassandra you haven't in the past so maybe this might be nice. If I can get things settled down south and get things done in October and November and be back by the beginning of December I think it will be nice to start a new tradition, goodness knows we are doing a lot of new things aren't we. I'm sure that Mitchell would be ok with a suit, and I know Maria has some nice dresses. The kids can dress up a bit, but I doubt they will be awake that long. I will let you know Cassandra and then we can go from there." The captain came over the intercom to let us know that we were about a half hour from landing.

Scotland was very nice, but it was good to get home. Roxie had plans to do Thanksgiving at her condo in the city which was when her family would meet Duncan. I don't think either one of them was worried about it at all now. Rachel came around one last time to see if anyone wanted more coffee or water. We said no so she took our cups to the galley. It was within ten minutes the captain told the flight attendants to prepare for landing. We buckled back up and waited for the plane to land. Touch down was smooth, and the plane pulled to a stop. We waited for the stairs to be pulled up, so we could disembark after Customs came on.

The luggage was being taken off as we were going down the stairs. The crew would be staying until after Thanksgiving. Even though James bought the real estate business, there were a few things that Duncan had to wrap up, so he needed to go back after Thanksgiving and work out the details with Catherine. He was going to be two days at most and then would return and go down south with Roxie. James said they could use the plane to go down and that way they could go last minute if they had to. Our luggage was put into the back of my car that was left parked at the airport. We dropped Duncan and Roxie off at her condo in the city and then off to my place. I told Roxie I would call her after Thanksgiving. They were going to be going out to look at the house that Duncan wanted to buy for them, so she said they would drop around and perhaps go for dinner. We started the drive to my place.

"Cassandra why not move into the house with me. I know that your condo holds a special meaning for you, but I thought since we are engaged and getting married, why not just move in together now." The thought crossed my mind. It would mean selling the condo, which I didn't think would be too difficult. The presales of the units in the new building were doing very well from what James said.

"I would need to stop by and get my mail and pack all my personal things to bring over. I don't need any of the furnishing obviously but perhaps your new chef could stay there until he finds a place of his own. I will need to get some packing boxes for my clothes, but I won't be able to do that until at least tomorrow." James said he would take care of getting that done. All I would need to do was tell them what to pack. We stopped long enough to pick up my mail and a few more clothes to do for the next few days and drove over to the house.

"I'm glad you agreed because I already arranged for George and Christina to be here to hand over the keys." We stopped at the caretaker's cottage and James got out to meet with Mr. Davidson. I got out to shake his hand as well. His wife and kids were out picking up cleaning supplies for the house. We continued up the drive to the house. It looked so impressive on the way up. There was still some colour in the trees and it looked like a fairy tale. George and Christina were waiting on the veranda for us. We got out and walked up the steps. George and James shook hands and Christina and I hugged.

“Glad you are both home and we want to congratulate both of you on your engagement. James, I want to thank you for entrusting me with building this home for both of you. I have truly enjoyed building it. Here are your keys and I hope you have many years of happiness and joy. Christina and I will go in with you in case you see something that needs changing.” Christina echoed George’s sentiments. James took the keys and opened the front door. He pointed out the alarm system to me and said he would show me later, but it was off for now. We walked in and everything looked amazing. We went from room to room taking everything in. There was so much to look at, we would have to go over it all again later. We went into the family room, and I saw the poppy painting hanging above the fireplace.

“James, you bought this.” I couldn’t say anything else because I didn’t want to cry in front of the others. We started out of the room, and I pulled James back. George and Christina continued on to give us a moment.

“Thank you, James, for buying that painting. It means so much to me that you would do that.” He smiled and kissed me and then we caught up with George and Christina. We continued on going from room to room. Everything looked perfect. The light shades and bowls were amazing, and the rooms were beautiful. The kitchen was like something out of a design book. There were things in this kitchen I had no idea what they were for, but I was sure that the new chef, Jonathan, would. We went upstairs to look at the bedrooms, each one was perfect. The master bedroom looked spectacular. The ensuite and the huge walk in closet which I didn't think I would ever even fill a quarter of one wall with my things. We continued on down the hall to the one bedroom that wasn't finished the last time we stopped by. James opened the door and ushered me in. On the back wall, it was painted a pretty purple with lighter shades in lavender on the other walls. There was a queen bed with her favourite animated animal comforter and pillows. It was made for Ayleen.

"Oh my, she is going to squeal when she sees this room. I am serious, you will have to cover your ears because her squeal hits a decibel you wouldn't believe." James thought of everything that Ayleen would like in this room, even having a duplicate Sparky for her. It was almost identical to her room at home.

"I wanted her to feel at home here when she comes at Christmas and any time after that. It's easy for adults to adjust but kids, I am told, find it harder in a new place. I wanted her to have familiar things around her." It was perfect. The house was perfect. We walked back downstairs. James gave George and Christina each an envelope.

"Bonuses, you both deserve them for a job very well done and ahead of schedule. I have no problem

recommending either of you if you ever need it."
George and Christina thanked James and they both left, and we were alone in the house, our home.

We went back through each room, taking more time to look at each thing that was in it. The paintings that we looked at in the different galleries, the glass pieces that James sent from his factory, everything down to the coasters were perfect. We took our bags upstairs and started to unpack. The boxes of clothes that James sent several weeks ago were unpacked, steamed, and hung up or put away. James had one side of the closet and I had the other. It was almost comical to see how little space all of my things took up.

"You know you can always do more shopping and fill up your side if you want. There will be functions that we have to go to, and you will see in no time, your side will flow over into mine." I said that I didn't think that would be possible. We both laughed and finished hanging things up and went back downstairs and out into the sunroom.

This was a perfect place for family gatherings. It was warm and inviting and with all the windows it made you feel like you were sitting in the outdoors. James debated about putting in a fireplace, but I said that this was where the Christmas tree would go, and the kids would be playing that it would be better if it didn't have one. There were already several fireplaces, so this room really didn't need one. There was a smaller dining room off the family room which would be where many of the meals would be. The larger one was for big family dinners. It was so relaxing sitting in the sunroom watching the birds fliting from tree to tree. Further back into the trees the deer were foraging.

"We will have to see if Mr. Davidson can make some bird feeders and houses. I know we could buy them, but I like homemade ones. We can maybe get him to build some sort of trough for the deer to feed out of. I know that they love sunflower seeds and different types of squashes. It will be fun to watch them, and I know Ayleen will get a huge kick out of it. Do you think Mr. Davidson does any hunting? I don't know if I would want any of the deer here shot but perhaps he could do moose and deer a little further north." James said he would look into all of it but right now we needed to decide about dinner.

"Jonathan isn't going to be here until tomorrow morning, so what do you say we head over to Jason's for an early dinner. I am sure that by the time 8:00 rolls around we will both be very tired." We got changed. James put on a black shirt with dress pants and a sports jacket, and I decided to wear my wool pants with my new royal blue cashmere pullover I bought. I had on my star necklace James bought with matching earrings. James pulled his sports car out and we went to the restaurant. It was early Tuesday evening, and the parking lot was almost empty at this time of the day. We got out of the car and went into the restaurant. Jason saw us and came over to greet us.

"Well, hello you two. How was Scotland? Did you have a good time?" I held up my hand for Jason to see my ring.

"Yes, we had a wonderful time but glad to be home." Jason was thrilled for us and seated us at our table. He brought out a bucket and champagne. I saw that it was my favourite champagne and was going to protest.

"No, my dear, I will not hear you say no to this. This is a special occasion and one that thoroughly delights me. I am so very happy for both of you and since the two of you started seeing one another, I had several bottles of this put in the wine cellar just in case such an event happened. Enjoy the champagne I will be back in a moment." As we drank the champagne, Jason came back out after a few moments. He was having the chef prepare a special meal for us. He got in some fresh bison tenderloin which was going to be prepared in a Saskatoon sauce, with roasted potatoes and grilled vegetables. For dessert and because he knew I loved caramel, there would a caramel cheesecake for the two of us to share. Jason left, and we continued to drink our champagne.

"I guess it will be Thanksgiving at our home and not your condo now. Do you think your sister and her family will be ok with that arrangement?" I was sure that it would be ok, but I would give her a call in the morning to talk to her. I didn't see it as being an issue.

"I think though I will wait until she comes to tell her about the engagement if you are ok with that. I don't see them not wanting to be in our home and all together. I will have to find out from her if anyone has any allergies or food likes or dislikes. I never met Nicole's boyfriend, so it will be fun I am sure." James would make sure that the chef was prepared for doing a larger meal.

"I can work out the menu with him for Thanksgiving over the next day or so. I ordered a turkey, but we may need to get a bigger one." I was looking forward to all of the holidays coming up.

"I do have one thing to ask. I have to go to Toronto a few days before Thanksgiving and meet up with my senior vice president of human resources and the director of marketing. They are not new to the company or Canada, but I recently brought them over from Germany. I'd like to invite them for Thanksgiving dinner if you are ok with that. I move people around from time to time so that people don't get bored in their jobs. I brought Richard and his nephew Mark in from Germany and moved two other people to Germany. I wish that I had thought of this earlier because I could have arranged to pick up your sister and niece in Ottawa and then come here but I am sure they already have their flights booked. If you think they won't object to them being here for dinner, I can let them know tomorrow so they won't have to be on their own. They won't be staying at the house; they will be at a hotel, and they are only staying for a day and going back to Toronto." I looked at him and knew that he was trying to play matchmaker and asked him as much. He said he remembered that I ask him if I knew of anyone that I could introduce her to.

"So, I thought of Richard who is sixty-three and a very nice guy. He lost his wife many years ago and his nephew Mark, who is forty-two was taken in by Richard and his wife when Mark was only fourteen. He lost his parents in an accident and his mother was Richard's sister, so he and his wife were the only family he had. I suggested the change and Richard talked Mark into coming as well. Even though I have not met your sister, I think that she and Richard would get along and who knows, maybe even your niece will like Mark, if she is not seeing anyone that is." I said I would talk to her about it tomorrow when I gave her a call. We finished our meal and dessert, had a cup of coffee, James paid the bill, and we went home. It was so nice to drive up that long drive and see the lights on outside the house. It was like a dream come true. Tomorrow we were going over to my condo to pick up a few more things and let Mr.

O'Leary know that I would be moving out and the chef would be staying at my unit for a short time.

"I will have to change my mailing address and my license, lots of things to do over the next few weeks." There was a very large gate at the entrance which James had an opener for. I wasn't keen on gates, but James said it would be wise for security.

"It will only be locked at night. During the day it will be left open most of the time as John won't be far away. So not to worry you are not going to have to deal with it each time you go in and out." We pulled into the garage and got out. James gave me the extra set of keys to the house and a garage door opener for my car. Lights came on as we approached the steps.

"I know you said you were tired, and I am a little but how about we have more coffee and go and sit in the sunroom and see if any deer come by." It sounded like the perfect way to cap off the day. There was lots of seating in the room, and all had good views of the forest. We sat in a very comfortable love seat enjoying our coffee and watching the woods. It was fairly dark, but we had the outside lighting on which projected far enough into the woods to see anything moving. After a short time, there was some movement. James looked as did I.

"Oh wow, there is a moose, a cow, and her calf I suspect. That's nice to see and I dare say it would look good in the freezer." I knew he was kidding because I already asked that nothing be killed on the property unless of course it was doing a lot of damage. The cow and calf looked healthy.

"I think they go through their rut soon. The cow will be chasing off her calf. I have never seen a bull moose and I wonder if we will get one coming through here. I'm glad to see that there are still a good number in the area. Not sure if John would be allowed to hunt on the property. He would have to look into that with the county and make sure he knows what the rules are. Moose can do a lot of damage to trees as can deer so if he gets permission to hunt here, the only thing I do not want to see is a young one shot." James agreed totally and said he would get John to look into it. We finished our coffee and went upstairs.

"Oh, damn I have a couple of emails to send out to Mina, go ahead up and I will be up shortly. I promise I won't be too long." James went back down to his study which had been completely set up. I went up, took a quick shower to get rid of airplane smell and got into my warm pjs. The weather was starting to change here too. The days were still quite warm, but the nights were getting chilly. I wanted to open a window, but I wasn't sure if the alarm was on. I would have to wait until James came up to ask him. Hopefully, I would

} be awake that long. The bed was unbelievable comfortable, and the sheets were so luxurious. The down comforter on the bed was light enough not to make sleeping too uncomfortably warm. I tried so very hard to keep my eyes open until James came in, but they were just too heavy.

James wanted to see if Mina had been successful in getting them into the observatory for Cassandra's birthday. They would be at the penthouse Nov 1st and go out for dinner and dancing for her birthday and then go to the observatory. He also wanted to make sure the Mina was able to get the emerald ring she tried on that Hans brought to the penthouse the night of the gala. If she wasn't able to get that exact one, it could have diamonds on either side of the emerald but not all the way around just as long as the centre stone was the four carat emerald. He would have bought her much more, but he knew it would have upset her. He would definitely get her some gold necklaces and earrings for Christmas.

While she was very easy to please she was going to be hard to buy for. She already said she did not need another car and definitely not one like his. Maybe next year he could convince her to upgrade her current suv to a newer model. As occasions came up he would make sure to splurge on her as much as he could. He would have to find out from Ross what it was he wanted to do other than what he was. He would like to see if he had any interest in working for him, but he had to see where his strengths were. Getting Lindsay, a job at a school where Ayleen would attend would not be a problem.

For now, though he wanted Mina to contact the principal of their school and offer up some free computers and techs to help them learn coding. James always encouraged his tech people to give back to their community by donating time. He willingly gave people time off to do that and with pay, so it was an incentive for them to show small kids how to be tech smart. His final email to Mina was to set up meetings for next week to discuss the new lab, the geothermal office and to look into the textile plant.

He was taking at least the time off before and after Thanksgiving to be with Cassandra in their new home. The following week he would be in the Toronto office as normal until the end of October and then off for the week of Cassandra's birthday then off to Germany, Austria, and Scotland. He wanted to make sure that nothing was booked for him for the full week prior to Christmas and the full week into the New Year. With all of these emails dealt with, which he knew that Mina would not see until morning, he shut off his computer and went upstairs.

Everything was locked downstairs, so he saw no need for now to turn on the alarm system. He would have to talk to Cassandra about it in the morning. He went upstairs, showered, and changed in the bathroom. She was fast asleep. He opened the window to let in fresh air. The nights were not quite as chilly here yet as they were in Scotland. He crawled in next to her, snuggled up close, put his arm over her and drifted off to sleep. The sun was shining through the window in their bedroom. There were no drapes on the windows because their bedroom was at the back. I could feel James close to me. I stretched and turned to look at him. He was wide awake and looking at me smiling.

"How long have you been awake? Maybe we should get drapes on the windows. The sun is up very early here in May and June, like 4 am early and I'm used to it, but it might be a shock to you." He said they would figure that out later. He wanted to relax for a few more minutes in bed with me beside him. For me, that was easy, being next to James snuggled up in bed was a no brainer. I gave him a wicked smile which started to make his body react.

"Ok things are getting a little heated, we should get up. I am sure that chef Jonathan is downstairs, and he knows we are here and is probably wondering what we want for breakfast. I will run down and let him know what we want while you get dressed. You can come down in your pjs and robe when you are ready. This is our home, and we can go down in our pjs if we want." James dashed into the bathroom and after putting on his robe went downstairs. I got up, washed my face, brushed my teeth, put on my slippers and robe, and went down to the kitchen. James was talking to Jonathan about breakfast. I went over to shake his hand and welcome him. Coffee for me was a medium roast and black. James liked his bolder and black as well. Jonathan had some muffins made and scones which he took into the small dining room.

"I suspect that you are still suffering from a bit of jet lag, so I thought I would do something up that wasn't heavy. I am preparing asparagus crepes with some fresh fruit. I hope you will like them. Perhaps after breakfast ma'am we could go over what you would like for lunch and then dinner." That sounded fine to me, and it gave me a chance to see what our plans for the day were. I told Jonathan I would see him later in the kitchen and that he could call me Cassandra. He nodded and went back to the kitchen to prepare breakfast.

"The coffee is excellent, how is yours? These muffins are delicious too, but I don't want to fill up on them. What are our plans for the day? I can ask Jonathan to do up salads for lunch unless you would like something more than that and maybe we can have a pasta dish for dinner. How does that sound to you?" James said it sounded great and that perhaps we could let Jonathan know what we don't like and then let him plan the meals as he wishes.

"After breakfast, I want to check on a few emails while you are in the kitchen. Then I suggest we go and get a few boxes and go over to your condo to bring over the things you don't want to risk having damaged. I will arrange this morning to have someone go in and do up the other packing unless you think that you can handle doing that yourself. I can get John to go over with the truck and pick up the boxes if you think that will work easier for you." It would be easier for me to pack and have John pick up the boxes and bring them into the house.

"It will give me a chance to purge anything I no longer want to keep although I did a lot of that when I moved into the condo, but there are a few things that I can probably give to a clothing charity. If we can pick up some boxes later today, I could start doing that tomorrow and then Jonathan won't have to keep driving in from the city, he will be able to move right in. I'll let him know that he can have the linens, but I will want to wash everything so that it is fresh." James went to his study when they finished eating and Cassandra went into the kitchen.

"Jonathan, that was a lovely breakfast. The crepes were the perfect choice. For lunch, we would both like to have a chef salad. For dinner we thought maybe a pasta dish with seafood perhaps. I don't like oysters although I know that James does but perhaps not in the pasta. James is fairly easy going when it comes to food.

He will try anything once but me I'm a little different. Things that I don't like are green split pea soup nor does James, sauerkraut I cannot even tolerate the sight or smell of it, neither of us likes eel or anything slithery like that, although escargot and squid don't apply because we both like that, we both love wild game. I don't like raw mushrooms, but I love them cooked. I hope this doesn't sound like I'm picky, but I think it is better you know." I discussed the rest of our likes and dislikes with him.

"There you have it; we are willing to leave all the meals up to you to change up and vary as you see fit. We will be having my sister and her family here for Thanksgiving. Her daughters Rhonda and Nicole and Nicole's boyfriend Austin. James is planning to invite two of his executives as well. I already ordered a fresh turkey from the butcher before I went to Scotland, but you may have to call to get one a little bigger. Either you can pick it up or I will. I did say to James that I would really like to do Christmas dinner. I am sure that you have family that you want to be with, but I will have to come into the kitchen to get you to show me how to use some of the appliances. The stove looks very daunting to me. The Thanksgiving crew all like desserts so a wide variety of them will be great and James's favourite is berry crumble with crème fraiche. Ok, so do you have any questions for me?" Jonathan was busy writing everything down.

"This is wonderful, and I thank you for allowing me to do the meal planning after today. Your likes are extensive, and I agree with you on some of the dislikes. I know how to cook anything and everything but I'm not a huge fan of green split pea soup either. As for Thanksgiving, it will be so much fun to cook for your family. I am sure everyone will have a good time. As for my family, I was an only child, and both my parents are gone. The few relatives I have are on the east coast and I don't go out there at Thanksgiving or Christmas. I just started dating someone, but she already made plans to go to Europe with her parents and since they have not met me yet, it would have been a bit awkward." I wasn't aware of his situation.

"I'm sorry I didn't know any of that. We know you come highly recommended so how about you do the cooking at Christmas, allow me to help if you need it and that will make me happy. You can sit with us at Christmas if you like. I will talk to James, and I am sure he will agree. We don't stand on formalities here. James is very much an employer who treats his staff like family and since you have none, you will be with us." Jonathan was touched and said that he would like that very much as long as James was ok with it.

"As long as I am ok with what?" I told James that Jonathan was going to be alone at Christmas. He is going to let me help cook at Christmas if I want. Are you ok with him sitting with us at Christmas dinner?" James totally agreed that it was ok.

"I am sure that Cassandra has told you we don't stand on formalities here the majority of the time. But Cassandra I want you to spend time with Ayleen and Ross at Christmas, not in the kitchen cooking. I will expect when there are important business people here, which won't be often, but there will be dinner parties, so I want it known now with all the staff that formalities are expected on those occasions. Being with us at Christmas is fine, we don't want you to be alone. I haven't had the chance to talk to Cassandra about this yet because a lot of things have been going on, but I usually have a lunch with staff on Christmas Eve. It is the time I give out bonuses and it gives me a chance to have a good chat with everyone." Jonathan was fine with that and went back to what he was doing but still listening.

"Sorry sweetheart I should have told you about that tradition, but we can start it here too. Now typically it is a Scottish affair, and I would still like you to incorporate some of the Scottish cuisine in meals and especially at that lunch. I hope you know how to make haggis. But not to worry if you don't. It can be tricky, and I can always have it flown in." Jonathan admitted that he never made haggis before, but he would give it a try and see if it measured up. We left Jonathan to doing things in the kitchen, and we went out into the sunroom.

I needed to give Sonya a call. James went to get some coffee for us.

"Hi Sonya, I'm back from Scotland. It was a lovely trip and James's family are so wonderful. I have lots of pictures to show you, but I have a couple of questions. Have you already booked your flights? No, ok then don't book them. James has to go to Toronto in a few days and he will fly into Ottawa and pick you and Rhonda up. How does that sound? I think you will like being on his plane better than a commercial flight. Ok good I'm glad that will work for you. Now, James's house was done a few weeks ago and he wanted me to move in with him, which I have done and am in the process of finishing. The house is big and there is more than enough room for everyone to have their own room. Will all of you be ok to come and stay here? Awesome now to my last question. James as I mentioned, is going to Toronto on business, he has a senior vice president of human resources that came in from Germany and also a director of marketing that he would like to bring for Thanksgiving. He moves people around a fair bit, so they don't get bored or tired in their jobs. Because they are coming back to Canada, he wanted to invite them for Thanksgiving. They won't be staying at the house. They will be at a hotel, and they are only coming in for a day. In fact, I think they will be on the flight with James when he comes to pick you up. Do you want me to be there, or will it be ok with just James? Great, that's good because it would have meant that he would have had to fly back here and then to Ottawa which would have been kind of silly." I knew that I rattled on very quickly about things.

"I have no problem with any of that and I am sure Rhonda won't either. We were holding off booking hoping to get a better fare but now we won't have to worry about it. I know you were going to pay for our flights but still we didn't want to book at full fare. I'll give Rhonda a call and tell her not to worry about booking flights. Now, I don't have a problem meeting James for the first time, but it would be kind of nice to maybe video chat before we go so that I can at least talk to him and see him. As for the two from his work, that's fine with me. I don't suppose they would be single, would they?" I could hear the laughter in her voice when she said that.

I laughed and said that actually they were uncle and nephew and that yes, they were both single. I gave her a bit of info on both Richard and Mark just, so she would know something, and I said that perhaps before James left for Toronto we could video chat for a bit. Plans for their stay were going to be casual except dressing up a bit for Thanksgiving which I knew she would have done anyway.

"Just make sure that all of you bring some workout clothes so that we can go for hikes. I doubt we will be going out for dinner anywhere since there is a chef here. I'm not bragging so please don't think that. James has always had a personal chef everywhere he lives." James came back with coffee, and I gave him the thumbs up.

"I know you are not bragging, and I am really happy for you. You seem to have found a really good man who wants to look after you and cares about you. A big difference from before." I said I would call her again tomorrow to go over the details of what they needed to do at the airport. I put my phone down beside me on the table.

"They hadn't booked a flight yet and since you said you would fly to Ottawa and get them if they didn't, I said you would. I hope that was still ok to say. I also mentioned about Richard and Mark and of course I have to give her more details tomorrow. She wants to video chat with you and I before you leave for Toronto, so she knows what you look like and at least will have talked to you. I hope that is ok with you too?" James agreed to everything and would have been happy to video chat now, but we had to go and get boxes and the rest of my things packed up after we finished our coffee. After the boxes were loaded in my car, we went over to my condo.

"I could have done this by myself James. I know you have a lot of business things to take care of." He wanted to come with me, so I wasn't going to refuse. The deal was that as I packed up boxes, he would close them and tape them and take them down to the foyer. When we were near to finishing he would call John and have him come with his truck to pick them up. I wanted to take some of the more breakable things in the back of my car.

When we got to the condo, there were a number of the residents in the foyer. They were happy to see me and James and when they found out we were getting married they clapped with joy. We went up to the unit and I started filling up the boxes, one after another. James picked up more than enough boxes and packing paper. For the most part, I was leaving a lot in the unit. It was only clothes and personal items that I was taking, at least for now. When the unit sold I would then look at perhaps moving the furniture to a model unit for the other building that was going up. But for now, Jonathan would need all of the things I was leaving behind. Mr. O'Leary came up to help James take down the boxes in the elevator and put them in the back of the truck. As they did that I threw all the bed linens in the wash and then dryer. It was going to take two runs to get everything moved. I was going to leave my mail key with Jonathan for now and he could bring my mail up each morning. That gave me a bit of time to get addresses changed.

"That is the last of them and it only took us three hours. I guess it is a good thing I am leaving mostly everything else." The last of the boxes went down and I took a moment to look around. This was an important place for me. It was really the start of my life over and into happiness. James waited at the elevator for me knowing that I needed a few minutes alone in my condo.

"You ok or do you want to take a bit more time in there. It is up to you I can wait downstairs." I said it was ok, and we went down in the elevator together.

"It's like a metamorphic feeling you know. I went into that condo as a larva, and I came out a fully formed butterfly. Sounds silly maybe, but that's how it feels." James said it wasn't silly at all and was a very beautiful and apt way to describe how things were happening. We put the last of the boxes in my car and drove home. Home, it was such a wonderful, warm, and comforting word and it was all because of James. John, Max, and Moira took all the boxes into the house and upstairs and put them in the hallway outside the bedroom. Moira said she would help with the unpacking, but I said I could handle it. It was mostly clothes and I needed to figure out where to put them.

"If it is ok with you I would like to get some things done in my study, but I can help if you want." I said no it was ok I could do this myself. Taking my clothes out of each box and putting them on hangars or in drawers was a good feeling. The dress I wore to the gala I left in the bag and hung it up. I wasn't sure yet how I was going to organize my things, but I could spend a day doing that when James was gone to Toronto. Of course, his side was meticulously well organized.

Maybe I would get Moira to help with that since she seemed to be so good at doing it for James. But for now, I wanted to take the time to put everything where, for now, I wanted it. There was one whole wall that was just for shoes and handbags. While I had more shoes and handbags now than I ever did before, I was sure that I would never occupy all those spaces. It was not who I was. The clothes taken care of I went down to see if lunch was ready. It was coming up on 1:00 so I checked to see if James was done in the study. He was hanging up as I was walking in.

"Good timing. Did you get everything put away? I think we should stop anyway and have lunch." We went into the dining room and Jonathan brought in our salads. They were a good size which was good because we were both hungry from doing all the moving. Dinner was going to be at 6:30 if that was ok, which it was with both of us. The salad was delicious, and we ate every bite. James went back to his study, and I went back up to finish the unpacking. There was only the toiletry stuff to deal with and that took very little time at all. I broke down all the boxes and brought them back downstairs and out into the kitchen. Jonathan said that he would put them in the mud room for John to deal with later. I hadn't gone through any of the cupboards in the kitchen, so I wasn't at all sure where anything was.

"Jonathan, I know that Christina got some beautiful china teacups, do you know where they are?" He showed me the cupboard that they were in, and I took down a beautiful blue one to make myself some tea.

"I see that you like herbal teas, from what is in the food storage and some other teas. If you like tea in the afternoon, I would be happy to make you a special blend that I came up with and I can bring it out to you in the sunroom. I know you are not into chamomile or green tea although both are good for you, but my blend doesn't have either. Let me make you a cup and try it. If you don't like it that's ok I can make you something else up." It sounded wonderful and interesting, and I went out to the sunroom and waited for him to bring the tea.

I unpacked my camera and brought it down to the sunroom. I took it out in case there were birds and other wildlife about. I turned one of the chairs around to face out into the woods. Jonathan came out with my tea which he put on the table beside me. I took a sip, and it was really delicious.

"I like this a lot. I will definitely have this again. It tastes rather like earl grey but not quite as strong. I hope that doesn't offend you." He said that he was happy I liked it and no it was not offensive. He wanted to create a tea that was lighter in taste. It was really good, and I asked him if he could bring out a small pot of it. He left to return to the kitchen.

I sat perched with my camera in one hand and a cup of tea in the other. There were lots of chickadees in the trees flitting about, but then I noticed a rosy grosbeak. I put my tea down and camera up, zoomed in and got a pretty good close up of the bird. Jonathan returned with the pot of tea and then disappeared again. I caught something further out in the woods. I put on my telephoto lens, and it was a red fox scrounging around for mice I suspect. It looked like it was hunting for them, so I watched it carefully through the lens. It leapt up into the air and I rattled off several shots on the camera hoping that I would have gotten a good one of it in midair. Not long after James came out and sat down beside me. He turned the other chair around to face out to the woods like me and I showed him the few pictures I had taken so far.

"Wow look at that bird, what did you say it was and look you caught that fox leaping in the air. Good job sweetheart. You should think about maybe framing some of these and we can put them in the rooms upstairs or in the hallway or even out here. We still have a lot of art to pick out and maybe some of these will do nicely." Jonathan brought out another cup in case James wanted some tea.

"You should try this; it's Jonathan's special blend. It's really good." James tried it and said that it was really good. We finished the one pot, and he brought out another. I took a few more photos, one of a deer and of more birds.

"I love to look at nature. I could spend all afternoon just staring out hoping to see a different bird or other animal. Roxie is the same. She had lynx and cougars at her country place, not that I want a cougar here, but it would be something to see a lynx. They are pretty elusive creatures. I think I must have been a naturalist in a former life and an astronomer. Did you get all your business taken care of? When are you leaving for Toronto?" He drank down the rest of his tea.

"I will need to leave on Monday morning very early but that still gives us the whole weekend together before I have to go. Maybe we can video chat with your sister tomorrow and get that out of the way, so it will give us time to be alone together." I thought that was an excellent idea. I took a few more pictures and then sat staring.

"It all seems a bit surreal." James looked at me quizzically.

"I mean meeting you when I did, becoming friends, the gala, going to Ottawa, Scotland and now in this beautiful home that has been a dream of mine for I don't know how long. I feel like I'm dreaming and I'm going to wake up and all this will have been just that, a dream. He pinched my arm softly.

"See, not a dream. I love you and I am so very happy you are here with me. I wanted this house to be all that you ever wanted, and I am happy in it with you. You make this a home for me. You made it an easy choice to move to Canada. Where you are I am." I don't know how he could be any more incredible than he already was, and I told him so.

"I hope you mean that because I seem to recall that someone was going to give me a massage and after moving all those boxes today, I think my muscles need a good massage." I looked at him and said I would give him a massage alright, yes indeed a very good one. We drank our tea, and I took more photos, even some of James. There was still a lot of daylight left and hours before dinner was ready. We decided to take a short walk into the woods and see what other things we could photograph. James got his camera out, which was way better than mine, and we went out for a walk.

He wanted to take some pictures of me with the trees and leaves that had fallen. It was easy to be with James, he never made me feel foolish so taking silly shots was fun. I put my camera down and picked up a bunch of leaves and threw them into the air. I could hear the camera clicking and clicking. There were more fun shots. There was a spot that we came up to where a tree had fallen and there was a tall part of the trunk still standing. James thought it would be good to get a photo of the two of us together near a stand of birches. He got me to stand in front of the trees and then came to stand beside me. He, of course, had a remote for his camera. We stood together in different poses and then continued walking. Sometimes James would fall behind to take a picture of a bird or squirrel. I was concentrating on trying to get a photo of a pileated woodpecker. They were a jumpy bird, so it was hard to snap one at the right time. I saw a grouse not far away and tried to get a photo of that. It was funny to watch it try to pretend it was hurt and getting away. It made me smile.

James caught up to me and I showed him the photo of the woodpecker. He never saw one like this before. We reached the ravine and went back around on the paved path. It was covered with leaves from the trees, and it was really quite pretty. I wanted to get a picture of James walking toward me. He gave me his camera and I jogged ahead a little and as he was walking toward me I started to take pictures. He had no idea that a beautiful buck came up a bit behind him and crossed the path. I was lucky that I was able to get it in one of the photos. Then he wanted to do the same with me. It took us a good bit of time to walk all the way around and back up to the house. It was a nice walk though. I hadn't unpacked my printer or laptop yet, which is where I kept all my photos, but I showed James the ones I took.

"Hey look at that. I didn't even hear him behind me. Wow what a good shot. I would love to have that one in my office here. Let me download mine and you can look at them on my tablet. It will be easier." It took a few minutes for him to download the pictures. He got some good ones of the birds and the squirrel and the ones of us were good as well.

"I like this one of us together. I'd like to put this one up in the bedroom on the table by the window. I didn't know you were taking these. Gee this one is not half bad of me. At least I'm not making a silly face." James said none of them were silly. He loved the one of me smiling at the grouse and the one where I had such peaceful look on my face.

"That one I am putting in my office as well as the close up one of us together. They turned out pretty good." There was a knock at the door. It was Jonathan letting us know that dinner would be in half an hour. We went upstairs to wash up and change into different clothes since we had been playing around with the leaves on the walk. The table was set with a pretty floral centerpiece. When we sat down, Jonathan poured us a glass of white wine and then brought out the pasta dish. It looked scrumptious. It had shrimp, muscles and even some lobster. The pasta was freshly made linguine he said, and the sauce was a white wine sauce. He hoped we would enjoy it and left the room.

"To you my darling and our new home and life together." We touched glasses and drank the wine. It was a wonderful Pinot Grigio that was quite delicious. We tasted the pasta and seafood, and it was superb. The fresh pasta made by him was so good.

"My word this is so good James. He's an excellent chef and I can't wait to try his other choices." After the walk we took, we were thoroughly enjoying the pasta. It wasn't too much for me but just enough to say I was full. Jonathan came back in to say that he had prepared an apple crumble with crème fraiche and coffee. He brought in the dishes of the dessert. I wanted a small portion because I didn't want to be too full. It was still warm, and it was so tasty.

"This is very tasty, and I would definitely like to have this at Thanksgiving if that were something you would normally have. I don't know what they have for desserts in Canada on Thanksgiving, but I really like this. It's not too heavy and the crème fraiche is excellent." Desserts on any occasion were whatever one wanted. There was of course the usual pumpkin pie but really anything was possible. We got up from the table and went out into the sunroom for a little bit. While it was still early I think I was still recovering from jet lag. We watched as the sun set in behind the trees and night started to come into the room.

"Come on James, I promised you a massage." Jonathan cleaned up and left. He was going to move into my place in a day or two, so he still lived in the city. We could see his car taillights going out the gate and the gate closing behind him. Everyone that worked here had an opener for the gate.

"We will have to talk about the security system tomorrow, so you know how it works. For the most part you shouldn't need to have it on but if while I'm away it makes you feel safer, at least you will know how to work it. It is very easy I promise. Jonathan has his code to get in as do the others. Your code is different. But I will explain all of that tomorrow. For now, I am ready for my massage." He shut off the lights and we walked arm in arm up the stairs. He went in to take a shower and I found some of the same massage oil that he used on me when we were in Scotland. I put some towels down on the bed cover. He came out of the bathroom with a towel around his waist. As he was laying down on the bed face down I took the towel away and he started to laugh.

"I hope it is going to be that kind of massage." He was still chuckling to himself but of course he knew it was going to be 'that kind of massage.' By the time I was finished, needless to say we were both relaxed. He went off to take a shower to remove the oil. As he was letting the water wash over him, I put my arms around him.

"Hope you don't mind if I join you, you know to conserve water." I took his soap and washed his back. He was leaning against the front of the shower. The motion was purposely slow and methodical.

"The second part of the massage." He was laughing but I continued to soap his body, from head to toe. When he rinsed off, I got out and took the towel to dry him off. The look in his eyes was steamy but he let me be the one to take this where it was going. I led him into the bedroom and pushed him gently back on the bed. I could tell he was enjoying every moment. I continued the massage on his chest, but this was more of a relaxation massage without oil. With each upward motion and then back, the passion in us was growing.

"And now the final part." We made love for the next while, slowly, tenderly and in no hurry to finish. We were in the house alone so there was no one to hear our cries of joy. It was the most wonderful moment I had ever experienced. James was tender and loving and a most skilled lover. We lay in each other's arms for hours, falling asleep. The sound of a buzzer woke me, and James was staring down at me.

"Good morning darling. I hope you slept as well as I did. Thank you for that spectacular massage." He was smiling from ear to ear. I kissed him and said that we should get up because the staff would be in the house shortly if they were not already. James went in to shave and then we got dressed because we planned to go for a long walk before breakfast. As we were coming down the stairs, Moira was busy with cleaning.

"Good morning Moira, it is a lovely day isn't it." She agreed smiling and said that the rest of the cleaning staff would be in shortly. We stopped in at the kitchen to let Jonathan know we were going for a walk and would have breakfast when we came back.

We decided to talk a leisurely stroll around the property. Most of the leaves were now down and the air was getting cooler. It was nice to walk hand in hand around the property. Grouse were flying off as we walked by, and blue jays were flitting from tree to tree. It took a good forty-five minutes to walk completely around at a slow pace. Back in the house, Jonathan heard us coming and put a pot of coffee for each of us on the table. We helped ourselves to a couple of cups. He then brought us in eggs benedict made with goat cheese and prosciutto with hash brown potatoes. There was freshly made toasted multi grain bread that was so delicious. I was enjoying every morsel. We took coffee out to the sunroom to cap off the wonderful breakfast.

"James why don't I give Sonya a call and see if she is free to video chat. We can get that out of the way and then enjoy the weekend since you will be leaving on Monday morning." He said it was an excellent idea. I put in a call, but she said she was going out the door to do some shopping but would call when she was back. We spent the next while sitting together looking out at the woods and enjoying the quiet.

"I need to check some emails, sorry hazard of the job, but I will be back as quickly as I can." It was fine, I didn't mind being alone and looking off into the trees. I had my camera and took some shots. A deer came right up to the window, and I was able to get off a couple of shots before it bounded away. James wanted to follow up with Mina on the emails he sent. He put in a call to her to see where things were.

"James, I am glad you called. I saw your emails and I have good news all around. The university has gladly agreed to give you a private viewing, of course, the donation you offered was a great incentive. They need to know the coordinates of her star so that they can get it all set up just before you arrive. Hans said that he has a four carat emerald with baguette diamonds on either side. He brought it by to show me and I think it is exactly what you want. I booked meetings for you for the following week and the week after or at least part of that last week. I spoke with Richard and Mark, and they said they would love to do Thanksgiving with you as they had no other plans. After Thanksgiving you are going to have to go to Germany to discuss the lab there and in Alberta with Quinn. He thinks the kiosks have great possibilities but would like to try it out in Germany to see how it goes. Unfortunately, you are going to be on the road for three weeks straight to get some things taken care of so that you can be off for Cassandra's birthday and the time over the holidays. I spoke with the owner of textile company in Scotland that makes all their own cashmere and other fabrics, and he would be happy to meet with you at your convenience to discuss the operation you want to set up. You also mentioned that you wanted to do a quick trip at the end of November to Germany and Austria to attend the Christmas markets and also to give Janet an opportunity to see the office in Germany. I made reservations for you at luxury hotel in Berlin, two executive suites of course and also a luxury hotel in Vienna. I will send you information on the Christmas markets in both cities. I think that covers all that you asked me to do but if there is anything else?" James was very pleased that everything was taken care of and thanked Mina. He had definitely lucked out when she came in for a job all those years ago.

"Mina, I know you and your family are getting together at Christmas, why don't you take them to my villa in the Turks. I will pay for you to go first class and you can spend two or three weeks there if you want. I would let you use the jet, but I will be using that to fly in Ross, Lindsay, and Ayleen, who would be very disappointed with me if she didn't get to go up in my plane." Mina laughed and said that she'd been talking to her family about the holidays and where to go. They always did a sun holiday because her parents and her husband's parents were not fond of winter.

“James thank you; I will take you up on that and we will have a wonderful time. I know that Cassandra and her friends are planning to go in April, so I can make sure that everything is in good shape for that.” James hadn’t forgotten about that trip either and said that he appreciated all she did. As he was going back out into the sunroom, Cassandra was on the phone.

“Sonya said she is back if we want to video chat with her.” James retrieved his tablet and put in the call. He said that it was nice to see her and that he was looking forward to them coming for Thanksgiving.

“It is nice to finally meet you. Cassie, sorry I know you prefer Cassandra, has talked a lot about you and we are looking forward to going. I have never flown before, so this will be quite an adventure for me. But I am really looking forward to seeing you in person and to see your new home. I hear that it is quite nice.” James spoke with her for a while longer. Sonya mentioned that her daughter Nicole and Austin would be arriving on Friday, and everyone was quite thrilled to be staying with them. We said we were looking forward to it as well and ended the call.

“You and your sister don’t look very much alike.” I said that she took after my Mom’s side while I took after my Dad’s. I showed James the new photos I took, and he laughed at how close the deer came to the house.

"I'm sure that once John puts out that trough we will see more of them. It is nice that there is such an abundant amount of does and that buck the other day was quite impressive." It was nearing lunch, and we went into the kitchen to see what Jonathan was going to make. For lunch today he was making bison steak sandwiches using the bread that he made this morning. He was making a special mustard base sauce for the sandwiches which he was going to serve with a creamy slaw. It sounded really good. We decided to take our sandwiches out to the sunroom, so Jonathan set up trays for us. Along with water, he was going to bring us more of his special tea. It was nice to sit together and enjoy the day in this very special room.

"I think this is my most favourite room in the house. I love the whole house, but this is where I think I will spend a lot of my time when I am home. I am planning to walk that paved path a lot and maybe even try to get into going up and down the ravine to work other muscles." James smiled.

"Please be careful when you are alone. I don't want you to slip if you try to go down that ravine and hurt yourself." I promised him I would always be careful. It was so nice to sit together and enjoy the silence, but I was getting a little restless and wanted to go for a walk.

"I know you want to go back to your study and work, so I am ok to go for a walk alone. But tomorrow I would like to go the art gallery in Edmonton. We have some walls that need artwork on them, and I thought we should have a look and see what they have." James kissed me and said he promised no work tomorrow. I put on my runners and a light jacket and took my camera with me. The sun was still shining brightly but it wouldn't be out for too much longer. It set pretty early at this time of the year. John and his son were working in the Quonset. The doors were open, so I could see that he was working on the trough. I stopped over to talk to them.

"Hello Max, it is very nice to meet you. John, I see you are working on the trough for the feed for the deer. Are you going to go by the feed mill and pick up the striped sunflower seed, if not I could do it? We've seen moose and I know they tend to eat the branches on trees, and I know they eat the roots of lily pads in the summer. Is there anything we can buy to also put in a trough for them? I don't want them to become used to being fed but it would be nice for them to stay long enough to get pictures." John said that they ate shrubs and lichen and bark off trees.

"I can strip some of the poplar bark off the next few trees we bring down for firewood, but they will mostly just walk through and eat what they want. I will protect the shrubs and things that are planted around the house of course, but they go pretty much where they want. James wanted to know if I hunted, and the answer is yes. Both Max and I plan to go out over the next few weekends a little north of here. We are hoping to get a moose or two since we both have tags and maybe we can get a couple of deer. That should fill the freezer in the house and even ours." I thanked him for the trough and went out on my walk. It was quiet, there wasn't even a breeze.

There were lots of red polls and purple finch flying around and the rosy grosbeaks were hanging around too. Once the bird feeders were put up on the trees near the house, they would be visiting often. I kept walking taking pictures of even the trees. There were a few shots that I hoped would look good so that I could try to paint them. I was a little more than halfway around the path and stopped to take a picture of a squirrel on a stump when a porcupine came out of the brush and startled me. It wasn't near enough to harm me, but I stumbled back and landed straight on a large branch right on my right butt cheek. I got up and it hurt like hell for a few minutes. I put my hand back and there was no blood, so I thought it would just end up being a bruise.

I hung my camera around my neck and finished walking around. It was hard to do because my butt was hurting like crazy. John and Max were still in the Quonset, and I didn't want them to see me limping, so I tried to walk as upright as I could and smiled and waved to them. I got up the steps and into the house and gingerly went upstairs. James had his head down, so I don't think he noticed me. I got into the bedroom and took off my jeans and my underwear. I wanted to have a look in the mirror to see if there was a bruise forming. I got myself positioned to look in the mirror when James came in.

"What in the hell happened? You have a very large bruise on your right side." I told him what happened and asked him to get the ointment out of the cabinet, so I could put it on to help with the bruise. He got it and told me to lay down on the bed. He carefully rubbed it on, and I tried very hard not to wince.

"This is going to be a very nasty bruise, but it is a bruise, and it will heal. It will hurt like crazy tonight though." He went into the closet and brought out a pair of my sweats to put on. At least they were loose enough not to apply any unneeded pressure on my skin.

"I feel like an idiot. I should be thankful. I guess that it was only a porcupine and I probably scared it more than it did me. I don't think I am going to be able to sit at the table for dinner at least not tonight. I can probably sit on a really soft chair in the sunroom as long as I don't put any pressure on my right side." James helped with the sweats.

"I will go and talk to Jonathan, and we can bring in tray tables and sit out there. I think it was going to be some sort of beef stir fry, so it should be easily set up out there. I'll get you an ice pack too to put on that." James went downstairs to the kitchen to have tables set up out in the sunroom. Dinner was not going to be for another hour, so I stayed in bed laying on one side with a pillow carefully tucked under my bottom, so I wouldn't roll. James came back up with some of Jonathan's tea on a tray and the ice pack. I really felt quite foolish.

"You know something like this happened to me once before only it was the door lock on my Dad's van. That got a colour purple I think even Ayleen would like." James saw that I was trying to be funny, but I could see the look of concern.

"James it's ok the ointment will help. I don't think it will be that bad." I could not have been more wrong. It was uncomfortable to sit and eat but I did and then James wanted me to go to bed. I said I wanted to have a shower before doing that and I would put on a nightshirt. He walked with me up the stairs and helped to get me undressed. I got into the shower and the warm water felt good. It was probably not the best thing for the monster bruise that was developing. I toweled myself off and put my nightshirt on. James was waiting to put more ointment on and see that I got into bed ok.

"Can I get you anything, more tea, a book to read, anything." I had my e-reader in the table on my side of the bed. I said I was fine and if he had other things to do, I would be ok alone. He reluctantly went back downstairs to his study.

The bruise was pretty big, and it was swollen but he knew that Cassandra was trying to downplay it. It was an accident, so he wasn't going to get all crazy and have John go out and remove every branch that was laying on the ground. He would have but he wasn't going to. He got back to what he was doing when she came in limping. He asked John earlier to find someone locally who had a Percheron horse and carriage. Cassandra said that her Dad loved Percheron, so he was going to try his best to get that breed. John said that there were lots of people not too far away that had Percheron, but they did not have the type of carriage he was looking for. James found one and showed it to John when Cassandra was on her walk.

"Please look into getting this and asking the owner of the horse if he can keep it at his place until Christmas Eve. Then I would like him to bring it here so that I can take Cassandra on a sleigh ride. If he has to put it on some sort of trailer to bring it that's fine. You can get him to unload at the side of the Quonset. There is more than enough room there and if you move a few things around in the Quonset perhaps he can put the horse in there until we are ready. Do whatever you need to, to make this work. I also wanted to see how the bird feeders were coming along. I know Cassandra wants to have them up as soon as possible." John said they were done and already hung up at the back like he asked and filled with bird seed. Max would make sure that they were filled at all times.

Now he was working on what to get her for Christmas. She already said she didn't want a lot of things. Because Ross, Lindsay and Ayleen were coming, this was going to be more about them than her and especially about Ayleen. James texted Ross to find out what they wanted for Christmas and what they could get for Ayleen. Since they would be coming on his plane there was no worry about how much they were taking back. Ross gave ideas for Lindsay and Ayleen and a couple of things for himself. Lindsay sent a list of things for Ross and Ayleen and a couple of things for herself.

They had a home which Cassandra bought for them and new vehicles. Perhaps he could get them newer models, but those would be waiting for them when they got back. He could easily go overboard on all of them, but he knew that he had to be respectful of Cassandra's wishes and concerns for the other grandparents. Cassandra didn't want them to be spoiled and James had to agree with that, but he could give them the things that they could never afford before. He knew that Cassandra had trust funds for them and perhaps he could bump those up. He would look into that when he went to Toronto. He would try to stick to the list even though he would have done more.

He looked at his calendar for next week and part of the following week. He had Mina make reservations at the hotel he had stayed at for a couple of nights for Richard and Mark. She confirmed that was done. He would mention to Richard that he was picking up Cassandra's sister and niece in Ottawa to bring them back with them on the plane. Hopefully, he wouldn't object too strongly to the obvious set up. He saw pictures of Sonya and her daughter at Cassandra's condo. Pictures that were obviously taken on some occasion because they were dressed up. He wasn't sure about Mark, but he thought that Richard and Sonya would hit it off. Jonathan came in to say that dinner was ready if he wanted to bring Cassandra down. James went up to get her. She was reading when he went in.

"Jonathan says dinner is ready. Let me get your robe and I will help you." It was a little awkward trying to get out of bed but once I was out I was fine. James helped me into my robe and slippers, and we went downstairs. Jonathan put trays in front of each chair. I could see that the bird feeders were up and loads of birds were at them. The food smelled great, but I was actually not very hungry. I ate as much as I could. Jonathan came to get my plate and I explained that it was excellent, but I wasn't hungry. He understood perfectly and said he would bring me another cup of special tea, a different one this time.

"He's really amazing with all these different teas he has. You know if there isn't anything else like it on the market it might be worthwhile to see if we could do that. I mean he could make the teas in the kitchen here and package them. Keep it simple of course in foil pouches so they stay fresh. Do samples maybe at a kiosk in a couple of the big malls here and see if they are a hit. It would give Jonathan his own product, but you could get a share of it because you could put up the money to get it started. We'd have to find out how many special blends he has though. It would have to be more than two. What do you think?" James pondered the idea and thought that it could work.

"I will speak with Jonathan when he comes back in and when Mark comes we can figure out a marketing strategy, but a share of the profits will go to you. Your idea and that is more than half of any business venture. I don't mind putting up the money, but you get the larger profit from it not me. I will agree to it if you agree to those terms." I said that I would and when Jonathan came back in James asked him how many different blends he had and were they his very own creation.

"I have about twenty plus different brews that I do up and they are all mine. I try different combinations until I find one that I like, and I know others will. But why do you ask?" James told him what we had been talking about and he became quite excited.

"Really, are you serious? I have thought about this so often. My mother used to love tea and I would try making her different ones even when I very young. This is awesome, and I can't believe you are doing this for me." James explained that they would discuss it further at Thanksgiving when his director of marketing would be here. They could work out a bunch of details then, but he wanted Jonathan to have samples of all the teas available for that meeting.

"I will be a guinea pig Jonathan and you can try each one of them on me. I will tell you honestly whether I think they are good. I think it will be fun." Jonathan went to the kitchen to start working on the teas. I had my camera beside me and started to take picture of the birds.

"Thank you, James, for agreeing to bankroll this idea. I know there are lots of tea places out there and some that do just specialty teas, but this would an interesting venture. I'm sure it will take off, but if it doesn't, I think it was worth a try, don't you?" James said the test run would give him a better sense of whether it would work.

"Let's see what happens then ok. I think it might take off, but we will see. I don't see it being a billion-dollar idea though, so I hope you don't have your heart set on that. It might end up being something local that, for Jonathan, makes him a good bit of cash, but we shall see." I agreed that we would wait to see how things went.

"Are you going to be ok to go to the gallery tomorrow or do you want to put that off for another time?" It didn't hurt to walk as much as it did. It still hurt to sit on my right side, but I thought that maybe walking would be good.

"I'm sure I'll be fine. I'll have a look at the bruise when I go to bed tonight. It will probably look a lot worse than it really is. I'd still like to go if you are still good to go. We don't have to spend hours and hours though. Maybe we should decide which walls we want to get paintings for and then focus on those. Does that sound ok with you?" James said it was a good idea. We sat for several more hours watching the birds. A few deer came through to have the seed that was in the trough that John put out while we were eating. The sun was setting, and it was so perfect sitting here. Jonathan left so it was James and I in the house.

"Before we go tomorrow, I want to walk you through the security system. We have an app through my company in Toronto that I will download for you and that way you can do everything from your phone if you need to. Maybe we can look to leave around 10:30 tomorrow morning, have lunch in the city and then get back here for 2:00. It will give me a chance to look over a few emails, yes, I know I said I wouldn't but then I can at least devote my Sunday to you before I leave. I promise to do that ok?" It was ok with me of course and I wasn't worried if he had to work Sunday. I was thinking maybe I would try a painting.

"I think maybe on Sunday I will try to do a painting from one of the photos I took. I can set my things up out here where there is lots of light. That way if you do have to handle some work you won't feel so guilty." He laughed and said he would enjoy watching me and perhaps he would read while I painted. I've been thinking since returning from Scotland what I could get James for Christmas. I mean what do you buy for someone who literally has everything he wants. Fenella showed me some pictures of when James was a child when his parents were still alive. There was one photo of them that was taken where James had proposed to me. Fenella said that James was around ten at the time and they were sitting close together on a picnic blanket. It was a family day at the estate, and everyone was on picnic blankets and Fenella took the photo.

She gave me a copy of it to have and I thought it would be a nice idea to have it painted. I would have to talk to the person who was showing me some tips and tricks for my paintings and see if she knew of a really good portrait painter that was local. While James was back in his study I gave her a call. She gave me the name of a very well-known portrait painter in the city. I contacted him next and asked if he could do a painting. I didn't want a huge one, something of a decent size that I could put in James's office, so he could look at it and remember that day. He asked me to email him the picture first, so he could see if he could work from it.

I emailed the picture to the painter who looked at it and said it was a pretty clear photo and thought he could paint from it easily. I saw other portraits he did, and they were really spectacular, so I had no hesitation when he said his price, which was quite high, but this was for James. He promised to have it done the week before Christmas which was actually good because I didn't want it around the house for too long just in case. I was sure that James wasn't the sort to want to know what his presents were just as I was not, but it would have been pretty obvious when he saw the gift what it could be. I discussed with James not to buy me lots and lots of gifts. We agreed on a few and that we would make sure to donate to the various charities in the area and in the city.

"I think I am going to head up to bed, are you going to come or stay here for a bit." James said he would come with me and make sure I got into bed ok. He would probably go and work for a bit in his study though. I had no problem going up the stairs. It twinged a bit but that was because I was moving the muscle. I went into the bathroom to have a look in the mirror to see how big the bruise was.

"Holy crap, that is bigger than I thought, but it was only a bruise and thankfully not a blood blister." James came in and I think the extent of the bruise worried him.

"Darling that is a lot bigger, do you think maybe you should see your doctor." I said it was ok but if it got very much bigger that I would look into going next week.

"The blood is not pooling into a blister so that is a good thing. It is a really nasty bruise, and it is going to look really ugly for several weeks, but I will get it checked if I think it is worsening, I promise." With that James helped me to get into bed and laying on the left side and putting a pillow behind my back so I wouldn't roll.

"If you are ok now I will head downstairs and I will try not to wake you when I come to bed." I gave him a kiss and said good night. He was such a wonderful caring man. I took out my cell and sent off a few texts.

Back in his study James looked through the material Mina sent him about Aruba. It was a beautiful place, and he could see why Cassandra wanted to go there. He liked the suite at the resort. He would ask Mina to book it for ten days and for some special things to be in the room when they arrived. This is where they were going to spend the first part of their honeymoon. Since they were so close to Curaçao, he asked her to book him ten days at a private villa as well. It was part of the Kingdom of the Netherlands and somewhere that he always wanted to go himself.

History of places always intrigued him, and this island had lots of rich history to it. Aruba was also part of the Kingdom of the Netherlands so it would be a bonus to also check out the history on that island as well. He hadn't asked Cassandra if she knew how to scuba dive, but he did recall her saying that she didn't like to go out on big water when it was choppy. It was a place that he had on his list to go scuba diving and he could always go with a guide for safety reasons. He was a skilled diver, but he never took chances.

He wanted to take Cassandra to his villa in the Turks. That was a place he bought many years ago where he would go to completely relax. He made it a rule that he would not do any business while he was there. He would go diving there with Duncan a lot when the two of them had put in long hours and months working.

Family members had gone as well when he was there, and he always had a good time. When it was only him and Duncan, women that would walk by their private beach would flirt outrageously with him. But they were either way too young or models and he wasn't interested. His thoughts went to the woman upstairs. He was scared when he saw that Cassandra had hurt herself. He'd never felt that way before. The love he felt for her was unlike anything he ever felt before.

He also asked Mina to find out if Gerard had completed Cassandra's wedding dress and he would arrange to fly to Scotland with Cassandra for a fitting in the middle of March. He would have to use that fitting to make sure the other dress he was having made for their Aruba trip fit her properly. He decided to tell her where they were going before she tried on the dress. With that squared away he went upstairs after shutting all the lights off. He went out to the sunroom for just a moment and there, not ten feet from the window, was that magnificent buck. They looked at one another and then the buck walked away. Cassandra was fast asleep, so he carefully crawled into bed and pulled the covers over him. He would have cuddled up to her, but he didn't want to risk hitting the bruise.

Chapter 7

It was morning and I was a little stiff getting out of bed. I tried not to move around too much so I was not completely relaxed. James was already up and downstairs. I put on my robe and my slippers and went down to the kitchen. James and Jonathan were talking and when he saw me come in he came over to me.

"How do you feel this morning? Is it still really sore? Do you still want to go to the gallery? Maybe we can sit in the sunroom, and you can put an ice pack on it again and maybe that will help a bit. Jonathan will bring in breakfast and coffee. The trays are still there from last night." I felt not too bad actually. It was hurting less but I was sure that the ice pack would help. It was a bright sunny day but cool. Jonathan brought in my coffee and set it on the tray. This morning we were having pancakes with maple syrup and some breakfast sausages that were freshly made at a local butcher. I asked for two pancakes which Jonathan said he would bring shortly. There were lots of birds at the feeders and the squirrels were busily trying to get into them to no avail. It was very peaceful watching them. Jonathan brought our coffee and James poured me a cup.

"You are being so sweet. I'm really not used to being pampered like this, believe me. I love it, but I am really ok. It isn't hurting as much, and I am sure in a day or two I won't even feel it. The purple is full blown now but it will eventually turn an ugly green. The coffee is good. How long did you stay up? I never even heard you come into bed. I must have been out like a light." He laughed because I was definitely out.

"It was late. I was finishing up a few details that I wanted to get out of the way, so I wouldn't have to wonder about them down the road. I love to pamper you, but I promise not to go overboard. I'm going to leave early tomorrow, probably before you are up. I want to get my meetings started as soon as possible in the morning. I will be there until Thursday of the following week. I hope you won't mind if I don't come home on the weekend. It will give me a chance to spend some time with Richard and Mark, kind of float the idea of meeting your sister and niece. If I don't have to run back on the weekend, I can get a lot more done. Is that ok with you? I will come back if you want me to." He was such a sweet man to be so concerned.

"James, I will be fine. I have no worries with you staying over the weekend. You are taking time off before Thanksgiving and a bit afterwards, so I am ok on my own. I promise you and I promise not to get startled by anymore wild animals." He knew I was teasing, and we both laughed. Jonathan brought in our breakfast and had another of his special teas for me to try. This one he said had a hint of lavender and a few other things in as well. It was a very pretty colour and it smelled wonderful. I took a sip, and it was so very good. I was trying to make out what the other ingredients were, but I couldn't.

"I don't need to know all the ingredients in fact I think it is better that you don't say what they are. That way nobody can copy it. It is really good, thank you." I dug into my pancakes, and they were very good. Nice and fluffy but once Jonathan was out of ear shot I told James that his were better.

"I'm not just saying that either. I do think yours are better. These are second best." He appreciated the compliment, and we sat eating and watching the birds and the deer.

"I saw that beautiful buck last night before I came to bed. He was standing right there beside that big birch. We stood looking at one another and then he walked off. Pretty nice to see wildlife so close like that." It was amazing and that is why I loved to live in the country.

Breakfast over I went up to shower and put on a pair of wool pants with one of the cashmere sweaters I brought back. This was a beautiful green, so I put on the star necklace and earrings, a little makeup and a spritz of my favourite French perfume and went back downstairs. James was waiting for me at the bottom of the stairs. We went out, got in his car that he had pulled up to the front door and drove to the gallery. Traffic was light, and I was glad that James knew where he was going.

"I haven't been in the downtown core since I retired, and it has changed so much. I'm glad you know where you are going. The art gallery is relatively new and quite a show piece, so I am looking forward to going in. Have you got anything in mind that you might be looking at buying." James looked online at what the gallery had and said that there were a few pieces he wanted to look at but didn't want to sway me so wouldn't say which. We parked in the parkade and went over to the gallery. So many changes to the downtown that I would have gotten lost. Walking through the gallery we stopped at several paintings and mulled over if they would suit us.

"I like this charcoal on paper, they are quite different. Perhaps one or two of these would look good in the living room." James agreed, and they were a couple of the choices that he picked. He also liked a few abstract ones which when he showed them to me I thought were really nice.

"I think these will look nice in the hallway upstairs and I think I might like this blue one in my study. What do you think." I thought they were all perfect, but I thought the blue would look better in the living room. James spoke to the gallery agent that was with us and the paintings we picked out would be taken down, wrapped and we could take them with us. We walked around for a bit more while that was being done.

With the paintings safely stowed in the trunk of the car we drove home. As we were driving James got a call from Duncan who wanted to know if we wanted to meet them for lunch at Jason's. He looked at me and I nodded yes. I called home to let Jonathan know we were eating out. We got to the restaurant just before noon. Duncan and Roxie were pulling into the parking lot as we got to the front door, so we waited for them.

"Hi, you two, how have things been going?" We went in and Jason seated us at our usual table. I sat down gingerly, and Roxie asked what was up.

"I was out taking pictures and a porcupine startled me and I jumped back and fell ass over tea kettle and hit my right butt cheek on a very large protruding branch. Ended up with a whopper of a bruise but it is getting better although it is still a little tender." I asked if they made any decisions on the house, and I could tell from their excitement that they had.

"We looked at the house the other day and it is really very nice. Nicer than anything I've ever had. It has four bedrooms and four and a half baths. Duncan has promised he will get a cleaning staff in a few times a week to keep it clean because I don't think I could handle it all. You will have to come and see it once the deal is closed. Duncan has been working on getting that done so we can move our things in as quickly as possible before we have to go down south. It looks like it will be done, and we can head down after Thanksgiving but after he comes back from Scotland. I am really looking forward to it. It has a nice large yard that backs up onto a wooded area. Nobody will be building behind us, and the neighbours are far enough away so that we are not passing sugar through the windows. Duncan is having painters come in to repaint the place as I'm not keen on the colours and he wants the carpeting taken out because he has dust allergies. That's ok with me and makes it easier to keep clean. He wanted to hire someone to do the cooking, but I love to cook. Maybe in a year or two I won't want to do the cooking so we can deal with it then." I was so very happy for them both and was really looking forward to seeing their home. Jason came in with the menus and water. He asked if we wanted anything to drink. Roxie and I declined but James and Duncan had a whisky. While Roxie and I talked, Duncan and James talked about work stuff.

"So are you looking forward to having your sister and her family for Thanksgiving. How is the house. I'll have to come over next week and see how everything is." I said that I was very much looking forward to Thanksgiving and my sister and her family coming but James was having a few colleagues come to dinner as well.

“Listen, why not after lunch come over and we can show you the house now that it is finished.” It was ok with Roxie if Duncan wanted to.

“Of course, we would love to come over. We would have been by sooner, but we’ve been doing so much running around trying to get things organized. Roxie and I would love that very much.” We had a wonderful lunch and then drove over to the house. We brought in the paintings as they were not too big and there were only four of them. Duncan and Roxie pulled up beside the car and we went in together.

“Wow this is really very beautiful. My what a grand entrance and I love this tile and the hardwoods, wow. But I really want to see that sunroom and then we can go to all the other rooms.” Duncan and James followed not far behind. James put the paintings in his office for now and would hang them later. We walked out into the sunroom and Roxie was thrilled.

“Wow look at how pretty this looks with the woods back here. Reminds me a little bit of my country place. Look at the bird feeders and all the birds and you have a feeding trough out there. How cool is all this. I love the furniture in here. It is nice and cozy, not too sterile. I love it in this room. Do you know where you are going to put the tree for Christmas? I just love everything. You’ll probably here me say wow a lot but you deserve this kid, you deserve it.” We hadn’t decided on the tree yet but probably just to the left of the door entering into the sunroom. We took them from room to room and into the kitchen. I introduced Roxie and Duncan to Jonathan. Then we went upstairs to all the bedrooms. When we went into the room James had designed for Ayleen, Roxie laughed.

"She is going to love this room. She's a lucky little girl to have a Grandpa who loves her and would do this. You deserve this kiddo. I would love this room." We laughed because Roxie actually would love the room and we went back down to James's study and to the downstairs where there was a workout area a big screen tv, movie room, games room, dry sauna, and wine cellar.

"What I like about this is that the windows are huge down here and you don't feel like you are in a dark basement. On those cold winter days or rainy days, it will be nice to exercise down here. James has a bunch of weights over in that area. I will use them but not to the degree he does. I only want to maintain my muscle tone." We showed them the wine room, where James had it pretty well stocked. Of course, there was lots of his own whisky and some bottles of bubbly.

"It's a pretty spectacular home and I am a very lucky person. James is so wonderful I can't even begin to tell you just how wonderful he is." Roxie hugged me, and we walked back upstairs. I asked if they could stay for tea, but they had to get going. Roxie had some running around to do still for Thanksgiving and she was trying to give Duncan an indication of where things were. For now, he was ok with Roxie driving but he hoped that he would get the knack of the streets and places before too long. We walked them back out to their car and waved as they drove off. We went back in, and James got out a hammer and hanging materials.

"Ok so let's decide where these are going. We can get them up for now and if we decide to move them we can." We hung up each one of the paintings and then went out into the sunroom to have tea. I had tea and James had a glass of wine.

"If it is ok with you, I think I would like to call Christina and see if she is free next week to come and help me decorate the house for Thanksgiving. I'd like to leave it more up to her to choose since she has a feeling for our taste." James was totally onboard with that.

"We should let her do it for Christmas and New Year's too. I know you want to decorate the tree yourself and that's what I like too, so maybe we can get her to do everywhere else. It's a big job and I think you should supervise and not try to do any of the actual décor. I don't want you to fall and hurt yourself." I said I was fine with supervising and would call Christina Monday morning. But the rest of today and tomorrow was for us.

"I'd like to go over and see if the seniors want to go for a walk. I don't want them to think I abandoned them. Do you want to come too, or do you have something else to do?" James said he would like to go so we got in his car and drove over. I still had a key to get in as I'd given Jonathan the spare I had. He moved in a day ago, but I was not going to go up to my unit. He was bringing my mail over and that worked out well. There were a few people in the lobby and when we came in they were so glad to see us. Apparently, Mrs. O'Leary had been taking them out for walks and the equipment in the exercise room had been updated and a number of the seniors were in there as well. It was wonderful to see them so happy and continuing to be active.

James and I took out those who were ready to go for a walk anyway. They were all walking at a good pace, and we talked as we walked. I was happy that Mrs. O'Leary was doing this for them and perhaps that is why James chose the O'Leary's to manage the place. The ladies loved James and were quite happy to walk with him and talk to him. It made me smile and I saw that he had a grin on his face too. We walked for about two kms and then back. It was a nice enough day for late September, and we had a good time. James and I waved goodbye and got back in the car.

"It feels good to know there is someone there to keep them moving. I'm pretty sure that was you who made that happen, so I thank you for that. At least I won't have to worry about them. I'll go over from time to time to keep tabs on them and see how they are doing. My butt is actually feeling much better now." Back home, James put the car in the garage, and we went for a long walk on the paved path. No cameras or taking pictures only the two of us walking hand in hand and enjoying the afternoon. It was nice to see the changes in the property from fall to preparing for winter. But there was a decided chill in the air. I hoped that snow would hold off until well into December but that never happened. It was about an hour or so until dinner, so we went to sit in the sunroom.

"James, we should discuss where we want the tree for Christmas. Have you given it any thoughts? I know we will get a fresh one but since we don't have anything here, we should think about how big and where." We walked back and forth and decided that between the door coming into the sunroom and the doors going out to the wrap around veranda on the left would be best. It was not near any heat source and there were lots of plugs to choose from. The furniture that was there could be easily moved and put in another room for the holidays. My phone buzzed at that moment, and I looked to see who it was. It was the artist about the painting of James and his parents. He selected a frame for the painting and wanted to know if I was ok with it. I texted back that I was and put my phone down.

"Anything important?" I said yes but it was a surprise so not to ask more questions. He smiled and didn't. We decided that a ten-foot tree would work best, and I told James where I always got mine in the Grove. He would look into getting in touch with the person who sold them so that we could arrange to get a tree that was fresh and not cut down weeks before. I went into the kitchen to ask Jonathan for some more of his lavender tea. He was getting the elk chops ready for dinner that he was going to have ready in an hour. He said he would bring out the tea shortly.

"We are having elk chops for dinner tonight. Can't say as I have ever had them. I'll be interested to see how Jonathan prepares them." After about five minutes Jonathan brought out my tea. James poured himself a glass of red wine. There were more colourful birds at the feeders.

"Birds are fascinating don't you think. I love to watch shows on tv and it always struck me the vivid colours of the different birds. The intense blues, reds, oranges, greens, and purples. So beautiful to see. I love all colours in nature and when you do get that textile company going, maybe try to look at the colours in nature for inspiration. I know you are not going to be doing the actual dyeing of the raw material, but it is a thought. I am sure that every manufacturer out there thinks the same way. You have been in Toronto in the fall and noticed the maple trees, the oranges that they get. It is the most beautiful colour of orange and when it is tinged still with that leaf green colour, it is amazing. I think an orange cashmere sweater with a dark green leather pant suit would be amazing. But I am already thinking of a fashion show. Sorry, I tend to get caught up in the moment." James didn't want me to apologize. He loved that I could come up with something and visualize its process from start to finish.

"It is what I do a lot of the time myself when I am trying to think what the consumers might be wanting. I like the idea of doing a fashion show at some point. I think once we have a lot of products we could certainly do something, perhaps even in the building. Would be kind of fun actually but that is a bit further down the road. I would like it though if you would write these ideas down and keep them. Since cashmere never goes out of style nor leather, I think that would be an interesting combination. Although using real leather is a bit tricky these days with the groups that are against it. Maybe you could fly some of your ideas by Gerard when you see him in March. Maybe get him a little buzzed about the idea." It was a wonderful thought, and I would definitely start writing things down. Gerard seemed to be able to pick up how I wanted things to look, and he wasn't offended in the slightest by it. But doing a line might be a bit different.

"Perhaps we could convince him to come up with some designs and he could put them in one of his shows or perhaps you could hire some local designers and Gerard could work with them. I agree, kind of exciting to think about. I presume you will find someone who has an extensive knowledge in the use of dyes. It would be fun to kick around colour ideas with that person." Jonathan came out to say that dinner was ready. I took my tea in, and James brought his wine. I put my teacup in the kitchen and asked Jonathan for a small glass of the red wine James was having. He did so and then brought in the meal.

"This looks very enticing. I can see that this is a blackberry sauce but what else is with it." Jonathan said that it was a blackberry port sauce with the elk chops, which were pretty big, and served with a celeriac mash and steamed broccoli. The flavor of the meat with the sauce was so delicious. The rest of the evening was quiet, and we made it an early night.

The next morning the skies were a bit gray, and the air cooled even more. James was already up and down having his coffee in the sunroom. I showered, got dressed and went down to join him. We had no plans for the day, so it was jeans and a warm sweater. I still had to pinch myself every day believing that this was my home too. James had his camera out and was taking some photos. I don't know how I got so lucky to have this man come into my life. He was kind, considerate, good looking, and so many other things that I could not have believed it. I could see that he was taking pictures of a deer, and as I got closer I could see it was the big buck he mentioned before. He'd been staring at James for a long time but when he saw me, his focus moved to my movement. I stood still because I didn't want to ruin the moment. James put his camera down. He must have gotten the photos he wanted. I went into the kitchen to grab myself a mug of coffee and went out into the sunroom.

"You were up early. I didn't even hear you get out of bed." He got up to give me a kiss.

"How is the bruise? Yes, my phone kept buzzing and I didn't want it to wake you up and since I promised no work today, I had to at least look to see if it was urgent. It wasn't so I came down and grabbed some coffee and waited to see if I could get some good shots. The pileated woodpecker was back. I guess Max hung up a suet ball which he or she was feasting on earlier. The big buck came back, and I got some photos of him as well." I said that I saw the buck. He was quite a nice one.

"My bruise is healing very nicely, and it doesn't hurt at all, well at least not very much. I'm going to miss you like crazy for the next week or so, but I know that you have a business to run, and I can't keep you all to myself. I think I will use the time to go to the spa and have a facial and maybe a massage and mani/pedi. I texted Christina this morning to see if she can come by first thing tomorrow and she said she would love to. I mentioned we would like her to decorate for Thanksgiving and she said she had lots of ideas. So that should be done by the end of the week." Jonathan came in at that moment to say that breakfast would be ready in about half an hour. It gave us more time to have more coffee and to talk. James was listening, but I could tell that his thoughts were preoccupied. He looked pensive.

"James is everything ok you look a million miles away." He was thinking about us and our home and how it all came about.

"Don't misunderstand me, I am not regretting anything, really I am not. My heart is filled with such love and joy that you are in my life. I know that I have family in Scotland, but I never thought that I would have a 'family' if you know what I mean. I have been so busy with my business, building it up more and more that I never really thought I was missing out, but since I have met you and Ross, Lindsay, and Ayleen, I realize that my life is very full now and being in this house, this home with you, knowing that your sister and her family are going to be here in just over a week, getting to know them and then having Ross come at Christmas, I just feel really blessed." I could see a tear escape and I went to him and sat on his lap and hugged him. We stayed like that for several minutes.

"I am happy that you are happy. I never thought, ever, that I could find someone like you. I mean I have dreamt of having someone with all your wonderful qualities, but I never thought I would be so lucky to have you actually in my life. I think that where we both are in our stage of life; it came at the perfect time. We still have things to discover about each other, but I think that is a good thing. I love that we talk to each other about things, and it means so much to me that I can trust you and that you respect me. I know that you would love to shower me with things every day, but you know that is not who I am. I don't need that sort of thing to know that you love me. I don't want to get 'used' to that sort of thing. I want it to always be something special. I know that you understand what I am saying, and I know that you know that I love you so much and I want us to be happy." James hugged me and said he loved me too and that our life together was going to be all that we wanted it to be. Jonathan came in at that moment to say that breakfast was ready. This morning it was Spanish omelets with more of Jonathan's freshly made multi grain bread. After breakfast, James said he wanted to talk to John about a few things. I decided to give Janet a call to see how things were going with her.

"Well, hi it has been a while since we spoke. How are things going with the two of you? I have to say I am so enjoying my job with James. It is such a joy to do this job and everyone at his office is being so wonderful. So, tell me, how was the trip, how is the new home?" It was hard to know where to begin. It was all so wonderful. I was happy to hear that she was enjoying her new job.

"You deserve a good job, not that your other one wasn't good but at least now you have a great pension, and much better pay. The house is so amazing; James is so amazing. I don't even know where to begin about the trip, the engagement everything. But we will be seeing each other at the end of November for the trip to Germany and Austria. I never thought I would be flying there to get Christmas ornaments of all things. But anyway, I had a mishap and fell on a big branch on my ass and bruised my right butt cheek. It got to be incredibly big, but it is starting to go away. James was wonderful and pampered me like crazy. I never thought I would be so lucky to find someone like him. I mean I wasn't even looking or thinking about it, but he is the most amazing person." Janet was thrilled that my life was so much better.

"We are getting the interior decorator in this week to decorate for Thanksgiving and then she will do Christmas and New Year's. James is picking Sonya and Rhonda up Thursday before Thanksgiving and bringing them back. Nicole and Austin will be here on the Friday. They will leave on the Monday because they have to get back to work on Tuesday." We talked for another twenty minutes and then she had to run because she was watching her grandkids.

I put in a call to Christelle but there was no answer. I changed into some workout clothes and went downstairs to get in a workout. I hadn't really been taxing myself, so I wanted to work up a good sweat. I was well into my work out when James came downstairs. He said he was going to change and work out as well. I wasn't a runner, but I walked fairly fast but today it was the climber and elliptical. I wanted to really work the muscles in my legs, butt and back. My right side was still sore, but I wasn't going to let that keep me from working out. James started out on the treadmill running. I then switched to some weights working out my upper arms and chest. As I was winding down, James was switching to the heavier weights.

Watching him workout was, to say the least, stimulating. He didn't quite have a six pack, but I didn't care. I was never impressed by men who were muscle bound. He was very well built, and he was nice to look at. James had a dry heat sauna put in, so I thought that I would take a quick shower and head in. I went into the bathroom next to the sauna, stripped off my sweaty clothes and jumped into the shower. I could hear James pumping away on the weights. I wrapped a towel around myself and went into the sauna. The red light in the sauna made it peaceful and serene. I laid my towel down and then laid on it. The heat felt great on my body. After about twenty minutes, James came in. Dripping wet from the shower and just a towel around his waist. He was devastatingly handsome, and I could feel my body reacting to him. He removed his towel and stretched out on the bench below me. I put my hand down to touch his body and he pulled me down to him.

"James, really sex in the sauna." He laughed as I laid on top of him.

"Our house, we have sex wherever we damn well please." I needed no further invitation. I laid on top of him, his hands caressing my body. It didn't take long for our bodies to react. The heat from sauna was making me feel incredibly aroused. I leaned down to James and kissed him. We have had very passionate love making sessions, but this was totally erotic. I wanted to stay on top bringing us both to ecstasy, but James put me under him.

"Woman you drive me mad with passion. I cannot get enough of you. I want you all the time and when you are like this I go crazy for you." We couldn't contain the passion in us. It was fast, unbridled, and exquisite. We both cried out and held each other for a moment and then sat beside each other catching our breath. I was still very much aroused.

"It must be being in this sauna, but I am so wanting to do that again. I feel like a horny little twenty-year-old." He laughed and said he would need some time to recoup but he loved my passion. I knew James needed time to recover but I couldn't help myself. I straddled him as he sat catching his breath, kissing him softly and teasing him, rubbing against him. I felt completely uninhibited for the first time in my life.

"I can't resist you, see what you do to me." James was more than ready but this time it was slow, burning and very passionate. We left the sauna and went into the shower. We put on the robes that were there and went upstairs. We could not stop touching each other but we had to get dressed. It was nearly lunch, and we knew that Jonathan was serving soup and sandwiches.

"Are you sure you don't want to make love again. I mean the soup won't spoil and the sandwiches won't either." James laughed but said he would take me up on my offer tonight. We went downstairs arm in arm.

"I adore you Cassandra. You are incredible and so damn sexy, but I need to check on the flight in the morning to make sure things are going as planned." We went into the dining room and Jonathan brought in the soup and sandwiches. It was a wonderful tomato and basil bisque and was very delicious. The small sandwiches were a variety of chicken salad, roast beef and horseradish and ham and cheese. James ate greedily. Lunch was very good, and we went out to the sunroom. Jonathan came in to tell us that dinner was going to be lobster rolls, crab cakes with a tossed salad and wild rice for James. I quit eating rice a very long time ago, but

James loved wild rice. Jonathan found a fish market that got fresh seafood in every Tuesday and Saturday.

"Lobster rolls I haven't had those in a very long time. I love them, and I can't wait to try Jonathan's version. What would you like to do this afternoon?" He thought for a moment and said he wanted to go for a drive after he checked on things.

"Where do you want to drive to?" He wanted to take me shopping at the mall. He knew I would try to resist but he wanted to go and buy me some things. I could see that it was going to be pointless to argue. After we finished eating and James checked on what he needed to, I went upstairs to get my handbag and James went to pull the car out. I grabbed a jacket and went out to the car.

"James, I really don't need to buy a lot of clothes, not right now anyway. I could do this while you were away." He knew all that, but he wanted to go with me and pamper me a little. He knew I would be reluctant, but he wanted to spoil me a little.

"I know, I know you can do all of this yourself, but I want to spend time with you, and I really want to do this. We can buy as much or as little as you like but I want to spoil you so please let me." I didn't argue with him. He was doing it out of love and nothing more. We got to the mall and went up to the top floor. After going into five or six shops, and after having tried on many different things, I came away with five new cocktail dresses, three new tops, a skirt, a vest which we both really liked, four pairs of suede booties, three pairs of high heels, three pairs of flats, a coat, eight pairs of dress pants, a very pretty teal gown, and some lingerie which I would not try on in the store and parade out in front of James. That would be for at home later. James would have bought me ten times more, but he knew he was pushing his luck.

"I have an idea, why don't you bring Sonya, Rhonda, and Nicole shopping on Saturday morning. The meal isn't going to be until Sunday. It will give me a chance to get to know Austin and I'm pretty sure we can find something to do. I think the ladies would like to go shopping knowing you are going to pay for it. Just remember to use the card I gave you. It will always be at the credit limit it was before." I knew Sonya liked shopping. I wasn't sure about Rhonda or Nicole, but they could always pick up something to wear for the meal on Sunday.

On the drive home, it started to rain and was almost a snow rain mix. It was coming a bit earlier than I wanted. I hoped that we would get some nicer weather before it got nasty. We'd been out shopping a little longer than what we expected, and it was very close to 5:00 when we went through the front door. James and I took all the bags upstairs and while I was putting everything away, he went downstairs. Dinner wasn't going to be for another hour. With everything hung up and put away, I went down to find James in the sunroom with a glass of white wine and one for me as well.

"Thank you for the shopping spree. You know we have got things arranged for Thanksgiving, but we have never discussed Halloween. I have no idea if kids will come down this far. I don't know if you like that sort of thing or not. We could always arrange to leave candy with John and Moira and let them give it out. What do you think?" James hadn't thought about it to be honest. He was never involved with Halloween because he travelled so much. It might be a nice to have them come up to the house.

"I've never handed out candy because I'm always travelling. We can give it a shot once and see how it goes. Are there any rules to this sort of thing?" I was happy he was going to do it.

"Well not really, they generally start to come around 6:30. That's when the little ones come out. I have noticed some kids in the subdivision up the road and I am sure they will come in. In past years, I've had as few as nine and as many as forty but that was in a more rural area. There are lots of houses in closer proximity, so we could end up with a lot. I don't know but I am one to always be prepared. I find that the older children who really shouldn't be going around, do so around 8:30. We can set an hour when we close the gate, but we'd have to leave a sign saying, 'out of candy' or something. I don't like it when fifteen and sixteen-year old's come around. If we have anything left over we can send it with Max, Marlene, and Julie for them to give out at school. We can put out some pumpkins and then see what sort of crowd we get. How are your pumpkin decorating skills? We can always get Christina to give us a hand. I'm sure she has done a pumpkin or two in her day." James thought it sounded like fun and was actually looking forward to it. The wine was excellent. The birds were fliting about, and deer were off in the distance.

"James, does it bother you that I don't ask a lot of questions about your businesses? Sometimes I think that maybe you don't think I'm interested. I am but I also know that you deal with some pretty secret stuff, and I know you can't talk about it." He took a drink of his wine and reflected.

"No, it doesn't bother me. You have shown interest in some things, those things that will be taking place here and that is fine. Yes, I do deal with some very secret things, and I know you know I can't talk about it. You have interesting ideas about possible ventures, like the tea and other things. You know, aside from the many, many reasons why I love you, I love that we are comfortable with each other. I don't feel like I have to explain my every absence from the room, you don't get concerned when I am working late because you know you will never have to doubt my fidelity. It makes what we have more relaxed, and I don't feel pressure or tension coming from you. You said once that we were both at an age where some things just don't trouble us, or something to that effect. It's true. We have amazing sex, but I don't feel like I have to perform. I love you and I love being with you in every way. It isn't a chore or duty for me to be with you or make love to you. I like the way we are together. Does that make any sense?" It made perfect sense to me.

"Oh babe, I do plan to make you a happy man tonight." He chuckled because he knew just what I meant. Jonathan came in at that moment and said that dinner was ready.

"Oh yeah I have been looking forward to these lobster rolls and crab cakes all afternoon." We went into the dining room and Jonathan put everything on the table. He lifted the warming lids for us to serve ourselves.

"Jonathan, I can't wait to try this. It looks so yummy." I took a lobster roll, a crab cake, which was a good size and a good helping of salad. Jonathan did a raspberry vinaigrette on the salad. James helped himself to a good helping of the wild rice. It looked delicious too, so I took a very little bit. Jonathan returned the warming lids and left the room.

The first bite of the lobster roll was heavenly. I knew that I was going to have another one. James liked them as well. I tasted the crab cake, and it was good as well, but I preferred the lobster roll. The salad was excellent, and the bit of wild rice was very nutty. We both cleaned our plates, and I had another lobster roll as did James and he had another crab cake. By the time I was finished I was pleasantly full. James had another lobster roll and another crab cake with more rice. He had a good appetite, but he worked out hard and had a busy job, so he needed to eat well. I had more salad while James finished up his plate.

"Wow, that was really good. We should have these again. I know Ross and Lindsay love seafood so maybe we can have them as part of the New Year's festivities. Jonathan would probably have to come up with some idea of a smaller bun to put all this good stuff in but I'm sure you will work that out with him." I said that it was a wonderful idea instead of having a great big meal.

"I must not forget to get them to pick up some of the egg rolls in Ottawa. You have to try these. They are so good, and I have never found any anywhere that compare. Their plum sauce is amazing as well. I'm getting a craving just thinking about them. We can buy them uncooked and freeze them and then put them in the oven to cook when we want them. My mouth is watering just thinking about them." James laughed as he had no idea that I liked Chinese food.

"For the most part I don't really, but these egg rolls. I'm telling you wait until you try them. If you know of better, then I want to try them." We finished eating and went back out to the sunroom. James refilled our wine glasses. The sun was just about down. He put on some music, a slow waltz and held out his hand.

"C'mon sweetheart, let's dance. We need to make sure that we are in perfect rhythm for our wedding." Dancing with James was like floating on a cloud. He was a beautiful dancer. We danced to three beautiful songs and by the time we finished the rest of our wine Jonathan left.

"Come with me, I promised you a night of passion." I took his hand and led him upstairs. Tonight, it would be long lingering kisses, warm embracing hands. We were in no rush and took our time. When our passion came to a height where we couldn't hold back, it was a sweet and exhilarating end to a very long love making session.

"I hope that will hold the both of us until you are home again. I think we've done pretty good today; wouldn't you agree?" James definitely had to agree but said that morning was going to be upon us before we knew it. We snuggled up together and fell asleep. James woke up early to take a shower. I heard him in the shower and crept in behind him. I put my arms around him.

"I'm going to miss you. Last night and yesterday were wonderful." My hands were exploring his body and I lowered them and got the reaction I was hoping for. His kiss was deep and passionate. The water was streaming down our bodies. His hands were up and down my body pulling me close to him. His kisses were making me dizzy. His lips found that spot on my neck that drove me crazy. My legs went around him, and he backed me up to the end wall of the shower. Our kisses became more urgent. James was more intense. I cried out with release, but James kept going bringing me to a point where my ears were ringing. My nails dug into his back only making his passion greater. Finally, he cried out with a release that left me too weak to stand. I held onto him. His breathing was rapid and labored. He looked down at me and kissed me.

"Now that, was incredible. I hope I didn't hurt you by pinning you against the wall?" I said that he didn't and was able to stand again. I took his soap and lathered him up. It was a sensual ritual for us after every love making session in the shower.

We got out and dried ourselves off. James went to the sink to shave and brush his teeth. When he was done he got into a pair of casual black pants, light grey shirt, and sports jacket. He put on some cologne and came back into the bedroom. I got back into my pjs and put on a robe, and we went downstairs. Jonathan knew James was leaving early so coffee was ready. He knew that James would be having breakfast on the plane so didn't prepare anything for him. We went into the sunroom to drink our coffee. There were several deer about, but they scattered when they saw us moving. The sun was still a couple of hours from coming up.

"Well, my darling I had better get going. The crew will be arriving at the plane shortly and I don't want to keep them waiting too long. I am going to miss you. I will call you every night to video chat and if I can at lunch. Please be careful when you go for walks, promise me." I promised I would be careful.

"This week I have a spa day planned and of course Christina is coming by later this morning to decorate. I will go for walks with the seniors, and I plan to do more shopping." We hugged and kissed at the front door and then he left. I went into the kitchen to talk to Jonathan.

"I'm not terribly hungry this morning. I can smell that you are baking muffins, so I will have a couple of those with more coffee in the sunroom. Christina will be coming here in a few hours, so I suspect she will be here for lunch. I am not sure how many people she is bringing with her so perhaps we could have a chef salad for lunch.

I doubt she will be here for dinner, but I will let you know. If it is just me, I'd like a pasta dish and for the time that James is away, can you keep all the meals on the light side." Jonathan said it would be fine and whatever I wanted he was more than happy to prepare.

I went out to the sunroom to have my coffee. Jonathan brought out a small pot of coffee and the muffins when they were done. I left my camera by the chair that I always sat in looking out at the woods. I noticed something moving out of the corner of my eye. I saw something stir again and from the far corner of the sunroom a big bull moose came around the corner. I'd never seen one before let alone this close. He was walking right up alongside the windows. I slowly grabbed my camera and started taking photos. He was in no hurry to leave. He was a magnificent animal. About hundred yards or so into the trees, I could see a big cow moose. He was obviously following her and as she moved off, he was not far behind. James would be at the airport in about another twenty minutes or so, so I waited until I figured he was getting on the plane, and I sent him the photo with the caption 'look who showed up this morning.' James texted me back about five minutes later.

"Wow he's massive. I love you. Talk later we are just about to take off." He said he would be in Toronto around 2:00 their time. He had a couple of meetings at the office and then a dinner meeting. The muffins were delicious, and I ate every last morsel. I took my plate, mug, and coffee pot back into the kitchen and went upstairs to get dressed. I put on a pair of jeans and a black V-neck cashmere pullover. I put on my star necklace and earrings, a bit of makeup, a spritz of my favourite French perfume and a pair of red suede flats and went downstairs. Just as I reached the bottom, the front doorbell rang. I knew it would be Christina and as I opened the door, I could see boxes and boxes of supplies and two of her staff with her.

"I came prepared to get started right away. I thought outside we could have some corn stalks tastefully attached to the railing here at the front and again at the gate. I've got some large resin pumpkins too that we can put out there and a few near the front door. I've got layouts for you to look at, but I think you will like them. I brought the stuff anyway just in case. We won't do every room to the hilt. I thought perhaps some touches here and there in James's study and the bedrooms. Maybe incorporate a fall type throw to put on each bed that is being used. I think you said three additional bedrooms plus yours. Anyway, have a look at the boards. If you are ok with it, the guys will start right now." I looked at each board and they looked great. She brought all the throws and the table runners for the dining room and bedrooms. The floral centerpieces would be arriving next week, so the flowers would be fresh. There were going to be small floral arrangements in the guest bedrooms too. She had beautifully decorated wreaths to hang on each door and the two huge ones for the front double doors.

"This is so great. I love it all. You have tapped into our style perfectly. I can't wait to see it when it is all done. We would like you to come up with designs for Christmas too. Bearing in mind of course that there will be a seven-year-old running around. James and I want to decorate the tree if you don't mind. We will try not to make a mess of it and have it clash. It will be only ornaments and lights. We hope to get a lot of the ornaments on a trip to Germany and Austria and there will be some very special ones from James's glass company in Scotland. Give Christmas some thought if you could. The tree will be in the sunroom, and it will be the only tree. We trust your expertise, so I will leave it with you." Christina was already thinking about Christmas but would work a bit more on the boards.

"Let's concentrate on Thanksgiving first. When we come back to take it down and pack it up we can go over Christmas. I presume you don't have any problem with using the same décor a few years in a row. We can donate it to a senior's home after a couple of years and get all new. But for now, my staff and I will get busy."

I let them know that we would have lunch in the small dining room, and it would be salads. They were fine with that, so I let them get to it. I had a text from the artist letting me know that he'd been working on the painting, and it would be done at the end of the week. That was way ahead of the original date he gave me. He said he was going on a long trip for several months with a bunch of artist friends and wanted to make sure that I approved of the painting and was happy with it before he left. I gave him a call.

"Hello, Michel, I got your text. I am surprised but thrilled that the painting will be done so soon. James is actually out of town right now. If you can bring the painting by on Saturday, I can look at it. I am sure it will be perfect. I've seen your work, and it has always been very impressive. I can show you where I want to hang it and see if you agree. Obviously, I will ensure suitable lighting, but I can't do that until after Christmas." Michel agreed to come by at 2:00 on Saturday.

I didn't want to hover over the decorators, so I went out for a bit. We agreed to eat at 1:00 so that gave them a chance to get a lot done before taking a break. I decided to get some prints done of the ones James and I took in the woods. I thought they would make nice gifts for his family. I had no idea what he usually gave them, but this could be in addition to that. I would talk to him about it when he called tonight. We already started a family photo wall in the upstairs hallway. I'd been thinking about getting a professional photographer to take some photos of me that James could put in his office here and in Toronto. I had no idea where to find a good photographer but perhaps Christina knew of one.

I picked up the frames I wanted at a frame store and drove back to the house. It was very near 1:00 and lunch would be ready soon. The front gate was already transformed with the corn stalks and the large resin pumpkins. The drive up I could see the wreaths on the front door and the corn stalks again at the railing. More pumpkins of different sizes and colours were on the steps and a large garland of fall leaves was put around the frame of the door. It looked very fallish.

Inside, there were a wide range of candles in large glass containers with decorative rings around the bottom. The candles were orange, red, green, yellow, and white. Some had beans of every colour glued around them. She did the same effect with a few of the pumpkins that she placed near the fireplaces. On one of the mantles, she put bunches of wheat in burnt orange containers with Give Thanks in white lettering on the outside. On another mantle there was a large metal container that she put resin mini gourds, and it had a number of candle holders. She put some white candles in these. In each room she and her staff did a beautiful job. They were finishing up in the dining room when I went in.

"Now bear in mind that we still have to put the floral centerpieces, but they will be all fall colours with a large cornucopia in the centre. Can you smell the pumpkin spice candles? I know you are not a huge fan of roses but in each of the smaller floral containers there will be orange, red and yellow roses. I also got some Scottish thistle brought in and that will be incorporated in the flowers. A little bit of home for James. The flowers will be here on Wednesday before Thanksgiving and I will stop by to make sure that they are put where they need to be. So, how do you like it so far?" I absolutely loved it.

"Let's go up and see what was done in the bedrooms. We gave a little more in the room your sister was going to occupy. You said she liked to decorate her home, so I thought we'd do a few more things in that room." We looked in each room and it was all so tastefully done. The throws were really nice colours that went well with each comforter.

"It is perfect. I love everything, and I know James will like it too. Christina, I don't suppose you know of a professional photographer. I want to get some good photos done of me for James's office. It has to be tasteful, but I want it a little sexy, you know classy. It will be in his office in Toronto, so it can't embarrass him." She knew of the perfect photographer. It was actually a school friend of hers.

"This gal is fabulous. She's done a lot of celebrities and influential people. I can give her a call and see if she can come by tomorrow. In fact, if she can, I can bring her as I have some last minute things to do for the décor. Does that work for you?" It sounded great. I had a spa day booked for the day after and a shopping day for the day after that. I mentioned that I thought maybe James and I would try carving a pumpkin but perhaps another year.

I knew James wanted a good photo of me in the black dress I wore at the gala so that was definitely going to be a photo I would have done. I had an idea for a photo of me wearing one of his white silk dress shirts and a pair of faded blue jeans. Probably sounded cliché but I wanted one for him. I had a few other ideas but would wait to see what the photographer thought. We had lunch together in the dining room. This room was looking very homey with what they did, and it was nice. James and I ate in here all the time and Christina did a great job of not making it too fussy. I took a few photos to send to James. By the time he called tonight it would be too dark to get the full effect, so I thought a photo or two would suffice.

Christina called her photographer friend, and they would be by tomorrow morning at 10:00. I went around again to each room admiring everything. Jonathan thought it looked really nice and loved what they did in the large dining room. It was late afternoon by the time everything was done, and they left. I went upstairs and changed into my work out clothes and went downstairs to get in a good work out. After an hour of sweating, I went upstairs to take a shower. I put on my jeans and a sweater and went back downstairs. Jonathan made up ravioli in a tomato sauce which smelled great. I pulled up a stool at the island and we were going to eat together. He put a bowl of ravioli with freshly grated parmesan in front of me and then made one for himself. It was very tasty.

"So how are the teas coming. We should probably set aside a morning for tasting while James is away. Why don't we do it on Sunday after breakfast." Jonathan was good with that. I finished eating and went into James's study. Jonathan left about an hour ago. I sent off a few texts waiting for James to call. I had a wicked thought. I ran upstairs and put on one of his white silk dress shirts with the only sexy black bra I had. I kept my jeans on and went back down to the study. I was alone in the house, so I wasn't concerned about being seen. I had on the light that was on his desk. It gave enough light for me to be seen. My tablet rang, and it was James.

"Hello, my darling, how are you?" I could see him looking closer into the tablet. He started to chuckle and sat back in the lounge chair.

"Are you wearing my shirt?" I smiled wickedly at him and said yes.

"I am but if you don't want me to have it on, I can take it off." I slowly unbuttoned the shirt and put it on the desk.

"Is that better James or should I take this off too." I knelt in his chair and had the tablet propped up against the desk lamp. I undid my bra and let it fall to the desk. I unzipped my jeans just enough so that he could see the black lace underwear. He was leaning back in his chair smiling at me.

"Is there anything else I should take off?" I could tell I was clearly getting to him.

"You are insatiable, and I love it but no don't take anything else off and you can put my shirt back on. I'm going to have to take a very long cold shower after this." I succeeded and smiled at him.

"I have been fantasizing about coming to your office wearing nothing more than a trench coat and a very slinky black lace chemise but since I'm not there, I thought this would do. I hope you liked my little tease." I could tell he was clearly uncomfortable.

"You are killing me here and you know very well that I liked it, a lot. When our company leaves after Thanksgiving I will reward you for that luscious display. Now aside from driving me crazy, how are you?" I told him that Christina finished the décor, but it was too dark now for him to get a feel for it. He saw the photos I sent and liked what he saw. I told him I had a spa appointment the next day and some Christmas shopping the day after.

"I've planned to keep myself busy pretty much the whole time you are away. I miss you like crazy, as you can obviously see. I think I will be taking a cold shower too." He laughed and said he wanted to do some Christmas shopping with me so not to do it all while he was not there. We talked for about an hour more and said good night.

I went out to the front entrance and set the alarm the way James showed me. I went upstairs, put the shirt back on its hanger and put on my pjs. I wasn't afraid to be alone. John was down the road, and I knew the gate was locked each night. I curled up with James's pillow which had his scent on it. I fell asleep and only woke up when the buzzer went off at 8 am. I jumped into the shower, dried myself off and did my hair. I put on a pair of brown wool pants with a white silk loose fitting blouse. Put on a bit of makeup, my star necklace and earrings and a pair of dark green suede booties and went downstairs.

Jonathan was already in the kitchen with the smell of coffee in the air. There were muffins left from the other day, so I had a couple heated up and took them on a plate to the sunroom. Moira was busy cleaning in the dining room, and I said hello as I walked by. The girls that she hired for during the week were upstairs cleaning. Jonathan brought me in a small pot of coffee. I texted Janet who was busy at work but so enjoying the challenge. She said she was heading off to Toronto Wednesday for a couple of days. I then texted Ross and Lindsay to say good morning. I asked Lindsay if I could video chat with Ayleen when she got home from school. She would let me know later on. I put in a call to Christelle because I hadn't talked to her in a while.

"Well hello stranger. I have been trying to reach you for a few weeks. What's going on?" She meant to call me. She had to watch the kids for her friend that lived a few floors down from her quite unexpectedly and was gone for two weeks.

"Every time I would sit down to try to call you the baby would cry. I'm pooped. I need a holiday. I'm not feeling great, so I will probably go and lay down after I talk to you. What is new with you? How is it living with James? I'll bet you are having a good time." She laughed as did I because we both knew what she was referring to.

"Let me just say that all those years of abstinence are being greatly rewarded. He is so amazing. He took me shopping before leaving for Toronto. He wanted to spoil me, but I am thinking maybe he wanted me to fill up my side of the closet. It is looking very sad compared to his side. He is so great. On Sunday we actually made love three times. We couldn't keep our hands off each other. I feel like a horny teenager when he is around. But we enjoy each other's company. We go for long walks holding hands, he's simply amazing." She was laughing but I knew she was happy for me.

"Listen, you deserve him. I know you love each other. I know you can trust him. He is not someone who will ever break your heart." I knew she was right. This was my true love. We talked more about what was going on with her. She hadn't been feeling well even before she had to watch the kids. I tried again to suggest that she say no to them, but she was helping them out because of a last minute thing.

"You need to think about your health first. I can't lose my best friend." She agreed she would take a break for a good long time. We talked about the house, and I couldn't wait for her to come and visit.

"When can we arrange it? I can have James pick you up when he's in Toronto. Oh, wait he has to take Sonya and Rhonda back after Thanksgiving. Why don't I go with him, you can come back with us and stay for the week and then we can take you back on Saturday." She said she would think about it and get back to me in a day or so. She was too tired to think about it now.

"If you are not there, you won't get asked to babysit and I really want you to come, but I won't press. Call me when you decide." I hung up with her and could hear the doorbell and told Moira I would get it. It was Christina and her photographer friend Jennifer. Christina introduced us, and we went into the sunroom to talk. I asked Jonathan to bring in more coffee and a couple of mugs.

"I have to say you have a very beautiful home. I love all the trees and my head is already bursting with ideas. What kind of photos do you want done?" I mentioned to her what I was thinking, and she loved the ideas. She liked the idea of the black and white with James's shirt and my blue jeans. She floated a few more ideas which sounded really good.

"I will take a lot of photos in different situations. We can go up and have a look at your wardrobe and I will pick out a few things. I assume you have something in particular you want to wear so show me. It will be very tasteful I promise. I don't do sleazy. I will bring a hair stylist, makeup artist and a fashion stylist with me. My schedule is usually pretty full at this time of year, but I can squeeze you in on Friday. We will start early so be prepared for a long tiring day. We will be here at 8 am and you will get hair and makeup done while I set up. I would like to have a look around outside too if I may. I have a couple of ideas for outside shots. If you are good with that, I will take a look around outside now." I said it was fine, absolutely fine. I was actually really excited about getting it done so quickly.

"I'm going for a spa day tomorrow and a bit of shopping the following day." She was getting ready to go outside.

"Good, make sure you get them to give you a really good facial. You have beautiful skin, but it always shows up well on the camera when you have a great facial. Please get them to do red nails and toes as well. Be well rested for Friday though. I'll be back in in a few minutes and we can have a look at your wardrobe." She was out the door and walking around. I thanked Christina for bringing her.

"I've seen her work online; she does some really beautiful photos. I can't wait to get them done. I'm going to give them to James for his birthday." Jennifer came back in, and we went upstairs. I could tell her mind was visualizing possible photo spots. I took her into my closet and showed her what I had. I held out the black dress for her to see.

"Yes, this will be a good shot. I gather you want the back to be the focus. I can make that work and it will be very nice. Gorgeous dress by the way and I love the shoes you have for it. Okay so I see the idea of the white silk shirt and the jeans you want to wear. Would you be ok with not wearing a bra? We can start with one but sweetie you are going to have to pick up some more sexy bras. Go to a lingerie store and get lacy bras in royal blue, red, pink and a dark green if you can. Get matching panties too. They can be briefs but I would prefer boy shorts; I wouldn't ask you to wear a thong. We can unzip the jeans and pull them down a bit to expose the panties. I'll bring along some costume jewelry as well. I'd like to see what a belly chain would look like on you. You have a great body and a great waist, so that would be quite sexy." I was a little skeptical about the belly chain.

"Don't worry Cassandra, you are very beautiful mature woman. I am not going to put anything on you that would look inappropriate. Your body is killer, and I would love to be in as good a shape. Trust me these will be done tastefully, and you will love them." I said I was only concerned because I wanted these to be in James's office and I didn't want him to be embarrassed if someone saw them. Christina assured me James would love them. Jennifer mentioned she had a couple of places outside for photos.

"We will bring along some other things for you to wear. My fashion guy is very good. I will show him a picture of you and get him to get a few things. I want something flowy for outside. I love that boiled wool vest with some brown leather pants if you have them and those green suede booties. Love those. If you don't have the leather pants please, try to pick some up. There is a really good leather place that just opened up at the mall and they have some very nice pants in there in all colours. Please get at the least a dark brown pair." After working out some details, they both left. I really had no other plans for the day, so I decided to do my shopping now instead of Thursday.

I went to a lingerie store first and picked up all the colours Jennifer wanted me to have and several extra. Then I went looking for the leather place. It was up on the top floor and in a far corner. I'd been looking for leather pants online for a few weeks now but couldn't find anything. The styles that they had for pants now were really ugly, so I was hoping this store would have something suitable. You could smell the leather when you walked in. Perhaps a marketing strategy but it worked for me. I went over to the section of pants. They had lots of different styles and colours just as Jennifer said. I wanted a straight leg and finally came across a pair in dark brown. They were in my size, so I tried them on. They fit like a glove. I asked the sales agent if they had any more in this style in other colours and maybe a bit of a different look. She said they just got in a new order.

"I probably shouldn't say this, but it's my store so I will. I don't like all these crazy styles and lengths. Maybe my age is showing but I like a good clean line on leather, not these skinny looking things that really don't look good on anyone. I'll be glad when that style has gone out the door." She brought me several different styles and colours. There was a dark green colour, which she said had a really nice blazer with it. In addition to the dark brown, I picked out red, dark green, royal blue, toffee, and black. I bought the dark green blazer as well.

"I could never wear leather before but since I lost weight I look ok in it." The lady said that leather, if in the proper size, looked good on anyone. But it had to be the right style and fit. I paid for my purchases and went back home.

I tried on the bras and panties, and they fit perfectly. I rinsed them out and hung them over the shower to dry. I hung up all the pants and blazer in the closet. Back downstairs it was well beyond lunch. My stomach was starting to growl a bit, but I didn't want to spoil dinner. There was a muffin left so I had that with some tea. Jonathan was making a seafood dish that he thought I would like. I was in the sunroom when my tablet began to ring. It was Ayleen.

"Hello Gramma. How are you? Is Grandpa there?" I said I was fine, but James was at work in Toronto, and I asked how she was and how school was. For both I got the answer of 'good.' She was learning more printing and was going to be able to print her own letter to Santa this year.

"Wow, so what are you going to ask Santa for? James will be sad he missed you, but we will video chat at Thanksgiving. She knew that Sonya, Rhonda, Austin, and Nicole were coming. I asked her how she liked her teacher." She rhymed off the usual things she wanted for Christmas. She was looking forward to talking to James. She was really smitten with him and that made me happy. She said she liked her teacher a lot, but she had something she wanted for Christmas that she wasn't sure Santa could bring.

"Gramma, I told Santa that I wanted to have a family picture. You, Grandpa, Mommy, Daddy, and me but I don't know how we are going to do that. We are only coming to your place for Christmas. Maybe I can ask Santa for that next year." I said that I had a wonderful idea. She was smiling and all ears.

"I can ask a photographer to come here the day after you, Mommy and Daddy get here. We can get dressed up in nice clothes and have a photo taken by the tree. Then, I can ask her to get it done up and framed and you can have it. How does that sound?" She liked that idea a lot, but she was not sure what she would wear.

"Well, I have this pretty dress I had made for you when I was in Scotland. It's in James's family tartan. You know what that is right, remember James gave you that outfit when he first met you and that had his tartan. So maybe you could wear that or the one I got for you. I think James would like that a lot. I can ask Mommy to buy a new dress and Daddy can wear his suit, so everyone will look really nice." She was giggling with excitement.

"Gramma I miss you. Christmas is too far away to see you and Grandpa. Can you come for my birthday, please?" I told her that when we took Auntie Sonya back that my friend Christelle was coming back with us for a few days but had to go back on the Saturday. We could come for her birthday if James could arrange his schedule, but I had to talk to him first. I heard her squeal, which of course nearly deafened me.

"Mommy, Mommy, Gramma and Grandpa are coming for my birthday. Yippee they are coming." Lindsay took the phone and was laughing.

"I told her I would have to talk to James first, but I am pretty sure he will re-arrange his schedule. I doubt he would miss her birthday." Lindsay understood but Ayleen was still going on about it.

"There won't be as many adults this time. She is having a few kids from her class, but they will only be here for a couple of hours. My parents are coming and that will be it. Everyone else can't make it." I said I would text her back tomorrow. She called Ayleen back to the phone to say goodbye.

"Goodbye Gramma, I love you. I have some schoolwork to do so I have to go." Lindsay said goodbye and we hung up. There was still about an hour until dinner, so I decided to go for a quick walk around the property. I put on my jacket and walked down to the gate. I saw John and waved to him. He came over to talk to me.

"Ma'am I will get Max to go around first on the quad. There's a bull and cow out there and I don't want you coming up on them unexpectedly. Just to be safe." Max drove out and I could hear him making noises. It was the start of the rut, and I didn't relish coming upon a horny bull moose. It took Max about twenty minutes to go all the way around and back.

"It's ok now. I scared them off and they went down into the ravine and up on the other side. I don't think they will be back for a while." I thanked Max for doing that and John as well.

"We can keep running them off but if the bull stays and draws another bull in, we may have to shoot him. I don't like the idea of doing that to such a fine specimen, but he could become quite destructive. We will wait and see. I talked to the county and fish and wildlife so there would be no problem if we had to shoot him. Max and I already have our moose tags, so I said if we did have to shoot the bull we'd use a tag. They said they were fine with that, and I also let the local police know just in case someone reported gunfire, so they could assure people it wasn't a problem. Please keep your phone handy and call me right away if you run into problems. Enjoy your walk but perhaps after this, it might be best to leave the outside walking till the rut is done." It was a little unnerving now to walk around but I didn't encounter anything. I agreed with John, I would do my work out downstairs for the next while. I got back in time for dinner. Jonathan remembered that I always wanted to try bouillabaisse. Since he found a very good fish market, he picked up the seafood to go in it. It made a rather large batch, so he let John and Moira know that he would bring some down to them for their dinner and he also made fresh rolls to have with it. He put aside enough for us to have a good sized bowl. It was really good, and I ate every bit of it.

I wandered out to the sunroom to relax for a bit. The bruise on my butt was starting to fade but it was now that ugly green. Jonathan brought me in a new tea he came up with this afternoon. He wouldn't say what it was. He wanted to see if I could make out what the ingredients were. It had a wonderful fragrance. I took a sip, and I could tell right away there was Saskatoon and maybe lavender, but I couldn't make out the rest. I told him it was good. We agreed that Jonathan would keep his ingredients to himself, so I didn't ask what else was in the tea. It was very good though. He returned to see if there was anything else he could get me, but I said I was fine. I put on a sweater and sat watching into the woods. The birds were busily eating away in the remaining light of the day. Jonathan was leaving for the day. I reminded him I was leaving at 9 am for the spa and they would be providing lunch. He would set the alarm on his way out. Now the house was quiet and peaceful. Squirrels were scampering about, and the odd deer came to the trough. There was no sign of the moose, at least not that I could see. It was getting darker in the woods, so I went upstairs and put on my pjs. I wasn't expecting James to call for a while yet, so I turned on the tv and watched the news. I must have fallen asleep because I woke with a start at my tablet ringing.

"Did I wake you; you look sleepy. I wish I was there cuddling up next to you. I got a text from John saying that he might have to shoot a bull moose." John told him it was starting to cause some damage to the trees but as long as none came down and he moved off, it would be ok.

"He told me Max made a round of the property because you were going for a walk, and he chased the bull and cow off. I think I would feel better if you exercised downstairs or went over to the gym just until the rut is over." I said that I was going to do my workouts downstairs. I was getting a better work out with the climber and weights anyway.

"So how is your work going? I hope you are not putting in really long hours. Janet mentioned she was going there on Wednesday. I also spoke to Christelle today finally. I was starting to worry but she'd been babysitting for her friend. I invited her to come back with us when we take Sonya and Rhonda back. I hope that was ok. She can't stay long though. She has to be back by Saturday. I also had a video chat with Ayleen. She misses us and wants us to come for her birthday. I hadn't realized it was coming so fast. She will be very disappointed if we don't go but I told her you were very busy so if we can't make it I think she will be ok." James planned on taking time off after Thanksgiving to relax a bit before he had a marathon of travel.

"I would never disappoint that sweet little girl. It would be great if Christelle comes out and since we are going to Ottawa anyway, we can bring her back with us and then go for Ayleen's birthday. I can rearrange a few things, but I can make it work. I will be going overseas right after we come back from her birthday. I have to go to Germany to meet up with Quinn to go over the results of the testing of the makeup kiosks. He said the numbers were pretty good. Then I have to go to France for several days of meetings there and then over to Scotland to deal with meetings there. But I will definitely be back for our first Halloween and then you and I are going to Toronto on the 1st, and we will be here for our birthdays. I know that I am going to be busy in Toronto while we are here, but I promise no work on your birthday or mine. We are scheduled to go to Germany and Austria at the end of November for little more than a week. It will be a quick trip, a few days in each city to get your ornaments then pop over to Scotland to pick up some special ones and then home. I will discuss that trip with Janet when I see her for lunch Thursday." The rest of the year was going to be very busy.

"Christelle will let me know for sure in a day or two. Ayleen will be over the moon that we are coming, but I think she wants to see you more than me. Lindsay's parents will be there too. Ayleen is having a few school friends over for a couple of hours, but they will be downstairs making a ton of noise I am sure. It will be a lot of back and forth on the plane. I know it is your plane but that must be getting expensive." I knew the plane wasn't strictly for business. James used it for pleasure quite often.

"I have a very large budget for my plane so not to worry. I'm glad you are going to exercise downstairs. Getting buff on me are you. Can't wait to see you naked and all those toned muscles, hmmm. Now I'm doing it to myself. I had better let you go. I know you have a spa day tomorrow, enjoy it. I love you sweetheart, good night." I blew him a kiss and said good night too.

I set my alarm, so I wouldn't oversleep, and I fell asleep not long after my head hit the pillow. I could hear my alarm and woke up with a start. I was having a wonderful dream about James. I hurried into the shower, dried off, put on some jeans and a sweater and the suede booties, dried my hair and went downstairs. Jonathan had the coffee ready. He made me some soft boiled eggs with English muffins and a glass of orange juice. I texted Lindsay to let her know we would be there for sure for Ayleen's birthday. She texted back the room would be ready. I ran back upstairs to tidy up and grab my handbag and then went out the door. It was a bit cool out, but the skies were clear, and it was going to be a nice sunny day. I brought my flip flops with me to wear home.

I got to the spa fifteen minutes before my appointment time. It was a pretty slow day the girl said so they took me in right away. I booked a one-hour massage, a facial, reflexology, and a manicure and a pedicure. The massage was great, and I was so relaxed when I came out and in for my facial. It was the same esthetician I'd been going to for a number of years. She really helped to rejuvenate my skin without doing chemical peels or laser work. I didn't want any of that or any chemicals injected. I mentioned I was having professional photos done so she did a combination of an organic and a hydrating facial.

"You have beautiful skin now Cassandra, even better than some half your age. Your skin looks at least twenty years younger, and you don't have bags under your eyes anymore. When you first came to me, you were, in all honesty, a wreck. But I nursed you back with care and now voilà you look beautiful." I thanked her for the facial. My skin felt dewy soft. It was now on to reflexology, and this was what I really needed. After being on my feet and working out so much, I needed this. I had it done many years ago and would get it done every month or so. I could really feel like it was repairing my body. Then it was on to my manicure and pedicure. I told the girl I wanted a really nice red nail, and she picked out a new colour. It looked very nice. I was definitely feeling very pampered today. The drive home was good with very little traffic. John saw me coming and came out to my side of the car. I asked him what was wrong.

"It seems we have a couple of bull moose now. They've been duking it out in the back for a few hours. Don't go near the back outside. They are really very unpredictable right now, crazed with testosterone. Since I already have the permission of the county, fish and wildlife and the authorities know, I may very well have to take one of them out. They will knock down trees and will even run into the house doing who knows what kind of damage when they are fighting each other. They already took out one medium sized tree that came very close to going through a window. I'm taking the chainsaw over and hopefully the loud noise will drive them off, but they are stubborn beasts at this time of the year." I went into the house and took off my flip flops and walked bare foot up to the bedroom. I put my handbag on the bed.

I went back downstairs still in my bare feet as I didn't want to smudge my toes. It was nearing 5:00 and I decided to have a glass of white wine. Jonathan was going to do some fresh BC sockeye salmon and a salad for my dinner. I took my wine out into the sunroom and saw the tree that had been knocked down. It was a good size and would surely have done some damage if it had come through the window. John was busy cutting it up and Max was taking the larger pieces down to the Quonset and piling them. The smaller branches I presumed they would burn down there. I finished my wine and went into the kitchen. Jonathan was getting ready to serve up my plate, so I hopped onto a stool, and he put my plate in front of me. He served himself up one as well and sat beside me.

"I never asked you how things were going with your new girlfriend." Jonathan and I talked about family, so I didn't think he would think this was invading his privacy. I could tell from the look on his face that things were not going well between them. I felt bad for him.

"I'm not devastated. We only went out a few times and it really wasn't working. She wanted to go out all the time and I wasn't free to do that. Don't get me wrong I love this job and I would not give it up for anything. She was a bit too demanding for my lifestyle, so we parted amicably." I decided not to ask anything further.

"This was very good Jonathan. I am going to have another glass of wine in the sunroom and then head upstairs. It has been a bit of a long day, relaxing but long." He said that he would clean up and then turn on the alarm when he left. I bid him good night. He left my mail on the corner of the island as usual. There was nothing much in there.

The sun was ever so slowly creeping down below the trees. Every day now the days were shorter and shorter. I finished my wine and went up to bed. My nails and toes were good now; they had a lot of time to harden. I got into my pjs and turned on the tv. I looked at the guide and they were doing a bunch of new shows on space and the cosmos. I loved to watch these programs because of the stars. Once again, my tablet startled me awake.

"Hey, oops looks like I woke you again. Sorry to be calling so late but I have been up to it in meetings. So how was your spa day? Anything new on the wildlife?" The spa day was fabulous, and I really had to start going more than once a month.

"Well, you are not here to keep me busy, so I fall asleep hugging your pillow." He laughed at me and said that he loved me.

"I do want to tell you though that we now have two bull moose in the back. They've been fighting like crazy and knocked down a tree that very nearly came through the windows in the sunroom. John cleaned it all up, but he feels he's going to have to shoot one of them or they could end up doing even more damage. Anyway, he will take care of it, so you don't need to worry. What has you so busy at work." It had been almost non-stop from the time he got back.

"We got another huge, huge contract. I can't even discuss how much money is involved and I can't even discuss it, but it is very good for the company. We've been working this deal for over a year, and it finally ended in a contract. I have a lot of very, very talented people who have been sought after by some other companies. They are very loyal to me and have said they won't leave. We have a lot of respect for one another, so they stay with me because not only do I pay them very well and offer great benefits, but they know that I trust them. Anyway, I can't say more than that. I am having lunch with Janet on Thursday; I may have told you that. She's doing really well, and we may look at getting her to train a few people to take over someday. I know she wants to retire in a few years, so I want someone to be able to step in right away. I miss you like crazy in case I hadn't already said. I am beat, so I am going to let you get back to sleep and I will call you tomorrow. Sweet dreams babe love you." I said good night too and I loved him too. But as soon as I put my tablet down, turned off the tv and put my head back on the pillow, I was fast asleep again.

I woke early the next morning to a very loud crash. I grabbed my robe and ran downstairs. I thought maybe Jonathan knocked over a bunch of glasses, but he came out of the kitchen looking around to see what was going on. He said he only came in when he heard the crash. We went towards the sunroom, but Jonathan stopped me.

"There's a lot of broken glass, be careful. We saw that a tree came through the window on the far right side of the room. It was clear that the moose did this. They were still visible a bit further back, fighting. Jonathan called down to John to let him know what happened. Moments later, Moira came into the room.

"I'll get a box and a dustpan and broom and get that cleaned up. Best to go into the kitchen, you don't want to cut yourself." Moira went into the mud room to get the broom and dustpan. She put on a pair of heavy gloves, grabbed a good sized box, and went in to clean up the glass.

John came in and started to curse. He said he would go and get a tarp to put up to keep any birds out. They were buzzing around Moira, and she had to keep shooting them away. He wasn't gone long and he and Max each had a ladder and were hanging up a tarp. Jonathan and I went back into the kitchen. I needed a cup of coffee. George gave us a very large binder with all the names of the companies he used when building the house, just in case something needed to be repaired. I put in a call to the contact at the window company. It was still a bit early, so I left a message for him to call me back.

John came in and let me know that it was just glass that was broken. The frame of the window was not damaged, so it wouldn't take long to repair. I said I called the people who installed the windows. He took the card from me and said he would follow up in about an hour. I had more coffee and some toast. I was glad that I did my shopping the other day.

Jonathan wanted to make me something more than toast, but I wasn't really that hungry. I went upstairs to get dressed. John was going to see where the bulls were, as they had moved off from when we first saw them fighting. I came back downstairs and went into James's study. I sent him a text letting him know what had happened. I wanted him to know everything was ok, nobody was hurt, and it was all being taken care of today. Within minutes my phone rang.

"Are you ok? Is John going to shoot the bull? When is the window being replaced? Damn I should be there." I told him not to worry, things were being handled. Again, I assured him nobody was hurt, and the glass had been cleaned up and nothing else was damaged.

"James, it is ok. It is being handled. John went out to see where the two of them were because when Jonathan and I went into the sunroom they weren't that far away and still fighting. Oops I just heard a shot, so I guess they were still on the property and John decided to shoot one. Maybe with one gone, the other one will leave and follow the cow. It could be that we have moose meat for the freezer." He knew I was trying to make light of the situation.

"Good, I'm glad it is being handled. I know you were planning on going shopping today. Are you still going to go?" I said no I did it the other day after Christina left.

"Good thing I guess since this happened. Oops I just heard another shot. I hope he didn't have to shoot the other one too. Maybe it was just a 'make sure you are dead shot' for the first one." I was getting another call, and it was from the window guy.

"James, I am going to have to let you go. I know you are busy, and the window guy is buzzing in. I love you talk to you tonight." I was glad the window guy called back as quickly as he did. He said he would come over shortly to have a look at the damage and see what needed to be done. If it was just glass, he could have a guy out later in the morning. I told him that John said the frame was fine, but he could meet up with John when he came.

John came up to the house and I met him in the kitchen. He looked a little shaken and I asked him if he was alright. He said he was but once he downed the one bull, damned if the other one didn't charge him, so Max had to shoot that one. I said that I had heard two shots, but I thought it was just to make sure the first one was dead.

"I'm a good shot ma'am, never had to make a second one to kill anything. No, the darn fool wouldn't just let it be that he was now the boss. He saw me as a rival and came at me. If Max hadn't been there to take him down I probably would have been trampled. I taught Max how to shoot so he brought the other one down with a single shot just like me. Did a good job. We will have to let fish and wildlife know we had to take down the two of them. It's good that we both have tags. I'll have to get out the big 4x4 tractor and drag them down to the Quonset. We will have to hang them right away, gut them and let them sit for several days. I have a couple of friends who run a butchery and they can cut up all the meat. I know that Max and I shot them, but would it be ok to give my butcher friends some of the meat. That's what we usually do when we bag game. We will have to dig a big hole to bury the guts though, can't let them hang not gutted. I'll get Max to go out on the far side at the back where he can dig a really deep hole and then he can take them out and bury them. It won't smell, and no animal will be able to dig them up." It was fine by me to share the meat. Jonathan would let him know which cuts of meat that he wanted for the freezer. I said I would like to be able to keep some steaks and roasts for my son and sister. They loved moose meat but never had a chance to get any. Jonathan would keep some aside for them to take back with them when they came. I let John know the window guy was coming shortly and that I asked him to look for him. He said he would take care of it. John went back down to the Quonset.

"Wow, what a day we've had here. Now that Moira has the sunroom completely cleaned up. I think I will set up at the other end and do a painting. I need something to focus on." I left Jonathan in the kitchen, and I went to get my painting supplies. I set everything up and then went up to change into some old clothes. I took a photo of the trees and setting sun a while back and printed up the photo. I thought I would give this one a shot. I always dreaded doing trees but the painter I worked with a few times showed me how to do them and it was much easier now.

It took me about four hours to do the whole painting to a point where I was satisfied with it. I took a photo of it and sent it to Ross and Janet for comments. Ross said he really like it a lot and Janet loved it. I left it on the windowsill to dry completely and I put my stuff away downstairs. Jonathan brought me in some sandwiches to nibble on while I was painting. When he came back in to get the plate he said that he thought it was very good.

When I came back from putting my paint stuff away, I saw that the glass was being installed. John was standing by to help if needed. It only took the guy a couple of hours, and it was done. John took care of the bill, which was part of his job and would submit it at the end of the month, like he did for everything else. It was after 2:00 by the time I finished the painting, and I was still a bit restless. I decided to do a workout and get myself 'buffed' for the photo shoot tomorrow. The bruise was almost gone and only a little bit of green remained.

I spent the next hour working my tail off and it felt really good. I liked this climber and it helped with my arms too. I would have to get Ross and Lindsay one of these. They had some equipment, but it was not as good as this and even though they'd lost weight, this would definitely tone them up. I would have to look into that soon, maybe get it for his birthday and an early gift for hers.

I ran up to take a shower and change into my jeans and a sweater that I had on earlier. My phone was ringing, and I ran back into the bedroom to get it. It was Christelle. She was calling to say she would love to come for a few days, but she still had to be back on Saturday.

"Oh yeah I am so happy. That will work out fine because Ayleen's birthday is on Sunday and she begged us to come, so James is rearranging his schedule to accommodate the little miss. James is arranging for a car to pick you up and bring you to the plane. We are bringing Sonya and Rhonda back and we should be in Ottawa by 4:30. So I will give the service your number and they will call you when they are at your apartment. I am so looking forward to seeing you again. This will be so much fun. We had to shoot two big bull moose today. Well, I didn't shoot them, the caretaker and his son did. They were fighting and knocking down trees and one of the trees came through the window. John only wanted to shoot one but the other one charged so his son Max had to shoot that one. Now we have lots of moose meat to eat. I'm sure you are going to tell me there is some symbolism there, but if it has to do with past stuff, I don't want to deal with it. Nothing from the past in this house." She said she was going to say what it meant, and it did have to do with the past, but she would leave it there. She was looking forward to coming but didn't want to do a lot of running around. I told her we could spend the entire time at the house, but maybe go out to dinner one night.

"Bring something a little dressy. We can get some photos done. James has started a family wall, and it wouldn't be complete without you." I mentioned about the photos I was getting done tomorrow; something really nice and one a little naughty.

"Oohlala he's really bringing your sexy side out; I'm kidding of course but I am so happy for you. I can't wait to see you and James in ten days." We laughed and said good night. It was late for her but just about dinner time for me. I was so happy she was coming. Jonathan kept dinner light. He made a garden salad with some grilled chicken. Tonight, we sat in the sunroom. I was telling him about Christelle, how we have been friends for so long and we were more like sisters. He asked if she had any allergies and I said no but she couldn't eat hot pork because it seemed to bother her.

"It is going to be a bit of a shock when my sister Sonya and her family come. I don't know if anyone has any dietary concerns, but I will find out and let you know." Jonathan was great company, but I suspected that James was behind him keeping an eye on me.

"That was another good meal, thank you but I have an early day tomorrow and I want to hit the sack early. Can I please ask you to put the alarm on when you go? Thank you so much and have a good night." I went upstairs and into my bedroom and into the bathroom and got my pjs on. I had a feeling James would call early since the past couple of nights he caught me almost asleep. Sure, enough my tablet started to ring.

"Hello James, how are you tonight? Christelle called to say she would love to come, and I am so very happy about that. I asked her to bring something a little dressy in case we decided to go out and I want to get some photos for the family wall." James was thrilled she was coming.

"I'm happy sweetheart but I wish you were here, so I could be with you at night. I really miss having your body next to mine. Things have been pretty busy here. I had to send one of my executives there to see how the buildings were coming along. What did you do today?" I said I did a painting of a photo I took out back a while ago and it looked pretty good.

"I'll send it to you, and you can have a look. I did a pretty good work out downstairs today, so I am happy to be relaxing. I miss you too and your pillow has been subbing in for you; but I can't wait to have the real thing home." I could see that he was tired, and I was a little worried. Maybe over the holidays I could convince him to ease up just a little.

"I am pretty tired, so I think I will say good night. Sleep well and I will talk to you tomorrow. I love you." I blew him a kiss and said I loved him too. Just six more days and he would be home for a bit. I set my alarm, so I could be up early. I informed John that I had people coming by early in the morning. He said he would be up at 6 am to make sure the gate was open. Jonathan was going to be in at 7:00.

I woke up and my alarm hadn't gone off. I looked to see if the power was on, and it was I just woke up early. I jumped into the shower and then put on a big terry robe. Jennifer said that they would be here by 8:00 but I wanted to get a cup of coffee in me and some toast. I was going back upstairs when the doorbell rang. It was just before 8:00 and sure enough when I opened the door Jennifer, and her crew were there.

"Glad you are up. Jess is the hair stylist, Mario is makeup, Jacob is fashion and I have Terry and Mike here to help with the equipment. Guys this is Cassandra. Ok let's get all the stuff upstairs. Terry help Jacob please with the clothing racks. Take everything up to their bedroom. She has a big bathroom and big walk in closet so put everything there. Terry when you have that done come back down please and help Mike set up the lights and camera equipment. Jess I want her hair in a messy French braid, lots of loose tendrils please. First dress is the black one you wore at the gala. Jacob get that ready make sure there are no lines. Mario, I want the makeup clean, classy, and flawless. She has amazing skin and bone structure, emphasize it. Jacob, she has crystal sandals for the black dress please put those on her. Cassandra did you get the things I wanted you to get?" I said that I did, and I even got a few other pairs of the leather pants in other colours just in case. As we walked into the bedroom and the closet I showed her the colours.

"I hope it is ok I got a straight leg. Each pant is a different style, but it is straight leg. That was what I was most comfortable in." Jacob took a quick look and said they were gorgeous. He looked at James's side of the closet.

"Oh, my God I have died and gone to heaven but what is this, you have nothing on your side of the closet and look at all these beautiful things on his side, designer, designer, designer, my dear lady why have you not gone crazy shopping. I love over here but this side is so sad and look you hardly have any shoes." I thought he was very amusing but had to let him know I was not into a lot of fashion just for the sake of having my closet full.

"I realize that I'm not typical, but I am who I am. I can rise to the occasion when needed but I am a jeans and sweater girl the majority of the time." He said not to worry, if I didn't have the right thing for the photo, he came amply prepared. I went over to sit on a stool, so Jess could do my hair. She was very quick, but it looked so pretty. Then Mario stepped in and gave me what Jen was asking for.

"You do have great skin, whatever you are doing, keep it up. Jen wants a dramatic eye and a red lip, that will show up best in the photos. I will choose what suits your skin, not to worry." I looked in the mirror and couldn't believe I was seeing me. He too was very fast. Jacob was waiting to put me in the dress and help me with my shoes.

"Clean lines my dear means no bra no panties. You can slip out of them when I pull the dress up. I have seen more than I care to ever talk about. You have nothing to worry about. I love these shoes. There, now go out into the bedroom, Jen is waiting." Jennifer had lighting set up and the full length mirror pulled into the centre of the bedroom.

"Ok Cassandra first I want you to look into the mirror like you are checking your makeup but don't touch your face. Jacob where is the jewelry." I said I had some that I wore with the dress. I had to get it out of the safe. James bought it for me after the gala. I gave the emerald necklace and earrings to Jacob.

"Let me put them on you so you don't chip a nail. These are stunning, and they look stunning on you." I went back out to stand at the mirror.

"Yes, love the jewels, perfect. Ok so I'm going to start taking pictures. Try to keep any hand movements slow, yes definitely put that gorgeous ring up there but remember not to block your face. Now I want you to look in the mirror like you are looking at someone who has come in behind you. Someone you really want to see but don't smile ok just look, perfect just like that keep looking. Ok now I need you get into the pink bra and panties and the men's white silk shirt and your faded jeans. Jacob put the belly chain on, use the delicate one. Jess take out her hair and slick it back a bit but not too much. Like she came out of the shower a few minutes ago and her hair is almost dry. Mario this time a smoky eye but not too much, keep it classy ok. Terry, Mike, I need to move everything downstairs to the front entrance. Let's go."

Jess took down my hair and used a water bottle to wet my hair and then sprayed it with hairspray to get the look Jen wanted. Mario removed the eye makeup and then gave me a very classy looking smoky eye and the red lip. This was the black and white shot, and I was going to be barefoot. Jacob took one of James's shirts off the hangar and grabbed my jeans that I set out. He told me to go get into the bra and panties. It was a little unnerving being around people in my underwear, but I was getting less nervous.

"Sweetie if it helps, Mario and I are gay, so you have nothing that interests us, so please don't be nervous. Now if your fiancé were here that would be a whole n'other party." I knew he was saying that to make me relax.

“Thanks, I feel better. I have a necklace and earrings James gave me that I really want to wear for this shot. I can let Jen know why.” I took out the necklace and earrings and told him what James had done.

“Oh my God I don’t know him, but I already love him. How sweet was that to do, you are such a lucky lady.” I put on the shirt which Jacob only did up one button on and then went downstairs. Jen was waiting by James’s office. She had the door open to his study only because she didn’t want the wreath in the shot.

“Ok, Mario, can you make the eye a little softer please, yes that’s better. Jacob, please unzip the jeans and pull them down just a little. I want them to lay open exposing just a bit of the panties and I want the belly chain to hang down between, yes just like that. Now Cassandra, I want you to stand here, leaning a little bit against the wall with one foot crossed over, just a bit ok not too much so we see the painted toes. Now I want you to look down and when you look up, I want just a bit of a smile, like a smirk but not a big smirk. Ok so when I say now lift your head, ok now. Yes, that’s great.” Jennifer was so quick.

“Now we are going to move the lights around because I want your ring in the shot. For this shot, we are going to open the shirt some so the bra is showing, not your whole breast, just enough of the bra to tease. I want you to put your ring hand on the wall but don’t block your face. Now, for this one, I need you to angle your body a little towards me, so we see that bra, maybe rest your chin on your left bicep, yes just like that, soft smile now, ok great. Ok last shot for this, I want you to lean against the wall again, and with your left hand lift the shirt back and let your hand rest on your hip. We want to see the ring, but we also want to see that bra again and the chain. That's perfect you are doing really well. Now for one more, I want you to stand out a bit from the wall not too much, put your shoulders back so they are on the wall and keep your head level, like you are doing a plank. I want you to let the shirt fall back, in fact Jacob undo the button so that one side of the shirt falls completely back. Now sweetie I need you to close your eyes and think about James but don't smile, yes, yes that is just what I want, keep that pose. Awesome. Now please go up and put the royal blue underwear on and come back down and we will do these same shots again. I want to see which underwear gives the best look. We did all the same shots again.

"Ok now I want the red ones on and please bring down your crystal heels." I ran up and came down as quickly as I could.

"Ok Mario, I need that smoky look a little more now but not too much. I don't want it to look like she's on heroin or anything. Jacob, please help her with the heels. Ok, into the study we go. I cleared some things off his desk but not everything, I hope that was ok. So here is what we are going to do here. I want you to lay your back on top of the desk and propped up on your elbows and forearms. Jacob can you go and crouch down and hold the chair, so it doesn't move in a sec. Cassandra, I want you to place your left foot on the back of the chair and push in a little but not too much and then cross your right leg over and extend your foot, yes just like that. Jacob try to pull the jeans down a little bit more, I want to have more of the pantie showing and let the shirt on the left side fall back. Now this is a theatrical cigar, not real but it does blow smoke. It isn't toxic or anything so if you can, and you won't cough or choke on it, take in a good drag and if you know how to blow a smoke ring, please do so. Ok so when you do, I want you to let your head fall back as you are blowing the smoke ring and once you have done that I want you to smile, but don't show teeth just a nice smile. Ok, so go with the smoke ring, yes that is awesome Cassandra good job. Try a couple more and if you want you can look at the camera and wink. These shots are going to be so great." We stepped out of the study, so the guys could get all the lighting out.

"Jacob, I want her to wear the brown leather pants, the boiled wool vest with a very loose white or cream colour blouse and whatever bra that won't show through, if she has a white one that will be good. Jess I want you to use a flat iron on her hair and keep it smooth, a casual look. Mario redo the eyes and lips. I want a soft look, maybe a rose colour lip. Jacob put her in the green suede booties she has. When you are ready, come out back." We went back upstairs. I showed Jacob two blouses that I thought would work and the wool vest Jen was referring to. He went with the cream colour one. Jess redid my hair and Mario my eye and lip makeup and then we went back downstairs and outside. We did the casual shot outside, and she seemed happy with it.

"Very good now go back upstairs and Jacob put her into the dress and pink sandals ready for the outside shot. Use the two strands of pearls around her neck and put some on her wrist, nothing on the left hand but that beautiful ring. Jess put her hair into a chignon please but not tight, let some strands come out, put a little curl in them but not too much. Mario we are now going to do a very dramatic eye, use plum shades which will bring out the green in her eyes and rosy, pink lip with gloss. Jacob the pink underwear will be fine as long as it doesn't show. I am trying to catch a certain light and I will only have one chance at it, so please hurry." We hurried back upstairs. Jess quickly did my hair and had the soft strands out. Mario redid my eyes and lips and put a bit more blush with a bit of pink. Jacob brought out the dress. It was stunning and looked like a soft pink cloud. The pink sandals were very pretty and not too high a heel.

"This is a beautiful gown, I love it." We knew Jen was waiting downstairs, so we went as quickly as I could walk in the heels. For this shot she was going to go for something very ethereal from what she described. She took a few shots waiting for the light to be what she wanted and then I had to get ready.

"I'm only going to get one shot at this with the light. I want you to look my way and beyond ok keep that pretty face like the one you had upstairs when you looked in the mirror at something behind me. I want you to make a motion like you are moving forward but obviously don't. I am waiting for the right light so when I say go, go and be as pretty doing it as you can. The guys will catch you I promise if you lose your balance. Ok the light is coming so get ready Cassandra. I'm going to be firing off a lot of shots so stay pretty the whole time ok. Ok, get ready, alright go Cassandra." I could hear the camera taking shot after shot after shot. Mike and Terry did catch me, but I wasn't worried that they wouldn't. Jennifer gave a shout of glee and said we were done outside now. Jacob helped me to get into the booties he brought out and we went back into the house. Jacob and Mario were holding the dress up, so it wouldn't drag on the ground.

"For the final shot, I want you to be coming down that beautiful staircase. I need the one fan that will be blowing on her guys but not too much. Mario touch up her lips maybe do a bit deeper shade. Jess fix her hair now, so it is all back but don't do tight, just everything in place. Jacob put the sandals on her and make sure the dress is clean of any debris from outside. We have a lot of beautiful shots, but I promise this will be a great one too." Everyone rushed to get me ready and the front entrance ready. Jess fixed my hair and Mario put a deeper rosy pink on my lip. With the sandals on we went back downstairs. Everything was set up.

"Ok so Jacob I want that dress fluffed out as much as possible. Ok this will be a regal pose if you will, no smiling but a smile if you know what I mean. I want that look in your eyes. I'm going to take a lot of shots and I will want you to take a step down so that we see the shoe. Just keep looking straight ahead though. Ok, so let's go. Cassandra you are looking magnificent. That's it, we are done." I went back up to take the dress off and put on the royal blue leather pants and put on the cream blouse and went back downstairs. Jen was set up in the sunroom.

"Cassandra, you were excellent, and I have a feeling those last few shots are going to be killer photos. Terry and Mike if you can pack everything up in the van and then come in and get the clothes racks. Jacob if you and Mario can put those at the bottom of the stairs so the guys don't have to go up that would be great. Let's sit and I will download these onto my computer, and we can have a look." I asked Jonathan to bring some wine if anyone wanted any and everyone wanted some except for Terry who was driving.

It was getting dark, and I couldn't believe we had been taking photos all day, but my body was sure telling me we had. Jonathan brought out some cheese, crackers, and bruschetta to nibble on. We hadn't eaten all day. I asked everyone to stay for dinner, but they had other commitments. Jen was finished downloading and went through the photos and put aside the ones that were fuzzy, or I was not making the right facial expression. She narrowed the shots down to four or five possibilities for each different wardrobe for me to choose from.

"Cassandra these are really good. Looking at these you would think you were a model; you took direction very well. So here are the ones that I think are the best, but you choose the ones from there that you like the most. You can have them all if you want but I know you wanted to do up special ones in frames for your fiancé." I looked at each one and had a hard time believing they were me. They were all really good. I asked her if she could make the small star blue like on my necklace. She did, and she liked the look even more. I looked from photo to photo and in each set picked out the one I wanted to give James for his birthday.

"Now this photo, Cassandra, this one is really remarkable. You had the perfect expression on your face, and you had the wherewithal to keep the material out of your face. I like that you let it wrap around your arm I think that this is the most exquisite of them all and probably the best photo I have taken in a long time." I was so flattered, and they all looked so good, but I chose the ones for James.

"Can I get you to come back out and let James see them all. I think he would probably want more of the photos, but I'd like him to pick them out." Jen said she would be happy to do so.

"I would like to use these two of you in the gown for my portfolio if you will allow me. They are really the most stunning pictures." For that I would have to talk to James, which meant that he would have to get this photo when he returned.

"If you want to do that, I can get this one enlarged. I think 12 x 14 in a beautiful frame would look amazing on his desk. It will be very stunning. I can get that done and have it back here on Tuesday. You can show it to James and then decide what to do from there. I won't pressure you and I promise you it won't appear on billboards or anything of that nature. It is strictly for my portfolio." I said that would be great, but I had a request.

"My son and his family are coming here for Christmas. My granddaughter told me she wanted to ask Santa for a family photo but didn't think he would be able to do it in time. I said that I would see what I could do because she really wants this photo. I hadn't known what I was going to do but now that I have worked with you I am wondering if it would be possible to have you here on December 22nd in the early afternoon to do a family photo. She would be absolutely over the moon about it." Jen asked if I wanted everyone to come and I said yes of course. I wanted everyone to look their best, so we set a date for the 22nd in the afternoon. I showed them a photo that we took at dinner in Ottawa. Jacob thought she was the most adorable thing.

"You know Jennifer, once James sees these photos he is going to be very impressed. So impressed he will want all of you to do our wedding in May. I'm sure you are booked well in advance, but James can be very persuasive." Jen laughed and said she would block it off but let her know if it was for sure. I walked them to the door and waved goodbye. I was beat. I went into the kitchen.

"Jonathan, I am starving, what are we having for dinner." He figured I would be hungry, so he was putting the final touches on a seafood pasta. He filled our plates, and we sat in the kitchen.

"Oh my God every muscle is aching right now. I could never do that for a living. This is so good, and I am so hungry. Thanks for hanging around a bit later. I finished my pasta and Jonathan took the plates to the dishwasher.

"Not a problem. I was watching a little bit. I hope you don't mind. That one of you in the gown standing on the log and the one on the stairs, James is going to die. You looked like a real pro." I said thanks, but I was beat and wanted to head upstairs. He said he would set the alarm when he left. I went into the bathroom and took off all the makeup. I hung up my clothes, took a quick shower, put some moisturizer on my face and put my pjs on and sat in bed waiting and hoping James would call soon. Bless him he was calling.

"Hi babe, how are you? How was your day?" I said it was very busy, but he couldn't ask me why. I would show him when he got home. He looked at me very puzzled and wanted to know if everything was ok. I assured him it was.

"I know that sounds mysterious, but you will be surprised I hope. How was your day?" His, he said was busy too and he was calling early because he wanted to have an early night. I said I was ready to drop so we said good night. I felt bad ending the call so soon, but I was so tired. I knew that Michel the artist was coming by tomorrow at 2:00 so I texted Jonathan to let him know I was going to try to sleep in until 9 am. He texted back ok.

I thought about all the photos that were taken and I was very happy with all of them. I had to admit that the one of me in the gown, especially on the staircase, was really beautiful. I really did like that dress, and I knew that James would ask me if I bought it and the shoes.

I would have to make a note to get in touch with Jacob to see if he could order me both. I wrote a quick note on a pad that was on my nightstand. I knew I was going to be stiff and sore tomorrow, but I wasn't going to have time to get in another massage. Maybe laying in the dry sauna for a while would help with my muscles. I was so tired, but my mind was still racing a bit. I was blown away at the fact that Jennifer wanted to use that photo in her portfolio. I thought things like that were only done with super models and famous celebrities. It was a bit of an ego boost and had me a little giddy.

I turned on the tv for a bit hoping that it would get me to relax more. But all there was on the news was bad things and I certainly didn't care to hear any of that. I switched it to a music channel of nature and set the sleep timer for twenty minutes. I loved the sound of nature and music, and I could feel that my eyes were getting heavy. I tucked James's pillow in close to my body and kissed it saying goodnight to him and drifted off to sleep.

Chapter 8

I woke up shortly after 9:00 and took a quick shower, got into some jeans and the dark green cashmere sweater and the green booties and went downstairs. I rounded the corner into the kitchen and could smell coffee. Jonathan was handing me a big mug of coffee. He was in the process of making me an omelet with some homemade multi-grain bread. I wanted to eat in the sunroom, so I took my coffee in there. Jonathan brought in my omelet and left me to eat. When I was finished I took my dishes back to the kitchen and went down to the study and put things back on James's desk.

I was feeling a little sore, so I went down to the sauna. I got undressed and spread out a towel and laid there for half an hour. The heat felt good, and I got out and got dressed again. I was still pretty tired, so I went back out into the sunroom and flopped into one of the big armchairs. I think I must have dozed off for how long I wasn't sure. I went into the kitchen and realized that I actually slept through lunch, and it was now 2:00. Jonathan said he came out, but he didn't want to wake me. I heard the doorbell and went to the front door. It was Michel and he was holding the painting. I was so eager to see it. We went into James's study, and he unwrapped it and held it up.

“Michel, this is unbelievable they look so life-like. I love it and I know that James is going to be blown away. Excellent job.” I showed him where I thought we would hang it and he agreed with the location. He suggested that type of lighting to have above the painting. I was very pleased. I paid Michel and walked him to the door and waved goodbye. I took the painting and put it up in one of the spare rooms that was not going to be used and safely wrapped it up in a blanket and put it in the closet. Taking a photo of it to send to Fenella was not the best option but I knew she would want to see it since I asked her for the photo. My tablet was ringing, and I knew it couldn’t be James. I was not expecting to get a video call from Fenella.

“Fenella is everything ok I was not expecting your call?” She said everything was fine and she just saw the painting.

“Cassandra, James is going to weep like a baby, just like I did. It is a beautiful painting, very beautiful. He will just love it. Thank you for sharing it with me. I promise not to show it to anyone but Callum. I hope you are doing well.” I said that I was and that I had some professional photos done yesterday. I didn’t have any to show her yet but would send her a few photos next week. She said she would look forward to seeing them. I knew it was very late for her, so I wished her a good night.

I decided to go for a short walk. It was still early, and it would be nice to walk around on the paved path. With no moose around it was an enjoyable walk. It was late enough in the day now to see if Ayleen wanted to video chat. Unfortunately, they were sitting down to eat, and she had some schoolwork to do. I gave James a call hoping I wasn't catching him in a meeting. He had in fact just finished one he said.

"It's good to talk to you. Been in meetings all day it seems but they are over now, and I have the rest of the day free. Going to go to the gym and get in a good work out and have dinner at the penthouse. We've had rain here most of the day, but it seems to be clearing out. What have you been up to today?" I so wanted to say something about the painting, but it was for Christmas.

"Just doing a day here, nothing much. Went for a walk and it was nice, no animals around. Wanted to video chat with Ayleen but she was busy. Going to do some tea tasting with Jonathan tomorrow. He has come up with a few new ones. I'm going to do another spa day on Monday, so I will be gone all day. Aside from missing you, nothing much else. But I am hoping that we can maybe talk about your schedule. James you are important I know, but you need some down time too." He knew I was concerned, and he was working on stepping back a bit. But he had to make sure that this last contract was handled by him not one of his executives.

"I will I promise. This last deal was very important and now that it is done, I can take things a little easier. I have a few more meetings that I need to attend over the next while and then, I can let my executives, whom I pay very well, play a more important part." I was happy to hear that, not that I thought he would completely step back.

"Maybe in the New Year, if you have to travel for more than a few days, I can go with you. I know you will be busy during the day but at least we can be together at night." James said he would like that very much. Jonathan poked his head around the corner to see if I was ready for dinner.

"James, Jonathan is letting me know dinner is ready. We can video chat later and talk more." He was heading off to the gym. I let Jonathan know that I could do the tea tasting at 1:00 the next day because I wanted to get to the gym and get in a really good work out. He said that worked fine for him.

Jennifer texted to say she had the one photo ready and framed and would work on the others over the next few days. I was very anxious to see them all. She was going to group some in a collage but thought she would put the one with the black dress and the black and white with the blue star in a double frame and the one of me in black and white and the smoke ring in a separate frame. I texted back that would be great and once James saw the rest, he could decide which ones he wanted for his office in Toronto. I had no idea what he would like so it would be best for him to choose. She was fine with that. I set up a time between Christmas and New Years to do that. She said it was fine with her as she was not going anywhere between the holidays.

I went into the sunroom to get myself organized. What a difference in my life. Now I had to keep things in my calendar to track my day. I laughed to myself because I was busier now than just several months ago. Later that night James and I video chatted. He said he worked out for an hour and a half and felt really good. He was going to have Richard and Mark over the following day for dinner to discuss a lot of matters some of which had to do with a marketing plan for the teas. I would let him know how many after tomorrow's tasting. James was tired as was I, so we said good night. I went into the kitchen and Jonathan was just leaving. I said I would set the alarm once he was gone down the drive. After setting the alarm, I went up got into my pjs and fell fast asleep.

The work out at the gym the following morning was great, and I did my best to incorporate more weights as Mason suggested. I had lunch and then sat down in the kitchen to start tasting. I tasted forty different teas but there were a few that I didn't like. Jonathan said he wasn't sure they would work so he was glad for the feedback. We settled on thirty that I thought would do very well. I sent James a text saying we had thirty teas. I told Jonathan I was going to go out to a movie, so he could go home if he wished. By the time I got back from the movie, it was very quiet. Some lights were left on, and John saw me come back in and then locked the gate.

It was still so pretty walking up to the house. Everything looked really nice for Thanksgiving. I went in, shut off the alarm and then reset it. I went to the early show, so I was back in lots of time to video chat with James. I wasn't tired, so I poured myself a glass of wine and went and sat in the sunroom. I had my tablet beside me. Max, I could see filled the trough for the deer with more sunflower seeds and they were out there eating away. My tablet rang, and it was James.

"Hi, I see you are not in bed yet. How was your day?" I said it was good. He talked to Mark about the marketing and discussed packaging. They thought going with small foil single serve packets would be best. He tasked Richard with hiring some top level executives so that the workload could be spread around a bit more and he wanted someone on site in Alberta. I mentioned I went to a movie, and he asked which one. I told him it was a comedy which unfortunately wasn't all that funny.

"Quinn is going to come over late October to have a look at the lab, so I won't need to go overseas right away. He would like to be involved in the final hiring process. I hope it is ok if he stays with us. He would have brought the family, but the kids are in school, and Charlotte is a lawyer and, on a case, right now. I've asked Richard to get the basics for the interviews set up, so Quinn can look over the resumes and then select who he wants to actually interview. He will only be with us for a few days, so I am trying to get the field of candidates narrowed down for him." I was very happy to have him stay and to meet him. We talked for another half hour, and I started to yawn.

"Sorry, must be the work out I did today. Tomorrow I'm going for a spa day so that I will be relaxed and refreshed for our visitors and you. I told Jonathan not to worry about making me dinner tomorrow, I will probably go to Jason's when I'm done for the day and have dinner there." James started to yawn now so we laughed and said it was time to say good night. He was going to be glad to be home in a few days. I took my glass to the kitchen and went up to bed.

The next morning, I made myself a coffee and some toast had a glass of orange juice and was out the door. My day at the spa was so relaxing and I took extra time for the massage. The hydrating facial felt wonderful as did the mani/pedi. The manicurist knew that I liked a lot of colours, so she made sure she had them all. We went with one a neutral enough shade but perfect for Thanksgiving. I sat waiting for them to be completely dry because I was going out for dinner.

It was a bit early for dinner but that was fine with me. Jason saw me coming and opened the door and took me to my table. He asked where James was, and I said in Toronto on business but would be home soon. I was having company come for Thanksgiving. My meal arrived, and I ate and then went home. John locked the gate behind me as I drove in. I turned the security system off when I went in and back on once I was in. It was a very relaxing day, but I wanted to go to bed. I took a quick shower and put my pjs on. James and I video chatted and then said good night. I fell asleep in no time. I got up the next morning, washed up and dressed. Jen was coming by today with the photo and I was anxious to see it framed. Jonathan was in the kitchen making coffee and muffins, which was all that I wanted.

"What did you do with the day off yesterday?" He met up with some friends and may have possibly met someone new, but he didn't want to say anything to jinx it. I wished him luck. I sent off some texts to Janet, Ross, and Lindsay as I did each day. Lindsay texted me that Ayleen lost a tooth in the front. She sent me a picture and I had to laugh. She would soon start losing more of them, but I hoped not until after Christmas. One wasn't too bad, but she would feel awkward smiling. I texted back to tell her to let Ayleen know I arranged for the family photo to be done when they came. Lindsay asked me to call her.

"Is everything ok. You guys are still coming aren't you." She said of course they were, but she wanted to know how dressed up they had to be. I told her that I had a silk dress for Ayleen in James's tartan made and it would be here for her. Ross could bring his suit with him and that only she needed to get something. She said she would go and have a look and I said I would too and send her photos. If I picked up something she would like I would have it here.

"I will get a few things with some shoes as well and you can pick and choose. I know how busy you are with school and then looking after the house on the weekend and getting ready for the holidays. Why don't you let me go look, I'll send you a bunch of pictures and you can say yeah or nay to them. I'll have them upstairs in the closet in your room and you can try each one on. I know your size for dresses and shoes so let me do the shopping if you are ok with that." She was definitely ok with it because she had so many other things to do over the next couple of months. She also mentioned that Ross had a surprise for me which of course she would not tell me about. We hung up just as the doorbell rang. It was Jennifer and she had an armload of things with her. I took a few from her and we went into the sunroom.

"Ok so I decided to get all the photos done we talked about and get them framed. I was just so jazzed with the photos that I kept working on them. I didn't do any airbrushing or touch ups, what you see here is all you and it is stunning." The first framed photo she showed me was of the tulle ball gown outside. It had a very ethereal look to it and the light was perfect in the background. It was so real looking. I think I must have stared at it for fifteen minutes. She handed me a double frame with the black and white one with my foot crossed and the blue star showing which also had me in the black gown beside it. It was quite something and I loved that touch of colour. The next framed photo was of me on James's desk blowing smoke rings.

"I had a very hard time choosing on this one because every one of your photos was that good, but I thought the one with you winking he would get a kick out of. But it was a hard choice between that one and the one with your head back blowing smoke rings. They were all so good." She brought out the rest of the photos too in 5 x 7 enlargements to give me an idea of what the rest looked like.

"Wow, you are really very good Jennifer. You make me look stunning in each one of these." She said it was not so much her as me. We looked through each one and I think the only one that I was not as keen on was the casual one. It was nice, but it didn't seem to fit with the rest.

"I love them all and I know James will too. Can I keep these, and do you mind if I send photos of them to a few of my friends and to James's Aunt? I said I would if I could." Jen had no issue with that at all.

"I was really torn whether to do the one of you on the staircase larger. It is an unbelievable photo, and I couldn't decide so I did them both up. Maybe he can put one here and the other in his office in Toronto." Jonathan came in and asked if he could look at them. I said of course he could.

"Wow Cassandra those are really good. I love that one of you on the stairs, but I also like the one that was done outside. James is going to be floored." He went back into the kitchen to make lunch. Jen said she could stay so we had chef salads and a glass of wine.

"Thank you so much for doing all of this so quickly. I am going to have a hard time keeping them until his birthday, but I will give him the two in the gown. If I don't I will probably burst wanting to show them to him." Lunch was wonderful, but Jennifer said she had to run. She enlarged the two ball gown photos for 12 x 14 frames. I took them upstairs and put them in the same spare room as the painting except for the two in the gown. Those I took and put in our bedroom and put them in the closet in one of my drawers. I gave Sonya a quick call to make sure she was still coming and Rhonda too.

"Oh yes I wouldn't miss this and in fact I just got off the phone with Rhonda and she said that she can get Wednesday off, so a day earlier. We could be ready to go then if that works for James." I said I would call him and then get right back to her. James answered on the second ring. I told him what Sonya said to see if he was able to finish up and come home a day early.

"Are you kidding, I will get Mina to arrange my schedule so that I can. I am glad they are able to do that because I miss you like crazy. Richard and Mark won't be able to come earlier though as they have meetings scheduled. They can come on a commercial flight on the day as planned." He said he would have their names at the gate, and he would be there to pick them up at 1:00 on Wednesday. I hung up with James and called Sonya back.

"He can pick you guys up at the airport at 1:00. You don't go into the airport ok; you go through a VIP gate for private planes. The security guard there will have your names and I assume Rhonda will be driving. She can leave her car parked in the VIP spot. James will probably be there a little before 1:00. You can bring however much luggage you need; he has no restrictions. James will be waiting for you at the top of the stairs to the plane. The weather has been pretty good here, not too chilly, but you should probably make sure you bring a warm enough jacket just in case. The flight will be about three to four hours. You will have lunch on the plane and whatever beverage you want. You will be getting to the house here around 4:30 and we will have a nice big dinner. I am so looking forward to seeing you both. It's too bad that Nicole and Austin can't come in a day sooner." She said she forgot to mention that because they were both coming in on Thursday now instead of Friday.

"This is wonderful. We won't feel rushed to go shopping now and I know James is looking forward to meeting all of you. I know you have talked to him on video chat, but he is so looking forward to actually meeting you. Now Richard and Mark will not be with you because James is coming earlier, which probably works out better because you won't have to deal with all the new people on the plane. Enjoy the flight, the plane is amazing, and James will take very good care of both of you." Sonya was now getting giddy with excitement. They would make sure they were on time tomorrow. I let Jonathan know that things had been moved up a day and that perhaps we could have a nice big dinner tomorrow night. He would take care of everything. He also let me know that the florist was coming by in an hour or so and that Christina was coming as well to make sure everything was as she wanted it.

"I know it is only Thanksgiving, but it feels like Christmas. I am so excited." I couldn't contain my joy. I poured myself a glass of white wine and went to the sunroom, but I was so excited I couldn't stay sitting. The doorbell rang, and it was Christina.

"Has the florist arrived yet, what has you so happy." I told her, and she was glad that she came by today. The florist brought all the flowers in through the side entrance to the kitchen. The boxes were laid out on the island and there were lots of them. So many that some had to be put on the floor.

"Before you start putting them out, I want to show you something. Come upstairs with me. I am so excited about this I can hardly contain myself." I took Christina into the bedroom closet and pulled out the framed photos. The look on her face said everything.

"Holy crap Cassandra these are so stunning. Did you get these for James, what am I saying of course you did? He will be totally blown away. My God this dress is stunning on you. I hope you bought it, but I don't see it." I said that I hadn't, but I would get it later. I took her to the spare room and showed her the painting and the rest of the photos. She laughed with joy when she saw the one of me blowing smoke rings and winking.

"He is going to love this one. It is tasteful and yet quite naughty. I love what you are wearing in everyone one these and being a little provocative showing a little of the undies, very sexy. I love this one with the blue star showing, that is so adorable. Thank you for showing these to me. You look stunning in every one of them. Now, I need to get the flowers put out." We went back downstairs, and I helped her with the flowers. I held the box while she put them out. They were so very beautiful, and I liked that she went with cream roses and not white. The thistle and heather were beautiful and just as I remembered when I was in Scotland. We took the flowers upstairs as well and I said that my guests were coming in a day ahead of schedule.

"It's a good thing that I had these delivered today then. I think they look really wonderful don't you." I agreed totally. The flowers in each room were so pretty. I loved the fall colours. I asked her if she wanted to stay for dinner, but she had plans with friends.

"Thank you but I have to run. Those photos are stunning. Jennifer is a very good photographer, but she had a beautiful subject to work with. Enjoy your evening and your holidays. I'll be back on the Wednesday or Thursday after Thanksgiving to take everything down and we can go over Christmas if you want." I said that I had my best friend coming to stay for a few days so perhaps we could wait until the week after to go over the boards. She said that was fine with her. I went into the dining room to look once again at the table. It was really pretty, and the flowers were really quite beautiful. The china was set out and it looked perfect. I almost cried at what I was looking at. I'd never had such a beautiful table set before. I was really so very blessed.

I was buzzing around like someone on speed, but it was pure joy that I was experiencing. I decided to go and do a workout and burn off some of this energy. It seemed to have worked because I was more relaxed now. I took a shower, dressed again, and went back downstairs. I poured myself another glass of wine and sat in the kitchen as Jonathan was preparing our dinner. When dinner was over, I went into the sunroom. Jonathan popped in to say he cleaned up and was leaving and would turn on the alarm on his way out.

I waved goodnight to him. I was so happy James was coming home tomorrow. It felt like such a long time since I had seen him. The woods were quiet, no deer milling about, and the birds were getting in the last of the feeding before the sun went down for the night. I put on some music to fill the room, so it wasn't so quiet. John called up to say that the moose was taken to the butcher, and it would be packaged by Friday. He was putting everything in the big freezers that were in the Quonset. It got quiet again. I decided to try James because I couldn't wait for him to call me.

"Am I interrupting anything? I am so anxious to see you tomorrow I couldn't wait to talk." He finished eating and was sitting by the fire with a glass of wine.

"I will be glad to be home. It has felt like a month that I have been away and not two weeks." I told him that Sonya and Rhonda would be at the airport on time and that they would be having lunch on the plane.

"Jonathan is going to have a nice big welcome home dinner for you. He didn't say what, but it doesn't matter, it will be delicious no matter what. Sonya might be nervous flying so keep her occupied with conversation." James was prepared for that, so he was going to keep her engaged. We talked for an hour, and he had another call coming in. He said good night and we'd see each other tomorrow. I went upstairs to pick out what I was going to wear tomorrow. I decided on the toffee coloured leather pants and the chunky steel blue colour cashmere sweater and the dark brown suede booties. With my wardrobe figured out for the next day, I got into my pjs and fell asleep having a wonderful smile on my face.

I woke next morning like it was Christmas morning. I jumped in the shower, did my hair and makeup put on my clothes and went down to the smell of coffee. Jonathan could tell by the smile on my face that I was happy. I had a nice big mug of coffee while he was doing up eggs benedict, a special day he said. I ate with relish and was so full of energy I had to do something. I told Jonathan I was going shopping and probably would not be back for lunch. He was going to do prime rib for dinner with roast potatoes and savory vegetables. He also was making up a berry crumble for dessert since he knew that was James's favourite.

I had hours and hours to burn so what better way to do it than shopping. The mall was decorated for Christmas and not Thanksgiving. I thought I would take a chance and give Jacob a call to see if he could meet with me to help me pick out some things for Lindsay and maybe a few things for me. He was free, and we agreed that he would charge me his rate on the hour because I didn't want a full time stylist. He said he would be at the mall in an hour. I told him I was on the third level and that I would be waiting. It didn't seem like an hour had gone by when I saw Jacob walking toward me. He took my arm, and we started walking.

"Ok, so can I see that picture of you guys again, so I can look at her features and skin colour. I know you said she doesn't wear a lot of dresses but for the photo you want her to wear one. Let's start here and then we will hit all the stores on the way down." We looked through every rack and picked out a few dresses. There was one in a dark green silk A-line that I thought would look very pretty on her. Jacob thought so too, and they had it in her size.

We held onto that and looked for another one in a different colour in case she didn't want anything dark. There was one in red with long sleeves in silk as well. I knew she would hate me for the silk but if I had to, I would pay for the cleaning. This one had a nice round neck, but it was plain which was okay. We looked through the costume jewelry and Jacob picked out a strand of big pearls, not too big but they had crystals. He wanted to get the matching bracelet, but I didn't think she would wear it, but I took photos and sent them to her to see what she thought.

She texted back after a few minutes that she loved both dresses and she even liked the pearl bracelet. She could wear the pearls with either dress. I paid for everything, and we went on to another store. We got her a pair of black suede shoes that she could wear with either dress that didn't have a high heel. She said she liked those too. I knew they weren't struggling financially as much anymore, but I wanted them to have some nice clothes when they came. I did have some cashmere for all of them for Christmas which I mentioned to Jacob. I texted her back again and asked if I could go crazy for her and Ross. Ayleen had clothes galore, so she was not an issue. She texted back the usual lol and knock yourself out. Having kept theirs sizes when we shopped in Ottawa, I looked at Jacob and said let's have fun.

"Lady you said the magic words to the stylist in me. Now, I think we will leave it with two dresses for Lindsay. You said you got her a brown cashmere pullover and a royal blue V-neck cashmere as well. Let's get her a pair of black leather pants, you can never go wrong with those and she's tall so that will look good and maybe a pair in dark brown. I am sure she will bring jeans with her, so let's pick up a few more sweaters and a few blouses that she can mix and match." We walked around the store together looking at different items.

"Since you got her cashmere, let's go with something that she can clean easily. These light wool mohair mixes are very nice, and they are hand wash so that will be ok. Maybe get her a really good pant suit that she can wear to work, perhaps even two or three. I know she works with little ones, but we will keep the fabric easy to clean. Let's get this navy blue one, this dark brown one and this black one. She can mix and match all the blouses and sweaters. I am sure she would appreciate flats when she is at work so let's get her a few pairs of those. I like the red suede ones, the green leather ones and of course the black leather ones. What about some boots. We can get her a really nice black leather pair and maybe a few booties in the suede like the ones you have only in black, navy, and brown. There that should do it for her." We had so many bags I didn't know how we were going to carry it all.

"Leave that to me, I'm good at managing a lot of bags. Let's go to the men's store and get that son of yours dressed to the hilt. Now I wish he would shave that beard off; it doesn't suit his face at all. He has your eyes, well his are brown but they are the same shape. Now I know you said he is a courier, so we know he is not going to be wearing designer dress pants to work, but he should have a few pair at least." We walked around the men's store and Jacob was looking at different things.

"I remember you saying you bought him a navy light weight wool suit, but I beg of you to buy him another suit maybe even two more. I highly recommend this designer wool suit in black and let's go with this really dark grey almost charcoal one. You said he tried on a light grey but the colour didn't suit him and I agree. He needs to stick with dark colours especially around his face. I would get at least two pair of black Italian lace up dress shoes, one in leather and the other suede. Let's get him at least three white silk shirts, three light blue, three light grey and some casual dress shirts in all of those colours again that he can wear with casual pants. We'll get these ties that he can mix and match with the shirts and suits. We'll have the suits tailored when he comes, no point guessing." Now there I knew I we didn't need to guess.

"I'm sure James can get him over here for an hour or so and then you can pick them up on another day. I suggest getting him chinos in black, dark brown, navy and perhaps in a light grey. As long as the grey is not near his face they can work, and I would get the stretchable ones, so he is comfortable. Again, with pullovers mix them up with V-neck and round neck, go with dark green, black, a light blue and I would even go with a red. He can wear a nice white t-shirt underneath and he will look amazing. Here get these t-shirts as well, you can never have too many of them. He doesn't look like the loafer kind of guy so perhaps a nice pair of sneakers. Ok so did we miss anything?" I looked at him with wide eyes.

"I know what his inseam is having bought him the suit, so we can get that done now and he won't have to run out. We can pick up the suits when we are done. I don't think we left anything in the store. I agree with everything you got, and I am glad that you made all the choices you did. I think they will love everything. I got Ayleen a dress and a few sweaters, but I know she is going to look at everything Mommy and Daddy got and wonder why I didn't shop for her. She would never say that, but I don't want her to feel left out. Also, that gown I wore for the photo shoot, I want to get it and the shoes, and I would like to get one for Ayleen but in a light shade of lavender with matching shoes. Hers should be a short sleeve though not spaghetti straps like mine. I will give you a cheque that should more than cover both but let me know if it comes to more." He saw the amount and said it should more than cover it.

"Be still my heart. I will order you the dress and the shoes and for Ayleen as well. I am so happy you are getting it. It looked stunning on you. Now for little Miss Ayleen, we will have to get her a few dresses. She has to look like a princess. I know you said her favourite colour is purple but maybe we can expand her colour choices a little. Let's head over to that store and have a look around." We had so many bags already that we had to take what we had down to my car. Fortunately, I had a big blanket, so we covered the packages, and the back windows were smoked so you couldn't see in. We went back in and up to the store for Ayleen.

Jacob pulled out a navy blue dress, that was velvet on top and tulle on the bottom. It had lots of sparkles in it. He also picked out a plum colour A-line for her that had some embellishments on it. They were both very pretty along with a few pair of cream colour tights and that was it for the dresses. I knew that Lindsay would be bringing run around clothes, so we picked out one pair of jeans that were adorable and a jean jacket and a Mandalay style tunic in a nice red as well as some velour tops and bottoms in navy, green, purple and red. We picked out a pair of red suede booties I knew she would love and a black pair as well. We got a pair of scalloped ballerina flats in gold that she could easily wear with any of the dresses as well as a black pair. I thought we were done.

"Oh no, now that I have the chance to take you shopping for you, I am going to do it. I am going to help you fill up that closet that is so bare right now. I know you bought leather pants and that's great and you have some nice wool and gabardine ones, but you need more in a few styles, and let's buy a few more gowns, you never know when you might need them." He obviously wasn't going to take no for an answer so after five hours of shopping I was pooped. Jacob was just hitting stride.

"You need to shop with me more often, you'll get your second wind, but I think for today, we did very well. Now let's go pick up your son's suits and get these packages down to your car." I could not have done all this without his help. While I spent a lot of money, I enjoyed doing it and as James's had requested many times, I used the credit card he gave me. I wrote Jacob out a cheque for his fee, which was not as bad as I thought. He deserved every penny. I would certainly think about bringing him along when I took Sonya, Rhonda, and Nicole shopping and mentioned it to him. I thought Rhonda would get a kick out of him.

I got home, and it took me several trips to bring everything in. Moira finished cleaning for the day and Jonathan was in the kitchen getting ready for the guests to arrive. James was due to be here around 4:30 pm, which was an hour from when I got home. I took everything upstairs and hung it up in the closets of the bedroom that they would be staying in at Christmas. I went and tidied up a bit and put on some lipstick. I went down and was going to have a glass of wine, but James texted they were on their way home. I stood in James's office waiting for them to drive up. It was silly, but I was anxious to see all of them. The car was coming up the drive, so I went to the front door and stood at the top of the steps waiting for them. James got out and waved with a big smile. I went down to give him a big hug and kiss.

"Welcome home James. Hi Sonya, Rhonda how nice to see you both." Hugs and kisses were shared all around. James said he would bring up the luggage and put them by the stairs. Sonya was looking at the house and so was Rhonda.

"Holy frig Cassie, oops, Mom said Cassandra, this is amazing. We had a good time on the plane. Mom did really well but James was keeping her busy. That's probably the sweetest flight I have ever been on. Love the plane and James is not bad either." Rhonda loved to talk, and it was nice to hear since I hadn't seen her in years. Sonya looked a little speechless.

"Come, let's go in it is a little chilly out." We walked in the front, and they were both speechless. I thought Sonya was going to cry.

"This is a very beautiful home and James is a very nice man. I'm happy for you, you have deserved this for a very long time. I love all the decorations." I said I hadn't done them myself that we had an interior designer do it. James came in with the last of the luggage which he left at the bottom of the stairs. I wanted to jump into his arms but refrained until we were alone. I think he knew that and smiled wickedly at me.

"Sweetheart do you want to give them the tour now, or shall we go into the sunroom, and I'll get some champagne and we can relax for a bit. Sonya did very well on the flight. I don't think she was as nervous as she thought she would be. I'll go get the champagne and glasses and join you shortly." I took them very quickly through the large dining room, living room and out to the sunroom.

"I do like this room a lot. You have a really nice view of the woods, and it is so quiet back here. I love the home; it is really very beautiful." Rhonda kept walking around looking at things. Sonya wanted her to sit.

"Hey, look around if you want. There is more to see. There is a games room downstairs, we have a really good work out room which I think you will both like and a dry sauna. There is a movie room down there too so if some night you want to watch the latest movie we can do that, all with popcorn if you want and a bar. We haven't really had a chance to use it yet. After we have some champagne, I will take you up to your rooms and let you unpack. Dinner will be in the smaller dining room on the other side of the kitchen. We'll be using the larger dining room for Thanksgiving dinner and once Nicole and Austin get here." Just at that moment James came back with the champagne. I knew he was going to bring up my favourite champagne which I didn't think Sonya would know anything about, but Rhonda did.

"Mom don't drop a bit of this it is very expensive, I mean really expensive." Her hand shook a little and I started to laugh.

"I was the same way the first time James bought it for me. It is really good, and I think you will like it. We will probably have some for dinner on Sunday. Now what shall we toast to." Rhonda said she would like to do it.

"To the two of you for having us in your home and being so kind and generous and holy crap Mom look at the rock on her finger. I guess we also have to say congratulations, may you have a long and happy life together." The toast was perfect, and I showed them my ring.

"James proposed when we were in Scotland. I was stunned when he gave me this, but he has been surprising me almost every day." They were both very happy for us. Jonathan came in to say that dinner was ready.

"Man, a personal chef too, this just gets better and better." I knew Rhonda would lighten the mood and make the conversation fun. She could get any room going in conversation and laughter and that's what I loved about her. I introduced Jonathan as he was bringing in the meal. He served up each plate asking for preference on the doneness of the prime rib. There was wine with the meal and coffee afterwards. Rhonda tried some of James's whisky on the plane and liked it. It was not something she would drink very often but she enjoyed it.

"Jonathan can make up any cocktail you would like, he's not only an excellent chef but he's a very good mixologist." Everyone decided to stay with wine. Dinner over and dessert eaten, we went to the sunroom.

"Perhaps we should take your luggage up first and I can let you unpack. Let's go upstairs. It's ok James we have it." I helped them take their luggage up and showed them each the room they were going to be in. We went into Sonya's first and she was very touched with the décor. Then I took them over to Rhonda's and she was tickled with her room.

"When you are ready, come down to the sunroom and we can have more wine." They said they would unpack as quickly as possible. I went down to the sunroom where James was and practically threw myself into his arms. He kissed me so deeply that I had to remind him they would be down soon. He held me close and kissed me again.

"I missed you so much and I can't wait to go to bed with you tonight." I laughed, and he went to get another bottle of wine.

"I like your sister and Rhonda although I have to say she is quite the talker. I loved it; she can spin the conversation around on a dime. I think she and Mark will get along very well and I know that Richard is going to like Sonya." That made me happy, but I didn't know what Rhonda's situation was. James said that he never thought to find out. They came back down in a matter of twenty minutes.

"My God, I love this house. I had to drag Mom out of the bedroom, she didn't want to leave. She loved it and I love the one I'm in. I can only imagine what this place is going to look like at Christmas. Geez we should come." I knew she was joking, sort of. I looked at James and he shrugged.

"You are more than welcome to come if you want. Ross, Lindsay, and Ayleen will be here, and I am happy to have more family. I know that it is usually only the two of you at Christmas, so why not come. We are going to pick them up and you know there is more than enough room on the plane and here." Sonya wasn't sure, but I knew Rhonda was onboard.

"Sonya, we would love for you to come. I would feel bad if you didn't and there is more than enough room." Rhonda was pleading with her and said she would even sleep on the floor if she had to. She thought about it for a few minutes.

"We would love to come, thank you for including us." So that was settled, and we would check with Nicole and Austin when they came. I knew that Sonya didn't get to spend Christmas with them often, so this was going to be very special.

"Plans for the time here, as I mentioned we have the exercise room downstairs but tomorrow morning if everyone is up to it we will go for a good power walk around the property. The path is paved and now we don't have to worry about sex crazed moose." I told them about the bulls fighting and how they had to be shot because they put a tree through the window.

"I hope you were able to keep all the meat." I said that we were at least most of it. The caretaker and his son shot them and tagged them, all approved by the property authorities and that the meat was currently being cut and wrapped and would be here on Friday.

"I'm going to send some home with you guys, so you can have roasts and steaks. We could probably have some steaks for dinner Friday night, but I will have to check with Jonathan when the meat is arriving. I think you probably noticed the caretaker's house as you were coming in. That is where John, Moira and their kids live. John looks after the grounds and maintenance. Moira and her daughters do the cleaning, at least the girls do on the weekends and Moira has a few girls that she brings in during the week. I still pinch myself. They are wonderful and like family." We sat and drank more wine. Sonya was starting to open up a bit more, laughing and participating in the conversation. Rhonda was wonderful making everyone laugh. It was a good time, but it was starting to get late, and we were going to have a pretty full day with Nicole and Austin arriving around noon. James was going to pick them up at the airport.

"Is it ok if I go with you James. Might be a good idea since Nicole and Austin don't know you." James said that would work well for him. Sonya started to yawn, not so much I think that she was tired. I think the champagne and wine were hitting her.

"Sonya, come I will walk you upstairs to your room. Rhonda, I know you are not sleepy yet so maybe you and James can share a glass or two of whisky and chat." I winked at James not really wanting to get Rhonda tipsy, but she could party for several more hours and I wanted to get James in bed.

"Do you really like the room. Christina the interior decorator put a few extra touches for you. I said you liked to decorate at home. I think you will be comfortable and warm." She gave me a hug which for Sonya to do out of the blue was rare.

"I'm happy for you, really I am. That ring, it is so gorgeous. It must have cost a fortune. That's a yellow diamond isn't it." I was hesitant to say anything because

I didn't want her to think I was gloating. She could tell I was hesitant.

"You don't have to tell me, and you would not be gloating. We are really happy for you, really, we are. I hope that I can have half as comfortable a life. Tell me about the ring." I told her that yes it was extremely expensive being a natural fancy yellow diamond. I had no idea what he paid for it, but I was sure it was well into the high six figures.

"On Friday, the girls are going shopping, and it will be on James. He made me promise to make sure that I would not let any of you pay for anything. He won't even let me spend any of my own money." She laughed and said I could give it to her.

"Sonya if you are having a hard time you know you can come to me. I will be more than happy to help out with anything, you know that." She said she did and was only kidding because she was quite comfortable financially.

"Right now, I want to hit the sack. That champagne was good, but I think with the wine it is hitting me. What time does everyone usually get up here. You know I am an early riser." I said that I was generally up at 6:00 as was James. She and I could go for a walk if she wanted. James could wait for Rhonda, who was not such an early riser, and have coffee together. I hugged her good night and said I would see her in the morning. James and Rhonda were still talking when I came down.

"I love this guy and I could talk longer but I am going to hit the sack too. I suppose Mom said she would be up at 6:00 but I don't think I will be. Maybe 7:00 for me and I will go for a run around the property if that's ok. I prefer to run than walk." James said he would join her if that was ok, which Rhonda said it was. The morning routine was set. Jonathan left hours ago. Rhonda went up to her room and now it was James and me. I went over to sit in his lap.

"Hi, I'm glad you are home. I have something I want to show you but it's upstairs." I took his hand and led him to our bedroom. He was looking at me with a questioning look. I went into the closet and took one of the framed photos out of the drawer. He was standing in the doorway, and I turned around and showed him the photo. His jaw dropped. He didn't say anything for a few minutes.

"That is stunning absolutely stunning. When did you get this done? I can't believe how beautiful you look in this photo. I mean you are always beautiful, but this is so beautiful." I pulled out the other one and he couldn't believe the photos. I explained that I had a bunch done, the others he wasn't getting till his birthday, but I wanted to show him these because the photographer thought they were so stunning that she wanted to put them in her portfolio. James kept looking at the photos. He was blown away.

"I can't wait to see the others if they are anything like this. What sort of deal did she want if she could use these in her portfolio." I said that she was going to wave her fee for the entire day, which was quite large and that she promised to only use them in her portfolio and not anywhere else.

"If you are ok with that and she is prepared to sign a document to that effect, then I am ok with it. These are so stunning. I don't know which one to put in which office." We put the photos down on the island in the closet and went into the bedroom. James took me in his arms and started to finish what he started downstairs. Clothes went flying and the covers on the bed were yanked back. He laid me back on the bed and started kissing me over and over.

"I have so missed you and I have so missed making love to you. I hope you rested while I was gone, this is going to be a long night." He was true to his word. We fell asleep in each other's arms in the wee hours of the morning.

I got up around 5:30 because I forgot to tell them that we had an alarm system, and I couldn't remember if James set it or not and I didn't want it going off. I pulled on my work out gear and went downstairs. Sonya was not down yet which was good. I sat on the bottom of the stairs with a bottle of water. Not long after, I saw Sonya coming down the hall dressed for a walk. I grabbed my jacket, turned on the lights on the path, handed her a bottle and off we went. I wasn't sure if she realized how long the walk would be. She said her head was a little fuzzy, so we slowed the pace a bit.

"This is a nice walk and it being paved and lighted makes it nicer. Will you plow it in the winter? This is a lot longer than I thought it would be, but it makes for a nice walk. Rhonda will love the run. She will probably go around several times though." We walked around two times and as we were going in, James and Rhonda came out at 7:30. I gave him a kiss and off they went.

"Don't forget you have to leave for the airport at 11:00 so take that into account on the laps." Sonya and I went in and went up to shower. I came down before her and had on a pair of jeans and the royal blue cashmere sweater with the black suede booties. She came down about ten minutes later wearing jeans and a burnt orange sweater with a pair of flats. We grabbed a coffee and went into the sunroom to wait on James and Rhonda. It was coming up on 9:00 when they came back in. They went up to shower and came down. James was wearing his jeans and a black cashmere V-neck with a white t shirt underneath and a pair of suede shoes. Rhonda came down in a pair of brown suede pants, cream colour pullover and brown suede boots. We went into the dining room and Jonathan brought out a large pot of coffee which he put by James who served everyone a steaming cup. Then Jonathan brought in hot trays that had scrambled eggs, bacon, sausage, eggs benedict, freshly made multi-grain toast, fresh fruit slices, yogurt, and some jams.

"Wow this all looks great. Do we go up and get what we want?" I told Rhonda to help herself. She did just that. James walked along beside her and then Sonya and me. I had the eggs benedict as did Sonya. It was all really good, and everyone enjoyed it.

"These are the best eggs benedict I've ever had." Jonathan appreciated Sonya's compliment. With our tummy's full, we grabbed more coffee and went to the sunroom.

"As you can probably guess this is our favourite room of the house, and, I might add, it was Cassandra's suggestion to make it run the full length of the back." I smiled with appreciation. James checked his watch and wanted to check on a couple of emails. He excused himself and went to his study. We sat and laughed about things from the past. It was nice to reminisce, but I didn't want to talk too much about other family. Sonya must have warned Rhonda about it because she never brought the other two up. James came back and said to

Rhonda that they should go. We walked out with them to the garage. I had a feeling that Rhonda was going to say something about the sports car. They went into the garage.

"Holy crap Mom look at this friggin sports car." Sonya shook her head, not that Rhonda shouted but that she nearly swore. I laughed.

"I'm glad it wasn't the 'f' bomb. Not that it would have shocked James or me. I was actually expecting it when you got here, so I'm happy she restrained herself." We walked down to the garage and Sonya saw the car. But they were taking the suv to the airport because of the amount of luggage. Rhonda and James went off to the airport and we went back into the house.

"I don't drive his car otherwise I would take you for a spin. I love the car, but I will never drive it and I told James not to buy me one. He wanted to, but I said no. Too much car for me and I would be so afraid of getting hit. What would you like to do until they come back. We can sit in the sunroom and have some tea. Jonathan creates his own which James is going to market. He has some very lovely teas that I think you would like. I think my favourite is the lavender, but he has a lot of them. She said that sounded good to her. I asked Jonathan for a pot of his lavender tea and the fine china teacups.

"I'm glad you are coming for Christmas. I originally wanted to do the cooking, but James said that I should spend time with Ayleen and to let Jonathan do it. He's an excellent chef and he makes the most amazing desserts. I told him what kind of stuffing I wanted though so he has agreed to do the one Mom always made. It isn't Christmas without her stuffing. When we go shopping I don't want you to back away from anything ok. I bought a whole bunch of clothes for Ross, Lindsay, and Ayleen for when they are here. Ayleen wants a family photo, so everyone has to get dressed up. I have a navy beaded lace dress James bought me that I am wearing. Lindsay is either going to wear dark green or red and Ayleen is wearing a silk dress in James's clan tartan that we had made for her. Ross will be in a suit as will James. I have this stylist friend who helped me pick out all the clothes for them and I know he would love to help all of you when we go. He's very amusing, gay and has impeccable taste. I spent a whack load of money that day, but James insists that I do. Does Rhonda even wear dresses?" Tomorrow was going to be a fun shopping day and Sonya was excited about going.

"I'm good with the stylist and I am sure Rhonda and Nicole will be too. It depends on what sort of dress Rhonda has to wear, so we'll see, but Nicole wears them for work all the time. I have no problem spending a little of James's money if that's what he wants. I could use some new clothes. I think Austin has a suit, but I doubt he brought it, so he would need one. Maybe he should come with us although I know he hates shopping." We were settled on the shopping spree.

"James can come along, and once Austin has a suit, shirt, tie, and shoes he and James can head back to the house and do whatever. Jacob has been dying to meet James. I think he has a crush on him." About an hour passed and we could hear people coming in the front door. We went out to greet them. Nicole gave her Mom a big hug and kiss as did Austin. Nicole came over to me.

"Cassandra, I was warned about the name, I haven't seen you in years. You look really good and wow the home is beautiful. Austin, this is Cassandra. She's my favourite aunt although I don't think I ever told her that." I gave her a big hug and kiss and Austin too.

"And you and Rhonda are my favourite nieces and I know I told you both that. Austin it is very nice to meet you. Come let's all go into the sunroom.

"Can I get anyone a drink. Rhonda would you like wine or whisky, Austin, Nicole, what about you. I see Cassandra and Sonya are drinking tea, do you want something else ladies." Rhonda told Austin that the whisky was James's own from his distillery in Scotland, so he said he would have a shot of that for sure. Rhonda and Nicole had white wine and Sonya and I continued with the tea. Nicole leaned over to smell the tea.

"It smells like lavender. It's a pretty colour. I might try some later if that's ok." I went to get her a teacup. James came back from the wine cellar with another bottle of wine and a bottle of the whisky. He poured Rhonda and Nicole wine and Austin and himself a shot of the whisky.

"Cheers everyone and thank you for hosting us in your beautiful home. Here's to a wonderful four or five days. What are the plans, or do we have any." Nicole sat next to Sonya on the sofa while Rhonda and Austin sat in the armchairs and James sat next to me.

"The plan is for the ladies to go shopping tomorrow. Oh yes, I forgot, would you and Austin be free to come for Christmas. Your Mom and Rhonda are coming, and I know that you have not had a Christmas together in a long time. We have lots of room and we would love it. Ross, Lindsay, and Ayleen are coming too. It will be the first time in a very long time I have been around family for Christmas so please say you will come." Nicole looked at Austin. I hoped I wasn't putting them on the spot.

"As it turns out the plans we had fell through. We were going to surprise Mom and say we would go to her place but since she is going to be here and Rhonda too, we would love to come. I can't even remember what

Ross looks like and I've never met Lindsay or Ayleen, so this will be a nice family reunion." I was so happy.

"Ok, so Ayleen wanted Santa to bring her a family photo, so I said I would help get her one. We are going to get dressed up for that part, the rest of the time everyone can be casual. As I was starting to say, tomorrow was going to be a shopping spree for the ladies, but Austin I would like to get you a suit for the photo. I'm sure you have a suit, but I would like to get you one. I bought two for Ross today, sorry honey, the credit card took a hit today." James laughed and said that was what it was for.

"If I can get you to come with us just long enough to get the suit. You and James can come in his car and once you are done, you guys can leave and come back here or go wherever. We'll go in the suv if you are ok with that James, it's bigger than mine." Austin said he saw the sports car when they pulled into the garage.

"James are you ok with that. I think you had some plans to do with Austin. If everyone is ok with that, we will have breakfast at 9:00 and then head out the. The mall doesn't open until 10:00. If you want to go for a run or power walk in the morning that's ok too. Does that sound ok with everyone?" Everyone was agreeable.

"Now I should warn you ahead of time that I have a stylist who is going to meet us. He was part of the team that was here last week to do a photo shoot. I should show you one of the pictures that was taken." James got up to say he would get it.

"Jacob is going to meet us at the mall and help pick out things. I know you know how to shop but this guy is really, really good, and he picked out a bunch of things for me. He's respectful and won't barge in when you are changing so wait and see whether or not you want his help." James came back with the photo and held it up for the others to see and Nicole commented.

"My God, that is a very beautiful photo of you Cassandra. You look gorgeous in that dress. If he can make you look like that, I'm in." James said he thought the photo was stunning and took it back to his office.

"There was hair and makeup as well, which I plan to have here on the 22nd as well. I thought we could get the family photo out of the way, and everyone could relax. Will you guys be able to make it for then." Nicole said they already arranged to be off the Sunday before Christmas, so they could be here any time after that. Rhonda said she would book off from the 21st and wasn't planning to go back to work until after New Year's. She and Sonya could come on the plane with Ross, Lindsay, and Ayleen. James was going to be in Toronto the week prior and would wait and bring them.

“What about you Nicole, can you and Austin stay until after New Year’s we can have a big New Year’s party. This will be such fun.” James was smiling. I could see that he was happy I was happy.

“Nicole and Austin, you should see his plane, you’d die. Too bad you guys live up north.” James said that something could be arranged at some point. It was then I guess that Nicole noticed my ring.

“Wow I just noticed your ring. Congratulations when are you planning to get married.” James told them that it was going to be May 1st in Scotland. He wanted them to come of course but we hadn’t gotten around to saying anything.

“I have a pretty large estate there and Ross and his family are coming and Cassandra’s friends, there will still be room for family if you want to go. My plane is more than big enough. Give it some thought and let me know.” Sonya said she would have to think about it.

Rhonda was game to go. Nicole and Austin would have to see. We left it at that. Nicole and Austin had lunch on the plane and the rest of us were still full from breakfast. I went to the kitchen to take back in the tray of tea and teacups. Jonathan was busy working on the plans for dinner. He wanted to know if everyone was ok with a moose roast. I said I would check and get back to him. I could hear the laughter coming from the sunroom. It was nice to hear, I missed that a lot.

"Does anyone have any dietary concerns; anyone a vegetarian." It seemed everyone was good to eat anything, so I let Jonathan know and returned back to the sitting room. James was going to take Nicole and Austin on a tour starting downstairs.

"I forgot to show them the wine cellar the other day and the movie room." Rhonda looked at Sonya and laughed.

"Mom no offence but Aunt Cassandra can you adopt me." Sonya laughed and asked if she could be adopted too. We took them on the tour. Rhonda was blown away by the wine cellar.

"Oh my God, look at the champagne, the wine, the whisky and other liquor. I could put a cot down here and be quite happy." We laughed because we knew she was kidding. Everyone was very impressed with the house. Dinner was going to be about four hours away. The light was starting to fade a bit. I took Nicole and Austin up to their room, so they could put their things away. Nicole took me aside.

"I am very happy for you Aunt Cassandra. I have to catch myself not to say Cassie. I'm glad that you convinced Mom to come out. Now that she has flown maybe we can get her to travel out to see us too. James is a really nice guy, and he is definitely in love with you. I'm very happy for you." I gave Nicole a hug and went downstairs. Sonya and Rhonda were thinking of going for a walk around the property, but Rhonda wondered if we had flashlights.

"No need for that." James turned on the lights that went all the way around. Rhonda laughed as did Sonya because she already knew but didn't have a chance to tell Rhonda.

"Of course, you have it lit. Does anyone else want to come?" Nicole and Austin were coming downstairs and said they were ok inside and maybe tomorrow. James went with Sonya and Rhonda, and I stayed with Nicole and Austin.

"Now that your Mom and sister have gone out I can ask you a question. Is Rhonda seeing anyone? The reason I ask is that when I started to date James, Sonya asked me if he had any rich single friends. James has many rich friends, but he also has some executives that are very well off too. He has two of his executives that are going to be joining us for Thanksgiving dinner. Sonya already knows about it and is fine with it, but I didn't say anything to Rhonda." I watched to see the expression on their faces.

"James thought that Richard, his senior vice president of human resources would be perfect for Sonya. He's a year or two youngers, is very well off according to James not only because he pays him extremely well, he pays all his staff very well, but James said he comes from a very wealthy family. He was in James's office in Germany, but he moved him to Toronto. He's widowed for some time now. He has a nephew who came with him that is the director of marketing. He's Rhonda's age and not married. James said he came close a few times, but it never worked out." They looked like they weren't upset that we were doing this.

"So, while we are not really trying to fix up Rhonda per se, from what James said, he thinks Rhonda and Mark would get along and if nothing else, have a great time together. But Richard he thinks would be perfect for Sonya. Your Mom wants to be with someone who appreciates her, treats her with respect and will be good to her. James said that Richard can do all of that. Now before you say anything, I would like you to wait until you meet them both and then see what you think. I am trusting James's opinion on this, and he is seldom wrong. If you don't think it's right, you can take James aside and let him know your views. I talk to Sonya at least once a week and while I know she is happy in her condo; I know that she is lonely, but I don't want her to settle. Are you ok with this because if Sonya sees that you are not she will feel awkward?" I wasn't sure how

Nicole was going to react. Was she going to think I was meddling. Did she want us to stay out of it? I wasn't sure.

"I think James is a standup guy and I have no doubt that his judgment is solid. He is obviously very wealthy, and he didn't get that way by luck I'm sure. I've been worried about Mom too and if you guys think this guy would be good for her then let's see what happens at dinner on Sunday. I am happy that you are looking out for her and if she can get even a slice of what you have, I will be very content. She deserves someone good." That made me very happy that she was ok with it. At that moment, the other three returned and good timing too because Jonathan came in to say that dinner was ready.

We ate in the small dining room. Jonathan asked Marlene and Julie to come up and help serve. I introduced them as they were going around the table. Jonathan let everyone know what they were being served. Everyone was commenting on how good the food was. Wine was served to those who wanted it. I was relieved as I wasn't sure if Nicole and Austin would like moose. I told the story of how we came to have them in the freezer. I could laugh about it now but at the time it was nerve wracking. Coffee was served with dessert, which James was happy with as it was his favourite. I looked around the table and got a little emotional. James wanted to know what was wrong.

"Nothing is wrong. I am so happy that all of you are here. It means a lot to me to have you as my family. Thank you for coming and sharing this holiday with us." James hugged me, and everyone laughed. By the time we finished eating and drinking our wine, it was nearing 8:00 pm. While it was closer to 10:00 for Sonya and Rhonda, it was only 7:00 for Nicole and Austin.

"I know for some; your internal clocks are telling you it is bedtime and others not so much. We can sit in the sunroom and have more wine and talk, we can go downstairs and watch a movie, or if you really want, you can go to bed. Whatever you like, we want you to feel at home." Sonya was tired I knew and said she was going to head to bed. The others were good to stay up for a while longer. I walked her up to her room and hugged her and said good night. She went in and closed the door. Back downstairs, the laughter was louder. I could see that James was really enjoying himself.

"James, I know you have a large company but what all do you do, if you don't mind me asking?" James didn't mind Nicole asking and he told her what he was involved in and about the businesses he was setting up here. Nicole seemed interested.

"I know that Austin is in sales in a large company up north and I think I heard Nicole that you work for an oil company in human resources. What other sorts of things have you done? I know that Rhonda is in internet security. Have any of you given any thought to maybe changing jobs or moving?" James knew that Rhonda had skills that could easily be incorporated in his Toronto office, but he wasn't sure what all Nicole and Austin did. If Nicole was more executive human resources, he could fit her in any number of places, but he was interested in what Austin had on his resume.

"I'm not sure if Cassandra told you I work in sales for a large mining company in Yellowknife but has its head office in Tofino. I've done a number of things over the years before I went into sales. Are you going to offer us jobs?" James liked that he was direct.

"The thought crossed my mind. Rhonda I could use you in my Toronto office easily. I have a major security and computer company there with a large cyber unit. We could talk if you are interested. Nicole I am not exactly sure what your job entails but if it is in executive hiring, I could definitely use you. I am trying to hire some top level executives to help ease the burden on me. I need smart knowledge people who can start on day one. Austin you sound like you have a lot of sales experience, but I'd have to run you through an executive program to see where your strengths are, but yes, I could easily offer all three of you jobs. Now, having said that, I know Rhonda that you have always stayed pretty close to your Mom, and I know from what Cassandra has said that she doesn't want you moving too far away. These are things we would have to work out. If you are interested, we can talk further." All three of them looked at each other as I walked in.

"Um what's going on in here. One minute you were laughing and now you look so serious." James said it was fine, he was talking job possibilities.

"They are going to think about it and let me know." Well folks I don't know about you, but I am beat. You are welcome to stay up if you want. Just know that the security system is on. I don't think you will be going out but if you do I can turn it off." They said they were tired now too, so everyone was going to bed. We hugged at the top of the stairs and said good night. James and I went into our bedroom. I went into the bathroom and took off my makeup and changed into my pjs. A cute little black chemise that I bought with him in mind. James came out in his pjs bottoms and had a huge smile when he saw what I was wearing.

"I have been waiting all day so patiently to make love to you. Now I can't wait any longer. I promise to be quiet if you will." He was teasing because we both knew that this room was soundproof for many reasons. We definitely missed one another because it was well after midnight before we fell asleep.

Jonathan was in early at 5 am. He knew some got up at 6:00 so he wanted to make sure the alarm was off and that he had the coffee going. Rhonda was up at 6:00 and went into grab some water and went for a run around the property. Jonathan turned the lights on around the path. Sonya got up about half hour later and she had some coffee and then went for a power walk. The rest of us were up at 7:00 and not so inclined to run or walk just yet. I told everyone the night before not to be shy about coming down in their pjs and robes. We didn't stand on formality here. James and I came down in our pjs, robes and slippers. We grabbed the coffee pot and some mugs on a tray and went into the sunroom. Nicole and Austin followed shortly after.

"Morning you two did you sleep well?" They said they slept like rocks. They loved their room a lot. We were working on a second cup when Sonya came back in. She was going up to tidy up and would be back down. When she came back down she sat beside Nicole and Austin on the couch and poured herself some coffee. Rhonda came in about a half hour later and said she was going to take a quick shower and would be right down. Jonathan was busy making fresh muffins and more coffee. He brought in a tray and said that breakfast would be ready shortly. Rhonda came down twenty minutes later and poured some coffee.

Everyone was hungry, and we ate quickly because we were off to the mall. I took the ladies and James and Austin followed. We got to the mall, and I could see that Jacob was waiting inside. All of the stores were starting to open so after introductions, Jacob took Austin and James to the men's store. Austin tried on two designer suits, black and dark grey, shirts, ties and shoes were also bought along with several pairs of dress and casual pants, shirts, cashmere sweaters and a couple of sports jackets.

The tailor would have the suits ready in an hour or so. We said goodbye to the guys and then Jacob took the ladies shopping. The three of them were open to whatever Jacob was handing over the change room stall. In each case, they came out and loved what they were wearing. For the dressy photo, Jacob gave Sonya a royal blue silk sheath, Nicole was given a deep rose organza A-line dress and Rhonda tried on a deep purple silk A-line. I thought that she wouldn't go for it but when she came out and saw it she loved it.

Jacob selected shoes based on what they were comfortable with in a heel. We continued shopping and bought lots of pants, sweaters, blouses and more shoes and boots. I wrote Jacob a cheque for his services and several hours later and many, many bags to carry, we went to pick up Austin's suits and went home. We got in the front door and Austin and James came out to help with the bags. James and I walked out to the sunroom where he had white wine ready.

"I'm glad we have that done. I seriously could not do this very often. I am beat. What did you and

Austin do after you left?" James took him by the new businesses, so he could see what was being done. The lab was pretty much set up and would need Quinn's final approval. The geothermal office still had some wiring to be done and the textile plant was getting the wiring and plumbing put in.

"You know that I talked to each one of them last night to see if they were interested in working for me. Rhonda and Nicole have the skills that I could start them right away, but I am not sure exactly where Austin's skills lie. He does a lot of sales, but he also has some management experience, and he has a strong work ethic, but I told him he would have to go through an executive program to see where he would fit in. Maybe none of them want to move which is ok I can always find other people. Nicole would have been an asset though with her executive skills, but it's up to them to decide what they want to do." I knew that he was doing this partly because of me.

"I appreciate you making them offers. I hope they will take you up on it, but I know that Rhonda will not move far away from Sonya. Sonya will be very upset if she does, but at some point, they both have to move on. I don't know if Rhonda is stifling her own career because of Sonya. They have a lot to think about." We sat sharing a few more thoughts and the others came in the sunroom. James gave everyone a glass of wine and said that dinner wouldn't be ready for several more hours.

"Is there anything anyone would like to do till then. You can borrow my car if you want to go out somewhere or you can go and work out, don't feel you have to stay here every minute if you would like to get out on your own." Sonya said she was fine.

"Well, there is actually a hockey game on, and I know you have the giant screen downstairs. Would you mind if we went down to watch the game?" James said he would go and show them how to use the remotes and they could use the bar down there if they wanted.

"We want you to feel at home here, so if you want to watch the game that's fine. You can watch a movie if you want. Do what you would normally do." James took them downstairs, and Sonya and I sat together.

"So, Richard and Mark are coming on Sunday, From the moments you have been with James, he thinks that you and Richard will get along really well. He is one of James's top vice presidents and he makes very good money, and his family had a lot of money. Mark, his nephew is about the same age as Rhonda and James wasn't sure if Rhonda was seeing anyone or not, but if she isn't, he thought they would, if nothing else have fun together. Are you ok with that? I don't want you to feel any pressure so if when you meet him, and you are not interested just take me aside and let me know and I will let James know ok." That seemed like a good plan for Sonya, having an escape route was wise just in case.

"What is everyone going to be wearing for dinner. Are we going to be dressy or is it casual dressy?" I was thinking about that myself and trying to figure it out.

"Why don't you wear that nice black pencil skirt with the burnt orange silk blouse and the black pumps. Maybe Rhonda and Nicole could dress likewise in the skirts and blouses they got, and Austin could wear a pair of the dress pants a shirt and sport jacket. I'm sure James will be wearing something similar, and I have a dress I was going to wear. We can work on hair and makeup for each other. I have lots of makeup for everyone to use. Too bad I couldn't get Mario and Jess to come out. I should see if that is possible. I can send them a text and see if they can come after 1:00. They are so fast they would be out of here in a couple of hours. Let me text them and see if they are free." James came back up to sit with us.

"Were you not interested in the game?" James hadn't caught on to hockey yet, perhaps later on when he was able to actually sit and watch some games.

"I was saying to Sonya that I was going to see if I could get the hair stylist and makeup artist to come on Sunday to do hair and makeup. I'm waiting to see if they are available. They just replied and said they can be here at 1:00 as long as they are out by 3:00 to go for family dinners." I texted back that was fine with us. We could hear hoots and hollers from downstairs. Sonya laughed and raised an eyebrow.

"Don't worry about that Sonya it is nice to have lots of activity in the house. It was pretty quiet when James was away, and I am happy to hear the noise." Nicole came up to see if there were snacks to have downstairs. I went to the kitchen and Jonathan already had a platter of finger foods for her to take back down.

"You keep treating them like that and they will never leave. They will want to come for every holiday." Sonya was much more relaxed now around us.

"James, I was talking to Sonya about Richard and Mark. She said Rhonda is not seeing anyone that she knows of, and I said that you thought perhaps she and Mark might get along. Sonya is looking forward to meeting Richard, but I don't know a whole lot about him, but I did say that if she was not interested to take me aside and let me know. I hope that is ok with you." I didn't want Sonya to feel obligated in any way to make nice with someone she couldn't bear to be in the same room as.

"That's fine with me Sonya I understand. I have a photo of Richard and Mark here on my tablet. Here have a look and see whether or not you like the look of him. As for his bio, well I have that on my tablet too. He is very accomplished in a number of things. I value him very highly as a senior vice president in my company. While Richard may be working out of the Toronto headquarters he is responsible for all of human resources in all my companies. He has a very important job, and he makes very good money. He has been with me for a long time and has some stock in the companies, so he's doing well financially but his family was quite wealthy as well. He has been widowed for a long time, but he would like to have someone in his life. He hasn't found the one he wants to grow old with as they say. Now as for Mark, well he's led a pretty wild bachelor life, but he too wants to get settled. He is director of marketing for a number of my companies and could probably make vice president if he was ready to settle down. Personally, I think that you and Richard would enjoy each other's company. I base that on what Cassandra has told me about you and in the conversations, I've had with you on the plane and since you have been here. But the choice, absolutely is yours to make." James didn't want to push so he left the conversation at that.

The three came upstairs, the game was over, and Nicole's team won, which Rhonda was not happy about. It was nice to see the two of them together. Jonathan came in to say dinner was ready. Tonight, we were having fresh arctic char with wild mushroom rice, tossed salad with an herb dressing and fresh homemade rolls with dessert being an assortment of petit fours. It was remarkable to see the chatter around the table. It reminded me a bit of when I was younger. James squeezed my hand and I smiled at him.

"So tomorrow we have a relatively free day, what would all of you say to going to Jasper for the day. Cassandra said that Sonya has never been there, and I don't know about the rest of you. We could leave here around 8 am and get there at noon, have lunch in Jasper, take some photos, see a few sights, and then come home. We would probably have to grab fast food on the way home because it would be too late once we got back to have a big meal. If there is something else you would rather do, we can as I am sure this will not be the one and only time that we get Sonya out here. The suv does have a third row seating so we could go together in one vehicle. What does everyone think about that?" Austin, Nicole, and Rhonda said they'd never been to Jasper either, so it would be a treat for them as well.

"Ok good, so we'll get up at 7 am, have a good breakfast and then hit the road." Everyone was agreed. We spent the rest of the evening drinking wine and telling stores. Everyone was very interested in all the stories James had to tell about growing up in Scotland, but it was now late, and everyone decided to turn in.

James would knock on everyone's door in the morning to make sure they were up. It was good to get into pjs and curl up next to James in bed.

"This has been quite a day, thank you again for being so nice to my family. I'm sorry about all the shopping though. I didn't mean for it to get quite so out of hand. Jacob and I went a little overboard." James wasn't at all concerned about the money and was happy that it was making me happy. We fell asleep in no time.

The alarm went off and James was already in the shower. I got up and went into the bathroom. I considered joining him in the shower, but it would have made us late. He came out dried himself on, shaved and put on a pair of jeans, sweater, socks, and sneakers and went out the door to wake everyone else up. I showered as quickly as I could and dressed in jeans as well and a dark blue cashmere sweater with my blue suede booties. I put on my star necklace and earrings a bit of makeup, put a flat iron through my dry hair and went downstairs.

Sonya was already down with James, and I could hear the others coming not long after me. We had coffee and breakfast, went upstairs to grab our handbags, came back down and everyone piled into the car and off we went. I was surprised at how much James knew of the area, kinda made me feel like I didn't know enough, and I lived here a lot longer. He was telling everyone about the places as we were driving along. Austin sat up front with James and then Sonya and I and then Rhonda and Nicole.

We had a wonderful time and got some great pictures. James brought his good camera and took photos of Sonya and her daughters and Austin. It was a great shot, and he was going to get it framed for her. We got back to the house around 8:30 that night. We did a lot of walking in the short time we were there. It was more for them to see the mountains and we took one jaunt to Maligne Lake. It was good to be home though. Nobody really did any shopping, so they took their handbags upstairs and came down for some wine. James had whisky as did Austin. It was a fun day, but I think everyone was a little tired and nobody was up past 9:30.

The next morning Rhonda and James went for a long run. Sonya, Austin, Nicole, and I went for a good power walk. I took them on a trail that I often went on and I think they were huffing and puffing a little when we were done. We had a great breakfast when we got back and decided to go to the museum and art gallery. We had lunch downtown and when we got back the guys had a very spirited game of snooker while the ladies watched. The rest of the evening after dinner was quiet, we decided to go and watch a movie which everyone enjoyed. We sat in the sunroom for an hour or so before going to bed.

Today Rhonda was going to go for a run in the morning and Nicole and Austin were going to join her. Sonya wanted to go for a walk so James and I said we would go with her. We were up at 6 am and out the door for our respective jaunts. We got back to the house around 7:00 and went to shower and ready for the day. Austin, Rhonda, and Nicole got back at 7:30 and they too went to have showers.

Everyone came down wearing casual clothes until later when we were getting dressed up for dinner. James said that Richard and Mark would be at the house for 5:00 so that we could have drinks and they could get to know everyone. We had a light breakfast of coffee and muffins or toast. Jonathan was busy getting everything ready for the dinner. The smell of turkey was in the air, or at least the prep for it. We went into the sunroom to relax and have more coffee.

"Does anyone have a best Thanksgiving story they want to tell?" James started and regaled us with some of the antics they had in Scotland. But in Scotland it was not called Thanksgiving. It was their Scottish Harvest Festival or Lammas which was held a month earlier. Then one by one everyone else said what their favourite moment was until it came to me.

"Honestly, I think this is probably one of the best. It could only be better if Ross, Lindsay, and Ayleen were here, but this is pretty high on my list." We laughed a bit and then the girls went upstairs to get ready for hair and makeup. Jess and Mario would be running from room to room. I knew that Mario was coming prepared for every skin tone, so I asked the ladies to put a chair in the bathroom, so he could do their makeup there because the light was best. It was a bit before 1:00 when the doorbell rang. I went downstairs to bring Jess and Mario up. We started with all of them in my bathroom so that they could look at everyone at once. Then Jess took Sonya first, then Rhonda, Nicole and then me. Mario followed suit. Jess and Mario came in to do me last.

"How is everyone looking? I really want Sonya to look stunning." Mario said that everyone looked lovely. Unbeknownst to me, James left the ladies some gold jewelry to wear and earrings, to finish off the new look. James was waiting on me to go down. They were very efficient and had everyone done by 3:00. I wrote cheques for them and walked them down to the door and waved goodbye as they drove out. Everyone else came down and we went back into the sunroom. I needed some tea, so I asked Jonathan for a pot and teacups.

"Bring a blend that will calm my nerves." He had just the blend in mind. It was a hit with the ladies. Nicole and Austin decided to go up and start getting dressed. It wasn't long after that Rhonda and Sonya went up. Dinner was coming along well. Marlene and Julie came up to the house to help serve the meal and Moira and John were coming up to join us. Jonathan got a really big turkey, so it had been cooking most of the day and the smell in the house was making everyone hungry.

"Looks like we are the last to go and get changed. It has been such fun having everyone here. I think they are enjoying themselves. I hope nobody is bored." James took me by the hand and said we should go and get dressed as well, which we did and came back down. The guys were wearing dress pants with a dress shirt and sports jacket, the ladies were wearing skirts and blouses except for me I was wearing the dress James bought me. The doorbell rang, and James went to get it. It was Richard and Mark. I don't know if Sonya was nervous, but I sure was. Nothing was said to Rhonda. We were going to see if anything would happen naturally. Richard was a very good looking man. The same height as James and build, maybe a little grayer in his hair. He had the bluest eyes I'd ever seen.

"Richard, Mark, let me introduce you to my fiancée Cassandra, her sister Sonya, Sonya's daughters Rhonda and Nicole and Nicole's boyfriend Austin. Everyone this is Richard Anderson and his nephew Mark Grayson. They recently moved from the Germany office to the Toronto office. We invited them here because Cassandra didn't want them to be alone for the holiday." Oh, you sly devil you put that on me. I gave him a look, which nobody else saw which put a big smile on his face.

"Shall we go into the living room; dinner won't be ready for another hour or so. I have white wine available or something stronger if you wish. Richard what can I get you." Richard said he would have a whisky. Mark said the same thing. The guys were having whisky, and the ladies were having wine. I was watching Rhonda eyeing Mark and vice versa. Sonya and Richard were a little subtler, but I could see that Sonya wasn't going to use the escape clause. I discreetly gave James the thumbs up. Since Nicole and Austin knew what was going on, they tried to engage Mark in conversation with Rhonda, who was giggling a little more than usual. James and I kept Sonya and Richard in conversation. This was the first time really that I got to see James use his talents. He casually brought up that Mark was an avid runner and did many local races in Germany.

"He's trying to find a good running group to do other races now in the Toronto area and beyond. Rhonda you said you race a fair bit, perhaps you could give Mark some info on that." It was a brilliant play because now they were actually sitting beside each other. I could see Nicole smile and nod at James. This was actually quite interesting to watch. I didn't have to lift a finger. But how was he going to engage Sonya and Richard in conversation. They were close enough to each other to talk. James was looking at me trying to think of something. Fortunately, Richard came up with his own opening line.

"Sonya, what do you do with your time. James told me that you walk a lot to stay healthy. I love to walk too, helps to sort out one's thoughts. When I lived in Germany the first few years I lived in the city and wasn't that keen on it, so I moved to a smaller village and commuted. It was a bit of a pain with the traffic, but it was nice to be able to go out for a walk in the morning or evening and not have to dodge cars." That worked like a charm, they started talking and every so often Sonya would laugh a little.

I looked at Nicole and Austin and then at James, we were all smiling. Jonathan came in to say that dinner was being served. The table setting looked so pretty. Christina suggested place settings which was perfect as it gave us the opportunity to put people where we wanted them. James sat at the head of the table, and I was to his right, Austin was on his left. Sonya was next to me, and Richard was beside her. Austin had Nicole next to him and then Rhonda and Mark. James brought up a couple bottles of champagne. Once everyone's glasses were filled he made the toast.

"Thank you to all of you for joining Cassandra and I in our new home for our first Thanksgiving. It means so very much to us that you have come, and we hope that you will enjoy the meal and the company." Cheers were made to that. It didn't take long for everyone to have their plates filled. Warming trays were set off to the side and Jonathan stayed nearby in case anyone wanted anything. John, Moira, and the girls sat on either side of the table to make things even. Jonathan then made a plate for himself and sat on the other side of Moira. We ate and there was a lot of chatter around the table. I leaned over to James to let him know that I thought it was pretty cute to implicate me.

"That will cost you a massage later. It is going really well, almost too well. Is that a bad thing or is it that they just like each other." James smiled and said not to worry. I was getting very full, and we had to have dessert and coffee. It didn't look like anyone was going to have seconds, so Jonathan took everything out into the kitchen and brought in the trays of desserts. He had pumpkin pie, made from scratch, pecan pie, and a berry pie, all that were served with crème fraiche. I had a very small piece of the berry pie with coffee. Everyone loved the food and the dessert. James turned to Jonathan.

"Jonathan, thank you for a great meal, everything was quite delicious. We will take our coffee into the living room." Everyone got up, taking their coffee with them to the living room. Now Mark and Rhonda sat together as did Richard and Sonya. Nicole came over to sit beside James and me.

"Wow, that worked well. Smooth job James. Mark seems a nice guy. We had a chance to talk with him, but I think we will go over and talk with Mom and

Richard for a bit, excuse us please." We took the opportunity to go and talk with Rhonda and Mark.

"Rhonda has told me of a race that is happening in a couple of weeks in Kingston and there is still time to sign up for it. We've agreed to meet and do the race together." Rhonda was glowing.

"That sounds great you guys. Rhonda, I know you have friends that you run with, so it will be nice for Mark to meet some of them." She said she would be happy to do that.

"Mark, you should invite Rhonda to the race in Toronto later in the month. It's 5k and 10k which I am sure is easy for both of you, but it sounds like fun. Rhonda you could stay at my penthouse if you like. Mark and Richard are in the corporate suites in the same building." Rhonda said she would love to do it.

"Sounds like fun, I've heard of it but never ran it, but I don't want to put Mark on the spot, he may have something else planned." Good play Rhonda.

"No, I would like nothing better. Perhaps we can go to dinner after the race." I tapped James on the thigh with my hand. We gave it a little shove and now it was up to them where it went. We went back over to Sonya and Richard, leaving Rhonda and Mark to talk alone.

"Richard asked me to go to the opera with him at the end of the month. I've never seen an opera before, so I am looking forward to it. I'm going to go down on the train." James said that wouldn't be necessary. He had to go to Toronto that week and he could easily pick Sonya up in Ottawa and she could stay at the penthouse if she wanted. He could arrange to fly her back when she was ready to go. James was doing everything he could to get these two couples together. It was getting late, and Richard and Mark had to drive back to their hotel. James walked them to the door. Nicole kept Rhonda busy because she could see I wanted to talk to Sonya.

"What do you think. He's more handsome than I thought. He seems very nice and the two of you were able to talk quite easily." She said he was nice, but she wasn't rushing.

"I'm glad James offered to let me stay at his penthouse. It saves any awkwardness. Will he be there; I think I would like to have him there." I said that he would be, he didn't want to say that at the time.

"Let's see how the date to the opera goes. He's a very nice man and I like his nephew too. I'll have to get something appropriate to wear, but I'm not going to think about it right now." Even though she said she wasn't thinking about it I could see that she was.

"Sonya, give the date a try and if you don't like his company then you don't have to see him again. He is very different from your late husband. He's not a heavy drinker, James assured me of that and he's extremely comfortable financially. Don't panic and back out is all I am asking. Promise me you won't do that." She promised she wouldn't.

We joined the others in the sunroom. Everyone was full from dinner and lazing about. We talked a bit about Christmas and if anyone had something that they wanted to do. Rhonda, Austin, and Nicole were talking about going skiing and snowboarding. I told them there were two areas in Edmonton they could go to.

"If you guys don't mind I might tag along with you; I haven't skied or snowboarded in a couple of years, but it sounds like a great time." Rhonda was surprised that James snowboarded. He said that he snowboarded in Europe quite a bit and wasn't bad. I knew that Rhonda and Nicole snowboarded, so the gauntlet was thrown down. I had to laugh because James told me that he was on the senior ski and snowboard team for Scotland but also tried out for the national team, but I wasn't going to say anything to them. We looked at each and laughed. It was still early but everyone decided to go up and start packing.

Nicole and Austin's flight back home was at 11 am. We were going to drop them off at the airport and then get on the plane to take Sonya and Rhonda back and pick up Christelle. Everyone decided to leave their fancy outfits for Christmas hanging in the closets. But they still ended up going back with more than they came, and I loaned Nicole one of my suitcases so that Austin's other suit wouldn't get crushed. The trip to Ottawa was uneventful. Sonya was more relaxed now. Rhonda and James got into a deep conversation. Sonya knew James made each of them an offer for a job. I was worried that she would be upset by it.

"If Rhonda does accept a job from James, you know she will be making more money than where she is now. You could always move closer but still be in an area where you can walk and feel safe. There are lots of very nice neighborhoods in the Toronto area." She said she and Rhonda talked about it last night.

"She came into my room to see if I would be upset if she took James's offer. I can't very well let her pass up that kind of an opportunity. It is pretty expensive to live in the Toronto area, so I will really have to think about it." I knew she was concerned. She was a frugal person and paying out a million for a place was not something she would do.

"I will help you with a place if that is what is concerning you. I will buy you a home if that is what it would take for you to be ok with Rhonda moving. Who knows maybe things between you and Richard will be such that you might be living with him, and Rhonda may be with Mark. I know, it is still very early but, you never know." James could see that we were in a very personal conversation.

"Rhonda, I would be very happy for you to accept my job offer. I know you will have to give your current employer an appropriate notice. Why don't we look at having everything take place in the New Year? That gives you time to sell your current residence and give notice. I can put you up in a corporate suite if you want or you can stay in the penthouse. But I think you should talk to your Mom and see how she feels about it. I don't want to be the cause of any ill feeling." Rhonda would do that but was sure Sonya would agree to the job change. James was doubling her salary and giving her an executive position, how could she refuse.

Rhonda came back to sit with us while James spoke to the flight crew. We had lunch on the plane and the rest of the flight was fairly quiet. We arrived at 4:30 and could see that the limo that brought Christelle was there. While Sonya and Rhonda's luggage was being taken off the plane, we went down the stairs. Christelle was getting out of the car and as I expected, she only had a medium sized piece of luggage. Introductions were made and then Sonya and Rhonda got in Rhonda's car, and they left. We went up into the plane while it was being refueled. James helped Christelle up the stairs. She was feeling ok she said, but we didn't want to take the chance of her tripping and falling.

"Wow this is a beautiful plane. Talk about flying in luxury, Oohlala." She and I went to sit down while James handled the details for dinner.

"So how was Thanksgiving? Did you guys have fun?" I said it was amazing and that Sonya and her bunch were coming for Christmas as well. James came back to sit down and buckle up. The usual security process taken care of, we taxied out and once up in the air, Maria came to take drink orders. I was going to have a small white wine, Christelle said she would as well, and James had a whisky. I showed Christelle the ring.

"You did good James; you did very good. I know the wedding is in May, but I may have to undergo another small surgery at the end of February, but we can talk about that later. I feel like royalty flying on such a beautiful plane." We laughed and talked and ate dinner. By the time we were getting ready to land, it was almost 7:00 pm Alberta time. James helped Christelle into the suv and we went home. She remembered some of the areas from her last visit years ago. The house was still decorated for Thanksgiving.

"Oh my God this is such a beautiful home you both have. I love the decorations for Thanksgiving." We got out of the car and James carried her luggage to the house, offering her his arm as we walked along. We got into the house and James took her luggage up to the room she was going to be in. It was the room that Sonya had been in. Moira changed all of the beds and did the cleaning. She took a few of the floral decorations from the large dining room and set them with some of the other décor in the small dining room. We did a short tour of the downstairs and then went to the sunroom. Since we had dinner on the plane, we weren't going to have anything else. Jonathan made up some canapes in case we were peckish. He came in briefly with a tray, we introduced him, and he left for the evening.

"I love this room. It is so nice with the woods back here. I'll bet you get to see a lot of wildlife." We said we had moose, which I told her about, deer, coyotes, fox, and lots of birds.

"We have yet to see a wolf, but I am ever hopeful. I know they roam in the area but so far I haven't seen one." We stayed talking in the sunroom for a few more hours. Christelle was tired so we walked her up to her room. The stairway was wide and the steps easy to walk. With her cane she said it was easy enough for her to navigate. James went back down, and I went with her to her room.

"This is such a beautiful room and I love the colourful throw and beautiful flowers. She took her things and put them away in the walk in closet.

“That closet is the size of my bedroom at home. Cassandra what a beautiful home. I am so happy for you; you have the man and the home that you have always deserved. I like him a lot and I know that he loves you.” That he did. Christelle was concerned about the height of the bed, but James took that into consideration and got her a small set of stairs to help her climb up. It was wide enough that she felt comfortable going up and down herself. She did it a few times, so I would feel at ease. She got herself ready for bed and I waited until I was sure she was ok to get up. She managed very well so I hugged and kissed her goodnight.

“There is an intercom right there by the bed, so if you need help at any time, just press this button and I will come and help you ok. Don’t try to do anything by yourself if you need help.” She promised she would but thought it would be ok. We spent the next six days talking, laughing, and showing her around. Most of the time we spent sitting in the sunroom watching the birds flit about. James said that he had some things to take care of which was fine with Christelle.

“Hey, you do what you have to, don’t worry about it. Cassandra and I are having a good time.” James went off to this study but came back with the photo that I had given him.

"I thought you should get to see this photo of Cassandra; doesn't she look stunning in the photo. She looks stunning all the time but even more so here." Christelle was blown away by the photo.

After James left I said I would show her the others when she went back upstairs. She loved the photos and especially the black and white with the cigar. That she said was probably the one she liked the most because it showed a side of me she knew that few other people did, the wickedly humorous side. She loved the painting I had commissioned for James too.

"He's going to love it all. I would even like a small photo of that one, if you can get me one. James is going to get a kick out of it." That was the goal and hopefully he would enjoy it. James took photos of us for the family wall and lots of candid shots of Christelle and I together. The time went by too quickly.

"It seems like you just got here and now we are going back to Ottawa. We will have to try to arrange for you to come longer next time." She didn't say much other than we would wait and see. We left for the airport on Saturday at 10 am. We got up at 8:00 and had a very good breakfast before heading to the airport.

The flight back to Ottawa was a good one. We talked and laughed lots, but I was so sad to see that we landed. We took Christelle to her apartment in the city. I wanted to go up with her, but she wanted to say goodbye at the limo. James and I gave her a hug and kiss. She hugged me a little longer and tighter. I cried when we got back in the limo that was taking us to Ross and Lindsay's. It was going on 5:00 and I texted Ross to let him know we were on our way. He said that Ayleen was anxiously awaiting our arrival. We got to their house before 6:00. James arranged for the limo driver to come back for us early Monday morning. Ayleen came running out of the house to greet us.

"Gramma, Grandpa you're here, you're here. I am so happy you're here." She was wearing a pair of jeans with a cute little purple sweater. I got down on my knees to give her a big hug and kiss and of course James picked her up to hug her and kissed her. Ross and Lindsay came out and we hugged and kissed. James of course was still carrying Ayleen as she didn't want down.

"She's been sitting in the window for hours waiting for the car to drive up. I trust your flight was good and did Christelle have a good visit?" I said we did; but it was too short. But what was the biggest surprise of all was that Ross shaved off his beard. His face was still a little pale, but it was so nice to see his face again.

"Why did you shave off the beard. I mean I am happy you did because I have missed seeing this face but why now?" There were a few factors which resulted in the decision he said. The biggest one was that Ayleen was now getting a bad rash from it which hadn't affected her before. He knew too that I never liked it, but Lindsay also said it would be nice to see his face again.

"The choice was clear. I found an excellent barber who gives me a razor shave once a week. I go every Saturday and it lasts about a week. I went this morning, so my face looks good right now." James said he thought it made him look younger without the beard. Ayleen was pulling at us to go inside. Lindsay put up decorations for her birthday tomorrow. Ross took our luggage up to the bedroom.

"Gramma show me the ring, show me the ring." I did, and she said it was very pretty in her cute little way of saying it. Ross and Lindsay liked it too. She wanted to know if we brought her a birthday gift and I said of course we did, we brought her a few. She wanted to see the packages, but I said not until tomorrow. We brought them some of the moose meat which Ross put in the freezer. I could smell that he had a roast in the oven.

"Dinner will be in about half an hour. I hope you don't mind having a roast of beef with roast potatoes, carrots, parsnip, and turnip. Finally Ayleen likes eating all of them. Tomorrow it is cold cuts and salads with cupcakes of course. James would you like a shot of your whisky while we wait for dinner. Mum do you want some white wine. We keep some in the house now for guests." I said that I would, and James said he would as well. Ayleen didn't know where to sit, so she sat between James and me. I had to tease her.

"You know Ayleen, it is ok if you want to sit on Grandpa's knee, Gramma doesn't mind." She looked at me and proceeded to get right up on his knee. We laughed. Lindsay said they invited Sonya to come over tomorrow too. Rhonda was doing a race, so she wouldn't be able to.

"Sonya said she would make up a tossed salad and she would make some chicken fingers for the kids. I have the cold cuts and fresh veggies with dip. My Mom is bringing along a pasta salad and I have all the plates, cups, cutlery, and extra coffee for everyone. I'm also doing up some fries for the kids." Ayleen was cuddling with James. It was a cute picture. Ross was going in and out of the kitchen to check on dinner.

"Dinner is ready, so if everyone wants to come into the dining room, I will put everything on the table, and we can pass it all around." It looked really good, and we took our seats at the table. Ayleen wanted James to sit on one side and me the other.

"That's ok Ayleen but you have to eat what we put on your plate, no stalling." Since going to school she was eating a lot better Ross said, not quite as picky as she was in the past. Ross made up a plate for her and cut up her meat. The rest of us served ourselves and we ate and talked.

"By the way, Sonya, Rhonda, Nicole, and Austin are going to be with us for Christmas as well. It will be a lot of fun I think. Ayleen wait until you see how we decorated your room. I think you will like it a lot." She'd been sleeping in her own room now for over a year. When they first moved into the house, she kept running back and forth into Ross and Lindsay's room.

"She's more settled now so I don't think she will have a problem sleeping in her own room at your place. Isn't that right Ayleen." She had her mouth full with food so couldn't say anything. She just nodded until her mouth was empty.

"Yes, Gramma I am a big girl now and I can sleep by myself. I'll bring my dolly with me. She sleeps with me all the time. Are we going to be able to go tobogganing when we go to your place?" We didn't really have a hill that was safe to slide down.

"Maybe Ayleen when some of us go skiing, you, Mommy, Daddy, Gramma and Sonya can come too and go down the toboggan hill that they have. But we will have to wait and see how much snow we get first. When you come, then we will make plans. Is that ok with you?" She said yes, she would say yes to James about almost anything.

"Maybe in another year, we can take out a few trees and make a hill for you to slide on, but we won't be able to do that this year. Maybe in a couple of years we will have some of James's cousins come over. He has a cousin Cailean and you and he are the same age. The two of you can go sliding together. Won't that be fun?" She had a puzzled look on her face.

"But why can't we go to your place for Christmas every year Gramma?" How was I going to answer that question.

"Ayleen, you have to remember that you have other grandparents who want to spend Christmas with you too. Grandpa and I have to be fair and let Grand'Mere, Gramps, Grandpa Jordan, and Sheila spend time with you as well. Some years we will come here for Christmas, but this year is special because we have the new house, and we want you to come and see it. I hope you understand why you can't always come to our place." She said she did.

"I know it wouldn't be fair to my other grandparents. I know but when we do come to your place it will be extra special." I looked at Ross and Lindsay hoping that I had not opened a can of worms.

“Don’t worry Mum we have already had this talk with her, and she said she understood why we have to do turnabouts, remember Ayleen, you said you understood that, so no more talking about it ok?” She said ok with such a sad little voice. After dinner, she went off to play with her doll. I was helping Lindsay load the dishwasher. James and Ross were talking in the living room.

“I hope we didn’t cause a problem. I would have you every year but even I know we have to do turns.” Lindsay said not to worry about it. Ayleen was only saying that because we were here. She understood the situation. Dishes loaded and dishwasher on, we sat in the living room talking.

“Ross, you don’t have to bring your navy suit with you when you come I have a ton more clothes that I bought for all of you, and even Ayleen. You will have a choice of things to wear, even casual ones. But bring other stuff with you too.” I showed them pictures of everything. Lindsay could not believe how much stuff I got them.

“We will need to pick up a couple of pieces of luggage to bring everything back.” I said we could get a couple of pieces at the retail store or the bag place. It didn’t have to be expensive luggage. Lindsay had to take Ayleen up for a bath and pjs. I know that James wanted to find out if Ross was looking to get into something else for a career and he knew I didn’t want it to be cooking.

I went upstairs with Lindsay and unpacked our pjs and toiletries. Ayleen was singing away in the bathtub. It was fun to listen to and she had a good voice. I wanted to give James a chance to talk to Ross, but I didn't want to stay upstairs too long.

"Ross how is work going. You must be getting ready for the busy time of the year? I've been watching how they are doing financially. I think that this time of the year is really boosting their overall profit margin. Have you ever thought about maybe doing something else? Is there anything you might like to do that would give you better job security and still provide you with lots of family time?" Ross hadn't thought about it he said.

"I've given up on any other ideas I might have. I'm getting a pension; I've got good benefits and I know that I will always have a job. At least for now unless they come up with some other way for people to get their packages. You sound like you had something in mind." James knew that he had to be careful how he approached this.

"I was just curious. Your Mom told me months ago that you took some security courses, but you never finished them. You know that I have a major security company in Toronto, and I have other businesses as well. I only wondered if there was something other than being a courier you would rather do. I would be willing to help you find that out if you want. But if you are happy where you are then that is fine too." Lindsay, Ayleen, and I came down just as they finished talking. I could tell from Ross's expression that he was thinking about what was said. Ayleen wanted a snack before bed, so Ross went to get her one. Lindsay was cleaning up the room she left strewn with toys.

"Um how did it go? He didn't look upset when I came down." James said it went fine and that he thinks he may have planted a seed for Ross to think about. For now, he was going to leave it and wait for him to come back to him. Ayleen came in and sat between us having her snack. She politely offered us some which we politely refused. After she was done, Lindsay took her upstairs after all the requisite hugs and kisses were given.

"See you in the morning. Can I come and wake you up, is that ok?" We said it was absolutely ok. I knew that Ross wouldn't say anything more until he and Lindsay had an opportunity to talk. I doubted very much that she would ever move away from her parents. It was getting late, and everyone went up to bed. We gave them hugs and kisses goodnight. It felt odd to be sleeping with James in this bedroom. I think we both slept a little restlessly. I woke a bit before James.

Chapter 9

"Morning, I don't think either one of us slept well, did we?" James smiled and said it was just a bit weird. We could hear a little knock on the door. A little tap, tap, tap.

"Is there a unicorn at our door?" I asked. We could hear a little giggle.

"No Granma, it's me Ayleen." I told her to come in and the door opened, and she came running and jumped up on the bed. She did this all the time, but it was a nice surprise for James.

"Morning Gramma, morning Grandpa. It's my birthday today. I'm having a party." She hugged me and then James and laid between the two of us.

"Yes, we know it's your birthday and you are having a party and some of your school friends over. It should be a lot of fun." She was definitely excited about it. I could hear Ross and Lindsay get up and they obviously knew where Ayleen was. She left the door open, and Ross stood at the door looking at her.

"Ayleen, what are you doing in bed with Gramma and Grandpa?" She lifted her head up to look at Ross.

"Gramma said I could, and we are talking about my party Daddy." He told her to come out, she had to have breakfast. James started to laugh because she didn't look like she was going to get up. Ross gave her a look.

"Oh, alright I'm coming. Are you getting up now too Gramma?" We said we would be down shortly. She sauntered out and Ross shut the door shaking his head. He was saying something to her.

"But Daddy, Gramma said I could knock before going in and I did that. She thought I was a unicorn, isn't that silly Daddy?" We could hear him laugh and say that it was very silly.

"She is so adorable, but we should get up. Do you want to shower first or shall I?" I suggested we shower together to conserve water, James laughed, kissed my nose, and went to the shower. We got in and out as fast as we could. James went about shaving and doing his thing while I went into the bedroom with a towel wrapped around me and put out what I was wearing today. James finished up and I went in to dry my hair, style it and put on some makeup, brush my teeth, and then dressed. James was already dressed and putting on his shoes.

"I will see you downstairs sweetheart." He left, and I hung up the towels to dry in the bathroom. I got dressed in jeans and a sweater, put on my star necklace and earrings, and put on my blue suede booties, made the bed, and went downstairs. James was standing beside Ross talking as he was cooking breakfast. Ayleen was having her cereal but still in her pjs. Lindsay was dressed in jeans and a sweater and getting coffee.

"I heard you had a unicorn at your bedroom door this morning." We laughed and so did Ayleen.

"It was fun. I love when she comes in and gives a big hug and kiss. James loved it too." Ayleen was nodding with a mouthful of cereal but said 'uh huh.' I sat beside her at the table to have my coffee. James came over and sat beside me. James asked her how old she was, even though he already knew.

"I am seven today. Mommy I have another loose tooth." Lindsay took a look; it was another front tooth. It didn't bother Ayleen to have already lost a couple of teeth. Lindsay reminded her to make sure she smiled with her mouth closed for a few photos.

"Yes, Mommy so we have a pretty picture. Gramma you should see the ones where I smiled and showed my missing teeth. It was funny right Mommy. But I will remember to smile nice for everyone." Lindsay said that it was funny. Ayleen finished her breakfast and Lindsay took her upstairs to get dressed.

She came downstairs wearing a pretty pink dress with sparkly shoes and a pretty necklace.

"Ayleen, you look very pretty in your dress, and I love your necklace." She said thank you and came over to show it to me.

"Oooh Gramma I like your necklace. It really sparkles. You have four big white stars and one little blue star. Why is this one blue." I took it off to show her our names on the back.

"James got this for me. See all our names are on the back. White stars are grown up stars and blue stars are baby stars. When stars are first born they are blue and then they turn white and when a star is ready to die it turns red. Maybe Daddy can show you all about stars on the computer, but not today." I put it back on, but she played with it in the sunlight and loved the way it sparkled.

While we ate breakfast, she played in the living room with her doll. We were having coffee and Ayleen came over to sit on James's lap. It was easy to see that she loved James. With breakfast finished and dishes in the dishwasher, we went into the living room to sit until everyone else arrived. The kids were due to arrive at 11:30 and would be leaving at 2:00. Lindsay had the basement ready for them with games to keep them occupied.

“I forewarned James about Ayleen’s squeal, just how high a pitch it is.” Sonya got there just before the kids arrived. Ross put the chicken fingers in the oven to stay warm and started the fries. Lindsay was going to get them to play one small game and then they would eat. After there would be more games.

“Hello, you two, nice to see you again. Have you recovered from Thanksgiving?” James said it was nice to have all of them. Ross handed her a coffee and the three of us sat in the living room. James’s phone had been buzzing all morning.

“James why don’t you deal with the calls before anyone else gets here.” He apologized and went upstairs to take care of them.

“Tell me, have you heard from Richard?” I could see that she was happy.

“We have been video calling every night since I got home. He sent me a big, beautiful bouquet of flowers. He wants to come and visit next weekend and said he would stay in a hotel, but I have a spare room, so I said he could stay with me. We agreed to take things slow since we only met. But I have to say I do like him. What is not to like, he’s tall, good looking, well off and he doesn’t drink a lot and is clean.” I said it was good that they were taking things slow, there was no hurry.

"Well not too slow though, I'm not getting any younger." We were laughing at that as James came back downstairs.

"Sorry about that. A few things have come up and I am going to have to go to Toronto tomorrow morning and then off to Scotland after the plane drops you off. I am sorry to have to let you fly home alone but the sooner I deal with these issues, the better." I said not to worry, I understood. The kids started to arrive. Lindsay was keeping Ayleen out of the basement until they all arrived, so she hadn't seen the decorations. There were ten kids in her class but only four of them were able to make it today. Lindsay shouted up that they were all present and getting ready to go in. That was the cue to cover our ears. Sonya and James thought we were being silly but as soon as they heard Ayleen squeal, they covered their ears too.

"I told you, that girl can shatter glass with that squeal." The kids were excited and all talking at once. Lindsay shut the door and the noise was barely audible. Their lunch was ready, so Ross got the juices and their plates on a big tray. When everything was done, he loaded up the food and took it downstairs. Ross had no sooner taken all the food down than Lindsay's parents John and Lisa arrived. I made introductions all around. I wasn't sure if Sonya remembered John and Lisa, but she said she saw them a few times in Almonte.

"We tried to time it to avoid the squeal. John has a bit of an earache, so we didn't want to chance it." Ross got everyone a coffee and we sat in the living room to talk. Lisa shook her head at the noise downstairs.

"Good thing Lindsay is used to that. I find it really noisy when the grandkids are together." She noticed my ring.

"Oh, my goodness are you two engaged? Congratulations to both of you. John, Cassandra, and James are engaged." They offered their congratulations, and we thanked them. Sonya got conversation going with Lisa and James struck up a conversation with John. The ladies and Ross got the food out and put it on the island. We were going to serve ourselves. Ross put a plate together and took it down to Lindsay. He was taking pictures each time he went down. The kids were eating off paper plates, plastic cups, so everything down there was being thrown out. We sat at the dining table to eat our lunch. John was sitting on the other side of James, and he asked when the wedding was.

"The wedding will be May 1st in Scotland at my home there. My family is pretty big, so we thought it would be easier to have it there." Lindsay told her parents about James which I said was ok, so they knew that he was pretty well off. James and John were talking about something. Lisa leaned over to me.

"We are very happy for you, you deserve this." We finished eating and took our plates to the kitchen. Ross loaded the dishwasher and said that it was time for the birthday cupcakes. We followed him down to the basement and the kids were sitting around a table waiting to sing happy birthday to Ayleen. She made a wish and blew out her candles. We took our cupcakes back upstairs. The kids were all pretty hyper by that time.

"Ayleen is going to open up the gifts from the kids downstairs. It is almost 2:00 so their parents should be coming shortly. Then she will come up and open up the ones from you guys in the living room." The parents started to arrive and went downstairs to pick up their child. Ayleen handed out gift bags for each one that came. She waved goodbye to all of them and then came running into the living room. While Lindsay relaxed and handed Ayleen the gifts to open, Ross went down to clean up. One by one she opened up all her gifts and said thank you to everyone.

"Auntie Sonya thank you for the chicken fingers. They were really good, and we liked them." Sonya said she was welcome. When she opened up the gift from us, James snapped off a few photos. She loved the hat, and it actually matched her dress, so she put it on and put the scarf on too. Once she opened all her gifts and said thank you to everyone, Lindsay's parents said they were going to leave. Sonya left next as she had a few things to pick up. We gave her a hug and kiss and said we would see her at Christmas.

Everyone was gone, and Ross and Lindsay could finally relax. Dinner was going to be at 6:30 and it was going to be burgers and leftover salad. That was fine with us. Ayleen was playing with some of the toys she got from her friends. Lindsay asked her to take all the toys downstairs and put them in her play area. It took a few trips, but she got it all done. Lindsay sat on the couch pooped.

"They had a lot of fun downstairs, but I am glad today is over. I'm glad it was only the five of them and not eleven." Ross brought James in a whisky. I didn't want anything. When Ayleen came back from putting all her toys away, she sat between me and James.

"Gramma I love my hat and the scarf it is so soft." I could tell she was getting a little tired as she was starting to play with her hair. As the rest of us talked, Ayleen fell asleep against James. Ross was going to take her up to her room, but James said she was ok where she was. We talked about Christmas, and they were both really looking forward to it.

Ayleen slept for over an hour against James. He was enjoying every minute of it. Ross went out to do the burgers and did up a mini one for Ayleen. He knew she probably wouldn't eat a lot because of everything she had eaten at lunch. She ate all of the burger and even some pasta salad, but she was clearly tired.

"Ayleen let's go up and give you a bath and put you in your pjs. You have school tomorrow, so you have to go to bed early." I think she was so tired she didn't protest. She came back down to say goodnight.

"Good night Gramma, good night Grandpa. Thank you for the presents and for coming to my party. I love you." She gave us each a hug and kiss and Lindsay took her up to her bed and then came down a few moments later.

"She was out before her head hit the pillow. She'll sleep right through to 6 am tomorrow." That was when they got up to get ready for school and Ross off to work. We had to leave at the same time. The limo would be here at 6:30 to take us to the airport. We cleaned up the kitchen and then everyone was off to bed.

We had another restless night of sleep and Ayleen came in to give us a hug and kiss and went down for her breakfast. We took time to have a coffee in the morning. When the limo arrived, we kissed and hugged them goodbye. James and I went to the airport and got there at 7:30. We boarded and took off within half an hour. I could tell James was still bothered at having to let me fly back alone.

“James it’s ok I know that things are pretty hectic for you right now. I know you wouldn’t be going if you didn’t have to.” James put his arm around me and kissed me.

“I appreciate that. Some things have come up at home in Scotland, so I have to deal with them, but I have things to take care of in Toronto before I can leave. I’m not happy about this at all.” I asked him what was going on at the estate that had him so furious.

“Fiona invited Victoria to the house. She absolutely knows better than that and she got into an argument with William who wouldn’t let Victoria in. Victoria threw a fit, Fiona was screaming at William, but he would not let her in. I’ll have to give him an extra bonus at Christmas. I’ve talked to Alisa, and she is going to have them move in with her until their house is ready. Fenella and Callum are going to go and stay at my place. They’ve been wanting to update their home, so this came as an opportunity. Damn Fiona she figured I would never hear about it I guess. Fenella went over right away when Victoria refused to leave. Needless to say, she left when Fenella arrived. I had a very terse conversation with Malcolm who had no idea what Fiona was doing. The two of them are going to have a conversation. This really perturbs me because I am trusting Malcolm to handle a lot. I will get it settled when I go back. I’ll be in Scotland for several days and then flying back to Edmonton for

Halloween. Richard is going to handle things in Toronto for me until the beginning of November. I love that you are being so understanding about this." I had no idea that the phone calls he was getting at Ross's had to do with this.

"Well don't be too harsh with Malcolm. I got the impression Fiona does what she wants but I agree she should know better, and she should have at least known you would be furious. Victoria has a lot of gall though. But don't let it bother you too much. Fenella took care of it and she and Callum are moving in now. I actually would have gone with you if I hadn't already arranged for Christina to come and go over Christmas decorations. I'm sure that there will be an excuse for it so don't waste a lot of energy on it." The plane was coming in for a landing in Toronto.

I gave James a long hug and kiss as he got off the plane. We had to refuel and would be taking off again shortly. Once back up in the air I asked Janine for a glass of wine. It would be at least three and a half hours before touchdown in Edmonton. I only drank half the wine and asked Janine to take it away. I closed my eyes for a little while.

The flight was smooth, and we got into Edmonton just after 10:30. I put my luggage in the back of the suv and drove home. I texted Jonathan to let him know I would be home for lunch and asked him to make me a chef's salad. I had to stop for gas on the way home. When I pulled through the gate, I waved to John and put the suv in the garage. I got my luggage out and took it into the house and put it at the bottom of the stairs. I waved hello to Jonathan and said that I wanted to have my salad in the sunroom. I gave Roxie a call to see how her Thanksgiving had gone.

"It was lovely and how was yours?" She said that Duncan and Mitchell got along wonderfully, and the grandkids liked him, even Maria liked him.

"Good thing you called today. We are leaving tomorrow to put the trailer up for sale and get rid of all the stuff down there. I don't have many things that I want to bring back but there will be a few things. I may have a buyer for the trailer though, but we'll see once we go down." I was happy to hear that things had gone well for them at Thanksgiving. The plane was staying in Edmonton to fly them down south and then heading back to Toronto to take James to Scotland.

"Ours was wonderful too. Sonya and her bunch are coming for Christmas too, so it will be a nice with Ross, Lindsay, and Ayleen here. I hope that you and Duncan will be back at Christmas and will come over for Boxing Day. I know you will be in your new home for Christmas, but I'd like you to meet everyone. They will still be here for New Year's and again I am hoping you and Duncan don't have any plans. It isn't going to be anything too fancy here but let me know once you are back and we can meet up." She said she would definitely call when they returned. I sent James a text asking him to call me tonight when he had a chance. It was nothing urgent. I gave Christelle a call to talk to her.

"Well how are you doing? Are you feeling any better after that very quick vacation?" She said she was fine, just tired. I told her about Ayleen's birthday, and I would send her some photos. But I wanted to talk to her about something else.

"James has to go to Scotland unexpectedly but he's working in Toronto for the next four days before he goes. I think I told you he was going to have his cousin Malcolm and his wife Fiona stay at his place while he was living here. Well Fiona is apparently a good friend of James's ex-wife, and she had the nerve to invite her over to James's home. She never lived in the house that I know of. I think she and James lived in a small apartment while the estate was undergoing some major updates. Fiona asked her over, but the butler William wouldn't let her in. He knew that James would not approve of it. But Fiona started yelling at him and Victoria refused to leave. William kept calling James while we were at Ayleen's birthday party. He had to ask Fenella to go over and get rid of Victoria because she would not leave. James also called Malcolm, Fiona's husband, and raked him over the coals. Apparently, he knew nothing of what Fiona was doing. I'm sure that

Fenella dealt with it and Fiona has been warned but I know James is going to ream her out when he gets back there. He wanted to spend a few days alone with me before he had some important meetings in Toronto. To say James is really angry would be mild." Christelle was flabbergasted.

"That was very rude of her and why would his ex-wife want to go to his home even if he wasn't there? Isn't she happily married to someone or is she looking to try and get back with James." I told her about the encounter the night we got engaged and at the spa. It seemed very strange that she would barge into a private room when we were having our celebration dinner and then when she barged into the private room when we were having mani/pedis. It was all very odd.

"I'm starting to think that maybe she is going to try. I know I don't have to worry about James. She tried to put her hand on him at the engagement dinner and he held her off. I don't think she liked that at all, and she was with her husband the Duke. Frankly from the look in his eyes I don't think the Duke cared if she stayed or left him. I wouldn't want to be in her shoes when James confronts her as I am sure he will." I said I would let her know what happened when I heard from James. I went into the kitchen to talk to Jonathan and to bring my plate back.

"Jonathan, I have been thinking about Christmas and New Year's Eve." We got into a discussion about whether he would be with this new girl or not and I hadn't yet talked to James about anything. I could tell he wasn't sure what to think.

"I appreciate the offer, I really do but the new girl I am seeing will, unfortunately, be on the west coast with her aging parents. They are not well, and she wants to spend the time with them as she is not sure if they will be here next year. I am grateful that you wanted to do this for me, but I am going to be here anyway." I was sorry to hear that about the girl's parents.

"Well, you can spend it with us then. I don't want you to be alone Christmas Day or New Year's Eve." He was grateful again but was going to meet friends later on Christmas Day and on New Year's Eve.

"Ok, I am happy you have plans. Can you look after getting the larger turkey then. I think we should probably have ham as well." He said he would take care of everything, and I went back out into the sunroom.

It was so good to be home again and while I didn't always like to be alone, I didn't mind it at the moment. It had been rather hectic over the last two weeks. I decided to give Janet a call to see what she was up to. I knew she would be working, but we hadn't talked in a little while.

"I won't keep you; I know you are very busy. I wanted to see how your Thanksgiving went. Ours was wonderful. It was nice to have Sonya and the kids here, well they are not kids, but you know what I mean. James had a couple of his executives for dinner. They are both very nice gentlemen. So how is work going for you?" Janet was loving the job and she had been back and forth to Toronto a few times training a couple of new girls.

"They are doing really well and catching on quickly. I'm glad you had a good holiday, and that Sonya was there. I remember you saying you hadn't seen Rhonda and Nicole for a long time, and you never met her boyfriend. But I guess he is more her common law husband than boyfriend right, they've been living together for years. It has been busy around here, even working from home I am on the go all day. But it will be nice not to have to drive in terrible weather in the winter. I probably won't be exposed to as many cold and flu bugs. The job has a lot of perks and not just the salary." I said I was going to have to go. I wanted to unpack and put some things in the wash. I decided to get dressed warmly and go for a good power walk. The air had a decided change to it. I was surprised though that we still hadn't any snow.

I felt better once I was back home from the walk. The fresh air was invigorating but it was nice to be in the warmth of the house. Christina texted that she would be by in the morning with her crew to take down all the décor. I said that we had taken apart the floral decorations and put them into a couple of vases. I wasn't terribly hungry, and I was feeling chilled. I told Jonathan that I would probably have some soup as I wasn't feeling that great. I thought maybe it was the travel in such a short time. He looked at me and came over to feel my forehead.

"You have a slight fever. Maybe it is all the activity you've had. I'll make up some chicken soup for you. Why don't you go sit in the sunroom for a bit, maybe take a couple of flu meds?" I went up to get my thermometer to check my temperature. It was elevated but only by a bit. I sat on the chaise and put a blanket over me and sat watching the birds. While bird watching was always a favourite pastime I really wasn't feeling up to it. I went back up to the bathroom to check my temperature again. It had gone up a bit. I went down to tell Jonathan I was going to go to bed and maybe have the soup later. I got into my pjs and crawled into bed. I stopped for gas on the way home from the airport and the attendant was coughing something terrible. I must have gotten something from him. I fell asleep and woke up to the sound of my phone. I answered groggily.

"Cassandra, what's wrong you don't sound good. Is something wrong?" It was James and I forgot I had asked him to call when he had a minute.

"Oh James, I'm ok I think I might be getting the flu or a cold. I have a bit of a temperature and I thought I should head to bed. Jonathan made me some chicken soup, but I don't have the appetite for it right now." I told him I took something for the fever.

"I'll come home and take care of you." That was such a sweet thing to say.

"I'm ok James. I know you have really important meetings for the next few days, and you need to go to Scotland as planned. It is just a silly cold and I'll be fine in a day or two. You need to take care of things over there so that it doesn't get worse. Really, I am ok. Jonathan is going to hang around for a bit and he's asking Moira to check on me from time to time. Really, I am ok, I am being looked after." He still wasn't convinced I could tell but he reluctantly agreed to go to Scotland as planned. I wanted to talk to him longer, but my head was aching, and I was really tired.

"Please video chat with me once you are in Scotland. You will see then that I am ok. Have a safe trip and make sure you text me when you arrive ok." He promised he would text me. He hung up and immediately called Jonathan wanting to know how I really was.

"It's a low grade fever. I've asked Moira to come up later and check on her. Moira will come up every few hours to make sure she is ok. We'll take care of her; you don't have to worry. I will call you if it gets any worse I promise you that." James said he was going to hold him to that. James put in a call to Fenella.

"Fenella I'm sorry I know it is late, but I need you to do something for me. I'm going to be arriving on Saturday. Can you please make sure William is there to pick me up? I also want you to tell Malcolm and Fiona to be at the house when I arrive. I know you spoke to them, but I am going to make it crystal clear to Fiona that she is not to do this ever again. I want meetings set up with every one of the executives for Monday and Tuesday. Make sure they have nothing else on as it will be an all-day meeting. We are going to get a few things settled because I intend to be back home Thursday or sooner if I can get things straightened out Monday and Tuesday. Thank you for taking care of this for me. I will see you Saturday morning. Good night Fenella." James poured himself a drink and looked out at the Toronto skyline. He should be home taking care of Cassandra instead of having to deal with Fiona and her stupidity.

Jonathan sent a text saying that Cassandra was sleeping soundly. Moira checked on her and her fever was still the same. James went to the office on Tuesday and met with Mina all day and for the next four days to go over every detail that needed taking care of for the next few weeks. He called every spare moment he had to check and see how Cassandra was doing but each time there wasn't much improvement. Fortunately, she was, for the moment, not getting any worse. This was the day he was leaving for Scotland, and he asked Mina to come into his office.

"Mina, while I am enroute to Scotland I need you to follow up with Jonathan on how Cassandra is feeling. Hopefully, it is just a cold or at worse the flu, but I need you to follow up with him hourly. If it becomes more serious get a message to me through the captain but only if it gets really worse. I know I'm being overprotective of her, but I shouldn't have to be flying to Scotland to deal with an idiotic wife of a cousin and an ex-wife, so please keep on top of that for me. I need to speak with Richard for an hour or so. See if he can come to my office for lunch. I want him to expedite getting the executives in place. I want you to sit in on the interviews with Richard. I trust Richard, but you know me better than anyone, so I want no less than six new directors of each department and no less than four vice presidents. I want the workload spread out so that I only have to take care of emergencies. I want to work from home as much as possible and only have to come to Toronto one week a month. I know, it will be a change for me because I am so hands on, but I need to start delegating more. Yes, I know you've been saying that for years, but I never had a reason to until now. So please contact Richard first and then when I'm gone the two of you start getting the interviews going. I will of course want a look at the final prospects before anyone is hired. I will make time for that." Mina left, and James was alone to stare into the photograph of Cassandra in the gown coming down the stairs. He called Moira to see how she was doing.

"She's staying in bed which is good. Her fever went down a bit, but it went back up again a little more. I'm giving her more medication and I'll wait and see if that brings it down. She keeps wanting to get up and go and sit in the sunroom, but I told her I would sit by her bedside to make sure she stayed in bed. I'll look after her James; you don't need to worry. I think it is a nasty flu bug she picked up. Everyone seems to have it." He thanked her and said he would call her just before his flight took off later that night.

"Damn it, damn it." He concentrated on getting work done. There were a lot of papers that he had to sign before lunch. Mina ordered lunch for James and Richard. He went over a lot of details with Richard.

"I want you to get everything in place Richard. I want to be able to run things from home and only come in here for urgent matters. So please get on those hires and send me a list of who you think should be hired as soon as possible. I'll be in Scotland handling some matters, but you can reach me by cell. So do you have any questions?" Richard said he did not and would get on things right away and have a list of candidates by the end of the week.

"I apologize Richard if I'm sounding demanding, but Cassandra isn't feeling well, and I had plans to stay home for a few days and then this crap in Scotland came up. I know it's a personal issue I'm dealing with, but it is one that never needed to happen. Are you and Mark settling in ok?" Richard had been with him since he took over his Dad's business, so not only was he a loyal executive, but he was also a good friend.

"We are doing fine James. I want to thank you for introducing me to Sonya. We have been in constant communication since Thanksgiving dinner, and I am very interested in her. I think Mark likes Rhonda, but I don't pry into his business. So go to Scotland, get things sorted out there and then come home as quickly as you can and spend some time at home. You are going to have a lot of travel coming up before Christmas. Things that only you can deal with so, as you so often say, do what you have to and get it done." James knew he could count on Richard, and he was happy that he and Sonya were hitting it off. James spent the next few hours finalizing some paperwork and then went to the airport. He gave a final call to Moira to see how Cassandra was doing.

"Her temperature has stayed the same. It hasn't gone up and it hasn't gone down, but she tried some soup and is taking lots of liquids. It will pass but it has to take its course." James said that he would call once he landed in Scotland. He drove to the airport and the plane took off within half an hour. For James that had to be the longest flight of his life, but he arrived in Glasgow at 7 am and immediately called to see how Cassandra was doing. Her fever had broken and now it was just a nasty chest cold.

"She coughed most of the night, so she is sleeping when she can. Jonathan is trying a few different teas to see what helps her, but she has had more soup and is still taking liquids. I will let you know if anything changes." William was waiting at the airport for him.

"William, I want to thank you for standing ground and not letting Victoria in my home. She had no right to be there, and Fiona had no right to invite her." They arrived at his estate within twenty-five minutes. Fenella was waiting for him at the door.

"James, I hope your flight was ok. Malcolm and Fiona are here and so is Alisa. I spoke with her, and she said that she hoped you wouldn't mind if she was present." He said that it was ok and perhaps it is best that she understands the gravity of the situation. James hugged and kissed Fenella. He told her that this trip came at the worst time because Cassandra came down with a terrible flu bug. The others were waiting for him in his study. Malcolm was nervous, and Fiona looked like she didn't want to be there. Alisa had no expression on her face.

"Ok so I am not going to beat around the bush. Fiona you had no right whatsoever to invite Victoria here, none, and then to start yelling at my staff and pitching a fit. I am extremely angry with you and very disappointed. Malcolm you should have known she was going to pull this stunt and stopped it from happening. I have given you a tremendous amount of responsibilities to manage my companies here with Angus, but I also expect there to be family loyalty. I will not tolerate this attitude of yours Fiona. I will never tell you who you can be friends with, but you need to grow up and understand the difference between what is right and what is clearly wrong. It offended me that I had to ask you to leave my home and ask Fenella and Callum to upset theirs lives and move in, so I would not have to let my staff go." Fiona started to cry but everyone knew they were fake tears.

"That won't affect me Fiona, you are being a selfish spoiled brat right now and it pains me to have to say these things in front of your husband. So here is how I am going to handle this. Fiona, you will no longer be allowed in my home until you can prove that you accept that you made an egregious mistake. Alisa I am sorry that it has come to this, but I will not tolerate this disloyalty. Malcolm if you feel you can no longer work for me, then I accept your resignation from my companies. Yes, I am sure that comes to you as a shock but as I said I will not tolerate disloyalty." Alisa was going to speak but Malcolm spoke first.

"James, I am truly sorry this happened, and Fiona and I will have a very long discussion at home. You have every right to be angry and I do not blame you for questioning my loyalty because of what Fiona has done. But I am loyal to you, and I do not want to resign. I want you to trust me James and in order to demonstrate that, I will make sure that Fiona doesn't step foot into any of your businesses. Security will be told that she is not allowed on the property. I too wish it had not come to this, but I do understand why you are angry. It was a complete slap in the face to you and the family." Fiona now was crying in all honesty. Now Alisa spoke.

"Fiona stop that sniveling. You brought this on yourself by maintaining a friendship with Victoria and I know you did it to be spiteful to James. I also know that you told Victoria about the spa day, and you did that on purpose because you wanted to cause a scene with Cassandra. Malcolm this is your issue to deal with and you had better deal with it promptly. This family has lost too much and I, for one, will not see it torn apart by you Fiona." All eyes were on Fiona now.

"James, I know you won't believe me, but I really am sorry for what I did. I will end my friendship with Victoria not because it is expected but because it is the right thing to do. I won't make excuses for what I did. It was wrong, and I was being a spoiled childish brat. But I ask you not to take it out on Malcolm. He really had no idea what I was doing, and he was furious with me when he found out. So please don't take it out on him. I accept being banished from your home and from not going to see Malcolm at work, but please don't take it out on him." It was now Fenella's turn to speak.

"James, you have made your position quite clear, and I think that Malcolm and Fiona understand the seriousness of the matter. While this situation is extremely serious it has been exacerbated for James because Cassandra became ill with the flu, and he cannot be home to look after her. Instead, he had to fly across the ocean to tend to the trivialities of your stupidity Fiona. So here is what is going to happen. Alisa and I are going with you to talk to Victoria. You will make it abundantly clear to her that you no longer want to be associated with her. You will block any calls from her and will avoid her at all costs, is that understood? We will deal with this tomorrow, so it is over and done with and perhaps James can go home sooner and take care of his fiancé. James, if you are agreed, once this has been dealt with, it will not be spoken of again. Have I made myself clear Fiona?" Fiona nodded that she had, and they were dismissed. James put in another call to Moira to see how Cassandra was doing. Fenella and Alisa were still in his study with him.

"James, the coughing got a bit worse, so we took her to the hospital. She has a little bit of pneumonia, but the doctor gave her some antibiotics and it should be cleared up in a week or so. Other than that, she is ok. The doctor gave her a good going over and her health aside from that is excellent." Fenella and Alisa were shocked. James's face turned white, and his lips became a tight line of anger. He said he would call again in a few hours.

"James, now before you do or say anything rash, I want you to take a few moments and think about what was said. Cassandra is ok and aside from the touch of pneumonia she is in good health. I know you want to punch something right now, but I am asking you to remain calm. The family matter here is being resolved. I know you are going to fight me on this, but I want you to have something to eat and then I want you to go to bed. Now James, listen to me, you are stressed out and you are exhausted. I will deal with any business matters with Angus and Malcolm. I will contact your flight crew to let them know that you are going to be returning to Alberta tomorrow night. The crew that flew over can rest and the crew that was here will be ready to go. James, I promise you I will take care of this for you, you know you can trust me, and you can trust Alisa." James let go of the breath that had been churning around inside of him since yesterday.

"Thank you, both of you. I appreciate that you are not fighting me on this. Alisa I was a bit worried you would not like what I had to say, but I think it has been coming for some time. So now it has been dealt with and

I do trust the both of you to handle things here. I desperately want to get home to Cassandra, so I will take your advice and have something to eat and then go to bed. Fenella, thank you for moving in on such short notice." Fenella laughed.

"I was happy to do it. I've been trying to get these renovations done piecemeal and now I don't have to, so you have helped us out. Callum doesn't like disorder, so he is happy with the arrangement as well." Alisa said she would be off, and Fenella went to the kitchen to get James something to eat.

I hated being sick and this really sucked. I let Ross know what was going on so that he wouldn't worry that I wasn't contacting him daily. I knew that James was calling Moira to keep tabs on me. I didn't want her to worry him, but I knew that James wanted to know and would not be happy if he wasn't told the truth. Moira came back in with some water and my pill.

"Your fever is down considerably, and the antibiotics seem to be working. What do you say about having a shower, getting dressed and coming down and sitting in the sunroom? You need to move about a little to get that stuff off your lungs." She saw me into the bathroom and got out some clothes for me to put on. A nice big sweater, some leggings, warm socks, and slippers. The shower actually felt good, and it was clearing out my head. Moira was waiting for me at the top of the stairs.

"I'll walk beside you in case you get dizzy. You've been in bed for several days, so your legs might feel a little shaky." I gave her a hug.

"Thanks for looking after me. I know you've been at my bedside a lot and I really appreciate it. James must be out of his mind with worry." She said that he was, but she was keeping him informed. Jonathan brought a tray of some soup and a new tea that I had not tried. It had healing properties in it but would not interact negatively with the antibiotics.

"I had Moira check with the pharmacist to make sure it was ok. The pharmacist thought it was a good idea." With a blanket on my lap and the tray up so I could have my soup, I watched the birds. The soup was good and so was the tea. The room was warming up with the light of the sun, but it felt good to be sitting up. Jonathan came back in and took the tray away.

"You must be getting a little tired of clear soups, so I made up a chicken barley that I can give you for dinner. It isn't too heavy, and it will be good for you." It sounded wonderful and I was looking forward to it. Moira put her hand on my arm to let me know it was time for another pill. I hadn't realized that I had dozed off.

“Didn’t I just take one a little while ago?” Moira laughed and said that was six hours ago. I’d fallen asleep for six hours on the chaise. Jonathan was bringing me in the soup he made. It smelled wonderful and tasted even better. My appetite was still not great, but I tried to eat as much of the soup as I could. Jonathan came back to take the tray and Moira said it was time for bed. I wanted to protest but she wouldn’t listen.

“Sleep is the best medicine for you now so no arguments. You have not had a fever today at all so let’s not push it by staying up later than you should. You are not coughing as much either so get sleep while you can and let your body heal.” I wasn’t going to argue with her because I knew she was right. I got into my pjs and got back into bed. Moira had completely stripped the bed and the fresh linens felt wonderful. I drifted off to sleep. It was almost 10:00 and Moira was going to head down to her home. She and Jonathan were taking turns staying in the house at night in case they were needed. She was getting ready to head out the door after talking to Jonathan when she ran smack into James.

“James my goodness you are home. I thought you were going to be gone another week.” He apologized for startling her but said he took care of what he needed to and hurried home to be with Cassandra.

"How is she doing?" Moira told him that she got her up today, just to move things around.

"She had a good shower, and I changed all the bedding. She had some nice soup today that Jonathan made and some medicinal tea that we checked with the pharmacist who said it wouldn't interfere with the antibiotics. She sat in the sunroom on the chaise and slept for six hours without even realizing it. She has been in bed for about three hours now, so she will be sound asleep. The pills make her groggy, but they are working. She has one in the morning around 7 am and in the evening around 7 pm. I'll let Jonathan know he can go home now that you are here. I'm glad you are back." James hugged her and thanked her for taking care of Cassandra. He ran upstairs and into the bedroom. She was, as Moira said, fast asleep. He went into the bathroom to get his pjs on and he carefully got in next to her. She moaned a bit and snuggled up to him. He wanted to wrap his arms around her, but he was afraid of waking her, so he lay next to her and fell asleep.

"James, you are home, why? I thought you were not going to be back for another week. You didn't come back because I had a little cold, did you?" He kissed her nose.

"Morning my darling, yes I came back early but I took care of what I needed to. Fenella and Alisa are going to look after everything else. You had more than just a little cold my darling, you had a touch of pneumonia and had to go to the hospital. Moira said that the pills are working so we are going to take it easy until they are done and then get you another checkup." Just having him home was the best medicine.

"The doctor at the hospital said that a nasty flu virus was hitting everyone hard and fast. I probably got it from the gas attendant when I stopped for gas on the way home from the airport. The doctor actually said aside from the flu and touch of pneumonia I was in extremely good shape for someone my age. I think he was a little jealous. But I am glad you are home, and it was so nice to snuggle up to you." He got up and got me a pill to take with some water. I took the pill and then said I wanted to take a shower. It was helping with the congestion.

"Want to shower with me, purely for safety reasons, I may still be a little weak." For half a second, he thought I was serious but the mischievous smile I had gave me away. The hot water felt good, not just for my congestion but on my aching muscles. James took the bath scrubber and put lots of body wash on it and washed me all over. If I was feeling weak, I was showing no signs of it. I found the soap that he always used, in a body wash and bought him a scrubber and washed his body.

"Cassandra, you are not feeling a hundred percent we shouldn't do this." His attempts to put me off were to no avail. I wanted him, and he was not going to disappoint me. It was not fast and primal like all the other times in the shower, this was slow and tender. I looked up at him and smiled.

"James, it is so good to have you home and I needed that so much." He kissed me softly whispering that he needed it too. He took me out of the shower and dried me down thoroughly. He put the big fluffy terry bath robe on me and then went to the sink to shave. I dried my hair and styled it a bit. I knew I was not going out, so I put on the least amount of makeup I could. I took out a pair of jeans, a camisole and a big warm sweater, a pair of nice warm socks and my slippers and went back in to brush my teeth. James was putting on jeans and a sweater as well. We went downstairs together. Jonathan was happy to see James and told me that I looked a little better. He had coffee ready for James.

"I'll have coffee too Jonathan. I know I have been drinking tea lately, but I feel ever so much better, and I have missed my coffee. I am not terribly hungry though, maybe just a soft boiled egg and toast." Jonathan said he would get that ready. He made eggs, sausage, and toast for James.

"We'll have it in the sunroom Jonathan, if you don't mind." James led me into the sunroom and seated me in a big comfortable chair with a tray in front. He put my coffee on the tray and sat down beside me.

"James are you going back to Scotland now that you see I'm ok?" He said he wasn't.

"I'm staying here until after Halloween, then we are going to Toronto for about a week. Then I will bring you home and be here for a few days and then I have to go back to Toronto until the middle of November. Then we will be going to Germany and Austria for the Christmas markets and then back home for several days. Then I am afraid I will have to go overseas until just before Christmas. I will pick up Sonya, Rhonda, Ross, Lindsay, and Ayleen on my way back. Can you please find out from Lindsay if I need to have a car seat installed for Ayleen or is she ok with a booster seat? I'd like to get that done before I leave so it is one thing off my mind." I said I would find that out for sure and let him know.

"Tell me, what happened with Fiona. I hope you weren't too rough on her. I know she screwed up but still, I don't want her to resent me." James finished eating and drank his coffee in contemplation.

"Fiona needed to know that I would not tolerate such disloyalty. She was never like that until she started to hang around with Victoria and frankly I'm not even sure how the two of them became friends. She agreed to stop being friends with her not because I insisted but because she knew it was the right thing to do. Until she can show me that she has changed, I've told her she cannot come to my home and Malcolm has barred her from going to his work. She is agreeable to this. I can only imagine what Malcolm said to her. Fenella and Alisa are looking after any important work matters along with Angus and Malcolm. I thought for sure Malcolm was going to fight me for being so harsh, but he knew that I was right." I felt badly for Fiona but didn't think it would be right for me to interfere.

"I feel badly for her. I have a feeling she might have been manipulated by Victoria. She struck me as the type to do just that sort of thing. But I don't understand what her reasoning would have been. She's married to the Duke; she knew you were clearly not interested in her. I think when she barged in on us at the engagement dinner and she saw my ring, well she had a look in her eye, and I thought she was going to say something to me. I know it might sound silly, but I think she still has feelings for you. I don't know if you noticed the way she looked at you or not, but I did." James smiled and then laughed.

"What are you laughing about?" He said he would like to have seen me toss Victoria out on her ass but only because he knew that I could.

"She might be several inches taller than you, but you are a hell of a lot stronger and tougher than she is. That's a compliment my dear. I know you can take care of yourself. Perhaps she still has feelings, but I clearly do not. You are the one and only woman I love and will ever love for the rest of time and beyond." He definitely knew how to make me happy, but I had to admit I was a little tired.

"I know that I said I was fine, but I am a little tired. I think it is the medication that makes me sleepy so if you don't mind, I think I will go back upstairs and lay down for a little bit." I gave him a kiss and went upstairs. James took the dishes into the kitchen.

"Jonathan thank you for looking after Cassandra. You and Moira went above and beyond, and I want you to know how much I appreciate it." Jonathan told him he was happy to be there, and James went into his study.

"Richard, I am back home. I took care of the family matter in Scotland and came back here. Cassandra was quite ill, had a touch of pneumonia but she is getting better. So how have things been going there?" Richard gave him an update which he was very pleased with. He told Richard he would look in on how things were going with the businesses operations in the industrial site.

"James, I have hired two executives for there so far. One of them has a lot of textile experience and the other one in the cosmetics industry. They come with impeccable credentials, and I think we were lucky to snap them up when we did. They are quite happy with the idea of moving to Edmonton and will in fact be going out there over the next week to look for houses. They have families so they want stability, and they viewed these new businesses as coming at just the right time for the market. Quinn said that he could come on the 27th but he would have to leave on the 30th to be home in time to take his youngest trick or treating. I said that I thought that would be enough time for him to interview the candidates we have for the lab. I found three chemists who have extremely good credentials and are willing to move there as well. I thought perhaps we could do a run at the university and see who in the chemistry program may be interested in working for us. One of the chemist suggested that and said that he would help since he was a graduate of the program. I've got other prospects for the other executive positions and will be nailing those down. We also have a job blitz that has been going the last few days for the textile plant and I will let you know how that fairs. It will be over today." James liked what he was hearing.

"Have you made any headway with the company in Edinburg being willing to train some people for us. I am sure that we can work out some sort of deal. I don't want to have to send fifty people to Scotland to learn the process. For the geothermal plant, we could probably get a lot of the workers from oil fields to come on board; you will have to first find someone highly respected in the field and see if they are willing to join the company. We will obviously be building a huge plant northwest of Edmonton and use the office in the industrial site as headquarters but keep on this and let me know when you have something more. With the move to go from fossil fuels we might be hitting this at a good time here. I know there are plants all over the world but let's see if we can be a forerunner here." Richard would keep in touch.

James sat for the longest time looking at the photo of Cassandra on his desk. Never in his life would he have thought he would meet someone like her. He had a family now but most of all he had someone he could share the rest of his life with, whom he trusted and valued and respected. He went upstairs to check on her and she was still sleeping. There was still an hour to go before lunch, so he went back and looked through some emails. As he was scrolling through his hundreds of emails he came across one that had him cursing.

"What in the hell is she doing emailing me." James read through the email and was absolutely livid. The audacity of Victoria to email him saying she was still in love with him and wanted him back. She would do anything to get him back. He looked at his watch and debated as to whether he should call or respond back to the email. He chose to respond to the email, telling her never to email him again, he was not interested in her and would never be interested in her. If she continued to harass him he would file a legal document against her.

“Of all the bloody nerve.” I stood in the doorway of his study.

“That didn’t sound good. Would you care to tell me what has you so riled up James?” He wasn’t going to lie so he told me about the email.

“Well well isn’t that interesting. She seems to want to up the game. Give me the phone number.” James wasn’t going to do it, but I held out my hand and insisted. I dialed the number and Victoria answered immediately.

“Victoria, this is Cassandra, I do not appreciate you emailing my fiancé telling him that you are still in love with him. I hoped taking the civil route with you would work but apparently not, so Victoria if you ever contact my fiancé again ever, I will kick your ass clear across the country. That is a promise that I will happily carry out if you do not stop. Leave my fiancé alone and I won’t tell you twice. Do you understand. Good.” With that I hung up the phone. James was stunned.

“Guess I don’t want to get on your bad side.” I slid down into the chair and sat on his lap and put my arms around his neck.

“She has a lot of nerve that one. But let’s not talk about her anymore, I am hungry, and I want to go out. Let’s go to Jason’s.” I told Jonathan that we were going out. We had a wonderful lunch at Jason’s and went for a drive over to Duncan and Roxie’s place to see how things were going.

“I guess they haven’t gotten back yet. Have you talked to Duncan to see if Roxie sold the trailer? I hope she did because I know she wants to move into the house as quickly as possible. I’m happy for them, aren’t you?” James was very happy for them. We drove for another few hours and went back home. It was good to get out of the house and be out. When we got back to the house we went into the sunroom. James had a whisky, and I had some water.

“Christina was supposed to come a few days ago but because I got sick Jonathan told her to wait. If you are going to be here tomorrow, why don’t I ask her to come out and we can look at what she has come up with for Christmas. Would that be ok with you?” James said it was a great idea. He wasn’t going back to Toronto until after Halloween.

“Are you doing that to keep an eye on me? I know you are extremely busy and trying to get people hired, so I will understand if you have to go to Toronto for a few days. Really James I am ok now and I only have another day of the antibiotics to take. I will see my family doctor and get a clean bill of health, so go if you have to." He said no, he was here till after Halloween.

"I've re-arranged my schedule until the first of the month. Then we are going to Toronto and while I am at work, you can go shopping. But if you don't mind being alone in the sunroom for a little bit, I will give Fenella a call to see how things are going there." I told him I was fine, so he went off to his study.

"Fenella, its James, how are things going there. Any further issues? She had the audacity to email me saying she wanted me back. I emailed her and told her never to contact me again, but Cassandra heard me cursing and she called Victoria." He chuckled.

"You should have heard her, told Victoria if she ever contacted me again she'd kick her ass clear across the country. I think Victoria got the message but if she didn't ask Gowan to file a restraining order against her. I presume that Malcolm has had his discussion with Fiona. I was thinking about how she could redeem herself and perhaps a suggestion that she do some community work might give her a reality check. I am not going to banish her forever, but I need her to know I was dead serious. What else is going on?" Fenella said that Fiona and Malcolm had a very long discussion about her behavior. Malcolm already suggested the community work and Fiona agreed.

"When Alisa and I went with her to tell Victoria that they were no longer friends, Victoria did not take it well. She called Fiona weak for allowing you to dictate who her friends could be, and she called us interfering old bats. But I will give Fiona credit, when Victoria said that she stood nose to nose with her and told her she was not weak, and that Victoria had only been using her to keep tabs on you. She forced Victoria to apologize to us. Honestly, James I thought she was going to punch her in the face. It was quite something to watch. I let Fiona know that what she did, I was very proud of her at that moment." James was very happy to hear that and said that he would get in touch with Fiona after the holidays.

"If I can find time to call her before then I will but right now I am too busy." He said he would call Fenella in a few weeks. James went back into the sunroom and sat beside Cassandra.

"The birds are going crazy in the feeders. It is so interesting to watch them. I wish we had cardinals here; they are such a beautiful bird. How were things with Fenella?" James laughed and told me about the confrontation Fiona had with Victoria.

"It's actually quite sad you know. I feel a little sorry for her. To be so unhappy that you try to go after your ex who is already engaged to another woman while you're still married to the man you cheated with. She must have a very unhappy life." James said probably so, but it was not his problem.

"I texted Christina to see if she could come out this afternoon. She said she could be here at 1:00. She and her staff will take down all the Thanksgiving things. She's going to leave the cornstalks up at the gate and maybe put a few of the pumpkins out there in addition to having them on the steps. It would be kind of fun to get dressed up. I don't know if you've ever done that. We can discuss it with her when she comes out." James's phone started buzzing. It was Richard, so he had to take it.

"Richard, how are you? What is happening?" Richard wanted to let James know that they finished the job blitz and found all the people James was going to need for the Toronto office and for the businesses in Alberta.

"For the textile company, I found a number of very qualified people in the processing of the raw product. Surprisingly, we had a number of people come to the job fair who worked at a heritage park who had to demonstrate how to do carding and weaving and they taught other people how to do it. We have a wide pool of people to draw from there. Quinn would be arriving in a day or two to give final interviews." James forgot about Quinn coming.

"Damn that's right I forgot about that. He's coming here on Tuesday. I know it is very short notice for you, but can you have the candidates here for him to do a final interview on. He is going to look over the lab and he can do the final interviews there. I really appreciate you getting on this so fast Richard. I will have to give Quinn a call. Talk later." James put his phone down and gave a huge sigh and went back to the sunroom.

"What's wrong James?" He said he forgot about Quinn coming.

"He will be here on Tuesday for three days. I told him he could stay with us. Are you still ok with that?" I was, and I was really looking forward to meeting him. James went off to his study to call Quinn and bring him up to speed on business matters. The doorbell rang, and it was Christina with her staff. She set them off to start packing up all the Thanksgiving décor.

"Do you and James want to sit, and we can go over the Christmas décor." James finished his phone call and joined us. We loved everything that she was showing us. She knew that I wanted to stay with the traditional Christmas colours and not go all modern. The house was going to look amazing and outside the amount of lighting that was going to be put up would be truly pretty.

"We will have to get on the lighting now before any snow falls. It will have to stay up until the snow melts, but you can decide whether you want to have the lights on throughout winter. It will be very pretty I promise." They were going to come back the next day and start putting up all the exterior lighting. It would take them several days to do and the forecast was going to be good for the next few weeks.

James and I sat talking in the sunroom about how nice it was going to look throughout the house. It was time for me to take another pill and James was tired from his travel, so we went to bed early. He admitted he was going on adrenaline when he first got home but jet lag hit, and he seriously couldn't do justice to making love. I laughed and said it was fine I wasn't expecting it.

The next day Christina and her staff arrived bright and early. She had the idea to put up wreaths on each of the lamp posts around the property. Something simple but festive. James was busy in his study, and I popped my head in to let him know dinner was ready. We ate and talked about the Christmas designs and the arrival of Quinn the next day. I was very much looking forward to meeting his best friend. We went back out to the sunroom. It was my last day of antibiotics for which I was thankful. I had an appointment to see my doctor tomorrow to ensure that the pneumonia was gone. I felt good and I wanted to get back to working out. It was getting late, and we went upstairs to bed. I could tell that

James was tired. With darkness now upon us we laid in bed, my head on his shoulder.

"James is everything ok you seem to be very distracted today?" He said things were fine, he was tired from the family drama and completely forgetting his best friend was coming.

"I've been worried about you too. Yes, I know it was a touch of pneumonia, but I was still worried. I am glad you are better now. I know Quinn is very anxious to meet you. I've been talking about you a lot to him." I said that I hoped it was all good. Joking of course because I knew that James would never say anything bad about me. He pulled me towards him and kissed me.

"I would never say anything bad about you ever. Now let's go to sleep shall we." We drifted off and woke early the next morning. It was a cool crisp day and Christina's staff were back putting up more lights.

James and I both went to the exercise room. I really wanted to get in a good work out. It was more than a few weeks since I was able to do so. James was working out rather intensely. I knew that he was angry about Fiona, but that situation righted itself. I knew also that my getting sick worried James because he was away so much lately. I wanted him to know that things were ok, so I asked him to come to my doctor's appointment with me. The appointment went fine, and I was given a clean bill of health. I could see the relief on James.

"You are going to need a doctor here. There are two male doctors here if you want to see at the front if you can get with one of them." He hadn't thought of that. He had a doctor in Toronto for emergencies and of course one in Scotland.

"You're probably right. We should check on the way out." Both of the male doctors were accepting new patients, so he had a choice which one to go with and would set up an appointment soon. He knew that he would have to pay until he got his citizenship but that was not a problem for him. Quinn was due to arrive in a few hours, so we went for a quick lunch and then out to the airport. His flight was delayed a bit, so we sat and had a coffee. The time passed quickly, and James checked the board and Quinn's flight finally arrived. We waited for him at baggage. James spotted him and waved.

"Quinn, how great to see you. Quinn this is Cassandra and Cassandra this is Quinn." He was every bit as tall as James and just as handsome.

"Cassandra so nice to meet you finally. I've heard so much about you I was starting think James made you up, but I see that he wasn't. You are as beautiful as he said." I said thank you and that I was very happy to finally meet him. We collected his luggage and went out to the car. I sat in the back, so James and Quinn could talk. The smile on James's face was so nice to see.

"I don't suppose James told you about all the trouble we used to get into at university. James may not look it, but he was quite the prankster in those days. I have to say that I am loving this area, and I am dying to see your new home. James, you look happy. I don't think I have ever seen you this happy before. You are obviously responsible for this Cassandra. You have made me happy for this guy right here." James was explaining things as we drove along. He went by the industrial site to show Quinn where it was. Quinn liked the location. Not too far from the city but enough so that they wouldn't have any issues.

"I like the location James and the building is a very good size. How is Richard coming along with candidates and lab people?" James informed him what Richard had so far. Quinn was impressed. It wasn't long before we were pulling up the drive.

"Wow, I love the property and this home is amazing. I'd like to take a tour around before dinner if we could. I need to stretch my legs and a good walk will do that." James pulled into the garage, and we took Quinn into the house. He was blown away by the home. James took him up to his room so that he could change into some work out gear. I ran up to do the same and James came in as I was finishing.

"It is so good to see Quinn and to have him here for a few days, we don't get that chance very often." We waited for Quinn at the top of the stairs and went out to walk around the property. James recounted the story about the moose. It was so good to hear him laugh, the two of them laughing a deep down belly laugh. It took a good hour to walk all the way around because we went slow. Quinn commented on the lamp posts and how it reminded him of some of the streets in the small villages in Germany. There was still an hour until dinner, so we went into the sunroom. Quinn was blown away.

"There is probably my favourite room in the house. Look at the view you have. It is like sitting in the outdoors." James poured them each a whisky and I asked for a white wine. My medication was done so I could now have a drink.

"It is so good to see you Quinn. I have missed you. You and Charlotte and the kids will have to come over next year and spend a few weeks with us." Quinn said he would like that and would talk to Charlotte about it.

"Richard sent me a portfolio of candidates and they come with extremely good credentials. Cassandra if you don't mind, I'd like to take Quinn to my study to go over a few business matters before dinner." I said that it was fine with me. It would give me a chance to go up and change out of my work out gear.

"James, she is lovely, and I can see that you are very happy with her. I am looking forward to the wedding and so is Charlotte." Quinn came around the side of James's desk and noticed the photo of Cassandra. He gave out a low whistle.

"James, she is stunning in this photo, really stunning. She looks like a top model in this photo. I have an idea and I hope that you will like it. The test trials for the mature cosmetic line went over very well in Germany. The product line has been selling off the shelves, so I hope that it will do as well here. But my idea is why don't we use Cassandra as a model for our ads. We could get her made up in our products and have a photo shoot. She is obviously very photogenic, and I think it would boost sales. I'm tossing it out as an idea." James thought about it, but it would be Cassandra's choice not his. He did agree that it would be a wise move to use someone of Cassandra's age and not someone in their thirties.

"I will ask her and see what she thinks about it, but it will be up to her." They looked up just as I was coming in.

"Up to me to what?" Quinn complimented me on the photo and said that he thought it would be an excellent idea to use me in the ads for the new product line.

"I am very flattered, and I will give it some thought, but I would also like you to think about maybe using a couple of the seniors from my old condo complex. They are all beautiful women and while they may not all look like models; I think that makes the point." Quinn had not considered that and had to agree. Jonathan stood at the door to say that dinner was ready. He prepared a roast of moose for dinner which I was looking forward to. All through dinner Quinn was telling me about the antics the two of them got up to. James wasn't embarrassed at all. Quinn knew that James went back to Scotland and was curious to know how the situation went.

"I hope I am not upsetting you by bringing this up Cassandra. She was not someone I cared for." James told Quinn what happened and about the email and about Cassandra calling Victoria and telling her to back off or else. Quinn was laughing and clapping with what he said was a newfound respect for me.

"Good for you; glad to hear you didn't let her intimidate you. James you have a great lady here and I am happy you two are getting married. We shall have to have a chat about a bachelor do." James said no to the bachelor party. He was ok with a few friends getting together but no wild drinking party. Quinn was ok with that. We took coffee into the sunroom and watched as deer walked by in the woods and the birds hurried to feed before night fell.

"Listen Quinn if you want to head up to bed, please do so. I know you've had a long day and a long flight. We usually have breakfast around 8 am and we can go over to the lab after, and you can have a look inside. At my last report it was ready to go but if there is anything else you need we can get it put in. We can come back and work in my study going over the field of candidates for a few hours. We will have lunch at 12:30 and then dinner at 6:00. We know you are leaving on the 30th and we need to get work done, but I want us to have some time together too." It was easy to see that they had more than a friendship, it was like two brothers together. Quinn said that he was tired and would head up to bed. James gave him big bear hug and kiss goodnight and he gave the same to me.

"I like him a lot James. The two of you are like brothers and it was so good to hear the two of you laughing together. I don't think I've heard you laugh that hard, so it was nice." James got me to come over and sit with him. We looked out at the woods and the wildlife.

"I feel truly blessed you know and even more so since you came into my life. I know that sounds corny but for years all I did was work and fly from one country to another. I had no real sense of home. I know I have my estate in Scotland where I grew up and that is home, but this here, this is my true home. I have you and that makes me feel whole. I know that Ross is not my son, but I feel a sense of fatherly protectiveness for him and of course Ayleen, well she just crushes my heart whenever I see her or hear her. I know I have family back in Scotland, but it is not the same. Maybe I am not making any sense, but I hope you understand." I said that I did understand, perfectly, and kissed him.

"James, I love you for saying that. I never thought I was ever going to be involved with anyone ever again. But you were patient and respectful. You made me laugh and feel at ease. I was at a point in my life where I was ok with being alone. I didn't feel the need to have someone to look after me. Perhaps that is why this feels so right, because I am not doing it in order to get away from something else. My life before you was happy and productive but my life with you in it is wonderful and exciting and so very special. I am so very blessed to have you in my life, to have you ask me to marry you and for you to build this home with the sole purpose of making me happy. You know I don't need all the expensive things in life, but you want me to have them because it makes you happy to give them. But the best thing about us is that we trust each other implicitly and that we love each other unconditionally. That to me is golden and worth more than anything." I bent down to kiss him and hug him.

"What do you say we head up to bed and we show each other just how much we love each other." I was all for that. We turned out all the lights and set the alarm. It was one of the sweetest nights we'd ever shared. Jonathan was in early, which was a good thing because Quinn got up early to go for a run. We forgot to tell him about the alarm, which Jonathan shut off just minutes before Quinn was heading out the door. Jonathan turned the lights on for the path. We showered and got dressed and went downstairs. Jonathan mentioned that he saw Quinn head out for a run.

"Oops we forgot to tell him about the alarm. Good thing you came in a bit early." We grabbed some coffee and went out to the sunroom. Quinn came in about an hour and a half later saying that he'd had a good run and was going up to shower and would be down shortly. After breakfast, James and Quinn went over to the lab to do the interviews. I decided to see if I could get in for a massage and a facial. I would have to book a mani/pedi for another day. I got back before noon and heard James and Quinn arrived shortly after.

"How was the lab Quinn. Does it meet your requirements and were you happy with the chemists?" He said it and they more than met his requirements. We had lunch and then they went into James's study to look over the rest of the candidates. James got Richard on the phone, so they could talk together. I decided to go for a walk around the property. When I got back they were still discussing things on the phone. I decided to give Christelle a call.

"Hey, you, how are you? What have you been up to?" Christelle said she was feeling pretty good. I told her that James's best friend was visiting and that they were going over some business matters at the moment.

"I'll bet they are happy to see each other. What are your plans for your birthday, or do you know yet?" All I knew was that we were going to Toronto for the week and that James would have to work a bit but at least we would be together at night.

"I'm sure that he will have something special planned. I don't know anything in case you are going to ask. Purely an assumption on my part but knowing James, I am sure it will be wonderful." I laughed and had to agree.

"He really is wonderful isn't he. I still have to pinch myself at times. I can't believe how someone like him came into my life. I am so very happy." Christelle knew that it was all the plan of the universe, and I could not be more thankful. We talked for about half an hour more when the guys emerged from the study. I said I would talk to her again soon.

"Have you figured out who the hires are going to be and when things will be up and running." They had indeed picked out all the executive staff and the other lab employees. They decided to hire all three of the chemists, that way they could have one looking after each division. In addition to the cosmetics lines, they were going to look at having two or three signature fragrances and possibly introducing a new one every other year.

"We'd like your help with that if you wouldn't mind. James told me that your preferred fragrance is a well-known French perfume but if we are going to come out with our own fragrances, we'd like to develop one that will be yours and we plan to develop one also that will be Charlotte's. There is a process involved in creating a fragrance which James will have the chemist involved in that division go over with you. He can start with what it is about your current fragrance that you like and build from there. Obviously, it won't be the same but perhaps you will like the new fragrance more. He can then come over to Germany and work with Charlotte. Would you be ok with that?" I said I would indeed and would look forward to working with the chemist.

"How exciting is this. The only thing I ask is you don't name it after me. I think that once the fragrance has been put together, I'll wear it and we will let James tell us what it invokes in him. Does that sound like a good idea?" Quinn was astounded because it was a phenomenal idea.

"I told you Quinn, she has some excellent ideas. Perhaps you should let Quinn know your preferred floral scents that you like?" I didn't have to think very long about that.

"I love plumeria, gardenia, jasmine, lavender, and freesia but I know all of those scents don't necessarily go together. I think the plumeria and lavender might be an interesting fragrance. I don't understand the whole process of making a fragrance but as long as there isn't any musk or heavy rose scent I am good with it. I'm sure that my current fragrance has the rose in it, but it isn't discernable to me and maybe that is the point. A perfume should have mystery to it and so many complex but relatable compounds in it, that it works. A woman should feel like a woman wearing it. Sensual, yet intelligent and her own person. I don't know if that makes sense or not." James and Quinn were looking at each other.

"Cassandra as a chemist and botanist that makes perfect sense and I know that you are wearing that French perfume now and while I am not trained in detecting the various scents of a perfume, I think that it does have rose in it but as you say it is not discernable. I like that idea that it should be a mystery. I think they worked that angle very well in their marketing so, once we have something, we shall have to really come up with a good market plan. You're right James, she does have very good ideas indeed." It was time for dinner, and we had a great time and laughed endlessly. Quinn wanted to video chat with Charlotte even though it was the wee hours in the morning for her, so he went into James's study. We waited for him in the sunroom.

"Wow a perfume for me, that is really something. Never in my wildest dreams would I have ever imagined that." We watched several deer at the feeding trough. We were getting lots of rosy grosbeaks and red polls at the feeders now. It was nice to see the different colour birds arriving. About a half hour passed and Quinn came into the sunroom.

"Quinn can I get you a drink, whisky, wine?" Quinn said he would have white wine and it was what we had as well.

"I just love this room; it is so peaceful back here. I mean the rest of the house is beautiful, but this room is so peaceful." We had to agree with him. We found it very peaceful as well.

"I noticed that you are putting up your outside Christmas lights. I guess you have to do that now due to the weather you get here. It is going to look really pretty I think." Most of the exterior lights were up so we thought we would give it a try and see how it looked. It was stunning. Each tree had one colour of lights on it but when they were all lit up it looked amazing. James turned on the lamp posts that went around the property. Quinn was very impressed. We turned them off and went back to the sunroom.

"I have been trying to think how to describe the two of you together. I've been married to Charlotte for a long time, and I love her more than anything. We complement each other in so many ways and I could never imagine being with anyone but her. But when I look at you two it is like the two of you have this aura or energy that grows and becomes more intense when you are together. I mean this sincerely. I have known James most of my life and I have never seen him this connected to anyone before. I think the two of you were meant to be together and it was to happen at this point in your lives. I'm very, very happy for both of you." James went over to hug his best friend. He even had a tear in his eye.

"Thank you for that Quinn. That was such a lovely thing to say, and I think that we both feel it as well. We were just saying last night how blessed we both are." Right at that moment the big buck came near the window. It looked at James and James looked at it. Quinn was stunned, and I was intrigued.

"Your friend is back. The two of you must have a connection, the way you look at each other." Quinn didn't know what to say.

"It seems that we do. He's watching over his domain just as I watch over mine. Not that I consider you to be property sweetheart, I hope you understand that." I said that I knew what he meant, and I understood the connection between him and the big buck. They sized each other up on the first encounter and acknowledged the determination in each other.

"That was amazing. Do you get wildlife like that coming this close all the time?" I showed Quinn the pictures of the two fighting bull moose and the window that they broke. We finished off a couple of bottles of wine and then we went to bed.

"Oh, by the way Quinn, we set the alarm system every night. Here is the password if you happen to get up before us again tomorrow and want to go out before Jonathan comes in." He appreciated the heads up but said that he was probably going to use getting up early to talk to his boys on video call tomorrow morning. He was scheduled to leave on the 30th and because they got their business done, he was going to use his last day to hang out with James. I could tell James was happy with that. We went into our bedroom.

"What sort of things are you and Quinn going to do tomorrow. I am going to see if I can get in for a mani/pedi and will be gone for a couple of hours. Maybe you could take him to pick up some things for his boys and his wife. I'm sure they would like something from Alberta." He said it was a good idea and they could maybe swing by the mall for an hour or so in the afternoon.

It had been a wonderful day, full of surprises and opportunities. James fell asleep almost as soon as his head hit the pillow. My mind was still going around about the events of the day, but I too could not keep my eyes open. James was up before me, and I think even before Quinn. I jumped into the shower and put on some jeans and a sweater and my black suede booties. As I was heading to the stairs Quinn was coming down the hall.

"Quinn, I want to show you something very quickly before James realizes we are up." I took him into the spare bedroom and took the painting out of the closet.

"I had this done up for James for Christmas. I love it but what do you think?" Quinn was looking at it and I could see that he was getting a little choked up about it.

"James and I have known each other since we were about thirteen. I knew his parents, his Mum more so than his Dad. James used to talk about the picnics they took as a family. They were the happiest moments of his life. He is absolutely going to be floored when he sees this. It is so life like, I wish I was here to see him when he opens it. Good job Cassandra, good job." I hurriedly put the painting away and we went downstairs.

"There you are. I thought I heard the two of you a bit ago. Should I be worried." We laughed knowing that it was clearly a joke. We had breakfast and then I had to get going to my appointment.

"See you both this afternoon. Enjoy your day together." I gave James a kiss goodbye and Quinn a hug and kiss on the cheek. I so liked him and was happy that they were going to have a full day together, just the two of them. The weather turned quite mild, almost balmy. I brought my flip flops with me to wear back home. My appointment was very relaxing, and I wondered what the guys were up to.

"I'd like to show you the other two operations that we are starting here. Then perhaps we can head over to the mall, and you can pick up something for Charlotte and the boys. You could always buy them Stetson hats to take back. Probably not something they would wear on a regular basis, but they are popular here. The provincial flower here is a wild rose and I know the jewelry store has some beautiful brooches because I got one for Cassandra for Christmas. I think Charlotte would like it, they are diamonds and what woman doesn't like diamonds." Quinn thought that was a really good idea and he was sure his boys would like the Stetsons. They first went to look at the geothermal office building. In it James had plans for the huge plant that was going to be built northwest of Edmonton. Then they went across to the textile plant. Progress on getting the equipment in and the various floor levels was already done. Quinn was quite impressed.

"I wouldn't mind being a partner with you on the geothermal and the textile plant as well. I think they are two areas that will do really well here. It will create tons of jobs and that's always a good thing." James would send him all the research information and they could talk when we went overseas at the end of November.

"We are hitting the Christmas markets in Germany and Austria. We will only be in each country a couple of days, but we will definitely get together with you and Charlotte. You can let me know what you think then. I know you will have to discuss it with her." They hit the mall at 11:30 am and picked up the Stetsons as they came in. The jeweler that James dealt with was on the top floor. Quinn was looking around at everything.

"This is a big mall, and it seems to be quite full for a weekday. Is it always like this?" James said that the few times that he had come it was always busy. They picked up the brooch for Charlotte and went back out. He took Quinn on a tour of the downtown which Quinn was also impressed with.

“The new arena has helped with the downtown core quite a bit. It has lot going on, not just in the city of Edmonton but the province as a whole. It took a hit with the downward spiral in the price of oil, but it is bouncing back. I don’t know for how long if they don’t move to other core industries but hopefully, I and possibly we, have timed it right and it is a profitable venture.” They drove back to the house. It was mid-afternoon, and I was waiting for them in the sunroom.

“I like that green on your nails, very pretty. I took Quinn on a quick tour of the city, and we stopped in at the mall and he got what he needed for gifts. But the rest of the day is for hanging out. We may go down and have a game or two of snooker. Did you want to join us, or have you got other plans.” I said that I was going to video chat with Ayleen. She had Lindsay text me a couple of times saying she wanted to chat.

“Well, make sure that you come downstairs so that I can say hello to her. Wait till you see her Quinn, she is the most adorable thing. But I’m a little biased.” Quinn couldn’t wait to see her. He and Charlotte had all boys. They’d been trying for a girl but when the fourth one was a boy they decided to stop. Charlotte’s law career was very important to her, as were her family, but she decided that four children was enough. I said I would come down because Ayleen would definitely want to talk to James. I put the call through, and Ayleen answered on the second ring.

"Hello Gramma, how are you? What have you been doing?" I said I was fine and asked how she was. I got 'good' and asked how school was and got 'good.' I said that I had the flu when I got home from visiting with her, but I didn't get it from her. She was sorry I was sick.

"I don't like being sick Gramma. It is not very nice." We talked about what she was learning in school. She knew how to print all her letters and was even doing lots of words and sentences. She knew all her numbers but now she was learning adding and subtracting.

"I like adding and subtracting. My teacher said I am very good at arithmetic and my printing was very good. I like school Gramma. I have lots of friends and Mommy and Daddy said that I can have a sleepover soon, but I have to wait until Halloween is over." I asked her what she was going to dress up as this year. She was trying to decide between a cowgirl and a princess or maybe a panda. She wasn't sure.

"Gramma, is Grandpa there, can I talk with him for a little bit." I said certainly she could. I said that he had a friend over visiting so she had to say hello to him too.

"His name is Mr. Drummond so be sure to say hello." She said that she would do that. I took my tablet downstairs as James and Quinn were finishing a game, which Quinn won.

"Ayleen wants to say hello." James took the tablet and as soon as Ayleen saw him she lit up.

"Hello Grandpa, how are you? Gramma said you had a friend there with you. Hello Mr. Drummond." James asked her how she was doing and how was school going. She reiterated everything she told me. Quinn stood behind James as he and Ayleen were talking. She asked him how he liked visiting Gramma and Grandpa.

"I am having a very nice time visiting Gramma and Grandpa. How old are you Ayleen?" She said that she was seven. She talked with the two of them about all the things in school.

"Grandpa, Mommy is calling me to go have a bath. I need to say goodbye now. Goodbye Grandpa, goodbye Gramma, and goodbye Mr. Drummond." We waved and blew kisses bye and said love you. She sent them all back to us.

“My word she is such a cute little girl and calling you Grandpa, you must feel very good about that. I can’t believe she is only seven though, she looks nine or ten. She must be very tall.” I said that she was very tall for her age and always looked a good two years older than she was. I left them to play another game.

“James, man you must be over the moon having that sweet little girl call you Grandpa. I presume you get along with Cassandra’s son. What a great thing for you, having such a wonderful family, something you always wanted.” James was very happy.

“Quinn, I tell you the first time she called me Grandpa I nearly cried. She already has me wrapped around her little finger, but I can’t spoil her too much. Cassandra wants to be mindful of the other grandparents. They know that we both have money, I think I told you she won money years ago and she has tried not to go overboard and make the others feel bad. Ayleen wanted to come here for Christmas every year, but Cassandra explained that it wouldn’t be fair to the other grandparents. Ross had the same talk with her. She’s a pretty smart seven-year-old. You can see her sitting there thinking about something, it’s really kind of cool to watch her little mind working.” They finished off three more games of billiards. James beat Quinn three out of five games and won a small sum of money.

They came upstairs arms around each other's shoulder. It was such a nice sight to see. Dinner was not going to be for another couple of hours, so we had some wine in the sunroom. I listened to them talk about their game and Quinn said James was losing his touch.

"I never used to win a game against you James, but I guess you don't get the chance to play much not like in our university days." I noticed something move in the woods but thought maybe it was a shadow. The sun was starting to set. I whispered to James and Quinn to look out into the woods. We looked, and a moose came out of the shadows.

"There is a cow out there and she's quite big. It must be finding good feeding areas." We watched as the moose came closer. It was like she knew the area and been here before. Quinn had his camera out and was taking pictures.

"If you keep your flash off she will probably come right up. Moose have bad eyesight, but their hearing is excellent. If you stay seated and don't move about a lot, she will walk right by. She, at least I think it is the same she, has done that before." Quinn sat quietly as did James.

"This is unreal. I can't imagine what it is like to have wildlife coming this close to you. Good thing there is a barrier between us. I don't think I've ever seen one in Germany. This is very cool." The moose fascinated James as well.

"This is such a cool place. If I didn't love Germany, I would be moving in next door." James laughed and said he would never leave Germany because Charlotte wouldn't leave. Quinn admitted he was right but said that was fine with him.

The moose walked away when Jonathan came in to say dinner was ready. We had wine and good food and lots and lots of laughter. I was sure that Quinn had lots of secrets he could have said about James but all I heard were some of their silly times and some of their great times together. His flight was pretty early the next morning. James was going to take him to the airport. I said that I would say goodbye to him now since they were going to be up and out of the house before 5 am.

Quinn's flight was at 8:00. I wanted James to have that moment with him alone. I knew they probably had said goodbye to each other lots of times, but this was a special time. I woke up around 7:45 and jumped into the shower. It felt good to be under the hot water letting it stream over my body. I already bought the Halloween candy a week ago and was going to sort it out and put it in small bags. I was thinking of James and felt hands go around my waist.

"James is that you?" I said it jokingly of course and his body connected with mine.

"Were you expecting someone else?" He laughed. I turned to look at him, all six foot three naked body of him.

"Am I mistaken or are we going to have shower sex?" He said we were indeed, and it was glorious, absolutely glorious. Dried off and dressed, we went down hand in hand to have breakfast. Needless to say, we were both very hungry. Jonathan decided to make up a typical Scottish breakfast, with smoked salmon omelet and black pudding. James ate with relish, and I even ate everything on my plate. There was lots of black coffee which we took to the sunroom.

I pulled out the bags to put all the candy in and while we drank our coffee and talked about Quinn's visit, I filled bags. I knew that there were a fair number of children in the surrounding subdivisions and so I made up enough for a hundred.

I put all the bags back in the box and took it to the kitchen and put it on the counter where it would not be in Jonathan's way. James was stretched out on the chaise lounge, and I went to lay down with him. It was so nice to have him home. I looked into his beautiful green eyes.

"James, I would like to make love again, are you up to it?" He looked at me and smiled.

"I am very up for it." He took my hand, and we went upstairs and once again our passion took over until we lay in each other's arms smiling. My thoughts drifted to the laughter that I heard from James, the laughter that was shared over Thanksgiving and to the laughter and joy that was to come. That's what this was, joy complete and undeniable joy. It made me feel very happy and I could not keep myself from smiling.

"Why are you smiling sweetheart?" I looked at him and said that I was profoundly happy right now. He pulled me into his arms and kissed me.

"That's good. I am happy that you are happy, but we really should get up. I've been trying to think what we can get Ross, Lindsay, and Ayleen for Christmas as well as Sonya, Austin, Rhonda, and Nicole. I know that we have to be mindful where Ayleen is concerned not to go overboard. I know that you have trust funds set up for them, would you be ok if I bumped those up. I mean they won't see it under the tree or anything, but it will be there for them whenever you have stipulated that they get control of it. Maybe we should go down to the sunroom and make out a list and get that done today if we can." He was so generous to have thought of doing that. We went down to the sunroom and started to think about each person. I brought them back scarves and sweaters from Scotland. We went through what I already picked up and James tossed in his ideas. We agreed on what to get and put the list aside.

"There is still time to go for a walk before lunch. Do you want to walk around the property or out through the subdivision?" We went out through the subdivision and saw that everyone was decorated for Halloween. We waved to people as we walked and stopped and talked with a few. We got back to the house in time for lunch. James went to his study to check on some emails after lunch and I used the opportunity to text Janet to see if she was free to talk. She was so I gave her a call.

"How are you feeling now and how is James? What is new? Are you ready for Halloween?" I said we were fine, and I was feeling much better. James was actually home but we were heading to Toronto after Halloween.

"James's best friend Quinn was here for a few days. It was nice to meet him, and he and James shared some great laughs. It was nice to hear. I made up a hundred bags of candy. I noticed there were quite a few in the surrounding subdivisions when we went for a walk so I was sure that we will get a good number. I'm looking forward to going to Toronto. I love it here, but it is always nice to be with James." We talked about her job and how things were going.

"I am so loving it. I don't regret for a minute doing it. But I have to let you go as I have to take Mom to the hairdresser. I'll text you later." James was still in his study, so I decided to do a painting. James liked the last one that I did, which I put in the room Ayleen would be in. I took out the photos I had and chose one. When I was done, I set it on the sill to dry and put my things away. James was still in his study working away.

"Am I interrupting?" I stood in the doorway waiting to see if he would stop. He looked up at me. He was so handsome, and it really made me catch my breath.

"I'm sorry, no you are not interrupting. I start going through things and I get wrapped up in it. I'm done now though. Why don't we go through the list of movies we have and pick something out and watch it down in the movie room. We can get Jonathan to make us up some canapes, not the usual movie watching food but neither of us likes popcorn. What do you say?" I liked the idea a lot. It would be nice to cuddle up together and watch a movie. We settled on a comedy and spent the next couple of hours laughing our heads off.

"That was very enjoyable, thank you for suggesting it. I loved those canapes, didn't you?" We agreed they were very good and would have to make sure those were on the list for New Year's Eve. We went back upstairs and out to the sunroom. James noticed my small painting and said that he liked this one a lot.

"I love the colours in the sunset, can I hang this one in my study?" I wasn't sure if he was humoring me, but I appreciated it, nonetheless. The walls in his office were not completely used up with pictures or paintings. He hung it up and asked me if I liked where it was.

"James, it looks wonderful there, but it isn't very professional. I love that you are being so thoughtful, but you really don't have to hang it here. I can put it up in one of the spare rooms." He said he wanted to hang it in his office.

"I love it really I do. I saw some of your earlier work and you have gotten quite good. I won't lie and say that you should do a show, but I like to be able to look up and see something that you have done. I eagerly await my first picture from Ayleen which I will display with equal pride." I laughed and gave him a kiss knowing full well that he meant every word of that. I already received a painting from Ayleen for James's birthday. I thought back to my conversation with her about it.

"But what shall I paint him Gramma?" I said for her to use her imagination and put lots of colours and to fill up the canvas. I bought some canvases and paints for her the year before, and we did up a painting together. She had fun and enjoyed it.

"Gramma I will make him a beautiful painting." She did exactly that. When I got it in the mail I was tickled to see that she did an abstract and used almost every paint colour. I wrapped it at home and put it with the photos I was bringing. I knew Ayleen would want to see him open it, so I told Lindsay that when he was ready to open it I would put in a video call. We went into the sunroom to relax. James poured us each a glass of wine. Jonathan mentioned we were having lobster pasta for dinner, and I was very much looking forward to it.

"Sweetheart you have not mentioned to me anything that you would like for Christmas. I know what you don't want which makes it a little harder, but I understand. I have some ideas, but you don't always drop a lot of hints you know." I knew that, but it came from years of not bothering so it was a hard habit to break.

"I know, I'm sorry I guess it would be easy if I said I wanted lots of jewelry and clothes and a big fancy car. But I am not like that although I have more clothes than I have ever had before. I just thought of something. I have always wanted a particular down jacket. I thought of buying one, but I wasn't sure if I wanted a short one, a car length or a long one. I put off getting one but those would actually make a nice gift for everyone. I have everyone's sizes from when we went shopping, so we could get those as gifts. But speaking of getting gifts, you are not exactly easy to buy for. You have more clothes than I do, and you have at least six very expensive watches that I know of. I think you are just as hard to buy for, so I need some ideas too." James couldn't deny that he had everything he wanted. He regularly gave to local charities. We talked about doing a sizeable donation of snowsuits to the snowsuit fund but giving to charities was something James always did.

"You are right, but this is our first Christmas together and I want to make it very special, so you have to allow me a little latitude in what I get you. I promise to keep it to something that you can wear more than once, ok." I agreed, and I knew that James was going to love the painting. I wanted it to be a memorable first Christmas for the both of us. We had dinner which was excellent and had more wine in the sunroom. Nightfall was earlier and earlier, and it was too cloudy to see the moon, so it was dark in the woods. It was still mild, but the forecast was showing that the temperature was going to change by the end of next week. Jonathan left, and it was getting late. I was going to head upstairs.

"I have a few things to check on darling, I will be up shortly." I kissed James goodnight and went up to bed. I tried to stay awake until he came up, but my eyes kept fluttering and I finally drifted off.

Chapter 10

James sat in his study contemplating a number of things. He reflected back on his life and all that he had accomplished. While he considered stepping back a bit, he hadn't thought about retirement. But he did want to spend more time with Cassandra. In all the times they had conversations about different things in life, he knew that she was interested in travelling to several places.

He decided on taking her to Aruba and Curaçao for their honeymoon. It was going to be twenty days of only them. No interruptions and it was one of the places she had on her bucket list. He booked a spectacular suite at one of the best resorts in Aruba for two weeks and a private villa in Curaçao for two weeks.

Richard interviewed a top security and IT executive who was very interested in taking the lead in the Toronto office. His bio sheet was quite impressive. Richard was quite confident that this guy could take over a lot of my duties in Toronto leaving me to run things here in Alberta. He was going to meet with him when he went to Toronto and work out a deal. Things were getting to the point where he would only have to go to Scotland once every six weeks for a week and in Toronto once a month for three or four days.

His thoughts drifted to the woman upstairs probably asleep by now. She was in remarkable shape and probably in better shape than he was, but he was very aware that she was seven years older than him. He could not imagine his life now without her in it and that was why he had been working so hard to get exceptional people in place so that he could spend more time with her. But right now, it was time to go upstairs and curl up next to her. She amazed him every day with her vitality and love of life. He enjoyed their sex life but knew that it would not always be the way it was now. That was something he could live with as long as she was happy, he was happy.

As expected she was sound asleep when he went into the bedroom. He quietly got into his pjs and crawled in next to her. She barely stirred. It was moments like this when she was sleeping peacefully that he felt most at peace. She was beautiful in all aspects, and he loved her more than he ever thought possible to love another person. He could see some of her in Ayleen and the thought of that little girl brought out such deep emotions in him. He developed a good relationship with her son which he knew made her very happy.

The full moon was coming through the window and shining on her. It was like he was looking at an angel and it made his heart swell up with such joy. He didn't want her to wake up, so he laid his head down and put his arm across her waist. James drifted off to a sound sleep. The next morning, I got up before James. He must have come to bed quite late because he was sleeping very soundly. I took a very quick shower and put on my royal blue leather pants with a white cashmere pullover and black suede booties. I went down to the kitchen to grab a coffee. Jonathan was going to make waffles this morning.

"James is still asleep so maybe hold off for a bit. I'm going to take my coffee into the sunroom." There was a light frost on the ground and the birds were feeding as always in the feeder. The squirrels were dashing back and forth picking up seeds that the birds had kicked out of the feeder. I sat for half an hour and heard James come down the stairs.

"Morning sleepy head. You must have stayed up pretty late for you to wake up after me. Jonathan is doing waffles this morning, but I asked him to wait for a bit. Do you want me to go and get you a coffee?" James leaned over and kissed me good morning but said he would run into the kitchen to grab a cup and let Jonathan know he could start breakfast in about twenty minutes.

"Yes, I was up late going over some work stuff which I am going to make a promise to you that I will delegate more to people and try to stay home more." I appreciated the thought but told him that I was ok that he was busy.

"James, I know you love what you do, and I would never ask you to stop doing that unless you really wanted to. You worked very hard to get yourself to where you are today, so don't stop that because of me. I would feel badly if I knew that's what you were doing." He could not love her more than he did now.

"I appreciate that darling, but it is not just me anymore. I knew that when I met you and asked you to marry me that my life was going to change, and I am really ok with that. Fenella has been telling me for years to delegate more and so has Mina. I don't need to be on top of things 24/7. Richard has hired some very well qualified executives and I know that Angus and Malcolm are doing an excellent job in Scotland running my companies there. I'm going to be meeting with a very highly respected security executive when we go to Toronto and if I think he can run the Toronto office, he will be hired. I will only have to go to Scotland every six weeks or so and only to Toronto once a month for meetings. This means that I will be able to look after the businesses here until they are well established, and I can then let the executives Richard hired run those. The whole purpose of this is so that I can spend more time with you. I can work from home as needed but we are both at a time in our lives when spending time together is important. I love you and I want to get to know you more and the only way I can do that is if I am here as much as possible. Maybe you will get tired of seeing my face every day but that's a chance I am willing to take."

He laughed because he knew I could never tire of his face.

"I will never get tired of looking at you, ever and shame on you for saying that looking for a compliment. I understand what you are saying. We are not twenty somethings and have our whole lives in front of us. I get that, but we are both healthy and in good shape and I fully intend on celebrating at least a thirty-fifth wedding anniversary with you. I may not be as spry as I am now, but I will hopefully still be in good shape." He took my hand and pulled me up from the chair and kissed me.

"Let's go eat, I am hungry, and we have a big day today don't we. Our first Halloween together. Have we decided whether we are going to dress up or not?" I thought perhaps not this year until we knew how many kids were going to show up.

"Maybe next year we can go all out on decorations. It is always dependent on the weather unfortunately. I'm hoping we get a fair number otherwise the last one who shows up at 8:30 is going to get a lot of candy." Breakfast over with, we went out for a walk around the property. It was a clear day but very chilly.

"James, after we come back from Toronto and if the weather is still good can we go to the mountains for a few days. It is a very spiritual place to be and the air there is so fresh and clean. I have always wanted to stay at this one hotel that looks like a castle. I know you have to go overseas soon after we get back, but I thought maybe for two or three days. What do you think?" James liked the idea and would book us a suite this afternoon when we got back. Back at the house, James went into his study to make the reservations for the nights in Banff. With that booked he went to join Cassandra in the sunroom.

"Suite is all booked for the nights of Thursday, Friday, and Saturday after we come back from Toronto. Now, what would you like to do for the rest of the day?" I texted to see if I could video chat with Ayleen before she went out for Halloween. I wanted to see her in her costume. Ross would get her to call just before dinner.

"I have all the bags of candy ready, and lunch is not for a couple more hours, but I'm not terribly hungry. We could watch a movie or have a sauna if you want." James said he wouldn't mind going for a sauna. The air had been chilly, and it was a good way to warm up. We went upstairs to take a quick shower and get into the big terry robes and then went into the sauna and set the timer for an hour. We got out of our robes and spread towels down to lay on. James was laying on his back on the seat just below me. I was lying face down looking at him. He had such a great body.

"I love being in this dry sauna. It's like nude sunbathing, makes you feel very uninhibited or at least it does me. Makes me want to do all sorts of things." James looked up and smiled at me. I slid down to lay on top of him.

"You are incorrigible do you know that, but I love it and you drive me crazy with desire." There was no restraining the passion that built up in the two of us. We teased each other until we couldn't restrain our need for release.

"That was so good James. You are an excellent lover and if we stay in here much longer I am going to want to do that all over again." I laughed at his expression, so I tossed him his robe and we went back upstairs to shower and dress again. I was about to go downstairs, and James pulled me close and kissed me so passionately my heart did flip flops.

"I love you so much I hope you know that, and I love that you want to make love as often as you do." I could feel that there was a but coming.

"But I know it isn't going to be like this forever and I am ok with that. I wanted you to know that ok. My heart will be full having you by my side." It was probably the sweetest thing anyone had ever said to me.

"James, I know that right now my sex drive is going a little crazy, probably because of all the years it was dormant. While I hope that it will not suddenly stop, I'm aware that we will not be making love three times a day every day. But for right now, I want to make love as often as possible. But if you don't want to, you have to say so." She completely misunderstood what he was saying.

"Are you kidding, I would make love to you all day long if I could, but work interferes with that. I am happy to make love to you whenever you want, well as long as I have some time to recover between. Don't get me wrong ok, I enjoy the shower sex, the sauna sex you drive me crazy when you get like that. I will happily keep up with you until I can't." We laughed and went downstairs. Lunch was light and delicious. We sat in the sunroom until James got a call and had to go to his study. He came back about an hour later to the sunroom.

"I hope everything is ok?" He said it was.

"It was Richard letting me know that he has arranged for me to meet with the new security executive. I hope it is ok that I will be going into the office on the Thursday and Friday. I promise that the rest of the time I will be with you." I was fine with it. I planned to do some shopping that day and maybe even a spa day on the Friday.

"I can get Mina to make an appointment for you at that exclusive spa for Friday if you want. You can text her and let her know what treatments you want." That would be great, so he texted Mina to make the appointment and then asked her to text me for the treatments.

"James, I know that Mina is like your right hand person in Toronto, but I have never had much time to talk to her aside from the short time at the gala. Do you think you could spare her on Friday, and she can come with me to the spa? If she wants of course." He said he had no problem with that and texted Mina to see if she wanted to go. Mina texted back almost immediately that she would love to and then she texted me.

"Thanks for thinking of me. I will book us for the works, massage, facial, body wraps, mani and pedi. If there is anything else, you want let me know? Haven't pampered myself like this in a while. Nice that James is offering to pay. Will have to request champagne and only the best caviar lol. See you when you come to Toronto. Looking forward to it!" I read out to James what Mina said and he laughed.

"You will probably have to start at 9 am to get all that in but I am happy to spoil the both of you. You because I love you with all my heart and Mina because she has been a loyal and very hard working assistant to me. I hope you both have a good time." I texted back to

Mina that I was looking forward to it as well and maybe if we could squeeze in a reflexology time as well, that would be all I needed. Dinner was going to be at 5:30 tonight simply because I knew that kids would start shortly after 6:00. My tablet rang, and it was Ayleen.

"Happy Halloween Gramma and Grandpa. I am a princess this year. Look at my dress, isn't it pretty and I have a wand and a tiara." We looked at her and said that she was very pretty indeed. She said she was going out with a couple of her friends and Mommy too of course.

"Daddy is staying home to give out candy with Freya. Mommy said we can't stay out too late because it is school tomorrow. Have you had any trick or treaters yet?" We said no not yet but it was still early for us. They got a dog right after Ayleen's birthday. It was more a present for Ross than anything. He had checked into this breed and knew that it was one that was good to have around kids.

"You have a good time and have fun with your friends. Make sure you don't run out onto the road. Bye love you." We blew her kisses, and she blew them back and said she loved us. James and I talked about the name they gave the dog. It was very Scottish indeed which made us both smile.

It warmed up considerably and we decided to sit out on the veranda and wait for the kids to arrive. The chill that had been there in the morning gave way to a chinook that had temperatures in the evening well into the mid-teens. Just as I predicted, the cars started to come up the driveway at 6:30. It was all the smallest ones, and they were so cute. By the time 8:30 rolled around we had ninety-five kids come through. There was another car coming up the drive with a couple of kids around age eight or ten. We handed them the bags that remained and once they left, we had John close the gate and put up a sign 'out of candy – sorry.' We watched to see how many other cars would drive up and there were at least another six cars. Next year we would have to be prepared for at least one hundred and fifty kids and we would try to get dressed up.

"Now that some have been here, I am sure they will put the word out at school, and we will get a lot more next Halloween. We should think about dressing up, nothing scary for the little ones." But that was next year, and we would think about it then. Lights were shut off and the alarm was turned on. We went upstairs to bed because we were heading to Toronto tomorrow afternoon.

The next morning we ate a good breakfast and went up to pack our bags. When James went down to his study to check some emails I went to the spare bedroom to get the black and white framed photos to give to him for his birthday and also the one from Ayleen. James went out to talk to John letting him know we were going to be gone for about nine days to Toronto. John would look after the place. James gave Jonathan the time off with pay. He would call him when we would be back. Jonathan actually found a place to live so he was going to use that time to move his stuff from my condo. He told James he would leave the key with Mr. O'Leary. I finished packing my bags. I decided to wear the dark green dress for dinner on my birthday. For James's birthday I was going to get something in Toronto. I brought my luggage down as it was only the one large piece. James already had his in the suv. He came in to ask if I was ready.

"I am, we need to take my luggage out." James grabbed it and put it in the suv. We drove to the airport. The crew was already onboard. We sat in our seats and Janine closed the door, went through the security procedure and we taxied out and took off. Maria came to see if we wanted anything to drink and we both said water. She brought back water bottles for the two of us and about two hours into the flight Janine brought our salads.

The weather was still good when we left, and it wasn't forecasted to change much. The weather in Toronto was slightly warmer. It was a late Indian summer for everyone. We arrived in Toronto shortly after 4:00. The limo was waiting for us and after our luggage was put in the trunk we drove to the penthouse. We arrived there shortly after 5:30. James advised

Antoine that we were going to be at the penthouse for dinner and was already in the kitchen when we arrived. We said hello and went to put our things away. It was my first time in his bedroom in the penthouse. It was larger than the others of course. It was very masculine. A lot of dark colour in the bedroom and bathroom. But it was James. He was waiting to see what I thought.

"I like it. It reflects your strength and confidence. It shows another side of you if that makes sense." He looked at me quizzically.

"Is that a good thing or bad thing?" I assured him it was a good thing.

"It's the primal you I think, and you know how much I love that side of you." He came up to me and hugged me.

"Oh yes, you do like that don't you." We kissed but knew dinner was going to be ready soon. I wrapped James's gift at home and took it and put it in one of the drawers he cleared out for me along with the gift from Ayleen. I went out into the living room. James poured us some wine which we took out to the terrace. It was a beautiful warm night, and we enjoyed the skyline. Antoine came to say that dinner was ready. We ate and talked about plans for the week. James was going to the office tomorrow and the next few days. I was going to go shopping tomorrow and possibly the day after and then

Mina and I had the spa day on Friday. We finished our dinner and went back out to the terrace and had more wine.

"It is nice being here just the two of us. It's like a romantic getaway." James agreed. Antoine left earlier and we were alone.

"Come let's go to bed. I want to be with you and make love to you." We put our wine glasses on the coffee table in the living room. James closed the bedroom door behind him. I turned to look at him and for the next couple of hours we explored each other's bodies, kissed, and made wild passionate love. We fell asleep naked in each other's arms. James was awake before me and was in the shower. I went in behind him and we knew what was going to happen. It was the most erotic sex we ever shared. We dried off smiling at each other. Antoine came in as we went into the living room. James had to go to the office and only had time for coffee. He came over to kiss me and whispered in my ear.

"That was great sex. I love you and will see you later." I had to giggle a little when he said that. Antoine was going to make me eggs benedict because he knew how much I liked them. After breakfast I freshened up and called for the limo to take me to the mall. It was after 9:00 when I arrived but stores were already open. It was decorated beautifully for Christmas. I let the limo driver know I would probably be two or three hours. He said he would go back to the penthouse and wait for my call. I went to the same store where I bought the black gown. Jackie recognized me and came over.

"Cassandra how nice to see you again. Can I help you with anything?" I told her that I was looking for a cocktail dress. I wasn't sure what colour, but I wanted it to be sexy but appropriate.

"I have a few new things in mind that I think you might like but please look around and see if you can find something. I will be back shortly." She went off to the back and left me to browse. I knew that I didn't want anything in white. I found a black dress in silk that I thought I would try. I didn't want beaded anything. I had jewelry to dress up whatever I bought. I looked at a long sleeve red linen dress with a v neck. I took the dresses to the dressing room. Jackie came back and asked if she could come in. I said of course, and she came in.

"These are new, just in and I want you to try them on." One was a royal blue organza sheath that had illusion long sleeves. It was very pretty. The other was a dark red organza A-line that had a jeweled belt and illusion long sleeves as well. The final dress was a black silk modified A-line that had a deep drape in the back. It was sleeveless and had a high neckline that sat under my collar bone. I tried the black on first and went out. Jackie helped with the side zipper.

"Wow, this is a beautiful dress but is it appropriate for me?" I was checking it out in the three-way mirror.

"Cassandra, you are a beautiful woman. You have a gorgeous body and your back in this is killer. I would never put you in something that was inappropriate. Trust me you look gorgeous in this." I went back in to try the other dresses. Each one just as beautiful. Jackie brought some shoes that would go with each dress. For the black dress she chose a pair of black sling backs. The heel was the right height for me. For the royal blue and dark red organza dresses, she had pumps that matched. I loved them all and couldn't believe I was going to buy all five dresses and the shoes.

"Jackie, do you sell negligees here?" She said they most certainly did. I told her I was looking for something romantic. She said she had lots that fit that, but she knew exactly what I wanted. She came back with five negligee outfits. They were all beautiful. There was a cream satin with a beautiful satin robe that would look good for the honeymoon, a black one that I wanted to wear the night of my birthday, a red one that I wanted to wear the night of James's birthday, a royal blue one and a pale pink one. While they were all different styles they were all lace or satin with lace or satin robes.

"We actually have all of these, as you will see, in a petite size so you won't be tripping over them." I decided to try on the black one to have a look. I came out and Jackie thought I looked stunning.

"Oh goodness, I love each of them." Jackie smiled and took them to the front and came back.

"I recall from your last visit here; you are not one to buy clothes just because. I know that Mr. Sutherland wants to spoil you and I am not saying that to make a sale. I don't operate that way. I can see that you are wearing a stunning engagement ring. I want to congratulate you on that. Would I love to dress you in lots of things, absolutely, but that is because you are beautiful and unpretentious." I told her that I did a lot of shopping back home and still my side of the closet was bare compared to James's. Jackie laughed, and I told her what I had as best I could remember.

"I know James likes to get dressed up to go out once in a while, but most of the time I'm in jeans around the house or work out gear. But when he is home I like to be a little more dressed up." She wanted to know if I would wear a suit and I said no because I was not sure where I would ever wear it.

"Ok so no suits, so let's look at some casual dresses and some skirts then and you can never have too many pairs of dress pants and tops. You said you bought leather pants in several colours, let's get some pretty blouses to wear with them. I know you don't like high heels, but if you have pictures of the leather pants, we can get some cute shoes to go with them."

Fortunately, any clothes I bought I took pictures of to keep on my phone for this very reason. She took my phone and went to pick things out. She came back with an armload of things for me to try on. She brought back shoes to go with everything. I tried everything on and some of the casual dresses I didn't like so she put those aside. At the end of it all I ended up with ten blouses in a variety of colours and styles, eight more pairs of shoes, seven casual dresses, eight pencil skirts, ten pairs of dress pants and ten pairs of casual pants.

"My goodness, I really do love everything but I'm starting to panic so I should stop." I put in a quick call to the limo driver to let him know I was almost done. Jackie took everything to the front and rang it through. James was very insistent this morning that I use the credit card he gave me, so I handed her the card. I was cringing waiting for the final total, but the majority of the items were on sale, so it wasn't as bad as I thought it would be. It was still a lot though and more than I ever spent on clothes. Jackie helped me down with my purchases and with them safely put in the trunk I went back to the penthouse. I hung up the two cocktail dresses that I planned to wear and put everything else away. I left out the black lace and tulle negligee and the red satin negligee and robe but put them where James would not see them. It was 12:30 when I got back, and Antoine prepared a salad for me. I knew James would not be home until this evening, so I sat on the terrace and texted Ross to see if Ayleen was free when she got home from school to video chat. He said he would let me know. I gave Christelle a call to talk with her. She answered on the second ring.

"Hi, how are you? I'm in Toronto at the penthouse. You will have to come, and we can see a show. I went shopping and spent a lot of money and I started to have a panic attack at the amount of money it came to." Christelle was laughing at me.

"Did you have fun? So, what is the problem. You said James gave you a credit card to use. He wants to spoil you so let him. The relationship is still new, and he wants to make you happy. He knows you are not materialistic, but he is an important businessman, and you will have to dress accordingly." I knew she was right. It was all so new to me being pampered like this. She laughed at me again.

"We both know why that was. James is a good man, nothing like the other one, not in any way, so for your first year be spoiled. You can slow it down later." I had to agree. She wished me a happy birthday and said she mailed us cards, which we would get when we got home. We talked for another hour and then she had to go. It was good to talk with her, she always had good advice for me. James texted to say he would be home in an hour. I went to freshen up a bit and waited for him on the terrace. Right at 3:00 James walked out onto the terrace.

"Hello, sorry I was longer than I wanted to be. I met with the new security executive. He is very impressive and wants the job and likes the terms. His name is Robert Harrison and his wife's name is Virginia. He's going to talk with his wife as they currently live on the west coast, so it will be a big move for them. He's young, in his early thirties and ambitious and I like him a lot and I think he will work out great. He likes the way things are set up and he's impressed with the high level contracts we have and the high level of staff. Richard checked him out thoroughly so there won't be any conflicts with the contracts we currently have. It would mean that I would only have to come here once a month for a few days. Mina has interviewed an assistant for him, which he was fine with. So that is another big matter taken care of. What did you do today? Did you buy anything?" I was happy for him because I knew he wanted to delegate more.

"Yes, I went shopping and I did some serious damage to the card. I bought a bunch of things but more importantly a dress to go out in for your birthday and a surprise for you afterwards. I almost had a panic attack at the store when I saw the pile of clothes and the final total. I won't have to go shopping for a good while now." James was laughing and said he was happy I went a little crazy.

"Good that makes me happy, and I know it is not something you like to do. I want you to feel you can go whenever you want, so I leave that up to you." We were staying in for dinner. Antoine was making a seafood dish with wild rice for James and a salad for me. We drank wine later on the terrace after Antoine left and stayed out there until well past midnight. It was a beautiful night, and the stars were beautiful, but it was late, and we went to bed. We were both very tired from the day and fell asleep quickly. James was off to the office again the next morning but had time to share breakfast with me. He wanted to know what I was going to do today.

"I think I will stop by Hans's shop today and have a look around if that is ok with you. I don't think I will buy anything, but you never know." James looked at me with a look of surprise on his face.

"I know, it so not like me, but I do like to look at sparkly things and I thought maybe I would like to get something nice for Christelle, if you are ok with that." James was very ok with it and would increase the limit on the card, so I would not have to worry. But that did make me worry but he smiled and said to have a good time.

"I must be off to the office. Tell Hans I said hello and buy whatever you want ok." I felt quite giddy at the moment. I had more than enough money of my own, but James insisted that I not touch it. I put in a call to the limo driver and asked if he could take me to the jewelry store in about fifteen minutes. He would be downstairs waiting. When I pulled up Hans was actually at the door with a customer and let me come through. He said goodbye to his client and came over to me.

"Cassandra how nice to see you. Let me see your ring. It fits beautifully, I gather you like it." I said that I absolutely loved it, but I was here to do a little looking around if that was okay. He asked me if there was something in particular that I was interested in.

"I'm looking for something for a friend of mine, she is actually my best friend and I want to get her something very special. I know this might sound weird to you, but her spirit animal is a wolf, and I was wondering if you had anything in diamonds like that." Hans looked at me and smiled.

"I understand spirit animals very well and I do have something to show you. I do have other clients who are animal lovers and of course they want diamonds in all shapes and colours on them, so let me go and get what I want to show you and I will be right back. Have a look around and see if there is something you want for yourself. Yes, I know you don't like to wear a lot of diamonds, but I do know that you like things that sparkle." He laughed, and I looked at him.

"Yes, James called and told me, so I have a few things I want you to try for yourself as well." He left the room and went into the back. The store was well protected, and I gather you could only get in by appointment, so I guess it was lucky he was at the door when I arrived. He came back after a few minutes with a tray which held the most exquisite pieces.

"Now here is a wolf head that is in black diamonds with a small blue diamond for the eye. It is a beautiful pendant and I think that your friend would like this a lot." It was very beautiful, and I loved it. The chain was 24 carat gold, and it was a heavy chain. It was stunning, and I knew that Christelle would cherish it. He brought me over to the counter to show me what he thought I might like.

"You know Hans, it is James's birthday on Tuesday, and I am taking him out for dinner. I bought this beautiful black dress that has a deep drape in the back." I showed him the photo of the dress. He smiled and held up his finger and said he would be right back.

"This would look stunning with that dress. It is all diamonds, and you wear it with the strand hanging down the back. It's called a lariat necklace. Here let me show you." He put the necklace on me and showed me how it draped down the back.

"It will fall just about here and will be beautiful on you. I encourage you to splurge and buy it." He was pointing to my lower back where it would fall which was just above the bottom of the drape. It was stunning.

"You can also double it up to wear as a regular necklace. Here I will show you how it goes together." He removed it and showed me how it would clasp together to form a double strand which I could wear on any occasion. He also suggested that I get a diamond cuff bracelet since the dress was sleeveless. He brought out a platinum cuff with diamonds. It was very delicate with lots of filigree, and it sparkled like crazy.

"You are making this incredibly hard for me not to choose this. I also want to look for something for my granddaughter. She loves unicorns, I don't suppose you would have one of those in diamonds, do you?" Hans scurried off to the back again. He came out with another tray. He had one that he thought might be suitable for her.

"This one has a platinum chain, and the unicorn is platinum with small white diamonds and a pink one for the eye. I think because she is small, going with platinum is a good idea. What do you think?" It was perfect, and I knew I was going to get her that from

James and me. I thought about the things for me and decided that I wanted to get them. Hans laughed and brought everything to the back and put them in velvet boxes.

"Cassandra, I know that you don't like to spend James's money, but he made me promise that I would make you use the credit card he gave you. I know that he upped the limit considerably, so you are going to be more than ok with what you are buying." I knew that Christelle would love the wolf, but I also knew she would scold me for spending that kind of money.

I gave Hans the credit card and steadied myself for the total. It was an amount that had my knees shaking but I did it. Hans saw me out to the limo, and I went back to the penthouse. I put the purchases away that I didn't want James to see until his birthday. The one for Christelle and Ayleen I kept out to show him. It was another warm day and after having a salad for lunch I took a glass of iced tea out to the terrace and sat in the sun. I would not have been able to do this back home right now. James gave me a call around 1:00.

"So how was your shopping. I hope you bought some things. I told Hans you would be stopping by. I forgot to tell you that you can only get in there by appointment, so he was watching for you." I said I was grateful he did that because I only realized that when I got there.

"I bought Christelle something and Ayleen something. I will show them both to you when you come home. The one for Ayleen we can give that to her for Christmas from the both of us. But it had me thinking that Ross might like to get something for Lindsay to have under the tree. I know they are going to bring things with them, but he has never been able to buy her a lot of jewelry and maybe I can take him when they come." James was happy that I got what I wanted for Christelle and loved the idea of giving something to Ayleen.

"Why don't you let me take him to the jewelers in Edmonton at the mall. I took Quinn there and he got a lovely brooch for Charlotte. I know he doesn't have a lot of money, but I will buy it for him to give to her. I'd like to do this with him if you are ok with that." I sensed that James wanted to bond a little more with Ross and I hoped that Ross would agree to it. James said he would be home in a couple of hours. He already told Antoine we were going out so that explained why after he cleaned up from lunch he was gone for the day.

"It will be a little fancy so pick out one of the dresses you bought the other day to wear." I said that I would probably wear the dark red organza. I sent him a picture of it as we were talking. He said he loved the dress.

It was a good thing that James had a clothes steamer because I had to steam out a few wrinkles on the dress. It was still very early, and I wanted to work out. There was a fitness room in the building, so I went down and went in. It was actually quite busy, but I saw the climber/elliptical similar to the one we had at home and went to work out on it. I put in an hour and was tired but pumped when I went back up to the penthouse. I jumped into the shower and took my time letting the hot water hit all my muscles. It felt really good. I dried myself off, dried my hair and styled it. I finished putting on my makeup and was sitting in my robe having a glass of wine.

"I love what you are wearing for dinner tonight. It must be something just off the runway in Paris." I laughed and gave him a kiss. He knew I was wearing the red dress. While he went in to take a shower, I finished my wine and then went in to put on my dress. James was out of the shower and had a towel around his waist.

"Here let me zip that up for you." He planted kisses all the way up my back. I turned to look at him and he could see he had started something.

"Oops no we can't do that now; we have reservations for 6:00 and it is already nearing 5:00 and it will take us a good forty-five minutes to get to the restaurant. Hold that thought." He went into the closet and put on a black suit with a white silk shirt and black and red tie. He was devastatingly handsome. He held out a box for me.

"I bought these for you to wear tonight. It made it easy once you showed me what you were going to wear." I opened the box and inside was a gorgeous gold and ruby necklace and earrings. They were stunning.

"James, oh my God these are beautiful. You shouldn't have but I am happy that you did." He helped me to put on the necklace. It was gorgeous with the dress. He took my hand, and we went out the door. The meal at the restaurant was very good and even better than when we'd gone before. James wanted to go dancing so we stopped at an exclusive club for an hour or so. It was so nice to be in his arms and I felt like a princess. When we got home, we went onto the terrace to have some wine. It was still a beautiful evening. It had been a magical day for me, but it was getting late, and I knew I was tired, and I was sure James was as well.

"If you want to put those back in the jewelry box I can put them in the safe." I hadn't thought about that and asked if I could put a few other things in as well, but he had to promise not to look at two of the boxes. I showed him the wolf pendant for Christelle which he really loved and the unicorn for Ayleen.

"They are both going to love these, and Ayleen is going to squeal I am sure when she sees her unicorn." I knew that she would for sure.

"You know James, I have been buying Ayleen a snow globe for Christmas for a number of years now and I was thinking that maybe when we go to Germany and Austria we could pick her out a couple of them. One to give her this year and one next year. What do you think?" He loved the idea and asked if I like them too. I looked at him with that look, which he knew meant something from the past.

"I do but if you don't mind I would rather that you didn't buy me one. The ornaments for me will be the biggest treat for me." It made him a little sad to think that so many things had been ruined because of the past, but he was not going to let that show. We went into the bedroom and James helped me undo the zipper on my dress. I wore my red lace bra and panties, something that I knew James liked. I was standing there in front of him with just the bra, panties, and my heels on. I was about to kick them off, but he put up his hand.

"Wait, let me look at you. You look so gorgeous and sexy like that it makes me crazy with desire." I went to him and kissed him with every ounce of passion I had. He hurriedly took off his suit and put it on the centre island in the closet and came back out to me. He laid me down on the bed and slowly took one heel off at a time, kissing my legs all the way up. It was driving me crazy with passion. He slowly removed my panties kissing me again all over and then my bra until I was pleading with him to make love to me now. We never had a night like that before. Nothing was held back, and we lay spent in each other's arms in the wee hours of the morning. We both started to laugh. James looked over at me.

"We are going to have to stop doing that or we are going to kill ourselves having the greatest sex ever." I laughed at him and told him it was only the beginning. He lay back excited at the idea but exhausted. We fell asleep shortly after.

James was up and, in the shower, I got out of bed and joined him. I said no shower sex as I was going for my spa day with Mina. He said I was no fun, but I knew he was teasing. I got dressed in a pair of black silk pants and a white silk blouse. I had time for a cup of coffee and some toast. Mina was picking me up at 9:00 and I would be gone all day. I gave James a quick kiss and went out because Mina texted she was downstairs. James was smiling to himself all morning and he could not stop smiling even when Richard came into his office.

"Well good manners prevent me from asking you why the big smile. I must say I have never seen you so happy James. You and Cassandra are really good together, and I'm not saying that as a subliminal message for the smile you have on your face. I'm happy for you and I think she is a wonderful woman. But I did not come here to talk about that, Robert called to say that his wife was all for the move, so he will be starting here in two weeks if that is ok with you." James was good with that and would be looking forward to having him take over.

"Richard, not meaning to pry but how are things going with you and Sonya. Didn't you go and spend the weekend with her and aren't you going to the opera soon?" Richard said the weekend went very well, very well and that the opera was next weekend.

"Mark asked Rhonda if she wanted to go and I was able to get four tickets seated together, so she is coming down as well. You did say they could stay here in the penthouse didn't you. I think Sonya would be more comfortable with that arrangement. We are taking it slow, and I am letting her set the pace of how things proceed but I think she is a wonderful lady, and I would not hesitate to ask her to marry me. I know James it is very fast, but I am not getting any younger and I want to enjoy being with a woman. You know when Cordelia died, I thought I would never fall in love again, but then I met Sonya and my whole perspective has changed. But we shall see what happens over the next few weeks. I think Mark is becoming serious with Rhonda. He never used to talk to me about such things, but he is looking to me for advice more and more and I welcome that. I know you offered Rhonda a job and she is thinking of accepting but I am hoping that doesn't come about until the new year. It will give Sonya and I a chance to see where this relationship is going. I hope that is ok with you?" James said he was fine with it.

"I am happy for you Richard. Sonya is a wonderful person and I think the two of you have some things in common and I really hope that the relationship does work out for both of you. As for Rhonda, she is very interested, but I already discussed with her not having anything done formal until the new year. She was ok with that because it gives her a chance to sell her condo. So good luck with everything and I am sure that it will work out for you." Richard left, and James got on with the papers in front of him.

"Mina I am so glad that we are getting this time together. You have worked with James for such a long time, and I want us to be friends." We got to the spa at 9:30 and taken into the back to change. I left my ring at the penthouse in the safe.

"I feel the same way Cassandra. I am so happy for you and James. Honestly, he is like a different person since he met you and I mean that in the best way possible. He smiles more and he's in better spirits. Before it was always about work and now, he and I can't get through a meeting without him bringing up your name half a dozen times. Don't get me wrong, I love it. I am happy that he has you and that he will slow down now. I see the massage therapists are ready for us. I will talk to you again when we have our lunch. Enjoy your morning." With that she was off in one direction and I in the other. The massage was wonderful, and I was so relaxed. Then it was the facial which was also very relaxing. I met up with Mina for lunch.

"How were things so far. My face feels like new again." I said the same thing and we both laughed. We enjoyed lunch and then it was off for the body wrap, then the reflexology and then the manicure and pedicure.

I was sure that I had fallen asleep when I had the body wrap. The girl had to touch my shoulder to wake me up. I apologized but she said it happens all the time. The body wrap is a very relaxing treatment. I got dressed back into my clothes. Then I went to reflexology and met up with Mina again. She never had reflexology done before, so this was going to be interesting. The reflexologist was explaining the treatment to her, and I was listening. I've had several of them, so it was nothing new to me. The treatments started, and Mina was oohing and aahing. She looked a little embarrassed when she saw me smiling.

"Hey, don't be embarrassed, you should have heard me the first time I had mine done. I totally embarrassed the reflexologist." It was male reflexologists, and they were both laughing at what I said because they knew what I was talking about.

"You guys know what I'm talking about I can tell. So don't feel embarrassed Mina, they've heard it all before." We both laughed and enjoyed the treatment. Then it was off for a pedicure. I chose a plum colour because I knew it would go with both the green dress and black one. But I chose a plum that was more on the pink side than purple. Mina was going with a lovely navy. I was telling her about my wedding dress but didn't have anything to show her. I did show her what I was wearing for my birthday.

"James is going to love that. I love the back of that, and you have such a beautiful figure. He will faint I am sure. Did James tell you that he is letting me, and my family use the villa in the Turks for our Christmas gathering. We always do a sun destination because my parents and my husband's parents don't like winter here in Toronto. I am going to make sure that it is perfect for when you and your friends go." We talked for two hours about when she first started working for James. I wasn't aware that he started off the company many decades ago.

"Oh yes, he wanted to branch out and he bought out the previous communications company I was working for and kept me on. That was not long after he divorced his first wife. He was not the easiest person to work for back in those days, but we got along, and I understood him. Now I can't believe the company that it has grown into. James has allowed me to train several other assistants so that I can sort of semi-retire. Now that James is stepping back a bit, so can I. It was long days for a number of years and now I can spend more time with my family. I don't begrudge a moment of working for him, not ever. I learned a lot from him, and he has been very good to my husband and me and my family. I owe James a lot and I will always be loyal to him. I will never hesitate if he wants me to do something for him although I am thankful now that he is not calling me in the wee hours of the morning when he is in Scotland. He would always forget the time difference. I can laugh about it now, but it used to tick my husband off when the phone would ring at 3 am." Our nails and toes were now done and just about completely dry and hard.

"Mina it has been so wonderful spending the day with you, and it makes me so happy that you adore James and would do anything for him. I hope you know that he feels the same way about you." She knew how James felt but it was nice to hear it and especially from me.

"I am so happy the two of you are getting married. You have given James a family, one that he wanted so much, and he talks about Ayleen all the time. He thinks of her like a daughter you know. I hope that is ok." I said that it was, and I often thought of her that way too. We went out to the front. Mina took care of the bill at the request of James. We laughed and laughed more in the limo. By the time I got home it was well past 5:30 and James was already home.

"You look like you have had a wonderful day. Did you and Mina have a good time?" I said we had a wonderful time and would do it again. Antoine was in the kitchen preparing dinner.

"I like the nail polish, very pretty colour. Would that be the colour of the dress you are wearing on Saturday. I said no but was now thinking whether this polish would go with the green dress. I decided it would look fine.

"No, I am actually wearing the dark green dress that I wore before, but I guess I could also wear the royal blue one I bought. I brought the brooch that I wore in Scotland and which I put in the safe with the other things. I hope it was ok that I brought it with me." James was smiling.

"Of course, it is ok, it is your brooch you know. I gave it to you, and you can wear it wherever you like. I love that green dress on you." We had dinner and then went out to the terrace. We had some wine and sat for a while watching the sunset and then the stars coming out in the darkness.

"You have had a long day and I suspect you are very tired. Are you going to shower before coming to bed? I am beat, so I am going to get into my pjs if you don't mind." I was going to take a very quick shower to make sure I got all the oil and seaweed off of me. I did take a shower at the spa, but it was a very fast one. James got into bed, and I was not in the shower long. I put on my pjs and climbed in beside him.

"It has been a long day and even though I am very relaxed I am tired. I love you James." He curled up next to me, kissed me and said he loved me too. Since it was Saturday we stayed in bed a bit longer. James told Antoine that he only had to come for dinner.

"I am going to take you out for breakfast today. We are going to go and tour the museum and the art gallery and then have lunch and we can decide what to do after that." It sounded like a fun day.

"James, can we go down to the waterfront and maybe go for a walk along the shore. I was talking to Sonya a little bit ago saying that there are some really nice neighbourhoods in that area. I know that housing is expensive here in Toronto and I know that she could never afford to buy a house, but I told her if Rhonda accepted your offer, I would buy her a place where she felt comfortable. If we can have a look around at where she might be comfortable if that's ok." James was happy to do that.

"I actually spoke to Richard the other day. He said that he spent the weekend at Sonya's, and she was coming next weekend to go to the opera and Rhonda and Mark were going as well. He really likes her, and I think he wants to ask her to marry him. Yes, I know that seems a little quick, but he said he wants to enjoy being with a woman while he can. Please don't repeat that to Sonya as I don't think they have slept together from the way Richard was talking. But I know he is serious about her, and he can make her happy." I was excited about this news.

"James, I would never repeat anything you tell me in confidence, but I know that Sonya is serious about him too. She is worried that people might think it is going too fast. But she said she doesn't want to wait too long and as she put it 'she is not getting any younger.' I think Richard would be safe in making a move. Although I don't think she will want to have Rhonda in the next room if you know what I mean. I know they are going to be staying here at the penthouse, and I know that Richard and Mark have separate suites on different floors, so maybe he could take her down to his suite for dinner or something. Maybe Antoine could make them a special dinner and take it down." James thought that was an excellent idea and would send Richard a text with the suggestion.

We toured the museum which had an exceptional exhibit on that we both enjoyed seeing. Then it was off to the art museum where we picked out four paintings to be shipped home to Alberta. We went over to the harbor front and walked around for about an hour or so enjoying the wonderful warm weather and the breeze off the water. We had lunch at a restaurant right on the water. Then we toured a few of the neighbourhoods. There were several very beautiful homes that I thought Sonya would love to live in. James made a note of them so that we could look at them online when we got home. When we returned to the penthouse, James took out his tablet and pulled up the houses we saw.

"I know you said she wouldn't be able to afford any of these so why don't we buy it for her. That way Rhonda can accept the job and she and Richard can be closer to each other and not have to rush their relationship. I am happy to buy it for her." They were all a million plus something I knew Sonya couldn't afford. We narrowed them down to three or four and I sent her the links to have a look at them. I called her just as she said she was opening my email.

"I want you to look at these places. James and I toured around, and they are all in really good areas and close enough that you can walk to the waterfront and get a good walk in there. There are grocery stores close by and lots of boutique shops and cafes nearby. Everything is pretty much within walking distance of any of the houses. Now I know you are going to immediately look at the prices and say you can't afford them, but James and I have been talking and we want to buy it for you. If you want to open them up and as you are looking through them we can look through them with you and you can ask about the outside. We didn't go into any of them because we didn't want to deal with the realtors." She opened up the email and the first link. All of the houses were bungalows which I knew she wanted. Some were brick exterior and others were stucco/stone exterior. We told her not to look at the price but to look at the interior and exterior and go from that. When she came down next weekend, Richard could take her to see them if she wanted.

"Well of the four you sent me I like all of them but if I were to say one it would be the one on Pinewood Trail. It is big, but Richard said he had a lot of friends who would visit and yes I know I was including Richard." James and I looked at each other and raised our eyebrows but said nothing.

"The price is too high though so if I had to pick a second best it would be the one on Cliff Road. I'm going to be with Richard next weekend so maybe he can take me out for a drive, so I can have a look at those two. I know you said you would buy it for me but that is a lot of money." James took the phone.

"Sonya if you absolutely love the one on Pinewood Trail I will buy it for you, and you can hire a cleaning staff to do the cleaning. I realize that it is a pretty big house, but I think you would be happy in that one. I've never seen your place, but Cassandra said that you've built the homes you were previously in and maybe this one will the perfect one for you. Say that you will go and have a look with Richard and if you really love it I will get it for you." Sonya was overcome with emotions and started to cry. I took the phone from James and went out to the terrace.

"Sonya, please don't cry, we want to do this, and it can be your home in case things don't go the way you want them to with Richard." She stopped crying.

"It isn't that it's because the two of you are being so kind to me and nobody has ever done that before. I really want to pursue a relationship with Richard, but I think any idea of getting married right now is much too soon. I would like to get to know him for at least six months, but I know Rhonda wants to accept the job with James and she won't do it if I stay here. If I get that house she can move in with me until she finds a place of her own if she wants. I know that she and Mark have been talking constantly since Thanksgiving, so I suspect that they might want to get a place of their own. But I want her to be sure too." She would go and look at the place she said and then let us know her decision. As long as the price tag wasn't too much of an imposition, she would seriously consider it. I said I would call her tomorrow. I went back into the living room because James gave me privacy to talk to her.

"Well apparently she is a lot more serious about Richard than I thought. She wants to get serious, but she said that getting married right now is too soon. She wants to wait for six months before she can commit to that kind of decision. She knows Rhonda wants to accept your job offer and she and Mark have been getting serious as well. She thought if she loved the house, and we didn't mind the price tag she would move and get Rhonda to move in with her. That is until she and Mark make up their minds what they want to do. I could see her having Richard move in and I think that she is going to sleep with him when she comes here for the opera. Maybe I shouldn't have said that, but I don't know if Richard would want a heads up. I don't know what guys think about that sort of thing, but I know that a woman would want to know. I think she wants that house, but the price tag scared her. I am more than willing to buy it for her." James would not hear of me doing that.

"No, I can easily afford that, and I don't want you to spend your money, remember, we already talked about that. As for a guy wanting to know, I can find a way of letting Richard know. We have never had those kinds of discussions, but we are close enough that it wouldn't be awkward. I know you are going to say you can pay half, but you don't need to, but we can always work out some sort of deal later on." His wicked smile told me it had nothing to do with money. We went off to bed because I was tired, and James was too, although he wouldn't admit it. I knew that the last few months were very taxing on him, so I said we were going to bed to sleep, no fooling around. But he wanted to play and started to tickle me, but I wasn't reacting. He wanted to know if I was upset he was doing that because I said sleep no sex.

"You are so silly James; I am not ticklish. I never have been but if you want to play we can." I stripped off my pjs and pulled his off and had my way with him. He was just a little out of breath when we were done.

"Wow, now I call that paid in full. I love you and that was very sexy. Maybe you can do that to me again sometime soon." He was chuckling as we were putting our pjs back on. I said maybe I would and perhaps sooner than he thought. We slept soundly until the next morning. James was wide awake and looking at me and he handed me a box. I sat up and asked what this was for.

"I seem to recall it is your birthday today and this is one of the many gifts you are getting today. No, you are not allowed to protest. Today is about you and doing what you want. So, Antoine is not here, I am going to make you pancakes with maple syrup and some fresh fruit, orange juice, and coffee. We are going out to dinner tonight, but we will be alone all day. Why don't you come out to the dining room, and I will make you some coffee? But first open your gift." I opened up the box and inside were beautiful gold bangles in yellow and rose gold.

"James, they are beautiful, I love them. I will wear them tonight when we go out." We went out to the living room and James went into the kitchen to make breakfast. Everyone knew that I didn't make calls or send texts on my birthday. My phone started to ring, and it was Christelle. She wanted to wish me a happy birthday and hoped that my day would be awesome. Then it was Janet who said the same. Then I got a video call from Ayleen.

"Happy birthday Gramma. I hope you have a nice day. Did you get a present yet? Can I see it? Is Grandpa there?" She sang happy birthday to me once she got all that out. James heard her and hurried over to say hello. She was thrilled to see him.

"Yes, Grandpa gave me these beautiful bangles aren't they pretty?" She oohed at them and giggled. James gave me the gifts from them that he brought in his luggage. They gave me a beautiful gold chain and earrings from the three of them.

"Gramma, is Grandpa making you breakfast? What are you having? I wish I was there." I said that he was making me breakfast and we were having pancakes. Ross and Lindsay wished me happy birthday and they told Ayleen she had to say goodbye, so Gramma could have breakfast.

"Oh ok, have a nice day Gramma, bye Grandpa, love you." James shouted back bye and love you. Ayleen hung up. James brought me a cup of coffee and said the pancakes would be ready shortly. It was going to be a wonderful day I could tell.

Breakfast was simply wonderful, and we took coffee out to the terrace. It was another beautiful day but a bit cooler, so I had to put on my robe. James came and sat down beside me and gave me an envelope along with a card. I opened the card first. It was beautiful and the prettiest card I had ever gotten. I opened up the envelope and it was the deed to the house. I looked at him not understanding.

"I had my lawyer draw up papers so that the house in Alberta would be in both our names. When I bought the land and built the house, it was all done in my name but now we are getting married I want it to be joint ownership. When we go back, we will have to stop in at the lawyer's office to sign the documents and then a new deed will be drawn up." I couldn't believe he was doing this, and I didn't know what to say.

"James, you didn't have to do that. I am overwhelmed that you did it and I love you so much for doing that, but it really wasn't necessary." He knew that, but he wanted to do it and he hoped I was happy about it.

“I am, please don’t take my surprise as not being extremely happy you did this. Thank you, and you know I love you so much.” He said he did, and we had more coffee and we stayed lazy for another hour. He mentioned the plans for the rest of the morning. We were going to the luxury spa that Mina and I had gone to, and we were going to have a couple’s massages and body wraps.

“They won’t be together, just the massages but I thought it would be nice to do something you enjoy. I can’t say as I’ve ever had a body wrap, but I will do it for you.” I was laughing trying to envision him in the body wrap. We were going to have a lunch out along the boardwalk.

“But we have to get moving because our first appointment is in forty-five minutes.” We got dressed rather quickly and went off to the spa. The couple’s massage was first, and it was really wonderful.

“I rather enjoyed that massage. How are you liking your birthday so far?” It was wonderful, and I was having such a great time.

“I loved it and I love you for doing this with me.” We went for our body wraps which were very invigorating. I took a good shower to get all the stuff off me and then went to the change room to get dressed. I waited for James to come out. He looked a little different.

"Are you ok?" He said he was and that he had no idea what a body wrap was. He felt like he was a mummy all wrapped up in seaweed.

"It was very strange, and I am not sure whether I like it or not, but maybe I will have a different feeling later on. Right now, I feel like I have seaweed everywhere and I took a really good shower." I was laughing at him but loving that he was being such a good sport about it. We went off to the waterfront and stopped at a small restaurant for lunch. When we got back to the penthouse it was going on 3:00. I got my ring back out of the safe and put it on. James poured us a glass of wine and we sat on the terrace. The sun warmed up the air now and it was nice to sit out. I wondered what we were going to do until dinner.

"I have someone coming over to do your hair and makeup for tonight. They will be here at 4:00, so we have a little time to relax and here is another gift for you to open." It was another jewelry box.

"James, you are spoiling me, but it is my birthday, and I am going to let you." I opened the box to the most beautiful gold and diamond earrings. They were absolutely stunning. I put them on for him to see.

"They look lovely on you, but you may want to take them off until you have your hair and makeup done. They will look lovely with the green dress and that brooch." I took them into the bedroom and put them on the dresser. It was wonderful the two of us together relaxing and nice that James wasn't doing something relating to work. He must have read my thoughts.

"I promised you no work on your birthday and I won't do any on mine either." It was getting very close to 4:00 and the hair stylist and makeup artist would be arriving soon. I went in to change my top into something that would be easy to take off, so I wouldn't ruin my hair. When I came out Tanya and Carmen were coming in.

"Hello, so it is the both of you that James hired to come and do my hair and makeup, how wonderful." They came in and wished me happy birthday and we went into the bedroom.

"Ladies, I hope you can do me a favour and come back on Tuesday as it is James's birthday, and I am taking him out for dinner, and I have this amazing dress I am going to be wearing. Let me show it to you and you can decide how you want to do my hair and makeup." They gasped when they saw the dress and loved it.

"You are going to look stunning but then you look stunning in everything. For tonight, you said you were wearing the green dress right, so perhaps we will bring it back and sweep it up a bit, leaving a few loose tendrils. Carmen can do your eyes with a plum shade to really bring out that green and perhaps a deep rose lip. What do you think Carmen?" She agreed completely.

"For Tuesday, we will curl your hair and bring it back in bunches and clip it at the back. It is hard to describe but it will look amazing with the dress. I have some really cute crystal clips. Carmen how do you want to do her makeup." Carmen looked at the dress again and had an idea.

"I know you are not big on a smoky look, but we can do one that isn't too extreme and do a really beautiful plum lip. I see your nails are a pretty colour so that will go well with both dresses. You will look awesome, trust us." I said I would, and they went to work. James took his clothes into another room to get dressed. He wanted to be surprised when I came out. They finished in an hour and a half and were very pleased with how I looked.

"Cassandra look at yourself in the mirror you look so beautiful." I looked and could not believe it was me. I put on my dress and Tanya did up the zipper. I put on my shoes and the bangles, earrings, and brooch. It looked really good with the dress. Carmen went out to see if James was waiting and he was. They went out ahead of me and stood aside as I walked into the living room.

"Wow you look stunning. Ladies you did an awesome job, but she looks beautiful no matter what." James paid them and before they left they took a few pictures of us with our phones, then they left.

"Cassandra, you look so pretty; you take my breath away. I have another gift for you, and I promise this will be the last one, for tonight." He handed me another jewelry box and when I opened it, I almost fainted.

"James oh my God this is beautiful, but you gave me a ring, why this one?" He took the ring out of the box and put it on my ring finger on my right hand.

"You said that you never got a 'going steady' ring. Perhaps we did this a little backwards, but I wanted you to know that you are my steady girl and my fiancée and soon to be my wife." I was so moved by his generosity that I started to cry.

"Nope you can't do that, you will ruin your beautiful makeup. Besides, we have dinner reservations and then we have somewhere special to be. So shall we go?" We went out and down to the limo. I couldn't believe this night; it was so unbelievable that I had to pinch myself.

We dined at one of the most exclusive restaurant in Toronto. James ordered what was now my favourite champagne in the year I was born, and we drank and toasted to my birthday. We finished the bottle and ate a wonderful meal. Then we went to what looked like the university. I wasn't understanding why we were here. The limo pulled up beside a huge dome shaped building. I tried to see what the name of the building was, but James blocked me from seeing it. Once we got in and went down a hallway and he opened the door, I understood where we were. I couldn't move, I couldn't believe that he'd done this.

"James, you brought me to an observatory, are we going to look at stars?" There was a gentleman over by the telescope. He got up when we approached him.

"Cassandra this is Dr. Alton Cooper; he is the head of astronomy here at the university. Is it all set up?" Dr. Alton said it was and he wished me happy birthday. I said thank you, but I was confused.

"James what have you set up?" He took me over to the telescope and sat me down in the seat that Dr. Cooper vacated.

"I want you to look through the eye piece and look at the star." I did as he asked it was amazing to look at an actual star. It was so beautiful. I looked over at him with a puzzled look on my face.

"Cassandra, you are looking at the star named Cassandra Lynn." I looked at him and I knew that tears were falling down my face. I looked in the telescope again and it was even more beautiful than the first time.

"James, you arranged for me to see my star, really. That is the most amazing thing you could have ever done. Even though it was my Dad who got it for me, you went to all of this so that I could see it. Thank you, thank you so much. I'm sorry Dr. Cooper if I got tears and mascara on your lens." He said it was easily fixed and took out a cloth and wiped it clean. I looked again at the star for a few more minutes. Dr. Cooper asked if I wanted to see Betelgeuse, the red star in the Orion constellation that was dying. I said that I would like that very much.

"I look up at that star all the time and wonder when it would finally explode. I know that it could have already done so but it takes so long for it to finally reach us. I love astronomy and star gazing." Dr. Cooper was thrilled that I loved stars so much. We thanked him for allowing us to use the telescope and went back out and back to the limo and home. It was like a fairy tale, and I was Cinderella. It was after 11:00 when we got back to the penthouse.

"James thank you for a wonderful night, a wonderful birthday. This has been one of the best days of my life and I am so glad I shared it with you." He was happy that I was happy. We went out to the terrace. He took me over to the railing and within moments there were fireworks. They were absolutely amazing, loud, and so pretty. I was clapping and jumping up and down laughing.

"I have never ever had fireworks on my birthday. This is such a surprise and I love it. Thank you so much." After twenty minutes the fireworks were over, and we went back inside. James was going to make some coffee and I said I was going to go to the bathroom. What I was really doing was changing into the black negligee that I bought. I went back out and James looked up as I was coming into the living room.

"Wow look at you, you look gorgeous. I was going to have coffee, but that negligee deserves more than coffee. Are you up to having a glass of wine. I don't have any champagne here, I'm sorry." I said the wine was fine with me. He took off his jacket and tossed it on the couch.

"To you my beautiful fiancée, a woman who took my breath away the first time I saw her, and I am still trying to catch my breath." It was a lovely toast and I kissed him to show how much I loved what he said.

"This is very beautiful, can I assume that this is not the only one you bought, and I can eagerly await to see you in another one, soon." I said it was possible, but he couldn't ask any more questions and ruin any surprises.

He was ok with that because he took my wine glass and set it down on the coffee table beside his and took me to the bedroom. I let the robe fall to the floor and I could see the lust in his eyes. That night was a spectacular night and there were all kinds of fireworks going off in my head. I wasn't sure when we finally fell asleep, but it seemed like the sun was starting to come up. My head was a little fuzzy from the champagne and the wine. It was still early, and James was still asleep. I got up and took a shower and then got dressed in my toffee coloured leather pants and a cream chiffon blouse. I took my black booties out to the living room. Antoine was in and making coffee. I took a mug and thanked him very much for the warm brew.

"Did you have a wonderful birthday?" I said that I did and that I got to see a star that I had named after me.

"It was a glorious day; the whole day and I wish that it would play over and over." James came out at that point, laughing and saying that he had a bit of a headache. I said I did as well, and it was probably from all the champagne. He knew he had to be in at the office for 9:00 but had time to have coffee and breakfast.

"Here have some coffee and you will feel better. I know I do." We sat on the couch in the living room drinking our coffee. Antoine brought over a pot and was laughing to himself.

"James, I have never seen you this relaxed and this happy. You should do whatever you did more often." James and I looked at each other and collapsed with laughter. Antoine did as well but in the kitchen. I knew that James was going to the office today for half a day. He promised he would not be any later than 1:00. Breakfast was light, and we talked about things as we ate.

"You know James; I appreciate that you have tried to tackle as many of the things on my bucket list, but you have never told me anything that you have on yours. Do you have a list?" He said he didn't really have one. He did a lot of things in his life so far and didn't feel that there was much he hadn't done that he wished he had.

"I know that is not the answer you were hoping for, but you are giving me everything that I ever wanted." I smiled and asked what that was.

"You are giving me a family, one that is mine and yours. Maybe not biologically but a son doesn't have to be of my own blood nor a granddaughter. I love them like they are my own and I will care for them as they are my own. You give me love every day and that is a far greater gift to me. Anything else is cream on top." I smiled wondering to myself if he was going to be shocked by the photos I was giving him tomorrow. I knew that there was nothing that I could buy him that he didn't already have five of or ten of. I knew that the photos would mean something to him, and I knew that the painting would be something he would always cherish.

He went in and showered and got ready to go to the office. He gave me a kiss goodbye and was out the door. I went out to the terrace to watch the sun come up. It was going to be another nice day. I was thinking of James's birthday tomorrow. I arranged with Mina weeks ago to take James to his favourite restaurant. Mina did her best to divert James from making reservations there for my birthday. He was a little surprised Mina said it was closed for a private party. Mina knew James would forgive her for that little lie. As promised, James was back at the penthouse shortly after 1:00. He wanted to go and work out, so I joined him. We worked out for a little over an hour. James showed me some exercises I could do with the weights to build up my biceps a bit and ones that would help to tone other muscles.

I did some of these same exercises years ago but hadn't done them recently. I was pooped when we were done. We took a long hot shower when we got back to the penthouse. We ate in tonight and enjoyed what was to be the last of the really warm weather in Toronto. We went to bed early because the day had been exhausting. My leg started to cramp a bit and James massaged it. He was so good to me. It made me flash back to all those times I had leg cramps before and had to massage them myself. James was still massaging my leg but watching my face. He knew that look meant she was remembering something from her past. He started to massage her other leg and she looked at him smiling.

"You are so good to me James; I am so lucky that you came into my life. I love you so much." He wasn't sure what to say.

"I love you too. Does that feel better?" I said it did and we laid back in bed. He decided not to bring up the past. We fell asleep and woke up to the phone ringing rather early. It was James's phone and he answered it, and it was Fenella. I could hear what she was saying.

"James, happy birthday. I hope I didn't wake you up. I thought that perhaps you would have plans with Cassandra today and didn't want to miss the opportunity to wish you a happy birthday." He thanked Fenella for the call but wasn't sure what the plans were for the day. I took the phone from him.

"Fenella, hello, how are you? I made lots of plans for the day, but I haven't had a chance to tell James, so it was a good thing that you called as early as you did. I will pass the phone back to James. Have a wonderful day." James was laughing because I told Fenella that she woke us up. He thanked her again for calling and said he would call in a few days. He was still laughing when he hung up.

"I'm sorry I know that was very rude of me. I will call her back and apologize." James held the phone away from me.

"She had no idea that is what you were getting at. I knew because I am around you more and understand your very subliminal messages. I don't think Fenella thought you were being anything, but cordial so don't worry about it." He kept laughing.

"Happy birthday James." I gave him a big kiss. "Now I can't say that I am going to cook you breakfast but I have asked Antoine to cook up something special for you this morning. Stay where you are, and I will bring you some coffee." I went out and Antoine was setting up in the kitchen. He made James's favourite coffee which I took back to him in the bedroom.

“Antoine said breakfast will be in about twenty minutes. So, the plans for today are, after breakfast we are going to drive out to a riding ranch about an hour’s drive from here and go horseback riding. Fenella told me you loved to horseback ride, so I found a stable near enough. I have not ridden in decades, but I am willing to suffer horrible embarrassment for you. Then we will come back here, shower and change and go for a wonderful lunch on a floating restaurant down at the harbour. Then we will come back here because Ayleen wants to video chat with you while you open up the present she sent for you. Be ready for the squeal because she is very excited about it. We will relax for a bit here and then Tanya and Carmen are coming to make me pretty again and then I will be taking you out for a wonderful dinner and some dancing and then we will come back here, and I will give you my gifts. Yes, that was plural. So how does that sound.” He didn’t know what to say. The fact that I went to the effort to find out he loved horseback riding was so thoughtful.

“I can’t wait to get the day started.” I went out to see if Antoine was ready and he said he was.

“Ok birthday boy let’s start your birthday adventure with breakfast.” James sat at the dining table and Antoine lifted the heating covers one by one. There was toad in the hole, smoked salmon omelet, black pudding, and a few other breakfast dishes that he loved and would have had in Scotland.

"Sweetheart, this is so wonderful. How did Antoine know these dishes?" I said that I asked Barclay for all his favourites recipes when I was in Scotland. I poured him more coffee and said to dig in. James ate and savored every bite.

"I feel like I am at home in Scotland. Thank you for doing this. Antoine you did an excellent job on everything." When he was done I took him to the living room and handed him a brown envelope. It came for him just before we left, and I put it in my luggage and forgot to give it to him. When James opened it he gasped. I knew what it was because Gowan called to say that his immigration had been approved.

"Gowan called to let me know that you would be receiving these. It's your final papers approving your immigration to Canada. You have to go before a judge in Alberta and it will be finalized. Gowan said that you were approved for dual citizenship because we are part of the Commonwealth, so you will still retain your Scottish birth rite. I hope it was ok that I didn't give it to you as soon as it came in." He looked over all the papers and the date he had to be in Edmonton at the courthouse.

"I'll have to adjust my trip over to Scotland but that won't be an issue. I want you to be with me at the courthouse. It is a big moment in my life, and I want you there." I said I would not miss it. James took the papers and put them in his briefcase.

"Ok, so let's get this started. Let's get changed into jeans and sweat tops and head out to the riding ranch." We had a blast at the riding ranch. James thoroughly enjoyed himself and I was lucky that I got a very easy going mare and easy to ride. My legs felt a little weird after riding for over an hour, but it wasn't too bad. I knew that they would be sore tomorrow though. We got back home around 11:30, took a quick shower and put on some casual clothes and went for lunch at the floating restaurant.

I booked the reservation a few days ago for 1:00 saying it was for a birthday. The waiters and waitresses brought over a cupcake for James with a candle and everyone around us joined in singing happy birthday. He really enjoyed it and wasn't upset that everyone sang to him. We got back to the penthouse just before 3:00. Lindsay was texting to see if Ayleen could call. I texted back that we just got in the door, so to give me about five minutes. I ran into the bedroom and got Ayleen's gift. James was sitting on the couch with my tablet and answered as soon as it rang.

"Happy birthday Grandpa." She sang the whole birthday song for him. James was laughing and a bit emotional at the same time.

"Have you opened my present yet?" James said not yet. I took the tablet and turned the camera around, so she could watch him open it. She started to squeal but put her hands over her mouth. I was laughing so hard I could hardly hold the tablet. James opened the gift, and he was so surprised.

"Do you like it Grandpa, Gramma showed me what to do and I painted from my imagination." James held it up like it was a Rembrandt.

"Ayleen, sweetie I love this. I will hang it in my office at home and when you come for Christmas I will show you. Thank you so much for this beautiful present. I really love it." She said he was welcome. Ross and Lindsay wished him a happy birthday and I gave him their gift. He opened that up and again was surprised. It was a framed family photo.

"This is really nice; guys I love it and I will put it on my desk at home in my study." I could tell James was getting a little choked up. They wished him happy birthday again. Ayleen came back on and blew him lots of kisses and then said goodbye.

"That was unbelievable. This is a great little painting she did, and I love all the colours and swirls. I love the family photo too." I could see a few tears escape and went to hug him.

"They love you James, you are a part of our family now too." He hugged me for the longest time. Tanya called up to say they were downstairs, so I sent the elevator down for them and waited in the door for them to come up.

James put a suit, shirt, tie, and shoes in the other bedroom once again because I wanted him to be surprised when I came out. I went to the safe and brought out the pieces I was going to wear with the dress. I showered not that long ago so my hair was clean. Tanya started to work on it, and I could see what she was talking about. It was going to look great with the dress. It took about forty minutes to get my hair done and sprayed so it would stay in place.

Then Carmen went to work on my makeup. She gave me a nice smoky eye and the perfect colour of plum lipstick. The end result was perfect. Carmen went out to see if James was in the living room, but he wasn't as yet. I put the jewelry boxes on the bed and got into my dress. They were both stunned at how low the back went but said it looked beautiful. I put on the necklace and got Tanya to place it just right at the back, then I put on my earrings and the diamond cuff bracelet. I looked in the mirror and could hardly believe it was me. Carmen went out again and James was in the living room.

"Wait until you see her, she is so beautiful." Carmen came back and then they both went to the living room. James was looking at me and I could tell that he loved the way I looked. Tanya told me to turn around, so James could see. His eyes nearly popped out of his head. I paid the girls, and they were off.

"You look so stunning and that dress my God, how am I going to keep my hands off you. I love the necklace, earrings, and bracelet. I am happy that you bought them, and they look amazing on you." I gave him a kiss and his hand ran up and down my back.

"James, we have a wonderful night ahead of us so if you continue to do that, we won't get to it." He smiled and said he was going to enjoy dancing with me and running his hands all over my back.

"I love this dress as you can easily tell. When did you say I get my gifts from you?" I knew that he was not talking about the ones I had wrapped in the bedroom. The limo was waiting for us downstairs and took us to his favourite restaurant. I ordered champagne and of course our favourite but his year of birth. We had a wonderful meal and then went dancing for a few hours. It was wonderful to be in his arms and people were watching us.

"I think it is because of your dress and the diamonds. I highly doubt they are looking at me when you look so beautiful." We got back in the limo and back to the penthouse. I wanted to change out of my dress, but James didn't want me to. I went to get the gifts for him. The first one I gave him was the double framed photo of me in the black dress and the black and white. When he opened them he had such a look of surprise on his face.

"You had more photos done. These are really beautiful. You know I love that black dress, but I think I like this one more. The black and white of you is really stunning and I like the pose and that you had the blue star done blue. They are beautiful photos of you darling and I love them very much." But I was not done yet and handed him the final framed photo. I was smiling but I was nervous too. James opened it and I wasn't sure about his reaction. Then he started to laugh.

"Wow I love this, and I love the pose and the sexiness of this photo. You look gorgeous and I love the cigar, was it real and the wink is just perfect." I said that the cigar was not real, and I had a lot of fun doing it. I was worried though that I was showing just a bit too much skin. He kept looking at the photo.

"I just noticed the belly chain, how sexy is that. No, you didn't show too much, it is just enough to be flirtatious, and I love it, I really do. Thank you for these beautiful photos and for a perfect birthday." I was happy that he liked all the photos but handed him the rest that were taken.

"I asked Jennifer for all of them, so you could see if there were any others you wanted. That was probably the toughest work out of my life. We spent the entire day doing the photos. He looked through each one and said he loved them all.

"I love all the black and whites and this one with your hand on you hip, wow that is very sexy and you are showing a bit more of that bra, wow. I think I would like this one framed for my bedside table. If I ever need incentive, this will certainly get me there in a hurry." I laughed as did he.

"Thank you darling for a wonderful birthday. It is the best one I have ever had, and you made it so perfect." He was going to get us some wine and I went back into the bedroom for his last gift of the night. I came out in the red negligee. I could hear him catch his breath. This one was very much sexier than the black one. James put down the wine and came to me.

"I think we should forget the wine." He slowly removed the satin robe and saw that the negligee was very different from the other one. He kissed my neck and then my lips, letting one thin strap fall. He picked me up and took me to the bedroom and stood me beside the bed. The negligee fell to my waist, James kissed me over and over. That night was a wondrous night of passion and love making. It was the perfect ending to a perfect day. I knew that we were heading home the next day and

Antoine would not be in. We drifted off to sleep but I woke up around 4 am and leaned over and kissed James all over his chest. He opened his eyes, and I was on top of him. He smiled and brought me down for a passionate kiss. It was the perfect start to a brand new day.

"That was wonderful darling, and I can think of no better way to wake up than you making love to me. But we are going home today, and we should get up soon." I said we would but not right now, right now I wanted him more than ever. A few hours later we got up. We showered and got dressed, packed our bags, and put them out by the door. James made us each a coffee and called for the limo. The driver took our bags down to the limo. We took one last look out on the terrace at the skyline.

"I have had a wonderful time James; I hope that you did too." He said that he most certainly did. We kissed and then went down to the car and out to the airport. There were a number of garment bags which Janine hung up in the storage area at the front.

James put all of the jewelry in his briefcase for safekeeping. The flight was uneventful, and it was nice to be back in Alberta and on our way home. It was much cooler here now and there was a hoarfrost overnight. It was so pretty to see with the sun shining on it. We carried our luggage into the house and upstairs to the bedroom. I put away our things and then went down to the sunroom where James was going through the mail. Jonathan was not going to be here until next week, so we decided to change and go to Jason's for dinner. When we got back we were both tired, so we went up to bed.

Next morning, we had coffee and some cereal and then drove to Banff where we spent three glorious nights in a two story suite with its own private pool. It was a very romantic time, but we had to get back because James was going to have his citizenship ceremony on Monday.

We got home late Sunday afternoon and went to the sunroom to relax. James's phone was ringing, and it was Duncan calling to wish him a belated birthday and to say that Roxie sold the trailer, and they were going to be heading back in the next day or so. James let Duncan know that his citizenship had been approved and he would probably be hearing about his soon.

"I have James, Gowan called me to say that mine was being finalized and would be approved but because I was down in the States with Roxie, he had to ask for an alternative date for the ceremony before the judge. It would have been nice to have had it done together but it couldn't be helped. We got the house in the subdivision near you. I am having some renovations done which hopefully will be done by the time we get back and can start moving in. When are you heading back overseas, I thought it was soon?" James said that he was going before the judge for his citizenship on Monday and then we would be leaving for Germany the following Monday evening. James said goodbye to Duncan and would see him soon.

"That's wonderful that everything went through on the house. I know it will make both of them happy and I think Duncan will like having you close by. It will be quite and adjustment for him." The trip to Banff was wonderful and nice way to complete our birthdays in a romantic getaway.

"James what time do you have to be at the courthouse tomorrow?" He thought it was 11 am but he would need to recheck the papers. He looked at the letter again and it was 11:00.

"Do you want me to put all your jewelry back in the safe? How are you going to get Christelle her gifts?" I was thinking about that.

"We are planning to go for a couple of nights to Ottawa for Ross's birthday and I thought perhaps we could meet Christelle for lunch and I could give it to her then along with the other things that I bought her for Christmas. We will be going on a weeknight, and I don't think Ross will want to go far or stay out late, especially for Ayleen as she will have school. Maybe we could go to a restaurant in Almonte. They have a few that are pretty good." James thought that would work out well and he would look online what was there and pick a location. But we were tired and could talk about it the next day.

We had breakfast and then we went up to change to go to the courthouse. James was going to wear his navy suit and I decided to wear my dark green leather pants and jacket with an orange silk blouse. James went down to his study to take care of a few things and then we left for the courthouse. He knew where he was supposed to go, and we arrived at 10:30 as had been requested in the letter.

There were only three other people participating in the ceremony, which didn't last all that long. On the drive home James was very quiet. I was trying to read what might be on his mind but couldn't. It made me a little worried that maybe going through the actual ceremony had him rethinking his decision.

"Cassandra don't look so worried. I am not having any second thoughts. You would not make a very good poker player you know. I can tell by looking at your face what is going on in your head." He laughed and took my hand.

"I assure you this was a very big moment for me, for us, and I was just thinking about it. There are a number of things I have to get taken care of, but the priority will be my passport. But it is all stuff I knew, and I know what and where to get it done. So don't worry ok." I said I wouldn't but wasn't sure if I was very convincing. We stopped at Jason's on the way back for a celebratory lunch and then went home.

"I have a spa day tomorrow, so what are your plans?" He was going to work on his passport. He was sure that he could get that done on a priority basis. He had some work to deal with as well. I asked Jonathan for a pot of his lavender tea and went into the sunroom. I decided to give Christelle a call.

"Hi, how are you? James got his citizenship today. It was a very happy moment." I knew she could sense something was wrong.

"So why don't you sound happy about it?" I said I was really very happy about it, but she could sense there was something and got me to talk about it.

"I don't know what it is. I have a very sad feeling and I don't know if it is related to that or what. Probably a lack of sleep." We started to laugh, and I told her about our birthdays and thanked her for the cards she sent us.

"He is such a great man. He bought me a beautiful ring, and said it was my 'going steady' ring. He had the deed to the house changed so that both our names are on it. He's so incredible I feel like I'm going to wake up and it will all be gone. I know, it's real and not a dream but I'm so happy and very much in love. We are going to Ottawa for a couple of days for Ross's birthday and we would like to meet you for lunch if that is ok. I have some early Christmas gifts for you." She said she would love to meet up, but I didn't have to get her anything.

"You bought me the condo I am in and furnished it and you paid off all my debts, you don't have to do any more than that." I knew she was going to say that, but I said I saw this while I was shopping, and I had to get it for her. We talked for a few more minutes and then said goodnight. James came into the sunroom as I hung up.

"Hi darling did you get everything done you needed to?" He said he did, and he heard some of what I said to Christelle.

"I wasn't trying to eavesdrop on your conversation, but I heard a little before going back to my study until you were done. I understand why you feel the way you do; I sometimes feel that way too. But I love you with all my heart and I know that you love me the same. I am trying to make up for all the bad moments you had, and I know that I don't have to do that, but I want to. I don't know if I can explain it, but I know that you have been hurt so bad in the past and yes, maybe some of that is on you but when I looked at that photo of you taken many years ago, I could see the pain and hurt in your eyes and in your body and I want to be able to erase it, make it like it never happened. I know that sounds crazy and I can't do that, but I love you so much that there isn't anything I won't do to make you happy." I understood what he was saying.

"James, I know you don't want to know what happened in my last marriage and I don't want to go into it in great detail." I told him all that happened and why I didn't want to get involved in the beginning when we first met. I wanted him to understand why I would have moments when I would reflect back on something because of something that was said or something I saw that would remind me of all that, but I always tried to push it away so that it wasn't affecting us. He took me in his arms and held me.

"I'm sorry you had to live that and that you had to tell me. I know it was hard for you and it was hard for me to listen to. Annie told me that you'd been hurt to your very soul and that if you wanted to tell me that I should listen and let you talk. I know you know I am not like that. I love you and I want to make you happy because that makes me happy. I know that you will probably never forget all of what happened to you, but I hope that you will let me replace all those bad memories with new and happy ones. I want to spoil you as much as I can, and I know that isn't going to be what replaces the bad memories, but I will be mindful of your concerns and do it within reason. Is that ok with you?" I hugged him for being so understanding and for loving me the way he did. I hugged him as hard as I could.

"This house, this life you are giving me is all I could ask for. I will let you spoil me within reason for a little while ok." He was happy with that. We went off to bed and slept in the comfort of each other's arms. I woke up at 8 am and James was already gone. I took a shower and got myself ready for the day. Jonathan was in the kitchen.

"Have you seen James?" Jonathan said that he saw him out for a run around the property when he was coming in. I had some coffee and toast and then left for my spa appointment. I wanted to see if I could catch James before I left. He was coming around as I was getting ready to head out the gate.

"James, I have to get to my spa appointment, but I didn't want to leave before saying good morning." I got out of the car to give him a hug and kiss, but he was already quite sweaty.

"Sorry darling, I forgot about the appointment. Been thinking about work matters. I hope you enjoy your spa day. I'll see you when you get home, I love you." He gave me a kiss and continued his run. My day was wonderful and relaxing. I got home right around 4:00 and found James in his study. He had the framed photos

I gave him on his desk, and he hung up the painting Ayleen gave him. He was looking through the other photos going through each one and I could see that he was getting emotional.

"James why are you getting so emotional?" He was thinking about what we talked about last night during his run and it was really hitting him hard.

"I am so sorry you had to go through that and that you felt so trapped." I went around the desk to hug him, and he really started to cry.

"James, you don't have to apologize; you didn't do anything to me. I survived it all. I have always been a survivor and I always will be. My life is great now and that is because of you. You have shown me such love, so very many times." I looked at him and we laughed. He hugged me and said I was incorrigible.

"Of course, I am, that's why you love me right?" He said it was and it was just one of the many things that he loved about me.

"Let's put these photos away or you are going to get all hot and bothered. Let's go downstairs and watch a movie. I'll ask Jonathan to make us some canapes and we can have some wine and eat a bit later." He thought that was a great idea. The movie was great, and it put the both of us in better spirits. While we ate a bit later than usual it was something light. We went out to the sunroom to have another glass of wine and watch the night descend on us.

"What are your plans for tomorrow. I was going to go for a walk with the seniors but if you have something in mind, I can change my plans." He had a bunch of running around to do tomorrow morning.

"I have an appointment at the passport office. They are going to expedite my passport which is a big load off my mind. I'm going to swing by the registry office and get my license changed. I have all the papers they are going to need so that can get done. Then I am going by Alberta Health to get my health card which will mean that I can finally make an appointment with the doctor and get a thorough checkup. I have been thinking about buying the sports car. I only got a one year lease on it, but I really like it and I know you do, so I am going to look at buying it. Once I have all that done and get back here, I would like for us to start doing up the Christmas list. Because we are going overseas soon, I would like to get the gifts for the family in Scotland as soon as possible. Are you ok with doing that today?" I said it was fine and probably best to get on it now and get it done.

Chapter 11

James went out to do his errands and I went over to the seniors building to go for a walk with them. They wished me a belated birthday which was so nice of them. When we got back I had a talk with Mr. O'Leary. He was interested in buying my place, or rather the corporation that owned the building. The unit they were given was on the small side for them and since I was putting it up for sale, they talked to their HR person to see if they could move up. It was agreed they could, and I needed to decided what price I was selling it for.

"I will sell it to the corporation for the same price that I bought it. I know the prices have gone up a good bit since then, but I am only looking to get back what I paid for it. If you want to have the corporate lawyer contact mine, here is the card. I will call her and let her know the price I have settled on and they can work out the details." He said he would get in touch with them right away. I sent some pictures from the trip to Toronto and the photos taken of me to Fenella, Christelle and Janet. My phone was ringing so I pulled over to answer it. It was Fenella and I remembered what I said to her the last time she called.

"Hello Fenella, how nice to hear from you. I hope all is well?" She said that it was, and she just opened her email to find the pictures.

"You both look amazing in the photos, and I love the ones that you got done. I am sure that James was quite blown away with them." We laughed, and I admitted I had fun.

"I know you and James, and your friends are stopping here for a few days enroute from Austria. I hope that you will be agreeable to a family dinner and perhaps we can do something of a pre-Christmas since you and James won't be here. Would you be ok with that?" I said that I thought it would be wonderful.

"Fenella that would be lovely and I am sure James would agree. My school friend Janet and her husband Wade will be with us. They've been to Scotland before, but we won't have time to really do a lot of sightseeing with them." We said goodbye and would see each other soon. I got back to the house before James, so I started writing everyone's name out on a separate sheet of paper. Then I got boxes out and put the things that I already bought in a box with that person's name on it. James came in shortly after I had that done.

"So how did it go with your errands?" He said it went well and showed me his new health card. He got a temporary driver's license and hoped that the real one would be in before we left.

"My new passport showing dual citizenship will be ready in a couple of days. I will have to go back downtown and get it. But aside from that everything went really smoothly. I see you have started on the lists and got boxes out." I said that I thought it might speed things up for us.

"Fenella called me to say she loved the photos I sent her of us and of me. I didn't send her the risqué ones though. She wants to do a pre-Christmas when we go, and I said that would be fine and I thought you would be ok with it. I was thinking about gifts, and we talked about getting those down jackets for the ones coming here but what about the ones in Scotland. I am sure they don't have them there and it would be something very Canadian and who can't use a nice down filled jacket." James liked the idea but was worried that we would not get them in time. He texted Fenella to make sure he had everyone's current size especially the kids because they had grown since last Christmas. While we were waiting for her to get back to us we went to their website. They had such cute things for kids and for adults as well. I picked out a few that I wanted for myself. James was laughing at me. Fenella texted back all the current sizes for everyone.

"I will send you this list off my tablet and you will have it for future. Let's get shopping and we already said that we would get ourselves a jacket or two, so don't hesitate. We can still get one to put under the tree." We spent the next three hours picking out jackets and snow pants for the younger ones and jackets for the older ones and parkas and car coats. It was unbelievable how many items we had sitting in our cart.

"I wonder if they give a discount for large quantities." I was only joking but when James was getting ready to pay for everything, we did get a discount. That had us laughing. He was going to do express shipping on everything, which rather destroyed the discount but at least we knew we would have them in three or four days.

"I was surprised at how much inventory they have on hand, but I guess at this time of the year they have to. I'm glad we will have everything in time. I hope that everyone likes the colours we chose. I'm glad that we are getting one for Janet, Wade, Duncan, and Roxie too. I wouldn't want them to feel left out. I know we have other gifts for them as well and we could probably give our gifts to them then." James said that everyone would like the coats as the colours available were all colours everyone liked. James printed out the confirmation invoice for safe keeping.

"Are you ready for all the wrapping we are going to have to do? I know that on commercial flights they don't allow you to wrap anything, do you face the same restrictions on a private flight?" James said that he didn't, so we could at least wrap all the items for

Scotland. The rest of the day flew by and after being hunched over his computer for several hours picking out coats, my back was in knots. We slept soundly, and James got up early to go for a run. I was awake though before he went out the door.

"Morning enjoy your run; I will see you downstairs for breakfast. I'm going to sleep a little more." I was out before he closed the door. I woke a half hour later, showered and got dressed and went downstairs. James was just coming in as I got to the bottom of the stairs.

"It is a little chilly out there this morning. I'm going to take a shower and change. I won't be long." I grabbed some coffee and went to the sunroom. It was a gray day, and it really did look chilly out. I was heading into the kitchen when James came downstairs, hair still wet but in jeans and a sweater.

"That didn't take you long." He whispered in my ear.

"I thought you were going to join me but since you didn't I saw no need to linger." I knew he was teasing me, but it was nice that he enjoyed our times in the shower. We had a wonderful breakfast and talked more about Christmas.

"I was going to work out today, but I think I will go for a walk a bit later." I knew James gave contributions to a number of charities, but I kept my donations to charities within my own community such as the food bank and with the children's hospital here. He said he would donate to them as well but would also give to a few others.

"We are going to need stockings for everyone that will be coming here. Some of the ladies over at the condo unit do sewing and quilting and every year they do up different crafts to sell. I'm going to ask them if they will do us up special stockings, ones that are unique. I know they will be happy to do them, and I will of course pay them for it. We will have to come up with some ideas for what to put in them." James was already thinking of what we could put in.

"For the ladies, we could put in some of our cosmetics. You have all of their skin types, so it would be a question of pulling out some different things to put in. We also do some men's products which we could put in for the guys." I said it was too bad we didn't have a fragrance ready yet, we could put that in as perhaps a trial to see if the ladies liked it, and the men too. James's phone was ringing, and it was Duncan.

"Duncan, are you and Roxanne back? That is great, the two of you should come to the house for dinner on Saturday and we can catch up. I've missed you both and so has Cassandra. Come by at 4:00 and that will give us a chance to have a few drinks and chat. Wonderful we will see you then." I knew that James missed Duncan and it was going to be great to see them both.

"I am going to go for that walk now. I know you have business to attend to. I'm going to put the lights on because it will be getting dark by the time I make the full loop." I went out and there was a definite change in the air. James put a call in to the chemist Dr. Rodney Shultz that was going to work on the fragrances.

"Rodney, James here, how long does it take for you to create a fragrance. I know you are going to create one for Cassandra. Do you think you could come over tomorrow and start the process? I know the cosmetics line is up and running and we have lots of product on hand and we also have some men's products now too, but I am hoping we can have the fragrance ready before Christmas." Rodney said he would come over tomorrow at 11:00.

"It would only be a small sample James until we can adjust the amounts needed to make a larger quantity." James was fine with that and said he was going to give it to family members that were coming at Christmas and this way it could be tested to make sure that the fragrance was truly unique to the wearer. He was going to get Mark to start working on a mockup for the bottle as well. Rodney thought it might be best to start with an atomizer as that would keep it simple.

"Rodney, can you check to see if there has or is a fragrance currently on the market called 'Uniquely Yours' and if not, we should patent it now so that nobody can claim it." As he and James were talking Rodney checked and there was nothing.

"I'll have the corporate lawyers work on getting the patent on the name and I will have Mark send you some quick mockups for the bottle later today." James was actually getting a bit excited about this now and it would be a good marketing test with the ladies. James said he would see Rodney tomorrow. The night air was very crisp, and I was glad to be heading up the steps. I was shivering when I got in and James came out of his study.

"Jeepers that is cold out there. My hands are freezing. I didn't think it was quite that cold or I would have brought gloves and a hat." James took my hands in his and they were like ice.

"Let's get you upstairs to the bedroom and I will start a fire and you can warm yourself up by it after you take a good hot shower." He started the fire right away and while I was in taking a hot shower he got my warmest pjs out and went down to get me a cup of hot tea. I dried myself off and my hair and put on the pjs

James put out. He pulled one of the big armchairs over by the fire and I sat there with a warm blanket over me. He came in and set the tea down on the table beside me.

"I should have brought my gloves and a hat, that was my own fault. I will know from now on to leave them in my jacket. The fire and tea feels really good but I'm getting a bit sleepy. It is probably from all the cold air and now the heat. Can you tell Jonathan I'm not up to eating anything? I think I will crawl into bed after I am done my tea. He gave me a very concerned look.

"James, I am fine, it was a combination of the cold air and now the heat that is hitting me. I'll probably sleep for an hour or two and then be up the rest of the night. I know you are hungry so go and have something to eat." He knew I was probably right but after the last time I fell ill he was going to make sure that he checked on me frequently. He went down and got his dinner and took it to his office. Not something he would normally do but he was going to try to get as much work done as possible.

He had an email from Richard saying that the Toronto office was running very smoothly. He also let him know that his weekend with Sonya went well and they did go to see the house. They both fell in love with it. He and Sonya talked about moving in but not sleeping in the same bedroom. It would give them a chance to get to know each other better without all the miles between them. Rhonda was going to accept the job offer and would also move in with them. The house was more than big enough they wouldn't be bumping into each other.

He knew that James was going to buy the house for Sonya but if their relationship was going to continue to progress as it was, and they decided to make the situation more permanent, he would give James back the money he paid for the house. James sent him back and email saying he was happy about how things were going in the Toronto office and how things were going with him and Sonya. He would accept being paid back at what he paid for it. He took his dishes back to the kitchen.

"Jonathan, I am going to head up, can you please turn on the alarm when you leave. Thanks, have a good night and drive safely. I think it has gotten a little icy out there." Jonathan said good night and he would be careful. When James got upstairs Cassandra was fast asleep. He went into the closet to get into his pjs and climbed into bed next to her. It always made him smile uncontrollably when she would snuggle her bottom into him. He fell asleep in no time and woke up moments before Cassandra.

"Did I sleep right through, I'm sorry. I was fully intending on waking up and spending time with you. I'm sorry I fell asleep." He said not to apologize, he actually went to bed not long after.

"I did get an email from Richard they love the house and want to move in. Sonya wants him to move in but not into the same bedroom. Being in the same house Richard said would give them more time to get to know each other. Rhonda is going to accept my job offer and she will move into the house as well. It's big enough they won't be on top of each other, and I think it will give Rhonda a chance to get to know Richard as well. Richard seems to think that their relationship is progressing quite well, and he feels that very soon he will be able to pay me back for the house. He knows the house will be in her name and he is ok with that. If they end up getting married, they can do the same thing we did and have the deed changed. I hope you are happy for them." I said that I was very happy. She deserved to have someone like Richard who was kind and respectful and treated her like a queen.

"Dr. Shultz, Rodney is coming by at 11:00 today to start the process for the fragrance. I hope you don't have anything else planned. He said you will need to shower but don't use any soaps or body washes, he wants to get your body scent, which I happen to think is intoxicating. He is doing this process the old fashioned way which isn't done much anymore. Yes, I know that was kind of corny to say that about your body scent, but true nonetheless." I hugged him and went to shower and did as instructed.

“Do I stay in a bath robe, or can I get dressed?” James wasn’t sure, so he contacted Rodney again.

“He wants you in a bath robe so perhaps you can get dressed and then take another shower before he comes. I’m sure you don’t want to walk around in a bath robe for the next three hours. I could think of something for us to do but apparently, we can’t do that either. It will skew the body odors. Let’s go and have breakfast. I made sure that was ok.” We got dressed and went down to the kitchen. Jonathan had coffee and breakfast all set. We ate in the dining room for a change and after we were done we went to the sunroom with coffee. It was almost time for Rodney to come by, so I went back upstairs and took another plain shower and then got into one of the big fluffy terry robes and went back downstairs. James already showed Rodney into his office which is where I found them.

“Ok so what is it that you have to do.” Rodney went through explaining the process of gathering some of my body oils and then got me to smell certain scents to see which I liked the best. I would be blind folded, so I couldn’t see what he was putting in front of me to smell. James was watching as the whole process took place. Rodney had all that he needed.

“I have enough different combinations to do a few fragrances. You surprisingly like quite a few florals and aromatic oils so it should be interesting to see how you like the end product. I can go back to the lab and start working on this now and perhaps in a couple of days I can come back and let you see what I have come up with." Now that was done I was going back up to get dressed and then returned to James's study. James showed Rodney out.

James was going to be interested to see what Rodney came up with. He watched Cassandra's face, and she was smelling all the different things Rodney put before her. But he had to look at the emails that kept coming into his inbox.

I went to sit out in the sunroom and was going to read but James came out and asked if I wanted to go over and have a look around the new sites. The lab was really quite interesting to go through and the textile plant still had a lot to be done but was coming along. James took me to the office for the geothermal and showed me the plans they had to build the plant but were still waiting on approval to put shovels in the ground.

When we got back to the house we went for a good long walk around the property a few times. After dinner we sat out in the sunroom having a glass of wine and watching the birds. We hit the sack early because we were both tired. Next morning, James went for another run, and I wanted to see if I could video chat with Ayleen. Unfortunately, she was at a friend's house, so I would have to try later perhaps. James got back after an hour and half running went up to shower and then went into his study.

"Duncan and Roxie will be here at 4:00 I've asked Jonathan this morning if he will do up a moose roast and he got one out of the freezer. We have a couple of hours to kill so I think I'm going to do a workout downstairs. Are you going to continuing working or are you going to join me? I think I'll do a sauna after." James's head came up when I said that, and he closed his computer and followed me up to change. We went downstairs and started our work out. I spent forty minutes on the climber/elliptical and James did some weights. We only had a little over an hour, so we took a shower and went into the sauna.

"Let's not pretend we are here for anything other than making love." He pulled me to him, and I was not denying him. It was quickly becoming our go to place for having exquisite sex. We took another shower and went back upstairs to get dressed as our guests were due to arrive in about twenty minutes.

"I'd like to say it is your fault for us running late but that last move you made, well, keep that in mind for later." James laughed and said he would definitely do that. I put on my red leather pants and white cashmere sweater with red pumps. James put on a pair of dress pants with a gray cashmere pullover. Duncan and Roxie pulled up in front of the garage and we opened the door to greet them. Roxie hurried up because it was chilly out and Duncan was not far behind.

"Look at you two with your tans, how are both of you? Come on in it is cold out. We are going into the sunroom." Roxie and I walked arm in arm to the sunroom and James and Duncan walked behind us.

"Boy I still love this room. We had a great time down south, but I am glad that I got the trailer sold as quickly as I did. It is good to be home and in our new home. The painting was finished last week, and the carpets were taken out as well and hardwood floors laid. It looks really nice. I'm checking on some cleaners to come by two or three times a week. We are having the kids over tomorrow night for dinner. So how have you been and what have you been up to?" I went to the study to get the photos that I had taken of me as Roxie had not seen them yet. Her eyes almost popped out of her head. Duncan was leaning over to have a look.

"I'm not sure I want you to see these love, you might have second thoughts about me." She was kidding of course and passed the photos to Duncan as she finished looking at them.

"Wow these are beautiful Cassandra and I love the one in the gown, that one is really stunning. But I like the black and white ones as well. These are very sexy, but I think that was the point right." I said it was, but they would not be on display for anyone but James. They were not being shown to everyone except those we knew who wouldn't talk about them.

"Duncan what can I get you to drink and you Roxanne what will you have?" Duncan was going to have a whisky and Roxie said she would join me if I was having some wine. James went to get our drinks and returned shortly afterward.

"To Duncan and Roxanne, congratulations on your new home. We are sure you will have many wonderful years and memories there." We sat talking about their adventure down south.

"Duncan how did you like being there. I know it can get pretty warm." It wasn't too bad he said, he'd been to hotter places.

"But perhaps if we want to get away in the winter, we can go to your villa in the Turks James." He said that would be fine, they could go whenever they wanted.

"We will of course be going there, the ladies that is, in April. I think we are going to do the middle two weeks. It will give us enough time to get back and then we will be off to Scotland for the wedding. I can't believe that it is not that far away." We talked more about what they did down south and then went in for dinner. There was lots of laughter, and it was great to see them again.

"Well love I think we are going to head out. We only got back the other day and are still getting used to the house. I have a ton of boxes to go through and unpack." After Duncan and Roxie left, James and I went up to bed. Lying in bed, I smiled and looked at him.

"Now about that move." He laughed under his breath and took me in his arms and replayed that move from earlier in the day, a few times. After breakfast, James checked on some emails and I went to do a workout. We had no plans for the day. After I was done my workout I showered and got dressed and went downstairs. I decided to send Ross a text to see if Ayleen was available to video chat given it was Sunday. Within seconds she was calling.

"Hello Gramma, look I lost another tooth. What are you and Grandpa doing today?" James could hear her and came out to the sunroom. He waved to her and said hello. She got the biggest smile on her face.

"Wow, how many teeth have you lost now? The tooth fairy must be busy with you. How is school going? You know we are coming to see you for a couple of days for your Daddy's birthday." Ross and Lindsay already knew this, but she shouted out to Ross to tell him anyway.

“Hi Grandpa, did you hang my painting yet?” I handed my tablet to him. It was cute the way she was with James.

“Yes, Ayleen I hung it up, but I said I would show you when you came for Christmas.” She looked at him with her big eyes like she’d been scolded. James melted and said he would show her now.

“I will show you now since I already have it hung up. Gramma is going to come along so we can both talk to you.” He showed her where he hung the painting, and she was happy. We talked to her for half an hour, then she wanted to go out and play. We sent kisses back and forth. I laughed at James.

“She doesn’t have you wrapped around her little finger at all.” He admitted that could very well be, but he didn’t care.

“I’m starting to think she likes you more than me now.” He knew I wasn’t serious.

“I think it’s because I’m new to her, but I am a devastatingly handsome Grandpa.” We laughed and decided to have tea in the sunroom. James went to the kitchen to get it. It was a different blend but one we both tried before and liked.

"I could get used to being at home like this. I can still check on things at my different companies and I'm glad that I'm here for a bit while the new businesses are getting up and running. I'm not sure if I mentioned it or not, but Quinn wants to partner with me on the other two businesses here. What do you think about that?" I was flattered that he was asking for my opinion on it.

"I think Quinn probably sees this as a way for him to branch out in some other areas much like you did. The two of you trust each other and you make good business partners. Unless you have a reason not to, I think it would be a great idea. I think the geothermal is going to make you both a lot of money and of course the cosmetics and perfume industry will never go out of style." I wasn't sure if that was what he wanted to hear or not.

"You are right, on all counts and I think that as long as Charlotte is ok with it, we will do it. I usually would bounce ideas off of Duncan but he's a little preoccupied right now. But that's ok, I trust your judgment even more." I was happy that he felt that way.

"By the way Mark is sending a few mockups of the perfume bottle and he has the foil packaging for the teas as well. He will be sending them by courier on Tuesday. I haven't seen them, so it will be a surprise for the both of us, but I have thought of a name for the perfume. How do you like 'Uniquely Yours'? I think it will suit what the fragrance is all about." I hadn't realized he had been working on a name.

"I love it and it will be interesting to see what Mark comes up with." Already in my head I was playing with the letters.

"I know you want to go back to work in your study so why don't you go ahead. I'm fine here by myself." He gave me a kiss and off he went to his study. He checked on the shipment of coats which would definitely be here by 5:00 tomorrow. He thought they were coming in individual Canada Goose boxes for each coat but wanted to be sure. The website indicated that they would be individually boxed so that was a plus.

James received an email from Robert Harrison, the new vice president of the security division. He wanted him to know that because of the large contracts they'd been getting, the office was getting calls of interests from some places south of the border regarding cyber security. He didn't want to say any more than that in an email and would discuss further when he went to the office in Toronto.

James let him know that he would be there the end of the first week of December and in the office the following day. James had to think about that for a bit. He wasn't sure given the recent climate in the US and with the current administration that he wanted to get into any business there. But he would see what Robert had to say and judge from there. James looked at his watch and decided to give Annie a call. He knew she would still be up having her evening tea.

"Annie, its James, how are you? How are things going?" She said that things were going well but James could sense that there was something in her voice but that she wouldn't say what it was. They talked for a half hour. He knew her well enough that unless she wanted to say it, she would not no matter how much he asked her. He wished her good night and said he would see her soon. James went out to the sunroom to get Cassandra to go up to bed. It had been a long day, and he for one, was very tired. He fell asleep as soon as his head hit the pillow.

All of the down coats order came in the next day, and we put the majority of them in the games room. We kept out the ones going with us to Scotland and the ones for Janet and Wade. We spent a few hours wrapping them up and put them in James's office. We went over to visit Duncan and Roxie in their new home and to bring them a housewarming gift. It was a beautiful home in a pretty spot, and it suited them both perfectly.

We got back home in time to get the package from the courier. The mockups for the perfume bottle and the foil packaging arrived. We picked the one we thought suited the fragrance best. James emailed Mark to let him know which one it was and what it was going to be called. We went with royal blue lettering on the bottle. We showed Jonathan the sample foil packaging for the teas, and he was very happy with it.

James went to pick up his new passport and I used the time to call Janet to confirm the time that we would be landing in Sudbury to pick her and Wade up for our trip overseas. While James was out I decided to go over to the lawyer's office and sign the papers to get the deed changed. It had been a very busy few days and we collapsed in bed early. We were leaving the next day to go to Sudbury. Jonathan was going to be off after we had lunch until we came back.

We got up early enough and had some coffee and breakfast and went for a good long walk around the property. James checked on some emails while we were waiting for our big lunch. We brought our luggage down and James put it in the car and then we loaded all the wrapped boxes. A light dusting of snow fell overnight but when the sun was fully out it would melt. We ate lunch, freshened up and left for the airport at 3:00. The luggage and packages were loaded, and we boarded the plane. We landed in Sudbury at 8:15 pm and waited at the top of the stairs for Janet and Wade.

“Hello, you two, how are you? Wow this is quite exciting, and this is a very beautiful plane. Talk about flying in luxury. Thank you for inviting us on this trip.”

James introduced them to the flight crew, and we went to sit in our seats. We got buckled in, listened to the security procedure, and then taxied out on the runway and took off. When we were up in the air, Drew came around to see what beverages we wanted. Everyone decided to have water.

"We will have snacks a bit later and then if you and Wade want to sit elsewhere on the plane to catch some sleep, don't hesitate. Drew will provide you with pillows and blankets and the lights will be turned off. We will have breakfast before landing." They said that was fine with them. Wade got up to use the bathroom and came back to tell Janet she should go have a look. She did and came back again amazed at the luxury.

"Not something you would get on a commercial flight that's for sure. But I'm sure with all the travelling you do James; you want to be comfortable." He said that indeed that was why he bought the plane. James went through the itinerary for the next twelve days. He outlined that we would be going to Germany first for three days, meeting with Quinn and Charlotte on the second day, hitting the Christmas markets and doing some sightseeing and shopping, then the same thing in Austria but without Quinn and Charlotte and then off to Scotland for four days.

"I thought you would like to go to Scotland again since we were coming this far, and it would give you a chance to do a little sightseeing and to also see my businesses there. I know you will want to have time to do some shopping in each country. I presume Wade that is ok with you. When we get to Scotland, my Aunt Fenella is going to have a family dinner on Saturday, and she wants to do it as a pre-Christmas party since we won't be there for Christmas. You will be with us, and you don't have to get anyone gifts. I know that you both have Scottish ancestry, so we will try to at least go to the towns where your ancestors came from because we won't be able to see all of Scotland in a few days. Is that ok with both of you?" Janet didn't know what to say so Wade spoke.

"It sounds perfect James. We are very much looking forward to it and it will be nice to see some of the places we saw a few years ago." Drew brought out some canapes for us to nibble on while we were going through the itinerary.

"James, I would like to at least give your aunt and uncle a gift since they are hosting the party. Perhaps you can give me some idea of what would be appropriate, and we can try to find something at the Christmas market. It would make me feel more comfortable if we could do that." James appreciated her thoughtfulness and said he would help them pick something out. Wade was starting to yawn so they went back to the middle of the plane and stretched out to sleep.

“I’m a little tired too, do you want to try to sleep or are you going to look over some papers.” James said he would sleep as well. It was about three hours into the flight, and we hit a bit of turbulence. Not enough to warrant putting seat belts back on but it woke Janet up. I could see that she was sitting up and as James and I were awake, we put on a light, and she came back to join us.

“Wade can sleep through anything. I have to thank you again for inviting us.” There was a little bit of nervousness in her voice. I touched James on the thigh under the blanket.

“If you ladies will excuse me; I’m going to look over a couple of reports. I won’t be long sweetheart.” He gave me a kiss and went up to the front of the plane so as not to disturb Wade.

“I’m so happy for you and I have to say I love that new ring James got you. I thought it was sweet that he got you your ‘going steady’ ring. He takes good care of you and that makes me very happy. It has been a long time coming for you.” I told her that I told James about my last marriage.

“Well not all of it in great detail but I felt he needed to know why I react at times the way that I do. I have agreed to let him spoil me within reason for one year, then we have to get more normal. His life is grand, he travels like crazy, does huge business deals and he is very wealthy. To go from what I was in, to have won the lottery and now to this, it has my head spinning a bit. He understands a bit more, but he has been so loving and caring. I keep saying it's like a dream and I'm going to wake up and he won't be there." She could see where I was coming from.

"I get it, I do, it would have me dizzy too. Speaking of which, I appreciate you talking to me through the turbulence even though it wasn't that bad. I'm going to go back and try to sleep again. See you in a few hours." James returned after she got back to her seat.

"Was she a little nervous?" I said that she was, and I talked to her about all of this and how it was a bit overwhelming at times. I think it got her mind off the turbulence.

"Thanks for getting the hint to leave us alone for a bit. I don't think she wanted you to see that she was nervous. But now that everything is calm, let's try to get back to sleep ourselves. We will be up in another few hours." We snuggled back up again and dozed off. James woke before me and before Janet and Wade. He asked Ian to get breakfast ready. I woke up to the aroma of coffee and so did Janet and Wade. They took turns using the front bathroom to freshen up. I let them know it had lots of toiletries to use. James and I freshened up as well and got seated as coffee was being put in front of us. Janet and Wade rejoined us for the rest of the flight.

"It is a good thing that you keep that bathroom well stocked with toiletries because I forgot to keep our toothbrushes and toothpaste out. Coffee smells great and I am quite hungry." The sun was just coming up and we were about an hour and a half from landing in Berlin. Breakfast was served with more coffee and juice. Wade and James got into a conversation about going for early morning runs and Janet and I talked about maybe working in a couple of hours at the spas.

"This is going to be a fun time, so let's enjoy the adventure ahead of us." We cheered to that. The dishes were cleared away when the captain was informing the flight crew to prepare for landing. We buckled up in our seats and the landing was very smooth. James ordered a limo to pick us up which was waiting in the VIP area. The driver loaded our luggage and we drove to the hotel. James checked us in and then sent a text off to Quinn to let him know we had arrived. Our luggage was taken up to our rooms. Our room was the presidential suite, and it was stunning and had great views of the city and the Brandenburg Gate. Janet and Wade were in the royal suite which had similar views. We arranged to meet in the lobby in about an hour. The plan was to do a little shopping, a little sightseeing and then come back and have dinner and go to the Christmas market in the evening.

"James if you and Wade are going to do a run tomorrow morning and the next day, perhaps Janet and I could book an appointment at the spa for a massage tomorrow, to work out the kinks from the flight and the next day a facial." James said he would arrange it with the concierge when we went down. We toured around the city by limo for a little bit, went to stand at the Brandenburg Gate which was quite an emotional moment and then did a little shopping. We had lunch, did a bit more looking around within the city and then went back to the hotel. We were going to have an early dinner and do the market so that we could go to bed early and not be too tired for the next day.

"Our room is amazing James thank you for getting us such a luxurious suite. It is going to be hard to try to sleep with all the beauty outside our window." We were happy they liked the room and went to the restaurant to have dinner. I was shocked to hear James speak German.

"You surprise me, I didn't realize you could speak German." He said he could get by ordering food and light conversation but was by no means fluent.

"Quinn is more fluent than I am obviously, but I am pretty fluent with French and of course Gaelic." He booked 8 am appointments for us for an hour and a half massage and the following day an 8 am appointments for facials while he and Wade went for a run. We agreed to meet in the lobby the next morning after we got back from appointments and runs. Dinner was delicious and when James signed the bill we went out to the Christmas market nearby. It was really something to see all the lights and everyone bustling about. We walked around for about an hour or so, but we were a bit tired and went back to the hotel and up to our rooms. We said goodnight to Janet and Wade and got ready for bed.

We slept really well and went down to the lobby the next morning. Wade and James took off on their run and Janet and I went for our massages. We felt refreshed after our massage and Wade and James felt good after their run. We went in to have breakfast and then we were going to head over to Mousa, and Quinn was going to take us on a tour. When we got there introductions were made and I was quite surprised at how big the building was. The tour was quite fascinating, and it took about three hours. Quinn recommended a place to go for lunch and said that he and Charlotte would see us later that evening. As we were having lunch in a very quaint German restaurant my thoughts went to my Dad and me wanting to go to where he was injured and the town he helped liberate. James must have read my mind.

"Perhaps in the fall next year we can come back and do that route you wanted to do that your Dad took during the war. I am familiar enough with the country to get us around. Would you like to do that?" I think the tear in my eye gave him the answer.

We got back to the hotel around 4:30 and went to freshen up for dinner. Because we were going to do the Christmas market after dinner we dressed warmly for it. We took many photos of us in our rooms, together and out and about. We got down to the restaurant at 5:30 and saw Quinn and Charlotte come in. It was good to see Quinn again and after James introduced us to Charlotte we sat, and James ordered some champagne.

"Not for me James, I have a court case tomorrow, so sparkling water if you don't mind." He ordered some sparkling water for Charlotte. James was going to make a toast, but Quinn asked if he could do the honours.

"Here is to James and Cassandra, may their life be filled only with happiness and love; and to Janet and Wade, may this not be your only visit to Germany." It was a wonderful toast. We ate and then went out to the market. Charlotte was a wonderful person and Janet and I hit it off with her immediately. While we were looking at items with Charlotte, Quinn and James stood back and talked.

"Are you still interested in being partners in my companies in Alberta Quinn? Is Charlotte ok with it?" He said she was very much in favour of it, and they agreed to work out a deal in the New Year. By the time

Janet and I were done, I had four dozen ornaments. Janet was only getting three or four ornaments, but Charlotte negotiated to get us a good deal. She did that with each item that we picked up at the market. But it was getting late, and Quinn and Charlotte had to call it a night.

"Thank you for coming to the market with us and getting us really good deals on what we bought. It was so nice meeting you Charlotte and I hope that you and Quinn and the boys will come and visit us in the new year." Janet thanked Charlotte as well and gave her a hug and kiss as did I.

"We would love to and sometimes it helps bringing a lawyer to help with negotiation. I have so enjoyed meeting all of you and Cassandra we should definitely keep in touch. We have each other's contact info now, but we must go, Quinn, kiss your boyfriend goodnight. Honestly, when the two of them get together I can't pry them apart." We laughed and hugged and kissed goodbye.

When we got back to the hotel and up to our suites, Janet and Wade said they were going to turn in. Morning was going to be here before we knew it and they were a bit tired from the day. We hugged and kissed them goodnight and went into our suite. I went out onto the balcony to look out over the city and the Gate. It was so beautiful, and I wished that my Dad could have seen it this way. James came out and put his arm around me and we stood in silence taking it all in. We hugged and went back in.

The following day was similar to the day before with James and Wade going for a run and Janet and I heading for a facial. James was able to use his negotiating skills in German to get us as good deals at other shops as Charlotte had the night before. We went back to the hotel for dinner and Janet and Wade came into our room for coffee. Tomorrow we were leaving in late morning to go to Austria. James mentioned that we would be doing almost the same things as we'd done in Germany, but he said that Austria's Christmas markets were even nicer. Janet and Wade went off to bed and we did the same.

We had breakfast in the restaurant and then James checked us out and the limo took us to the airport. We loaded our luggage and packages on the plane. When we landed in Vienna there was a limo waiting to take us to the hotel. James had the presidential suites booked for us. We decided to do a short tour since we got in a bit later. The city had so much history to it, and it was stunningly beautiful.

"I think that I could spend a couple of weeks here easily. This city is so beautiful, and restaurants are playing the Viennese waltz, it makes you want to dance, but I won't. I don't know the Viennese waltz but maybe it is something we can learn James. What do you think?"

He knew I was teasing. He was right about the markets though; they were much better than Germany. The ornaments were so much more delicate than what we bought already. Buying another four dozen had Janet laughing. But the German ones were still very pretty.

I decided to get a couple of snow globes here for Ayleen. The ones here were so much prettier than the ones that I saw in Germany. I still got Ayleen a couple in Germany, so I was covered for the next four years with globes. We had a wonderful three days, and we enjoyed one another's company. While James and Wade went running Janet and I spent time at the spa. The first one was a massage; one can never get too many of those and the last one was a mani/pedi. We wanted our nails and toes done for Scotland.

"It's nice don't you think that our guys are becoming friends. Wade really likes James and is very impressed with him." James commented to me on how much he liked Wade as well.

"This is such a beautiful city I hate to think about leaving it late tomorrow morning, but Scotland awaits, and you are going to love it at the estate. This has been such a wonderful trip so far and I am so glad that you are here with me. It means a lot to me that you could come." Janet was feeling the same way.

The next morning, we had a late breakfast and then packed up our luggage and other bags and drove to the airport. The flight to Scotland was going to be a little over two hours. When we arrived, William was waiting for us. We left the Christmas ornaments stowed in the plane but took out all the gifts that we were giving to the family and Wade and Janet.

James introduced Janet and Wade to William, and we drove to the estate. Barclay was, we were told, preparing us a lunch. Fenella and Callum were staying at the house and could possibly be for at least another year. James would have to decided what to do after that time. I sent Janet pictures of James's estate, but nothing is as good as the real thing. They were both blown away at the size and extent of it.

"Oh my gosh everything is so green here still." I laughed because I'd said the same thing to James when I came in September. We arrived, and Fenella was waiting on the steps for us. William was going to look after the luggage and packages and see that it was put by the stairs. Mrs. O'Toole was in and would see that it got upstairs. James ran up to hug and kiss Fenella.

"Fenella, this is Cassandra's school friend Janet and her husband Wade, this is my Aunt Fenella. I assume that Callum is at the hospital. They will meet him at dinner then." We went inside, and Janet was speechless. It was like looking in a mirror at how I reacted when I first came.

"It's beautiful isn't it. Fenella it is so good to see you again." I hugged and kissed her, and we went into the small sitting room. William put on a fire as it was chilly out. It was almost lunch, but we had time for coffee.

"It is so nice to meet both of you. I hear that you both have Scottish ancestry. It must be quite something to be in the land of your ancestors. I'm sure that James will be taking you around to see some of the sights. It is so good to have you and James here again. You both look wonderful, and I loved those photos you sent. You looked amazing in them." She noticed the ring that James got me for my birthday and said that it was quite stunning.

"He has been spoiling me and I am letting him for a short time. What is Barclay preparing for lunch. Something traditional Scottish I hope. I think we need to immerse Janet and Wade into it right away." Fenella laughed and said that they were having something quite traditional. James was happy about that.

"Barclay is doing up a soup called Cullen Sink and a Smoked Goose and Papaya salad. Fenella asked how the trip was going so far and we told her about the Christmas markets and how beautiful the cities were.

"James, I believe you are going to be taking them to tour your businesses here. Alisa has been working on some special ornaments for you and for you as well Janet. Alisa is an amazing artist. We both took art in university, but she was so much better than me. She is the head artist at Sutherland Glass Company. She comes up with the most exquisite designs doesn't she James." He had to agree wholeheartedly that Alisa was truly a talented artist. Barclay came in to say that lunch was ready. We went into the small dining room, and it was set beautifully.

"Fenella, you set a lovely table thank you so much for doing that for us. Janet this is what the heather here looks like, isn't it beautiful and the thistle too." The pale pink roses were also stunning. The meal was wonderful, and Janet and Wade loved it.

"If this is typical Scottish cuisine I am loving it. I love fish at any time and the salad was delicious. I can't say as I have ever had smoked goose before but that was very good." We returned to the sitting room and had tea.

"Fenella, I brought along some of the teas that Jonathan has been making up and would like you to try them. Perhaps tomorrow we can try the lavender tea. It is really good, and I am sure you will like it." I gave her the packages of all the teas that I brought.

"Your luggage has been taken up to your rooms. James, Janet, and Wade are in the green room, so if you could show them up, I will take these teas out to the kitchen and ask Barclay to make another pot of tea. I am quite anxious to try the lavender and don't want to wait until tomorrow. I will see you back down in the sitting room once you have unpacked." We went upstairs, and I showed them the room they were going to be in. The rooms had all been redone since we were gone, and they looked amazing. I took Janet around to the other rooms, except for the room that Fenella and Callum were in. She loved them all.

"My word this is a big estate; I think I would have been a little overwhelmed with it all too. Fenella is lovely, and I can't wait to meet the rest of your family." I left her to go to her room and unpack. James was waiting for me in ours.

"It is nice to be back here isn't it. This room has some nice memories don't you think?" He was being coy, and I told him we didn't have time, but I would take him up on it later. We went back downstairs and rejoined Fenella in the sitting room. She was having a cup of the lavender tea.

"My goodness this is very good. I hope you brought me lots of it." I said that I did but the others were equally as nice. James told her that we were going to put them on the market soon.

"The idea was Cassandra's and of course our chef back home, Jonathan is the creator of them. You won't find these anywhere else in the world. He makes them up in the kitchen, testing different combinations. We will make sure you get a supply." Fenella was on her second cup. When Janet and Wade came back downstairs we took them on a tour of the house and then outside to see the grounds. I pointed out the gazebo where James proposed to me.

"It is also the same spot where James's Dad proposed to his Mum. The gazebo wasn't there then but they put it in some years later and it has been where they have had many family picnics. It is a beautiful spot and maybe tomorrow we will take a walk over. It overlooks a lake, and it is so peaceful there. We will be getting wedding photos taken out there." We gave them a tour of the grounds and the gardens, which was another area where we planned to take photos.

"People come here all the time for wedding photos, but James won't have weddings done here." Janet and Wade were amazed at the size of the estate.

"I am dumbstruck, but I have to tell you I am very anxious to go out for a walk on the moors. It would not be a trip to Scotland if we didn't do that." James figured as much and ensured that they had the proper hiking boots in their rooms. Janet hadn't realized they were for them and thanked James.

"It's a challenging walk on the moors so perhaps we will give you a day to catch your wind and then we will go. Tomorrow is the family dinner and Christmas party so perhaps we should wait until Sunday to do the moors. I hope that will be ok." They said it would be perfect. We went back into the house and Fenella was getting off the phone.

"Callum is on his way. He was in surgery early this morning and it was a difficult case. It went well, and the patient is doing good considering. He will be home in about an hour, so if you want to freshen up we will be sitting down for dinner at 6:00." Fenella liked to dress appropriately for dinner. I let Janet and Wade know so that they brought suits and dresses to wear.

"I went on a bit of a shopping spree before we came. Now that I am making so much money, I splurged a lot on me and Wade. I was glad you told me about the dress code for dinners because I would not have thought to pack enough dresses and suits." When I went shopping in Toronto, I picked up several dresses to bring with me.

James already had suits hanging up in the closet along with other clothes, so he packed light. I put on the purple silk beaded dress with matching shoes. James put on a charcoal suit with lavender shirt and dark grey tie. We met Janet and Wade coming out of their room. Wade was wearing a navy suit with light blue shirt and navy tie; Janet was wear a deep gold organza dress with embellishments and matching shoes. We arrived downstairs to the sitting room and Fenella was wearing a beautiful black lace A-line dress with matching shoes and Callum was wearing a black suit with white shirt and multi-coloured tie.

"Hello Callum, good to see you. Let me introduce Cassandra's school friend Janet and her husband Wade." Callum gave me a hug and kiss and shook Janet and Wade's hand.

"Very nice to meet you both. I hope that you will enjoy your stay in Scotland. I am sure James will take good care of you as will my lovely wife Fenella." Callum was having a whisky and James joined him. Wade, Janet, and I had wine and Fenella had sparkling water.

"You look very nice; I love your dresses. Janet that colour looks lovely on you and I love the shoes that match it. Cassandra, you look lovely in anything you wear but that purple is very stunning. Dinner was another typical Scottish meal which went over well. We adjourned to the sitting room where William already started a fire, and we sat having coffee and talking.

"Janet, James said that you are now working for him. Are you enjoying your work?" Janet said she was loving and wasn't just saying that because James was right beside her.

"I really love it and he has been so nice to me and he's great to work for." Fenella asked Wade what he did.

"I retired not that long ago from the provincial government in the grants program. I did that for a number of years, and I still do some work for them on a part time basis. I am retired but not fully retired. Now I do a lot of running, watch my grandsons play hockey and garden. I am learning to relax more now." It was getting late, and I knew that I was tired, and I was sure that Janet and Wade were too. We decided to head off to bed. James stayed up for a bit with Fenella but the rest of us went up. William put all of the wrapped boxes in the games room that we still had to put bows and ribbon on.

"It is good to be home Fenella. I have missed you very much, but I love living in Canada too. You and Callum will have to come over for Christmas next year. I am sure Angus and Catherine can do without you for one year. Thank you for stepping in and living here. I really do appreciate it. I'm going to have to figure out what to do once you leave though. I know that Malcolm and Fiona still have major work to get done on their home, so perhaps if you think she has learned her lesson, I will ask them to come and stay." Fenella did not have to think long about what he said.

"James, I truly feel that Fiona has learned her lesson and I know that she is really sorry for having disappointed you the way she did. She has become the old Fiona now that she is not seeing Victoria anymore, who by the way got divorced from the Duke but she is now, I've heard engaged to some oil magnate in Finland, so I don't think you will be running into her again. Callum and I would love to come and spend Christmas with you in your new home. Next year they spend with Catherine's family up north anyway, so we would be on our own, so we would love to come. I saw Annie the other day and she was delighted to hear that you were coming. She wants to see you when you have a moment or two, alone she said." James said that he would see her before they left. They went up to bed and turned out the lights. The next morning everyone was up early. James and Wade went for a run and Janet, and I went for a walk. Fenella had to run into town to take care of a few things. We met up with James and Wade on their way back to the house.

"Did you guys have a good run?" They said yes but it was a bit chilly. Wade was thoroughly enjoying the fresh Scottish air.

"Well let's head back for breakfast shall we. Fenella has gone out to run some errands, so we will be breakfasting by ourselves." This morning Barclay made fresh scones and we are having toad in the hole. Janet was very much enjoying all the names of the different foods.

"I should put in a video call to Mom and Dad, they will get such a kick out of the fact that I am here in Scotland again." After we finished breakfast, we went into the sitting room, so she could make the call on her tablet. She got them a tablet months ago and showed them how to use it. She made a bunch of video calls for weeks ahead so that her Dad would know how to answer the call.

"Hi Dad, is Mom around. We are here in Scotland at James and Cassandra's home. It is so beautiful here you would not believe it. I can't get over how green it is." She took the tablet outside so that they could see the moors and the green hills. Her Mom was over the moon that she was in Scotland again. She didn't talk to them long but at least they got to see the area.

"I'll bet your Mom was thrilled and your Dad too. They've never been here have they?" Janet said no, and it was not going to be possible now because of their ages and her Mom's heart condition.

"I will take lots and lots of pictures and videos to show them and they will be happy with that. They laughed when I told them we had toad in the hole this morning. Mom said she remembers her grandmother talking about that." It was nice that she was able to show them some of Scotland. So today we were going on a tour of the companies.

"They've finished the Saudi Prince's yacht, so we can actually go onboard now and see what his money has gotten him. We will stop by the distillery but won't stay long, but we will go by the glass company. Alisa has the ornaments ready for us." James asked Alisa to make up ornaments with our names on them; James, me, Ross, Lindsay, Ayleen, Sonya, Rhonda, Austin, and Nicole. He called her later to ask her to do two of the same for Ross, Lindsay, and Ayleen and also to make up one for Janet and Wade. He wanted to make sure that Ayleen could take one home with her. They were both fascinated by the distillery and how the whisky was made. The yacht was something else to see. It was luxurious and maybe more so than any of the presidential suites we'd stayed in.

"They've been working on this yacht for nearly two years. He kept wanting to upgrade things. It cost him a hundred and sixty-five million dollars for this yacht, and it is worth every penny. He will be getting delivery of it in the spring when the threat of serious weather won't hamper delivery. We've done up yachts for other Arab royalty which they had their own crew sail without incident, so I am not expecting this one to be any different. They are sending over their own crew so if they sink it, it will be on them." The last stop was the glass company. I couldn't wait to go back inside and see what they were working on now. They were working on a magnificent window for a church. It was stunning to see how they brought the pieces together and the painting that was done on the glass. Alisa came out to meet us.

"Hello James, Cassandra, how nice to see you both again and back in Scotland." James introduced Janet and Wade to Alisa. She took us up into the office to show us the ornaments she did for us. They were exquisite and so delicate. I love that she decorated Ayleen's with unicorns pulling Santa and his sleigh. It was very cute, and I loved all of them. Janet was very surprised that she did one up for her and Wade.

"Thank you so much we shall treasure these always." James took them on a tour of the rest of the plant. I stayed back with Alisa to talk with her.

"Did Fenella tell you that Victoria and the Duke divorced, and she is now living in Finland engaged to an oil baron?" I told her I hadn't heard but it was nice to know that we would not be running into her now.

"I hope she is happier now. I love the ornaments Alisa, thank you so much for doing all the detail work on them. I love that you made each one different. You are a very talented artist and I know that James truly appreciates that and your loyalty." Alisa seemed to be very touched by what I said. Perhaps she didn't truly understand how much James appreciated her. The others came back and were talking endlessly about the work that was being done. I mentioned that Janet and Wade did a bit of stained glass as well, so this was a place that we appreciated very much. We left and went out on a bit of a tour. James took us to where Wade's ancestors came from and to where Janet's Moms' ancestors came from. Oddly enough they were not that far away from each other.

"Small world isn't it. James is going to take us up to Arnprior tomorrow. You will get a kick out of it. I know I did and there is also Renfrew which is not too far from his estate." By the time we did all the driving around it was close to lunch. James called Barclay earlier on to say that we would be out for lunch.

"You can't come to Scotland and not have lunch in a pub." James was taking us to the same restaurant that he took Roxie and me. Janet laughed and laughed when we pulled up and saw the sign. We had a great lunch. We went back home after stopping at a few more places. We were going to do some shopping the next day as well as touring. Dinner tonight was going to be roasted grouse, which was not something that Janet and Wade had eaten before.

We dressed a little more casually tonight as Fenella realized that we don't always dress formally for dinner. Janet wore a navy pant suit with a white blouse, I wore my dark green leather pants and blazer with a bright orange blouse and Wade and James wore dress pants, a shirt and sports jacket. The meal was wonderful, and Janet and Wade thoroughly enjoyed it. We adjourned to the sitting room to have tea. Fenella wanted to try more of the blends, so we had some with her. James mentioned that he was going to go and see Annie in the morning. Tomorrow was also the family dinner and Christmas party so there would be no touring tomorrow.

When we finally went to bed, I asked James to give me a massage. My legs were cramping up from all the walking we did, at least that was the excuse I gave him. The massaging led to other things, and we made love once again in Scotland. We fell asleep well after midnight. James was up and out the door before the rest of us got up. He had some errands to run he said last night so would see us for lunch. After breakfast, Janet, Wade, and I put on our hiking boots and hit the moors. I wasn't sure if they knew how challenging it would be because Janet was a little out of breath when we got to the point I wanted to take them. I was a little out of breath too but Wade being a runner wasn't.

"Isn't it spectacular up here. The air is so much different out here on the moors than it is down by the estate." There was a good wind blowing by the time we got to where I wanted us to be, and everyone's cheeks were nice and rosy.

"We should head back down. I have a bunch of wrapping to do and I hope you will help me with it Janet." Wade said that he was going to walk around the estate and take pictures and would meet up with us later.

A tree was put up and decorated in the large living room. Fenella was in there putting gifts under the tree. Janet and I went into the games room to put the ribbon and bows on all the boxes. I marked on the outside which ones were hers and Wades. I put the ribbon and bows on those myself but kept off the name tags until I took them to the other room. I wrapped hers in a yellow shiny paper and Wade's in green with colourful ribbons and bows on them, so I would know which ones were theirs. When Janet wasn't looking I put the tags on.

There were quite a number of gifts under the tree already. With our nineteen boxes it took up quite a bit of space, but we spread them around, so they wouldn't be lumped together. I knew that James went to see Annie and that she would be joining us for dinner. James returned after lunch with a bunch of gifts of his own and some he said that were from Annie. I looked at him quizzically because I thought we were only giving the coats. He laughed at me and took the gifts to put them under the tree.

"No peeking either of you." He knew that I never did such a thing, but I had to admit I was curious. Janet went out to meet Wade and to have some pictures taken of them outside. I used the opportunity to ask James why Annie wanted to meet him.

"She wanted to talk to me about her will." I looked at James finding that hard to believe. I got the sense that wasn't completely true, and it would have been the first time that James had not been entirely honest with me. But perhaps it was something between him and Annie and it was none of my business. I let the matter go. James went over in his mind about his visit with Annie. She was so very happy to see him, and she wanted to tell him something but could not go into great detail because she was not supposed to. James played the conversation back in his head.

"James, I have been getting messages of something that is going to happen. I can't tell you exactly what that is because I am not being shown the whole thing. But I do know that it involves Cassandra and a sadness. I know that it has nothing to do with you, her son, daughter in law or granddaughter. I would definitely tell you that. It will happen in the New Year but not immediately. That is all that I can say, so please be there for her when this happens. She is going to need your strength and love more than she has ever needed anything before. Be strong for her James and be compassionate, I can say no more. You must not say anything to Cassandra, it will only make her worry and fret until things do happen. I am only telling you this now because you will need to be there for her. The message was for you James not for her. Now you don't need to come and pick me up for dinner. I have arranged for a driver to take me up, but I will ask you to take these gifts with you, so that I don't have to worry about them. I need you to look over some things that I have in my will to ensure that I have it right." After he went through the things in her will with her he said he had to get back.

"I'm glad that is taken care of. I will see you at 5:30." She hugged and kissed James, and he was out the door. Annie wished that she could have told him what was going to happen, but things must play out as they were designed. She would send Cassandra healing energy when the time came.

We went upstairs and got changed into evening wear for dinner. I decided to wear the dark red organza dress. James made sure to bring all the jewelry that I would need in his metal briefcase where he carried important things. He helped me with the gold and ruby necklace he bought me. He was wearing his black designer suit with light grey shirt and black tie. We were going down the stairs when Janet and Wade came out. She was wearing a dark grey embellished silk A-line dress with long sleeves and Wade was wearing a charcoal suit with white shirt and grey tie.

Everyone was starting to arrive, so we waited in the foyer to greet everyone and introduce Janet and Wade as they were coming in. Angus, Catherine, Fiona, Laren, Skye and Cailean were the first group to arrive. I hadn't met Fiona and Laren the last time. They were identical twins, so it was going to be hard to tell them apart. But James pointed out to me that Fiona had green eyes and Laren had blue eyes. It was the only way he was ever able to tell them apart. We introduced them to Janet and Wade. Not long after Malcolm, Fiona, Cameron, and Donald arrived and then Alisa, Glynnis and Gowan, Errol and MacKenzie. Cameron and Donald were not identical twins, but they had similarities about them. The last but not least to arrive was Annie. James escorted her into the living room as she could not stand in the foyer while everyone was introduced. James introduced Janet and Wade to Annie.

"Annie is like a grandmother to me in many ways. I love her dearly." Janet was pleased to meet her as was Wade. Annie looked at the two of them and then said something to Janet.

"You had a dear old friend who died not long ago. She watches over you and is very proud of you. Ah, I see that both you and Cassandra have both had something similar happen to you in your childhoods.

They apologizes for their actions. In time perhaps you will forgive it, but I see that you are not ready yet. Cassandra has forgiven long ago. She has forgiven much in her life, so sad. Anyway, this is a happy time so let's enjoy shall we." Janet was stunned. I thought I told her Annie was a medium but maybe I forgot. She pulled me back and let me know that I hadn't told her about Annie, but she was floored when she had brought up the elderly friend who died. Dinner was loud and joyous. It was a typical Christmas meal except with goose. There were several kinds of potato, many different dishes of vegetables and the trays of desserts were endless. I was glad that we went for a good walk on the moors earlier, so was Janet.

"My word this is so wonderful; you are so lucky to have such a wonderful extended family." I knew that was true for sure. After dinner we took coffee and tea into the large living room. Fenella asked Annie to try the lavender tea as she knew she would like it. Annie loved it and asked for some to take home. James, Callum, Angus, and Malcolm were in charge of handing out the gifts. James spoke first though.

"I hope you won't mind if I hand out the gifts from Cassandra and I first, then we will get to all the others which will be easier to get to I think once ours are out of the way." They did take up a lot of the space around the tree. Once all of the gifts were handed out and to Wade and Janet too, they opened them. They let out gasps when they pulled their coats out. James let them know that these were made exclusively in Canada. They were busy trying them on and each one said how much they loved them. Janet and Wade were surprised with theirs. Janet gave me a hug and whispered in my ear.

"My God I know how expensive these coats are, you guys must have paid out a small fortune for all of these." I smiled and said that we thought it would make great gifts. Everyone loved the colours we chose for them, and they fit perfectly. I was happy about that because I was not looking forward to having to take a bunch back. Then the men started handing out gifts as they came to them. Everyone remained seated and when the guys came to give gifts for them they put them beside their wives and wife to be. Once they were done, everyone started to open them up. Fenella and James made sure that Annie had some gifts as well. I had no idea what he got anyone when he went out, but he wrote on the tag that the gift was from the both of us.

Annie was the first to open the gift from James and me. He whispered to me what it was quickly, so I would not be surprised. He got her a beautiful diamond necklace with angel wings as the pendant. She loved it and James helped to put it on her. Then everyone else started unwrapping theirs. James bought Janet and Wade each a very expensive watch. They were both stunned with the gift. They loved all the cashmere we got them too and Janet loved the four-leaf clover pendant. Fenella gave a gift on behalf of her bunch and Alisa gave one on behalf of hers. From Fenella she got several beautiful cashmere shawls and Wade got several cashmere pullovers. From Alisa's, she gave Janet and Wade beautiful paintings of the areas where their ancestors came from. They were moved to tears with the gifts.

Alisa wanted her to know that James mentioned where their family came from, so she went out and took some photos and chose a spot that they thought they would love to have in a painting. They went over to Alisa and Fenella and hugged them and then to each of the family members. I opened up the gift that Annie gave me. It was a box that held four crystals that she had made into different shapes and put on a charm bracelet. The bracelet was 24 carat gold, and it alone was beautiful. She wrote down what the power of each crystal was and would talk to me about it later she said.

I thanked her very much for the thoughtful gift. James bought me a beautiful multi-gem cuff with diamonds, emeralds, rubies, and sapphires. It was lovely, and I could wear it with anything. James was not expecting a gift from me, but I saw him more than once looking at this really expensive watch online. It was new and would not be available until late next year, but I asked Hans to get one for me, which he did. James was blown away by the watch.

“How did you get this; they are not even available for buying until next fall. I couldn’t even get one with all my connections.” I said that I got Hans to pull in a few favours and told him that if you asked for his help to get it he was to tell you it was not possible.

“Hans told me he could not possibly get it for me no matter how much I was willing to pay him. Well played my dear, I was not expecting to be able to get this for another year. Thank you so much I love it.” Now that all the gifts were opened, and the wrapping paper, bows and ribbon dispensed with, we sat around while Callum played the piano and he and Fenella sang songs. It was a wonderful party.

Skye and Cailean were starting to get very tired, so the parents got them to get their coats on and they went home. The rest followed them as it had been a long day for everyone. We wished them good night and thanked them for coming. There was Fenella and Callum, Janet, Wade, me, and James left. Callum continued to play softly, he found, he said, that it kept his fingers nimble. He was an excellent pianist and studied classically in school, but medicine was his first love. Janet and Wade took their gifts up to their room and wished everyone a good night. We stayed downstairs with Fenella and Callum.

“Fenella, it was a lovely party and it truly felt like Christmas. Thank you so much for doing this.” It was her pleasure she said, and she had to admit that she thoroughly enjoyed it. We took any dishes out to the kitchen and then went up to bed ourselves. Callum and Fenella were right behind us.

"I was quite touched by Annie's gift. Did you know that the crystals she picked out have to do with strength and courage, recovery and regeneration, spiritual connection, and spiritual protection? I think she is trying to tell me something in a roundabout way, but I will wear the bracelet every day because I believe that is what she wants. I know that we are going to be doing more touring around, but I would like to spend a few hours with her alone if she is willing. Perhaps you can take Janet and Wade into Edinburgh and Glasgow for a tour around there." James knew that if he protested she would become suspicious, so he said that he was sure Annie would love that.

"I will give her a call tomorrow and see if it can be arranged for Monday morning. Tomorrow we are going up to Arnprior and we can also show them the royal yacht while we are in that area. Perhaps we can also have dinner at that Italian place we went to with Duncan and Roxie. I think they might like a little change in meals." James laughed at that.

"Not everyone can enjoy smoked salmon for breakfast. I know they were being good sports, but I agree with you perhaps a dinner out for Italian will be welcomed." We cuddled up and fell asleep within a few minutes.

The next morning after breakfast we were off and wouldn't be back until evening. Janet got a huge kick out of seeing Arnprior and going around the town. It was much smaller than the Arnprior where we came from, but she said she liked this one better. I knew what she meant. We went further north than we had before, and it was beautiful to see the seas. There was quite a wind coming off of them and we went back to the warmth of the car. We got to the Italian restaurant which both Janet and Wade appreciated.

"We thought perhaps you would like something more typical than what you would get at home. The food here is amazing so be prepared." They both said they had never eaten anything like it before and they had a lot of Italian restaurants back in Sudbury.

"This is leaps and bounds above any of those and I am not just saying that." We believed her because it was better than anything James or I had as well. When we got home it was dark. Fenella waited up to see how our day had gone. Callum had surgery in the morning, so he went to bed hours ago.

"We had a wonderful time. Got to see a little more of the north than I did before. It was quite breezy and cold though. We are going to have some tea; would you like to join us Fenella." She said she would and wondered which tea I was going to make. I wanted to surprise her. I made a pot of the one with the Saskatoon in it. It was a bit sweet, but the lavender helped to break that down a bit.

"Oh my, this one is quite lovely too. This chef that you have is quite talented where teas are concerned. You could probably do quite well James if you sold some of them here. I doubt that anyone has any of these combinations." James thought of that and was going to work on getting a deal with some of the stores locally and in the surrounding areas.

"My dears, I am going to head up to bed and hopefully I won't wake Callum. He has another big surgery tomorrow. I will be glad when he steps back a bit, but he loves what he does, and he saves so many lives. Until the morning then." She gave everyone a hug and kiss goodnight.

"Tomorrow James is going to take you to Glasgow and Edinburgh in the morning and early afternoon. I am going to see Annie for a little bit. I want to talk to her about the crystals she gave me and get some instruction on how to use them. I know you are in good hands with James. We said goodnight and went to bed. James was a bit restless in bed, so I leaned over to ask him what was up.

"I'm sorry, I am feeling a bit out of sorts. I'm not ill, I think I miss our home. Kinda crazy isn't it when this is the home I was born in and lived most of my life. I know that Malcolm and Fiona are still living with Alisa because their home won't be ready for years. It's a heritage building I think I told you and it needs major structural repairs, so I think I will ask them to move back in when Fenella and Callum's home is ready. Do you think that is a good idea?" James was diverting me from what was troubling him.

"I know that you have something going on that you don't want to talk to me about and I am going to respect you and not keeping asking. I love it that you are thinking of our home as home and that you miss it. I do too but I love it here too. I can understand why you might feel a little conflicted. I do, however, hope that if it has anything to do with your health you will tell me and not keep it from me. So now that I have said that I agree that you should let them move back in. I know you don't want to let staff go, but there is a lot of time to think about that. Right now, I am tired, and I want to curl up next to you." He kissed me and promised that his health was good.

We woke the next morning to bright sunshine and a bit of a warming up. After breakfast, James got out the suv and took Janet and Wade to Edinburgh and then they would go to Glasgow. I waved bye to them and went upstairs to gather my things. William was taking me over to Annie's home. When I arrived, she opened the door and welcomed me in. She had a really nice home. It looked more the Scottish home that I had been thinking about. She had two sitting rooms, one which she kept strictly for her readings. There was a very warm energy when I walked by. She noticed the smile on my face and asked me why.

"I got a warm feeling when we walked by your reading room. Is that not a good thing? It felt positive and not negative." Annie said that was good.

"You have keen awareness about you. You wish to talk to me about the crystals and why I chose them for you. First, I want to assure you that I see nothing bad happening to you, James, your son, daughter in law or granddaughter. You will live for a long time and see your granddaughter marry and have at least two children maybe more. You have had a lot of sadness in your life and the crystals that I gave you will help that to heal, but there will be other moments of sadness. It is the way of life is it not. The agate and epidote will help you in those areas, the labradorite and Tibetan quartz will help you with your spiritual connection and protection. I know that you don't want to develop your intuitive ability, but it is there in you and whether you wish to believe it or not, you know things and see things. These crystals will help you so wear them often, every day if you can." She knew exactly why I was coming to see her, which did not surprise me at all.

"Annie, I do have some things I would like answered if it is possible. These are things that I have wondered about for years. Do you want me to go into detail about them?" Annie said no it was not necessary.

"Your mother does apologize for what she said to you when you were seven. She knows that you saw her in a dream but that you could not hear her. Sometimes, when those who pass over they speak at such a frequency that we don't understand, and they don't understand why we don't understand what they are saying. It takes patience on both ends until it becomes easier. She thanks you for forgiving her and admiring her and all that she went through when she was young. Your father holds no anger towards you for not going to his funeral. He understands why you didn't and appreciates that you were thinking of him and all the others who came. He knows what you went through now when you went to stay with him. He is not upset with you and loves that you did what you did. Now with the other question you have, I know that the only answer you were ever looking for was either a yes or no. I think that you have known the answer for years but somehow you wanted it confirmed. They didn't want to tell you and make the life you were in at the time more difficult than it was, but the answer they say is yes. I too am sorry that you had to live with that all those years. But it was a path that you took with the best of intentions and love in your heart, and you did all that you could. Even he apologizes for all the lies and betrayal and is happy for you now." I felt like a knot that had been in my shoulder for decades and decades was now gone. I could finally let all of that go.

"I want to thank you for telling me all that. I know that sometimes you are not supposed to do that, so I hope that you will not get in trouble with the spirits on the other side. I know that my intuition is pretty good and generally I can look at someone and know if they are not the nicest people. Sometimes it takes more than one look for me to see it. I was always doubted but I was never wrong. You are right that I don't wish to develop my abilities further. Maybe if I had met you forty years ago, I would have been very proud to have studied under you. But now, I am happy with James, and we have a good life together." Annie brought us tea and we sat in front of the fire.

"You and James were meant to meet now, at this point in your lives. It would not have worked if you met earlier. He has worked so very hard for so many years, he does need to slow down a bit, but not all at once. It will be too much of a shock to his system. James is feeling a little guilty that he loves his home in Canada with you more than he does the home that he was born and raised in. The two of you will find a way to keep the estate here going. Cailean is still very young, but he will be like James when he grows up. He will have the same keen sense of business that James has and maybe even a little better and when he is old enough, James will turn the estate over to him. Cailean will raise children in that home, and it will be full of life. I have not told this to James but perhaps you can tell him to help ease his mind. Cameron will work for James. He has a good head on his shoulders, and he has a girlfriend and is already thinking about marriage. It will be a good marriage, but they will eventually move into Alisa's home when she dies. This is all some years down the road and Alisa will be into her late nineties. James's heart and soul are with you now in your new home but for now that is all I can say." I was with Annie for a couple of hours, and I could tell she was getting a little tired. I called William to ask him to come back and get me. We walked back to the reading room and Annie invited me in. The room was still warm, and I could sense energies.

"You feel energies and you see ones who have passed on, like your aunt on your mother's side. I can tell you that Cullodina and Patrick are here, and they are very happy you are with James. They love your new home, and they will be at your wedding. All is as it should be, and the other side is very happy for you and James. Many of them are clapping and cheering." We left the warm embrace of the room and walked to the front door. William rang the bell to let me know he was waiting outside. I hugged Annie tightly and gave her a kiss on her cheek.

"We will be back in mid-March for dress fittings and then back a week before the wedding. I would love for you to meet my son, daughter in law and granddaughter." Annie said that she would look forward to it. I got in the car and went back to the estate. I was not expecting the others to get back until well after lunch. I decided to go for a good long walk and ended up at the gazebo. The swans left for warmer climes and the lake was now still. While the breeze was quite cool, I felt warmth around me. It was like I was getting a big hug and it felt good. I got back as James, Janet and Wade were getting out of the car and heading into the house.

"Did you guys have a good time and see lots of things." Janet was quite excited with all that they'd seen today.

"James took lots of pictures of Wade and I together so that we will have lots to show the folks at home. How was your visit with Annie?" I said that it was wonderful, and we had a great chat. We walked in and went to the sitting room. Wade took the bags of things that they bought today up to their room.

James offered Janet a glass of wine and I had one as well. James had a whisky and poured Wade some wine when he came back downstairs. They told me about the places they went to and loved all of it. They were definitely going to come back again and stay for a longer period. Dinner was ready, and we went in to eat. James was unusually quiet, but Janet kept the conversation going. It had been a full day and at 9:00 they went up to bed. James was looking out the window and I went up to him and hugged him.

"You have been very quiet today James? Is there something on your mind?" I knew that there was something he wanted to tell me but couldn't.

"You know when Annie and I were talking about the crystals she gave me, she said that I had been through a lot of sadness and that I would undoubtedly go through more. She said that it had nothing to do with you, Ross, Lindsay, or Ayleen, but it was life, and it would unfold as it would. Knowing that nothing bad will happen to any of you gives me peace of mind. She would not say any more on the matter and we talked about other things like the estate. She knows you feel conflicted, but she said that I could tell you that Cailean will move in when he is old enough. He is going to be like you with your keen sense of business and maybe even a bit smarter. He will marry and have lots of kids and the house will be filled with laughter and joy. She mentioned that Cameron will work for you. He has a girlfriend who I gather he hasn't told anyone about, and they are talking about marriage in a few years. Cameron and his wife will move into Alisa's place when she dies, which will be when she is well into her late nineties. The estate will flourish and stay in the Sutherland name. That should help to ease this guilt that you feel about our home back in Canada." He was greatly relieved to hear all of this. Annie never told it to him before.

"I hadn't told you this, but I left the estate to Cailean in my will. He isn't a Sutherland, but he will maintain the Sutherland name of that I am sure. It eases my mind a lot knowing all this. Cameron will do a good job running the company when Angus and Malcolm are ready to step back. I hope that Donald will too, but I sense that he is a little less focused than Cameron. But I am happing knowing this and feel a weight off my shoulders." I asked him if he wanted a massage.

"You know I'm not going to say no. You know what always happens when we give each other a massage." I did indeed and was looking forward to it and it got us both very relaxed to say the least.

Today we would be going home but not until 10 pm so we still had the day to do a little touring and shopping in Dumbarton. A few more gifts were bought, and we drove back to the estate for lunch. Afterwards, we packed all of our things and brought the luggage downstairs. We went for a long walk down past the farm and up the road. It was a leisurely walk, and we were well dressed for it. Tonight's dinner was a relaxed one. Fenella asked for a venison roast for dinner which was very good. James brought over some of the moose meat for them to enjoy at a later date. We sat in the small sitting room waiting on Callum who came in late and ate his dinner in the kitchen and then joined us.

"I'm glad you made it home in time to say goodbye to us Callum. I would have missed that if you hadn't." James gave him a big hug and Fenella as well. We gave them hugs and kisses and said we would be back in mid-March for the dress fittings. It was going to be a very quick trip though, probably only three days. William took the luggage and packages out and waited for us in the limo. We hugged Fenella and Callum again and said goodbye and got in the limo.

"I am going to miss those two. They have been wonderful hosts and Wade and I have enjoyed ourselves immensely." The ride to the airport was quiet. The plane was fueled and ready to go. Once our luggage was stowed, we got onboard. We went through the usual routine, James filled out the duty free forms for Canada and looked after anything that was owing for tax. We got into our seats for takeoff and once we were up in the air, Janet and Wade moved to other seats on the plane to go to sleep. James and I did the same. I woke up before James and went to the bathroom. When I came out James was awake, and he gave me a soft kiss and went into the bathroom. Ian was getting the coffee ready, and Janet and Wade were starting to stir. Breakfast this morning was going to be omelets and fresh fruit. When Janet and Wade freshened up they came to the back of the plane to join us.

"We'll be home in a few hours. I don't know about you, but I will be glad to sleep in my own bed tonight." We each looked at one another and burst out laughing because James had been sleeping in his own bed for the last four days. It seemed to relieve any tension that was in the air, and we laughed and joked the rest of the flight. We landed in Sudbury and walked off the plane with Janet and Wade. With hugs and kisses and their luggage and packages loaded in their car, they drove out of the airport. James and I got back on the plane for the remainder of the flight home. Drew brought us each a salad and some water. It was eerily quiet now on the plane.

"We will have a few days' rest at home and then the trip to Ottawa then you have to leave for Toronto and then you bring everyone back with you for Christmas. Time has flown by. Christina will be coming in to decorate the house so there will be a certain amount of chaos. I hope you will be ok with that." James said he would be fine because it would be happy chaos in their home. We landed in Edmonton two hours later, unloaded our luggage and packages and drove home. We both let out a collective sigh when we started up the drive. It took a couple of trips to get everything into the house and upstairs. I said that I would unpack in a little bit.

"Let's have a glass of wine in the sunroom. I have missed sitting there and watching out the windows." James wholeheartedly agreed with that and got a bottle of white wine up from the cellar. We sat with the bottle between us and stared into the woods. The quiet is what we both realized that we had missed.

"I have an idea, why don't I text Jonathan and give him tomorrow off as well. We can sleep in until we are ready to get up if we want. We can get dressed up and go out for dinner at Jason's and then have an early night. I have been wanting to have you all to myself for days and days." It sounded like an awesome idea. James texted Jonathan and then made reservations for 6:00 at Jason's. We went upstairs and unpacked and put everything away. James put my jewelry back in the safe, but I kept on the bracelet Annie gave me. I could feel the energy from the crystals.

We were both pretty beat by the time our heads hit the pillow that night and we slept in until 10:00 the next morning. James was in no hurry to get out of bed. He had that look in his eyes and I knew what that meant. By the time we got into the shower it was 11:30 and of course it was the shower, so when we finally got dressed and downstairs it was almost 1:00. I made us up a chef's salad and we ate in the sunroom.

I hadn't worn all of the dresses that I brought to Scotland, so after fixing my hair and putting on some makeup, I put on the dark pink embellished dress with long sleeves with the dark pink pumps that I bought to go with the dress. The dress was already heavily embellished, so I wore the jeweled cuff bracelet James gave to me in Scotland and the star necklace and earrings he gave me. James wore a dark grey designer suit with a pale blue silk shirt and blue and grey tie. He got out the sports car and we drove over to Jason's. Because it was a weeknight, there were hardly any customers and those that were in the restaurant, Jason kept in the main dining area. He cleared out the tables in the private room and it was only the two of us in there. We had champagne and a lovely pasta dish that was new on the menu. It was delicious, but we had no room for anything else. We finished off the champagne and went home. Once we were in, James turned on the alarm and we went upstairs. It was another glorious night of making love and we fell asleep after midnight.

We got up, showered, dressed, and went downstairs. Jonathan was in early, and we could smell coffee once we left the bedroom. Christina texted me early to see if she could get started on the décor today. She had a lot more than she thought and would appreciate the extra day. I said that it was fine, and she was going to be at the house around 9 am. We had breakfast and James went into his study.

I followed him, and we looked at all the photos we took. I picked up a number of frames when I went to the frame store weeks ago just in case we needed them. There were several photos that Janet took with James's phone of the two of us that he wanted to print out and frame. We also took a family photo of everyone at the Christmas party, which James also wanted to frame and hang up on our photo wall. While he was doing that I answered the door and let Christina and her crew in to do the decorations.

"Thanks for letting us come a day early. I had more decorations than I realized, and I am grateful to have the extra day to get everything done. It will be absolutely beautiful." I left her to go about getting things done. They were going to hang a wreath on James's office door because any other decorations would have been in the way. They worked like busy beavers and had the entire entry way and stairs done by the time they left. Tomorrow they were going to work strictly on the large dining room and living room. Nothing was being decorated downstairs. James and I agreed to keep that area clear, so people could go down and have fun without having to worry about knocking something over.

James and I went out to pick up our tree at the lot. He found out who the dealer was and requested a ten foot Fraser fir, which was only delivered yesterday, so it was very fresh. We took it home and put it up in the sunroom. We let it sit for a few hours to open out and then we spent the next several hours decorating it. I picked up lights months ago and some other beautiful ornaments from another store that I loved to get ornaments from. They would look really nice with the ones we got overseas. With the tree completely decorated, we asked Christina what she thought.

"You know I like it with only the ornaments and lights. I thought it was going to look a little bare, but you have lots of ornaments on there and it looks beautiful. I'm not just saying that either. If I thought it needed more I would tell you, trust me." With the tree approved by the decorator we sat down with a glass of wine. The smell from the tree was evoking thoughts of Christmas. Even James thought it smelled great.

By the time Sunday rolled around they had the entire house decorated. They worked early and late and got everything done. I was amazed at how quickly they got all of the decorations installed. The upstairs was done similar to that of Thanksgiving. There were different wreaths on each door and a Christmas themed throw on each bed. Christina bought tall metal glittery elves to put in each room along with a few other decorations. They looked so cute. In Ayleen's room she had Santa and his reindeer in her window and similar metal glitter elves throughout the room. It was enough to say Christmas without cluttering up the rooms. It looked amazing and even James was quite thrilled with it.

"Now, the floral centerpieces won't be here until the 18th. I went with a lot of red and white carnations, holly, and button mums, pinecones. I tried to stay away from spruce greenery because that tends to drop so I went with pine greenery. I think you noticed what we used on the railings is soft, so it won't be bristled if anyone touches it. I was thinking of your granddaughter when I chose it, so I hope that works out ok." It looked breathtaking. I thought I was wandering around in one of the big stores that decorated at Christmas.

"John will water the tree while we are in Ottawa. Then I will be home while James goes off to Toronto to handle some work related matters. I will be here when the floral centerpieces arrive." Christina said that she wanted me to text her when they came, and she would come and make sure they were exactly what she ordered. I was getting very excited now about Christmas.

But I was wondering what else I could get James. I was giving him the painting which was a pretty big gift. I gave him the new watch in Scotland. We got each other the down coats for Christmas but I wanted to get him a few other things to open. I would have to think about it. We left for Ottawa late morning and arrived in the afternoon.

We arranged for a limo so that Ross, Lindsay, and Ayleen would not have to come and get us. There was a bit of snow on the ground but only just to say it was there. Because his birthday was on a weeknight, we agreed to go to a local restaurant in Almonte for dinner. There was one I knew they liked so that is where James made reservations. After making a brief stop in Ottawa for egg rolls, the limo pulled up to their house and Ayleen and Freya came running out. It was cold out and she didn't have a coat on, and she was wearing her slippers. James picked her up and wrapped her inside his new down coat. We both decided to wear one when we left.

"Ayleen, you are going to catch your death of cold coming outside like that." I told James I could manage the luggage and he took Ayleen back in. Freya sat looking at me, so I gave her one of the smallest bags to take in. She had it between her teeth and I thought it was so cute. Lindsay got quite a laugh out of it.

"The both of them were waiting in the window for you. I think that Freya realized you were coming before Ayleen and kept jumping up and down. I see you are helping Gramma in with the bags. Good Freya." I took our luggage up to the bedroom. Ayleen was still tucked inside James's coat.

"Ayleen why don't you get down and let Grandpa take off his coat." She reluctantly got down and Ross hung the coats up in the closet.

"Sorry we are a little late, but we went into the city to pick up some egg rolls. It was a little bit out of our way, but they are so good, I had to get them." Ross was going to put on steaks but waited. Lindsay was preparing a potato and vegetable. While we were waiting we had a few egg rolls. Now James understood what I was talking about.

"Wow these are really good. We will have to get more frozen ones to have at New Year's. We are having mostly finger foods and canapes instead of a great big meal. I think after the big meal at Christmas we will appreciate something a bit smaller. But I have to say I love these egg rolls. We should put in an order for when we go to see Christelle tomorrow and pick them up on the way back home. I think we will probably need at least ten or twelve dozen with lots of that plum sauce. We can put them in the freezer here and then in coolers with ice to keep them frozen." Dinner was ready, and we sat down to eat. Ayleen had lots to say and pointed to her teeth that were missing. She did not feel awkward about them at all.

"Gramma I can feel my other teeth coming in, but I don't think they will be here before Christmas." I said that was fine, they would be in when they were in. We were telling them about the trip to Germany and Austria.

"Austria is so beautiful; I am hoping that James and I can go back again for a few weeks. Germany was beautiful too, but Austria was something else." It was getting late, and they had to go to work and school the next day. We were going to have lunch with Christelle and pick up the egg rolls and plum sauce.

Chapter 12

The next morning Ayleen knocked to see if she could come in to say good morning and give us a hug and kiss before she went off to school. We said she could come in and she jumped up on the bed and gave us both a big hug and kiss.

"See you after school. Have a nice day." She was off. They left and then James and I got up, showered, got dressed and had some coffee before we went to the city to see Christelle. We told her we would pick her up at her place. I was so happy to see her. James got out and gave her a hug and kiss and helped her into the limo.

"Gee talk about driving around town in style. I could get used to this." We were going to a favourite restaurant of hers. She told the driver which one and he knew where it was. On the drive over, I gave her the gift that I bought her. She wasn't going to open it, but I wanted her to. Her eyes popped, and she couldn't believe what it was.

"Wow are these diamonds, wow. This is so beautiful, and you know of course it is my spirit animal. Thank you so much for this but you shouldn't have done this. I mean I love it, but you shouldn't have done it." She then opened James's gift which was an expensive watch. I thought she was going to faint she was so surprised. She thanked James over and over and I helped her to put the watch on. I told her she could open the other gifts at Christmas.

"You guys have been so good to me, and I can't thank you enough. I mailed off your presents before you told me you were coming, and you should get them soon." Over lunch we told her all about the trip overseas and the house was now decorated for Christmas. She was going to be at her weekend place for Christmas and not doing too much. James went up to pay the bill while we sat and chatted a bit more.

"Cassandra these gifts are too much. What I got you guys for Christmas is nothing compared to what you gave me. I feel a little awkward." I told her that any gift she gave James, and I would be priceless because it came from her.

"Christelle, please don't feel that way ok. I am having hard time myself trying to think of things to get James. It's not easy to buy something for someone who has everything. I know he is going to go crazy for me at Christmas and I did get the painting done for him, but I still want him to open more than one gift. I am in a bit of a hard place too. I didn't know he got you the watch, really, I didn't, and you know that as soon as I saw this wolf I had to get it for you. As you so often told me, let him spoil you, well, let us spoil you. James knows how important you are to me, and he would do anything for you, you know that right?" She said she did and would not feel guilty about the gifts. James came back to the table. I would have kept her for longer, but we had to get back and she wasn't feeling that great. We called in our order for the egg rolls before we picked up Christelle and after we dropped her off home we picked them up.

We put them in Ross's freezer until we were going home. There were still a few hours until they came home from work and school, so we gave Sonya a quick call to meet her for coffee in Almonte. When we got there she was already waiting inside. We got a few looks getting out of the limo and going inside. Sonya was laughing a bit when we walked in.

"Did you have a nice trip overseas. I saw some of your pictures. Austria looks quite nice, very historic." I said that it was, and I thought she would like it.

"We had a wonderful time, the four of us. While James and Wade went for a run each morning Janet, and I would have a spa treatment. It was wonderful, and the Christmas markets were everything I thought they would be. So have you had anyone interested in your place?" She said there were three different couples who came back a few times.

"The possession date is for February 1st if it sells now. I want to thank you both for buying me that home in Toronto. I am taking all the furniture from here because it is a big house. Richard is moving in with me, I think you both knew that. He has agreed to let me go furniture shopping to fill up the rest of the house and he is going to pay. I can't say as I have ever had that happen before. I want him to come with me, which he said he would. I'm looking forward to it and I know Rhonda is looking forward to the job with you James." James was pleased that he could do this for her. The house was bought and would close the middle of January. There wasn't a thing that Sonya wanted to change to the house. Even the paint colours she loved, so she would be able to move right in when she sold the condo. Richard was having a cleaning company come in to give the house a thorough cleaning.

"Have you got your house ready for Christmas. I can't wait to see how you have it decorated." I said that Christina and her crew were out for the last four days working from early morning till late at night. She had a much larger crew this time, but they got it all done.

"Wait until you see it, it's like the most amazing decorations ever. All the rooms look so nice. I can't wait until you see everything. I guess I get a little excited about Christmas." James laughed at me.

"Nah you are not showing your excitement at all sweetheart." Now he and Sonya were both laughing but I knew it was in good fun. We spent an hour with her and then went back to Ross's. We got home before they did, and we let ourselves in. We were not getting dressed up for dinner. I was going to wear my dark brown leather pants with a light blue cashmere pullover. James was wearing his black wool pants and a pale lavender shirt. When Ross got home he went up to shower and change right away. Lindsay and Ayleen pulled in about a half hour after him. Lindsay went up to shower while Ross changed Ayleen into her purple cotton pants and purple sweater that she got from her grandparents for her birthday. Lindsay came down in a pair of brown wool pants and a cream coloured sweater.

We went to the restaurant in the limo. Ross told the driver which restaurant and how to get there. Ross and James sat at the front of the limo and the ladies sat at the back. Ayleen was now in a booster seat, no more car seat. She sat between Lindsay and me. The restaurant was not overly full, so we got to our table and water and menus were brought.

The dinner went well, and we even had a birthday cupcake for Ross, which he didn't mind getting at the restaurant. We went back to the house; James told the limo driver what time to be here the next morning. We went and sat in the living room and gave him his gift. I picked up the Scottish Skeen for him because I knew that he collected knives. James picked him up a brand new tablet that was not even out on the market yet. He opened up my gift first and was rather surprised.

"Wow Mum this is really cool. Don't you wear these with kilts James?" James said they did indeed and that he, Quinn, and Duncan would have theirs when they wore their kilts for the wedding. I hadn't really asked Ross whether he was willing to wear a kilt or not. It was only going to be for the ceremony and then they were changing into suits.

"I guess if you, Quinn, and Duncan are wearing kilts I would look a little out of place if I didn't. If it means a lot to you, I will wear one as well but not for the whole night." James was pleased that he was willing to do this.

"It is only for the ceremony, then we are changing into suits. I am very pleased you are willing to do this. I know that for Duncan, Quinn, and me it is a normal thing, so I hope you won't be too uncomfortable and so you know, you can wear underwear." Ross was happy about that. Then he opened the gift from James and couldn't believe that he got him a new tablet. It was much bigger than his other one, which Ayleen was always using.

"It is fully loaded with every application you will need and every app. My tech team has created a fool proof firewall that nobody will be able to penetrate so you can feel easy using it for any banking or online purchases. They will also be sending you updates to install to keep it current. You are completely secure on this tablet." He thanked James very much for the gift.

He studied the Skeen a bit more and realized that it was carved from a rare stone. James was telling him all about it which made Ross even more impressed. He gave me a big hug and kiss and James as well. It was getting late and time for bed. We were leaving for the airport at the same time they were going off to work and school. Ayleen gave us big hugs and kisses and would see us in the morning before she went to school. Everyone turned in.

Morning came pretty fast, at least that is what it seemed to me and James. We didn't bother to shower in the morning, just washed up got dressed, packed up our luggage and put it in the limo. We gave Ayleen a great big hug and kiss and said we would see her in a few days. We said goodbye to Ross and Lindsay and said the same. We left before they were ready to head out. The plane was there and ready to leave when we got onboard. The crew that flew us over from Scotland went back on a commercial flight. It was now the Toronto crew that would be flying.

The limo driver took our overnight bags out of the trunk of the limo and placed them by the stairs. The egg rolls and plum sauce were in several large coolers that went in the cargo hold. We didn't have much luggage, so we had it stowed in the front storage area.

Martin closed the door; Rachel went through the security procedure, and we were taxing out the runway and preparing to take off. It was a clear day for flying and there was little to no turbulence. Rachel brought us coffee and Martin was busy with the eggs, sausage, and toast. When we were at altitude, Martin brought our breakfast. Rachel refilled our coffee, and we talked about last night.

"I am glad Ross is going to wear a kilt. I know that means a lot to you. He was very impressed with the tablet. Did you get one for Lindsay for Christmas? Ayleen can have Ross's now, and Lindsay will probably give hers to her Mom." James did in fact get Lindsay one that was the same as Ross's. He contemplated getting Ayleen one but thought he should wait for another year. She started taking coding in class, thanks to James and the volunteers from his office. They would go to the school on rotations of teaching for a three-week period and then they would rotate and go back to the office and someone else would do a three-week rotation. Doing it this way allowed the school to give them the program for an entire year. We got back to Edmonton around 5:00 pm and went home. James was leaving the day after for Toronto. He was going to leave the next morning but pushed his meeting back because he wanted a day at home with me before everyone arrived and we still had a lot of gifts to wrap.

We had a lovely dinner and then had some wine in the sunroom. We went up to bed around 9:00 but neither one of us was terribly sleepy which led to us having a passionate night. Eventually we fell asleep around 1:00 and slept in until 9:30. Jonathan was in and made coffee but saw that we were sleeping in and made up some fresh muffins.

We spent the morning relaxing a bit and then set about wrapping all the gifts. By the time dinner rolled around we finished wrapping every one of them. I took some wrapping paper, ribbon and bows upstairs to wrap the painting I got for James. I was still trying to think what else I could get him. It was so difficult because he had pretty much everything. I put in a call to Hans to see if he could help me. James did not wear anything other than a watch.

"Hans, I want to get James a few more things for Christmas but I am struggling to come up with ideas. I thought maybe you might be able to help me. I was looking online for ideas and saw some rather unique cuff links. They are called Tateossian cuff links, I don't suppose you would have them, would you?" He said he did and that he had a few different ones. I said that I would like as many different ones as he had, and that James would be in Toronto so if he could wrap them up in Christmas paper and wrap them again in brown paper, so he wouldn't know what they were. They would be unique and not something he already had. Most of his cuff links were plain gold or platinum so these would be a nice addition. Hans said that he would be happy to do that.

"Since I have you on the phone Cassandra, have you thought about a wedding band for James? We have some interesting new ones that I think he would like." He said he would send me some pictures to my phone to have a look at. I agreed I wanted something different for James but not with any stones. As we were talking the pictures came in.

"Wow I like the ones with the rope design and the inlay design, what are they made of?" Hans said that they were palladium with platinum inlays.

"I think James would like the palladium with a hammered or braided platinum inlay. They are very beautiful bands. But you can have a look whenever you come to Toronto again. These will not be going out of stock any time soon." We were planning to go to Toronto right after we took everyone home after New Year's, so I would come by and have a look then. I found James in his study going through some emails.

"Rodney called, and he wants to come over to show us the new perfume. It isn't in the bottle yet, but he's excited to see what you think about it. I told him to come right over, I hope that was ok." I said yes, and the doorbell rang. I answered the door and welcomed Rodney in. We went back into James's study.

"I have two samples here and I will put some on a card for you to smell and then you can let me know which fragrance you like the most. I have the atomizers ready to put the fragrance in, but I need to know how many you want for Christmas." Rodney waved one card in front of me. It was such a pretty scent, and I knew it was one I would wear. He gave me a minute for my nose to clear of the first scent and then he waved the second one in front of me. I loved this one even more.

"I don't need to know what all went into the making of it, but I think I could detect plumeria in the second one and I love that. It has a kind of heady fragrance to it which I also love. Now, will this one react differently on each person or is the first one more likely to do that." Rodney thought my guess on the second one was very good.

"Yes, the second one does have plumeria in it and it is quite a heady fragrance. It has the same characteristics as the other fragrance you wear but not all of the same combinations. This one is less likely to react differently with each person who wears it. The first one however will do that more easily because of what is in it." James and I both said we did not want to know what the combinations were.

"Rodney can you have four of the two ounce atomizers of the first fragrance ready for the 19th. I realize it is a very short time frame, but it is a small quantity, so I think it is doable. That is the fragrance we will call 'Uniquely Yours' and the fragrance that Cassandra loves will be for her, it will not be sold anywhere. I know you still have some of your favourite French perfume, so we can wait until that is used up and then you can have your very own fragrance. I like the scent of it, and this might sound like a very proprietary term to use but when I smell it I think of when you are wearing it that you are mine, so if you don't object, we can call it 'Mine' and get Mark to come up with a bottle that is yours. Would that be ok?" Rodney said that he could easily get four bottles done up for that date and he would keep the second scent as Cassandra's. I was very much ok with the name and that I would pick out a bottle shape and colour after the holidays. Rodney left a small sample of the fragrance that was mine and then left and it was now James and I alone in the house.

"You really liked that second scent, maybe after I take a shower I should put some on and you can let me know how much you like it." James smiled and followed me up to the bedroom and into the shower. He showed me how much he liked the fragrance over and over and over again. James woke early and showered and got dressed. He was leaving for Toronto and last night was amazing. He could still smell her perfume. He leaned over to give Cassandra a kiss and hug.

"James have a safe flight and give me a call when you land." The smell of her perfume was so intoxicating to him that he very nearly got back into bed with her.

"That perfume is very arousing, but if I don't leave now, the crew will be wondering where I am. I love you and I love that new fragrance. I will call you when I land, so go back to sleep for a little while." He did not have to ask me twice; I fell asleep thinking of last night and the passion. I must have slept another hour before finally getting up.

When I stepped into the shower there was a box on the taps with a note from James 'a small token for all the wonderful times we have shared in the shower, love James.' When I opened the box it was a beautiful gold rope chain with matching earrings. When I finished showering, I put them on with my jeans and sweater and the star necklace and the bracelet from Annie. I sent James a text to thank him for the gift.

I grabbed some coffee and muffins and went out to the sunroom. I wasn't very hungry for anything else. Jonathan was busy making desserts and the food for Christmas and New Year's. Anything that he could prepare in advance and freeze, he was doing. All the baking made the house smell great. I sent a text to Roxie to confirm that she and Duncan were still coming on Boxing Day and that they were coming at New Year's.

She texted back they would be coming for both parties, but the kids were going to Maria's parents for New Year's this year. I gave Christelle a call to see how she was doing.

"I'm ok just tired a lot lately. I really love my watch and pendant. I will be at my other place over the holidays, so you can reach me there if you want. I'm going to have to let you go, I want to go and lay down for a bit." I told her to take care and would call again soon.

I spoke to Jonathan about hiring some help in the kitchen over the holidays. He was glad that I suggested it and was going to contact some of the students at the college. I went over to visit with the senior's, but they were all out for walks. I saw Mr. O'Leary and asked him how things were going with the sale of my unit. He said that all the paperwork was done, and it was with my lawyers. I apologized because I'd been so busy lately but would stop in there on my way home.

"A couple of the ladies left this box for you. They thought you would be by today." It was the Christmas stockings that I asked them to make for me. I would look at them at home. I went to the lawyers and signed the papers that I needed to for the sale of my condo, and they would courier me the cheque tomorrow.

I booked myself in for a facial and mani/pedi today. I didn't have the time for the massage but maybe between Christmas and New Year's. After the appointment was over I decided to get silly things to go in the stockings along with some chocolates and the perfume and makeup. Since we were giving them other gifts, I thought it would be fun to go this route for the stockings. I picked up enough stuff to go in everyone's stockings including mine and James's. When I got home, I hung up the stockings which were really pretty. I then wrapped all the stuffers with people's names on it so that I would know which stocking to put it in. I completely forgot to eat lunch, so Jonathan brought in some milk and a couple of muffins. I got a call from Lindsay, which was unusual, and asked if everything was ok.

"Oh yes everything is fine. I wanted to know what else I needed to pack for us. I know you have lots of clothes there for Ross, Ayleen, and I, so I didn't want to bring anything dressy when I knew you had things already there. I will bring the obvious things like pjs, robes and slippers and of course other clothes for Ayleen to play in. I will be bringing her snow suit, so she can play outside as well." I told her to bring some casual clothes like jeans and maybe something that they could work out in if they wanted.

"The others like to go for walks or runs but we also have exercise equipment downstairs if you don't want to go out. There will also be the days going tobogganing and skiing. Everyone will be dressing up for the photo and Christmas dinner, but New Year's is going to be very casual, so you have the list of things that I got you, Ayleen, and Ross, so fill in from there." I let her know that we had some movies for Ayleen if she wanted to watch them and others for the rest if anyone wanted to see a movie.

"I am going to order the limo to pick you guys up, so you don't have to leave your car at the airport. I'll get Sonya and Rhonda to go over to your place and you can leave from there. I think that will work out better don't you think." She said Ross was coming in and mentioned about the limo.

"He said that was a great idea." They were leaving Freya with her parents. I put in a call to the limo service that James was dealing with and requested the same driver because he knew where to go. It was arranged that they would be picked up at home on the 20th at 2:00 and taken to the airport. The plane was due to arrive at 3:00 so they would not have to sit around and wait.

So that was another thing off my list of things to do. I was still trying to think of something else that I could get James. I sent a text to Quinn asking him if he could help and hoped that I wasn't waking him up. He called and said I wasn't waking him up. The boys had nasty colds and had been up coughing. He told me that

James loved Shakespeare's plays when he was in university and read all his works but could never get his hands on a first edition. He knew James was hard to buy for because he had most of anything he wanted. He wished me luck on finding a first edition. I checked James's office to see if he had a first edition, but he didn't, and I texted Fenella to see if he had one in his office there. She let me know that he didn't. I did a lot of reading when I first moved into the condo and got to know the librarian at the local library. I decided to go there tomorrow morning and see if she could help me out. James called as I was getting into bed.

"Hello James, thank you again for the gift. How was your day?" He said that he was glad I liked it and his day had been crazy busy. He wanted to talk longer but he was so tired, he had to hit the sack. I told him I loved him and wished him a good night. The next morning, after breakfast I went over to the library. I went up to Miranda to see if she could help me with the first edition of the plays.

"Those are very hard to come by and they can be quite expensive. But I do know of a gentleman who is an avid collector. I only know him because when I was working at the main library in the city, he came in often to look over the classic collection we had, and we would often talk about books. He is a sweet old man and I keep in touch with him because he is alone. I can give him a call to see if he would be willing to have you go over and talk to him." I said that I would really appreciate that. When Miranda got off the phone she gave me his address and said that he would be expecting me at 1:00 today.

I hurried home to freshen up and change into a dress because I thought if he was old fashioned he might not appreciate seeing me show up in jeans. I put on a little makeup and then went out the door. I found his home easily which was a very small place, but it looked well maintained. I rang the doorbell, and it took several minutes for him to come to the door. I introduced myself saying that Miranda spoke to him about me. He looked to be in his mid to late 80's. He asked me to come into his sitting room where it was much warmer. There was a light snow overnight, but the roads were fine. I didn't want to stay in the city too long and face a lot of traffic going home.

"Please come in and have a seat by the fire. Can I get you anything?" I said that I was fine.

"Miranda tells me you are looking for a first edition of Shakespeare's plays. I am happy to say that I have several of his first editions and I do have the plays. Do you enjoy books Miss Harris?" I said that I did but I hadn't done much reading lately and that he could call me Cassandra.

"My fiancé is an avid reader, and he has loved Shakespeare since his university days. I don't know if you are willing to part with any of your first editions, but I would pay you whatever you were asking for it. I can see that you love books, you have so many of them and I understand that it would be hard to part with any of them." I wasn't sure if I was overdoing it, so I stopped talking.

"Cassandra, I am an old man, and I am not well. I live alone, never married and I have no family. Books are all that I have to take me places that I have never been, and they are good company. Shakespeare was a favourite of mine as well and I have spent many years collecting all that you see here. I am planning on donating the majority of my books to the library. I know that Miranda will be very pleased about that." My shoulders sank, and I thought that I hit a dead end. I was ready to give up and head home.

"But I will sell you his first edition plays, in fact all the ones that I have of Shakespeare, and I have a few others that I think your fiancé may also enjoy. I know that these are worth a lot of money, but I didn't buy them as an investment to sell at a later date to make money. I bought them because I loved them, and I think, from what you say, that your fiancé feels the same way. I will sell them to you on the condition that they are never sold at an auction. You must agree that they will end up at a library for them to retain." I said that I would definitely promise him that. He wrote down on a piece of paper what he wanted for the ones he was going to part with. I looked at the amount.

"Mr. Jones, these are worth way more than this, even I know that, and I am willing to pay considerably more for them." He said that he was not interested in the money, he wanted them to go to a good home and to someone who would appreciate them as much as he has all these years. He would not let me write him a cheque for a penny more than he had written. I wrote him a cheque and he went to get boxes to put them in. The way he touched each book as he took it from the shelf and ran his hand over the cover, I knew it was difficult for him to part with them. I asked if he was sure he wanted to part with them and he looked at me and said he trusted me that they would be very well taken care of. They filled four big boxes, and I took each one out to the car, one at a time. As I was doing so I asked him if he was going to be spending the holiday with friends. He said that he had none and would be alone at home.

"Mr. Jones, it makes me sad to think that you will be here alone. I would like you to join us for dinner on Christmas Day. You have done me such a wonderful thing by selling me these books. I can send a car for you to bring you to our home. We would really love to have you." I could tell that he was a little emotional at my invitation.

"I have not celebrated Christmas since my parents died when I was twenty. It is a very generous offer, but I would not want to impose on your family." I told him it was no imposition and that I would not take no for an answer.

"It will give you a chance to talk to James about an author you both admire. I know it would mean a lot to him, so please say that you will come." He said that he would not refuse such a kind gesture.

"It will be mostly adults, but I do have a seven-year-old granddaughter, so I hope that children do not upset you." He said it would be a joy to be around my family. I would arrange for a car to pick him up Christmas Day at 4:30. We were going to have dinner at 6:00 if that would suit him. He said that was fine, he normally ate at 6:00 so it would not be an adjustment for him. He did, however, want to be home by 9:00 as he had medications to take and went to bed early. I promised I would have him home whenever he wished, I hugged him and thanked him for the generous gift and would see him on Christmas Day.

When I got home I took the boxes up to the bedroom. I had a variety of large Christmas boxes that would be perfect to hold the books. There were eight other individual first editions, which I wrapped and put in the safe. The Shakespeare ones, I put in a couple of the boxes and wrapped them and put them in the games room with all the other gifts. I was finally done shopping. I had dinner and a glass of wine and sat in the sunroom. Jonathan hired three students to help him out in the kitchen. They were busy helping him to prepare for the next few days when everyone would be here. After Jonathan and the students left, I went up to bed waiting for James to call. He was right on cue.

"Hello darling, how are you? What have you been up to today? I got a package delivered to the penthouse for you. It doesn't say where it is from, were you expecting something?" I said that I was.

"Can you please bring it with you when you come home. I have had a very productive day, and I met a very interesting gentleman. He is all alone, so I invited him to Christmas dinner. I hope you are ok with that. I can't tell you anything about how I met him, or it would ruin a surprise." James laughed and said that it was fine with him.

"Don't forget we are having the Christmas Eve lunch with the staff. Jonathan knows and is preparing something light. I know he is joining us for the meal on Christmas Day. What did you do that you can tell me that made it such a productive day?" I told him that I bought silly gifts for the stocking stuffers along with some chocolates.

“The stockings the ladies did up are so festive, wait till you see them. I thought going with silly gifts would make it fun. I got some for your stocking and mine as well. So how have your meetings gone?” He was in meetings the last two days with Robert the new vice president of security. Robert wanted to discuss some queries that the company had been getting from south of the border.

“I gave my reasons to Robert why I didn’t think it was a good time to do any deals right now and he agreed with me. Perhaps we can look at it again at a later date. Rodney said he had the fragrances ready and would be bringing them over tomorrow. Mark got really nice gift boxes done. Speaking of Mark, I have a feeling that things have changed between him and Rhonda and Sonya and Richard. I got the impression that they were going to be joining us for the holidays. Have you heard anything?” I said that I had not but would give Sonya a call in the morning.

“I can hear the fatigue in your voice James, let’s say good night and we can talk tomorrow.” He agreed and said he loved me and wished me good night. The next morning, I was raring to go. I grabbed some coffee and went to the sunroom to call Sonya.

“Morning, how are you? Anything new on your end?” I could hear the giggle in her voice.

"I was going to call you this morning. Richard gave me a ring, not an engagement ring but one that said we were a couple. He came down the other day and said that he didn't want to put off telling me his feelings any longer. I admit that I was glad and was in fact holding my feelings back as well. I didn't think things would move as quickly but Richard pointed out we were not getting any younger and he didn't want to be a guest in the new home. He spent the night and not in the spare room." I was speechless but happy for her.

"Well good for you. He's a good man Sonya and he will look after you and you won't want for anything. I presume that you want Richard to come with you for the holidays. That is fine with us, we don't have any problem with that at all. What about Rhonda, how are things going with her and Mark?" She said that they too had taken a more serious step and Mark also gave her a ring, again not an engagement ring, but it was the first step for the both of them.

"She was hoping it would be ok for Mark to come as well for the holidays. I was sure you wouldn't mind so I told her I would ask." I said that was fine as well. The more the merrier. After we hung up I texted James to let him know. He called back within moments.

"Wow, that's great. I'm happy for the both of them as I am sure you are as well. I will pick up watches for both Richard and Mark as a gift from us. It is too late to get them coats like everyone else I think. What about your gentleman friend should we get him anything?" I told James that he was quite ill and really didn't have a need for anything, but an idea popped into my head.

"I know, we can take a group photo with him, and you can print it out and we will put it in one of the extra frames that I have in your office. I know that will mean a lot to him and he will treasure it." James didn't respond for a bit.

"You have such a big heart Cassandra. That is such a thoughtful gift for him. I hate to cut this short, but I do have to go to a meeting, and I have an evening meeting, so I may not get the chance to call you tonight, but I will send you a steamy text." I told him I loved him and would await the text. Later that night as I was sitting in bed, I got the text from James and the text was very steamy and it had me having wonderful dreams all night long. The next morning, I was coming down the stairs and Christina was at the door.

"I apologize if I am too early, but I wanted to get all the flowers placed. The florist actually arrived right behind me and is taking the boxes in through the kitchen." We went into the kitchen to see and once the boxes were laid out on the floor, Christina started taking them to where they belonged. It looked like chaos but wasn't really. Jonathan said that he was picking up the bird on the 23rd so that there wouldn't be last minute rushing. The students were a great help and would also be doing all the serving of the food on Christmas Day and New Year's Eve. I checked on Christina who finished putting all the flowers in the rooms.

"We are now having thirteen for Christmas dinner, so we will need to set those places." Christina bought more than enough china and cutlery to set the table with so adding three more people was not a problem. She did up cards for place settings and I gave her the names and she wrote them out in calligraphy. With the flowers and centerpieces placed, it was smelling very much like Christmas. The tree looked beautiful, and the house looked perfect.

After Christina left, Rodney stopped by with the fragrances. The gift boxes were beautiful, very Victorian. He brought an extra bottle for me because my fragrance would not be ready until the New Year. Now everything was set for the holidays, and it was to wait for the arrival of everyone. I was so excited. James had the suv at the airport but texted that he was going to order a stretch suv because he knew that not everyone would fit in our suv. Jonathan and the students were very busy in the kitchen, but he made me up a salad for lunch, which I took to the sunroom to enjoy.

Snow was falling now in big, beautiful flakes and it was starting to build up. The flakes were huge, and it looked so pretty. I checked on the news and it was forecasted to be about ten centimeters, enough to cover the ground and it be a white Christmas. It was only forecasted to snow today and then not again until after everyone got here. I checked on the ski hills and they were running at full capacity, so that would make some very happy.

I sent off a Christmas floral centerpiece to Christelle, Roxie, Judy, Janet, Fenella, Catherine, Alisa, Fiona and Glynnis from James and me. They would be delivered tomorrow. I went through my list of things to do to make sure I hadn't missed anything. James was giving all the staff bonuses, so that would take care of them.

The doorbell rang, and it was a courier with an envelope. It was probably the cheque for the house. When I opened it, that is what it was, but I didn't have time to go to the bank today. So now that chapter of my life was closed. I was getting ready to head to the sunroom when the doorbell rang again. It was another courier with a much larger box. I took it to James's study to open.

It was the gown and shoes I wore for the photo shoot and the one for Ayleen. I forgot that I asked Jacob to order them for me. They were already paid for, but it completely slipped my mind. Ayleen's was simply adorable, and I thought perhaps I could get a photo of her and I in them when Jennifer was here. Jacob enclosed a note 'I hope you will both get a chance to wear this on a special occasion, enjoy, Jacob.' I took the gowns and the shoes upstairs and hung the gowns in my closet and put the shoes on the shelf. I remembered that I bought Ayleen the diamond unicorn and thought it would look perfect with the dress.

I knew that James was not going to be calling this evening, so I took a glass of wine out to the sunroom, turned on the Christmas lights and put on some Christmas music. I was blissfully happy. James sent me a text that had me blushing a little. I told him he was being very naughty and would end up with coal in his stocking. He sent back a laughing emoji. I couldn't wait until he came home tomorrow. I had another glass of wine because I knew I was going to be too excited to sleep. The snow was coming down heavier now and there was a good amount already on the ground. I thought I was going to have trouble sleeping but the wine had me out like a light.

The next morning the snow stopped thankfully, and the sun was coming out, but it was cold. John was busy plowing the driveway but was leaving the paved walkway with snow on it. Perhaps he was waiting to see how much more snow he got before doing it. Jonathan was going to do a big dinner tonight with roast moose, roast potatoes and vegetables and a Yorkshire pudding. He would do up a different dessert for Ayleen because I wasn't sure she would like the Yorkshire pudding.

Dinner tonight was set, and the kitchen was busy. Moira was in to do a cleaning and had all the beds made up. I checked on the flowers and they were well watered. Ayleen's room was ready for her. I think for the rest of the morning I was walking on a cloud.

James texted that he picked up everyone and they were heading home. I wish I could have been on the plane with all of them. James, Richard, and Mark arrived in Ottawa before 1:00. When the stairs were pulled up he got out to see that Ross, Lindsay, Ayleen, Sonya, and Rhonda were getting out of the limo. He went down to greet them. Ayleen went running into his arms.

"Grandpa, we are going on your plane today. I am so excited." She stifled a squeal and James laughed. He gave her a big hug and kissed her. There had been snow in Ottawa but not enough to cause any issues. Although Ayleen did not want to get down, he put her down, so he could hug Ross, Lindsay, Sonya, and Rhonda. Richard and Mark came down the stairs to come and meet them.

"Ok, let's get everyone's luggage onboard because I know Gramma is at home and is probably climbing the walls with excitement to see everyone." Ayleen wanted to sit beside James at the window. He explained that they had to listen to the security procedure and get buckled in. Ross and Lindsay were smiling because she was paying attention to everything he said and to what Janine was saying. The plane started to taxi out on the runway. Ayleen was getting very excited. Ross told her not to squeal and she had to cover her mouth if she was going to. James had to laugh because she was not nervous at all. Richard and Sonya, Mark and Rhonda sat across the aisle. Although Ross and Lindsay and Ayleen were on the plane before they hadn't been up in it, so it was exciting for them. Once we were up in the air Maria and Janine came around for beverage orders.

"Ayleen, would you like some juice, I made sure that we got some orange juice if you would like some. Ross, I have whisky on board and wine, but you can have what you like." Ayleen happily accepted the juice and was looking out the window amazed at seeing everything below. James knew that there was no point in trying to have a conversation because she kept pointing things out. Once they got above the clouds she was amazed.

"Grandpa we are above the clouds, look at them and it is sunny out." Ross explained to her that the sun always shone above the clouds. She was thoroughly captivated. Her eyes were glued to the window.

"Well now it gives us a chance to talk while she is mesmerized by the clouds. We don't really have any formal plans as I am sure Cassandra has told you other than the photo shoot and Christmas dinner. We are having a big dinner tonight, but meals will be rather relaxed. Breakfast will be laid out in the morning, and you can have what you want. Lunches will be kept light, and dinners will be at 6:00. If you have plans to visit anyone, you are free to use the suv to go where you want. Cassandra sent me a text as I landed to say that we got a good bit of snow so for the skiers and snowboarders I am sure that is good news. We have a stretch suv picking us up at the airport in Edmonton because my suv would not be able to accommodate everyone and luggage. I'm sure Ayleen will get a kick out of that. I'll be going in the suv, and you guys will be following me in the limo." At the mention of her name, she turned around to look and smile but went right back to looking at the clouds.

Maria and Janine were getting ready to serve a late lunch. For Ayleen they had chicken fingers and salad and for the rest of it was salad with grilled chicken. Ross switched to water, but Lindsay had a glass of wine as did Sonya and Rhonda. Once lunch was over James, Richard and Mark had a bit of business to discuss.

"If you will excuse us for a little bit, we need to get a little business out of the way and then it will be all fun and games." Ayleen was still looking out the window but turned around as James moved to another seat.

"Mommy, I have to use the bathroom." Lindsay went with her while Ross talked with Sonya and Rhonda.

“Rodney dropped off the fragrances at the house. Mark you said you had some mockups for the bottle for Cassandra’s fragrance.” He pulled out his tablet to show me the bottle. It was beautifully shaped and a lavender colour glass. The lettering was in a deep purple.

“I think she is going to love this one. The fragrance won’t be ready until the New Year though. Rodney wants to concentrate on creating enough of the ‘Uniquely Yours’ to have it ready for some local stores for the last minute Christmas shoppers.” Richard indicated that they now had the staff needed for the textile business to start up and had a list of applicants for the geothermal office.

“That is good news. We can start the interview process in the New Year. Now unless you guys have some other more pressing business, I say we put anything else on hold until after the holidays. Let’s go back and join the others and have fun.” They got up and rejoined the others. Ayleen was still looking out the window.

“I can’t believe how quiet she is being, who knew all it took was clouds.” Ayleen turned back around in her seat and wanted to watch a movie. Ross selected one from the onboard server and she sat with earphones on watching her favourite show.

"She's a good traveler, most kids are fussy and hard to control. I'm glad about that because the flight over to Scotland will be much longer. Fortunately, most of the flight will be at night and she will be sleeping." By the time her movie was over, it was almost time to land.

"Ayleen, we have to put your seatbelt back on, we are going to be landing soon and then it will be off to see Gramma." She sat back while James got her buckled up again.

"Grandpa, I love flying on your plane and seeing all the clouds. They are so pretty and fluffy from up here." The captain advised the flight crew to prepare for landing. Maria came around and gathered up all the dishes and drink containers. The landing was smooth. Lindsay told Ayleen to hold her nose and blow so that her ears wouldn't get blocked from the change in altitude.

James texted me to let me know that they landed, and they were going to load up the suv and limo and drive around to pick up Nicole and Austin and then home. It seemed like he just called, and they were pulling up the drive at 3:30. I put on a coat and boots and went out to meet them. Ayleen ran up into my arms and gave me a big hug and kiss.

"Gramma I love your home; it is so pretty. The plane ride was so much fun, and I got to see all the clouds from up high. They were very pretty to look at." I hugged everyone else, and Ayleen and I went hand in hand into the house. Moira and the girls came up to help with coats and things and then went back down to their house. Sonya, Richard, Rhonda, Mark, Austin, and Nicole went off to the sunroom with James to get everyone drinks. I started showing Ross, Lindsay, and Ayleen around. I showed them the large dining room first.

"Wow Gramma, that's a big table and look at all the pretty flowers. Where am I going to sit Gramma?" I showed her that her place card was right next to me, and Lindsay was on the other side. James came back to join us, and we went to his study where he could show Ayleen where he hung her painting.

"I like it on that wall Grandpa." She went around to the other side of his desk to sit in his chair.

"Gramma you look pretty in this picture. I love your dress." I had a surprise for her but was not going to tell her today. The tour continued, and we showed them their rooms. First Ross and Lindsay's, which they loved, and then Ayleen's.

"Everyone get ready for the squeal." I opened the door and I think it was probably the loudest squeal yet.

"Gramma it is so pretty, and I love the purple and look there is a Sparky here and I have my favourite animal blanket. I love my room; can I play up here with the toys." I told Lindsay that it would be fine.

"Ayleen, we are going downstairs first to show you around more and then if you want to come back up and play, you will know where to go when you want to come down. Is that ok?" She said it was and we showed them the living room, small dining room and then out to the sunroom which went past the kitchen. We introduced Jonathan and he introduced the students who were helping him. We went out to the sunroom where the others were already seated. Everyone loved the tree and the decorations.

"Ross, Lindsay what would you like a drink?" Ross said he would have a whisky and Lindsay was going to have a white wine.

"This is a beautiful home Mum; I love the real tree. You can smell it as soon as you come in the room." Ayleen went up to the tree to smell it and touch it.

"Is this a real tree Daddy?" Ross told her it was, and she had to be careful of all the ornaments. It was then that they noticed the ornaments on the tree. Ayleen loved her ornament.

"We had the same ones duplicated so you could take them home for next year. Ayleen look out at the bird feeders and all the pretty birds." She did for two seconds and then asked if she could go back up to her room to play. I asked if she wanted me to go with her and she said no she knew the way. James watched to make sure she didn't get lost.

"She's good, she's up the stairs already. Dinner will be ready in an hour so if you want to take your luggage up to your room and take some time to unpack, we can have another drink before dinner." I told Sonya, Rhonda, and Nicole that they were in the same rooms as before. It gave us a chance to say hello. James pulled me into his arms and kissed me.

"Hello darling it is so good to be home and I love all of the decorations. The tree looks really nice all lit up and I can't wait to see the driveway." I told him that I had them on last night.

"By the way I have several things in the safe, you must promise not to touch them or pick them up." He said that he wouldn't touch them. I put them at the very back of the safe and moved everything else up. James remembered the package and went to get it from his briefcase.

"Oh, thank you, I will take that upstairs, no touching or shaking." James was laughing. I went down to see how Ayleen was doing.

"May I come in." She looked up and said yes.

"It's your house Gramma of course you can come in. I love my room and I put my dolly on my bed see. She likes it here too. I am glad that Mommy and Daddy's room is right across the hall just like at home." I showed her the bathroom and that there was her favourite animated animal night light for her. She said that was nice, but she wasn't afraid of the dark. I went to put the package in my room. I knew that Hans already wrapped them, so it was not something I had to get done. Ayleen was happily playing with the toys that we got her. Sonya and Richard came back down the hall.

"I love all the decorations, everything is very Christmassy, and the flowers are beautiful." We went back down to the sunroom.

"James, I forgot to show Ross and Lindsay downstairs and maybe Ayleen might like to see the movie room." He went up to her room and she came back down with him holding his hand. He took Ross and Lindsay downstairs to show them around. The only room out of bounds for the moment was the room with the arcade games in it. I poured myself a glass of wine and sat down. When they came back Ayleen was still with James, holding his hand.

"Ayleen would you like something to drink, a juice or water." She asked for a juice, but Lindsay said it was going to be her last because she had a lot on the plane.

"You know what happens when you drink too much juice Ayleen." She promised she would not do that. She whispered in my ear.

"I won't pee in the bed Gramma, I promise. I will run to the bathroom." I told her I appreciated that. I let Lindsay know that I bought the sheet protectors anyway, just in case.

"You have a lot of nice decorations Gramma." I said thank you. Jonathan came in to say that dinner was ready. We would be eating in the large dining room while everyone was here. Jonathan and his students brought in the meal and served everyone. Lindsay made up Ayleen's plate. As far as she was concerned it was roast beef.

The meal was wonderful, and Ayleen ate everything on her plate, and she loved dessert. I told Jonathan she loved chocolate, so he made her a chocolate mousse. The rest of us, or those who wanted it, had the Yorkshire pudding. After dinner, we went into the sunroom again to have coffee or drinks. Plans were being made for tomorrow. Rhonda, Mark, Austin, Nicole, and James were going to go snowboarding. When Ayleen heard that she wanted to know if we could go tobogganing.

"You have the mind of a steel trap. I didn't think you would remember that Grandpa said when they went skiing we could go tobogganing." Ross said she didn't forget anything. Sonya and Richard said they would go for a walk around the property.

"James, you will have to see if John has cleared it. There is quite a lot of snow on there and it might be difficult to walk." Ayleen started to talk to me about something. James stood in front of Sonya and Richard talking to them. After a few minutes, they said that perhaps they would walk out and around the subdivision instead. They didn't want to trouble John. I thought no more about it.

"James, we can't fit everyone in the suv; I can stay behind here as I have a few things I can do." He said it wasn't necessary as they talked about snowboarding on the plane he asked the service to send the stretch suv to come back tomorrow.

"If everyone is agreeable we will leave here at 8:30 tomorrow morning to be on the hill at 9:00 and come back at 1:00. I have arranged for the women to go and have facials and mani/pedis at 2:30 for the photo shoot. We will be done by 5:30 and home in time for dinner." Ross, Lindsay, and I will take Ayleen tobogganing while the others went to the ski hill.

"We can grab a quick bite at the ski hill, but we have to be back no later than 1:00. Richard, the suv will be here in case you want to take Sonya out for lunch, or you can stay in, just let Jonathan know." It was agreed we would get up at 7 am, have breakfast and leave for the hill. We talked and laughed until it was time to go to bed. James and I had a very heated and passionate night. It was breakfast buffet in the morning. Ayleen ate well and then Lindsay got her ready to go. She brought her snowsuit, and the others had the proper gear for the snow. Even Ross and Lindsay had snow pants.

"I forgot to say that tomorrow morning, all of the guys the photographer would like very much if you would go to the barber in town to get a proper shave please. I booked appointments for you starting at 9 am. James is going to take you." When we got to the ski hill Ayleen wanted me to go down the hill with her. When we got near the bottom we tipped over, but we were laughing like crazy.

"Ok, Ross you go now. I don't want to hurt my back." He and Ayleen and then Lindsay and Ayleen made many trips up and down the hill.

I could see Rhonda, Mark, and James snowboarding. Nicole and Austin chose to ski. I was very impressed by James's skill with the snowboard. After a couple of hours in the snow, everyone came down to the lodge to have something to eat. Rhonda was laughing.

"You've got skills there James. Where did you learn to snowboard like that?" James had to fess up and tell them that he was on the senior ski and snowboard team in university and that he tried out for the British national ski team. They did very well and won quite a few medals. That broke Rhonda up laughing. After lunch, we went back home. Richard and Sonya were enjoying sitting and talking in the kitchen with Jonathan. It got chilly out and it started to snow a bit more.

"I'm glad we came back without any bumps or bruises. That would not have gone well for the photo tomorrow. Ok so for tomorrow not to come across bossy but I have been asked by the photographer that you wear what she has on this list." I read out to everyone what she requested.

"I promise I will not tell you what to wear after the photo is done." Everyone was in complete agreement because they knew that was why I took them shopping in the first place, so nobody argued.

"Now ladies we have to scoot out the door for our spa appointment. Lindsay I can look after Ayleen while you are having your facial. I had my appointment a couple of days ago, so I am good for tomorrow." It was an enjoyable afternoon for the girls. They got polishes that would go with what they would be wearing. I asked for Ayleen to have a lavender colour put on her nails and toes. They came out of their facials feeling really good and sat down in a private room for the mani/pedis. Ayleen was having a lot of fun. I let them know that I booked a full day after Christmas to have the works.

"Ayleen, since you already have your nails and toes done, this is going to be an appointment for the adults. You won't mind staying at the house with Daddy and Grandpa will you." She said that was ok with her. When everyone was done, we went back home. It started to snow a little bit more.

"We have hair and makeup coming for the ladies at 11 am, gents you will be at the barber's. Jennifer will be here at 1:00 and she wants to be out of here by 3:00. She will be taking photos of Ross, Lindsay, and Ayleen; me and James, then the five of us together, then the group photo, then Sonya and Richard, then Rhonda and Mark, then Nicole and Austin, then the six of you, then just Sonya, Nicole, and Rhonda then I will be having her do some of Ayleen and me. While she is doing Sonya and her group, Ayleen and I will be changing. Ayleen I will show you the dress after and you can try it on, but you can't say anything." She promised she wouldn't.

Jonathan let us know dinner was ready, so we went into the large dining room to eat. When we finished we went back into the sunroom to have coffee. Ross, Lindsay, Rhonda, Mark, Nicole, and Austin went down to watch a movie. Ayleen wanted to stay with us, and I took her up to try on her dress. She loved it and didn't want to take it off, but I said it was for tomorrow. We went back down to the sunroom talking away and I told Ayleen to look out at the trees. Several deer came out to feed at the trough. She was fascinated to see them so close.

"Gramma look at the little one." I told her that it was probably born this year in May or June. She thought they were so cute. She was starting to get tired, so I passed her over to James and went down to let Lindsay know.

"Ayleen come with me it is time to have a bath and then pjs and bed. You can come back down to say good night to everyone after you get your pjs on." After half an hour she came back down, hair dried and ready for bed.

"Grandpa will you come up and read to me until I fall asleep." I knew that must have made James feel so good. I was not going to feel bad because she asked him. It made me very happy.

"I would love to. Do you have a favourite story? Did you notice that we got some story books for you and put them in the bookcase in your room?" She said she did and picked one out before coming downstairs. Lindsay said she would head back downstairs then. James took her up and got her tucked into bed and started to read her the story. I quietly went up because I wanted to video tape some of it. Not all of it, just enough so that he could look back on it as a good memory.

"James is sitting on this little chair in her room. It is hysterical. He is reading away to her, and she is having such a hard time keeping her eyes open, poor thing, she's had a full day." Richard went into the kitchen to get another pot of coffee.

"Are you upset that she wanted James and not you. I can only imagine that you've been looking forward to that moment." I said it was fine. I read stories to her at their place.

"It will mean a lot to James, probably more than it would me, so I am happy for him." Richard came back with the coffee, and we had another cup. James came down about twenty minutes later.

"She is out cold. I left the nightlight on in the bathroom, she said that would be ok even though she wasn't afraid of the dark. I doubt that she will wake up until mid-morning." Sonya and I looked at one another because we knew that would not be the case. The others came up from the movie room and said they were going to turn in. Richard and Sonya decided to head up as well. Now it was James and I alone in the sunroom.

"I think we should move all the gifts to the spare bedroom. I think we should have done that in the first place because I know they will want to use the arcade games in there." It took us several trips, but we got them moved. I printed out a sign that the room was off limits. The next morning there was a knock at our door. James started to laugh.

"Is that a unicorn knocking at our door." We could hear her giggle outside.

"You'd better come in little unicorn." She opened the door and came bounding into the room and jumped up on the bed.

"Gramma I slept the whole night in my room. I only had to get up once to go to the bathroom. I was a little scared and knocked on Mommy and Daddy's door and Mommy came in and stayed with me until I fell back asleep. You have a very big room Gramma and I like your big bed, there's lots of room for the three of us."

She nestled down in between the two of us. I could see the delight in James's eyes. Lindsay came to the door as Ayleen left it wide open.

"I'm sorry to bother you but I seem to have lost Ayleen. Do you know where she is?" She started to giggle under the covers, Lindsay held back a laugh.

"I guess I will have to call out a search party to looking for missing Ayleen." She flew up out of the covers laughing.

"I'm here Mommy I was hiding." Lindsay couldn't hold back the laughter.

"You are such a monkey, come on, we have to get you dressed and ready for breakfast. It is photo day today." Ayleen jumped up and slid down off the bed. We both fell back laughing our heads off.

"Doesn't she just crack you up. I have so missed being around a little one. Ross was exactly like that when he was small, the very same. He and Ayleen have the same expressions; it is like looking into the past." We got up and got dressed and went down to join the others for breakfast.

"Everyone make sure you eat lots because we will only have something to nibble on at lunch because of the pictures. Ayleen did something that I think caught everyone by surprise. She stood up on her chair and waited until everyone was looking at her.

“Thank you for being part of my family photo. Thank you, Gramma and Grandpa, for doing this for me.” She sat back down, and I could have cried.

“You are very welcome Ayleen; we are very happy to be able to do this for you.” She gave James and I a hug and kiss. We finished breakfast and went to freshen up.

“Oh, by the way, we cleaned out the games room, so if anyone wants to play pool or any of the other games in there you can.” Ross and Lindsay went down to take a quick look before the guys had to leave for their appointments at the barbers. The ladies sat in the sunroom having coffee while we waited for the stylists to come. Jess texted that they were going to arrive around 11:00 to get an early start. It was nearing 11:00 and right on cue, the doorbell rang, and it was Jess, Mario, and Jacob. I introduced them to everyone and as we were heading upstairs the guys came back.

“How did it go at the barbers? Did you guys enjoy being pampered?” They said they enjoyed it and looked wonderful. They went into the sunroom while we went upstairs.

"Mario, I suggest you start with Lindsay, then Ayleen, then Sonya, then Nicole, then Rhonda and then me. I have the shortest hair so mine won't take quite as long. We can do the makeup in the same order and Jacob can you make sure please that everyone's dresses are wrinkle free. You and Mario can decide what looks to go with for with them. Can you help with necklaces too please, we don't want anyone to chip a nail? Also please make sure that all the men's ties are tied the same." I knew I sounded anxious, but Jacob assured me things would be perfect. One by one they were getting done and getting dressed. Lindsay was the first to come out and she looked so pretty, then Ayleen.

"Gramma, I love my dress, thank you for getting it for me." She looked so cute with the curly hair and Mario put a little lip gloss on her lips. In three hours, everyone was done. The guys also got dressed. Jacob made sure that everyone's tie were done properly and were straight. He was so happy when he saw that Ross shaved off his beard.

"He has such a nice looking face; I am happy for you he shaved it off." I was the last one to get ready and went downstairs. Jen arrived about fifteen minutes before I came down. She decided that we would take all the shots on the staircase. The lights were set up and she got Ross, Lindsay and Ayleen placed to take the first photo. It proceeded on from there and once the group shot was done, Ayleen and I went up to my bedroom to change into our dresses. I helped her into hers and Jacob fluffed out the dress and I gave him the unicorn necklace to put on her.

"Gramma this is so pretty, thank you." I put on the diamond necklace that altered to make it a two strand necklace. Jacob helped to put that on me. We were ready to go back down to take some photos of the two of us on the stairs. Lindsay and Ross waited and when they saw Ayleen they gasped.

"Ayleen, you look very pretty in your dress. Mum you look very pretty too." Ayleen was a natural with the photographer. Jen was amazed at how well she took direction. We got a dozen or more photos of the two of us. Then we were done. Ayleen ran into the sunroom to show James her pretty dress. Everyone loved it.

"Wow look at you two. You look very pretty in those gowns. I hope you got some good pictures." Ayleen went over to sit on James's knee.

"Ok Ayleen we have to go back up and change, the photos are done so if you guys want to change too you can go ahead. Jen said the photos turned out great. She would get them back to me in frames on the 27th." I took Ayleen back up and helped her out of her dress. Lindsay brought in some jeans and a sweater for her to put on. While I was getting changed, James took care of paying everyone. He came up to change out of his suit.

"I think the photos are going to be really nice and everyone will be pleased with them. That was a nice idea to get photos done of you and Ayleen. She was very happy with her dress." We got changed and then went back downstairs. Ross, Lindsay, and Ayleen went to the movie room to watch one of Ayleen's movies. Rhonda, Mark, Austin, and Nicole went into the games room. Sonya and Richard were waiting for us in the sunroom. Jonathan brought in some coffee which I really needed.

"Thank you for doing up family photos for us. I haven't been able to get any of us dressed up for decades, so it will be nice to have something to put in the new home." Richard handed James a cheque. James looked at him quizzically.

"We agreed that I would pay you what you paid for the house. Now that Sonya and I are going to be living together as a couple, I wanted to pay you back. We both love the house a lot and until Rhonda and Mark figure out where they want to live, they are going to stay with us. The house is more than large enough that we won't be under one another's foot." Sonya thanked James as well and gave him a hug.

"So now that the family photos are out of the way, we can sit back and relax. Dinner will be in about three hours." It started to snow again, big, huge flakes. I for one wouldn't mind going for a walk around the property. The four of us got bundled up and went for a walk.

"James why hasn't John cleared the snow off the path. It is making it more difficult to walk." He said that he had to fix something on the machine, which James knew was a bit of a lie. Sonya could see that he felt awful about it and helped him out.

"This give us a better work out don't you think. I enjoy walking on the snow, and it isn't that bad. It's packed down a bit and the new fresh layer is not much." James gave her a look of thanks that I obviously did not see. When we got back, Ayleen was looking around for us.

"Where did you go, my movie was over, and I came looking for you." She had a worried look on her face. James picked her up and gave her a hug.

"We went for a walk. Why don't you put on your coat and you, and I will go for a little walk down the driveway? It isn't cold out, so you won't need your snow pants." Ayleen ran to get her coat, boots, hat, and gloves. I put them on her and she and James were out the door. They walked up and down the driveway a few times. I waved down to them to let them know that dinner was nearly ready.

As we ate, the discussion came up about tomorrow. Everyone wanted to go skiing and tobogganing again, so James booked the stretch suv to pick us up at 9:30. After dinner there was going to be a game of snooker with James and Ross taking on Austin and Mark. Richard was going to be bartender. There were four arcade games off in one corner of the room. Rhonda and Nicole were playing against each other. Sonya and Lindsay got on another one and there was one that was strictly for the smaller kids which Ayleen and I got on.

Everyone was having a good time. The guys were having a very spirited game of snooker. Lindsay played with Ayleen while Sonya and I went to watch. James and Ross were beating Mark and Austin. James was laughing because Mark said he was going to beat him this time. Richard was laughing behind the bar, so we went over to sit on the stool and have a glass of wine.

"Ross is not a bad player, but James is very good. Mark is going to eat his words I'm afraid." It was twenty dollars a game which James and Ross won two out of three so far. The guys were having fun and getting along so well. Ross was laughing because James was now making a run on the table. Mark and Austin were trying to throw him off his game by jeering him in a fun way. Austin started to tease James now because the next shot he was going to have to make was difficult.

"Oh, James man, I don't think you are going to make this one buddy. It's a pretty tough shot, you can toss in your money now if you want." Sonya and I were laughing. James was concentrating on the shot. Austin was still trying to get under his skin, so he would lose focus. James looked over at me and winked. He made the shot and Austin and Mark laughed because they couldn't believe it.

"He's a pool shark, Mark. He's been playing with us." But it didn't stop them from playing a few more games. They had a great time. Lindsay came over with Ayleen who was clearly tired and ready for bed.

"Give everybody a hug and kiss goodnight." She did and Lindsay took her up to bed. After twenty minutes she came back down.

"It was the excitement of the day and then the fresh air, she is out like a light. She was even asleep before I got her pjs on." Lindsay paired up with Ross and Nicole with Austin to play some snooker. Mark joined Rhonda for a spirited game of arcade at which he was also losing.

"Man, I can't win at anything tonight." James, Sonya, Richard, and I sat at the bar having wine. I couldn't get the smile off my face I was so happy. James gave me a hug. It was a very nice day all around. Around 11:00 everyone started to head upstairs. James turned off all the lights but left the Christmas lights on the driveway on. He turned on the alarm and we went off to bed too.

"Thank you for such a wonderful day. I think everyone had fun playing downstairs." James said that he thought so too. Tomorrow would be another fun filled day. We got up the next morning, had a wonderful breakfast, loaded everyone into the limo suv and drove to the ski hill. Ross, Lindsay, and I went tobogganing with Ayleen and the rest went skiing. Sonya was a beginner, so she and Richard stayed on the easy hill. The others went off to the bigger slopes. We met up at 12:30 for lunch and then went back at it again. We got home shortly after 3:00 and I think everyone was rather tired. It snowed at home some while we were at the hill.

We were hungry at dinner time, even Ayleen. Ross, Lindsay, and Ayleen were going to use my car to go over to her aunt and uncle's for lunch the next day. Everyone was pretty tired from the day at the ski hill, and everyone was in bed by 10:30.

It was Christmas Eve, and today we were having the staff lunch. Sonya, Richard, Rhonda, Mark, Austin, and Nicole decided to go to the mall and do a bit of last minute shopping. They would be home around 5:00. The luncheon went well, and James handed out the Christmas bonuses to everyone. He even had a small bonus for the students that Jonathan hired. After lunch James went to his study to look at his emails and I went to the sunroom. While it was wonderful to have all the hustle and bustle with everyone in the house, it was nice to have a bit of quiet time. James came into the sunroom and handed me a gift. I looked at him wondering why he was giving me a gift. I opened the box, and it was a double strand of multi-coloured pearls with a matching clustered multi-pearl earrings.

"They are Tahitian pearls and I wanted you to have some pearls from me. I think they will look lovely with the dress you plan to wear for Christmas dinner." They were very beautiful, and I gave him a kiss in thanks. I took them up to the bedroom and put them in the safe. The others were starting to return. Ayleen came running into the sunroom to tell us about her visit. It started to snow again, a little heavier so I was glad that everyone was back. Sonya came in from putting things away up in their room.

"The mall was insane, but it was fun." Dinner was going to be tourtiere, potatoe pancakes and grilled carrots with chocolate mousse for dessert.

"After dinner, we would like everyone to come into the sunroom. We are going to let you open up one gift from us. You will see why we are doing this and there is a special surprise." James wanted everyone to gather first in the living room and wait until he went to get them. Then James and I went up to the spare room and started to bring down the large boxes that had the coats in them. The plan was to give each person their box and let them open it. But James had something else up his sleeve. He asked me to go and bring everyone in but not for ten minutes. When we returned there was a Santa Clause sitting in the armchair waiting to hand out the gifts. Ayleen was the first one to go up and get hers and then me. I looked at James knowing that he did this more for me than for Ayleen.

Of course, Ayleen tore through the wrapping paper to open up the box. She was the first to take out her down jacket and snow pants and then her big boots. One by one they opened them up and were shocked. James unbeknownst to me express couriered in a coat for Richard and Mark and put it with the other coats. They stood up and were trying on their coats. The snow started up again and it was nice big flakes. It was fairly mild now too, with the temperature hovering around minus five. We thanked Santa who left by the side door in the sunroom. James waited long enough for him to go down the drive.

"Ok sweetheart, I need you to get your long coat on and bring your warm mitts. I have a surprise for you." We got dressed warmly and went to the door. When James opened it, I couldn't believe it.

"James, a horse drawn carriage for a ride in the snow. This is so perfect." It then dawned on me why the path hadn't been cleared.

"This is why John never cleared the path." James admitted that he had to tell a few fibs to keep me from finding out. Ayleen saw the horse and carriage and she wanted to go too. We got her dressed up in her new coat and pants, her boots and warm mittens and took her with us. James turned on the lights for the path. The carriage was a beautiful red and gold and the horse was a black Percheron. It was absolutely perfect.

"Gramma it looks like Santa's sleigh." I said that it did indeed. James helped me in and then put Ayleen between us and we were off.

"James this is the most perfect surprise. I love it, thank you so much." We had a blanket over our laps and Ayleen was thrilled to be going for the ride. We went around a couple of times and when we got back, the others had their coats on and lined up for their turns. It was the most perfect night.

"Gramma that was so much fun and that horse was very big." I said what breed it was and explained a little about the breed.

"Ayleen, do you know that this was Great Gramps favourite horse. He had one many, many years ago when he and Great Nanny lived way up in the bush and Great Gramps used to haul big trees out of the bush using a horse like that. Ross and Lindsay came back from their turn around. It was going on 9:00 and it was well past Ayleen's bedtime. She said goodnight to everyone, and we went in with them.

"Santa is coming tonight Ayleen, so you have to go right to sleep. When you wake up in the morning, you have to wait for Mommy and Daddy before you can come downstairs ok." She said ok and they took her up.

By the time everyone had their turns, it was almost eleven. The horse and carriage were taken down to the Quonset, where I didn't realize they'd been for most of the day. James thanked the owner of the horse and asked if he could come back again on Boxing Day to do it during the day. He said he would be happy to. Now that Ayleen was up in bed and safely asleep James, and I brought the gifts down. The others were doing the same and when all the gifts were under the tree, there was very little room to walk around. We sat together in our pjs and robes and had a glass of eggnog and rum.

"You see guys why we did the coats earlier. We would never have been able to get in the room otherwise." James turned on some Christmas music very low. The snow was falling steadily. James checked his watch.

"Merry Christmas everyone." We realized that it was now Christmas Day and gave each other a hug and kiss. James and I stood in the doorway watching everyone enjoying the eggnog and laughing. He pointed up and I looked up and I could not believe he had mistletoe.

"Where on earth did you get this? You can't get it anywhere in Canada because it's actually illegal to have it." He brought it back from Scotland and had been hiding it in the kitchen fridge. We kissed under the mistletoe and that was my very first time. It was now almost 2:00 in the morning and we went up to bed knowing full well that Ayleen would be up bright and early which meant that everyone would have to be up bright and early. I think seeing all the gifts under the tree, it wouldn't be a hardship to get them up. Everything was set for the morning, so we turned in. I knew that Ayleen would be up early so James set his watch for 6 am. Sure enough, there was a knock at our door. We knew it was Ayleen, so we told her to come in. She came running into the room and jumped up on the bed.

"Gramma, Grandpa it's Christmas morning. We have to go see if Santa came." We said that we would have to wait for another little bit because it was a bit too early to wake any of the others. We talked to her about the things that we did over the last few days. At 8:00, we couldn't hold Ayleen back any longer. We got up and put on our robes. I told her she had to go and wake

Mommy and Daddy up which she did. Then I whispered in her ear. She giggled and went half way down the hall and shouted at the top of her voice.

"Come on everybody, Santa was here, it's Christmas morning." We forewarned everyone the night before and one by one they came out of their rooms with pjs on and robes and slippers laughing. Ross picked up Ayleen and waited until we went into the sunroom first, then he let her down. She came barreling into the sunroom and stopped at the door. James was taking pictures of her as she came into the room, and I was doing video. Her eyes were like saucers and then it came out, the squeal. Sonya forewarned her bunch, but I don't think they thought it would be that loud. James was busting a gut laughing.

"Well, I guess everyone is awake now. Ayleen, can you sit there with Mommy and Daddy, James is going to bring coffee in for everyone and then we can start with the gifts. So you have to be patient a little bit longer ok." She was so excited she couldn't sit on Ross's knee. She was jumping up and down. While James was getting coffee, I ran up to get the painting. The other gifts I tucked in with the rest when we were bringing them down.

James played Santa and handed out the gifts starting of course with Ayleen. Ross indicated which one was from them and he handed that to Ayleen first. There was nothing lady like about the way she ripped through the paper. Ross asked her not to squeal again, once was enough. She opened the gift from them, and it was a bunch of games and toys. She did her best to muzzle the squeal. While she played with those for a little bit, James handed out other gifts from us. He handed out the gifts that were the watches for everyone. He gave me one also and I gave him one.

It was interesting to see the looks on everyone's faces when they saw the watches. They couldn't believe it. They put them on right away and thanked us for the great gifts. James opened his from me and loved the cuff links and matching tie clips. He got me a diamond necklace and earrings. I handed James the gift which contained the first edition plays by Shakespeare. He opened it carefully and there was shock on his face.

"Oh my God, oh my God, how, where did you get these. I have been trying for years to buy these and have never been able to get them. I don't know how you did this but thank you. You have no idea how much these mean to me. I have loved Shakespeare for years; how did you even know?" I said that Quinn told me how much he loved the plays, and I did a little bit of searching and found someone who was willing to part with them. When everyone else finished opening up their gifts, I handed James his last gift which once again he opened carefully. When he finished opening it I took it and stood in front of him and held it. I could see tears streaming down his face. Ayleen went over to him.

"Grandpa why are you crying?" He picked her up and explained about the painting.

"I don't know how Gramma did this Ayleen, but this is a painting of when I was ten years old and this is my Mum and Dad and we were on a picnic in Scotland, in the same place where I proposed to Gramma." Ayleen got closer to the painting and said that she like it and that he looked a lot like his Mommy.

"How did you get this done? Where did you get a picture of this?" He composed himself and I told him that I asked Fenella for the photo and got the name of a pretty famous portrait painter here in Alberta. He worked on the painting for weeks as he was getting ready to go on a long vacation. I was very happy that he liked his gifts.

"The painting is exceptional, and I feel like my parents are right here." Jonathan came in to say that breakfast was ready. While the others went off to the dining room, I took James with the painting to the study.

"Michel, the painter, and I chose this wall to hang it on. He told me what lighting to get for it but obviously I couldn't get that done until after Christmas. The gentleman who sold me the first edition works is the one who is joining us for dinner, so you will be able to talk with him. He, like you is an enthusiast of Shakespeare. Now we should join the others for breakfast." He pulled me towards him and kissed me.

"Before we go I have one other gift to give to you." He handed me a set of keys and I looked at him.

"It isn't for a sports car only because you wouldn't let me buy you one, but I got you a new suv which I know you will like. It is the top of the line of the one that you already have. I knew you wouldn't let me get you anything else." It was in the garage and said we would go look later. Right now it was time to join everyone else.

It was fun to listen to the chatter of everyone talking about their gifts. They loved the cashmere pullovers, scarves, and hats that I got them. Ayleen said that she loved her teddy bear that James gave her and would bring that to bed with her tonight. After breakfast everyone took their gifts up to their rooms and we cleaned up all the wrapping paper that was all over the place.

I put in a call to Christelle to wish her Merry Christmas, she thanked us for the beautiful throw and the flowers that we gave her. I said that I would call her again in a few days as it was quite hectic today. I then called Janet to wish her and Wade Merry Christmas, she thanked us for the flowers. I told her as well I would call her in a couple of days. I put in a quick call to Judy but there wasn't any answer, so I left a message on her machine wishing her a Merry Christmas and I would call in a few days. Ross and Lindsay came downstairs before any of the others.

"Ayleen fell asleep with her bear under her arm. I don't think she will sleep long but it was an exciting morning for her." There was coffee on the table, so Lindsay grabbed a cup. Ross had some water. James went to his office and came back with a small pouch for both of them.

"These will be waiting for you when you get home. You will need to change the plates and decide what you want to do with the other cars." I knew that James got them each an upgrade in their vehicles. They were blown away and gave us a hug and kiss.

"My God, thank you for everything. It has been a great Christmas for Lindsay, Ayleen, and me." I gave Ross a hug and said he was welcome, and we were happy to have made it great for them. I could smell the turkey cooking. Jonathan was busy in the kitchen and his students were there as well. While breakfast had been substantial, lunch was going to be very light.

Chapter 13

It was a beautiful sunny day and Rhonda and Mark went for a run. Sonya and Richard went for a walk as did Nicole and Austin. Ross and James went to work out downstairs while Lindsay and I sat in the sunroom watching for Ayleen. She came downstairs at 12:30 and we went in to have soup, sandwiches, and a salad. After lunch, Ayleen went up to play with her toys, the rest went down to watch a movie in 3D. James and I sat in the sunroom having a glass of wine. I let everyone know that our guest would be arriving at 5:00 or shortly after, so if everyone could be changed for dinner prior to that I would be grateful. It was a nice relaxing afternoon; Ayleen came downstairs after playing wondering where everyone else was.

"They are watching a movie downstairs, but it should be finished soon. Are you happy with your Christmas Ayleen, did you like your gifts?" She climbed up on James's knee and said she was very happy with her gifts. The movie finished at 3:30 and everyone came back upstairs. We sat talking for a bit then everyone went up to change. I asked Lindsay if she would put Ayleen in the navy dress or the plum one.

"Hopefully, she will like both of them and will be happy wearing it. She can wear which every necklace she wants, the one she got from James or the one we gave her with the unicorn." James and I went up to change. I was going to wear the royal blue organza with the pearls James gave me. He put on a charcoal grey suit with a pale blue silk shirt and grey tie.

"This gentleman who is coming, you never said what his name was." I stood for a moment and realized that I hadn't told him his name.

"It's Mr. Jones and he is in his mid to late eighties I think. He's a very nice man and quite an avid book collector. You should see all the books he has and some of them are quite rare." James stopped tying up his tie and stood in front of me.

"You don't mean Albert Jones, do you? He has one of the largest rare first edition collection in the world. He's the one that I have been trying to get to sell me the first edition Shakespeare plays. How on earth did you meet him?" I said that I wasn't sure what his first name was, but James opened up his tablet and showed me a picture of him.

"Yes, that's him. I had no idea he was famous. The lady at the library knew him and that he had a lot of first edition books, but she never hinted that he was famous to me." James was excited all over again.

"My God I am going to get to talk to the one man who knows more about Shakespeare than just about anyone else alive. This is almost as good as getting the first editions. He never talks to anyone, ever, and nobody even knew where he lived. I can't believe he will be coming to our home." James hugged me and thanked me. He was now, he said, actually nervous. Everyone gathered in the sunroom, James and I came downstairs as the doorbell rang. When James opened the door, it was Mr. Jones standing there. I went up to him and brought him into the foyer.

"Mr. Jones, I am so glad that you were able to make it. This is my fiancé James Sutherland. He loved the books and I believe that he knows something about you." Mr. Jones head went up when he heard me introduce James. They shook hands.

"Ah yes, Mr. Sutherland, yes I know who you are. You've been trying for years to get me to sell you some of my rare first edition Shakespeare. I guess now you have what you were looking for. I am happy that it is going to such an avid admirer of Shakespeare." I took his coat from him and put it in the closet. James continued the conversation.

"Mr. Jones, I am great admirer of yours as well. You have the reputation as one of the leading experts on Shakespeare and I am very honoured to meet you and have you in our home." I could tell that there was a change in Mr. Jones' attitude towards James.

"You may both call me Albert and it is a great pleasure for me as well to finally meet the man who has been quite persistent to get in touch with me. Your fiancée is a very charming woman and very hard to resist a request from. Now that I know who you are, I will be more than happy to entertain the idea of giving you further editions but let us not talk about that now. You have a very beautiful home, and it sounds like you have a large family." We showed him into the sunroom and introduced him to everyone. Richard was the only other person who had any idea who he was.

"Albert, can I get you anything to drink, I have a very fine whisky here that you may enjoy, but we have wine or whatever you would like." He said that he would very much like a small shot of whisky. Ayleen was sitting with Ross and Lindsay and was being a bit shy.

"Cassandra is this your granddaughter." I brought her over and introduced her to Albert.

"Ayleen, do you like to have stories read to you. Your Grandmother told me that you would be here, and I brought you something very special. You must promise to take very good care of it. It is a story that I published many, many years ago. I guess you could say that it is a first edition. The book is no longer in issue, so I hope that you will enjoy it." Ayleen took the gift and said thank you. She went over to Ross and opened it up carefully. It was a story about a unicorn, something that she really liked.

"I wrote that children's book when I was in my thirties. It is the original which they made plates from. I did all of the illustrations myself, which I was very proud of at the time. It did very well and made the best seller's list, but I would not allow it to be reprinted. Books are meant to be treasured so I hope that you will treat it with care and someday you can pass it down to her children." Ross opened the book and carefully turned the pages so that Ayleen could look at it. He promised Albert that they would take very good care of it. Ayleen took the book back over to Albert.

"Would you read me the story Mr. Jones?" I think Albert was very surprised at the request. I told him that dinner was not going to be for a little while, so if he wanted to, there was lots of time. Ayleen sat down on the couch beside him.

"It would be my pleasure to read the story to you." Ayleen sat as close to him as possible while he took the book and went page by page, reading the story and explaining the pictures. Ross was sitting across from him and videoed the whole thing. When the story was completely read Ayleen said thank you.

"Thank you. Mr. Jones, I loved the story and I promise I will be very careful with the book." She took the book back over to Ross for him to look after. James sat beside Albert when Ayleen left.

"She's a delightful child, you must be very fond of her." James smiled and said that he was indeed very fond of her. The conversation went on for another few minutes and then Jonathan came in to say that dinner was ready. Before we went to sit in the dining room, I asked if everyone would come for a photo. I lined everyone up on the stairs. I asked Jonathan to take several pictures. He showed me the ones he took and there was a very good one, so I said we could proceed to the dining room. James helped Albert into the dining room and into his chair beside him. Once everyone was seated, Jonathan and his students brought out the food. James had champagne brought up earlier so that he could make a toast.

"Cassandra and I want to thank all of you for coming to be with us on our first Christmas in our new home. Here is to family, to old friends and to new ones." The food was passed around and the conversation became like a steady hum. I watched Albert as he looked around at everyone and I thought I saw a tear, which of course he quickly wiped away. He and James were talking about Shakespeare, but they got into other topics as well. Albert commented on the whisky and James told him it was from his own distillery.

"You don't say. You seem to have quite the business empire James. I did read up on you, you know. I was very impressed but until meeting you today, I would not have been willing to part with my collection." James had a request to propose to Albert.

"Albert, you mentioned that you might be willing to part with other first editions. I am willing to build a wing onto the local library and name that wing after you, if you would be willing to sell me your entire collection, with the agreement that the collection would reside in your wing. If that sounds agreeable to you, perhaps we can go to my study and talk a bit more." Albert said that he was very flattered.

"I appreciate the offer of dedicating a wing with my name on it. Books have been my life and as I am sure you are aware, I have quite a collection. Perhaps it might be best to continue this conversation in your study when dinner is finished." They spent the rest of the meal having an enjoyable conversation. When dinner was over I took everyone back into the sunroom while James and Albert went to this study.

"James, your offer does intrigue me. I know that you are very wealthy but at my age now, money doesn't matter to me. I am sure that Cassandra told you I was ill. The truth of the matter is that I have maybe three or four months to live maybe a bit longer. My heart is not able to keep going and I have no desire in having an operation that may or may not work. I've had a good life and I have my books. Cassandra is a very charming woman as I said once already, and I hope that the two of you will have a wonderful life together. I will agree to your terms on two conditions. One that you promise none of my collection will ever be sold ever and that the cheque that you write me will instead be put towards reading programs in schools in rural areas and small towns across the country. I know it sounds an odd request, but children should have every opportunity to read and explore through books and gain knowledge. They should be able to hold a book in their hands and feel the pages. If you will guarantee me that James, I will sell you my entire collection." Albert wrote down the amount on a piece of paper and handed it to James. James was stunned. He knew that his collection was worth more than that amount.

"I will have my lawyer draw up an agreement that we shall both sign. I will build a wing on the library with my own personal money and dedicate it to you. I will have your collection reside there and it will remain with that library in perpetuity. In addition, you will agree that the sum that I am paying to you will be given to schools in rural and smaller towns throughout the provinces and territories to enhance their reading programs and libraries so that other children will have every opportunity to read as many books as they choose, and it will also be used to help maintain the wing in your name. However I will also add the same amount to the reading program so it will get to all the schools. If you agree to this, we can shake hands and you can trust that I will have the papers drawn up this week for you and me to sign. I will bring them to your home personally if necessary." Albert was in complete agreement and was very happy about the idea for the schools.

"You are a smart man James. I am sorry that I never took the opportunity to meet you previously. Now why don't we rejoin your family." James took him back to the sunroom and then excused himself. He went in to print off the photo that was taken and put it in a frame. He stuck a bow on it and took it back to the sunroom. He motioned Ayleen to come over.

"Ayleen, this is a gift that I would like you to give to Mr. Jones, from all of us. You know how you wanted to have a family photo taken so that you would have it, well Mr. Jones doesn't have any family, but Gramma wants very much for him to think of us as his family now. Can you do that for me?" Ayleen nodded and took the frame over to Albert.

"Mr. Jones, I have something for you. Gramma says you don't have a family but now you have us as a family." She handed him the photo which he took with tears in his eyes. He pulled out a hanky to blow his nose.

"Ayleen, you are such a sweet girl and I think you take after your Gramma a bit. It is very generous of all of you to share with me your Christmas dinner. This photo means more to me than any rare collection that I have, and I will cherish it for the rest of my days. Thank you all of you for being so kind and generous to me." Everyone else was pulling out a tissue to wipe away the tears. James stood up to speak.

"Ok, so no more tears, this is a joyous occasion. Richard, in case none of you knew is an excellent pianist and if we would all like to go into the living room, we will have coffee, tea or whatever you would like to drink while he entertains us." Richard said he would be happy to play. We went into the living room, James got a fire going in the fireplace, Richard began to play, and we had a great time. I noticed the time and I knew that Albert wanted to be home by 9:00. I let James know and we walked Albert out to the foyer and James helped him with his coat.

"Albert, you know you are more than welcome to stay, we do have a spare room that you can sleep in." He took my hand and kissed it.

"Thank you my dear but all my medication is at home. This has been an evening I will not forget for many reasons. Perhaps another time." I looked at James and he knew exactly what I was thinking.

"Albert, everyone is going to be here to celebrate the New Year, why don't you come and stay with us on

New Year's Eve, and I can bring you back home the next day if you wish. I will personally come and get you. You can stay overnight or for a few days if you wish. I have to fly everyone home on the 2nd, but we would love to have you here." Once again Albert shed a few tears.

"You are both being so very nice to me, and I really do appreciate it. I don't want to impose on your holiday. It was nice of you to invite me to dinner, but I can't impose further." James looked at me with frustration on his face.

"Albert, James is going to come and pick you up on the 31st and bring you here to spend New Year's Eve and Day with us. It isn't going to be a formal occasion, canapes, and other small foods. We are not getting all dressed up, so you don't need to wear a suit. James will help you pack if you want when he comes to get you, but you will come and spend it with us. You are family and I won't see alone at New Years." Albert looked at James.

"I don't suppose there is any point in arguing with her." James said there wasn't. Ayleen came out right at that moment.

"Then I would be happy to accept your invitation. So James tell me, do you own your own plane. In all my years of living I have never flown. I suppose you find that odd, but I never felt the need to go anywhere." Once again, I looked at James.

"Then you shall fly with us when we take everyone back to Ottawa. We won't be staying of course, just dropping them off refueling and returning. It will mean a long day, are you up for that?" Albert started to chuckle.

"I am sure that if I get tired I can close my eyes. This will be a wonderful adventure for me. I look forward to it. But for now, I am ready to go back to my home." Ayleen took Albert's hand in hers.

"You can sit beside me Mr. Jones. I like flying and if you get nervous, I will hold your hand. The clouds are so pretty up in the sky." Albert bent down to give Ayleen a kiss on the cheek and said he would very much enjoy that. James took Albert down to the limo that was going to take him home. He told the driver to make sure that he escorted Mr. Jones safely into his home. Ayleen went back into the living room where the others were.

"That was the most amazing Christmas I have ever had. Thank you, sweetheart, for everything, for the first editions, for the most amazing painting and for Albert. I know that you know he is quite ill; did he tell you that he has only about three or four months to live maybe a little longer. He has a very bad heart and wasn't willing to undergo surgeries. I think he has lived a pretty full life even if it all happened within the last six hours. He agreed to sell me his entire collection, but we can talk more about that later." We went back inside to join the others. Richard was playing some Christmas songs that everyone was singing to, and we joined in. It was probably the best day of my life…so far. Ayleen was getting very tired. Lindsay took her up to give her a bath and put her in her pjs. She brought her down so that she could say goodnight to everyone.

"Gramma will you come up and read me the book Mr. Jones gave me." I said that I would love to and hand in hand we went up to her room. Ross showed James the video he recorded of Albert reading the story to Ayleen.

"That will be a keepsake for her Ross, one that you will want to preserve for her so that she will have it." He said that he would definitely take care of that when he got home. The night rolled on with songs and laughter but one by one, everyone started to head off to bed. Ross and Lindsay were the last two aside from James and I to go up. Lindsay gave us a hug and kiss goodnight and thanked us for all the great gifts. Ross gave James a hug.

"Thanks Dad for everything, Mum you too. Night." I gave him a hug and kiss. He took Lindsay's hand, and they went upstairs.

"You're welcome son, sleep well." I looked at James who was visibly moved. They turned and waved. When they went down the hall to their bedroom, James hugged me.

"He called me Dad; did you hear that. I couldn't be happier." I said that I heard, and I was very happy for him.

"It is getting late, and we know a certain someone who will probably be up early." We went off to bed with hearts that were full. The next morning after breakfast, the bunch went skiing. Sonya and Richard went for a walk and Ross, Lindsay and Ayleen relaxed with us. It was a full day; a full few days for Ayleen and they didn't want her to be overtired and worn out, so today they were sticking around the house. While they went down to watch a movie with Ayleen, we sat in the sunroom having coffee.

"It was wonderful yesterday wasn't it James. I think everyone enjoyed their gifts and the food was amazing, and it was a fun evening." He said it was indeed a great day.

"What time are Roxanne and Duncan coming by, do you know." She told me they would be by after lunch.

"They will be staying until after dinner. I am taking the girls to the spa on the 29th and I'm going to ask Roxie to come too. You and Ross will have to entertain Ayleen because we are having massages, facials, body wraps, reflexology and mani/pedis, the works. I think they will enjoy them. Thank you, James, for making all of this possible for me. I am so happy being here with you and knowing that you love my family." He gave me a hug as we sat together looking out at the birds flitting about at the feeder. The movie must have been over because Ayleen came bounding into the sunroom and sat with us. She said nothing but was quite happy to sit with us in silence watching the birds. After a little while I asked her what Mommy and Daddy were doing.

"They said they were going to try out the sauna. What's a sauna Grandpa?" James explained what the sauna was but that she was much too young to go in it because of the heat. Sonya and Richard came back from their very long walk and joined us in the sunroom.

"We don't want you to get ill, so the sauna is not something you can try. What would you like to do?" She looked outside and said she would like to go out and play in the snow. I went down to let Ross know we were going outside with Ayleen. While we went out, Sonya and Richard sat having a glass of wine. We got her dressed up in her new down jacket and snow pants and did likewise and went out with her. She and I made snow angels which James took pictures of. The snow was not good enough to make a snowman, but it was ok to have a snowball fight. We had James on the run, but he got us both good with a big armful of snow. It had both Ayleen and I falling on the ground giggling. James took a picture and video. It was getting close to lunch, so we went back in and freshened up.

"Our friends Roxie and Duncan are going to be here soon. They are coming after lunch to meet everyone and will be staying for dinner. Duncan is Grandpa's uncle, so you should call him Great Uncle Duncan and the same for Roxie because she and Great Uncle Duncan will be getting married. Ross and Lindsay came up in terry robes and went upstairs to change. They loved the sauna. Just as they were coming back down, the doorbell rang. James went to get it and it was Duncan and Roxie. They came into the sunroom and James introduced them to Ayleen, Sonya, Richard and to Ross and Lindsay who came back downstairs. Duncan already knew Richard, but Richard didn't know Roxie. Roxie was looking around at all the decorations and loving everything.

"Hello Ayleen, your Gramma talks about you all the time and I have seen lots of pictures of you. We have a belated Christmas gift for you. We hope you like it." Ayleen opened it up and it was a sweater with her favourite animated animal. She wanted to put it on, but we said maybe tomorrow.

"Thank you, Great Uncle Duncan, and Great Aunt Roxie. I love this character. How did you know?" Roxie laughed and said that Santa told them. Ayleen's eyes got big, and she went to sit on James's knee.

"Duncan would you like some whisky, Roxanne what will you have?" Of course Duncan knew Richard and was happy to meet Sonya.

"Ross, would you mind pouring Duncan a glass of whisky, and Richard and James." Ross got the men their drinks and poured one for himself. Lindsay took Ayleen's sweater up to her room.

"Lindsay, Sonya, and I were actually going to have some white wine, would you like a half glass Roxie?" She was fine with that.

"So how was your Christmas with Mitchell, Maria, and the kids?" They had a great time she said.

"They love the house. The boys wanted to stay over but one had a hockey game early this morning. We went when it was later in the game. I didn't want to get up that early. Tomorrow some of my old neighbours are going to stop by for lunch and then we are going to relax. We still have a lot of unpacking to do and a bit of furniture shopping. Duncan is going for his citizenship in the New Year and so am I. Duncan worked with the lawyer to get all my papers straightened out. It was too much bother before, but we are taking it on the same day, the 19th. Duncan and I are going out to dinner, and we'd like you and James to join us, if you can." I was so happy for her. I knew how hard she had tried to get all the proper papers done before, so I was happy it was working for her now.

"We would be happy to. Let us know where you want to go, and it will be our treat." Duncan said it would be their treat and it would be at Jason's since it was so close by. Ayleen was starting to get a little sleepy and dozed off sitting beside James.

"If you will excuse me, I'm going to take this little one up and put her in bed." James carried Ayleen, who was out like a light, upstairs to her room. He came back down ten minutes later.

"It must have been the snow fights we had. She never woke up at all. Now, you must come and see the painting Cassandra gave me." Ross, Lindsay, Sonya, and Richard waited in the sunroom while we took Duncan and Roxie to James's study. He hung the painting up but hadn't yet had the lighting installed. Duncan was stunned when he saw the painting.

"My word, Cullodina and Patrick, James you would swear she was right here and Patrick too. Cassandra, I don't know who you got to paint this, but they did a phenomenal job. James you must have been blown away." James said he was but that was not the only thing. He showed Duncan the first edition of the plays. Duncan was flabbergasted.

"James, you have been trying to get your hands on these for decades. How did you do it Cassandra?" I told him about Mr. Jones, Albert and he was completely blown away. Roxie was looking at the painting.

"James certainly does take after his Mum, doesn't he? He has her hair colour and the same green eyes. She's very beautiful." Duncan came up behind Roxie.

"Yes, my dear, she was very beautiful and yes James takes after her in many ways. She had a heart as big as Scotland itself and she was such a generous and kind person. She helped out in the community, and she is very much missed." Duncan and James both got a little choked up. They were also shown the wonderful work of art by Ayleen.

"This is also a priceless piece of art and I love it." We went back into the sunroom. Ross was pointing to a moose that came out of the trees.

"Lindsay and I have never seen one this close up. Too bad Ayleen is asleep she would have loved to have seen this." The cow wasn't in any hurry to leave, and it seemed like it knew that it was supposed to stay. It decided to lay down and doze off.

"Well I guess as long as we don't make a lot of noise it might be there when Ayleen wakes up." Roxie struck up a conversation with Lindsay and Ross, I was talking to Richard and Sonya and James and Duncan were talking about the citizenship ceremony. I noticed Ayleen coming towards the sunroom and I went to get her.

"Ayleen, if you are really quiet, you will see a moose just in the trees." Her eyes got really big.

"A moose, what is a moose?" I explained that it was part of the deer family only they were much, much bigger. She went to James, and he picked her up and pointed to the moose, which decided that it had been dozing long enough. We stood still, and it came right up to the window and then walked away.

"Grandpa that moose was really big, and it had a big nose." We laughed and had to agree, it did have a big nose. She stayed with James on his lap.

"Boy she sure loves James, doesn't she?" I said to Roxie that she definitely did. Ross and I went into the kitchen to get some canapes that Jonathan was making up. The others were returning from there ski trip. James introduced them to Duncan and Roxie. They went upstairs to change out of their ski gear and came back down to join us in the sunroom. Ross poured Mark and Austin a whisky and Nicole and Rhonda a glass of wine. Roxie and I were sitting together watching everyone.

"I am happy that you have family here with you. They seem to be having a great time together. I like your sister Sonya and Lindsay is so nice. You must be on cloud nine right now." I said that I was and had been for a long time now since James came into my life. As if sensing that I was talking about him he looked over and smiled and mouthed the words 'I love you' and I said them back. Ayleen was quite happy sitting on his knee listening to him talk to everyone.

"You know Roxie I don't think it is possible for me to be any happier than I am right now. Ross even called James Dad the other night. James was so moved by it. I am so relieved that they like each other so much." Ayleen came running over.

"Gramma, Grandpa said we were going for a sleigh ride before dinner." She dashed back over to James and got up on his knee again.

"That's right, James took me on a horse drawn carriage ride Christmas Eve, Ayleen was with us, then everyone went for one. It was after eleven by the time everyone had a turn. He asked the gentleman who owned the horse, which is down in the Quonset right now, if he would come back over today. Which reminds me, I have yours and Duncan's gift from James and me. They are under the tree." I went over to get them, and Duncan came and sat by Roxie to open them.

"Oh my God a down coat. These are beautiful thank you so much. Duncan aren't these great." He said they were, and Roxie went over to the tree to bring James and I our gifts from them.

"I didn't even see you put this under the tree." It was a beautiful woven native basket from a Yuma native basket weaver.

"We took a drive to a native arts centre, and we thought it would be something different for your home. I know you have a bit of Aboriginal ancestry so I thought you would like it." It was beautiful and we both loved it.

"Now there is something that I didn't know about you, that you have Aboriginal ancestry." I said that I was not exactly sure if it was true or not.

"I have been meaning for a few years now to hire a professional genealogist to actually do up the family trees but never got around to it. Perhaps one day soon." James took the basket and for now put it on the buffet in the dining room. Ayleen was patiently waiting for the gifts to be opened because she wanted to go for a sleigh ride. The owner of the horse, Mr. Wright arrived, and

James took her out to go around a couple of times. Then Ross and Lindsay went with her. Roxie said it looked like fun, so she and Duncan went with her. James went out to talk to Mr. Wright, he took the horse back down to the Quonset. Dinner was ready, and we went to the dining room to enjoy the meal.

"Cassandra the decorations are lovely; I really love how the table is set." After dinner we had drinks in the sunroom. Around 8:00, Duncan and Roxie said they were going to head off home. We walked with them to the door and hugged and kissed them goodnight. The others decided to go and watch a hockey game on tv. Lindsay took Ayleen up for a bath and put her pjs on. She had a big day and was already sleepy. She gave everyone a hug and kiss goodnight and Lindsay took her up to bed.

"Now sweetheart, you and I are going to go for that carriage ride, just the two of us." We put on our warms coats and gloves and went outside." Mr. Wright was back and now it was the two of us riding around under the full moon. I snuggled into James.

"It has been the most wonderful Christmas. I loved having all the family here and Albert too." James said it had been a wonderful time. We went around three times and then went back into the house. Mr. Wright took his horse down to the Quonset and then left. We could hear the cheers and laughing downstairs, but we enjoyed being in the sunroom, just the two of us. We sat watching as the moon came around and dipped behind the tree line. The others started to come back up as the game was over. They came in to say goodnight and went up to bed. We were alone once again.

"What is on for tomorrow?" I knew that Jennifer was coming by mid-morning to drop off the photos that she took but I did not have any plans.

"I suppose the others will want to go skiing again but we can find out at breakfast what everyone's plans are. For now, I think I am ready to hit the sack. What about you?" James agreed; it had been a long day, so we went up to bed ourselves.

The next morning over breakfast, Austin, Nicole, Rhonda, and Mark were planning to go skiing. They asked Ross and Lindsay if they wanted to go along. They both took some skiing lessons over the last few years but never had much of a chance to go out. They didn't want to go without Ayleen, but she hadn't started her lessons yet. I knew that Ross really wanted to go and so did Lindsay.

"We can look after Ayleen if you want to go. Ayleen do you want to stay with Gramma and Grandpa while Mommy and Daddy go skiing with the others?" She looked up from eating her pancakes.

"Yes. Can we play in the snow again?" We said of course we could. So it was settled, the others would go skiing.

"Sonya have you and Richard any plans? You are more than welcome to use my car to go anywhere if you want to." They decided to go for a walk after breakfast and figure out what they wanted to do after that. Breakfast over with, the others went to change and took off. Since it was the six of them they used the suv and Mark knew how to get to the ski hill, so he drove. Sonya and Richard took off on their walk. We got Ayleen dressed up in her warm coat and snow pants and big boots that we bought her for Christmas. It was a sunny day today but a little chilly. When Sonya and Richard came back they decided they wanted to go for a drive, so I gave them the keys to my car, and they were off. James was swinging Ayleen around and she was laughing as was he. After throwing snow at each other I suggested maybe we take a walk around on the pathway.

"Maybe we will see some deer or other wildlife. You haven't been around in the daytime Ayleen, so you might like it." She was all for that and challenged James to catch her. It was fun to watch the two of them together. I brought my camera along to take pictures as we went. Ayleen would see a squirrel and try to go up to it, but it would always take off. She would pick up some snow and throw it at James and he would chase her down the path. I was snapping off pictures like crazy and even some video. They did this about three quarters of the way around, then Ayleen got tired.

"Grandpa can you carry me on your back. I'm tired." Of course James hoisted her up on his back and we walked back side by side. Ayleen did very little talking the last bit back to the house. At one point I actually thought she was asleep, but she wasn't.

"I'm not sleeping Gramma, but I am tired." We got back to the house and got her out of her coat and pants.

"Ayleen would you like some hot chocolate. I'll get us some." James and Ayleen went out into the sunroom, and I went to the kitchen. Jonathan had some hot chocolate ready and poured us three cups. When I got back to the sunroom, James and Ayleen were in one of the recliners and she was starting to fall asleep. I sat beside them in the other recliner. She took a couple of sips of her hot chocolate, but I think the combination of the walk, the fresh air and now the warm air had her tuckered out. She dozed off on James.

"James, you have such a look of contentment on you right now." I took a picture of the two of them.

"I am very content right now. She is the most adorable thing and I love her so much. I feel so very blessed right now. She might not be my blood, but I love her as though she were." We sat drinking our hot chocolate while Ayleen slept on James's chest.

We weren't expecting any of the others to come back until dinner, so it would be the three of us for lunch. Ayleen slept for almost two hours. I think she only woke up because she had to go to the bathroom. I took her upstairs and sat on the bed waiting for her to come back out. She came out and sat on the bed with me.

"Ayleen, do you know how much Gramma and Grandpa love you. We love you a whole bunch and we have had so much fun with you. So now, we are going to go down and have lunch and then after lunch we will watch one of your movies. Grandpa has a bit of work to do and then he will join us when he is done. Does that sound ok with you?" She said that it did, and she wanted to watch her favourite movie.

We went downstairs, had some turkey sandwiches with cheese and pickles. We finished lunch when the doorbell rang, and it was Jennifer with all of the photos. We took them into James's study and went through them. Ayleen loved all the photos. I looked at the ones that were done of Ayleen and me. They turned out really well. Jennifer said that she really liked the one of us sitting on the stairs with our heads together. I asked her for duplicates of the ones of Ayleen and I because I was sure Lindsay would want them or at least some of them.

"That is such a sweet photo of the two of you. Have you decided about me using the ones of you Cassandra in my portfolio?" I said that I had and that I was fine with her using it as long as it she agreed to the terms we had talked about before. She said she agreed with it. James wrote her a cheque to cover the photos and frames. James asked her if she would do our wedding and since I already forewarned her she said she blocked it off as I had previously mentioned it to her. She was happy and thrilled to do it.

"I am sure that the others will want copies as well but until they see these we won't be able to say for sure." Jennifer said to let her know and she would print them up and send them to me. After she left Ayleen, I went off to watch her movie while James did some work. The movie was about half over when James came down. He sat beside me and of course Ayleen climbed up into his lap. We both smiled while we watched the rest of the movie. When the movie was over Ayleen wanted to go and play with her toys in her room.

"That's ok. We will be in the sunroom if you are looking for us." She ran upstairs to her bedroom. We sat in the sunroom having a glass of wine.

"I hope the others are having a good time because I know we are." I pulled out my camera to look over the pictures that I took earlier. James loved the video of the two of them chasing each other.

"I'm going to print out the pictures and we can put them in a collage on the family wall. There's one of the two of you that is really nice, do you want that for your desk." He said he did, and he would like one for his desk in Toronto as well.

"I'm going to print off a bunch of the photos and send them to Fenella, so she can put it up on the family wall there, if that is ok with you?" Of course James agreed so we went through all the photos and picked out the ones for the family wall. Ayleen came back down and sat with us.

"What would you like to do Ayleen, we can watch another movie, or play a game, or watch tv, what would like?" She wasn't sure what she wanted to do.

"I have an idea, why don't we go into the kitchen, and we can make cookies with Jonathan." Her face lit up when I made that suggestion. We went to the kitchen and Jonathan and Ayleen got together to make cookies. He put one of his aprons around her which looked so funny.

"Grandpa and I will be the taste testers." She laughed, and I think Jonathan actually enjoyed having her help him make up the cookies. He was very patient with her showing her how to do everything. She listened carefully and followed his instructions. The cookies were now in the oven to bake. We sat on the stools waiting for them to be ready. The timer went off and Jonathan took them out of the oven. I poured each of us a glass of milk and we sat on the stools, and each had cookies and milk.

"I liked making cookies Gramma. Can I help Jonathan with more baking?" I looked at Jonathan and he smiled.

"Maybe tomorrow you can help me make muffins. How does that sound?" Of course Ayleen was thrilled and said yes. After we were done, we went back into the sunroom.

"Grandpa will you colour with me. I will go and get my crayons and colouring book from my bedroom." She ran upstairs and came back down in minutes, crayons and colouring book in hand. For the next few hours she and James coloured. The others came back from skiing and Sonya and Richard called to say they were going to have dinner out.

"Mommy, Daddy I helped Jonathan to make cookies and tomorrow he said I can help him make muffins." Lindsay said that was wonderful and she would have a cookie after dinner. They had a great time skiing.

"She didn't give you any trouble, did she?" I said we had a wonderful time and showed her the pictures I took. Ross came in and said they were going to play some games downstairs. I told them dinner would be in an hour. James and Ayleen continued to colour.

After dinner Mark showed us pictures of them skiing. He took them with his camera and then downloaded them to his tablet. They were good pictures and there were some of each of them having fallen but they were laughing and having a good time. Sonya and Richard came in about an hour after we finished dinner. They went back to the mall and then drove around.

"We got lost for a little bit but got back on the right road. It's actually a very nice city here and the surrounding towns and cities are quite nice too." I showed them the framed photos that Jennifer brought by earlier. I gave them their individual photos and if they wanted additional copies to let me know. I showed Lindsay and Ross the ones that were done of Ayleen and me.

"These are really pretty, and I like this one of the two of you on the stairs with your heads together. Can I get copies of that one?" I said I had doubles of all the ones of Ayleen and I and just Ayleen in her dress because I figured she would want them. Ayleen was very happy with her family photo.

"Thank you, Gramma and Grandpa, for giving me this. I will hang it in my bedroom at home." It was getting late and time for Ayleen's bath. She had a full day and even though she slept a bit during the day she was still very tired.

"All that fresh air is doing you good. You will sleep well tonight, and I think Grandpa will too." Ayleen laughed and gave everyone a hug and kiss. She gave an extra big hug to James.

"Thank you for all the fun today Grandpa." He hugged her back and said she was welcome. Lindsay took her up to bed. The rest of us had wine or whisky and we heard about the skiing adventure. I was glad that nobody got hurt. Eventually everyone went off to bed. Tomorrow we were going to Jasper for the day. We were going to drive up in my car and James suv.

We left right after having a big breakfast and got to Jasper at lunch. We had a quick lunch and did some looking around. Ross and Lindsay wanted to take Ayleen up in the gondola, so we joined them. Sonya and Richard went off with the others to shop and look around. I was a little nervous going up in the gondola, but I didn't want Ayleen to see that. James held my hand the whole time. Ayleen was looking out the window amazed at how high up we were and how big the mountain was.

James explained to her how the mountains were formed. When we got to the top we looked around and took pictures and then took the gondola back down. It felt good to be down on the ground. We drove back into town and met up with the others. We did a little shopping, got some souvenir sweaters and t shirts for Ayleen, and then went back home. We stopped on the way home at a restaurant to have dinner. Ayleen enjoyed seeing all the goats and the elk. It was a fun day, and I was glad that she got to see the Rockies. We took tons and tons of pictures, so she would have something to remember. Ayleen fell asleep in the car and Ross and Lindsay took her right up to bed. The rest of us went into the sunroom.

"Well guys, tomorrow the ladies are off to be pampered for an entire day. What plans do you have, remembering of course that you will have a seven-year-old with you?" Ross and Lindsay came back downstairs and joined us in the sunroom.

"Listen if you guys want to go skiing tomorrow I am happy to look after Ayleen. I don't mind that at all." Ross said that he couldn't let James be with her by himself.

"I'll stay around the house with you. I'm not as good at skiing as you guys so I don't want to hold you back. Maybe we can build her a snow fort tomorrow. She will like that." James agree that was a great idea.

Richard said he would join the guys if they didn't mind. He was an excellent skier, so they could hit the more experienced slopes.

"Well that's good, now the day is laid out for everyone. We will be leaving here at 8:30 so we can have breakfast and then go. I know it will be an early rise at 7:30 but unless we want to wolf down our breakfast I suggest that is when we get up. We will go in my car. James, we should be back here by 5:00." It was going to be a wonderful day of relaxation for the women.

"I hope you have a good time because I know Ross, Ayleen and I will." The ladies decided to head up at 9:30 but Ross and James stayed downstairs for a bit. They never had a chance to talk alone since Ross called him Dad. I gave them a hug and kiss goodnight and went upstairs. James poured both him and Ross a whisky.

"Ross, it meant a lot to me when you called me Dad the other day. I want you to know that I never expected you to do that, but I really appreciated hearing it." Ross took a sip of the whisky and put it down.

"I didn't know I was going to say it either, but it felt right to do it. I may not always call you Dad but at least you know that that is how I think of you. You've made Mum very happy and that makes me happy. I guess you must have heard that her late husband and I did not get along, which is rather an understatement.

Ayleen never knew him and that was fine with both Lindsay and me. But I can see how much Ayleen loves you. She has latched onto you almost from the beginning. I think she found it odd that there was Gramma and no Grandpa but there is now and that is all that matters. I don't know about you, but I think I am going to turn in. Goodnight Dad see you in the morning." James smiled and hugged and gave Ross a kiss.

"Goodnight son, sleep well." James sat for a while longer finishing his whisky and thinking about what Ross said. He turned off all the lights, turned on the alarm and went up to bed. I was still awake when James came into the bedroom. I wasn't going to ask him about what may have been said between him and Ross. James crawled in beside me and put his arms around me and I cuddle into him. We laid like that for several minutes then James leaned over and kissed me and said goodnight.

The ladies were downstairs and having breakfast. Some of the guys got up too but Ayleen was still asleep as was Ross. We finished eating and went out the door. We arrived at the spa with ten minutes to spare. Massages and facials were being done first and then we would stop for lunch. After that it would be the rest of the treatments. Rhonda said she was starting to love all the pampering.

"I could get used to this on a pretty regular basis, which I am sure surprises Mom. Maybe when we get back home we can do a mother/daughter spa day once a month or so." Sonya said she would like that a lot.

"Well if Austin and I move to Toronto, maybe we can make it mother/daughters. I think I am going to take James up on his offer and Austin would really like the opportunity to go through the executive program. It probably won't happen until the spring. We both have loose ends to tie up." I could tell that Sonya was very happy and shocked.

"Well when you do come to Toronto you can stay with Richard and me until you find what you want." I saw a smile on her face that I had not seen in a very long time. We got home a little after 5:00. I saw that there were a couple of snow forts built, so James and Ross had their hands full. Ayleen came running out to Lindsay when we got back.

"Mommy did you see my snow fort. Grandpa and I built one and Daddy built one and we had snowball fights. It was fun Mommy. Did you have fun at the spa?" Lindsay said she had a lot of fun. The guys were back from skiing, and they were in the sunroom. James poured the ladies some wine.

"So how was your day James. Did you win the snowball fight?" He said that it was a lot of fun.

"Ayleen got Ross pretty good a couple of times. She has a good arm on her and she didn't cry when she got hit. Of course we made sure that there were no snowballs in the face. We played outside with her for four hours I think. She had lunch and then crashed and only woke up about half hour ago." I hoped that he got pictures which he said he did when he could. We had dinner and then more wine out in the sunroom. By 9:00, Ayleen was ready to go to bed. Lindsay gave her a quick bath; she ran down to say goodnight to everyone and then she ran upstairs and to bed. Lindsay came down only long enough to say she was going to bed as well. One by one everyone else went upstairs as did James and me.

"You had fun with Ross and Ayleen today. I'm glad the three of you were together. I probably shouldn't say this to you, but Nicole is leaning towards accepting your job offer and Austin wants to go through the executive program. Sonya is beyond happy that they will be in the same area. I think this will be the first time ever since they were kids." James was surprised but happy and would wait for them to say something to him.

"I don't think I laughed so much in my life. Ayleen was like a little soldier trying to pick Ross off. You could see her mind plotting out a path to sneak up on him. She is a very smart little girl. She got me good a couple of time too when we traded sides. I made the mistake of pretending to be hurt and she came over starting to cry thinking she actually hurt me. My heart sank when she did that. When I told her I was just pretending she washed my face with snow. I learned my lesson. Ross was laughing and so she hit him with a snowball. It was a lot of fun, but man am I beat. I thought I was in pretty good shape, but she really puts you through your paces. Did you enjoy your spa day?" I said that I did enjoy it very much.

"I think I will get gift certificates for Lindsay and her Mom to go for a spa day every once in a while. I think that she has been enjoying the times we have gone since they have been here, and I know that she loves getting massages, so I'm going to arrange that for her when she goes back." James thought it was a great idea. Tomorrow there were no plans, it was going to be a day of relaxing around the house. I heard a knock on the door. I looked at the clock by the bed and it was 6 am. James stirred when I moved. I knew it was Ayleen, so I told her to come in. She jumped up on the bed and laid down between us.

"Gramma did Grandpa tell you he made me cry?" I said that he had and that he shouldn't have done that.

"Grandpa you are not allowed to play tricks like that, it's not nice." James promised her he would never do anything like that again. He kissed her nose and she started to laugh. I saw Ross come up to the door.

"Ayleen, it is time to go and have breakfast. Let's go." She put her head up and looked at Ross.

"Daddy can I come down with Gramma and Grandpa?" I nodded to him that it was ok for her to do that. She looked at him with her big eyes.

"That might work on Grandpa, but it doesn't work on me. You can come down with Grandpa and Gramma but just this one time." Ayleen laid back down giggling. Of course, the giggling had everything to do with the fact that James was tickling her. Ross laughed and walked back down towards his bedroom. We got up after a few minutes and then went downstairs. Ayleen was on James's back and the two of them were laughing. Jonathan had coffee ready as well as orange juice. Breakfast would be ready shortly. Ross and Lindsay came down as did Richard and Sonya.

"Are the others coming down or are they going to sleep in for a bit." Sonya thought they were going to sleep in for a bit. I let Jonathan know the others would be down later. After we were finished breakfast Sonya, and I went for a walk. Ross, Lindsay, and Ayleen got dressed and went to play in the snow forts. James and Richard went into this study to talk about business. Rhonda and Mark came down and went to have something to eat and then Nicole and Austin came down not long after. Mark and Rhonda were going to go for a run. He poked his head in James's study.

"Rhonda and I are going for a run but if you have business to talk about and need me, we can go for a run later." James said it wasn't anything important and could catch him up later. He and Rhonda went out. After they ate, Nicole and Austin went into James's study.

"James, Austin, and I would very much like to take you up on the offer you made at Thanksgiving. Austin and I have been discussing it and we both feel that it is an offer that neither one of us can turn down. We would not be able to do anything for a few months yet though. I have to give my employer a month's notice. It was part of the signing agreement with them. Austin also has to give a month's notice to his company, and we have to sell our condo. It can all be done but it will take at least two or three months. If you can give us that time, we would be happy to accept." James looked at Richard and said that he was very agreeable to the terms.

"Richard will be in touch with you over the next month or two and work out the arrangements. I am very happy that you are coming on board, the both of you." They shook hands and Richard said that Sonya would be very happy. They went out for a walk around the property.

"Sonya, everything seems to be coming around for you. You and Richard look very happy together, Rhonda and Mark look happy, and she will be moving to Toronto with you, and it looks like Nicole and Austin will too. You are happy about all of that aren't you?" She said she was extremely happy.

"It has been a long time since I have had my kids living close to me, not that they are kids anymore, but you know what I mean. Now if they would only make me a Grandma too." I said it will happen.

"Nicole and Rhonda are still young, maybe a little older than you would want them to be for a first child, but it happens all the time now." She was crossing her fingers that Rhonda would be first.

"She and Mark really get along and they love so many of the same things. He treats her really well and she adores him. I would like to see her pregnant sooner than later, but I don't know if that is in either of their plans right now." I put my arm around her as we walked up to the house.

"Well Sonya you never know. Maybe Mark will actually propose to her on New Year's, and they may want a child right away. Not saying I know anything, but you never know." I'd been watching the two of them together and clearly, they were in love with each other. I don't know why I thought Mark was going to propose but I had a very strong feeling. We walked back into the house and James and Richard were still in the study. We waved at them as we walked by. I asked Jonathan for a nice big pot of tea, something different this time.

"I think that I am going to abstain from drinking today. We will be drinking tomorrow for New Year's and probably lots of champagne, so I am going to give myself a day's rest." Sonya agreed that she was going to do the same thing. Jonathan brought out a tray with the tea and tea cups. She loved the cups.

"I'll find out where Christina got them and send you some if you like. It can be a house warming gift from James and I." She said that would be great. James and Richard came out to join us.

"We are abstaining from drinking today, taking a little break. There will be lots of bubbly tomorrow so today is a day of rest for us." James said that it sounded like a good idea which Richard also agreed with. I went to get some more cups and returned to the sunroom.

"Richard, do you think Mark is going to propose to Rhonda tomorrow night?" He nearly choked on his tea. He looked at me with a strange look.

"How could you possibly have known that. I haven't said a word to Sonya or to James for that matter." James just laughed and told Richard that I have my ways. Sonya was elated.

"You must not let on, none of you. I have no idea where he is going to do it, but I know that it will be done privately. He is not into public displays." We promised not to say a word. Sonya looked at me and I could tell she was wondering if I knew anything else. I shrugged my shoulders. Nicole and Austin returned and came out to the sunroom. Nicole had tea and Austin had some water.

Ayleen came around to the back and stood far enough back so we could see her. She tried to throw a snowball at the window but wasn't able to. Ross came around to get her and then they came in. When they got her out of her snow suit she came in to join us. She sat on the couch between James and me. James got her some water and one for Ross and Lindsay. Mark and Rhonda came back from their run and went up to shower. We tried not to look at them differently when they came in.

"For lunch, we are having a treat, lobster rolls and crab cakes with salad. Jonathan's lobster rolls are amazing. He's going to do a smaller version of them and the crab cakes for New Year's. It is going to be an interesting menu." James got more water from the kitchen and gave them to Rhonda and Mark. There was a bit of an awkward silence which, thankfully, was saved because lunch was ready. Ayleen loved the lobster rolls.

She thought it was like having hot dogs that were all cut up, so we let her think that. After lunch Mark, James, and Richard went to his study to go over a bit of business. Ross and Lindsay took Ayleen downstairs to watch a movie. Rhonda, Nicole, and Austin decided to go down for a sauna.

"My goodness it was hard to keep a poker face, but I think we did it. Maybe Mark will say something to Richard and James while they are in the study. I'm not going to ask, and I don't think you should either. You have to look surprised when it happens." We agreed to look surprised but not too surprised because that would look phony. Ross came back upstairs; Ayleen fell asleep. He put her in bed and was going back down to join Lindsay.

"What I wouldn't give to be a fly on the wall in James's study." We sat drinking our tea and talking about other things. After an hour passed, Rhonda, Nicole and Austin came back up and went upstairs to change. They weren't long and came in to the sunroom.

"I love that sauna; the dry heat feels really good. Mom you should get one of those put in your new house." Sonya said she would think about it. I poured Nicole some tea and Rhonda had some water. Ross and Lindsay came upstairs as their movie was over.

"Thank you, all of you for coming here for the holidays. I know I've said this already and will probably say it again, but it means a lot to me that you came. It has been very different since Mom and Dad died and we split off for various reasons but I'm glad that you came here." They knew what I was talking about and didn't need me to go into any detail.

"Aunt Cassandra we are happy to be here. I can't remember when I spent Christmas with Mom and Rhonda or New Year's for that matter. We have enjoyed being here and you have been the greatest hosts to us. It is all of us who should be thanking you for inviting us." I could feel myself starting to choke up.

"Before we all start crying, let's change the subject. I think John is going to clear the pathway tomorrow, so you will be able to walk and go running there without problem. I wish we could have fireworks but with all the trees it isn't the best idea. I'm sure we will be able to see any from the veranda at the front if they let them off in the small park. Jonathan gave me the list of foods we are having tomorrow. I don't think you will object to anything. We will of course have a good lunch and breakfast. Mr. Jones will be here with us too; I think you know that I invited him to join us." I passed the menu around and everyone liked what we were having.

"Wow, caviar, lobster, prime rib, egg rolls, can't say as I've had these on New Year's Eve, this should be a lot of fun. Do we have party favours as well?" I had everything, and it was on the dining room table.

"We are hiring a bartender because Jonathan will be a little busy putting all the canapes together. There will be champagne but if you want a particular cocktail you can have that too." Sonya could see that I was a little worried about that.

"Just because there is a bartender, don't anybody get silly and drink too much. It has been a wonderful holiday, and we don't want to end it with somebody falling down drunk. So know your limit." They said they would behave. James, Richard, and Mark came into the sunroom at that point. Ayleen also came downstairs and went over to Ross.

"Mum can I speak to you for a minute." We went out into the hallway to talk.

"Ayleen tell Gramma what happened." She was looking very sad.

"Gramma I know I promised I would not pee in the bed, but I accidentally did. I'm sorry." She started to cry, and I took her in my arms.

"Ayleen don't worry, Gramma put down a protective sheet so its fine. Come we will go up and change the bed and wash the sheets. No harm done." Ross went back into the room and Ayleen, and I went up to change the bed.

"I'm really sorry Gramma." She still felt badly.

"Ayleen, I promise you I am not upset. You have been so good, and you have been playing a lot and you were really tired." We got out more sheets and put another protective sheet on, just in case, and fixed the bed. Everything was good now. She came and gave me a big hug.

"Now, dinner should be ready so let's go downstairs and join the others." She held my hand the whole way down and stayed pretty close to me. She was quiet all through dinner. I didn't want her to be embarrassed but I didn't want to draw attention to her either. James asked her if she wanted to play a board game after dinner.

"I think that is an excellent idea. We have a bunch of board games, and we can play or those who want to play can do so. For those who are not interested you can go to the games room and play down there." I picked up a number of games in case that was what everyone wanted to do. James and Ayleen played connect four. I bought a rummoli game which the rest decided to play. It was a game we used to play back in the day, and I thought they would enjoy it. The only two who were not familiar with the game were Richard and Mark. Austin explained the game to them.

The rummoli game was set up in the small dining room. I bought lots of nickels for the occasion since pennies were no longer available. I had enough rolled nickels to give everyone four rolls after that they would have to dig into their own wallets. We set up the table putting in the extra leaf and brought out the extra chairs. I put a deck of cards on the table, and they were all set. We took the connect game to the sunroom where it was quieter, and James and Ayleen played while I watched, and helped her a little. Once she got the hang of the game, Ayleen didn't need me to help her. She was actually beating James and he said he was really trying to beat her. She laughed and laughed every time she beat him.

"Grandpa I win again. Do you want to play more?" James thought that I should play against her for a little while.

"Why don't you play with Gramma and see if you can beat her." She won the first game, but I won the next few games. I tried to challenge her to think more strategically even though she didn't know that is what I was doing. James saw what I was doing. He'd been trying to beat her when he played.

"Ah Ayleen, Gramma is better at this than I am. Oh, oh she has you now. How are you going to win?" It made her look at the board and where the chips were. She dropped her chip, and it went the right way and she won.

"I won Gramma I won. I beat you and Grandpa. Can you read me a story Grandpa?" James said he would but first she had to get her pjs on. I took her upstairs to get changed and then brought her back down. She sat in the recliner with James, and he read her one of his favourite stories. I went to check on the others.

"Well it looks like Ross and Sonya are doing well, the rest of you not so much. Can I get anyone anything? Jonathan made up cheese trays and crackers in case." They said that would be great and everyone wanted water. I made each of them up a small plate and put it beside them with their water and then went back out to the sunroom. Ayleen fell asleep, but James kept reading for another page.

"I think I read all of four pages and she couldn't keep her eyes open. I'll take her up in a minute. How is it going out there?" I said that Ross and Sonya were doing well, and they were having a good time. Every so often we could hear a roar from the dining room. It wasn't bothering Ayleen; she was out like a light. James took her up to her bed and I followed. I let him tuck her in and then we went back downstairs. I let Ross know Ayleen was already in bed. James and I went out to the sunroom.

"I'm glad I got that board game. It was a game we played when we were in our teens and then as adults. Many a weekend we spent playing that game, but we used pennies back in those days." I smiled thinking back.

The group played rummoli until 11:30 with Ross and Sonya being the main winners. They went up to bed as we did after putting all the dishes in the dishwasher and shutting off the lights. Arm in arm we went upstairs to bed. I was not sleepy, and neither was James. He leaned over to kiss me, and I kissed him back and then it was a night of sweet passion.

The next morning at breakfast we talked about what everyone was going to do until this evening. Tonight was the New Year's Eve party and while they were free to go about doing what they wanted, I asked that everyone be back and dressed, casually, for 6:00. James was going to pick up Albert at 5:00 and he was going to spend the night.

"Albert has never been in a plane before, so he is going to fly with us when we take all of you home. We are not going to be able to stay overnight though like we first planned. The first stop will be to drop Richard and

Mark off and then on to Ottawa. The limo will be there to take you back to Ross and Lindsay's." Everyone agreed they would be back in lots of time. Sonya, Richard, and her bunch went skiing. Ross, Lindsay, and Ayleen went to see her aunt and uncle to wish them Happy New Year. Ayleen didn't want to go but I explained that they had to go and spend time with Lindsay's relatives too. Lindsay told her that they were not going to stay long, which seemed to make it ok. They left around 10:00 and it was James and I in the house. Jonathan and his students were busy in the kitchen getting things ready for tonight. We decided to go and have a sauna. We took a shower in the downstairs bathroom and then went into the sauna.

"This feels really good, and my muscles are relaxing. It has been a wonderful time having everyone." James said that it was indeed. It was nice to relax in the warm heat. We got out took another shower and went up to change.

"That is probably the first time we haven't done anything but a sauna in there since we have been in the house." We both laughed about that.

"I'm going to tell you something, but I don't want you to say anything to Sonya. Mark asked me if I could call Mr. Wright to take out the horse carriage. I think that is how he plans to propose to Rhonda, but you can't say anything, and you can't let on. He's going to sneak her out hopefully without anyone noticing." I had a feeling that was what he was going to do. I promised not to say anything.

The rest of the day went on without much fuss. Ross and Lindsay got back around 3:00 and went up to get changed. It was going to be dressy casual for tonight. The rest came back from skiing around 4:00 and went up to change. James and I went up to change as well. He put on a black pair of dress pants with a dark green V-neck cashmere pullover and a white t-shirt underneath. I decided to wear my black leather pants, red cowl neck cashmere sweater with my red suede booties. Everyone else was coming down to the living room. Ayleen was wearing a pair of black pants with red blouse and her red suede booties.

"Gramma we have the same kind of shoes on and same colour of clothes." James left to go and pick up Albert. Duncan and Roxie arrived while he was gone. It was 6:00 when they got back. He and James joined the rest of us in the living room. He introduced Duncan and Roxie to Albert. He sat down beside Ayleen and me.

"It is very nice to see you again, both of you." We said that it was nice to have him here again. James let everyone know what the plan was for the evening.

"Because not everyone will be able to stay up until midnight here, Cassandra and I decided that we would do an early version of New Years for those who would be going to bed early. I got John to construct our version of a ball drop which he has just put up outside the front door. We will do that at 9:00 and then again at midnight for those who plan to stay up, if anyone does we will do it again. There is a small park not far from here and it is almost in a direct line from the house. I arranged with the other subdivision owners to have fireworks set off at both 9:00 and midnight. I believe everyone is having a large lunch as we are only going to have hors d'oeuvres and nibbles throughout the night. I think with what Jonathan is preparing, it will more than fill anyone up. There will be champagne of course and we also have a bartender. While we want everyone to have a great time, I encourage you to not overindulge in the alcohol department. So let's have fun and ring in a New Year." A portable bar was set up at one end of the living room. Champagne was on ice to toast in the New Year.

Richard entertained us by playing the piano and the students were wandering around offering up food. Albert and Ayleen got into a conversation about unicorns. Nobody noticed that Mark and Rhonda slipped out. It was wonderful to see everyone having a good time. Just before 9:00 we gathered around the front doors, which James opened up.

I saw Rhonda and Mark come walking back to the house. John and his family were also out to watch the ball drop. It was quite ingenious how he did it. It had lots of flashing LED lights and dropped down perfectly. We had a glass of champagne and toasted to the New Year. Fireworks went off right on cue and there were lots of expressions of excitement at them. When they were finished, Lindsay took Ayleen up to bed. Half an hour later, James escorted Albert up to his room. He showed him where everything was and left him, closing the door behind him. Duncan and Roxie took the opportunity to head off home. They said they had a wonderful time.

The rest of us continued on with the party, being mindful of the two sleeping upstairs. I could see that Rhonda and Mark pulled Sonya, Austin, and Nicole off to one side. Then they announced to everyone else that they got engaged. There were more toasts and best wishes given to them. Her ring was very beautiful. While Sonya was overjoyed at the news, she and Richard opted not to stay up until midnight. Ross and Lindsay decided to go to bed as well. The rest were going to hang in until midnight to ring in the New Year for real. Jonathan and the students left at 10:30 pm. We let the bartender go home at the same time and at midnight we did the same thing all over again. There were a few more glasses of champagne and then everyone else went to bed. James and I tidied up a bit and then went upstairs.

"Happy New Year darling. It is the first of many that we will celebrate together." James kissed me, and I kissed him back. We were both very tired from the day and it didn't take long for us to fall asleep. James got up early the next morning before anyone else.

Unbeknownst to me, he had a tradition on New Year's Day of putting a gift outside everyone's bedroom door. Even though it was a Scottish tradition his family did for decades, he decided to start the tradition here. He got up and went to his office where he had small gift bags for everyone. He quietly put the gift bags at each person's door and even one for Ayleen and for me. I got up not long after he left the room and when I opened the door I saw the gift in front of our door and one in front of everyone else's door. I took my gift and went downstairs. James was in the sunroom having coffee. He poured me a cup.

"What is this?" He explained the tradition and I thought it was wonderful. I opened my gift, and it was gold and diamond bangles. They were beautiful, and I thanked him with a kiss. Ayleen came into the sunroom holding her gift.

"Look Gramma, Grandpa this was on the floor at my door. Is this for me?" James said it was and told her about the tradition. She opened her gift, and it was a cute charm bracelet with a charm of her favourite animated animal. She squealed in excitement.

"Well if that doesn't wake the others nothing will." Sure enough one by one or rather two by two, they came downstairs. Each one asked the same question and James explained the tradition. For the ladies he got them a bracelet with diamonds and for the guys he got them diamond cuff links. Everyone had a cup of coffee and then went back upstairs to get dressed. James took a quick shower and got dressed and went to see if Albert needed any help. I took a shower and then got dressed myself. Today was going to be a relaxing day. James came downstairs with Albert who said that he slept very well. James told him about the tradition which he thought was wonderful.

"I was very comfortable and had no problem getting around in the morning." Ayleen came bounding downstairs and into the dining room.

"Good morning Mr. Jones." Albert wished her good morning as she sat down beside him. He changed I thought since Christmas. There was not the look of loneliness in him anymore. He was relaxed and smiling. Everyone else started to come down and into the dining room. Nobody had hangovers, which I was very pleased about.

"Albert, Rhonda, and Mark got engaged last night. Isn't that wonderful news." He said it was indeed and congratulated them. Albert was sitting on one side of James, and I was on the other.

"What are everyone's plans for today?" Rhonda, Mark, Austin, and Nicole were going to get in one more skiing trip. Sonya and Richard were going for a walk after breakfast but had no other plans for the day. Ross, Lindsay, and Ayleen were staying around the house.

"We are going to play out in the snow fort again today, right Daddy?" They said that is what they were going to do but not right away. James was going to take Albert over to show him the new businesses as he voiced an interest in seeing them at Christmas. I was going to do a work out when they left.

After breakfast, the skiers took off, Sonya and Richard went out the door and James got Albert ready to go to the industrial park. Ross and Lindsay were going to take Ayleen down to watch one of her tv programs for half an hour and then go outside. I went up to change into some workout clothes and got in a good work out for an hour. I took another shower and got dressed again. As I was coming downstairs, Ross and Lindsay were taking Ayleen out to play. I put in a call to Christelle to wish her Happy New Year.

"So how were your holidays? Has everyone been enjoying themselves?" I said that it was going wonderfully but everyone was going home tomorrow. I told her about Albert and that he was coming with us on the plane as he had never been on one. Her New Years was quiet much like it always was. She went to bed at

10:00 just like always. I said that I would call her after everything settled down and back to normal. I put in a call to Janet to wish her and Wade Happy New Year. They had a quiet night as well and didn't stay up until midnight either. I told her what we did and that I thought everyone enjoyed it.

"The food was perfect, enough to fill you up but not be stuffed. The caviar went very quickly which did not surprise me, but the food Jonathan made was wonderful. James and I stayed up until midnight with the ones who wanted to do so but everyone behaved. Nobody overindulged which was great." I told her I had to go and would call her in a few days. Sonya and Richard came back from their walk and went up to start packing their suitcases. Ross, Lindsay, and Ayleen came back in too. They were playing outside for over two hours, and she was getting a little tired. Ross took her down to watch a movie while Lindsay went up to pack their suitcases. She came back down after about half an hour.

"I think I'm going to need a couple more suitcases." We both started to laugh, and I went to get her a couple of mine to use. When she went back up James and Albert came in. He thoroughly enjoyed the tour. Lunch was nearly ready. Those who were home went to the dining room where Jonathan served up a soup, sandwiches, and salad. He made up a small pizza for Ayleen which she loved. Albert looked a little tired after lunch and asked if we minded if he went to lay down until dinner.

"Are you feeling ok Albert?" He said that he was just a little tired. James took him upstairs and saw him into his room.

"Albert are you sure you are alright. I can have a doctor come if you feel the need." He said it was not necessary. He was not used to all the excitement, which he said he very much enjoyed, but it was not something he was used to.

"James don't worry; I am ok just a bit tired. I have all my medications with me so please don't worry." James left him to lay down and rest.

"Is he ok? Do we need to call a doctor?" James said no, Albert was ok but needed to rest. Ayleen also went up for a nap. Lindsay had the majority of their bags packed. Sonya said the same. It was going to be sad to see them all go home but life had to go back to normal.

"Jonathan mentioned that tonight's dinner was going to be all wild game. John and Max went hunting and got a couple of deer and they sent up a few roasts. Of course we already had the moose in the freezer and one of John's friends got a lot of ducks and grouse, so I hope everyone likes wild game. Of course, we won't let Ayleen know what it is, or she won't eat." Ross said that was a good idea not to say anything. We sat around in the sunroom talking and having wine. The rest came in from their skiing and said they had a great day. They went up to change and rejoined us in the sunroom. Ayleen came down still a bit sleepy and sat with James. I went up to check to see if Albert was up. As I was going down the hall, he opened up his door.

"Did you have a nice rest Albert?" He said he did and took my arm and we went downstairs. When we reached the bottom he stopped.

"I want to thank you for your hospitality. You and your family have made the last months of my life the happiest they have ever been, so thank you so much." He gave me a hug and kiss on the cheek. We went out to the sunroom where everyone was in conversation. James got up to get Albert a small whisky. Ayleen went over to sit with Ross. I think she knew she was going home tomorrow because she had a sad look on her face.

"Ayleen, why so sad? Haven't you enjoyed your holiday?" She nodded yes but a few tears started to fall.

"I don't want to go home. I want to stay here." I picked her up and gave her a hug and she clung to me.

"Ayleen, you know you and Mommy and Daddy can come back any time you want. But you have to go back to school, and I am sure that Freya is missing you a lot. Won't you be happy to see her again and all your friends at school?" She nodded yes and dried her eyes saying that she missed Freya too. There was an hour to go before dinner, so Rhonda, Mark and Nicole went up to do some packing. They came back down as we were going in to the dining room. The meal was wonderful, and everyone complimented Jonathan. We went into the living room, sat and talked. The evening was a wonderful one and it was going to be hard to say goodbye. That night James and I talked about the holiday.

"It was wonderful, and I am so glad everyone came. I know we talked about having Fenella and Callum over this year, but don't you want to go and spend Christmas in Scotland?" James thought about that but would prefer to have Fenella and Callum over and perhaps Alisa if she wanted.

"I have spent a lot of Christmases there. I think for a few years, I would like to spend them here and have my family from Scotland come here. Perhaps in a few years you and I can go there. Maybe we can even bring Ross, Lindsay, and Ayleen. I think she would get a big kick out of that." I thought she would also, but we would have to plan it right.

"They applied for their passports last fall and got them before Christmas. That is an important item out of the way. Because of school, Ayleen and Lindsay are always off so it would be Ross to work around. He could probably swing it if they don't take holidays in the summer. They will be coming for the wedding so perhaps once they see your home, they will be more than happy to go again." James said he would talk to Ross about it at another time.

"But it is our home my darling not just mine. It is as much your home as it is mine." We drifted off to sleep to once again and for the last time for a while, awakened to a knock at our door. While James entertained her I showered and got dressed. Then he did the same. I took Ayleen downstairs for breakfast. Ross and Lindsay were already down. They knew Ayleen was with us. James came down with Albert. He had his overnight bag with him which James put by the stairs with all the other bags.

Nicole and Austin's flight was at noon, and we planned to leave to fly back at 11:00. James ordered the stretch suv again to take everyone to the airport. Once all the bags were loaded into the limo, we left at 9:00. We dropped Nicole and Austin off, so they could go through to get their flight. Sonya, Richard, Rhonda, and Mark got out to hug them goodbye. They got back in the car, and we went through to the gate to James's plane.

The luggage was set out at the stairs to be loaded. James took Albert up the stairs into the plane and got him seated. He asked Janine to look after him while everyone else was coming onboard. Ayleen sat across from Albert and reached over to hold his hand. Everyone else took seats in the middle of the plane. Ross and Lindsay sat across the aisle from us.

Maria went through the security procedure and then we taxied out onto the runway and up. Ayleen was amazed at the ground below us. There were a few clouds in the sky but not as many as when she came. I thought she would be disappointed, but it gave her a chance now to see the ground below. I think she was as fascinated by that as she was the clouds. She leaned over to point out things to Albert which he thought was quite fascinating. We made the stop in Toronto to drop off Richard and Mark and then back up again. The flight was wonderful, very little turbulence and Albert looked like he was enjoying himself.

We had a light lunch on the plane, and it was not long after that the captain was telling the flight crew to prepare for landing. Janine helped Albert to straighten his seat and re-buckle himself. The plane came to a stop in front of where the VIP area was. The luggage was unloaded and put into the awaiting limo. I had to brace myself to say goodbye. Ayleen gave each of us a hug and kiss and she was crying because she didn't want to let go. She hugged James again so long that I thought he was going to break down in tears. I could see Lindsay starting to cry, which was causing a chain reaction.

"Let's all cry and get it over with." Everyone started to laugh, and I was glad that my comment broke the moment. Albert stayed onboard while we said goodbye. He waved at everyone from the door. There were more hugs and Ayleen tearfully got into the limo. We went back onboard and waited for the plane to be refueled. Albert was wiping away a few tears. I was concerned about him.

"Is everything ok Albert?" He was a bit choked up when he spoke but said he was fine.

"I have never had a family, not since my parents died when I was quite young. But the two of you have made me feel like I was a part of this family. It was hard to wave goodbye to them and especially to Ayleen. She is such a sweet child, and she definitely loves the two of you. It is good that she has lots of family around her being an only child." We said that he was now very much a part of our family. James echoed what he said once before.

"Albert, you don't have to be blood to be family. I feel that Ross is like a son to me and Ayleen very much my own granddaughter. Cassandra and I consider you to be like a Great Grandfather in the family. You are welcome in our home any time you want to be with us." Albert thanked James for the sentiment and said he wanted to keep in touch. It took a half hour to refuel and make sure that everything mechanical was fine and we changed flight crews.

We taxied back out onto the runway and once again we were going home. We arrived late in the evening, and we drove Albert home. We walked him up to his door and got him inside. James put his overnight bag by the sofa and hugged him and said goodnight. The drive home was quiet. We were both feeling quite drained emotionally. The lights were on when we pulled up to the house and it was so pretty. But it was decidedly quiet now. Going from the living room to the dining room to the sunroom, it was all quiet. James poured us each a glass of wine and we sat staring out at the woods, in silence. We went up to bed and fell asleep almost immediately.

Something made me wake up. It was very dark out, there was no moon, and I could not see what time it was. Everything was pitch black around me and I couldn't even see my hand in front of my face. The power must have gone out for some reason. I flopped back down in bed trying to remember what I was dreaming about. It had been a wonderful dream. I felt the bed beside me, and it was empty.

"Well, I guess it was a dream after all." I laid back in bed recalling what happened in the dream. I felt the covers moving and gasped in fright. A light came on and I looked at who was beside me.

"Darling what's wrong? The power went out for about an hour, but it is back on now. Why did you jump when I got back into bed?" I looked at him and realized that I hadn't been dreaming. This was real, and James was in bed with me in our home. I looked around the room letting it all sink in.

"I thought this was all a big dream I was having. When I woke up and the lights were out and it was so dark in the room, I thought that I had been dreaming all this. But you are here, and it is real." James took me in his arms and kissed me.

"Yes, it is all real, you are not dreaming and to prove it." He had that look in his eye which I knew meant it was going to be a long night, a long, glorious passion filled night.

www.ingramcontent.com/pod-product-compliance
Lightning Source LLC
Chambersburg PA
CBHW020243030826
48979CB00030B/2506/J